Praise for
Cordelia Underwood, Or the
Beginnings of the Moose

"An amiable, richly populated first novel . . . that should soothe even the twitchiest reader. . . . Diffuse and leisurely, the novel seems designed for long afternoons in a hammock . . . Reid's gazillion characters sparkle." —*The New York Times Book Review*

"Reminiscent of John Irving at his hilarious best . . . a charming, old-fashioned romp through Victorian New England."
—*Boston Herald*

"Nothing passes idle hours in lazy summer days better than an old-fashioned tall tale. Whatever the season, readers will enjoy Van Reid's debut novel and its collection of eccentric Yankees . . . Reid's story offers a lemonade-at-the-fair freshness that will delight readers of all ages." —*The Christian Science Monitor*

"An affectionate homage to Charles Dickens's masterpiece by the first-time novelist Van Reid . . . [with] adventures and mis-adventures galore. . . . If the next installment resembles this amiable Dickensian romp then it will prove, to quote Mr. Pickwick himself, *'delightful—thoroughly delightful!'* "
—*The Cleveland Plain Dealer*

"A decidedly entertaining read. . . . This Maine native writes with such authenticity about the turn of the last century one wonders if he's not a time-traveler. . . . Ultimately, how the pieces fit together doesn't much matter because the pieces themselves are so funny and so crisply written and so Maine. . . . Old-fashioned, rollicking good fun." —*Concord Sunday Monitor*

"It's refreshing to read a story with no sex (just a little ro-mance), hardly any violence, and absolutely no naughty words. Recommended." —*Library Journal*

PENGUIN BOOKS

CORDELIA UNDERWOOD

Van Reid, whose family has lived in Maine since the eighteenth century, has for the last seven years been assistant manager of the Maine Coast Book Shop in Damariscotta. He lives with his wife and two children in Edgecomb, Maine.

VAN REID

Cordelia Underwood

OR

The Marvelous Beginnings

of

THE MOOSEPATH LEAGUE

PENGUIN BOOKS

PENGUIN BOOKS

Published by the Penguin Group
Penguin Putnam Inc., 375 Hudson Street,
New York, New York 10014, U.S.A.
Penguin Books Ltd, 27 Wrights Lane,
London W8 5TZ, England
Penguin Books Australia Ltd, Ringwood,
Victoria, Australia
Penguin Books Canada Ltd, 10 Alcorn Avenue,
Toronto, Ontario, Canada M4V 3B2
Penguin Books (N.Z.) Ltd, 182–190 Wairau Road,
Auckland 10, New Zealand

Penguin Books Ltd, Registered Offices:
Harmondsworth, Middlesex, England

First published in the United States of America by Viking Penguin,
a member of Penguin Putnam Inc. 1998
Published in Penguin Books 1999

1 3 5 7 9 10 8 6 4 2

Map by James Sinclair

THE LIBRARY OF CONGRESS HAS CATALOGUED THE HARDCOVER AS FOLLOWS:
Reid, Van.
Cordelia Underwood, or, The marvelous beginnings
of the Moosepath League / Van Reid.
p.   cm.
ISBN 0-670-88097-3 (hc.)
ISBN 0 14 02.8010 3 (pbk.)
I. Title.
PS3568.E47697C6   1998
813'.54—dc21   98–5623

Printed in the United States of America
Set in Electra
Designed by Francesca Belanger

To Mom and Dad,
who kept me safe

CONTENTS

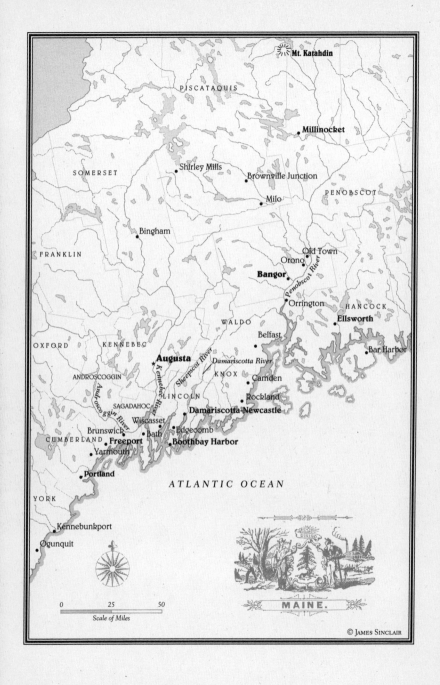

Mt. Katahdin

PISCATAQUIS

Millinocket

Shirley Mills

Brownville Junction

SOMERSET

Milo

PENOBSCOT

Bingham

FRANKLIN

Old Town

Orono

Bangor

Penobscot River

Orrington

HANCOCK

WALDO

Ellsworth

OXFORD

KENNEBEC

Belfast

Augusta

Sheepscot River

Damariscotta River

Bar Harbor

ANDROSCOGGIN

KNOX

Camden

Kennebec River

LINCOLN

Rockland

Androscoggin River

SAGADAHOC

Damariscotta-Newcastle

Wiscasset

Brunswick

Bath

Edgecomb

CUMBERLAND

Freeport

Boothbay Harbor

Yarmouth

Portland

ATLANTIC OCEAN

YORK

Kennebunkport

Ogunquit

DIRIGO

MAINE.

© James Sinclair

0   25   50
Scale of Miles

Prologue: The Mariner
JULY 1, 1896

HE EMERGED, when night had fallen, from the rough end of Portland's wharf district, where illegal liquor was peddled, where sailors and coarse landsmen and hard women caroused, and where well-meaning people did not linger. He rose from that ill-lit place and began his ascent at the foot of High Street, a shadow between the street lamps with a hesitation in his step.

Another solitary walker—one George Selby of Danforth Street—crossed the street to avoid meeting him. *"Walking to my brother's this evening,"* Selby would write in his journal (dated that same night, July the first, 1896), *"I believe I saw, on High Street, the ghost of the German who is said to haunt the perimeters of his ancient grave site."* Selby was referring to the legend of an early casualty of the Revolutionary War—a man killed by British arsonists, who in October of 1775 burned what was then known as Falmouth in retaliation for the town's support of the Rebel cause. Never identified by name (he was thought to be German because of an address in his pocket), the man was buried in a nearby field and said to trouble the area with his sad presence.

So George Selby (by all accounts a cautious man) gave a wide berth to this apparition, which he reported as *"hunched and dark and silent."* It was an apt choice of words, for one would not need to believe in ghosts to see something mysterious in this figure.

Hunched and dark and silent, he stopped where High Street meets Spring Street and considered the large house upon the corner. Tall curtains masked the first-floor windows, partially obscuring the light from two front rooms. He stood at the end of the walk and watched the slivers of light reach across the lawn. Great elms on either side of him soughed in the warm southwesterly breeze as he pulled a small card from his coat pocket. It read:

MR. JAMES UNDERWOOD III
CORNER OF HIGH & SPRING STREETS
PORTLAND, MAINE

His footfalls sounded upon the walk and upon the steps as he approached the front door. At the top step he paused some minutes, the card still in hand, then removed his hat before raising his fist to knock.

Cordelia Underwood was gratefully startled by the knock on the front door that evening; for the better part of the day—indeed, for the better part of several days—she had been plagued by an unfocused sense of restlessness.

At twenty-three, Cordelia was older than most women still living in their parents' houses—most women her age were married by now, or at least occupying a suitable *position*. Her seeming lack of prospects was not due to any want in character or appearance; her hair, more red than auburn, was thought a liability by some, it is true, but as many others considered it more than a little attractive, framing her dark eyebrows and green eyes.

As for character, she had a good deal of it.

But, purely through the fault of circumstance, she found herself, on the evening of July the 1st, 1896, in the overfamiliar surroundings of her parents' home, with no prospect of employment, and very nearly as little of social recreation. Everyone she knew below the age of forty and above the age of seventeen was *gone for the summer!* To be truthful, her parents were not, in their late years, lions of society.

So when a knock came at the front door—unexpected at this late hour—she jumped at the sound of the sharp rap as if she had been physically prodded, and was grateful for it.

Hurrying to the main part of the house, she reached the front hall at the same time as her father, who inquired with raised eyebrows whether she was expecting a visitor. Cordelia, with similar expression, shook her head. Her father, James Underwood III, then stepped forward and opened the door.

Evening entered first—a scent of new-mown lawn and roses on a cool breeze that felt more of late spring than early summer. It seemed the night itself had knocked; no figure was immediately discernible beyond the light of the hall. Then the shadows materialized into a short, dark-clad man, who stepped cautiously into the doorway. He wore a peacoat and held a shapeless hat in his hands, wringing it like a wet washcloth and hunching over it as if someone might take it from him. He was nearly bald and his beard was short and patched with gray. Everything about him bespoke the sea—the fresh smell of salt, the windburn in his cheek, and the uncertain manner with which he stood on dry land.

"Good evening to you, sir," said the fellow, before James could speak.

He nodded to Cordelia. "Ma'am. I apologize for the late hour, but I had a trouble finding your address, and my ship sails with the first tide tomorrow."

"That's quite all right," said James. "As you can see, we have not retired. How can I help you?"

"It's more that I might help you, sir. It's to do with your own brother, Captain Basil Underwood."

"Basil?" said James, who had himself risen to the rank of naval lieutenant, serving aboard a blockade ship against the Confederacy during the Southern Rebellion. In his sixty-sixth year, he still maintained much of his military bearing. He straightened, considerably, however, at the sound of his brother's name. "Perhaps you have not been informed, Mr. . . ."

"Stimply, sir. Charles Stimply."

"Mr. Stimply, my brother has been dead these past two years."

"Aye, and I was with him when he did die."

Not a little surprised, James searched Mr. Stimply's face for motive, but sensed that this last statement was only a means of introduction. "Come in, Mr. Stimply," said James. He stepped back and ushered the seaman past the door. "Let me take your hat and coat, sir."

"I won't be staying long—I thank you just the same," returned the man.

Cordelia's father glanced at her briefly before waving the man into the front parlor. "You'll take a cup of tea," he conjectured. "My wife has just taken a pot from the stove."

"Anything more would be prohibit, wouldn't it, then."

James Underwood smiled. Mr. Stimply was referring to the fact that the State of Maine had been without legal recourse to liquor since before the war. "I think we have some medicinal claret in the house, don't we, Cordelia? This is my daughter, Mr. Stimply."

"A pleasure," said the man. It was clear that his pleasure would be greater if the medicine cabinet was not found wanting.

There was a dark and undisclosed crime in the Underwood family history, some iniquity so terrible as to be buried by those closest to it from the knowledge of successive generations. All that Cordelia Underwood knew was that some ancestor—a great-great-grandfather, she thought—had barely escaped from the south of England with his life just prior to the first American Revolution.

In Cordelia's mind, that ancestor had always represented a small island of dark fascination amidst a sea of dull, if respectable, genealogy. Her late uncle Basil, her father's younger brother, occupied a similar geography in her imagination; the two, in fact, were almost the same person in her memory.

Cordelia had known her uncle when she was a child, and then not well. Basil was a handsome man, darker than her father, and not as tall. Papa had told her more than once that life at sea was rough, but if it was (and she had no reason to doubt him), her uncle showed no outward sign of it. He had a gentle manner, almost shy, when he visited his brother's family, and it only occurred to her in later years that he was unused to women and small children.

He was a man of strong opinions, however, if careful in his expression of them; and there was about him a sense of latent energy that she imagined to be a product of his career at sea, where quick invention and instinctive deeds could prove the difference between life and tragedy.

She had been in awe of him, linking him in her mind with that wild ancestor who fled for his life to the colonies. She had transmuted that dark and undisclosed crime into an act of personal integrity and put her uncle Basil's face upon it.

An untimely death in a far-off land had only added to Uncle Basil's mystique; and through the dearth of detail regarding his demise his family had come to a single and erroneous conclusion: that they would never learn very much about his last days.

Cordelia feared to miss something important between her father and Mr. Stimply in the parlor and, in her haste, came close to dropping the bottle of claret from its shelf in the pantry cupboard.

"Ah, that would buck up a man greatly!" declared Mr. Stimply when Cordelia offered him a glass of the requested spirit. Her mother, who had arrived in the parlor while Cordelia was gone, declined to join Mr. Stimply in a drink, but James took a glass in order to be polite. Mr. Stimply silently saluted the ladies and took a great gulp of the stuff.

Cordelia sat upon the sofa beside her mother, as the seaman perched awkwardly on the edge of a chair. James Underwood, who had settled himself in his favorite seat by the dormant fireplace, leaned back and crossed his legs. Cordelia studied the contrast between Mr. Stimply and her father.

James Underwood was long and thin, and handsome in a long, thin sort of way. His hair was still full, now a brilliant silver, as were his thick mustaches. His attire was elegant; his manner was quiet and his bearing authoritative.

Charles Stimply was thick with muscles, his back so broad for his size that it look hunched. He was not a tall man, but he exuded a large presence in their front parlor. He could defer to the amenities proper to such a place, but it was plain that he was accustomed to rougher ways. His voice sounded permanently hoarse, perhaps from bawling over high winds and crashing seas. He was missing the two last fingers of his right hand.

"Mr. Stimply worked for your uncle Basil in Venezuela," Cordelia was informed by her father. "And sailed with him before that, it seems."

"Aye, for four years," intoned the man.

"Have you been this long returning to the United States, Mr. Stimply?" asked Cordelia's mother. Mercia Underwood was tall for her sex, though still some inches short of her husband. She was twelve years younger than James, and her hair retained much of its color, a handsome auburn that had never been as bright as Cordelia's. Though smiles came easily to her pleasant features, they always came softly.

"In a roundabout way, Mrs. Underwood," said the man.

"It's very good of you to make this effort to visit, Mr. Stimply," said James.

"Well, sir, it's by way of a promise, you understand."

"I see." James leaned forward in his chair, his eyes alight with interest. "Did my brother have any last words he wished brought to us?"

"He did charge me with passing on his greatest affection," returned the seaman. He finished off his claret and looked at the empty glass with regret.

"Let me," said Cordelia, hurrying to fill it again.

"I am obliged." He sipped carefully this time, and smacked his lips lightly. "There was James, which is yourself, sir," he continued. "And Mercia, which would be your lovely wife. And James the fourth, and Brendan."

"Our two sons," said James the third. "They are not home now. Jamey is in Boston; Brendan is due within the month, aboard the *Franklin*."

"Ah, yes," said Mr. Stimply. "Your brother sent his greatest affection. And to you, ma'am," he said to Cordelia, whose face had betrayed some hurt. "Captain Underwood was quite adamant that I deliver his greatest affection and best wishes to little Cordelia."

The young woman sat back in the sofa. *Little Cordelia*—the words touched her in a way that news of her uncle's death had not. Mercia placed a hand on her daughter's.

"There is more," said Mr. Stimply. "And I would have delivered, too—Captain's sea chest, which he directed me to pack whenever he came out of his fever long enough to know what he was telling me—and I'd have delivered it but for Mr. Pue at the wharf."

"Nathaniel Pue? The Custom House inspector?" asked James.

"The same. A bother to all order and government! He's held up the chest till next of kin come to sign for it." The man finished off his second glass of wine, then placed it carefully upon a doily on the table beside him.

"You were there, then, when my brother died," said James.

"Aye, *and* I dug his grave."

"His partner's letter said that it was yellow fever."

The fellow nodded.

"Mr. Stimply, I think you have been a great service to my brother, both before and after his death. If there is anything I can do to—"

The sailor stood then, before James could finish. "Charles Stimply," he said, "was falsely accused of a grave crime before the mast, and only Captain Basil Underwood cared enough to find the truth of the matter. If not for your brother, sir, I would have been hanged from the yardarm, ten years ago, day after tomorrow. It's a pleasure to meet you. He did speak often, and fondly."

The Underwoods rose as one when the sailor moved toward the hall. "You're not leaving so soon, Mr. Stimply?" asked the mother.

"Well . . ." said the man. He turned and looked at each of them carefully. "Yes, I am. Sail tomorrow. The *Merlin*," he added, to answer the next obvious question, "for Liverpool."

"Godspeed, Mr. Stimply," said James, shaking the sailor's hand. "And thank you."

"And for your hospitality. Ladies."

James held the door while Mr. Stimply stepped past it and into the darkness beyond. They could see his silhouette when he reached the street. He paused there for a moment, then disappeared in the direction of the harbor.

In the parlor once again, the Underwoods were silent while they considered this brief apparition. Though not so greatly troubled by this news of an uncle who had been more real in her imagination than in life, Cordelia was yet aware of her father's feelings toward his younger brother—the two had been close in their youth—and she was concerned to know how this unexpected remembrance affected him.

"It's a shame that Mr. Stimply couldn't have stayed," said Mercia. She touched her husband's arm, and he took a breath, as if suddenly waking up.

"Yes," he answered, though it wasn't clear that he had heard her.

"Shall I have one of the boys at Mr. Spurling's drive me down to the Custom House tomorrow morning?" asked Cordelia. "To get Uncle Basil's sea chest?"

"Not at all, dear. I can drive down," replied her father, retrieving more of his natural animation as he spoke. "You can come with me, if you like." He turned to his wife. "Mercia?"

"Let's all go," replied Mrs. Underwood.

There was something cheery in the thought, the momentary gloom dispelled by the prospect of an outing. Curiosity played a part, as well, in the sudden change of mood. There was an image in Mr. Stimply's story—Basil rising from a fever to direct the packing of his sea chest, the gnarled seaman respectfully following his instructions—that radiated with a dramatic charm as much as it hurt with its sense of pathos. How would a man, sure of his immediate destination, pack luggage that could not travel with him? Would he store away remembrances of himself, or forward his own remembrance of those he loved?

Sitting on the edge of her bed that night, her keepsake box opened beside her, Cordelia searched through moments of her childhood, collected in the form of simple jewelry, bits of ribbon, a tiny New Testament, and a seemingly out-of-place slingshot. She took from the box an oval brooch that held a delicate cameo.

She traced a finger over the mountain that was etched into the small piece of agate. There was a lake at the foot of the mountain, and trees—pine trees—she thought—in the foreground of the scene. She touched the stone with the back of her finger, then laid it against her cheek, where it felt cool, like water. Uncle Basil had given the cameo to her on her seventh birthday; she had been quite grateful for what she considered to be her first piece of grown-up jewelry.

She remembered seeing Uncle Basil only a few times during her childhood, but it had always been plain that he enjoyed his niece and nephews. "Have you been to the Marquesas?" asked her brother Brendan during Uncle Basil's last visit, some twelve years ago, when Cordelia was eleven years old.

"Yes," answered Uncle Basil. It was a crisp autumn evening, and a fire snapped on the parlor's hearth. Uncle Basil crossed his legs. There was something elegant about him—his dress, his movements. "With Captain Hartung," he added, "in '72. We stopped at one of the islands for water."

"Did you see cannibals there?" pursued Brendan.

"I saw natives. I didn't inquire about their eating habits. They seemed civilized enough, in their own way."

"Were their teeth filed?"

"I'm sure your sister isn't interested in such things," said Uncle Basil, which showed how little he knew about eleven-year-old girls. Cordelia, with some presence of mind, excused herself from the parlor, then asked her brother about the Polynesian cannibals when Uncle Basil was not within hearing. Looking back on it, she was sure that Brendan had embellished the tale.

Papa had taken the news of his brother's death with an outward calm that did not deceive his daughter. Neither of her brothers was home at the time, and she had felt the weight of silence as if she had borne it alone. Mama said little, but spent a large portion of several days with her husband in their room. It wasn't till after the memorial service that Papa began to seem like his old self. He wore a black armband till the first anniversary of Basil's death.

Sitting on her bed now, Cordelia gazed at, only half-seeing, the brooch: the mountain and the trees in white, the sky and the lake in blue.

"Uncle Basil," she said to the brooch, quietly aloud.

The clock in the kitchen struck midnight, and she had not yet heard her father climb the stairs.

Book One

JULY 2, 1896

1. The Custom House Wharf

PORTLAND'S CUSTOM HOUSE WHARF was a place of steady commotion in the worst of weather; but on such a day as the 2nd of July, 1896—when the sun was strong enough to warrant a parasol for strolling ladies, and the sea breeze brisk enough to suggest a shawl—sightseers and ship spotters, brightly dressed sweethearts and gallant beaus, sailors, shoremen, lads, swags, and lollygaggers made of the great quay a swarm of movement and sound.

It was a quiet place when Nathaniel Pue, customs inspector, arrived at six in the morning. There was little traffic on the wharf before the Custom House opened—the odd thoughtful man on his early-morning constitutional, the occasional sailor nursing the effects of the previous night's revel, an indigent curled upon one of the wharf-benches. (One cold spring morning, Inspector Pue had discovered a man frozen to death there.)

In warm weather, Pue often saw the idle and unrepentant Horace McQuinn leaning with his short, bony frame against a piling. Horace would turn, slowly—with mock severity—and simply raise his hand in the air. Nathaniel would wave back, oddly gratified by Horace's notice. From his office in the Custom House he could watch Horace watch the ships at anchor; but as the morning proceeded, Horace would be swallowed up by the great crowds, and similarly swept from the inspector's mind during the business-filled day.

Most who knew Horace McQuinn did not realize that he had worked in his younger days. There was a sense of idleness about the man, a humor toward the labor of others, that characterized him as a lifetime loafer. He could stand for an hour without shifting his feet, or drawl a long tale—filling his listeners with belly laughs or their hearts with horror—while never raising his voice above the level of confidential speech. Even his one-handed pipe filling gave the impression of a man who moved no more than he had to.

But Horace McQuinn had driven logs on the Kennebec; he had sailed before the mast, and for several years driven a coach from Bath to Rockland along the old King's Highway. Horace McQuinn had worked in his youth—he just hadn't liked it much. Now—gray-haired, weathered of face, his fingers yellow with smoke—he quite preferred the labor of others.

To be fair, Horace sympathized with those fellow creatures who passed him with a heavy burden. "Don't be straining yourself, now," was his most common form of advice, and he delivered it with immeasurable concern. There were times, indeed, when he would go so far as to offer the services of any particular gentleman or sailor who might be standing nearby.

At Horace's elbow this morning—while the traffic on the quay increased—was the untidy figure of a man in rumpled clothes, whose hair stood in a cowlick at the crown of his head, and whose expression never changed from that of the utmost astonishment. Mouth open, eyes wide, Maven Flyce was nearly thirty years old, appeared thirteen (for the look of wonder on his face), and reacted to the entire world as if he had just been born.

"Gory, Hod!" he piped. "It sure is a choice morning!"

There was a ladder several feet away that reached to low tide, and Horace, leaning against his favorite piling, was gazing down the ladder's length, idly considering the shadow of a nearby boat, fractured on the surface of the water. He lifted his head to consider the truth of Maven's statement. Certainly the day was fine enough to draw the crowds that were his principal form of entertainment. The sun was warm on the back of his neck, and the southerly breeze was fresh in his face. "It will do," he said.

A stern-faced matron trundled past, and something haughtily unforgiving in her glance caused Horace to shiver slightly. Maven, who had no hat to tip or touch, inclined his head and raised a hand to an imaginary brim. The woman recoiled slightly, as if unsure of his meaning, and threw a dark frown in his direction. Maven made a sound like a frightened hiccough. With her own noise of dismissal the woman continued down the wharf. Twice she looked back, sure that she had been insulted somehow, and each time Maven let out a small sound of astonishment.

"So help me, Horace!" said Maven. "What was that?"

"Her expression did have a certain tone of voice," said Horace. He snickered quietly and, after a moment, declaimed the following:

> "A *stare from that one passing there,*
> *Could petrify the bravest spirit;*
> *On summer days it cools the air,*
> *And freezes anything that's near it.*"

Among his many unheralded talents, Horace possessed a gift for verse, though he was never a poet on demand. His rhymes seemed to form from thin air, find expression through his voice, and return to the ether unhindered by art and unrecorded for posterity.

"Honestly!" exclaimed Maven.

Movement and sound on the wharf increased with every minute. Sometimes Horace would laugh without explanation, and Maven, amazed, would search the crowd for something amusing; finding nothing, he would shake his head in honest wonderment and return his attention to the few swift clouds above, or the water lapping against the pilings below, or a particularly pretty face passing by.

A man sauntered through the press and approached Horace with a knowing smile. He would have been well-dressed if he had ever thought to wash his clothes. His teeth were a misfortune, his hair was matted beneath a dusty hat, and his face was dirty. But if he was dirty, his smile—somehow—was dirtier still. There was something beneath that smile, a hint of almost sinister potential. Horace himself was no model of public virtue, but standing next to this fellow he looked like a social aristocrat.

A barque with the name *Follow Me* at its bow lay at anchor several lengths out from the wharf, and Horace was watching as a boat was lowered from her near side. An inner sense must have told him of the newcomer's steady gaze, however, for he turned and looked the man in the eye, undisturbed by that distorted smile. "Adam," said Horace, with his own sly grin.

The man jingled something in his pockets. "There is an old fellow," he said, "would like to see you up on Martin's Point." His eyes didn't blink; his smile never shifted. He glanced once at Maven (whose mouth hung open) before resting his gaze on Horace.

"I'll get up and visit him," said Horace. He matched Adam's unblinking stare. Finally the man broke away and continued down the wharf.

"My goodness!" said Maven. "You sure do know a lot of people!" He was about to ask Horace about this exchange, but watching the man's unappealing swagger disappear into the crowd, he caught sight of something that straightened his posture.

A break in the immediate crowd revealed a statuesque, dark-haired beauty striding with confidence and grace toward them. Her head was up so that the brim of her elaborate hat did not shadow her dark eyes, which seemed to miss little of her surroundings. There was something of the patrician in her straight nose and the near-angularity of her face. Her mouth was wide, and set primly, though not lacking a modicum of humor.

Then the break in the crowd grew and a man was revealed at her side, escorting her, arm in arm. He was handsome, and though not short, still only a couple of inches taller than she. He was as dark and patrician; and to Maven's way of thinking, they made a striking couple.

"Goodness sakes!" said Maven, almost shouting. "Aren't they handsome!"

"They'll do," said Horace.

"Aren't you just surprised at the number of handsome people, Hod?"

"It does make the day pass quicker."

"Well, I certainly am surprised!"

"It surprises me to hear you say it," said Horace quietly.

Looking past Horace, Maven saw a new point of interest—a pretty green dress and a head of red hair that dazzled in the sunlight.

Horace, meanwhile, watched the boat from the *Follow Me* tunk against the pilings below; a portly gentleman with a valise in one hand was helped by the crew to the foot of the nearby ladder. Despite the roundness of his girth and the hindrance of his baggage, the fellow climbed with little difficulty, and was just making the top of the wharf when the redhead and the striking couple crossed paths in front of him.

Without warning, a sudden breeze lifted the gentleman's hat from his head, and Maven hollered as the fellow began to step out into thin air in an attempt to retrieve it.

A groom from Spurling's Livery arrived with the Underwoods' horse and carriage at ten o'clock and was combing Melody's brown mane when Cordelia and her parents emerged from their house and came down the front walk. The unexpected melancholy of the previous evening had proved too hesitant to take hold, and now it evaporated in the face of a bright July morning. The elm trees along the street sifted a light southerly breeze, the sun blinking through their shifting leaves.

The private residences on High Street, which they followed to the waterfront, bloomed (as did their own house) in reds, whites, and blues—flags, striped buntings, and patriotic symbols fluttered from doorposts and windowsills and trellises.

The carriage did not linger by these sights. Something in the air this morning dictated a brisk pace. There were mixed feelings amongst the Underwoods concerning their errand; it was natural that some regret would be attached to the claiming of Basil's last worldly possessions. But curiosity is not a low sensation, and the interest that they felt in the mystery of this unexpected delivery raised their mission above the merely sad.

James did not expect to find an empty hitching post in the vicinity of the Custom House; but commerce will solve what circumstance poses, and here commerce showed itself in the form of several enterprising boys, one of whom, for a short coin (that is, a nickel), would act as a migratory tether, watching horse and rig while keeping them from the flow of shifting traffic.

Leaving Melody and their carriage in the care of a boy whose gap-toothed smile engendered an instant trust, the Underwoods negotiated the crowded walk arm in arm. There were several temporary stalls along the way, and hawkers of silk scarves, and roasted peanuts, and penny-dreadfuls called to them as they passed. Gulls oared their wings overhead, catching the sun on their white backs and swooping past the wharfside tower of the Custom House.

Cordelia turned when they reached the dark oak doors, to gaze back at the activity on the wharf across the street. "Perhaps I'll walk along the wharf, Papa," she said, thinking that she had spent too much time, as of late, surrounded by walls.

"Do be careful, dear," said Mrs. Underwood, before her husband had the opportunity to consider the propriety of their daughter walking unescorted among the general press. Cordelia realized that her mother had cut short discussion and allayed James's inevitable doubts with four simple but elegantly placed words. Taking her mother's parasol, she hurried through the slow-moving traffic, pausing only to wave and smile from the other side of the street.

Feathered hats and bright parasols rose above the crowds like blooms reflecting the morning sun, but Cordelia's parasol hung unemployed upon her arm—the July light was too glorious. More than one hat was touched in her direction, and more than one head turned as she passed—but Cordelia, unaware of the latter, took the former as common civility. These gallant acknowledgments were, in truth, reflections of her smile, which itself was not common.

One young man, approaching through the crowd, evoked a corresponding admiration in Cordelia, and the presence of a beautiful woman on his arm did not discourage her from timing a potent glance in his direction. He had, indeed, caught sight of her already—and was, perhaps, preparing a glance of his own—when a singular event occurred in the dwindling space between them.

A rotund man of medium height and middle years climbed from a ladder to the surface of the wharf, and promptly lost his hat to a sudden and unheralded gust from the north. The light breeze had given no indication that headgear was in danger; this notwithstanding, some impish curl of wind met him at the summit of his climb and neatly lifted his hat into the air.

Reaching for the hat as it left his head, the portly fellow would have stepped off the wharf if not for Cordelia, who had the presence of mind to grab him by the elbow. She, in turn, found her own center of gravity suddenly over the harbor water, and was endeavoring to right herself with several wild arm movements, when another quick mind revealed itself and she was pulled, first by the back of her sash, then by her waist, to safer footing.

The handsome young man released Cordelia once she had regained her balance. He nodded with mock formality. "Thank you!" said she, stepping aside for foot traffic as onlookers recommenced their activities.

"My pleasure," said the young man, who did not suffer from close scrutiny—indeed, he was a list of good looks: dark brown eyes, a straight nose, strong jaw, and curly black hair. (Horace, still leaning against the nearby piling, thought it was the young fellow's pleasure indeed, and let out a short sneezelike laugh.)

"Thank *you!*" said the portly gentleman to Cordelia.

Cordelia laughed, one hand over her heart. "It's a wonder I didn't pull us both off." ("I was so surprised!" said Maven Flyce, though no one seemed to hear him.)

The portly man laughed with her. "If I hadn't attempted to walk on air . . . ! Sir," he said to the young man, who was backing away, "I am much indebted to you for rescuing this young lady to whom I am indebted."

The young man bowed again, and Cordelia was aware, suddenly, of the woman waiting for him a few feet away. The older man raised a hand to tip his hat before realizing it wasn't there. The woman smiled as her companion took her arm, expressing both humor and admonishment with the lift of an eyebrow. They disappeared amongst the pedestrians on the wharf.

He only glanced back once.

"I am indebted, miss," said the portly fellow, reaching in vain for his hat again. A remarkable jollity flashed behind his spectacles. One could believe that smiles came easily to his round face. He was in the flush of his middle age; his eyes were dark, and what small fringe of hair left to him was chestnut brown. He stood on short legs and his round shoulders shook when he laughed.

"Oh, dear," he chuckled, but his humor stopped short with an involuntary sound of pain when he turned to find his dropped valise. He stood precariously on one foot for a moment and waggled his right ankle.

"You've been hurt," said Cordelia, touching him gently on the shoulder. The man's pained expression disappeared as he regarded the beauty before him. The green eyes and slightly upturned nose, which was dusted with freckles, struck him first; then the moderate mouth lit with fine teeth, the delicate chin and dark eyebrows. From beneath a simple straw hat, her red hair had come loose on one side. She was small boned and the hand that she held up to him was slim and graceful.

"Oh, no, my dear," he assured her, "it's fine." But his smile had a wry quality to it as he tested the suspect ankle. Hoping to appear at ease, he bowed. "Tobias Walton, at your service."

"Cordelia Underwood, at yours," said she, not fooled by his gallant denial. She held her hand out and grasped his firmly. She had taken notice of the two men watching this scene just a foot or so away—one grinning candidly, the other staring openmouthed.

"Your hat's on its way," said Horace McQuinn.

"Excuse me?" said Mister Walton.

Horace pointed down at the water, and when they looked over the side of the wharf a swimmer was just reaching the ladder, the wayward hat between his teeth. In another minute a sailor—stripped to the waist, barefoot, and dripping—gained the top of the ladder.

"You have rescued my hat!" announced Mister Walton. "Why, I shall be indebted to the entire city before lunch." He took the proffered article and barely stopped himself from putting it soaking upon his head.

"Pardon me, ma'am," said the sailor, who seemed awkward, suddenly, with his lack of clothing. He glanced toward Horace, recognized him, and gave him a nod. Then he turned about and took a splendid dive from the wharf.

"Oh, my!" said Cordelia.

"Dear me," said Mister Walton. "I would have liked to have given him something for rescuing my hat."

"He should be careful," said Horace, peering after the diver. "There are old pilings down there."

There was nothing about either Horace or Maven that encouraged a reply from Cordelia, but Mister Walton waggled his wet hat, by way of salute, and said a cheery "Good day." In another moment he and the young woman were moving toward the street, chatting happily as if they had known each other for years. Mister Walton limped slightly, as they disappeared in the crowd.

"Well, I never!" exclaimed Maven, and he was quite sure that he hadn't.

Horace regarded his friend for some moments, gazing at Maven's extraordinary cowlick as if noticing it for the first time. Suddenly, he said:

> *"Maven's hair is quite the sight,*
> *Inspiring this unworthy sonnet;*
> *It adds six inches to his height,*
> *A shame to wear a hat upon it."*

"My land!" said Maven. "I don't know how you do it!"

"That fellow came as near as he could to swimming without getting wet," said Horace, his extemporized verse already forgotten.

"He was kind of baffled," suggested Maven.

"Now he's losing his baggage."

"What?"

"Forgot that bag of his," informed Horace.

Maven looked, but the valise was not where Mister Walton had left it.

"That young fellow seems to have taken a liking to it," said Horace, indicating with a slight incline of his head a ragamuffin figure disappearing with Mister Walton's valise into the passing crowd.

"Hey!" shouted Maven.

The boy turned his head and saw Maven with his neck craning and his cowlick waving in the air. The boy's jaw dropped and his eyes widened—then he was gone, the bag with him.

"Goodness sakes, Horace!" said Maven. "It's been clapped and run off with right under our eyes!"

"Why don't you go get it, Maven?" suggested Horace.

Maven's already wide eyes widened considerably. He stretched his head forward like an angry rooster and finished off this expression with his own rendition of a determined frown. Though he lived his life in a state of perpetual astonishment, Maven seldom astonished himself. He did just that, however, by wading into the crowd in pursuit of the thief.

"Pardon me," he said as he stepped on a sailor's foot, and "I'm very sorry," upon kicking the cane out from under an elderly gentleman, and "I can't tell you how doleful this makes me," when given a harsh glare from a matron whose feathered hat he had dislodged. His path through the traffic was punctuated with a sort of bobbing gait, so that Horace was able to monitor his friend's progress by continued sightings of Maven's cowlick.

Maven, by means of these vertical oscillations, was attempting to catch sight of his quarry; what he caught instead were inquisitive, even suspicious, glares from other pedestrians. A dog, fascinated with Mavin's eccentric progress, separated itself from its owner and barked at the pursuer's heels. The crowd thinned unexpectedly, and Maven had a brief glimpse of Mister Walton's valise dwindling before him just as he fell over a wheelbarrow.

He traveled in this conveyance for several feet, in the company of a large sow, before the stevedore trundling them dropped wheelbarrow and all in a shuddering halt and filled the air with waving arms and a cloud of foreign verbiage. Effusive with apologies, Maven attempted to shake the dog's teeth from his pant cuff, and shouted abruptly as the sow nudged him lovingly in a ticklish place.

"Haste causes difficulties," said Maven to himself, deciding that furtive creeping might win what speed and agility could not. So adopting a posture of stealth—head down, knees bent—he dragged the growling dog after him through the crowd.

Leaning against his piling, Horace continued to track Maven's activities by noting the migration of confusion and indignation down the length of the Custom House Wharf. He could not see exactly what transpired, but he could imagine well enough. A lad appeared, sent by Mister Walton to find his valise, and Horace told the fellow what he knew. He had little hope of the bag's recovery.

He was surprised, therefore, a good half an hour later, to see Maven emerge from the traffic on the quay with the valise in hand. His hair was wilder than before, and he was missing a good portion of one pant leg, but the look of wonderment on his face was as plain as ever.

"Gory, Hod!" said Maven. "I have never, I promise! I caught the bag and lost the thief! Goodness sakes! I had to explain the whole thing to a passing law officer! He made me pick up everything I knocked over!"

"Funny how people meet," said Horace McQuinn to a respectable-looking fellow who happened to stand, for a moment, beside him.

The man looked down his nose at Horace. "I haven't the slightest idea what you're talking about, sir."

"That's just what I mean," said Horace.

2. Pigs, Not Contraband

As James and Mercia stepped from the street into the Custom House, their senses were assailed by the thunder of business within. The smokes of many cigars and pipes were accumulated in a blue haze; and the shouts and orders that echoed in the cavernous interior had more the quality of the barking of dogs than the speech of men. To the unschooled eye, all was chaos—captains of ships and captains of industry coming and going between knots of gesticulating activity, inspectors mulling over cargo manifests or stamping documents with their official approval, messengers scurrying between correspondents.

There were lines before each of the clerk-windows, and James led the way across the marble tiles to the shortest of these.

"What *is* wrong, Mr. Underwood?" rose a voice above the general din. A figure separated itself from the crowd and approached James and his wife.

"Wrong, Mr. Pue?" asked James Underwood.

"Wrong," said that man. "Untoward. What is wrong with this establishment?"

James saw, now, that the question was academic. He smiled. "I have always found the Portland Custom House a model of efficiency, Mr. Pue—especially under the influence of your administration."

"You are very kind, sir," said Mr. Pue. "But you have not observed."

Nathaniel Pue, official customs inspector, was as neat a man as you could want for such a job—from his dress, to his posture, to the cut of his hair and the trim of his beard. He was not tall, but this attribute lent him an air of brevity that must be admired in any public official. He did not seem short, but compact. Somewhere between forty and fifty, he was a handsome man—carrying himself with the authority of the latter age, and looking the former, despite a hairline that had answered its own call to brevity.

James exchanged an amused glance with his wife and looked about the main room of the Custom House—at the marble countertops and tall, light-filled windows. For a moment, he was baffled; then he caught sight of the flags at either end of the room.

"You are not decked out, Mr. Pue," said Mercia, before James could speak.

"No Fourth of July bunting, Mr. Pue?" asked James.

"It's well you should ask," said the man. "Mr. Prie!"

"Yes, sir," said a young man, who stepped up to Mr. Pue's side.

"Mr. and Mrs. Underwood, here, have noticed a certain deficiency in our institution," informed Mr. Pue.

The young Prie did his best to hide his exasperation. "Yes, sir. The decorations have been ordered and should arrive within the hour."

"A model of efficiency, Mr. Underwood," said Mr. Pue, with some irony. He left his subordinate and led the way back to the hall. "Sir, ma'am—if you would come with me, I have kept your claim under my personal supervision. Mr. Prie, please send two of the boys to my office."

James turned for a moment, before following the customs inspector, and winked at Mr. Prie. The young man smiled, a short laugh escaping him.

"A governmental establishment should be festive on such an occasion, don't you think, Mr. Underwood?" wondered Mr. Pue as he led the way up the stairs.

"It does seem reasonable."

"He's a good lad." The inspector paused at the first landing and turned to regard them. "A cast-iron pot on one side of his head and a sieve on the other. He can remember the document number of a six-month-old manifest, and couldn't tell you what day of the week it is. Yes, Mr. Murning?"

A clerk standing at the bottom of the stairs said: "There is a discrepancy in one line item of the *Humboldt*'s cargo list."

"After working here awhile, Mr. Murning," said the inspector, "you will find that most manifests need some adjustment. If only a single item is off, then Captain Pelf has made a good account indeed. Does it amount to more than five percent of said item?" inquired the inspector.

Mr. Murning stared into his eyebrows in search of a calculation. Then his face cleared, and he said: "Yes, sir."

"Does it look like contraband?"

"Contraband?"

"Might he be harboring distillates—drink, man, alcohol!"

"It's pigs, sir."

"Pigs?"

"Small ones. Pound-wise it might not be more than five percent."

"What are you talking about, Mr. Murning?"

"There were three litters born since they left Charleston."

"Charleston pigs," said Mr. Pue, as if committing the phrase to memory.

"Pigs do have litters, don't they?" asked the clerk.

"You can't stop them, Mr. Murning. Record the discrepancy as *acquired in transit*."

"In transit?"

"It's either that or an *act of God*."

The clerk frowned and shook his head before hurrying back to his desk in the bustling main room. "Charleston pigs," said Mr. Pue again, before continuing up the stairs to the second floor. "One never knows, ma'am," he added, with a glance in Mercia's direction.

"I'm sure one doesn't, Mr. Pue."

Another clerk met the inspector at the door to his office. "The constable at Yarmouth has reported several crates, with the name *Castalanara* on them, washed up on the beach there."

"That will be the wreck off Cape Cod, last March. Take the first train down and make an accurate accounting. Find what sort of claim has been made for the registry." Having answered "Yes, sir," while his superior listed the details of his mission, the clerk hurried down the stairs.

"Will there be anything to claim?" asked the inspector as he ushered the Underwoods into his office ahead of him.

"I have no idea what's in the chest, Mr. Pue," said James. "It contains my brother's personal effects."

Mr. Pue nodded. "I met your brother, once. Under memorable circumstances. Yes, Mr. Prie?" he asked of the young man, who stood, out of breath, at the door.

"The decorations have arrived, Mr. Pue."

"Well, raise the flag! No, the flag is raised. Raise the bunting, then— or hoist it, or whatever you do."

"Yes, sir," replied the clerk, and he was gone.

"It's quiet here in the winter," averred the inspector. "There it is," he said, pointing.

The trunk stood under a tall window in the office; such a wandering object that it looked at home even in this temporary place. James had the fleeting fancy that Basil's sea chest would fit in any nook or corner that it briefly occupied, but that it would grow out of place the longer it remained in one spot. It was typical of its sort, but he imagined that he would recognize it amongst a hundred like it. Mr. Pue had placed it in plain view, not in a dimly lit corner, or behind a desk, but where it might hold court in his bright office. Looking past it, out the window, they could see Portland's Observation Tower on Munjoy Hill.

"Thought it must be your brother's. His initials are spelled out in brass studs on the top."

"Thank you," said James. "We appreciate your looking after it for us."

"Not at all. When I was a clerk, years ago, I was coming off a ship one night, after a day of reconciling a list of goods, and I heard a commotion in one of the holding sheds on the wharf. It wasn't very wise of me, but I was young, and I surprised three men rifling the unclaimed stowage. About as hard a looking crew as you would want to startle, and I was sort of sorry for it.

"Captain Underwood happened by just then. Poked his head in, saw what was about, and asked the three burglars for help with his trunks— calm as church on Sunday. They helped him, too. He gave them a lecture for a tip and sent them on their way. Wyatt Earp never handled himself with such ease. Got into his carriage and drove off without a backward glance.

"I was kind of worn out after that one. Never did get to thank him properly. Just sign right there, Mr. Underwood." Mr. Pue had found the proper document on his desk. He dipped his pen and handed it to James.

"Thank you, Mr. Pue," said James as he signed the paper. "I hadn't heard from my brother in a long time."

There was a sound of fluttering behind the inspector and he turned to see a stream of red, white, and blue rippling outside the window. "Ah, the bunting," said Mr. Pue. "Won't do without it. The holiday must be served. The lad can get some work done when he puts his mind to it, but I think he's in love."

"One never knows, Mr. Pue," said Mercia.

"I'm sure one doesn't, ma'am."

Cordelia watched with amused sympathy as Mister Walton took stock of his waterlogged hat. "Do you know of a good haberdasher, Mister Walton?"

"If Alfred Hill is still in business, yes."

"His son, I think."

"Ah, yes. Well, it has been some years." He elected to carry his hat in his hand, and continued to falter down the wharf on his sore ankle. Cordelia took his arm and managed to lend him support without appearing to do so. He was grateful for her assistance and not unconscious of the quiet manner in which she rendered it. It occurred to him then that, except for himself, she was without escort.

"My parents have business at the Custom House, Mister Walton," she said, seeming to read his mind.

"The wharfs can be a dangerous place, Miss Underwood. Why, when I was a lad, I once—"

"Oh, there's a scad of people about, and I'm not shy with this," she said, raising the point of her furled parasol. To several people, frowning suspiciously as they moved in the opposite direction, it looked quite like a weapon as she brandished it before her.

"I am sure," said Mister Walton with a smile.

"Besides, there are people like you . . . and that nice young man who kept me from falling overboard. I wish I had gotten his name." She looked back over her shoulder, as if she might catch sight of him. "You've been to Portland before, then?" she asked, when they came to the street.

"Oh, yes, my dear. I was born and raised here."

"Are you related to the Waltons who own the shoe factory?"

"I *am* the Walton whose family once owned the shoe factory."

"I'm wearing shoes from Walton's! Have you come back to visit your family?" asked Cordelia.

"As a matter of fact, my aunt died recently, and I have come back to decide what to do with the family estate."

They were crossing the street now, and Cordelia very nearly stopped at midstream to convey her condolence. "Oh, I am sorry. I didn't mean to pry."

"Not at all," insisted Mister Walton. He patted her hand as he urged her forward. Changing the subject, he said: "Your parents won't be alarmed, I hope, seeing you on the arm of a strange man."

"Oh, Mister Walton," she said with a laugh—a reaction he found cryptic and, yet, somehow pleasing. The truth was that he was so amiable, with his cheery smile and deep chuckle, his rolling gait (hindered now by injury), his round face with honest brown eyes appearing large behind thick spectacles—he was so unclelike, even fatherly, that the thought of anyone being alarmed at the sight of him made her laugh. Her laughter was infectious, and he laughed as well, the very innocence of which delighted her.

It wasn't till they reached the carriage that Mister Walton remembered his valise. Cordelia would have gone back for the bag herself, but he insisted on paying the boy who had been watching the Underwoods' horse and carriage to retrieve it.

While they waited for this mission to be completed—Mister Walton seated on a nearby bench and Cordelia holding the horse's bridle—two men emerged from the Custom House with the sea chest. Followed by Cordelia's parents and Mr. Pue, they descended the steps to the street and carried the trunk to the back of the carriage.

"Mama, Papa," called Cordelia from the mare's side. James and Mercia were surprised to find her tending the horse, but she gave them little opportunity to ask questions. "I want you to meet Mister Walton," she said; then: "Oh, Mister Walton, don't get up. Your ankle."

"Oh, not at all," he said and, rising from the bench, extended a hand to James, who shook it with polite firmness. "I'm pleased to meet you, sir," said Mister Walton. "Your daughter saved me from going overboard."

"He lost his hat," said Cordelia.

Since he was holding a hat, albeit still in a wet condition, it seemed proper to explain. "It went overboard," he said.

"A sailor from one of the ships brought it to him," said the young woman. "There was a nice young man who kept me from falling off the wharf."

"A very capital fellow, I am sure," assured Mister Walton.

"And Mister Walton has hurt his ankle. And he forgot his valise."

None of this was very illuminating to Cordelia's parents, and their bemused expressions indicated the confusion caused by such a bewildering string of unconnected detail.

"Good heavens!" said Mister Walton, chortling happily. "I've been a complete disaster since stepping on dry land!"

The sight of the portly gentleman, so pleased with his disastrous state, caused Cordelia to almost shout with laughter. James and Mercia smiled themselves, so disarming was Mister Walton's humor over his own misfortune. "Oh, good heavens!" he said again, still laughing.

"Is it Mister Walton, of the shoe factory, then?" asked Mr. Pue. "Jacob Walton's son?"

"Yes, sir," said Mister Walton, wiping tears from his eyes. "I am pleased to meet you."

"Nathaniel Pue," said the inspector. "Shall I hail a carriage for you? Perhaps you would like to have that ankle looked at."

"That is quite all right, Mr. Pue," said James Underwood. "We should be glad to take Mister Walton wherever he needs to go."

"Oh," he said, waving a hand. "I have been far too much trouble to your lovely daughter already."

"It's no trouble at all," said Mercia. She was quite taken with him.

"All tied in then, sir," said one of the workmen. He tugged experimentally at the ropes that held the chest to the back of the carriage, and nodded, satisfied.

"Now, where is your valise?" said Cordelia, still holding the horse's bridle. The boy was crossing the street without Mister Walton's bag, his expression apologetic as he approached them.

"The fellow on the wharf says a kid took it," he said simply.

"Not a goat, I'm sure you mean," said Mr. Pue, who was a stickler for accuracy.

The boy tossed him a frown. "He says his friend chased after him."

"Who is this fountain of information?" wondered Mr. Pue.

"Mr. McQuinn."

"Oh, well, then. I daresay, nothing much gets past Horace McQuinn." The boy shrugged profoundly.

"Are you still at your family's place, Mister Walton?" asked the inspector.

"Why, yes, I am."

"Well, I know where that is—and if your bag shows up, I'll have it sent to you."

"I am very much obliged."

"Should we talk to this McQuinn fellow, and see what else he knows?" wondered James.

"No, no," said Mister Walton. "It's taken up far too much of everybody's time already."

"Here you are, son." James put a generous coin in the boy's palm.

"The gentleman's already paid me," said the boy.

James merely waved a hand, and unlooped the reins from the knob on the carriage headboard. The boy tipped his hat and scurried across the busy street. The ladies climbed in; then Cordelia and her father helped Mister Walton onto the front seat.

"We should look after that ankle of yours, Mister Walton," said Mercia.

"I really do believe it's getting better," said he.

"Mr. Pue," said James, with a salute.

"Happy Independence Day to you," said the inspector.

"I am so glad for your bunting," said Mercia, as Melody picked up the shake of the reins and the carriage pulled away from the curb. Mr. Pue and the two workmen watched them disappear in the traffic.

"A kid *might* have taken the man's valise," said the inspector to no one in particular. "Goats will eat anything."

3. An Almost Empty House

"I'M SO SORRY ABOUT YOUR AUNT, MISTER WALTON," said Mercia Underwood as James pulled the carriage up to the walk that led to the front door of the Walton family home.

"Thank you," he replied. "I wish you could have known her—she was such a grand lady. She lived a full life, though, and passed quietly, I am told. I am only sorry that I wasn't with her when she died."

"Are you celebrating the Fourth with anyone?" inquired James. "We're picnicking in Freeport with Mercia's aunt Delia, and there is sure to be plenty of good food to go around."

Mister Walton was touched by the offer. "Oh, you are too kind. But I couldn't impose upon your generosity any further."

"Not at all, sir," said James.

"Nonsense, Mister Walton," said Cordelia.

"Mister Walton may have other plans," said Mercia, patting her daughter's knee. "But if you find yourself at the fairgrounds in Freeport, Saturday noontime, I hope you watch for us, and join us for lemonade and a sandwich."

"I will most certainly, ma'am," he said as he stepped down to the street. His ankle seemed much better now. With heartfelt thanks, he waved goodbye and watched, with an unexpected pang of regret, as Mr. Underwood turned the carriage about and shook Melody's reins. He had grown to like these generous people during his short acquaintance with them, and especially felt a paternal fondness for Cordelia, who turned and waved one last time as they drove out of sight around the next corner.

So Mister Walton came home with little more than his wet hat in his hands and the key to the front door in his pocket. His stomach grumbled as he turned up the walk.

The house on Spruce Street was an example of the Federal style—his father, Jacob, had once termed it "modestly grand"—a brick building, with gardens along the south and east walls. Except for the black wreath on the front door, it was little changed since Mister Walton had last seen it; the lawn had recently been trimmed, and the flowers of early summer were bright in the midday sun. Mr. and Mrs. Baffin, who had been in the employ of his family for as long as he could remember, lived now on the other side of town, but had continued, obviously, to watch over the grounds and keep house.

He paused on the walk, momentarily disheartened by the prospect of seeing his family home uninhabited for the first time since it had been built. Until now, there had always been someone to greet him—his parents, his sister (before she went to Africa), his aunt. He turned and looked back at the street: the tops of the elm trees shifted with the breeze; a robin bobbed quickly on the lawn and flew off.

It occurred to Mister Walton, while turning the key in the lock, that he had never had to let himself in in this fashion. The tumblers boomed in the tall oak door and, swinging it open, he was conscious of an echoing space in the hall beyond, though it was as filled with a stairway, a hat rack, an umbrella stand, and two chairs as it had ever been. A great wave of memory met him as he caught the scent of waxed floors and polished furniture. Long-stilled voices rushed to greet him like lonely friends, and he was suddenly filled with a sympathetic melancholy for these phantoms.

He closed the door behind him, and could not keep himself from one small (and, perhaps, superstitious) greeting. "Halloo," he said quietly to the empty house. Dust—stirred by the movement of the door and a brief exposure to the day's light breeze—ascended in graceful spirals, lit by a shaft of light that slanted from an unseen window in the upstairs hall. Mister Walton half-expected someone to appear at the head of the stairs.

Hanging his wet hat in the hall, he moved into the noiseless parlor, where the drapes were closed and the resulting shadow breathed with a strange chill. The old folk were still here somehow. He could almost see them; certainly he could sense them—his father in his chair by the window with his head buried in a book, his mother crafting mittens or tatting doilies by the fireplace—and he was in the midst of conjuring these images (and doing so with such a degree of success that goosebumps rose on his forearms) when an unidentifiable sound came from the further precincts of the house.

Mister Walton's eyes, already wide behind his spectacles, were larger yet with an unpleasant thrill as he paused in midstep and keened his ear. *Perhaps*, he thought, *it was a mouse*. True, it hadn't sounded like a mouse; and if it was a mouse, it was a particularly large one. Strange, that his old familiar home could seem so uncanny to him; that a single creak of an aging timber, or bang of a loose shutter, could paralyze him so. He was poised on one foot; his mouth was open and his shoulders were hunched in fear. He forced himself to relax, scoffing at these whim-whams.

Then came the sound again, this time more definitely. Someone had shut the door to a cupboard—a pantry cupboard, he would vow. The noise, a seeming ghost of life in this silent place, brought back all his gooseflesh and petrification. Was this a ghost indeed; or a thief, unaware of being heard in his search for felonious gain? *Well,* thought Mister Walton, *if a ghost, better to meet it; if a thief, better to frighten him away.*

"Halloo?" he questioned the rear portion of the house, but the word sprang out in an apprehensive squeak. He listened for a moment, then said "Halloo?" again, with more of his natural voice.

Something like a low human utterance reached his ears, and Mister Walton crept forward, cringing at the complaint of a noisy floorboard. The room that in later years Aunt August had used for a bedroom was just behind the parlor, and he stood in this doorway, peering through the draped gloom to the hall beyond. He heard footsteps now, and was tempted to retrace his path with greater speed than he had originally taken it.

"Who is there?" came an uncertain voice behind him, and despite his lack of height, Mister Walton came within an inch of hitting the top of the door frame as he jumped with fright. He landed a full one hundred and eighty degrees opposite the position from which he had taken off and nearly repeated this gymnastic feat at the sight of a head suspended in the doorway to the front hall. He let out two whooshing gasps in the midst of his physical gyrations, and was barely heartened by a similar sound emanating from the face in the doorway.

It occurred to him then that the head was not disembodied (which had been his first impression) but attached to a form that was crouched in similar fright behind the door frame. "Master Toby?" came a familiar voice, and the bent form of Cedric Baffin, the Walton family's ancient retainer, established itself beneath the gray head.

"Mr. Baffin?" said Mister Walton with a gust of relief.

"Master Toby?" came the question again. Cedric Baffin stepped cautiously into the parlor and peered through the gloom to be sure of his eyes.

"Mr. Baffin," said Mister Walton, "I cannot tell you how grateful I am for the sight of you." He actually laughed then—partly with relief, partly with joy at seeing the old fellow, and partly with a hilarity that shook from the foundation of his great heart as he imagined the figure he must have cut, pirouetting his stoutness in midair.

"Toby! Toby!" shouted the elderly servant. He embraced Mister Walton where they met in the middle of the parlor. "Lucinda said you'd be home soon!"

"How is Mrs. Baffin?"

"Suffering from the rheumatism, I fear. Rather more than she lets on, as you might guess."

"Yes, of course."

"Ah, young Toby, let me look at you! Are you just back, then?"

"Yes, but I hadn't expected anyone to be in the house. The door was locked."

"I came in by the back, you see."

Mister Walton laughed again to think of the fright he had just experienced. Mrs. Baffin, it seems, had been prescient in her expectation of his arrival and for the past week had been sending a basket of food each day so that *young Toby* might not be greeted with an empty larder. Mister Walton was greatly moved (the more so since the Baffins were no longer in the employ of his family) and doubly gratified when Mr. Baffin led the way to the kitchen and laid out a plate of cold meat, warm bread, pickled beets, and a slice of strawberry pie.

Cedric Baffin sat at the table next to his young Toby and watched delightedly while each morsel disappeared. He told Mister Walton of recent news and local gossip — of the strange incident of the highwayman on Vaughan Bridge and the next-door neighbor's visiting cousins, of the riot that nearly destroyed the Saco Town Hall and the recent ordinances passed to discourage the smuggling of demon rum — and whenever he was momentarily stumped for something to say, he would simply repeat: "Well, Lucinda said you'd be coming home soon."

"She is a fine woman!" said Mister Walton with great sincerity as he sized up the piece of pie before him. "And the house! Dear me, Mr. Baffin, you must be spending as much time at it as ever."

"Well, Toby, things shouldn't go to seed."

Mister Walton leaned back in his chair and took a deep breath. He felt both hurt and joy in his heart; to come home to an almost empty house, to see these rooms without the warm presence of his family, but to be greeted by this beloved friend, and now to have Mrs. Baffin's famous cooking placed before him — it all rushed in upon him in a disorder of emotion, and tears came to his eyes before he knew what he was about.

Old Cedric smiled, but a tear showed on his own cheek and he felt no shame for it. He put his hand over Mister Walton's and they sat for some moments nodding and smiling and wiping their eyes.

4. The Sea Chest

"YOU HAVEN'T WASTED ANY TIME," said Cordelia. She had half-expected some sort of ceremony to commemorate the opening of Uncle Basil's sea chest. Instead, she and her mother found James in the parlor with the trunk flung open, and the first of its revealed contents in small piles at his feet.

"I'm sorry," said her father. "Should I have waited for you?" He looked up from a bundle of letters. They had been tied together with a red ribbon, which lay now, with the loose envelopes, on his lap. James filed through these, noting the postmarks and the handwriting.

"Are those from us?" asked Cordelia. She and Mercia stood each to one side of his chair and looked over his shoulder.

"Some of them, yes. Look at this one. From the handwriting, which is mine, and the date of the postmark, I would guess that this carries news of your birth."

"Oh, really? You wrote to Uncle Basil about me?"

"Of course I did."

"He kept all his correspondence?" wondered Mercia.

"A good deal of it, at any rate; there are four more bundles of letters in there. Now whose handwriting is that?" James lifted an envelope past his shoulder and his wife took it from him.

"It's a woman's hand," she said. "Postmarked from Hallowell. Whom do we know in Hallowell?"

"Or, more to the point," suggested Cordelia, "whom did Uncle Basil know in Hallowell?"

Her mother flipped the envelope over several times, as if some clue might reveal itself. "Hallowell—that's near Augusta, isn't it."

Mercia had given up the envelope, and now James looked at it, front and back, several times over. "Hmm," he added, after several silent moments. Clearly curiosity was tugging at him.

"Should we read it?" Cordelia asked.

"I wonder why Basil had Mr. Stimply pack these letters." James fidgeted with the envelope absently. "Perhaps, in his sickness, he didn't remember that this was among them."

"Do you suppose there are others?" wondered Cordelia. It wasn't entirely admirable, she knew, but she felt no compunction about opening the letter and reading its contents.

James slipped the envelope back amongst its companions and laid the unwrapped letters on the round lamp table beside his chair. "Let's see what else we have," he said, and leaned over the trunk again.

This time he produced three fat books, looked about for a place to put them, and, finding none, handed them to his daughter. They had the look of hard use—their covers battered and indented, their pages brown with age and dampness and sea salt. Cordelia cocked her head and peered at their bindings, but any information once printed there was now worn away.

"*The Anatomy of Melancholy*," she read aloud from the title page of the first book. Her mother looked over her shoulder.

"Ah," said Mercia, "Robert Burton. Your uncle could quote from this at length."

" '*So oftentimes it falls out a great book is a great mischief,*' " quoted James, showing his own familiarity with the volume in question without looking up from the depths of the trunk. He lifted a box made of dark wood into the lamplight. It was as long as his forearm and perhaps a foot wide; the light behind him shone upon its smooth surface with a warm luster. The initials *B.U.* were inlaid in black upon the top.

"These will be his Navy Colts," he said. He shot the hasps at the front of the box and raised the lid. Two long-barreled pistols lay in their own impressions on a bed of dark velvet. James lifted one, ascertained that the chamber was empty, then weighed it thoughtfully in his hand.

Cordelia set the first book on a table beside the sofa and inspected the second volume. "*The Life and Opinions of Tristram Shandy, Gentleman,*" she read from the title page.

"That was your uncle's favorite book," said her father.

"Really?" She flipped through its pages with interest.

"Yes, and not to be yours, I hope."

"Really!" she said again, with more interest still. "Is it as bad as all that?"

James laid the Colt back in its box and looked up to consider this.

"You've read it?" inquired his daughter.

"Yes, I have."

Cordelia made a silent O with her mouth and laid the book aside.

A strange object covered in green, white, and yellow beads came out of the trunk next. It was the size and shape of an acorn squash, with one small flat surface on which it could be set without rolling. It seemed a sort of receptacle—a fancy jar, perhaps—but James searched in vain for a way to open it. Something rattled within it when he tipped it.

"A musical instrument," was Mercia's guess.

"Perhaps," replied a skeptical James. He shook it carefully. "It's not very musical." Indeed, whatever rattled inside the object sounded like dice in a cup.

"A percussion instrument," ventured Cordelia. She took the beaded globe and perused it with a frown. She placed it against her ear and tipped it slowly from side to side. "It must be," she said, finally. "I can't think of anything else." Her mother took a turn with the thing next, while Cordelia picked up the third book, and her father reached back into the trunk.

"*The Pickwick Papers*," said Cordelia, with a note of warm familiarity. It pleased her that she and her uncle had had a favorite book in common.

Mercia set the odd object on the floor beside James's chair and peered into the trunk. She unraveled a small roll of fabric and lifted a small figurine into the light. "Ivory," she said, and passed her fingertips over the smooth cream-colored surface.

The statuette was of a young woman, dressed in the high fashion of the previous century. The details of her face were not entirely articulated, and yet she wore a definite smile—a coy smile, perhaps—and the suggestion of her features, and of her expression, were so masterfully rendered to give the observer the impression of seeing more than was materially there. The little figure held a fan modestly over her bosom.

Mercia handed the statuette to her daughter. There was something libertine about the figure (despite the coy expression and the demure attitude) which quietly pleased Cordelia. "Was Uncle Basil a Romantic at heart?" she asked.

"Is there any other place to be one?" replied her father dryly. "Now what is this?" He took from a corner of the chest a small envelope with his name, brown with time and distance, written on it in Basil's hand. It looked the sort of enclosure one would send with a gift, and perhaps, thought James, that was just what it was—attached to these artifacts of his brother's life.

He opened the envelope, slipped a card from it, and frowned at what was written there. His mouth formed a word that Cordelia could not apprehend.

"Whatever can that mean?" said Mercia, who was reading over her husband's shoulder.

"Minmaneth," said James, as if trying to recall an indistinct memory.

"What is it?" asked Cordelia, her curiosity peaking. Her father handed the card to her. In Basil's plain and steady hand, it said:

Our Minmaneth is a young goatt.

"Well, that certainly clears the matter up," said Cordelia.

"I am glad you think so," said her father.

"What is Minmaneth?" asked Mercia.

"Who, really," said James. "It was a game we played when we were young. Minmaneth was a figure from an ancient legend that our mother used to tell us. I haven't thought of him for years."

"Was he a young goat, then?" asked Cordelia.

"He wasn't a goat at all. In fact, I don't remember that the story had anything to do with goats."

"Did Basil like mysteries?" wondered Mercia.

"No more than you or I, I suspect. "No," said James, reaching into the chest again. "I fear this is simply a symptom of Basil's fever."

"That would explain the second *t* in goat," suggested Cordelia. She did not feel that the issue was properly explained, however, and her face showed it. She looked up from the cryptic sentence to gauge her father's expression, but his face was hidden behind a long, legal-looking piece of paper. She leaned forward and read the word *Deed* on the back of the document. Her mother hovered close beside him, scanning the paper with a look of surprise. James watched his wife while she read, and when she was finished, she turned and looked at her daughter.

"What is it?" asked Cordelia.

"It's a deed," said her mother.

Cordelia had already discerned this much. "A land deed?"

"Yes," said her father. "Quite a large tract of land in the interior part of the state." He folded the document once and held it out to his daughter. "It all looks proper and legal, drawn up by an American law firm with a branch office in Caracas. Your uncle has signed it, but it has been made out in your name."

5. Enter Ephram, Eagleton, and Thump

THE GLORIOUS FOURTH WAS APPROACHING, and—while Mister Walton settled himself in his family home, and Cordelia Underwood read the first chapters of *Tristram Shandy*—Mr. Ephram, Mr. Eagleton, and Mr. Thump (of the Exeter Thumps) were gathered not far distant from any of these people, and they were in a state of genial enthusiasm. Bachelors all, they had met and had been meeting at the Shipswood Restaurant every Thursday night for fifteen years—and for fourteen years they had joined together in Fourth of July revelry.

Enthusiasm, indeed, was a byword for them, and they entered into whatever events and observed whatever entertainments the holiday offered with a sort of masculine robustness that quite pleased the older ladies. But this, their fifteenth Fourth as a trio, promised a level of excitement previously unmatched—thanks to a seemingly insignificant discovery on the part of Mr. Thump.

It is interesting to note that these three men—each hovering around the age of thirty-nine—had as little in common, beyond their age and family fortunes, as three men could.

Mr. Ephram (the beneficiary of a highly successful cartographic company) collected timepieces, Mr. Eagleton (the scion of prosperous jewelers) was an amateur meteorographer, and Mr. Thump (whose father had formed one of Portland's flourishing shipping firms) enjoyed contemplating the art of sailing.

Ephram was a Baptist, Eagleton a Methodist, Thump an Episcopalian.

Ephram was a Democrat, Eagleton a Republican, and Thump a Greenback Silver Standard Bearer despite the party having more or less dissolved ten years before.

They were of different heights, breadths, facial features, and preferred tailors. Ephram (the tallest) wore a large pair of dark mustaches to go with his gray suits, Eagleton went clean-shaven and wore tan suits, and Thump (the shortest) wore black and was facially inundated by a great explosion of brown beard and mustaches.

They even read separate newspapers: Ephram searching for truth in the *Eastern Argus*, Eagleton sure that he found it in the *Portland Daily Advertiser*, and Thump quite pleased to find whatever he could in the *Portland Courier*. It was Thump, in fact, who caused the enthusiasm aforementioned by reading aloud an item from his preferred organ.

Harriet Beecher Stowe had died the day before—the papers, all the papers, were full of news concerning the accomplishments of her life and the details of her passing. The three friends had spent some of the evening contemplating the great lady in silence as they ate, and the rest of the evening reading to one another what their respective journals had to say concerning the authoress.

Meaning no disrespect to the departed, Thump briefly changed the subject (and thereby changed the tenor of the entire evening) by reading from a short item that described the formation of a club in Portsmouth—the Bywater Club.

If ever these three men held anything in common, it was the thought that simultaneously dawned upon them while Thump idly read this item aloud. Once finished with the article, he lowered the *Portland Courier* and looked to his acquaintances, who (in turn) were looking at him and each other.

"A club," said Ephram.

"Indeed," said Eagleton.

"What?" said Thump.

"What, indeed!" said Ephram.

"Most certainly!" said Eagleton.

"A club!" said Thump.

And thus it was decided—they would be a club, or they would have a club, or they would form one—whatever it was you did with a club, they would do it. It was a magnificent idea, and if the State of Maine had not prohibited the sale and drink of alcohol they might have raised a toast. Ephram clapped the table with the palm of his hand several times, applauding this stroke of sagacity.

"Where shall we meet?" wondered Eagleton, who was precise in his wondering. His questions were often to the point.

"Why, here," suggested Thump cautiously.

"Here?" said Eagleton.

"The Shipswood?" said Ephram.

"Well," said Thump with a defensive frown.

"The Shipswood!" shouted Eagleton, so that nearby patrons looked up from their meals to see what the noise was about. "Of course, Thump," he said in a smaller tone.

"Well," said that worthy, his expression clearing.

"Wonderful," said Ephram. "The Shipswood it is."

"Yes, sir," said a waiter, who paused at their table with their menus.

"When shall we meet?" pursued Eagleton, when the waiter was gone.

Thump leaned back in his chair. The eyes of the other two men were on him—they weighed upon him with their expectation: he had, after all, come up with a place for them to meet; he had, without a doubt, engendered the whole capital idea with his timely reading from the *Portland Courier*. Thump wondered if he had run out of inspiration, when an answer occurred to him. "We could . . ." he began.

"Yes?" said Ephram.

Thump frowned with concentration, but because of his extraordinary beard, Ephram and Eagleton had to lean forward to see his expression. The effect was that of two birds of prey searching out their next meal, but Thump was unshaken.

"What?" asked Eagleton.

"Do you think?" wondered Ephram.

Thump raised an eyebrow.

"Yes," said Ephram.

"Of course!" shouted Eagleton.

"Thursday night!" said Ephram.

"Ha, ha!" laughed Thump. He banged the table, then glanced about uncertainly.

"A club," said Ephram, not to be disconcerted by public scrutiny.

"What sort of club shall it be?" wondered Eagleton.

"What sort?" asked Ephram.

"What sort of club? What sort is this Portsmouth group?"

Thump referred to his paper. "A merchants' club, it seems."

"Hmm," said Eagleton. "Won't do for us."

"What sort," said Ephram, as if to himself.

Thump shrugged elaborately, and they did not press him. The answer to this question was not so easily gotten. It could not be a trade guild: being of independent means, they had no trade between them. It could not be a religious brotherhood: their churches, they were told, were quite separate on matters of doctrine. It certainly could not be political in nature: not with a major election raising its disuniting head in the fall.

Thump looked down at his menu. "What sort," he mused.

It was a silent meal. Thump, with his perspicacity, had gotten himself into something of a corner, the two sides of which were ably represented by the expectations of his comrades. He hardly tasted his meal (which was scrod) and ate with an attitude of abstraction.

Ephram (who dined on roast beef) and Eagleton (curried lamb) did their best not to watch their friend as he thoughtfully chewed his food. An answer to this third question was not forthcoming, however, and—like the proverbial teapot—seemed to delay itself the more for being anticipated.

"Well, a club," said Ephram, after the check had come and the bill had been paid, and the three of them were retrieving their jackets and accoutrements from the cloakroom.

"Yes," said Thump, disappointed in missing the hat trick. "What sort, though."

"Well," said Eagleton, "we'll meet as a club whether we have *sorted* it out or not." He was the wag of the trio. They were outside now, pausing on the top step to take stock of the evening. "Expected fair tomorrow," said Eagleton, looking up at the night sky.

"Six and a half minutes past nine," said Ephram, consulting his watch.

"High water at 4:48 A.M." said Thump, though not with his usual enthusiasm.

"The Fourth is on Saturday," said Ephram, as they descended the steps. "Day after tomorrow, you know."

"Ah, yes," said Thump.

"Where shall we meet?" wondered Eagleton. "Deering Oaks again?"

"Balloon ascension at Freeport," said Ephram; he shook out his paper, and by the light of the street lamp outside the Shipswood he read: " 'Mrs. *Roberto — in an attractive suit of tights — will repeat her popular 2,500-foot parachute jump from an ascended balloon.' "*

"Good heavens!" said Eagleton. He looked at Ephram's *Eastern Argus* to see for himself.

This news revived Thump considerably, and it was decided that they would celebrate the Fourth in Freeport. The 7:00 A.M. Express out of Union Station was chosen as their mode of transportation, and they shook hands, parting in three different directions.

As they walked home, Ephram, Eagleton, and Thump each did his best to contemplate the sad departure of Harriet Beecher Stowe and the great effect she had had on the abolition of slavery. We should not harshly judge them, however, if these instructive thoughts were sometimes interrupted by visions of the brave Mrs. Roberto in her attractive suit of tights.

Book Two
JULY 3, 1896

6. A Deafening Silence Hushed by the Smell of Bacon Frying

It had been a long night for Mister Walton, alone in the old residence. He had insisted that Mr. Baffin set out for home well before dark, and even managed to hail a cab for him, while they walked a ways together down Spring Street.

Once he returned to the house, however, he regretted the loss of Cedric's company, and he spent the evening restlessly pacing from room to room. His own steps were loud in his ears, the rooms all too familiar in their furnishings and all too strange in their lack of population. Another person at the other end of a house can give the entire structure life; one person alone makes a home large in its emptiness and loud in its silence.

Mister Walton gazed at the backs of books in the study, shuffled through stereopticon slides in the parlor, and listened intently to scurryings in the kitchen walls. In the parlor he sat for a while in his mother's favorite chair and paged through an old album of tintypes. He wondered about his sister—who was in Africa, the last he knew. He thought about his brother, lost off Cape Hatteras. He wandered into the front hall, where he could converse with ancestors framed in ranks along the stairway.

He had gone upstairs with a cup of warm milk, found a nightshirt in the bureau in his old bedroom, and climbed beneath the covers, weary and sad. Mr. Baffin had told him of Aunt August's last months, and Mister Walton drifted off, thinking of her and wishing, for the thousandth time, that he had been closer to home when she had taken ill. He slept the entire night, but dreamed contrarily that he was wakeful, that people whom he could only vaguely see were dragging heavy objects through the room, scraping huge chests along the floor and bumping massive furniture against the doorjambs. It was several minutes after he woke the next morning before he realized that he had indeed slept through the night, though he did not feel very rested.

He sat for a while in bed, feeling logy, regarding the little hills that his feet made under the covers and wiggling his toes. He got his spectacles from the nightstand beside his bed and put them on. He regarded his feet again.

For a moment, he thought that the smell of cooking wafted from the kitchen below; perhaps he was still dreaming, after all. He breathed a deep stretching breath and the aroma of bacon caught his attention fully. "Of course," he said aloud, and bounded from bed, the restive night instantly forgotten.

He could move quickly for a portly man, and was half-dressed before a knock at the door announced Mr. Baffin, who carried a basin of warm water. He had never in his life been so grateful for such a simple amenity, and he splashed happily as he shaved and washed his face.

Mrs. Baffin was taking a pan of biscuits from the oven when Mister Walton trotted into the kitchen, and she nearly dropped them in her eagerness to embrace him. "We took a carriage in first thing," she said, eyes brimming. "I could hardly sleep last night, just waiting to look at you." There was a slight burr in Lucinda's speech, redolent of the Nova Scotian coast, where she had spent her girlhood. Her husband came in with some fresh strawberries, purchased from a peddler who had been passing by, and laid them on the table beside Mister Walton's breakfast. The Baffins had already breakfasted at home, but Mister Walton insisted that they sit with him and have a cup of coffee.

The back door and the kitchen windows were open to the promise of another gently warm day, and the song of a sparrow could be heard in the tall oak behind the house. An overwhelming sense of gratitude filled Mister Walton up to the top of his balding pate, and he found that he could not stop smiling as he ate the large breakfast that Mrs. Baffin had cooked for him.

Three-quarters of an hour had passed in this fine manner, with genial talk and a soft breeze and birdsong, when Horace McQuinn appeared at the back door.

"Good morning," said Mister Walton; then, recognizing Horace from the day before, he rose from the table and went to the door. "Well, goodness sakes! It's the gentleman from the wharf. How may I help you?"

"Morning," said Horace. "I think I have something here for you." He lifted the missing valise into view.

"Why, my goodness sakes!" exclaimed Mister Walton. "My bag! Come in. Come in." He stepped up to the door and shook the newcomer's hand. "Tobias Walton, and I am at your service, sir."

"Horace McQuinn," said the man. As he entered the kitchen, he brought with him the acrid scent of tobacco, which hung about his clothes and his person, and clung to his hands with a tenacity that any *eau de cologne* would have envied. He handed Mister Walton his valise, then nodded to Cedric and Lucinda.

"Have you had breakfast, Mr. McQuinn?" asked Mister Walton. He ushered the man to the kitchen table, but Horace preferred to stand beside the stove.

"I don't tend toward breakfast these days," he said. "But that coffee smells likable." In another moment he was leaning against the kitchen counter, coffee in hand, as if he'd done it all his life; and from this vantage he commenced his tale of the prodigal valise—which was more or less accurate.

"It has been a terrific inconvenience to you," insisted Mister Walton.

"Oh, it was nothing," said Horace with a wave of his hand. He took a drink of his coffee and smacked his lips.

"I would like to give you something for your trouble," said Mister Walton. He was reaching into his vest pocket for some coins.

Horace made a face and waved his hand again. "Oh, ridiculous," he said, and "No, no, no," when Mister Walton tried to press him with a reward. He pushed the offer away with his hand, saying:

> *"Wise men all around the world*
> *Are met on one accord:*
> *An honest favor asks no prize;*
> *It is its own reward."*

Mister Walton thought on this. "I like that very much. Who wrote that?"

"I don't think anybody's written it yet." Horace made a sound that Mister Walton first took to be a wheezing cough, but the man was only laughing with a short snicker.

In the next moment, Mister Walton understood Horace's meaning and laughed himself. "You don't think anybody's written it yet," he repeated as he chuckled, patting Horace's shoulder.

"Good coffee," said Horace, by way of thanks. He set his cup in the sink and saluted the Baffins with a nod before turning to leave. "Glad to meet you folk."

Mister Walton followed him to the back door. "If there's ever anything I can do for you, Mr. McQuinn . . ." he began.

Horace paused for a moment with his back turned. He had sized up his man. He turned slowly, his face filled with the expression of someone who doesn't like to ask, but . . . "Well," he said slowly. "There is one thing, if you were to know how to drive a rig."

"Why, yes," said Mister Walton. "I can drive a rig."

Horace rubbed his chin. He had even shaved for this occasion. "I've got a sore shoulder, you see, and it hurts to chuck the reins. I drove over, you know, to drop off your bag, but I've got to go up to the Mariners' Hospital, you see, and . . ."

"Say no more. Say no more." Mister Walton raised his hand like a defendant being sworn in. "Just give me a moment to get my coat."

The rig that waited for them was a large wagon with crude sides built like a split-rail fence. A gray mare—indeed, an old gray mare—stood sleepily in the harness and gave no visible notice when the two men climbed onto the rough bench that served as a seat. It took Mister Walton something of a running jump to secure his position at the reins, and then he had an uncomfortable sensation that the seat might tip backwards. He didn't see Horace mount the wagon; the man was simply sitting there beside him once he had stationed himself firmly enough to look around.

"Well," said Mister Walton, blinking through his spectacles. He resituated his hat, which was dry by now, though not entirely recovered from its recent trials. "She seems a nice old horse."

"She won't frighten you," averred Horace.

Mister Walton looked at the somnambulant creature before him and almost laughed. "No, I don't suppose she will," was his response. He clucked at the old horse and shook the reins. The mare raised her head and yawned, which was something Mister Walton had never seen a horse do; he was quite fascinated. Again he spoke to her and chucked the reins, and this time they began to move, though not at any great speed. Indeed, *speed* would be something of a misnomer, unless the pace of the mare was considered in terms of geological time. Eventually they did reach a rate of movement that Mister Walton might have matched on foot if he was tired.

Horace seemed content; he wouldn't miss much, traveling in this fashion. He pointed ahead of them, saying: "Saw a moose once, on this street."

"Goodness sakes! When was that?"

"I was just in long pants, I guess," said Horace. "Oh, he was a brute. His rack was six feet if it was an inch. Miss Vandemeer lived in this place then." He pointed to a grand old colonial home on their right.

"I know the name," said Mister Walton, "but she died, I think, before I was old enough to remember."

"No wonder," said Horace gravely. "That moose went and peered in through her parlor window. Scared her half to death while she was putting a jigsaw puzzle together. A week later, when she had partially recovered, she finished that puzzle, but was missing a single piece, and it was finally decided that the sight of that moose had somehow caused her to swallow it."

"Goodness sakes!" said Mister Walton again, almost laughing.

"She was old even then, you know," continued Horace, "but she was sweet on Humphrey Cleaves, who lived on the corner of Winter Street here. . . ." And on Horace went, filling an appreciative Mister Walton with whimsical history and old gossip. There was hardly a landmark that did not have some memorable incident attached to it, and rare was the house that they passed in which some eccentric character had not lived.

The gray mare pulled the wagon in the direction of Munjoy Hill and, following it, one could have heard Horace's broad methodical speech punctuated by Mister Walton's surprised and delighted exclamations of "Goodness sakes!"

7. Minmaneth

CORDELIA ROSE EARLY, that Friday morning, with the intention of writing a long-overdue letter to her cousin in Ellsworth. She had slept surprisingly well, when one considered the curiosity and excitement of the night before, and had wakened with a confidence that the day promised something pleasant.

She descended the back stairs to the kitchen and quietly found some cold remains of last night's dinner to nibble on before proceeding to the front room and her self-appointed task. Mrs. Feeney, their cook four days a week, had not yet arrived, so the stove was cold and there was no hot water for coffee. Feeling only moderately ambitious, Cordelia did without.

The front room was unexpectedly airy when she entered it, and from the sound of bees buzzing in the philodendrons, she realized that the windows were open. Her father, sitting in a chair by one of the windows, looked up from a letter unfolded on his knee and smiled at her.

"And I thought I was getting the worm this morning," said Cordelia. "Or have you been up all night?"

"No, no," said James. "But I've been up an hour or so."

"Looking through Uncle Basil's things again?"

"Yes. Trying to make some sort of story out of them."

"And the results?"

"Brilliantly unsuccessful."

Cordelia saw, then, the card with the odd inscription upon it on the table beside her father's chair. She took the card and read it, trying once more to make some sense of its single enigmatic sentence.

Our Minmaneth is a young goatt.

"It means no more by the light of day, does it," said she. "You said that you heard about this Minmaneth from your mother."

"She was full of stories about him. It wasn't till years later that I realized she must have invented most of them. I have yet to meet anybody besides my brother who had ever heard of him, and I've only found a brief mention of him in a single history."

" 'Minmaneth,' " she said, reading from the card again. "It has an Indian sound to it."

"He was a Scot, actually. John McOrm was his real name, and Minmaneth was the title of his family estate, which his father lost through bad debts and gambling. According to my mother's stories, the house was burned by his father when the law came to turn them out, and the elder McOrm died in the fire. John went to the New World in search of his fortune, and took on the name of his family lands with a pledge to win them back."

Cordelia found a seat opposite her father and encouraged him, with her obvious interest, to continue.

"These events, you understand," said James, "occurred in the days when France and England still vied for this part of the world. Portland was known as Falmouth then, and the forest was close by. It was the early part of the last century.

"John—or Minmaneth, as my mother always spoke of him—eventually found himself on these shores and was soon involved in the war between the colonists and the natives. He was captured by a band of Abenakis, but it turned out that his adopted name—or some variation of it—held a mystical significance to the Indians, and he was spared."

"At the last moment, I am sure," said Cordelia.

James held a thumb and forefinger in front of one eye to indicate just how thin that last moment had been.

"It's no wonder that you and Uncle Basil played at this," said his daughter. "There are no end of possibilities."

"Ah, but there is better still. Minmaneth, you see, was an invaluable liaison between settler and Indian, and eventually became more like an Indian himself. He shaved his beard, his hair grew long, he wore buckskins. His days of hunting as a boy in Scotland served him well, for he became like a force of nature in the woods—a formidable tracker and a deadly shot with both musket and bow. He was feared as much as respected by the colonists, and he was not always quick to choose sides between the two people, but weighed his opinion where he thought justice rested."

"My goodness!" said Cordelia. "He is Ivanhoe, Robin Hood, and Deer-slayer in a single suit!"

"But there is better still," said James again, and he smiled when his daughter laughed aloud. "Minmaneth never forgot his pledge to regain his family estate, and with this end in mind he pursued the legends of ancient treasure and lost cities. He struck further into the interior than any European before him and had more adventures than Arthur's knights."

"I want to hear them all!" declared Cordelia sincerely.

"Somewhere, the fruit of his labor lies buried—gold and jewels and ancient works of art. My brother and I tore up a good deal of countryside—half playing, but half believing we would find Minmaneth's treasure."

"Did he never return to Scotland?"

"He disappeared, you see. Something to do with an Indian maiden and a battle between warring tribes at the foot of Mount Katahdin." James's demeanor grew quiet as he looked into the middle distance of his memory. "I can remember night after winter night, sitting in the parlor of the old house at Cape Elizabeth, the fire the only light in the room and my mother never looking up from her needlework as she told her stories. She was lonely, I think—my father was out to sea so much.

"But she told these marvelous tales—and very landbound they were too, now that I think of it. Marvelous tales: the French and Indian Wars, lost cities, blood friendships, the dark woods filled with game and lurking with danger. You would have thought she had been there, she was so vivid in her descriptions of hiding amongst the fern from an enemy tribe, or chasing game over the ancient hills. I think she enjoyed them as much as we did."

Cordelia was thinking about the end of Minmaneth's story. "Isn't Mount Katahdin somewhere near the land that Uncle Basil left me?"

"You've been studying a map."

"But don't you see? The land being so close to the mountain and the story of Minmaneth's treasure?"

James laughed, not unkindly. "I've thought about it myself, sitting here the last hour or so. But it doesn't fit. Why would Basil be so cryptic? And a young goat? That's not very romantic, even spelt correctly. It's just not like my brother to be recondite. The answer is simple, I fear: our boyhood games returned to him in his last hours. Minmaneth must have been a product of his memory, but the rest a product of his fever."

Cordelia looked at the card again. "Our Minmaneth is a young goatt." "Well, I am keeping my eye out for buried treasure," she said, though this sounded something of a contradiction in terms.

"I hope you do," said James, thinking to himself that his daughter was treasure enough. It was clear, however, from his smile, that he would be looking too.

From: Miss Cordelia M. Underwood
High & Spring Streets
Portland, Maine

To: Miss Priscilla Morningside
Ellsworth Falls, Maine
Care of Mrs. Henry Morningside

July 3, 1896

My Dear Cousin,

I have been thinking for a long time of writing you and now have really set myself about it. I wrote Emily and Charlotte more than a month ago, and thought I should have had an answer before now. How are you getting along in this beautiful summer weather? They say rain perhaps on Saturday, which is too bad. I do wish you could come down with Aunt Delia for the Fourth, but I suppose your mother could not make the trip and would be desolate without your company. At any rate, the Fourth will be a memory by the time you receive this, and it does look likely that we will be getting together later in the season.

One reason that I have not written before this is that it is so difficult to put pen to paper when there is nothing to say. Nothing, unfortunately, is what has happened to me since I wrote you last (in May, I think)—nothing, that is, until yesterday. Let me tell you.

An old sailor came to our house the night before last with news that my Uncle Basil's last effects had been sailed up from Venezuela and were waiting at the Custom House to be claimed. Yesterday Mama and Papa and I went down to do just that, and I left them to it, in order to take the air on the wharf. (Don't tell your mother that I went unescorted or Mama will never hear the end of it!) Well, the most extraordinary thing happened to me. An older gentleman, about Papa's age, had just stepped onto the wharf from a ladder and his hat blew off! When he reached for it, he very nearly stepped off the wharf itself, and I very nearly went off, as well, when I grabbed his elbow.

The most handsome man caught me by the waist, however, and rescued me. He was dark and tall, and there was something merry about him—his brown eyes positively struck me! Unfortunately, he was not without escort—a woman who was every bit his equal. I do wish I could have disliked her, but she was pleasant as well as beautiful, and quite ready to lend her beau over for a timely rescue. My red hair and freckles paled beside her, I am sure, and were not to be considered any sort of threat. I do have green eyes, however, as you know, which I have always thought my best asset, and I gave him a shot with them, I can tell you. (Perhaps you had better keep this letter away from your mother altogether.) He returned to his lady, which was to be expected, and they disappeared amongst the crowd. The worst of it is that I did not even get his name.

I did make a friend, though. Mister Walton, the gentleman whose hat blew off, is one of the most delightful people I have ever met. He is rather round, and wears spectacles, and laughs a great deal—mostly about himself. I would have been disconsolate over my too brief encounter with that hand-some man if not for Mister Walton's jolly company on the way back to the Custom House. There is more to tell, but I want to get to the most surprising news, which has to do with the contents of Uncle Basil's sea chest.

Have you ever heard of a town named Millinocket? I have, but only in passing, till yesterday. It seems that I own land there—a parcel purchased years ago by Uncle Basil and signed over to me in a legal document after he had taken ill. It is very sweet and very sad to think of him leaving me such a remarkable legacy, even as the yellow fever took him away. He never seemed very comfortable around me, but Mama says it was only the natural reticence of a bachelor and a sailor toward a young niece whom he thought (mistak-enly) to be highly breakable, but for whom he enjoyed a great fondness from afar. And since Mama said this I have remembered a time when we were all having Christmas dinner together, the only Christmas that I remember him spending with us, and he said to me: "If I had ever married, I would have wished for a daughter like you." Looking back on it, it makes me think that he was a little sad.

Papa himself seemed surprised that Uncle Basil left the land to me, rather than James and Brendan. Millinocket is in the northern interior of the state and he expects it to be somewhat rough and unsettled. It has been a settlement since around 1830, though—according to our almanac—and something of civilization must have creeped in by now. (I hope not too much.) I am in the process of talking Papa into bringing us up to see my land—imagine it, my land!—and I give him about three days before he acquiesces. So, keep a good thought. Such an expedition would send us first in your general direction, and I am sure I can wheedle a few days' rest in Ellsworth Falls, coming and going.

I am more than a little excited, as you can imagine, and cannot wait to see you. Give my love to your mother, and tell her to be well for I plan to be *like a brisk wind when I arrive. No lack of energy will be allowed. Perhaps we can talk her into letting you go with us to Millinocket. Mama and Papa send their love, and I send mine.*

Your Loving Cousin,
Cordelia

8. Curiosity by the Barrel

LIKE MANY OF THE CITY'S INHABITANTS, Mister Walton had only seen the Mariners' Hospital from the tree-lined road below it. The hospital and its grounds, however, were at their best that day, as the old mare pulled Horace's rig into the curving drive: the sunlit lawns were freshly cut; the middle-aged oaks were dense with leaves, restless in the breeze from the sea; the rhododendrons were bright with pink flowers; and the roses overlooking the rocky shore were just peeking from their bonnets.

At Horace's suggestion Mister Walton pulled the rig next to an outbuilding, where several posts offered hitching rings, and by the time he had clambered to the ground, Horace had the old mare tethered. Mister Walton stroked the horse's neck and smiled out at the expanse of harbor and ocean visible from the knoll.

"Come on in and meet Mr. Privy," said Horace.

"I wouldn't want to intrude," Mister Walton said.

"Ridiculous. You couldn't intrude on Mr. Privy if you were carrying a barrel of bait."

"Well, if you're sure."

Horace made a face and waved one hand in mock disgust. With a speed and method equal to the old mare's, he led the way to the hospital's entrance. In deference to Horace's sore shoulder, Mister Walton opened the great oak door, and they stepped into a magnificent and echoing hall. An older woman at a large desk greeted Horace. "How are you today, Mr. McQuinn?"

"No better," said Horace, with a short snicker.

"No better than you ought to be, you mean," she returned with a sort of good-humored severity.

"Well, it has been said." He laughed again. "How's Mr. Privy?"

"He's quite well today, Mr. McQuinn. He'll be very happy to see you."

Mister Walton followed Horace, who led the way to a side corridor, stopping occasionally to peer in on an acquaintance or to inquire of someone's health—he might have been a doctor making his daily rounds.

Once, he simply halted in the doorway to a patient's room and pointed at the man. "You be good!" he insisted.

"*You* be good, you old dodger!" returned the man with great delight.

Horace laughed to himself as he continued down the hall, and Mister Walton was both gratified and amazed at the goodwill spread simply by the pointing of Horace's smoke-stained finger.

At the last room off the corridor, Horace knocked lightly, though the door was ajar. Then he stepped inside and Mister Walton quietly followed him. Propped up on several pillows, his bed by a bright window that overlooked the green lawns and broad ocean, slept an ancient white-bearded man, long in limb and large of frame, yet somehow small in his great age.

The room was spartan in its accoutrements—a bed, a chair, and a small table, but little else. The rhododendrons by his window might have been planted just for him, however, so insistently did they peer in with their young flowers. For all its bareness, the room was bright and cheery.

By an accident of their circuitous route through the hospital, they could see Horace's wagon and the old mare pulling lazily at the grass, which only added to the peacefulness of the scene.

"Sit down, sit down," said Horace. He pointed to the single chair in the room, and when Mister Walton protested to take the only seat, Horace propped himself on the windowsill and said it again: "Sit down, sit down."

Mister Walton did sit down, and together they watched the ancient gentleman gently sleep.

"This is Mr. Privy," said Horace.

"He seems to be resting nicely," observed Mister Walton.

"Oh, he will."

They watched Mr. Privy some more. There was something beautiful about the ancient fellow—his snow-white beard, the smooth crown of his head shining in the light of the sun, the magnificent wrinkles of his face, his peaceful slumber. Several minutes passed, in which this peaceful slumber was the single object of study, and it occurred to Mister Walton that this was Mr. Privy's normal state. Softly, he asked Horace if the fellow ever wakened.

"Once or twice a day," said Horace. "He eats a little boiled fish and milk, nibbles a bit of a cracker, thanks you, and nods off."

"Does he ever know you're here?"

"Perhaps" was Horace's only answer.

"And you visit him often," said Mister Walton.

"He was a carpenter aboard the first ship I sailed on. I was more than a little wet behind the ears—and proud, you know. Mr. Privy made things a little easier for me. He was a great strapping fellow, but kind of gentle. Never heard him so much as say 'damn.' "

"He sounds a wonderful fellow," said Mister Walton with great feeling.

"I've known a lot like him, one way or another," replied Horace.

It was true—often there is a sort of unstudied gentility to the hard workers of the world; Mister Walton had seen it himself among seamen and lumpers, loggers, and farmers. And he was thinking of some of these gentlemen laborers, when a man appeared on the lawn between the window and Horace's wagon. Mister Walton might have taken little notice of this fellow except for a frown that the man threw in his direction, followed by a satisfied nod in Horace's.

The man wore a blue vest, a red neckerchief, and the sleeves of his striped shirt were rolled up. With the crook of one finger he held a short jacket over his shoulder, and in the other hand a brown hat, with which he waved to someone below him, nearer the shore.

Horace was talking of his days before the mast, and how a storm had once blown his ship off course to Greenland. Mister Walton listened with great interest, though he found himself occasionally distracted by the man on the lawn. Horace was painting the picture of a small community of Eskimos, and explaining how a Micmac Indian who sailed with him thought them primitive, when a second man appeared just outside the window—then a third, and a fourth, each of them mimicking the first man's glances at Mister Walton and Horace. All told, there were five of them when they spoke among themselves, agreed on some point, and advanced to the door of the outbuilding next to which Mister Walton had left the horse and rig.

The Micmac, according to Horace, had finished his sailing days in England, where he was hired by a merchant's wife as a butler. Contrarily, Horace claimed to have also sailed with an ex-butler, who was of the express notion that high tea was the most significant sign of advanced civilization.

"Pardon me," said Mister Walton at this juncture, "but there are some men out there who seem to have mistaken your rig for another's." Indeed, the five men were carrying, in shifting pairs, a series of large barrels from the outbuilding and loading them onto the back of the wagon.

"I'm just delivering something for a friend," explained Horace. "He's up country, tending to a sick aunt."

"Oh, I see," said Mister Walton, though it seemed to him that there was something surreptitious about the loading of the wagon. Perhaps they did not have official sanction to be using the outbuilding. "I hope she's better."

"She's mending."

Mr. Privy made a snorting sound in his sleep and they thought he might wake, but soon it was obvious that he was enjoying himself too much. A nurse came in and shifted his pillows, and Horace bantered with her good-naturedly, suggesting to her that Mister Walton might be looking for a wife. Mister Walton blushed wonderfully and laughed aloud.

"Oh, good heavens!" he said as he laughed. "I wouldn't wish myself on any good woman!"

"Perhaps Miss Helen, here, isn't so good," suggested Horace, finding it necessary to ward off a playful cuff from the woman. "Ooh!" he protested. "Such violence."

Mister Walton was so diverted by this rambunctious scene that he did not see where or when the five men disappeared, after they had finished loading Horace's wagon.

But he wondered briefly, as he climbed onto the bench seat of the rig, what was in the barrels behind them. "Pickles, perhaps," said Horace, glancing back from his perch, but offered no explanation why five unidentified men would appear from nowhere to load his wagon with eight large barrels of pickles. "A favor's a favor," he added with a profound shrug.

The old mare sauntered them down the drive to the road and pulled them back in the direction of the city. The day had reached a senses-filling zenith with the height of the sun. Even the air over the mouth of Back Cove had warmed considerably, and the horse's methodical pace, along with the peaceful watch they had taken over Mr. Privy's sleep, conspired to lull Mister Walton into a placid state of mind. Horace was less talkative on the return trip, but his good-natured driver was content to amble along in comparative quiet. It was only afterwards that Mister Walton remembered passing a policeman, who looked with some interest at the cargo in the back of their conveyance.

Horace hummed to himself absently as they descended Munjoy Hill. "If you don't mind," he said, when they neared the corner of Smith Street, "I'll drop off here and meet you at the end of the line."

"Drop off here?" said Mister Walton, pulling up on the reins. "But where am I going?"

"She'll take you there, no mistake," assured Horace. He was already standing on the street, and he reached out to gently pat the horse's flank. "It's just the other side of town. I have to stop by a friend's and look at his new dog."

"But how will she take me there, if I don't know where I'm going?" asked a thoroughly flummoxed Mister Walton.

"She knows the way. You'll see." Horace waved once, then turned and shuffled down Smith Street.

Several carriages, pedestrians, and a man on horseback passed Mister

Walton, while he pondered his odd circumstances. There was no mistaking his deep perplexity, even when approached from behind, so it was not unusual that a constable, walking down Cumberland Street, would stop to offer his assistance.

"Are you lost, sir?" asked the officer.

The mare swung her head around with such wide eyes and greeted the officer with such a *cusnorf* through the nostrils that Mister Walton simply gaped at the creature and never got a look at the man—which, in hindsight, seemed a remarkable stroke of luck, since it meant that the officer never got a look at him.

For in the next instant the horse had snapped her nose forward, jerked the reins from Mister Walton's hands, and bolted down the street like a felon in fear of her life. Mister Walton heard the officer speak, then shout, as they rattled away. Groping for the reins, the bespectacled man caught them at his feet, which gave him something to hang on to; but no amount of pulling or whoa-ing discouraged the mare from her sudden burst of speed. Again he heard the officer shout, but with each command to stop, the mare only increased her exertions, till houses were flying past too swiftly to count and picket fences sped by in a solid blur.

The Roman Catholic church was quickly visible, coming up on his left, and Mister Walton realized with horror that they were charging toward a major crossing at Franklin Street. Again he pulled back at the reins, but the mare was plunging forward without regard to oncoming traffic. She let out a great blustering whinny as they neared the crossing, and a carriage pulled up in time to let them by. The driver of the carriage shook his fist and cursed the air blue behind them, but they were soon out of earshot and charging past scattering pedestrians and barking dogs. Mister Walton felt his hat lift with the wind of their movement and he barely clapped a hand upon it in time to keep it on his head.

The steel-rimmed wheels drummed like thunder beneath him, and the shadows of overhanging oaks and elms and maples swept past like storm clouds in a high wind. He attempted to articulate some warning as he plummeted down Cumberland Street, even as he tried to remember the crossings that approached with such dangerous speed. What he managed was to whoop out the name of each street as he came to it, like some mad tour guide, shouting: "Pearl!" and "Chestnut!" to a series of amazed onlookers.

Round about Cedar Street, a young man on horseback joined into the spirit of things and attempted to charge alongside of him. "Is it a fire?" shouted the lad. "Is it a fire?"

"Elm!" shouted Mister Walton, and outstripped the fellow four lengths before they reached Preble Street, losing the equestrian in a near-collision of several vehicles.

A passing drummer helped the young man to steady his rearing mount and asked, breathlessly, what the ruckus was about. "He's got his hat crammed over his eyes!" was all the lad could say.

Indeed, Mister Walton's litany of streets was culled purely from memory by the time he reached the corner of Cumberland and Alder. Somehow he had managed to cram his hat so far down over his face that it had caught on his spectacles, and with one hand on the reins and the other on the seat below him, he dared not let go long enough to extricate himself from the resulting blindness.

It was while nearing the Free Will Baptist Church that the mare began to moderate her pace. The choir was practicing, and the loft windows were open to the summer breeze, so that Mister Walton, with his hat stuck over his nose, could not be blamed for wondering if rescue was arriving from on high. *"To journey's end, oh speed my troubled heart,"* they were singing. By the time they passed the church, the mare had slowed from a gallop to a fast trot and he was able to disengage his hat from his head.

The mare still would not respond to the reins, however. *Well,* he thought, *Horace did say that she knew where she was going.*

That seemed to be the case. The mare almost slowed to a walk at the next crossing, broke into a trot again along a less populated avenue, turned east, took a hairpin turn north, and after giving herself a nice walk pulled into a barn on an unmarked street.

Mister Walton did not move immediately from his seat, but sat frozen, one hand gripping the reins, the other still pressing his hat to his head. Light from the westering sun spilled through the barn doors onto the horse's sweating back, and Mister Walton thought that the comparative shadows inside the barn were playing tricks with his eyes. The horse appeared now, not gray, but brown.

He blinked, removed his somewhat fogged spectacles, and replaced them after a good wiping. No, the horse definitely looked brown. He climbed down then, somewhat unsteadily, and passed a hand over the mare's flank. His hand was besmirched with a grayish residue, which had shed from the animal's back as it had worked up a sweat.

"I don't know where that horse goes to get so dirty," came a booming voice from behind. A large man, respectably dressed, lifted a fedora from his head in greeting and stepped into the barn. "Somewhere she gets this white ash on her, till she's as gray as Martha Washington. Her own mother wouldn't recognize her."

"I don't suppose she would," said Mister Walton, still astounded by it all. "Nor officers of the law."

The man looked quickly over his shoulder. "D. C. Pembroke," he said, when he saw that Mister Walton was not speaking of any immediate presence. He held out a hand.

Mister Walton shook the hand with as much goodwill as he could muster. "Are you the fellow with the sick aunt, then?" he asked.

"No, my aunt's dead. Is that what Horace told you?" The man laughed heartily, shaking his head. He proceeded to unharness the mare. Mister Walton simply stepped aside. "That Horace!" said D. C. Pembroke, chortling to himself. "He might lie, you know, but he'd never steal. He has told me so himself many a time." This amused him and he began to laugh all over again.

Mister Walton wandered out into the sunlight and surveyed the well-tended grounds of a handsome house and barn. There was a chair-swing under a widespread oak and he settled himself into it. Several minutes later a carriage pulled into the drive and Horace stepped down from it.

"Didn't take *you* long to get here," said Horace, wide-eyed as he ambled over to the chair-swing. Wavering between indignation with the man and thankfulness for having survived his ordeal, Mister Walton was somewhat mollified by the look of honest wonder on the old fellow's face. "You going to make it?" asked Horace, which, coming from him, was almost a tender inquiry.

Mister Walton was nearly as put out with himself as he was with Horace. He hadn't traveled most of his adult life without encountering the occasional scoundrel, and he had hoped that he might recognize one when his path was thus crossed. Looking at Horace, however, he found it difficult to count the man a scoundrel. "You are a rascal, Mr. McQuinn," he announced.

"So Mother would have it," replied the man.

"What is in those barrels—rum?"

"You mean it wasn't pickles?"

Mister Walton was not practiced at looking stern, and found it difficult to arrange his features in a reproving fashion. "Isn't this sort of activity best conducted in the dark?" he asked.

"You're apt to bump into people at night," said Horace.

"I very nearly bumped into several in broad daylight," returned Mister Walton. "That horse knows very little about moderation." Oddly enough, he thought he might laugh out loud.

"She did pick up a bit of a tail wind. I had to close my eyes when you hit Franklin Street."

Mister Walton did laugh, then, at the absolute sincerity of Horace's expression. "*You* had to close your eyes! I had my hat down over my face for six blocks!"

"Well, no one will recognize you, then. I hadn't any notion she was so nervous about the law."

"Mr. McQuinn," said Mister Walton. He shook an admonitory finger. "It has been a diverting tour, but I will thank you, in future, not to involve me with your trafficking in illegitimate goods."

"Old Horace owes you one," said the man with great seriousness.

"And what about Mr. Privy? I suppose he is just a convenient dodge for your operation."

"Oh, no," insisted Horace. "That's just mixing business with pleasure. Everything I told you about him was God's honest truth."

Mister Walton almost laughed again. He was thinking of himself careening down the middle of Portland with his hat crammed over his eyes, and it was just too wonderful.

"The honest truth," repeated Horace. "I might steal, but I'd never lie."

Book Three

INDEPENDENCE DAY, 1896

9. What's Good for the Soul

" 'AT LEAST A DOZEN CITIZENS *were witness to a remarkable one-wagon race down Cumberland Street on Friday afternoon at about 2 o'clock.'* " Mr. Eagleton read this sentence aloud from the July 4 issue of the *Portland Daily Advertiser,* his accentuation fitting nicely with the rhythm of the rails as he and his colleagues trundled north toward Freeport.

"Yesterday?" said Mr. Ephram. He had lowered the *Eastern Argus* so that the upper half of his face could be seen above it. His eyes traced the passing landscape through the windows on the opposite side of the train.

"One wagon?" said Mr. Thump, from behind the *Portland Courier*.

"A one-wagon *race,*" said Eagleton.

"Irony," suggested Ephram.

"Remarkable," said Thump, lowering his paper.

"So it says," said Eagleton. He read from the sentence again: " '*a remarkable one-wagon race.*' "

"No race with only one participant," said Ephram.

"No, I don't suppose," agreed Eagleton.

"Unless, of course," said Thump, "it was a race against time."

This brought a pause to the conversation. Half a mile of rail went beneath them as they considered this possibility.

"Perhaps there is more to this item," suggested Thump. Clearly the fresh air outside of the city had done much for his perspicacity.

Eagleton lifted the *Daily Advertiser* and read aloud from the article. " '*Calvin Drum, of the Portland Constabulary, was at the onset of the event and tells this reporter that he was making the rounds of his beat, when he spied a portly man of middle age perched upon the seat of a wagon at the* corner of Cumberland and Smith. The back of the wagon was laden with eight or ten large barrels, the contents of which the reader will not discover in this story.

"'Officer Drum noticed a melancholy aspect to the figure on the wagon, and was convinced that the man was lost. With that desire to serve so characteristic of our Police Force, Officer Drum stepped up to the wagon and inquired if he could be of assistance. What transpired next, by all accounts, surprised the driver as much as it did the constable. The mare attached to the wagon—a creature that had given no outward appearance of ambition—suddenly bounded forth in a cloud of dust.

"'Sensing something dangerous, if not downright suspicious, in this sudden flight, the perceptive officer gave a great shout for the man to stop the speeding transport, but was not given the satisfaction of seeing his orders obeyed. Indeed, the horse increased its efforts as each of the officer's shouts reached its ears, and soon Drum was horrified to see horse, wagon, and driver careen toward the meeting of Cumberland and Franklin Streets without a hint of moderating their pace!'"

"Good heavens!" interjected Thump.

"I should very much say!" added Ephram.

"Speeding wagon," said Eagleton to Mister Walton, who was listening from his seat on the opposite side of the train.

"Oh, yes," said Mister Walton, reddening with embarrassment. "Do forgive me, please. I couldn't help but hear."

"Not at all," said Eagleton.

"First-rate reading voice, has Eagleton," said Thump.

"I would certainly say," said Mister Walton.

"Thank you," said Eagleton. "Thump's own narration has a certain dramatic flair that I have often admired."

Thump was gratified to hear this, and said so, bringing the honors full circle by adding: "Ephram, of course, enunciates with exquisite precision."

"Oh!" said Ephram, denying the compliment with a wave of his hand.

"True," said Eagleton. "True."

"I have yet to misunderstand a single word the man has said," insisted Thump to Mister Walton.

"I do strive for accuracy," admitted Ephram modestly.

"*Enunciator Emeritus!*" announced Eagleton. "No less a title is deserved." He lowered his paper now, and peered at the ceiling of the car with such intensity that the others, Mister Walton included, craned their necks to see what he was looking at. This was unfortunate since Eagleton had only lifted his gaze so that his jaw might jut more nobly as he appointed his comrade with this grand rank. With the other men staring at the ceiling, the effect was somewhat lost.

It was Ephram who first recovered from this impasse, stating his name and extending a hand across the aisle to Mister Walton.

"Tobias Walton," came the reply as they shook hands, and similar ceremony was observed with Eagleton and Thump.

"Did the wagon meet with an accident?" wondered Thump aloud.

"No one was hurt, fortunately," said Mister Walton, then looked as if he had been pinched when he realized what he had said.

"Eyewitness!" said Ephram.

"Firsthand observation!" said Eagleton.

"Extraordinary!" said Thump. They each insisted on shaking his hand again.

"Yes, well," said Mister Walton. He was not deft at manipulation, but managed, awkwardly, to change the subject by inquiring of the three men's destination.

"We are traveling to Freeport," informed Thump.

"Plan to partake of the celebration there," added Eagleton.

"Fourth of July, you know," finished Ephram.

"Why, that is my own destination and purpose!" said Mister Walton.

"Capital!" exclaimed Eagleton.

"Fate!" said Ephram.

"Destination derived from destiny!" insisted Thump. They each shook Mister Walton's hand again, enthused to discover a fellow traveler who had been witness to great events. He was invited to join them, and he shifted across the aisle to sit beside Ephram.

"Little sequel to this story," said Eagleton, glancing down his nose at his paper. "*Daily Advertiser* has no clue as to the wagon driver's identity."

"I hope . . . !" said Mister Walton. "I mean, it seems he disappeared somewhere after the Free Will Church." Mister Walton's discomfort was obvious, as he strove to speak, and the three men feared he had taken sick. He looked from one to another of them, and was so seized by the honest concern in their faces that he suddenly said: "Actually, *I* was the driver of the wagon."

"Good heavens!" said Ephram. He sat up straight beside Mister Walton.

"Extraordinary!" said Thump.

Eagleton was positively dumbfounded. "Wild horse! Runaway wagon!"

"A man of action!" insisted Thump.

"Slowed in the nick of time!" asserted Ephram. "Possibly saving lives!"

Mister Walton could not say whether he was shaken more by the rhythm of the train or by the renewed pumping of his hand. He was rather confounded by the delighted reception given to his confession, and had every intention of spilling the entire tale (though leaving out Horace's name), but was frustrated by his companions' great excitement and a new tangent in the conversation.

"We are beginning a club, you know," said Thump, who turned to Eagleton: "And he's just the sort of man."

"A club?" said Mister Walton, not understanding.

"Ground floor," said Ephram. "Members wanted."

"You have a personal invitation," said Eagleton.

"A club?" repeated Mister Walton.

"Haven't a name, yet," said Thump. He tapped a forefinger at his temple. "Hasn't come."

"What sort of club?"

"Undecided," answered Ephram.

"Inspiration pending," explained Eagleton.

"Inspiration pending," repeated Ephram. "I like that very much."

"Thank you, Ephram."

10. Freeport

THE WINDOWS OF THE TRAIN that pulled into the Freeport Station at 11:10 on the Fourth of July, 1896, were decked in red, white, and blue; streamers fluttered from the engine, and even the cow-catcher was festooned with the colors of the day. From near and far, the noise of firecrackers and rockets rose above the ruckus of the crowd and the chuff of the engine. A band greeted the train with a stirring, if vaguely sharp, rendition of the "Battle Hymn of the Republic."

The engineer, as instructed, blew his whistle a good mile from the station, and the band leader, decked out as colorfully as any worthy contemporary of John Philip Sousa, scurried about like a mother hen, gathering his horn players and flutists and drummers, who drank lemonade in the shade and did their best to flirt with the local girls. Soon they were fashioned into a presentable formation and playing with all their might to be heard over the wheels and steam and final whistles of the approaching locomotive. A sort of auditory battle ensued, with cheers and shouts adding to the confusion. The engineer, carried away by the sheer abundance of noise and revelry, blew superfluous hoots of his steam whistle; and young boys passed out small flags, courtesy of the Harraseeket Hotel, to passengers as they stepped down.

After the conductor helped her onto the station platform, Cordelia received one of these tokens with a bright "Thank you" to the smudge-faced lad who held it out to her, then looked for her great-aunt Delia while her parents stepped down.

White was the predominant color of dress among the throng, though the men might sport stripes; the women brightened the station's prospect like white lilies. Flowered hats and colored sashes and ribbons accented the sunny aspect of their dress. Parasols bloomed in the sun, and laughter and shouts filled the air once the engineer's steam whistle and the band had called a truce. Peddlers hawked fireworks among the crowd.

Aunt Delia Frost was waving from the seat of her carriage, which was drawn up alongside one end of the station. Cordelia saw her first, and looked half her age as she beamed at her aunt and waved emphatically. Aunt Delia looked pleased, somehow, through her usual wry expression, as they approached.

"Delia" was short for "Cordelia," and her great-niece was her name-sake. Aunt Delia was seventy-eight years old and drove her own carriage, even if a man was aboard, which in 1896 explained quite a lot about her—including, some said, why the husband of her youth had left her for the Gold Rush of '49. Cordelia thought this bit of gossip unfair, and once had said so to her great-aunt, when Cordelia was no more than six or seven. "Run away?!" Aunt Delia had exclaimed. "Good heavens, child, I threw him out!"

Aunt Delia did not dislike men—on the contrary, she was ready to like anyone. She had loved unwisely, however, and simply tired of it. She never mentioned her husband of two years without some touch of affection soft-ening the contours of her disregard. She had heard from Abner Frost twice in forty-seven years—once after the War Between the States, to let her know he had survived. The last she knew of him, he was living in Wyoming, and she secretly suspected him of having an Indian wife.

"Don't try to kiss me till you get into the carriage," she said as they came to the end of the station platform. "I'm too old and I can't bend over ... though, James, you're tall enough—come over here while the others are getting in and it will save time." During moments such as this, Cordelia's great-aunt could make her almost giddy with suppressed laughter. "I told you that I would have everything we needed," Aunt Delia was saying as they piled several blankets and a hamper of food among her already abundant provisions.

"We did invite someone to join us," Cordelia's mother replied, "and if he is able to come, we wanted to be sure to have enough."

"Well, I hope he is either good-looking or clever," said the older woman, and James had barely gotten himself seated beside his wife before Aunt Delia whipped up the horses and wheeled into the gathering traffic.

Cordelia righted her hat after the first lurch and smiled happily into the sunlight. They followed the general flow of carriages, riders, and pedestrians to the fairgrounds. Cordelia's gaze swept the people that milled about the storefronts, and suddenly she was looking into the face of the handsome young man who had saved her from going overboard two days before. He was leaning against a porch post, and his own face turned as they moved past. He smiled appreciatively at her, and she, struck by the frankness of his admiration, only stared back in return. Cordelia turned to keep him in sight, but soon they had descended the hill and he was gone.

"No, I came alone," Aunt Delia was saying, in answer to a question from Mercia. "Certainly your sister wouldn't make the trip."

"How is she?" asked Mercia.

"As pale as ever. Grace is so prone to the vapors that she is in danger of turning into a cloud and blowing away on the next stiff breeze. She needs a husband, I think."

"Well, it hasn't been very long, Aunty," said Mercia, over the clop and trundle of the carriage.

"Good heavens, Henry has been dead for five years! Your brother's first wife had been gone hardly a year before he remarried, and he didn't burst into flame. Now his second wife is ailing as well. You children do seem to be attracted to people of weak constitutions. James, how have you been feeling?"

"Breathing regularly, Aunt Delia," said James. "Thank you."

"I'm glad to hear it. I've always been fond of you and don't look forward to any more funerals before my own."

"I'll do my best to oblige, certainly."

"I liked your brother too, though I must say, he disappointed me by passing on when he did."

"We just heard from Uncle Basil!" said Cordelia, sounding to her aunt more excited than sensible.

"Are you conducting séances now?" wondered Aunt Delia, and James explained.

Aunt Delia listened in silence as they neared the fairgrounds. They passed by the last of the houses and trees so that the harbor and waterfront were visible beyond the sloping fields. Already crowds of people were defining the boundaries of upcoming events, with great numbers milling about the hot-air balloon that bobbed on its tether in the light breeze. Nearby, speakers declaimed to the assembling throng. Clouds gathered out to sea, and the sun was only just escaping from behind them as it rose.

11. The Political Fray

THE BALLOON ASCENSIONIST, Mrs. Roberto—*in her attractive suit of tights*, as the newspapers had advertised her—was perhaps as responsible for the crowd milling about the hot-air balloon as the hot-air balloon itself. The fact that she was wearing an attractive suit of tights might have escaped many of the spectators if the word had not already gotten out, for little more than her ankles were visible beneath a skirt that, admittedly, was shorter than some (that is, some women) thought it ought to be. The only other portion of her attractive suit of tights visible was on her lovely forearms, which were gracefully evident from beneath a short-sleeved blouse.

Mister Walton had read nothing of this personage (or her wardrobe), and could not be blamed for following his newfound acquaintances directly to the hot-air balloon as soon as they arrived by hired carriage at the fairgrounds. Ephram, Eagleton, and Thump expressed the greatest interest in balloon ascension as they walked—some might say trotted—across the field, past picnickers and children with sparklers and firecrackers, and Mister Walton quite admired the enthusiasm of his new companions.

There was an eerie quality about the enormous red, white, and blue gas bag as it swayed and shifted in the rising breeze; it seemed alive with a breath of its own, its basket whispering against the grass as it stirred. It dominated the immediate vicinity like a tethered elephant, restless and watchful, its festive colors obstructing the sky.

It was not enough, however, simply to observe the balloon from behind the gathering crowd; nothing would do, assured Thump, but they gain an interview with the ascensionist *herself*. The gender of the pronoun surprised Mister Walton, as did her costume when they finally gained the front of the crowd. He was afraid she might be cold.

Mrs. Roberto was a woman of some maturity—though young for a widow—and there was a type of wisdom in her eyes that made most men quickly forget the more nubile members of the fairer sex. Her hair was black and lustrous, falling down her back in a style usually acquainted with younger women. There was a certain exotic cast to her face—her nose prominent, her lips heavy and, by the way, more red than God had made them. She was not a small woman, but what she missed in nymphlike grace she more than made up for with a sort of languid warmth. She sat in a chair upon a low platform, legs crossed indelicately at the knees, and held court. Many of the men, once they had reached the front of the crowd, did their best to pretend they didn't see her. Suddenly the balloon's basket, and the great winch and cable that held the balloon to the ground, merited intense scrutiny.

Mister Walton, having arrived with less intention than his companions, was able to look Mrs. Roberto in the eye with an honest smile and greet her. "Do you suppose the weather will hold off?" he asked.

"That would be very kind," she said, as if he might have something to do with it. Mrs. Roberto's voice had the resonant tone of a cello, lending a suggestiveness to her speech. Mister Walton found his ears blushing.

"Some opportunity for precipitation by this afternoon," said Eagleton. "Though the chances for weather increase sharply as the day progresses." He squared his shoulders and delivered this pronouncement with unexpected authority; as soon as Mrs. Roberto's attention fell upon him, however, he appeared regretful. "Meteorographically speaking," he mumbled and turned to inspect the knots that held the balloon to its basket.

Mister Walton was fascinated by Mrs. Roberto's history—he had known a balloon ascensionist after the war, but it was news to him that anyone would willingly parachute from one, particularly when that person's spouse had taken, in a similar feat, a fatal plunge. In the course of their conversation, and with polite curiosity, he heard from her a brief autobiography.

Though standing at safe distances from the lovely Mrs. Roberto in her attractive suit of tights, Ephram, Eagleton, and Thump hung upon every word spoken between her and Mister Walton, and were further impressed with their new acquaintance as a man of action. They were disappointed, therefore, when he wished Mrs. Roberto a soft landing and expressed to them his goodbyes.

"Must leave?" asked Eagleton, shaking Mister Walton's hand.

"I have been invited to join a picnic," he explained.

"Other engagement," said Thump.

"I'm sure I'll see you again before the day is out," said Mister Walton.

"Consider our club," said Ephram, handing Mister Walton his card.

"I most certainly will, thank you." Mister Walton shook the man's hand, then trundled through the ever-growing crowd with a wave.

"Extraordinary," said Thump, watching Mister Walton's portly figure disappear amongst the throng.

"Purposeful," insisted Eagleton. "Certainly purposeful."

"He's a man for our membership, I'm sure!" said Ephram. He briefly caught Mrs. Roberto's eye and flinched.

Mister Walton found the Underwoods relaxing on a piece of ground they had claimed for their picnic beneath a tall oak in the corner of the field.

Cordelia saw him first, and greeted him happily as he moved up the small slope, through the gathering cliques of families and sweethearts to the foot of the tree.

"Good morning, good morning!" he called as he approached, for the sun had not yet reached its zenith.

"This must be Mister Walton," said Cordelia's great-aunt.

"And you will be Aunt Delia," he said playfully.

"I am Delia Frost," she confirmed.

"Tobias Walton," said he, with a bow. A sudden rattle of firecrackers punctuated his self-introduction and startled him into a wordless exclamation. Then with a laugh he shouted, "You'll make rain, young man," to the boy who had set off the chain of explosions.

Rain did threaten as the day progressed, and Mrs. Roberto hastened her balloon ascension by two hours in order to avoid the storm. She and her pilot, who was dressed as Uncle Sam, waved to the still-accumulating crowd while rising majestically into the clouding sky.

Speeches were being delivered at a podium close to the balloon's point of departure, and Mrs. Roberto took flight just as Cornelius Blithewaite, Democratic candidate for governor, had reached (by his own reckoning) the dramatic apex of his thunderous declamation of piety and patriotic fervor. "Even as the human race shines, beaconlike—the grandest of God's works—" he exclaimed, "so does this vast nation, wrestling for morality in the pulpit, fencing for justice in the rostrum, and taking aim through the bead of honor, represent the finest expression of human will!"

Blithewaite was shouting into the sky, his fists raised, his eyes squinted shut, like an Old Testament prophet pulling down the word from on high; and having finished with this potent sentence, he dared a small peek at his audience, only to find the entire assemblage craning their heads after the movement of Mrs. Roberto's balloon. Blithewaite was a broad-shouldered man, of medium height, with a great shock of white hair capping his head. He had thick spectacles, and a full beard that wagged when he spoke.

Ephram, who had been as interested in Mrs. Roberto's activities as anyone, turned back to the speaker, when silence from that quarter became apparent. Seeing Blithewaite's pained expression, he realized that he had, perhaps, missed a salient point in his favored candidate's speech and, feeling that some reaction was necessary, instigated a round of applause.

Vexed with the delayed reaction, Blithewaite continued. "Such emphatic will can only be carried out with the utmost courage, and the complete willingness to put one's own well-being in the path of our enemy's deadly fire!" Blithewaite, of course, was speaking in metaphorical terms of the opposing candidate, whose earlier speech had sounded (to the untrained ear) almost metaphor for metaphor alike.

"You forgot to wear your uniform!" shouted someone in the crowd, and Blithewaite snapped to attention.

"What?" he said, breaking the first rule of rhetoric by reacting to a heckler.

"You forgot to wear your uniform," repeated a dark-haired young man who stood next to Eagleton. The fellow's words were not expressed in strident or sarcastic tones, but were delivered as if only Blithewaite's best interest were being considered.

"Uniform?" snapped the man on the platform.

Though a Republican, Eagleton gave the young man his own version of a hard look; this sort of interruption, after all, was not courteous.

"Surely such a warlike fellow as yourself," the young man was saying, "must have done great damage in the name of freedom during the War Between the States."

"Yes!" shouted someone from another corner of the crowd. "What's all this about courage and deadly fire? You don't look like you've peered down the barrel of a popgun!"

Blithewaite let out a terrific *harrumph* that only precipitated a general clamor and laughter. The local Republican candidate for governor, Henry Van Smooten, then stepped forward with hands raised and spoke, seemingly in his rival's defense. "I am sure that my esteemed opponent was worthily employed during the Great Conflict. Not all men are called to risk life and limb for freedom's cause."

Blithewaite's eyes widened in indignation, for Van Smooten had spoken so backhandedly, and with such a smile on his face, that nothing but insult was gotten from his declaration of support. Van Smooten was a thin, gray fellow, with large ears, a jutting chin, and spectacles as thick as Blithewaite's perched on the end of his sharp nose. The two candidates were of a height, and their eyes met directly when they turned to one another.

"What are you saying?" demanded Blithewaite.

Van Smooten gave his rival a friendly pat on the shoulder. "I am just saying that no one can besmirch your reputation for your failure to show on the field."

"Looks like you're not wearing your stripes, either!" bellowed someone.

Van Smooten, whose speech had been as bellicose as Blithewaite's, turned with sudden fire in his eye and searched the crowd. "I was the secretary to Senator Highgate, helping to govern our nation in its darkest hour!"

"Buying your way out of the draft, you mean!" came another voice.

"Bad form, bad form," said Thump.

"Questionable situation," said Eagleton.

"Not in the best interests of an enjoyable outing," said Ephram.

"On the contrary," said the young man. "Just watch." He winked at Ephram, Eagleton, and Thump and pushed his way to the front of the crowd.

"I was working for a mercantile exchange, supplying our regiments with coats," Blithewaite was insisting.

"War profiteer!" came the shout from the crowd.

"I am ready, at any time," declared Van Smooten, "to defend my ideals to the last drop of blood!" He threw his chest out and set his jaw defiantly. For some reason, he directed this statement to Blithewaite, who took it as an immediate challenge.

"I'll stand against the swiftest tide of evil and corruption, even though I drown in the process!"

"Gentlemen, gentlemen," said the young man as he stepped onto the platform. "All this can be solved very simply."

"Who are you?" demanded one of Blithewaite's attendants belligerently.

"I am John Stewart Benning. Who are you?"

The man appeared confused by this question; he stepped backwards and immediately faded from the crowd's attention.

"Mr. Blithewaite . . . Mr. Van Smooten." John Benning proffered his hand to each of the men, who eyed him with suspicion. The crowd had gotten unruly, and the young man raised a commanding hand to indicate the necessity for quiet. "This can all be solved very simply," he repeated.

"It can?" said Blithewaite and Van Smooten.

Some in the crowd laughed. "Now, now," said John Benning. "Mr. Blithewaite, in listening to your speech, I was struck by your description of certain evils against which we must take arms, even to the detriment of our physical safety."

"Of course," said Blithewaite. He looked ready to say more, but John Benning spoke before him.

"Now, am I mistaken in deducing that Mr. Van Smooten is representative of those very evils—that this is the very reason for your candidacy against him?"

Mr. Blithewaite opened his mouth twice without speaking, then said "Yes" with sudden conviction.

"Evil?" hollered Van Smooten, as if he had been bitten. "Why this . . . this political malefactor is a veritable snake in the garden!"

"Exactly," said John Benning, stepping between the two before they could close in on one another. "And so I propose a bout of fisticuffs—best out of three rounds."

The roar that greeted this motion was deafening. Mrs. Roberto (even in her attractive suit of tights) was forgotten. Sums of money were raised in the air as men made wagers, not on the proposed bout, but on its likelihood of coming to pass.

"This is ridiculous!" said Van Smooten.

Blithewaite, before he could stop himself, said: "I thought you would say that."

"Are you impugning my courage?" asked Van Smooten indignantly.

Blithewaite seemed to realize, at this point, that he had just closed the door on a graceful exit. If he had thought quickly, he might have claimed to have been referring to Van Smooten's good sense. Instead he stuttered excitedly, and Van Smooten was free to interpret the statement as he wanted.

"I'll fight you!" declared Van Smooten. "And consider it a blow for the veritable Rights of Man!"

Again the crowd roared, and this time, as the commotion died, the Freeport band, marching onto the fairgrounds, could be heard trampling the Grapes of Wrath. A great sense of martial purpose filled the two candidates, and as one they turned and strode down the steps of the platform. Men and women parted for them, and John Benning led the way to an unoccupied portion of the field, where the ever-increasing throng made a cordon to describe an improvised ring.

Not everyone in the crowd was happy with these proceedings. "This can't be legal," said one stern-faced elder.

A man who was in uniform—indeed, he looked remarkably cool on this summer day in his woolen blues—stepped forward. There were the stripes of a sergeant on his shoulder, and the sleeve of one arm was pinned to the side of his coat. He had an ancient scar across his cheek, and his face had the ruddy look of someone unimpressed with the state's prohibition against drink. But he had a gentle strength about him, and the crowd let him through to the ring with deference to his age and his service.

"Now what's all this?" he demanded, not without humor. "You don't really mean to promote a boxing match between these two?"

John Benning smiled. "Well, Sergeant, they seemed so ready to spill their blood for any number of worthy causes, I thought it cruel to deny them."

"That's the way to fight a war," averred a man in the crowd. "Let the politicians have it out."

The veteran turned an appraising gaze on the two combatants. Blithewaite and Van Smooten had divested themselves of their jackets and were limbering themselves up, their faces frozen in attitudes of heroic determination. Van Smooten looked, as he shot his fists at imaginary foes, like a man who had fallen asleep on a nest of ants, while Blithewaite gave several experimental pumps into the air and followed each jab with a triumphant "Ha!"

Perhaps the old soldier couldn't imagine that either man had any real ability to cause the other harm, for he turned back to John Benning with a soft smile. "You'll need a referee," he said simply.

"The honor falls to you, sir," said John Benning respectfully.

"No," said the sergeant. He indicated his empty sleeve. "If they get tangled up, I couldn't separate them with one arm."

John Benning scanned the crowd, and his eyes fell upon Ephram. "You, sir," he said. "You look like a fair-minded man."

"Democrat!" shouted Ephram in a tone higher than was natural to him. "Decline on grounds of partiality." He turned to Eagleton, with no intention but to see how his friend reacted to this.

"Republican!" shouted Eagleton, and together they turned to Thump, who belonged to a party that had been dissolved for ten years.

12. A Descent into the Maelstrom

IN A SMALL FOLDING CHAIR that the Underwoods provided for him, Mister Walton sat at the edge of the picnic linen and dined happily on cold beef, potato salad, boiled eggs, and numerous breads, chutneys, and jams, while Cordelia's great-aunt Delia entertained him with tales of her niece's early signs of single-mindedness. Cordelia, of course, was delighted to hear of all the contrary things she had done as a child, and Mister Walton beamed as Aunt Delia described how she and her great-niece had conspired to put bow ties on the necks of her South Freeport neighbor's ducks.

"You have not seen a drake properly dressed, Mister Walton," she was saying, wiping tears from her own eyes, "till you have seen him fitted with a black bow tie."

"The picture is not complete," said James dryly, "till you have imagined your neighbor as she watches them waddle in a line through her backyard."

Certain nearby picnickers had enjoyed the story as well, without crossing the bounds of courtesy; indeed, there was much good-natured banter between groups as they ate and played. The lighting of firecrackers was presided over by fathers, who did their best not to look like they were having as good a time as their children. A game of croquet had begun some yards away, and the immediate population had dwindled accordingly.

The news skipped across the field that Mrs. Roberto (in her attractive suit of tights) would expedite her balloon launching in order to make her famous parachute jump before the weather turned. While they watched this intrepid lady rise with her pilot into the graying sky, it was remarked that the speeches at the other side of the field were inaudible from where they sat, and, inevitably, a discussion arose over the pros and cons of this state of affairs. During just such an exchange with a particularly pleasant gentleman, Mister Walton introduced himself.

"Dr. Patrick Moriarty," said the man, shaking Mister Walton's hand. "I see, by your expression, that you are an enthusiast of the great detective."

Indeed, a surprised light had risen in Mister Walton's eye at the name *Moriarty*. Two years ago he had read (along with every other devotee) of Sherlock Holmes's death, and nearly wept to think of that grand character, however fictitious, plunging over Reichenbach Falls with the evil Professor Moriarty. "Why, yes, I am. Forgive my lack of tact."

"Not at all," said Dr. Moriarty. He was a genial, middle-aged fellow with a wife and two young daughters, all three of whom had joined the croquet match. "I had one patient," he said, with complete seriousness, "who refused treatment from me for a year and a half after Holmes died."

"Oh, my."

"I'm an admirer of the detective myself, and not a little perturbed with this previously unknown relative of mine for causing his demise."

"Ah, well, you can pick your friends, you know," said Mister Walton, with no more of a smile than might be called sly.

Dr. Moriarty was looking down the field, past Mister Walton's shoulder, and it was clear that something unusual had caught his eye. Mister Walton turned to see a large crowd gathering at one side of the speakers' platform. "Which event is that, do you suppose?" he wondered aloud.

"I don't know," said Dr. Moriarty. "It has more the look of a mob than an event." He had been sitting against the oak tree, but he stood now. Cordelia came forward and peered after the throng. "If I didn't know better, I'd say that a bout was being set up," said the doctor.

"A bout? Do you mean a fight?"

"Yes, and perhaps I *don't* know better. If that isn't a boxing match . . ."

"Who could it be?" said Cordelia. "It isn't legal to set up an unscheduled fight, is it? Aren't there licenses and such?"

"Exactly," said Dr. Moriarty. "Perhaps I had better take a closer look, in case anyone is hurt. Maybe, by the power vested in me as a physician, I can call it off. Care for a walk?" he asked Mister Walton.

"Perhaps I will stretch my legs, if the Underwoods don't mind."

"Not at all," said James. "But do come back and help us finish all this food."

As referee, Thump had not the slightest idea what was expected of him. He had read of prize fights in the *Portland Courier*, but had never actually seen one, and judges only merited a passing mention in such articles. He was more than a little daunted, therefore, to find himself surrounded by a boisterous crowd with Blithewaite, Van Smooten, John Benning, and the one-armed veteran.

Blithewaite and Van Smooten eyed each other like two aging tomcats, circling sideways with their fists waving threateningly in front of them. Shouting above the babel of the crowd, Benning declared the Queensberry rules, which Thump knew only by name. The old soldier, who could see the confusion on the face of this unenlightened referee, patted Thump encouragingly on the back, saying: "Just keep them apart if they start grappling with each other, and don't let either of them hit where it's not polite."

The noise of the crowd rose to a deafening level as John Benning and the one-armed soldier took to the sidelines. The two combatants knew enough to shake hands and take opposite sides of the ring, but Thump only stood between them, looking from one to the other.

"Give the word, sir," said John Benning to Mr. Thump.

Thump hadn't the slightest notion what that word might be. He considered saying "Ready, aim, fire!" but this seemed out of place. "On your mark, get set, go!" was equally inappropriate. Finally, he shouted, like an emperor at the Colosseum, "Let the game begin!" and tripped in his haste to remove himself from harm's way.

The crowd roared with cheers and laughter as Blithewaite and Van Smooten circled, tigerishly, several paces away from each other. They had divested themselves of coats and hats and rolled up their sleeves in a businesslike manner; now they were fired with blood and determination. Thump scurried from one side of the ring to the other.

The combatants made several circuits of the ring, glaring with express dislike—jaws jutted, eyes wide with fierce intensity, mouths constricted in frowns that would have been painful in lesser men. The noise of the crowd increased as its numbers grew and Blithewaite and Van Smooten were so filled with pugnacious resolve that they began to throw jabs into the air, though they were not within six feet of each other.

Thump was soon out of breath and red in the face as he moved his short bulk back and forth, covering more ground than either of the fighters. Twice he backed into a flailing blow, and once he thought he heard a growl emanate from Van Smooten's throat.

The battlers shot dangerous looks over their fists. The veneer of civilization had fallen; all pretense to human charity was tossed aside, all tolerance of an opposing view sloughed off like so much useless clothing. Perhaps ten feet away from one another now, they circled the ring with concentrated emotion.

So far they had endangered no one except Thump, but their continued circling had a heroic quality that spurred the raucous clamor of the crowd.

"Yes, sir," said the one-armed sergeant to John Benning. "This may be the way to fight a war."

"Do you suppose that either of them knows whom he's fighting?" wondered Benning over the din.

Indeed, so relentless were the two combatants that they were unaware of stretching the limits of the ring. The crowd retreated slightly as one of them backed into someone or the other trod upon a toe. Somehow the distance between them had grown rather than lessened, and this only seemed to increase the terrible volatility of their stares and give greater accent to the violent fluctuation of their thrusting limbs.

Then came the moment of truth, for Van Smooten unexpectedly stepped on Blithewaite's hat, an action that (to be fair) was undoubtedly accidental. Blithewaite, however, was renewed in his martial anger, and being in the vicinity of Van Smooten's hat, he purposely crushed it with the heel of his boot. Van Smooten was so thunderstruck by this gesture of disdain that he stepped back. Blithewaite followed suit, impelled as he was by the force of Van Smooten's wild expression.

They were now a full fifteen feet away from each other.

The surrounding tumult reached an almost unbearable peak, and without further prodding the throng fell back. Blithewaite and Van Smooten sensed in this mass retreat an awe, perhaps even a fear, of their grisly purpose. Thump stood alone in the center of the ring, and glanced helplessly from one violent politician to the other. There was a new sound to the crowd, a sort of warning, even pleading, and Blithewaite and Van Smooten, each convinced that this sense of fright and awe was directed at himself, closed ranks with one another—stiffly, and with strangely agitated steps.

Thump watched in horror as they neared the center of the ring, their faces contorted with animal ferocity, their minds twisted with the approbation of the crowd and the memory of their pulverized hats. The throng cried out again, but Blithewaite and Van Smooten were past any change of heart. They were nearly upon one another, no longer flailing the air with their dangerous blows. A great shadow fell over them, as if the sky itself took on the aspect of impending doom.

Thump thought that he could hear his name being called from the crowd, and he turned to see Ephram and Eagleton pointing at the sky. He looked up then and found himself directly below Mrs. Roberto's gracefully billowing skirts. He thought, as she descended upon him, that it was, without a doubt, an attractive suit of tights. He was quite taken, really, and didn't exactly mind when he and she became entangled, first in her gracefully billowing skirts, then—and Blithewaite and Van Smooten disappeared as well—in the red, white, and blue canopy of her gracefully billowing parachute!

13. The Veiled Invitation

MISTER WALTON AND DR. MORIARTY ARRIVED at the outskirts of the crowd in time to see Mrs. Roberto and her parachute descend over the figures in the improvised boxing ring. Dr. Moriarty opened a way through the throng and Mister Walton followed him till they came to the edge of the inner circle. Already John Benning and the one-armed sergeant were directing the gathering of the parachute, so that the fate of those beneath could be discovered.

Mr. Thump was the only one who had sustained any real injury; a large bump was visible on his forehead—possibly inflicted by the heel of one of Mrs. Roberto's black boots. Mrs. Roberto was already tending to the stricken man when they were revealed from beneath the lifted parachute. His head was resting gently in her lap; he appeared unconscious, but was breathing, and there was a look of peace upon his face that few did not envy.

Blithewaite and Van Smooten were not to be found. Like rabbits beneath a magician's cape, they had vanished.

Ephram and Eagleton hurried to the side of their stalwart friend; Dr. Moriarty called for some water, which was brought, and some medicinal spirits, which were quickly produced from the crowd. Gathered around the still form of Thump, John Benning remarked to the one-armed soldier how much they must appear like Benjamin West's painting of *The Death of General Wolfe*.

"It was an heroic action, Thump," said Ephram to his unconscious friend.

"In the fray," said Eagleton. "Ever in the fray."

"Dear me, was he fighting?" asked Mister Walton.

"He was referee," said the sergeant, with a wry smile.

"None more suited to balancing the scales of fair and sportsmanlike play," said Eagleton.

"Insistent upon his duty," said Ephram, forgetting that Thump had to be restrained from dashing off when picked for the office. But there was absolutely a tear in Ephram's eye as he looked down upon his fallen comrade.

"He is undaunted by the prospect of danger," added Eagleton.

Thump heard all this from a beatific haze. It was gratifying to hear the voice of Mister Walton, who seemed to have recognized someone in the crowd that had gathered around the stricken man. "I am delighted to see you again, sir," came another familiar voice in answer to Mister Walton's greeting.

Mrs. Roberto was tender in her attentions to Thump, who took a deep sigh, as if sleeping upon the softest pillow. "My," said Mrs. Roberto, "he has a magnificent beard!" She brushed the hair back from his forehead. Dr. Moriarty had bathed the man's face in cool water, and now he applied a flask of brandy to Thump's lips.

Thump's eyes opened dreamily. He hadn't, until this moment, the slightest notion where he was; and now he found himself looking past certain of Mrs. Roberto's physical endowments, which were considerable, and into her soft brown eyes as she gazed upon him with the utmost concern.

"High tide at eighteen past six," said Thump, and without warning he sat up.

Eagleton and Ephram were greatly agitated by their friend's agitation. Ephram produced one of his pocket watches and announced the time. "Two twenty-three," he said, looking at the watch critically.

"Showers expected," said Eagleton, ever the meteorographer. "Late afternoon, early evening. Possible thunderstorms scattered throughout the southern part of the state."

Thump was on his feet now, brushing himself down. Mister Walton and the sergeant helped Mrs. Roberto to her feet. "I hope you are not hurt," she said to Thump.

"One piece, I think," he said. He was so shaken by his physical contact with the woman that he couldn't even think to thank her for her concern.

"He seems quite fit, really," said Ephram.

"Tremendous descent," said Eagleton. He turned red in the face. "In the parachute, you know."

"It was a remarkable performance," said Mister Walton to Mrs. Roberto. "We were quite thrilled."

The crowd, by this time, had dispersed to other events, and even John

Benning, who had instigated the great Blithewaite–Van Smooten bout, shook Thump's hand and wandered off to other pursuits. The one-armed sergeant went to join his regiment. Mrs. Roberto's crew was carefully folding her parachute and she thanked Dr. Moriarty and Mister Walton for her rescue from under her equipage, then returned to her balloon, which had been winched back to earth.

"I can't say that I am surprised to find you here," said Ephram to Mister Walton.

"Ever in the thick," added Eagleton.

Thump was returning to the dwindling group, after retrieving his hat, which had blown some yards away. "Forming a club, you know," he said. "Not to forget."

"I will certainly keep it in mind," said Mister Walton. The three men insisted on shaking his hand once more, and they stood looking from Mister Walton to Dr. Moriarty, till Mister Walton excused himself on the grounds that he must return to his hosts. Dr. Moriarty gave Thump a final once-over, declared him hale, and accompanied Mister Walton across the field. Ephram, Eagleton, and Thump went off in search of a booth that would serve food.

"Did you understand what any of that was about?" asked Mister Walton.

"Not entirely," said the doctor. "The sergeant said that the two speakers decided to have their differences out in the ring."

"How extraordinary!"

"I suspect an outside agency might have influenced them. Good afternoon, Tom."

This last was directed to a boy of about ten or eleven years, who stepped out from under the oak, near which the Underwoods and Dr. Moriarty's family had laid their picnics. The lad was hatless, and his corn-silk hair stuck out at several angles. "Uncle Enoch is poorly, Doctor," he said, his solemn expression not attuned to the celebration of the day.

"Your uncle Enoch has been poorly for some time now," replied the doctor.

"He's gotten worse, and he told Mama they're coming for him."

The doctor nodded seriously. "You know what my rig looks like, son. Go drive it up by the field and I'll meet you there."

There was something that Mister Walton had wanted to tell Cordelia, but in the face of this new concern he promptly forgot about it. "I hope your patient is not as ill as his family fears," he said to Dr. Moriarty.

"Tom's mother is a practical woman and not given to exaggeration," said the doctor. "If she sent for me, Enoch must be near his time. He's her husband's uncle and ninety-six, after all. Dear," he said to his wife, who had been sitting with Mercia and Aunt Delia, "I'll send Tom back with the carriage, so you can go home after the fireworks."

"Nonsense," said Cordelia's great-aunt. She waved a negligent hand from her seat beneath the oak. "We will bring them home, Patrick."

"That's very kind of you, Mrs. Frost, but will you have room?"

"Certainly. The more the merrier, and if it's a little cozy, so be it."

The doctor was thinking that Mister Walton would be taking up a lot of room in Delia's rig; and sensing this, Mister Walton informed him that he had not come with the Underwoods. Dr. Moriarty rummaged through his family's picnic hamper and found half a sandwich. He gathered his coat and hat and called to his two daughters, who were still playing croquet, and who were used to their father being called away at all hours and events. He bade goodbye and looked ready to leave—Tom had already driven the carriage up to the edge of the field. The doctor stood for a moment with his hat and coat, as if inwardly debating something.

"Mister Walton," he said, turning to the bespectacled fellow. "Have you any plans for this evening?"

"Why no, Doctor. Is there any way that I can be of assistance?"

The doctor moved in the direction of his carriage, indicating that Mister Walton should walk with him. "I am guessing that you're the sort of man who wouldn't turn down the opportunity to witness an uncommon occurrence."

"You intrigue me, Doctor," said Mister Walton, falling in beside the man, and adjusting his spectacles on his nose.

"Good. Your friend beneath the parachute—when did he say the tide would be high?"

"Eighteen past six, I believe, though I must admit to some confusion over his reasons for announcing it, just then."

"That would put low tide at something past midnight. It was a bit of a non sequitur, wasn't it. Now, there will be dancing, early in the evening—at the town hall, since rain is expected—and fireworks at nine, I think. I should imagine that you might take a turn or two on the dance floor."

"If I can find a willing victim to accompany me."

Contrary to this self-deprecation, Dr. Moriarty thought to himself that the portly Mister Walton would cut a pleasing figure in the gambols and waltzes. "I'll send my carriage for you at about half past ten, then, and have it meet you at the hall."

"Yes, of course," said Mister Walton. He was vastly curious, but did his best to appear otherwise.

"I'm sorry to be mysterious, but I find myself with the chance to have an . . . uncorrupted observer." Dr. Moriarty stopped for a moment and regarded Mister Walton seriously. "I should warn you that I am inviting you to a death watch."

"I thought, perhaps."

"You must not feel obliged to join me."

"I am sure you have reasons for asking me along."

"Good. You might say that this has been a case I have been working on for some years." And finishing the distance to the carriage by himself, he called over his shoulder: "If Holmes can have his Watson, Moriarty will have his Walton."

14. Tolerable and Moderately Good

THE STORM SENT THE FOURTH OF JULY BALL indoors, and simultaneously solved the problem of overcrowding by driving away those who had come in open rigs. Aunt Delia's carriage had a collapsible top, which had already been raised to keep the seats dry, and so she and the attendant Underwoods were among those who remained. It was a genial mob—for there is seldom a more satisfied group of revelers than those who revel in spite of the weather.

Mercia and James sped the dance floor with precision and élan. Their daughter, from her chair against the wall, watched them with a mixture of pleasure and longing—longing for the simplicity of her childhood, longing for some unknown but eventful future, and longing for a present in which she would find herself part of such a couple. James and Mercia were leaving the dance floor, glowing from their exertions, when a waltz was called. James took his wife's hand, gently swept her toward him, and led her gracefully away again as the first notes plaintively sang from the lead fiddle.

Mister Walton had been speaking with Ephram, Eagleton, and Thump on the other wide of the room, but as the new song struck up, he hurried his round self to Aunt Delia's chair and offered his hand. Aunt Delia's seventy-eight years weighed very lightly upon her as she accepted his invitation. Soon they vanished among the twirling crowd.

Cordelia watched for them or her parents to appear again as the dancers revolved past her in a blur. The faces, mostly unfamiliar, shifted one to another, and she had become almost hypnotized by the sweep of outstretched arms, the confidential expressions, and the swirl of skirts, when she was conscious of the handsome young man whom she had seen this morning walking toward her—the very same handsome young man who had prevented her from falling overboard at Portland's Custom House Wharf two days before.

Conflicting notions chased each other through Cordelia's mind as she watched the man approach: one was to absent herself from his immediate trajectory; another was to pretend that she did not recognize him; several quickly conceived plans incorporated various witty (or hopefully witty) things she might say once he was within speaking distance. *You can see that I have stayed well away from the water since I spoke with you last.* No, that wouldn't do; it made it sound as if she didn't bathe. *You will be glad to see that there is no height here for me to fall from.* That sounded as if she were clumsy, or constantly in need of rescue.

He was looking directly, and frankly, into her eyes, and smiled warmly as he came to her. Did it really take as long as it does to tell about it? Looking back, Cordelia would certainly doubt it, for she hadn't arrived at a satisfactory plan before he stopped in front of her seat and bowed with comic formality.

"Oh, please, don't get up," he said, as she rose from her chair. She did think, perhaps, that she had appeared too eager, so she returned to her seat, but with such a loud sort of landing that he couldn't be blamed for wondering if she hurt herself. It was not gracefully accomplished, and Cordelia was, by this time, red to the tips of her ears.

"I haven't had the opportunity to properly thank you," she managed to say, referring to his timely rescue of her two days before.

"Perhaps, then, you might thank me by putting my name on your dance card." There was a sincere hope in his brown eyes that struck a chord, almost painfully, within her.

"To tell the truth, I hadn't expected to need a dance card," she said; and to look at her soft features, her freckled nose and dark eyebrows, her green eyes and red hair glowing in the lamplight, one might think— though mistakenly—that the statement was dishonest. Cordelia had imagined herself, from childhood, to be plain, and all the admiring glances that had come her way had not convinced her otherwise.

"I can't imagine that you haven't more than one card, already full," said the handsome man. He reached into his jacket. "But I have come prepared for just such an eventuality." He took from an inside pocket a dance card, with the legend *Freeport Fourth of July Celebratory Ball*—1896 on its front cover. Two middle-aged ladies who were seated next to Cordelia watched, without pretense to minding their own business, as he handed this to the young woman.

She took the dance card and unfolded it. It had room for a dozen names—six to each side—and every line was filled with the name *John Benning*.

Cordelia laughed aloud. "Are you sure that you have given me the right card? Someone seems to have been practicing their signature on this one."

"An admirer," he answered, "hoping to get the steps right by the last dance."

The two ladies were absolutely giddy by this point, and could hardly contain themselves in the vicarious pleasure of watching this romantic badinage. "This John Benning," asked Cordelia, "is he in the room?"

John Benning reached out his hand. "Come," he said. "I will introduce you to him. He is said to be a moderately good dancer."

"I am only tolerable myself, so perhaps it will be to both our benefits." She accepted his hand and allowed herself to be whirled upon the dance floor.

John Benning proved to be something more than moderately good as he led her into the revolving crowd. When they had waltzed halfway around the room, and she had caught a glimpse of her mother's curiosity as they passed each other, he said: "All that I lack now, ma'am, is your name."

She felt out of breath, suddenly, as the events of the last few moments had caught up with her. Through the crowd, she could see the two older women pointing in her direction and talking enthusiastically to their neighbors. She realized that she had not answered him, after a moment, and said, simply: "Cordelia Underwood."

The titillated onlookers disappeared behind the circle of dancers. "Well, Miss Underwood," said John Benning with the frankness that had already startled her so. "When I saw you across the dance floor, *tolerable* was not a word that came to mind."

15. A Storm at Mast Landing

THERE WAS NOT MUCH that Dr. Moriarty could do for Enoch Dill. However commonplace, the forces at work here were deep and mysterious, and in Enoch's case merciful as well. Enoch's final hours were warm and snug in his own bed; and if they were not quiet, with the rain pummeling the attic roof, they were nonetheless peaceful.

"Would you like another lamp, Dr. Moriarty?" asked Mrs. Dill.

"This is fine, thank you." He took the dying man's wrist and felt for a pulse; but finding life too faint to register there, he laid a gentle hand against the side of the dying man's throat. The artery thrummed weakly, sluggishly, as the doctor kept time with his pocket watch. "I have asked a friend to join us tonight," he said conversationally.

"Tom said that you asked him to pick someone up at the hall."

"I hope you and your family don't mind. No disrespect is intended."

"I understand . . . your reasons."

"Thank you. I say 'friend,' and yet I met him only today."

"Uncle Enoch always welcomed a new acquaintance," said Mrs. Dill without smiling.

The doctor did smile, however. "Yes." He put his watch away, glancing at the rain-streaked window at the other end of the attic room. "That window looks out at the bay?"

Mrs. Dill nodded, and after a period of rain-pattered quiet, she said: "I've never seen it before," speaking of something else.

"I have seen it twice. If it comes tonight, however, it will be for the last time, I think."

"I understand why you asked someone to come."

An uncorrupted observer, thought Dr. Moriarty.

"My daughter will come up so that I can make something to eat when he arrives."

"That's very kind."

When Mrs. Dill was gone, before Annie came to replace her, Dr. Moriarty went to the window and looked out into the rainy night. Even with his face pressed to the glass he could see little more than shadows beyond his own lamplit reflection.

In his bed, ninety-six-year-old Enoch Dill dwindled peacefully.

When Mister Walton stepped out of the Freeport Town Hall, Dr. Moriarty's carriage awaited him. He had spent his evening dancing reels and quadrilles, and even the occasional waltz, with several mature women, and delighted himself and his partners in doing so. While dancing, Mister Walton would express an hilarious anecdote, or pretend to be confused with the steps expected of him, and invariably his companion would be escorted from the dance floor in great gales of laughter.

It proved just what an agile dancer he was that he could add two or three capers to a step without overshooting his partner, or come close to missing a cue without ever quite doing so. Once, while dancing with Mercia, he walked a promenade backwards, as if he were carried away by a high wind, and the entire hall roared with delight.

There was something almost contradictory about the man—portly, gracious, and seemingly quiet even in his jollity. His round face, his wide eyes behind magnifying spectacles—even his nearly bald head—expressed something of the child in him; and yet, there was a wisdom in his joy of life that seemed ancient in its philosophy.

Whenever he waited out a dance, in order to rest, he would sit with the Underwoods, who deliberated on the handsome young man monopolizing their daughter. Cordelia and John Benning (who had been briefly introduced to her parents) seemed to need less rest than other folk, and when they did wait out a dance, it was by the punch bowl on the opposite side of the room.

Mister Walton did recognize John Benning from two days before on the Portland wharf, and had recognized him earlier in the day at the aftermath of Mrs. Roberto's unexpected parachute landing, which is what he had meant to tell Cordelia.

Outside, the night had darkened, and a fitful rain increased as clouds choked the sky. The wind picked up, and heralded the coming of electrical flashes with the smell of ions.

Mopping his brow, Mister Walton looked up at the schoolhouse clock that hung above the small proscenium at the other end of the hall. It was ten-thirty. With regret he bade his dance companions good night, added thanks to the many he had already expressed to Cordelia's great-aunt and to James and Mercia, and stepped out onto the front steps.

Dr. Moriarty's carriage awaited him, and though lanterns burned on each side of the rig, they did little to dispel the wet darkness. He cocked his hat against the wind and rain, pulled his coat tight about him, and descended the steps to the carriage. "Mister Walton?" inquired young Tom, who sat upon the driver's bench, almost invisible in a black slicker.

"Yes, my boy," he said, above the rain. "How is your uncle?"

"I fear he's dying, sir."

"I am very sorry to hear it." He squinted through the damp, but couldn't see the boy's expression.

"Thank you, sir. But he had a good long life, and knew the Lord."

"There's comfort in that, son. I hope I won't be intruding."

"Ma's expecting you, sir. She knows why Dr. Moriarty asked you to come. Besides, Uncle Enoch was always one for company."

Mister Walton saw the flash of a smile with this last thought, and he climbed into the carriage. A flicker to the east silhouetted buildings on the other side of the street, and, several seconds later, a soft rumble carried over the sound of carriage wheels and horses. It occurred to him that he had no idea where they were going.

It was a classic squall coming in from the northeast—a great swirl of wet and chilly weather backing up over the mainland—and though it was relatively mild for a nor'easter along the immediate coast, Mister Walton suspected that those out to sea might be having a bad time. The rain was loud on the top of the carriage, and he was sorry for the boy in front of him, hunched against the driving weather; more than likely, though, the lad was too young to think of it as anything but an adventure. Lightning illumined the sky in cold flashes, and thunder—a little closer now—shivered the air.

The carriage was turned north, but soon they were twisting east and south again. Tom slowed the horses as the road grew wilder and steeper. Through the rain, his single passenger could see lights a mile or so across several hills and a dark body of water. Mister Walton wasn't sure how either Tom or the horses could see the road, and as the way led along the edge of a headland, he tried not to think about it. Twice the carriage took a lurch toward the water and he was sure they would tumble into the river.

He was content, therefore, to feel the carriage draw to a halt, and hear the horses nicker with that sound of recognition that marks the end of a journey. Tom snapped the brake against the rear wheel, then jumped down to throw a chock against it. Mister Walton was about to open the carriage door and step down when the boy called out: "I wouldn't go out the right-hand side, sir."

Mister Walton had been gripping the right-hand door—which was the side he had got in on—and he glanced out the window, surprised to see nothing but sky and water, barely demarcated from one another in the rainy blackness. A fork of lightning snapped at the opposing arm of land and nicely lit the gulf that yawned beyond the water side of the carriage. He laughed wryly. "My aunt August insisted that it was bad luck to leave by a different door than the one through which you entered, but I think I'll chance it."

Tom opened the left-hand door with an efficient snap. It was clear, even in the dark, that his passenger was slightly disconcerted. "Sorry, sir, I should have spoke sooner. It's a long step—and a swim, I think—on that side."

"That's all right, my boy. A miss is as good as a mile, they say, and I suppose that goes for long drops." Climbing out the other side, Mister Walton could see the small hulk of a modest cape standing amongst several windswept trees some yards away. Lights burned in two windows, and in one window he saw the shadow of someone peering out.

Flagstones led past a row of rosebushes that rushed in the wind and rain; Mister Walton could smell them in the heavy air. He picked his way carefully along the wet rock, Tom bringing up the rear. The door opened before they reached the back step, and Tom's mother ushered them into a warm, dry kitchen.

The reason for his being here was still not apparent to Mister Walton, and he stood awkwardly in the middle of the room as Mrs. Dill took his coat and hat. There was just enough fire in the old iron hearth to trouble a pot of tea, which burbled quietly with a steady puff of steam.

A door opened on the other side of the room, revealing a narrow stairway, leading up. Dr. Moriarty appeared from the shadows and stepped down into the kitchen. "Good evening, Mister Walton," he said in a normal tone, the volume of which surprised the newcomer. It had been expected, with a man dying upstairs, that the whole house would be speaking in whispers.

"I do hope," said Mister Walton, in something below a normal voice, "that this is not an intrusion."

"The doctor said you'd be coming, Mister Walton," said Mrs. Dill, as if that explained everything. She was a weathered-looking woman, though he could see the beauty of her youth peering through her years. She was trim from her labor, and her fingers were dexterous as they flipped the collar of his coat up—the better to dry—before hanging it behind the stove, and she proceeded to arrange a cold meal and hot tea at the kitchen table.

"Come have a bit to eat," said Dr. Moriarty, pulling a chair up to the table. Tom scooched a chair up beside the doctor and waited politely for the rest to sit. Mister Walton found it hard to figure that he was sitting down to eat here with strangers and near-strangers, Mrs. Dill calmly pouring tea, with a man dying somewhere above them.

Mrs. Dill did not smile, but her features softened slightly. "Come sit, Mister Walton. Uncle Enoch did love a new acquaintance, and would have been grieved to think that anyone wasn't well fed at his table."

"Thank you, Mrs. Dill," said the bespectacled fellow. And, trusting that he would eventually understand the mystery of his being here, he pulled a chair up to the table and gladly accepted a plate of cold meat, a handful of bread, and a cup of tea.

A Storm—July 4th, 1896

The storm upon the landing shook
Each creature in his den or nook;
Each from his sleep or duty took,
That all might pause in prayerful wonder.

And whether sea or land was hit,
Whatever frozen moment split,
The shocking incandescence lit
That very instant torn asunder.

A mystery sailed the wind-swept rain,
And, peering from a storm-lashed pane,
I glimpsed St. Elmo's fiery chain
Along the coast it meant to plunder.

And there I felt my heart-strings tightening
Thinking with each peal so frightening
What a fearful lamp is lightning
And what a spectral herald thunder.

— TOBIAS WALTON
December 12th, 1896

16. It Was Their Duty

EPHRAM, EAGLETON, AND THUMP were ecstatic over their discovery of Mister Walton. Standing in their own small group in a corner of the Freeport Town Hall, they smiled at the prettily dressed ladies who waltzed past them, and discussed amongst themselves the man's extraordinary virtues.

"I believe it is safe to say that he is first-rank," insisted Ephram.

"Quite, quite," added Eagleton, by way of enthusiastic accord.

Thump rubbed the bruise on his forehead. He had been uncharacteristically silent since his accident on the fairgrounds. Ephram and Eagleton were sure that he had been stunned, and this was near to the truth, for he *had* been stunned—not by the blow to his head, but by the still-vivid recollection of Mrs. Roberto in her attractive suit of tights as she descended in her parachute drop upon him. The image was burned into the cornea of his memory, and he found little in his present circumstances, however prettily the waltzing women were dressed, to distract him from contemplating that instant in which he glanced up at the plummeting woman.

Ephram repeated his assertion that Mister Walton had the stuff for a position in their undefined and nameless club, hoping that this contention would rouse their friend from his baffled state.

"I do hope she wasn't injured in the collision," said Thump.

Ephram and Eagleton exchanged concerned glances. Clearly something needed to be said. "I shouldn't worry," said Eagleton. "She did seem healthy."

This was, perhaps, an unfortunate choice of words, for it put Thump in mind of waking with his head in Mrs. Roberto's plush lap, and looking up at her soft brown eyes, past certain *robust* endowments. Thump agreed that she did seem healthy, and said so. He had, in fact, seen her soft brown eyes with only one of his own, somewhat in the fashion of a mountain climber who sees with one eye the pinnacle he hopes to reach from under a rocky overhang.

"There are a good deal of charming ladies in attendance, this evening, don't you think?" wondered Eagleton, to neither of his friends in particular. "We should, perhaps, put to use our skills upon the dance floor, eh?"

"I was thinking just that," said Ephram, when it was clear that Thump was not going to respond. "And you, Eagleton?"

"I am thinking of it as well. Yes, indeed."

All three of these men had taken lessons in dance, stiffly learning how to maneuver the latest steps in the arms of Mrs. De Riche, an eighty-two-year-old matron and patron of the arts, who was accustomed to younger students. Since graduating from Mrs. De Riche's Academy of Ballroom Sciences, they had attended twenty-three functions in which dancing was the primary event, and not once put to use the fruits of their learning.

It seemed that even the possibility, however doubtful, of a dance would not draw Thump from his state of quietude, and to lift the uncomfortable silence between them, Eagleton, in an extraordinary moment of levity, suggested to Ephram that a woman on the other side of the hall was watching him.

"What?" said an astonished Ephram.

"I think your prospects have decidedly improved," said Eagleton.

"No!"

"Oh, yes, I do," teased Eagleton. He winked broadly at Thump, who simply said: "Hmmm?"

"Who?" demanded Ephram.

"There—just in front of the second window from the left."

"Is she standing?"

"That's the one." Eagleton was rather proud of his choice.

"In the pink dress?"

"Oh, I think, most definitely." Eagleton was bobbing with excitement, having rather forgotten that he had fabricated the entire idea.

"No!" said Ephram again.

"Without a doubt!"

Ephram considered the young woman across the dance floor. "No!"

"Oh, yes!"

"Oh-ho!" said Ephram, unbelieving; but the thought so delighted him that he laughed when he said it, which animated his face quite handsomely. The young woman in the pink dress, who was idly taking in the room, caught sight of Ephram's smile and smiled in return. The two friends reddened to the ears and chortled giddily to one another. Ephram felt as if someone must be tickling him. "Good heavens! I think you're right!"

Eagleton poked his friend in the ribs. "Quickly, you must wave to her!"

"What's that you say?"

"Wave! Wave to her!"

"Wave to her?" Ephram threw his shoulders back, lifted his jaw, and, with an expression of utter terror, shot a hand in the air.

The young woman, who thought Ephram was being terribly funny, laughed prettily and flickered a delicate hand in his direction. She then caught the attention of another young woman standing next to her, said something, and pointed, upon which this second woman looked, laughed, and waved as well.

Eagleton was saying something that sounded like "Hoff, hoff, hoff!" as Ephram poked him in the ribs. "I think *she's* looking at *you*," said Ephram.

"No!"

"Oh, yes, I really do! Look, she's waving again!"

"Oh-ho, Ephram, you're right! Good heavens, what do I do?"

"Wave!"

"What?"

"Quickly, man—wave to her!"

Eagleton lifted an arm with as little grace as his friend, like a wooden soldier volunteering for hazardous duty. The second young woman seemed to have caught the giggles from her friend and waved with obvious pleasure to Eagleton.

Eagleton felt weak in the knees, just contemplating his next sentence. Ephram caught him by the elbow as he sagged slightly. "Perhaps . . ." suggested Eagleton, "perhaps we should actually make an approach and speak to them."

"Opportunity knocks but once," said an inspired, if perspiring, Ephram. "Well, twice in this case."

"It would be impolite to ignore charming prospects," added Eagleton, quoting dance mistress Mrs. De Riche.

"And here we have charming prospects of the first rank, I say," agreed Ephram. He turned to Thump and took the man's hand, shaking it vigorously. "You must wish me luck, my friend," he said.

"Hmmm?" said Thump.

Ephram took Eagleton's hand and shook it vigorously.

Eagleton took Thump's hand and shook it vigorously. "Perhaps they have a friend," he hoped aloud.

"Hmmm?" said Thump.

The current waltz had ended, the musicians paused for breath, and, shoulder to shoulder, Ephram and Eagleton marched across the dance floor. Halfway to their intended destination, however, a certain palsy affected their limbs, so that neither of them could actually put one foot ahead of the other, unless that foot was headed in the direction of the punch bowl, exactly ninety degrees from the two young women, who smiled at their eccentric approach.

They did not see the expressions of the two young women as they turned away, but no punch, however tasty, could quell Ephram and Eagleton's sense of disappointment as they filled their cups. "Feeling a bit dry," said Ephram.

"Hot weather brings on thirst," philosophized Ephram. He was checking his timepiece.

"How *did* you know that we were *dying* for a glass of punch?" came a feminine voice, from behind Eagleton. He swung about on one heel and, magically, managed not to spill his cup by extending it at arm's length. The young woman took the cup deftly from his hands, as if it were meant for her. "Thank you so much."

The second female raised an eyebrow in Ephram's direction.

"Twelve minutes past ten," he said. He dropped three cups before managing to fill one, then gingerly handed it to her.

"Continued thundershowers and heavy rain expected till morning, followed by partial clearing," said Eagleton.

"No telling what the tide is without Thump," said Ephram, ever ready to remember an absent friend.

The young women, delighted with this information, laughed so uproariously, some people thought that Mister Walton had returned. Ephram and Eagleton glanced at one another, each hoping that the other might have the slightest idea what to say next. Fortunately, the two young ladies, Sallie and Ophelia, were more than ready to do the talking for them. Ephram and Eagleton stood at the punch table and nodded and smiled at everything the young women said. Sallie and Ophelia were flattered by the gentlemen's kind attention and quite sparkled the rest of the evening.

In their own profound pleasure, Ephram and Eagleton did not, at first, see a more-than-stunned Thump gliding past them on the dance floor with the extraordinary Mrs. Roberto.

17. The Wake of the Dash

THE STAIRWELL THAT LED to Enoch Dill's bedroom was steep and dark and narrow; and it was airless with that musty stillness often found in places in between. Two small pictures from an old calendar hung upon the right-hand wall: the first was of a barefoot boy leading a cow along a meadow path; the second, of a young woman sitting beneath a willow tree by a brook.

A peal of thunder rumbled softly through the walls of the stairwell as Mister Walton followed Dr. Moriarty to the second floor of the house. A door at the head of the stairs opened with a short creak and they ascended the last steps to an unfinished chamber where nothing but roof boards and shingles lay above and the downpour sounded loud and comforting. One window at the end of the house was opened just a crack, letting welcome drafts of cool air into the close space and rain upon a sea chest beneath the sill.

A single lamp sat upon a stand by a bed. Mister Walton was almost startled to see a young woman sitting nearby, an open book in her lap. It had not occurred to him—though it seemed sensible—that someone would be with the dying man at all times.

"Good evening, Annie," said the doctor in a conversational tone.

"Good evening, Doctor," said the girl. She laid a ribbon in her book and closed it.

"This is Mister Walton," explained Moriarty.

"Have you come to keep the doctor company, Mister Walton?" she said, after a gentle nod of acknowledgment.

"Yes, ma'am, if it is not an intrusion."

"Well, I'm glad, for the doctor's sake, that you could come. Uncle will be keeping other company tonight." She rose from her chair now. "Will you be needing anything, Doctor?"

"Another pot of tea, perhaps. In an hour or so, Annie. What do you say, Mister Walton?"

"That would be fine."

The door closed behind the girl and they could hear her light footsteps on the treads. Dr. Moriarty found a chair in the corner of the room and drew it up for his companion, then sat down in the chair beside the bed. He reached beneath the covers, gently drew out a thin arm, and gazed toward the window as he felt the dying man's pulse.

Mister Walton could see little of the quiet form in the bed but a nose made prominent with age and a short gray beard. "He's weak," said Dr. Moriarty. "I can hardly feel his pulse."

"Has he been sick long?"

"He's been old long. Old and tired. I wonder he lasted till now." The doctor smiled down at the man. "I certainly don't think he wanted to. Enoch Dill is the last of an unusual fellowship."

"Indeed?"

Moriarty slipped Enoch's hand back beneath the covers. "I think the storm is blowing past," he said, and the thunder did seem to have sneaked away when they were not listening. There was only rain now—still insistent upon the roof—and the occasional low rumble to the west. "That window looks over the water, Mister Walton. Can you see anything from it?"

Standing by the window, Mister Walton could see the darkness of the water as a separate darkness from the land. Strangely, he could sense the motion of the river—the surge of the wind-driven swells—though the night was dark enough to hide even the froth of the whitecaps, and that intuition of movement carried with it an understanding of the water's depth and chill. One corner of the window reflected the light of the room's single lamp, warm in contrast to the wet night, and in that reflection he could see the doctor watching him. Moriarty lowered the shade of the lamp so that Mister Walton might better see.

"Nothing but rain and the night," said the man at the window. He adjusted his spectacles on his nose and squinted through them. A brief glimmer of lightning barely delineated the contours of cliffs and trees, making the resurgent darkness more inscrutable than before. "Nothing," he said again, turning back to the room.

The doctor glanced at his watch and tucked it back into his vest pocket. "It's early yet, perhaps. We'll keep an eye closer at the turn of the tide."

Mister Walton pulled at his own watch fob and checked the hour as he returned to his chair. It was nearly half past eleven and low tide had been predicted to occur shortly after midnight. He was more mystified than ever, but was amused rather than bothered; Dr. Moriarty inspired trust, and with that trust was the understanding that all would be revealed in its time.

He watched the small form in the bed, trying to discern some indication of breath, but the man's respiration was so shallow as to leave the bedclothes undisturbed. "He seems peaceful," said Mister Walton.

"Yes, I truly believe he is," said the doctor. "As I hope I will be, when my time comes."

"You say he is the last of *an unusual fellowship*."

"He is indeed."

Mister Walton glanced about the room for some clues, and his eyes fell upon the netting of an ancient ship's hammock folded neatly on a shelf in one corner. That, and the sea chest beneath the sill, made him think of Mr. Privy sleeping soundly in his bed at the Mariners' Hospital. "Was he a sailor, then?" he asked.

"No, he was a shipbuilder, though he had family who sailed. Have you heard of the *Dash*, Mister Walton?"

"Ah, the great privateer! Was Mr. Dill a builder, then, upon the *Dash*?"

"He may have seen some work upon it, though he was still young." The doctor glanced for a moment over the quiet form of the dying man, as if to include him in the conversation. "Mr. Dill was born with the century, so he would have only been thirteen or so when it was built, and hardly fifteen when it disappeared."

"I remember, now, that it came to an unknown end. My father, who was just the smallest sort of lad when it disappeared, used to tell me about it."

"The fastest and deadliest ship ever built on these shores, or so I've been told," said the doctor. "She was long since gone before my own father was born, so I have had to take other folks' word for her history. No equal in speed, it was said. She never attacked an enemy ship in vain, and was never injured by a hostile shot."

"I have heard those exact words on my father's lap."

"She foiled the British blockade, outran His Majesty's ships, and captured fourteen vessels in less than two years. Saved the Porter family from bankruptcy, and any number of Freeport families from consequent penury."

"She simply disappeared, if I remember."

"On a cruise to test the speed of a new privateer, called the *Champlain*. In a squall, much like this one, perhaps, though earlier in the year, the *Champlain* lost sight of her, and she was never seen again. A Porter himself was her captain, then, and it was thought that he underrated her speed and that she foundered off George's Bank."

"And Mr. Dill is the last person left to know something particular about the *Dash*?" asked Mister Walton.

"He is the last to have known someone who was lost with her."

"This is the fellowship, then, of which you spoke."

"Yes. His beloved older brother, Chandler, was only nineteen when she sailed her last. And some portion of Enoch's heart has been waiting to see him again ever since." The physician reached beneath the covers to touch Enoch Dill's wrist. A small sound came from Moriarty and he lifted his medical bag from the floor next to his feet and rummaged through it till he found a small mirror, which he held beneath the dying man's nose. The smallest mist appeared there to indicate that the thread of life had not yet been severed.

Mister Walton was thinking of what the doctor had said, still not sure why he had been asked to accompany him at Enoch Dill's deathbed. They talked some more of the *Dash*, of her short but extraordinary career, of the sixty men who were lost aboard her, and of the many families (in the Freeports) and in Porter's Landing and Mast Landing—even where they now sat—who were bereaved by her untimely and unknown demise.

At just a few minutes shy of midnight, footsteps could be heard on the stairs and the door opened to reveal Mrs. Dill with a cozy-covered pot of tea and three cups. She arranged these on the stand beside Uncle Enoch's bed and served the two men before joining them.

"Have you seen anything, Doctor?" she asked as she raised the cup to her lips.

"Not yet. But perhaps Mister Walton would not mind taking another look. It's less than an hour before the tide begins to turn."

Mister Walton still hadn't the slightest idea what he was looking for, but went, with his cup of tea steaming before him, to the window and stood so that his own round silhouette formed a shadow against the light of the lamp. It was still raining, though not so hard as before, but the wind drove sprinkles against the window in wavelike rhythms. Outside, there was only darkness—if anything, blacker than before.

"I can't see a thing," he said. "I must admit to some surprise that you expect me to, looking out over the river on a night like this."

"Just such a night as this," said the doctor.

"It won't take long, I'm thinking, with the wind as it is," said Mrs. Dill.

Mister Walton wondered if they were waiting for some sight of her husband, coming in with the tide before the storm, but there was no look of concern to accompany that sort of vigil. He returned to his seat while the doctor and Mrs. Dill talked of local matters, not bothering to speak below normal tones. It seemed a shame, thought Mrs. Dill, to send her uncle out from a hushed house.

Mister Walton fidgeted with his watch; he was anxious, now, to tend his place at the window. When another quarter of an hour had passed he rose, without being asked, and peered into the night a third time. The conversation behind him fell silent as he gently pressed his forehead to the cool glass and gazed out over the water.

At first he saw nothing but the same black night as before; then, when his eyes had adjusted slightly to the gloom, he thought he saw, through the erratic sheets of rain, the slightest hint of something gray in the distance—

in the narrows between Porter's Landing and Wolf's Neck. Then the rain fell between in a great gust and the undefined shape was gone.

"Is something there?" asked the doctor, when Mister Walton continued to gaze into the rainy night.

"Yes," came the bespectacled man's reply. He set his cup of tea down on the floor, for fear that it would steam the window. Then "Yes!" again, as he returned to his vigil, and caught a second glimpse of something gray and amorphous on the turbulent waters. He glanced back to see Dr. Moriarty with the mirror, testing the dying man's breath again. Mrs. Dill took her uncle's hand and held it, her expression thoughtful and distant. A chill of premonition passed through Mister Walton as it occurred to him that Enoch's last moments and the object on the Harraseeket River were somehow linked.

He watched through the stormy dark, catching an occasional glimpse of gray whenever the curtains of rain briefly parted. It was another, almost phosphorescent, glow—following the first—that made him realize what he was seeing; the pale line was a running wake, and the gray object was a ship at full sail, tearing before the wind of the storm and up the wide bay of the river. The vessel seemed unheedful of the strength of the wind, or the propinquity of the shore, crashing through the swells of the river, blown up by the storm, its prow piercing the water with a courageous determination.

Mister Walton wondered how he was seeing this ship at all; he perceived no particular light aboard her, nor could he imagine any light on shore strong enough to illumine her through the driving rain. But there she was, running before the storm—so clear to the eye that he could see her for a three-masted schooner, oddly rigged like a brig at her forward mast; and there were men, perhaps, upon her deck, no more daunted by the storm or their approach to land than the vessel herself.

"Good heavens, they shall crash!" he said.

"Never fear, Mister Walton," said Mrs. Dill. "They are a skillful crew, as well as gallant."

Such seemed to be the case, for the schooner was suddenly becalmed, though no sail was shortened, and no gust of wind decreased—indeed, the storm sounded larger as the vessel loomed below the steep shore and the small cape atop it. She rolled and tossed upon the waters, and Mister Walton gasped as a longboat, as gray to look at as if seen through a fog, was lowered from the schooner's port side. In the gloom he could see oars shipped from the boat, and stalwart backs, small and gray in the distance, pulling against the waves.

"The tide is turning," said Dr. Moriarty.

Mister Walton watched as the boat was oared toward the shore, disappearing from sight behind the small bulk of land between the house and the water. All the while, the great schooner held its place, tossing with the wind and waves. A stillness behind him caught Mister Walton's attention and he turned to see the doctor arranging Enoch Dill's arms upon his chest.

"He is gone," said the doctor, more quietly than he had spoken the entire night. Mrs. Dill pulled the sheets over the still form, while the doctor joined Mister Walton, for the first time, at the window. "Ah, yes," he said, looking upon the river. "You have joined another sort of fellowship, my friend."

"So I suspected," said Mister Walton. "But I am confounded to think what that fellowship might be."

"You have entered a small society among the living, Mister Walton, that have laid eyes upon the mighty *Dash* herself."

"The *Dash*, Dr. Moriarty?" Mister Walton tried vainly to suppress a shiver. Mrs. Dill's reflection darkened the window further as she appeared at his shoulder.

> "*She was manned by a crew of gallant lads* [the doctor recited],
> *As ever a vessel's deck had trod.*
> *Three score and two, and brave men all—*
> *And their fate is known to none but God.*
>
> "*They all belonged to the towns around,*
> *There were brothers and cousins and comrades, too,*
> *Full armed and equipped to put to sea,*
> *And the skies were never a softer blue.*"

Mister Walton could see the gray longboat, now, pulling back toward the gray vessel. He peered to see the name upon its prow, but she was still tossing too swiftly, too far away, the night and the rain were too thick, and his eyes were misting slightly as he watched the figures in the longboat brought aboard and the longboat raised.

> "*But weeks and months and years sped on,*
> *And hearts grew hopeless and cheeks grew pale,*
> *And eyes are dim that watched so long*
> *To catch a glimpse of her home-bound sail.*
>
> "*But when any of those who loved the lads*
> *Are ready to slip their moorings here*
> *And sail away to that unknown port,*
> *You will see the Dead Ship gliding near.*"

"Do you suppose," wondered Mister Walton, "that his brother was one of those manning the longboat?"

"The old folk always spoke of Uncle Chandler as a great hand at the oars," said Mrs. Dill.

When boat and crew were all aboard, the ship hung in her place for a bit, shouldering the swells that splashed like surf against her bows; and Mister Walton could imagine that she and her men might care for one last look upon the shores of Earth. The wind and rain slowed for a moment, then picked up with a strange roar, shifting suddenly in the opposite direction—a westerly wind to blow the storm back over the coast. The ship heeled about and caught the wind square in its sails. In a moment it was scudding down-river for the ocean and—if Dr. Moriarty was right—for eternity.

> "And the ship and the life go out with the tide,
> And those who are left have thought and said,
> We are most of us gone and the Dead Ship soon
> Will come no more for the souls of the dead."

Book Four

JULY 5-6, 1896

18. The Unasked Question

THERE HAD ALWAYS BEEN OAK TREES on Delia Frost's land in South Free-port: grand and solitary watchmen, spreading their presence and their shade over the grounds. But since her husband had left (never to return) in search of gold during the rush of '49, and since her father and brother had left for the War Between the States (never to return), other growth had mastered the borders of the family property.

The stone walls were partly hidden now; small trees and bushes cloaked them against the weather, and the leaves of many years lay banked like foot warmers along their windward sides. One stretch of stonework alone remained uncovered, and that was along the eastern border of the property, which overlooked Staples Cove and Bowman Island.

Cordelia's father had often wondered if someone should be hired to reclear Aunt Delia's land, but the old woman was uninterested. Her father and brother had built several of the walls, yet she did not mourn to see them disappear beneath the cover of tree and bush; she knew where they were.

She could see part of one of these obscured walls from her bedroom window, even in the first days of July when the verdant growth of summer had taken hold. She stood for a moment in her nightdress and robe on the Sunday morning after the Freeport Fourth of July Celebratory Ball, gazing down at the stones that remained visible, searching out the personality of the day, when Cordelia appeared in her line of sight.

The young woman looked nothing less than a vision dressed in white and green, her red hair let down upon her shoulders. Delia was struck by this sight of her great-niece, there was such an air of romantic distraction about the girl as she shuffled the leaves of past autumns still wet with the night's storm. Delia was also struck by the fact that she knew next to nothing about John Benning, the man with whom Cordelia had danced almost the entire night.

"You had little to say when we got home last night," she said as she approached the stone wall where Cordelia sat now, looking out over the cove and the island. The old woman had made a quick business of dressing, and put off breakfast in order to interview Cordelia before James and Mercia were up.

Cordelia turned away from the sea breeze and the sunlight to watch her great-aunt step along the flagstone walk. "Did I?" she said brightly.

"Yes, if nothing at all counts for little," said Aunt Delia wryly.

Fearing that her aunt was not very agile, Cordelia offered her hand, but Delia waved her away and plunked herself unceremoniously onto the wall. "I came down and sat on this very wall," she said, "almost fifty years ago to consider Abner's proposal of marriage."

"Well, I haven't a proposal of marriage to consider," said Cordelia, with a certain relief in her voice that her aunt was glad to hear.

"You look like I did, though, I'm sure."

"Why, how did you look, Aunty?"

"What were you thinking of just now, when I spoke to you?"

"Do you see that gull?" said Cordelia. She pointed down the slope of the land to an outcropping of rock fifty yards away. A herring gull sat with his feathers ruffling against the light breeze. He had a hunched, expectant look, and his head darted from one side to the other as he watched for some sight of either breakfast or company. "I was thinking that if I could memorize his markings and see him the next time I am here, I would name him."

"My goodness!" exclaimed Aunt Delia.

"Why, what were you thinking when you sat here fifty years ago?"

"I was thinking that if I moved to another town my German was good enough to convince people that I was from Bavaria."

Cordelia laughed. "Well, they are almost the same thing."

Aunt Delia smiled.

"Why did you come down here, Aunty?"

"You know very well. I want to hear about this beau of yours before your father wakes up and demands to know what the young man does for a living."

"John's father is a surveyor. Quite successsful, I might add."

"And what does *John* do?"

"He's been to Cambridge. And he's traveled. He's done the Tour."

"He uses his time well, it seems. Does he not have to work for a living himself, then?"

"He works for his father, as a matter of fact."

"Hmm," said Delia. She shifted herself on the stone wall before asking the important question. "Is he interesting?"

"He's very funny."

"That's a beginning."

Cordelia leaned conspiratorially toward her aunt. "He misbehaved terribly at school."

"I like him better still."

"But my beau he is not." Cordelia herself could not say how this thought affected her. She broke the conversation for a moment by looking away, seaward, so that the breeze blew the loose strands of red hair away from her face.

Delia admired the freckles on the young woman's nose, then admired the nose itself. *She has my nose, the lucky girl, but she's prettier than I was.*

The pause in their talk did not last long, but it does not take much time for the mind to riffle through pages of experience; Cordelia, in the space of several breaths, relived the pleasures and frustrations of the evening before. The pleasures had derived from the dance itself, as well as from the company of John Benning, his humor and interest, and her own ability to keep up with him both in repartee and on the dance floor.

The frustration came from having seen John Benning on the Custom House Wharf two days before in the company of a beautiful woman, and from not having the nerve to inquire of him who this potential rival was. For if he was not Cordelia's beau, he was at the very least a likely one.

Of course it was foolish, this hesitancy; but asking him about this other woman seemed somehow uncouth once he had promised to call on her. Their talk, too, had not made a great deal of room for such a query.

John Benning had an ease of character, an ability to disarm with frank admiration; indeed, he made no secret of his admiration of Cordelia, though that openness was always tempered with a humorous glint in the eye and the sort of smile that might be sported during an enjoyable game of cards. It was this that both drew her toward him and gave off a certain sense of danger, which admittedly might also have drawn her toward him. But only once had he said anything that she had the least objected to, though her objection had been expressed with her own well-formed sense of drollery.

"If I had known," he said between dances, "how many beautiful women had blossomed near my old haunts, I would have come home much sooner."

"In the plural," she volleyed, "that statement might be considered too broad, and therefore too vague to safely express to a single person."

He fell serious, or half-serious, and she wondered if she had talked herself out of a happy culmination to the evening. With hardly a smile, though with that same glint in his eye, he said: "Form the statement in the singular, Miss Underwood, and it may, truthfully, be applied to yourself."

"Does he plan to call on you?" asked the great-aunt.

"He did say he would."

"Here, I hope. I would like to meet him again."

"No. He had to leave Freeport last night. He had some business to tend."

"On Sunday? Well, he might have to wait, then. Your father is talking about taking you north to see this land your uncle left you."

"Is he?" Cordelia's focus of thought shifted entirely. "That didn't take very long. I hardly had the chance to badger him about it." Then the two topics of their conversation joined together in her mind. "It isn't because of Mr. Benning, I hope! Papa didn't take such a dislike to him that he's whisking me out of harm's way, is he?"

"No, I don't think your father is all that quick to judge. But he did bring it up last night."

Cordelia made a face. "I do want to go . . ."

". . . but Mr. Benning merits your presence as well."

"It *was* pleasant to meet someone. I think he deserves a chance, don't you?"

"If he's smart enough to ask for it."

"But Aunty, please don't refer to him as my beau in front of Papa, or Mr. Benning will have to declare his intentions the first time he crosses the threshold."

"I will be circumspect. But his attention to you did not go unnoticed."

"Were we an awful curiosity?"

"Not awful in the least. People couldn't keep their eyes off you because you were so handsome together. *And* because you were having such an obviously good time of it."

Cordelia reddened. She looked for the gull she had been watching and saw that it was gone.

"Besides," continued Delia, "your Mister Walton was entertaining enough to merit his own attention. He covered for you very nicely. I do like the men you met on the wharf the other day. Perhaps I should take a stroll down there myself. I might run into some retired salt who'd like an old woman."

"Aunt Delia!"

"Well, my dear, just because there's snow on the roof doesn't mean the fire has gone out in the hearth," said Delia Frost, and she slapped her niece's knee with a laugh.

19. The Vote Is In

EPHRAM, EAGLETON, AND THUMP BREAKFASTED that Sunday morning at Freeport's Harraseeket Hotel, where they had spent the night—Ephram and Eagleton sharing a bed with a farmer from Casco, and Thump occupying a narrow cot in the corner of the same room. Uncharacteristic of his race, the farmer was still snoring long after daybreak, when the three friends rose and repaired to the dining room.

Thump exhibited little enthusiasm for the previous night's events as they set to a meal of short biscuits and sausage and eggs and pancakes and syrup and fried potatoes and herring and sour cream and milk and apples and several jams; his appetite had obviously not suffered from the excitement, however, for he ate with a seriousness and concentrated effort that would have done well for several men of larger parts.

"A fine young woman, Miss Riverille," said Ephram with feeling as he paused over a helping of herring and potato. He dolloped a bit of sour cream upon his plate with a flourish, as if to exclamate his point.

"Without a doubt," said Eagleton. "She is a fine young woman."

"*Exceptional* might be an appropriate term."

"I couldn't agree with you more."

"That is, not to put too fine a point upon it."

"Not at all."

"She was not disagreeable, to my mind."

"I found nothing to make me think so."

"Rather pleasant to look at, wouldn't you say?"

"I was, indeed, ready to say just that."

Ephram turned to their laconic friend. "You're quiet, Thump."

Thump looked up from his plate with sudden interest, though the workings of his ruminant muscles never ceased. "Hmm?" he said. The bruise on his forehead had lessened somewhat, but it still concerned his friends.

"Quiet, I say," said Ephram.

"Yes," said Thump. "It is."

Conversation came, momentarily, to a halt. The clatter of silverware upon china rose to a position of primary sound as Ephram and Eagleton considered the train of discourse. Thump had done a great thing last night, dancing with Mrs. Roberto, and they would have liked to talk with him about it. They themselves had *not* put to use the lessons learned at Mrs. De Riche's Academy of Ballroom Sciences, though they had spent most of the evening in the company of Sallie Riverille and Ophelia Simpson.

Ephram and Eagleton had not said very much, either, leaving the lion's share of talk to the two females, only occasionally interspersing the conversation with announcements concerning the time and weather.

"Miss Simpson is a remarkable sort of person," said Eagleton to Ephram. "Or so she seemed to me."

"She is most definitely," said Ephram. "Most definitely."

Like a Roman citizen displaying the senate staff, Eagleton raised a fork in the air as he spoke. "She is, if I may say, uncommonly affable," he declared.

"I could not help but notice," agreed Ephram.

"Not unlike her friend Sallie in quantity and quality of favorable characteristics."

"We could not be more in agreement if we were each saying the exact same thing."

"I do feel inspired," said Eagleton suddenly.

"As do I," said Ephram. "Eh, Thump?"

"Hmm?" said that worthy. He looked up from his plate as if just now realizing that his friends were at the table with him.

"This idea of yours concerning a club is capital," said Ephram. "Simply capital."

A light dawned in Thump's expression. "Yes, well," he said.

"Ephram?" said Eagleton with a sort of intensity that could not escape the notice of the man addressed.

"Yes?" said Ephram.

"Thump?"

"Hmm?" said Thump.

"I have an absolutely enormous notion!"

"Inspiration?" wondered Ephram, eyes wide.

"Yes, I think most certainly. Something in the nature of a proposition."

"Really?" said Ephram. "Let us hear it."

There was dramatic pause as Eagleton sat straight against the back of his chair and squared his shoulders. He began what follows in a deliberate fashion, growing more excited and speaking more rapidly as he continued. "I propose," he said, "that in recognition of his qualities as a man of action, in acknowledgment of his sterling character, so obvious at our first meeting, and in appreciation of his unselfish aid in rescuing our charter member, Joseph Thump, from the tangles of a descended parachute, I move that we nominate the Honorable Mister Tobias Walton as chairman of . . . our club!"

"Good heavens!" cried Ephram. The clink of silverware died for a moment as those at other tables in the dining room turned to see what had caused this outburst.

Ephram and Eagleton took little note of this attention, however; their eyes were upon Thump, who rose from his chair with a wild expression upon his bearded face. "This is a time for deliberate action, my friends," he said. "We are at a veritable crossroads, from which the future of our club's destiny will be forever affected. I, therefore, move that we vote this very minute to install Mister Tobias Walton as chairman of . . . our club!"

"Good heavens!" said Ephram.

"Can we do that?" wondered Eagleton.

Thump raised a single eyebrow.

"Is it in the rules?" wondered Ephram.

"There are no rules!" declared Thump.

Eagleton stood, his napkin raised to one shoulder like an epaulet. "We are writing the rules!" he realized aloud.

"We are writing the book!" declared Ephram, rising to his feet to stand with his friends.

"All those in favor!" demanded Thump.

20. The Ghost in the Garden

NORTH EAST TELEGRAPH
COMPANY
OFFICE — FREEPORT, MAINE

JULY 5 AM 9:00
PORTLAND, MAINE
MR & MRS C BAFFIN
12C ADAMS ST

STAYING WITH FRIENDS THE DR MORIARTYS S. FREEPORT.
EXPECT HOME MON. REGARDS.
TOBY

MISTER WALTON WOKE SUDDENLY with the distinct impression that some-one had spoken his name. For a moment he blinked myopically at his unfamiliar surroundings—the nightstand, the pitcher and wash basin, the greenish-blue wallpaper; even as he reached for his spectacles, however, he realized that he was in the guest bedroom of the Moriarty home. He peered up at the ceiling and imagined pictures in the imperfections of the plaster.

Good heavens! he thought, as the memory of the previous night's eerie vigil returned to him. *Could it really have been?* He shivered slightly beneath the sheets, though it was a warm July morning and the sun shone upon the carpet in elongated panes.

What a series of events had brought him here! Imagine that such a simple and ridiculous act as losing his hat from the Custom House Wharf could lead him to new friends and uncommon experiences!

Three days. Well, things come in threes, they say. Life will quiet down a bit now. The thought made him sigh; it was too bad, somehow, that things must quiet down. For one thing, it meant that he would have to finally decide what he was to do with the family house. Despite the excitement of the past few days, despite his new friends (and, in fact, perhaps in reaction to them), he felt a wave of loneliness pass over him. He wondered where all his life's wanderings had got him—under a strange roof, with no family left him but a sister who was (the last he knew) in Africa.

Optimism was a keystone to Mister Walton's soul, however—optimism, faith, and goodwill. There are few things more healing than a cheerful imagination, and before long he had cheerfully imagined several fine scenarios that might carry him through this next day and the rest of his life.

He stretched with a small groan and sat up in bed, looking at the carpet; it occurred to him that the spill of sunlight was not long enough to indicate an early hour. He and the doctor had retired in the wee hours, but he had not meant to sleep the morning away. It was Sunday morning and the Moriartys were no doubt expecting to go to church.

Mrs. Moriarty and the two little girls had already gone, as it turned out, and the doctor, who had only just risen, was banging around with some pots and pans in the kitchen. The smell of fresh coffee, of bacon frying and biscuits warming drew Mister Walton in the right direction.

> *"Ah! Breakfast—most noble meal!*
> *No day should be without you.*
> *Your groaning tables soon reveal*
> *The cheer you spread about you."*

"Good morning!" said the doctor, when his guest entered the kitchen. "Mary and the girls will be home soon. Have a cup of coffee."

Mister Walton happily availed himself of this amenity and sat down at the kitchen table, while Dr. Moriarty busied himself with bacon and eggs. "Sunny side up," he replied to the doctor's question, then thought of the voice in his mind that had drifted away with his first waking thought. He could hear it in his memory now saying "Mister Walton," and it sounded not unlike Mr. Thump announcing the hour when the tide would be high.

"I hope you were not disappointed in our phantom ship last night," said Dr. Moriarty to Mister Walton at breakfast that Sunday morning.

"It was the most singular thing," admitted the older gentleman. He laid down his fork and knife and considered his next statement. The doctor's wife and their daughters, Aria (who was ten) and Emily (who was seven), were at the table, and Mister Walton was concerned that the subject might frighten the children. "I have traveled a good deal, Dr. Moriarty, and heard of . . . similar occurrences . . . but I have always taken such tales with a grain of salt."

"And is your opinion still seasoned?"

"I must say that it all seems a little unreal, sitting at breakfast with your lovely family, and the sun shining through the window."

"It is the third time I have seen that particular apparition, Mister Walton, and it is no more real for the repeat performances." Dr. Moriarty reached behind him for the coffee urn on the sideboard and poured his guest and his wife a second cup.

"Was it a frightening ghost, Daddy?" wondered Emily, her eyes wide, and her shoulders slightly hunched with expectation.

Dr. Moriarty glanced at his wife, who had chided him in the past for speaking carelessly before their daughters. It was a certain flaw of his to voice an honest wonder about any subject occupying his mind, regardless of company. Now he realized that the present topic of conversation was not, perhaps, conducive to pleasant dreams in young children.

"No, dear," said the father, "I couldn't say for sure that it was a ghost at all. Mister Walton is quite right in considering it an interesting experience without wholly accepting it for what it seemed."

"Believe none of what you hear," said Mary, "and only half of what you see." Her smile was ironic and indicated that she herself was not to be taken with complete seriousness.

"But were you frightened?" wondered Aria.

"No, dear," said Dr. Moriarty. "It was a strangely comforting vision. Wouldn't you say, Mister Walton."

"Oh, yes, I would indeed." And it was, he thought, strangely comforting for an apparition that raised the hair at the back of his neck.

"Mommy has seen a ghost," said Emily, and now it was Mary's turn to be caught out.

"Has she?" said the doctor, returning to his breakfast with his tongue in his cheek.

"Well," explained Mary. "They wanted a ghost story last Christmas."

"Ah, yes! The prisoner of war." The doctor patted Emily's head.

"Mommy saw him in the garden," Aria informed Mister Walton.

"My goodness!" said the portly fellow, unable to resist a quick glance through the window at his shoulder. The gardens of the Moriartys' backyard looked all too cheerful and sunny to harbor a specter.

"Not our garden, Mister Walton," said the doctor. "This was at Mary's family home."

"Oh, I see." The older gentleman was a little sorry to have exhibited such obvious curiosity.

"Another phantom of the War of 1812, it seems. You shouldn't keep our guest in the dark, my dear." Dr. Moriarty was pleased to have been let off the hook for his own indiscretion.

"Oh-ho!" laughed Mister Walton.

Mary smiled slyly at her husband's conspicuous motive for encouraging her story. "It may prove a dull experience to tell, Mister Walton, compared to your encounter last night."

"Told by you, Mrs. Moriarty, I am sure that it could not be dull." Mister Walton spoke with complete sincerity, and would have appeared courtly even if he had said this merely to be polite.

Mrs. Moriarty was not a beautiful woman—her features were a little too strong to be considered comely—but her smile was always true, and she had fine hazel eyes that shone with an attractive intelligence. Mister Walton, who had a natural sympathy for women, liked her very much.

"Mommy thinks the ghost was in love," said Aria, her face solemn.

"He did fit a particular historical description, it is true. But my suspicions concerning his identity are only a whimsical conjecture. Please, Mister Walton, do continue your breakfast." She sipped from her coffee with the air of an orator wetting her lips for a speech.

"My family is from Wiscasset," she said. "My father was a merchant captain, and his father also. My mother, in fact, was a daughter of a captain, so my being landbound, you see, is only an accident of my sex." She flashed a look at her husband. "The house in which I grew up was smaller in my grandfather's day, but there were beautiful gardens dating back to his time. My grandfather's sister, Cressida—Aunt Cressy, I called her—tended them till the day she died, when I was thirteen years old. She never married, and though she was very kind to me and my brothers and sisters, the gardens took most of her time during the warm months, and occupied most of her thoughts during the cold.

"She seemed to derive little pleasure from the gardens, however—they were an occupation, almost an obsession, though I must admit I never thought very much about this side of her character till after she was gone.

"The year after she died Aunt Cressy's gardens saw little attention; and as summer came to an end the flowering bushes needed trimming, the roses needed pruning. The annuals had never been planted that spring, and their usual beds were suddenly the home of weeds and grass. It distressed me to see her beautiful gardens gone to seed; it was too much like forgetting Aunt Cressy herself, and I determined to remedy the situation with my own two hands when spring came around again."

Mary had warmed to her tale now, and far from finding it dull, Mister Walton was as charmed with what his hostess told him as with the natural grace with which she told it. She was gazing at her own gardens now, and it was obvious to him that she was looking out at roses and flowerbeds that he could not see.

"I spent a great deal of the following winter planning the resurrection of Aunt Cressy's garden, and when spring arrived I went to work, begrudging every day of rain, and wishing that I had paid more attention to my aunt's horticultural gifts when she might have passed them on to me. I don't think I had the natural talent for flowers that she had, and I certainly didn't have the experience, but as summer leafed out, the garden took on something of its old life.

"My father was away most of that season; he was at sea a great deal, of course, when I was a child. My mother was not well then, and she seemed to enjoy the garden from her sickroom window, so it seemed to me that there was double purpose in my labors. My brothers and sisters took no interest, however, and I spent much of that summer—my fourteenth— alone with the primroses and daylilies.

"It was early in August, on one of those mornings when the heat of the previous day has never been fully dissipated by the night between. The garden was still, almost breathless, damp in the humid air and heavy with the scent of its own flowers. The bees and the early cicadas created a wash of monotonous sound that was pleasant, almost dreamy, to hear. I had been watching a cluster of shoots among the nasturtiums for some days, and recently decided they were weeds, so I was down on my knees in my best sun hat and working gloves, when I distinctly heard my aunt's name spoken aloud.

"My first response was simple surprise, and I merely straightened up without a thought to turn and see who had spoken. Then the voice came again. 'Cressida,' it said: a man's voice filled with such warmth and longing that I blushed, as if I myself had been called by someone who loved me in the most hopeless and romantic way.

"And then I did turn. And I can't say that I was frightened or even very shocked to see a tall, rather handsome man, dressed in the uniform of a British naval officer, but a uniform that had not been seen in practical use for years. He stood at the other end of the garden, and his eyes, I thought, might drink me in, they were that expressive of love and devotion. Tears sprang to my own eyes, I was so struck by the force of his emotion.

"He was more shocked to see me, I think, for a strange cloud fell across his expression. And as I tried to squint my tears away—quite actually in the blink of an eye—he was gone. And I stumbled over to the bench where my aunt had spent so many waking hours watching her beautiful garden, and I wept as if I had lost my most beloved friend."

There were tears, even now, in Mary Moriarty's eyes as she spoke; Mister Walton felt himself misting up, and he doffed his spectacles to brush at his closed eyelids. "This was an apparition, then," he said.

"Yes. It seemed so to my eyes—and to my heart."

Mister Walton put his glasses on again and blinked. He had forgotten where he was, for a moment, and he looked around to see that Mary's family was not unmoved by her tale, though they had heard it before. Her daughters were filled with honest wonder, but Dr. Moriarty watched his wife with a seriousness and a love that might have been the picture of that phantom's own passionate expression.

"Was this the ghost of some lost love of your aunt's?" wondered Mister Walton.

"It was my first and only opinion on the matter," said Mary.

"There is a sequel to this story," said the doctor.

"Oh, my goodness!" said Mister Walton. It was almost too much to hope for. "Did you see him again?"

"I didn't," said Mary. "But my mother did."

"Oh, dear me! And she was ill, you say."

"Yes. In fact, I had no intention of saying anything to her about what I had seen. She was actually on the mend by the beginning of August, but I feared that she would fret either over this presence on the property, if she believed me, or over my state of mind, if she didn't. I realized that this man I had seen must be someone from my aunt Cressy's girlhood, and that I would have to wait patiently for my father's return to inquire about him—if indeed my father would know anything.

"But it was my mother who brought up the subject, for the next day she fell asleep in her chair in her room, and woke in the late afternoon to find the very same figure—by her description—standing in the doorway, with the look of someone who is on a profound search. She said there was something purposeful in his gaze, as if he himself had only just wakened to some new truth. And when she spoke to him, he was gone.

" 'Mary,' my mother said, 'Perhaps you shouldn't spend so much time in the garden. Your aunt, I think, kept it for her own reasons, and maybe those reasons need to rest.'

"So I abandoned the garden, left the flowers to the encroachment of weeds, and hardly walked there. For a while I felt as if I had betrayed a trust, but I was fourteen, and in late August I went to a church picnic at Fort Edgecomb, where I met Patrick. I was very young." Mary gave each of her daughters a deliberate look. "And I saw your father only rarely the next two years, but I was also very much in love, and I began to think less about Aunt Cressy's garden and the apparition that my mother and I had seen."

Mister Walton was absolutely overflowing with curiosity by now, and waited upon Mary's every word.

"By the time my father came home, late in September," she continued, "I had decided not to say anything about the man in the garden. The memory had grown unreal, just as your memory of last night, Mister Walton. I willingly stayed away from the garden as fall approached, and half-believed that what I had seen had been a product of my self-imposed loneliness there. It was my father who raised the subject, one unseasonably cold night, when he had built a fire in the parlor.

"Mother, still not fully recovered from her illness, had retired early, and Daddy and I each had our nose in a book, when I sensed from the corner of my eye that he had set down his reading to watch the fire. 'There was a reason, you know,' he said without preamble, 'why your aunt Cressida never married.'

"I said I had often wondered, and he thought it remarkable that I had never been told. My mother, for some reason, was always a little quiet about family things.

" 'Your aunt was in love once, you see. She was only sixteen, I think—years before I was born. Her brother—your grandfather—was first mate aboard a privateer, the *Thomas*, and in May of 1813 they captured two British vessels, the ship *Diana* and the brig *John Peate*. The *Thomas* was out of Portsmouth, but there were several Wiscasset men aboard her, and since these vessels were captured not far from the mouth of the Sheepscot, the captain was induced to give his Maine men an extra measure of glory by delivering the captured vessels and crews to the Wiscasset dockside.'

"The commanding officer of the *Diana*, my father told me, was Captain Solomon Jennings, a gallant sort of gentleman, and he and the captain of the *John Peate* were given their parole, a standard practice in those days. Officers, when captured, were often allowed to roam within the town of their confinement, if they would simply give their word not to attempt escape. Captain Jennings gave his word, along with the other officer, and they were granted their freedom as far as the limits of the town.

"Then one evening, Captain Jennings was invited to my grandfather's for dinner, and it was there that he met my grandfather's younger sister, my aunt Cressida. She was barely sixteen years old, but already thought of as the most beautiful young woman in town. This reputation had not gone to her head, I've been told; an elderly friend of my father's had once told him that she had been as beautiful to know as to look at.

"Well, Captain Jennings had sailed the world and fought in a dozen naval conflicts, but he was not prepared for Cressida, and he fell like a great towering oak. You could hear the crash, they said.

"Things were different then; they might be at war with Captain Jennings, but that didn't mean they had to dislike him. Neither Cressida's father nor brother stood in the way of these two spending time together—always at the family home and always, when weather permitted, in the garden.

"But a dilemma arose between Cressida and Captain Jennings. They were deeply in love by the end of June; barely a month had passed. Captain Jennings got word that an exchange of prisoners had been agreed upon, and that he and his men were to be sent home under the stipulation that they not sail American waters for three years. Solomon Jennings was beside himself. He had two choices, and he knew that he could not live with either of them.

"The first was to return to England and, at best, not see Cressida for three years. It was an impossibility, he said. The second was to renounce his loyalty to the British Crown and Navy—equally untenable.

"So Captain Jennings devised a third desperate plan of action. He would break his parole, escape to Boston, where he was sure he could arrange secret passage, then return to Wiscasset for an elopement. Explaining his plot to Cressida, he promised to return. 'I swear to you,' he said, 'on my love, I swear, that I shall meet you again in this very garden.'

"Your coffee is growing cold, Mister Walton."

"Oh, no, no," he said, and took a quick sip from his cup. It was indeed lukewarm, but he did not want her to take time away from her story to fill it. "It's fine, really it is. But Captain Jennings? He never returned, then."

"Oh, yes, Mister Walton, he certainly did—and many times, I think. But he was caught almost at once, you see, in Portsmouth—a British sailor out of uniform."

"Good heavens!"

"They hanged him, of course, and official word of his death did not reach Wiscasset for several months. But it was only a week after his escape, the story has it, that he fulfilled his promise and met Aunt Cressy in the garden. Grandfather found her in a dead faint and she was unconscious for three days. It was during her convalescence from this tragedy that she began to tend the garden herself, coaxing buds from the soil, and filling the backyard with the most beautiful blooms the town had ever known. You could smell their fragrance all up and down the street.

"And every summer Captain Jennings' soul, like a butterfly, was drawn by those flowers, and their fragrance, and the work of his beloved's hands, to repeat the fulfillment of his vow."

"I have traveled in every state of the Union," said Mister Walton, "and never stopped to think that there was so much to see, and so many stories to hear in the very state that gave me birth."

"Between the *Dash* and Captain Jennings," said the doctor, "it does give one something to think about." They were in the Moriartys' own garden now, strolling among the roses and the philodendrons.

"But really, I have been remiss," said Mister Walton. "This Fort Edgecomb that you mentioned—I take it, since you were picnicking on its grounds, that the military no longer occupies it."

"Oh, no," said Mary. "Not for years. It was decommissioned, I think, soon after peace was reached with the British."

"It's not a very large affair," said Dr. Moriarty. "Just a simple blockhouse, really, across the Sheepscot River from Wiscasset. It looks a bit like Fort McClary at Kittery Point. The stockade is gone, but the gun emplacements are still visible."

"Well, I've heard of it, but never seen it."

"It's quite handsomely situated," said Mary, "as most forts are; the point being to command an important view."

"Really, I must appear quite ignorant."

"Not in the least, Mister Walton. On the contrary, you seem remarkably well traveled."

"But not in my own home, Mrs. Moriarty." Mister Walton brought his portly figure to a halt and his hosts stopped on either side of him. He clasped his hands behind him and regarded the top of an elm tree. "Yes, it shall be remedied," he said, and it was clear to the Moriartys that he was speaking to himself as much as to them. "Since returning home, fate has gently nudged me from one pleasant or extraordinary encounter to the next. I have let the winds of whim take me where they will, these past few days, and I have not been disappointed. Now I feel the suggestion of Fort Edgecomb coming upon me, and who knows what I shall discover there."

"You are an adventurer, Mister Walton," said Mary with a quiet smile.

"My dear sister is in Africa with her missionary husband. That, I think, qualifies as adventure. No, Mrs. Moriarty, I claim no bravery—only curiosity. I do love to meet new people, and see new sights."

Dr. Moriarty had moved a few paces ahead of them and was admiring a blossom with his nose. The girls appeared around the corner of the house, playing tag. Mary took Mister Walton's arm and with the doctor they recommenced their saunter through the garden.

"Did you ever see the captain again?" asked Mister Walton. "Captain Jennings?"

"I never did," said Mary. "I think he must have gone over to the other side, Mister Walton, once he realized that his love was waiting for him there."

NORTH EAST TELEGRAPH
COMPANY
OFFICE—FREEPORT, MAINE

JULY 6 PM 2:00
PORTLAND, MAINE
MR & MRS C BAFFIN
12C ADAMS ST

PLEASE SEND SMALL LUGGAGE W/CLOTHES TO MEET AT
FREEPORT. TAKING RR NORTH. IF NEED CONTACT WISCASSET
HOUSE TONIGHT. REGARDS.
    TOBY

21. The Game Was Big in Wiscasset

IT WAS TWILIGHT OF THE NEXT EVENING when Mister Walton arrived in Wiscasset.

A ribbon of royal purple shone above the courthouse at the top of the hill, and the trees along Main Street were black against the sky. The street lamps seemed hindered by the fading light, or unwilling perhaps to shed their brilliance till they were wholly unrivaled by the greater light of day.

Up ahead of the station platform the train's engine chuffed impatiently, and further back a ramp was dropped with a crash from the local feed store to an opened boxcar. Waiting for his bags, Mister Walton watched as the silhouettes of men with wheelbarrows passed from store to car and back.

Walking to the corner of the platform, he peered down the narrow alley of buildings to the bridge and the dark waters of the Sheepscot River.

Barely a yard away from him was a single dray horse and wagon backed up to the side of the feed store. A great broad-shouldered fellow emerged from a doorway and stepped into the rig with a massive sack in each fist. Trudging to the head of the cart, he laid these down and picked up the reins before straightening as best as he was able.

"You haven't got that bear working for you up there, have you, Peter?" said a second man standing at the doorway.

"I haven't seen him," said the man in the cart.

"I thought, perhaps, you'd yoked him to the plow."

"I haven't seen him," came the serious reply again. "I wouldn't know what to feed him."

"What do you feed a bear?" wondered the man in the doorway. He was merely a shadow in the gathering dusk, and it was a moment before Mister Walton realized that the question had been addressed in his direction.

"Oh," he said. "I think they are omnivores."

"Really," said the shadowy figure. "I didn't know bears were religious."

"They are very quiet about it," said Mister Walton, without blinking.

"Your bags, sir," said a porter, setting Mister Walton's valise and a second bag at their owner's feet. "Can I get a carriage for you?"

Forgetting, for the moment, the subject of bears, Mister Walton asked how far the Wiscasset House was, and since it proved a reasonable walking distance he decided to travel shanks' mare. A towheaded boy materialized at his elbow and offered his services for the expedition. Mister Walton handed the boy his valise, but the enterprising fellow insisted on taking both bags.

The train's bell rang and the whole line of cars lurched forward—north, toward its next stop. The western face of the station was pinked by the last light of the sun when Mister Walton glanced back at it, but there was a morning sort of spring to his step. A breeze off the river curled past him and sharpened the air with the tang of salt, and evening strollers were compelled, by his amiable expression, to smile as they passed, or tip their hats, or even speak.

"Have you ever seen a bear, sir?" asked the young boy, nearly breathless from the portly man's energetic pace.

"A bear? Yes, I believe I have seen a bear once or twice, in captivity."

"Is that near Boston?" wondered the lad.

Mister Walton chuckled. "Well, there are those who think so. No, my son, captivity is where a *captured* animal is kept; in a circus, you see, or a zoological garden, perhaps. Here, let me take the valise at least. That bag, I fear, is heavier than you thought."

"That's where this one came from. A circus."

"A bear, you say?"

"Yes, sir."

"I wondered what was meant by that conversation at the feed store. Is someone displaying a bear hereabouts?"

"Not yet."

"But you're expecting one, then?"

"As soon as someone catches it."

Mister Walton did not feel enlightened by this discourse, but even in perplexity he was pleasant and with another chuckle he led the way.

Lights burned in the windows of the Wiscasset House and a small crowd could be discerned in the parlor, and these facts made the building instantly pleasing to Mister Walton as he and the young boy mounted the front steps and entered the foyer.

"Come in, come in," said a tall man holding court in the parlor.

Mister Walton stepped inside and bade good evening to the dozen or so women and men spaced about amongst ornate furniture.

"Please, join us," said the man. He was thin, with large features and a prominent Adam's apple; his hair was sparse, but his eyebrows were jet black, and they arched ironically when he spoke. "We have been holding forth on a number of important subjects," he said, "and we are greatly in need of a new opinion." General laughter followed this declaration, and he added: "We'll send for a man to take your bags."

An attendant appeared, just then, and offered his assistance to Mister Walton, who introduced himself. "Yes, sir," said the attendant, taking the bag and valise. "We have been expecting you." This did not surprise Mister Walton, since he had wired ahead for a room, but it did engender a small buzz of excitement amongst the small group in the parlor.

While the new guest was thus engaged, the tall man looked down his nose at the young boy. "Do you know who he is?" he inquired.

"He's the one they said was coming, I think," replied the boy. "He spoke of capturing bears." As if smelling something unpleasant, the tall man waved the boy away, and Mister Walton barely caught the young fellow in the hall in time to press a generous gratuity into his hand.

"Alfred Lofton," said the tall man, when the new guest returned to the parlor. "I'm sorry, I didn't catch the name."

"Tobias Walton, at your service, sir."

"You know what is on our minds tonight, then, Mister Walton," said Lofton, loftily.

The room fell silent in order to hear Mister Walton's response. He thought it an odd question, really, but felt up to the task of answering it. "Well, since I arrived, bears seem the subject of popular discourse."

"I am to understand that you've been informed of the details?"

Mister Walton didn't know when he'd had such a succession of extraordinary conversations. "Concerning bears?" he ventured.

"Indeed," said Lofton.

"I don't believe I have." Mister Walton blinked at the rest of the company, who waited upon his every word. "The boy *did* intimate that one needed catching."

"Let us hope it is not to be caught anywhere nearby," said the *grande dame* of the group. "We ladies are quite alarmed, I promise you, sir."

"I am certainly sorry to hear it, ma'am."

"I don't think that she's a particularly dangerous creature, Mister Walton," said Lofton. "The bear, I mean," he added, when Mister Walton threw an astonished glance in the direction of the older woman.

"Oh, of course," said the puzzled man. "The bear."

"She's quite used to people, we are told, but that in itself rather complicates the matter."

"It does?"

"She isn't so apt to simply disappear into the forest, is she."

"Oh. But she's used to people, you say? The bear?" Mister Walton was doing his best to understand. Meanwhile, the man from the inn waited.

"You *haven't* been informed, have you?" said Lofton, a hint of irritation in his voice. When Mister Walton — eyes and mouth wide — confirmed this suspicion, the tall man said: "She belongs to one of these Wild West circuses that the yokels love to patronize; and while the special train carrying this horde stopped here briefly yesterday morning, some simpleton in charge of the animals allowed the bear to escape. The sheriff doesn't seem very concerned over the matter, but our ladies here at the inn dare not venture forth for a walk in town or a round of croquet."

"That is distressing," said Mister Walton. He gave the man from the inn a look that indicated the need to be rescued.

"Shall I show you to your rooms, sir?" said the attendant.

"Yes, that would be fine," said Mister Walton. Hat in hand, he nodded to each of the women and shook hands with the men, including Alfred Lofton once more. They did seem interested to meet him, which was very nice, even if their conversation was eccentric.

When the man from the inn had led Mister Walton away, a buzz went up among the occupants of the parlor. One man got up to stand beside Lofton, saying: "He's not exactly what I expected, you know."

"He is very prompt, however," said Lofton. "I was told that we shouldn't expect anyone for three days."

"He is very much a gentleman," expressed one of the women. "I do hope he is cautious."

"But it is true," said another, "he did not impress me as a man of action. I was looking for a younger man, I suppose; or at least a rougher one."

"He is rather, shall we say, stocky?" said the fellow beside Lofton.

"And those spectacles of his," said someone. "I thought these fellows had to have tremendous powers of sight."

"Perhaps he isn't what we had in mind, it is true," said Lofton. "But appearances can be deceiving. The Big Game Club wired that they would send one of their best men, and this Mister Walton may prove hard as nails beneath that . . . exterior."

22. It Was a Shame About Maude

"A TRAINED BEAR HAS ESCAPED," said James Underwood as his daughter scurried down the stairs with the last of her bags. He stood in the front hall with the day's edition of the *Portland Daily Advertiser* unfolded before him.

"She wasn't very *well* trained, was she," suggested Cordelia, balancing a hatbox and a portable writing desk on a portmanteau that stood upended by the door. She stood back and surveyed the luggage that she had collected. "I am not sure that I packed enough."

"Only enough for the entire crew of a *small* vessel," suggested her father without looking up from his paper.

"I'm sure there are quite enough petticoats there for a small crew," she admitted. "Where did she escape from?"

"The bear, you mean?" said James, who had gone on to other items. "From her cage in Wiscasset."

"Who escaped from her cage in Wiscasset?" asked Mercia from another room, where she was closing the drapes to keep the rugs from fading in the summer sun.

"A bear escaped, Mama," said Cordelia.

"Who barely escaped?" demanded Mercia.

Cordelia was about to try again, but her father shook his head and rolled his eyes. *Don't humor her* was the connotation of this wordless idiom, for in his expert opinion his wife was having fun at their expense.

From the beatific innocence of Mercia's expression when she came into the hall, Cordelia judged her father's assumption to be correct. This pleased Cordelia, for Mercia's playful manner revealed her excitement over the forthcoming journey.

Cordelia herself smarted a little at leaving home now that John Benning had promised to pay her a call, but the anticipation of an adventure overshadowed her doubts. She was thrilled with the notion of seeing her newly inherited land, and her father's assurances that there were no proper roads to take her the entire way only heightened her interest.

Most of all she was keen to see her cousin Priscilla, whom she had not visited since their mothers had quarreled last Christmas. Aunt Grace was a sweet person as a rule (when she was not suffering from a headache or a bout of *nerves* or some form of ague), but she was a great worrier, and her unbounded anxieties often encouraged her to put her own oar in somebody else's bay.

The picture of unselfish concern, Grace had not been shy of expressing to Mercia her anxiety over Cordelia's marriage prospects. Mercia, with as much tact as can be expected of a sister in these circumstances, had told Grace to please trouble herself with her own daughter's outlook, then listed several of her own concerns, most of which touched upon Grace's nature, which was described as nosey and high-strung. Grace denied the former and fulfilled the latter by having an attack of the *vapors* and disappearing into her room for the rest of the day.

Relations between the sisters were cordial, if strained, for the rest of the Underwoods' stay, and it had taken the intervening months for their succeeding communications to properly warm again. Mercia insisted, whenever she brought the subject up, that she had forgotten the entire thing.

"Did they capture her?" asked Mercia, as she entered the hall.

"The bear, you mean," said James dryly, but before he could answer, a man came to the door to say that he had brought their carriage. Cordelia and her mother instructed the driver as to how to load the luggage, and James listened to this short course, the newspaper forgotten in his hands.

"You haven't told us about your bear, Papa," said Cordelia, when the driver had staggered back to the carriage with the load they had given him.

"I had the distinct impression," said James, "that the creature had no fascination for you."

"On the contrary," assured his wife, and she and Cordelia each took a seat upon one of the lower steps of the front hall stairs.

"Contrary" would have been just his choice of word, but with a flick of his wrists, he snapped the paper open to the proper page and proceeded to read in a dramatic tone of voice.

" *The wire from Wiscasset is humming these days with news of a truant bruin.'* "

"I like that," said Cordelia. " 'Truant bruin.' "

"It is a felicitous phrase," he agreed before continuing. " *The beast, it seems, is the property of Colonel Cobb's Wild West Show, which performed to enthusiastic audiences in our own fair city last September. Those who have patronized Colonel Cobb's entertainment will remember Maude, the less* than statuesque bear who goes under the stage name of "Kodiak." Maude, as we prefer to think of her, provided some of the most uproarious moments of the show by covering her eyes with her paws whenever Colonel Cobb pointed his famous Remington rifle in her direction. The ursine actress, upon the colonel's command to behave like a proper bear, brought the house down by standing on her head.' " James looked up from his paper. "I'm sorry to have missed that."

"I am sorry to have disparaged her training," said Cordelia, who was enjoying her father's theatrical reading. "It's obvious that I spoke too soon."

"Ah, but listen to this. Her abilities are manifold. 'Maude,' it says here, 'proved to possess talents, however, that even the colonel did not suspect, for during a short stop at the Wiscasset Station, on Sunday afternoon, she made good her escape. It was not till the touring company's personal train reached Bath that Maude was missed, and a certain amount of deduction, i.e. when was she last seen, led to the conclusion that she had deserted her post at the County Seat.' " James didn't bother to look up from his paper to add his own commentary. "In the end she de-trained, as it turned out."

"I resisted saying that myself," said Mercia.

" 'Sheriff Charles Piper, leader of the local constabulary, suspects that Maude will prove more nuisance than danger; and there being a reward of fifty dollars for her safe capture, he doubly suspects that fortune seekers will be more nuisance still. With the understanding that actresses are famous for their nervous temperaments, Sheriff Piper has ordered that hunting dogs not be used for the task, and has himself led two forays into the surrounding countryside in hopes of ending the fugitive's run before either bear or populace come to harm. At the hour before this edition went to print Maude was still on the loose.

" 'This journal suggests that, upon sight of the bruin, a harsh command might encourage her to stand on her head, in which position she may be susceptible to capture. We await further word from Wiscasset, and promise the sequel to our readers.' "

"Does our train take us through Wiscasset?" wondered Mercia.

"I certainly do hope so!" said Cordelia earnestly.

"Yes, it does," James informed them. He delved several pages into his paper till he came to the railroad schedules. "I'm afraid we don't stop there, though. Perhaps we'll get a glimpse of Maude as we trundle by." He folded his paper methodically.

It was in the afternoon that a private carriage stopped before the Underwood home, and John Benning stepped onto the sidewalk. From top hat to spats, he was nothing short of impeccable—every line and lineament carefully orchestrated for its greatest effect on a young woman's heart and a parent's sense of decorum.

There was nothing unsure about John Benning—no last-minute inventory of his appearance, no second look at a written address to be convinced that he was at the right place, certainly no hesitation in his step. Several minutes later, after a series of polite knocks and a patient wait by the front door, his return down the walk and back to the street was just as confident. He climbed back into his carriage, spoke to the driver, and his face revealed no hint of surprise or disappointment.

The carriage moved out into the light traffic of High Street and hurried down the hill in the direction of the harbor.

23. Sundry Moss

WISCASSET WOKE THAT TUESDAY MORNING and peered from its windows for any sign of Maude. Mrs. Althea Pool, who had sat on her glasses the previous spring, stared out her back door at something black for several minutes before she realized that the object was closer than she thought. Her cat, it turned out to be, sitting on the fence.

William Nute caught sight of something that had a substantial chance of being a bear. He stood on a knoll behind his house and shielded his eyes against the bright sky, but the object of his attention was too far away and too quickly gone to be sure that it wasn't a dog or a trick of the light.

The river, as it happened, proved the better venue for bear spotting; Joseph Jones, puttering down from Sheepscot Village in his bargelike vessel, the *Northstar*, had a very good look at something ursine making its way just above the western bank.

This news touched land at the Wiscasset waterfront and did not tarry on its way to town, where most individuals were philosophical. Bears, said George Turner at the telegraph office, were reasonable creatures—not like a sheep or a rhinoceros. Bill Gibbs reminded George that this reasonable creature made a living standing on her head in front of audiences. Dr. Cushman expressed interest in George's expertise regarding rhinoceroses.

"I wouldn't trust one," said George.

The news quickly reached the county jail, where Sheriff Charles Piper was overseeing a visitation. Geoffrey, the son of the jailer, Seth Patterson, arrived out of breath and bursting to tell what he had heard in town.

"Should we go look for her?" wondered Seth.

The sheriff thought a moment. "If Colonel Cobb's man shows up, we'll take some men out in the heat of the day when she's apt to be lying in. I suppose word has gotten all over town," he said to the boy.

"George Turner says that bears are more reasonable than rhinoceroses," said Geoffrey.

"Rhinoceroses?" gasped Mrs. Patterson.

The news was received with more excitement at the Wiscasset House. Many of the hotel's patrons were at breakfast when someone rushed in to announce that Maude had been sighted. Alfred Lofton rose from his table with a grim look in his eye and asked if the big-game hunter was up. A servant was directed to make inquiries in this line and returned minutes later to say that Mister Walton had not yet made an appearance.

Lofton was irritated but undaunted, and he proceeded to organize a hunt so that they would be ready when Mister Walton deigned to rise. Lofton himself retreated to his rooms, and when he returned to the parlor, fully rigged with knee breeches, wool stockings, tweed jacket, and deerstalker, he was gratified by a hearty round of applause.

But the big-game hunter was still not in attendance, and Lofton, spurred by the approval of his friends, demanded that the man be roused; easy enough to demand, of course, though it smacked a bit of belling the cat. Nobody quite wanted to be the one to rouse a big-game hunter.

A young man who odd-jobbed about the hotel was hired for the duty, after some discussion concerning a fee. While the fellow clambered up the stairs with Mister Walton's room number and many bits of advice following him, a small crowd of men gathered in the front hall.

There is a rare moment between sleep and the waking state that all too often escapes humanity. Generally, this state follows a good night's rest and almost always precedes a day in which the sleeper is liberated from social obligation. It is that territory of consciousness in which the individual is still deep enough in the arms of Morpheus to be blissfully unaware (or at least undisturbed) by his corporeal self, and just awake enough to appreciate this freedom.

Mister Tobias Walton was possessed of such a moment that morning. His bed was exceptionally comfortable, the breeze through the open window almost warm, and the blankets pulled over his shoulders were of a perfect weight and insulative value. The science of man could not devise a situation of greater comfort.

But a simple knock on the door might drive it away.

It says something of the depth of Mister Walton's paradisiacal state that it took several knocks (and, in the end, great thumps upon his door) to rouse him. It says something of his good nature that he did not throw a shoe at the first head that afterward peered into his room.

"Good morning, mister," came a deep voice, resonant with missing *r*'s.

"Yes, good morning," said Mister Walton, blinking with his unspectacled eyes at the blurred figure that entered his room. With a grunt, he swung himself into a sitting position and his feet to the floor. "Have I slept past the check-out time?" he wondered aloud.

"Wouldn't have the slightest," came the reply.

Mister Walton's hand hovered over the nightstand by his bed and eventually he came in contact with his eyeglasses. Once he had these perched upon his nose, he blinked again at the man who had disturbed his sleep.

The stranger (for Mister Walton had never seen the man in his life) had draped himself in the large chair opposite Mister Walton's bed. It was difficult to say just how tall he was, but he looked extremely long with his feet stretched some distance in front of him. He had accomplished as horizontal a position as was possible in that piece of furniture, and his hands were folded behind his neck, his elbows akimbo, completing the picture of complacent ease.

Mister Walton guessed the fellow to be something above twenty years of age. He had brown hair of a medium shade, and his eyes were darkly set in a pleasant, if not handsome, face. His nose was a tad too wide and his chin, which had not been shaved this morning, was a mite too square. If not for the obvious interest which he showed in Mister Walton's pajamas (made of silk with a pattern of red Chinese dragons), the stranger's relaxed demeanor would have given the impression that he was going to sleep.

During the course of several awkward moments, Mister Walton waited for the young man to declare his motive for rousing him. The young man, however, looked perfectly content to contemplate Mister Walton's ornate nightclothes, and gave no hint as to the nature of his visit.

"Can I help you?" asked Mister Walton.

"Well, I've been sent to get you," said the man.

"Really!"

"Oh, yes. They are waiting for you down in the dining room."

"How extraordinary!"

"They are concerned over your rising late."

The pronoun *they* was not descriptive enough for Mister Walton, and he asked the fellow to define the term.

"*They* are the other guests, aren't they," he said.

"Other guests?" returned Mister Walton.

"And Mr. Alfred Lofton, pacing the floor."

"Alfred Lofton," said Mister Walton to himself.

"Spoke to you last night, he says."

"The gentleman in the parlor?"

The man in the chair shrugged elaborately.

"And you say they are waiting for me?"

"Absolutely no doubt about it."

"Well, I shall certainly get dressed and see what this is about."

"I knew a Walton once," called the young man when the older fellow had shuffled into the small dressing chamber annexed to his room. "He couldn't pronounce his *w*'s, and for three years I thought his name was Alton."

Mister Walton chuckled as he filled his washstand and washed his face and hands. "My family name," he said over the sound of splashing, "was actually Walnut two generations ago."

"Someone dodging the law, eh?"

"Gambling debts, actually. It was my grandfather."

"Try not to gamble myself," said the fellow in the chair.

"Very wise. My grandfather was nearly ruined."

"Did the change in his name save him, then?" wondered the young man.

Mister Walton appeared in the doorway, half of his face lathered with shaving soap. "It was a hole in his boot that saved him, actually."

"I've never had much use for a hole in my boot," said the fellow, "but perhaps I have been hasty." He contemplated one of his soles with interest.

"It has just dawned upon me," said Mister Walton, "that you have the advantage of me, sir."

"Sundry," said the young man.

"Yes, well, I am sure you have many advantages," agreed Mister Walton good-naturedly. "But I was speaking of your name."

"That *is* my name," said the fellow, rising to his feet. "Sundry Moss."

It took a moment for Mister Walton to realize what the young man was saying, and another moment to be sure that his leg wasn't being pulled. "Sundry," he said, trying the name on his own tongue. "It's quite likable really. Sundry." He stepped forward and extended his hand. "I am Tobias Walton, though you seem to know that already."

"I am pleased to have your acquaintance," said Sundry, shaking his hand. "You've missed a spot there."

Mister Walton retreated to the washroom to reapply his razor, and in a few minutes he was dressed and ready to meet those who, for their own mysterious reasons, waited below.

"Did you get those fancy nightclothes hereabouts?" asked Sundry as he closed the door behind them.

24. Oddly Hunting Maude

Mɪsᴛᴇʀ Wᴀʟᴛᴏɴ ᴡᴀsɴ'ᴛ sᴜʀᴇ how he came to be included in the hunting party; but as it turned out, Alfred Lofton and his colleagues in leisure were under the conviction that he was eager to join them in their chase of the escaped bear. He had, on the contrary, wished for nothing more than a late sleep, a leisurely breakfast, and a quiet tour of Fort Edgecomb. And yet the men of the hunting party were so impatient to make their pursuit, while so selfless in waiting for him, that he had not the heart to disabuse them of the notion.

Lofton, decked out in his hunting gear, was waiting in the foyer when Mister Walton and Sundry Moss came down the stairs; and several other anxious faces appeared from the main sitting room as soon as it was announced that the late sleeper was roused.

"I had imagined," said Lofton, testily, "that you would be an early riser."

"I am sorry," said Mister Walton. He couldn't imagine why Mr. Lofton had imagined him to be any sort of riser at all, but was too polite to say so.

"We have been waiting for several hours now."

"She has been sighted," said one of the men.

"She?"

"Maude, Mister Walton," said Lofton, and when the perplexed expression did not leave the bespectacled man's face, he added: "The bear, sir."

"The bear!" said Mister Walton.

"And we are off!"

"Well . . ."

"I took the liberty of having a breakfast packed for you," said Lofton, and he placed a small tin box in Mister Walton's hands. "Mr. Moss!" and here the word *mister* had the sound of a ship's captain addressing his subordinate.

"Yes, Mr. Lofton," said Sundry, without the slightest hint of the subordinate in his voice.

"The guns are ready? The way is chosen? The front runners are beating the bushes?"

"I think we are all set," said Sundry.

"Come, Mister Walton," said Lofton. "Let us bag this beast."

A baker's dozen of them congregated on the back lawn of the inn, glorying in the brilliant sunshine and the smell of salt from the river. They could not have looked less like a group of men preparing to track down a bear. There was a singular lack of physical prowess about them that would have suggested, to the unenlightened eye, nothing more strenuous than a grueling round of croquet. Even Lofton, who was tall and thin, gave an air that suggested his unfamiliarity with the rugged arts of outdoorsmanship.

But their wives and sisters and aunts came out to see them off as heroically as if they were Myrmidons off to hunt the wild boar.

Standing to one side of this assemblage, Sundry Moss alone—in his youth and India rubber boots—looked the part. Mister Walton, whose portly figure yet retained a certain degree of robust vigor, was perhaps second in the appearance of readiness: a standing that was greatly enhanced when the party's single weapon—a 32.40 Winchester—was put into his free hand.

Sundry eyed the rifle with speculative interest. "You didn't bring anything of your own?" he asked Mister Walton.

"Seeing that you arrived unequipped," explained Lofton, "I took it upon myself to secure a weapon for you."

"That's very kind," said Mister Walton, mystified beyond further response.

"Are you planning to get intimate with that creature?" wondered Sundry.

Mister Walton looked doubtfully at the rifle. He was not ignorant of sporting matters and realized that one would have to be close and extremely accurate to bring down a bear with something less than a 30.30. His response, which would have indicated that he had planned nothing at all in this regard, might have ended the misunderstanding concerning his identity then and there, but he was interrupted again by Lofton's impatience.

"Come, my friends!" declared the self-imposed master of the hunt. "It is time we were apace of the game!" He brandished a riding crop, which appeared incongruous with his hunting togs, and led the way up Federal Street, in the direction of the place where Maude was last seen.

The men, unarmed save for Mister Walton, did their best to look brave and sporting, throwing back their shoulders and waving to their womenfolk with resolute smiles. The wives and sisters and aunts were effusive in their goodbyes, and one older woman, weeping, insisted upon pressing her handkerchief into her husband's vest pocket for a token.

Sundry relieved Mister Walton of the rifle as they set out. "I'll hold this for you," suggested the young man, "so you can eat your breakfast."

Peering into the tin that had been given him, Mister Walton felt conspicuous as they marched up the street, but he and Sundry lagged behind the rest of the company and he was able to pick at his breakfast—consisting of a sandwich of cheese and sausage and an apple—in relative peace.

The men ahead of them were a noisy lot, considering their mission; they talked in loud voices and bantered amongst themselves like schoolboys. Sundry theorized that a quieter approach might be in order if they were at all interested in catching their quarry—laying a certain emphasis on the word *if*—but the rest of the party (besides Mister Walton, who was eating his breakfast) must not have heard him, for their general volume following this observation actually rose.

Some paces beyond the county jailhouse, two of the party—Mr. Swelter and Mr. Blick—began to argue the finer points of bear hunting, their opinions unbiased by any practical experience in the matter. The gist of the disagreement was difficult to ascertain, but it was violent enough to bring the party to a brief halt, whereupon Lofton berated Swelter and Blick for their dissension. "United we stand, gentlemen! Divided we fail!"

This statement engendered its own round of debate, which brought them to the crest of the hill where Federal Street ends and the road north from Wiscasset begins. "Now, Mr. Moss," said Lofton, raising his voice above the hubbub. "Where was this creature last seen?"

"She was crossing the field, and disappeared in those trees by the riverbank." Stretching before them, on either side of the road, were rolling hills of field and farmland. To the right the land lowered itself gently to the Sheepscot River, where a small grove of pines and a single oak cast their shade. "Mr. Jones saw her, coming into town. Mr. Jones was coming into town," he added. "We're not sure where the bear was going."

Mister Walton found this last qualification amusing, but Alfred Lofton frowned purposefully. "It is as we suspected. She is unafraid of human proximity, and is dangerously close to the loved ones we have left behind. We need a plan," he announced.

All eyes leveled on Mister Walton, and he realized that, for some inexplicable reason, this plan was expected to originate with him. Raised eyebrows surrounded him. Sundry also watched, his face expressing a more general curiosity.

"Yes, a plan," said Mister Walton.

"We're not a very stealthy gathering," said Sundry.

"Hmm?" said Mister Walton. "No, no. Well, I guess not."

"Perhaps we can use that to our advantage."

"I think we'll wait for Mister Walton to speak up," sniffed Lofton.

"I know just what Sundry is saying," said Mister Walton, which was not entirely the case. "Very good, Sundry. What do you think?"

"We should make a line, perhaps, along the road," said the young fellow. "And spreading out to the farm on the next hill, the man furthest from here will begin to walk toward the river. When he's a ways off, the next man will do the same. Then the next, and so on. That way, we can be as noisy as we like and drive the bear toward those of us with the rifle."

"Hear, hear," said Lofton. He shook Mister Walton's hand.

"Excellent," said Blick. Swelter was already hieing down the road, shouting excitedly to a passing horseman.

It took several explanations before they all understood the concept, but soon the company was strung out along the road and down the opposite slope of the hill (with Lofton himself at the near end of the line), waiting for Mister Walton and Sundry to take their position.

Mister Walton was by nature a brisk walker; but Sundry kept pace with him, his own gait long and gangling, as they moved toward the group of trees overlooking the water. They could hear the liquid trill of a veery from a nearby bush, and three crows launched themselves from a tree by the riverbank, chortling the news of their approach.

When they reached the trees, the trunk of a large oak afforded Mister Walton's shoulder a welcome place of rest, and its crown of leaves a canopy against the brilliant sun. He looked over the lovely surface of the Sheepscot River and sensed the tug of the outgoing tide.

"Perhaps you will want to man the gun now," suggested Sundry, and he passed the rifle to Mister Walton.

Mister Walton hefted the gun uncertainly. He had handled firearms since he was a child, but never in such odd circumstances. He glanced in Sundry's direction and found the young man observing him with a quizzical expression. "That was a very good plan you had, by the way," said Mister Walton.

"It only meant that you and I didn't have to do so much walking as the rest of them," explained Sundry. "It's going to be a warm day."

"I hadn't thought of that," said Mister Walton.

The drive had begun; the man at the further end of the line proceeded to cross the field, taking two or three steps before tripping. The diagonal row of drivers took shape, the shadows of clouds lazily tumbling by them in the waning breeze. The news had been that Maude had disappeared near the shore, and as each of the men approached the bank of the river, their progress slowed almost to a complete halt. What had begun as a rather clodhopping, stumbling line eventually metamorphosed into a queue of gracefully tiptoeing men mincing their way forward.

It was pleasant to be out of doors—to be within reach of the river's salty tang, glorying in the sunny day while standing in the shade of a friendly tree. Mister Walton breathed deeply and caught, in one draft, the scent of salt and pine and grass and wild strawberries.

A shout came down the line and from his position by the tree he peered through the shade and sunshine and keened his ears. "What's that they're saying?" he asked Sundry.

One of the men furthest away, whose path had taken him onto a small knoll, was jumping up and down and waving his arms. "Maybe the bear is below him," said Sundry. He stepped past the trees where the bank grew steep, and scrutinized the narrow line of shore. He was convinced that their exertions would come to nothing; and so, turning back to Mister Walton with the words "I don't see her" on his lips, he was more than a little surprised to discover the bear standing just above him on the bank.

Maude had been dozing, in fact, on the opposite side of the tree against which Mister Walton had rested his shoulder—lying with her belly in a hollow between the massive roots of the ancient oak and blending nicely with the contrasting shade. But she was on her feet now, blinking sleepily and yawning soundlessly as she sauntered around the oak to see what the noise was about.

Sundry gaped helplessly as first her nose appeared to Mister Walton, then her face and her round ears, her bulking shoulders and muscular forepaws. To Mister Walton, whose eyes grew rounder as the bear's presence increased, she seemed to be germinating from the tree itself.

She was no more than medium-sized, but any bear must seem large enough when met at such close quarters. Mister Walton took two steps back, raising the rifle to his shoulder, and tripped over a protruding tree-root. He landed with a thud and a gusting exhalation of breath, raising the rifle to accommodate his sudden lack of height.

"Mister Walton!" shouted Sundry, who had been temporarily frozen.

"Stand back, Sundry!" commanded the bespectacled gentleman, and as he squinted past the rifle's sights, he was astonished to see the bear tuck her head between her forepaws and raise her hindquarters into the air. Gaping up where he fully expected to behold gnashing fangs, he saw instead a pair of swaying bear's feet. Lowering his gaze to Maude's face, his eyes grew wider still, and he said: "Good heavens! She is standing on her head!"

"What is it?" cried Sundry, as if he had been pinched. He was scrambling now, back up the bank and through the trees.

"Good heavens!" said Mister Walton again. "She's smiling at me!"

Indeed, if a bear cannot smile, then Maude was doing a very good job of trying. She could see very little with her eyes buried in the grass, but her teeth were bared in a very ingratiating grin. She gave a low, cowlike moan.

On his feet now, his rifle lowered, Mister Walton nearly laughed with a mixture of nervousness and delight. He stood his ground but looked cautious. "I have never, Sundry . . . never."

"Truth to tell, Mister Walton!"

"But why is she standing on her head?"

"It's what she does, I think. When you told me to stand back, she just upended herself."

"I've never seen anything like it!"

Maude lost her balance at this point, and for a moment they thought she might somersault down the bank. Her claws dug in, however, and she righted herself, startling the two men with a sudden cough. Her black arms waved at Mister Walton as she sat back on her haunches.

"Stand back!" said Mister Walton, taking a step or two back himself.

Maude gave a mournful groan, laid the top of her head on the ground, and upended herself again.

Mister Walton let out a single amazed "Ha!"

"Shoot her!" came an angry voice. "Shoot her, before she gets away!" It was Alfred Lofton, who had drawn closer to the strange scene; he halted his progress several yards away.

"Shoot her?" Mister Walton had forgotten the rifle in his hands.

"Yes, I have a claim on the pelt! Your people distinctly told me I could have it if I was present at the kill! Shoot her!"

Mister Walton glanced from the angry Lofton, to Sundry, to the upside-down bear, and back to Lofton. "Mr. Lofton," he said, never raising his voice. "I have bagged my share of ducks, and in my thin youth successfully tracked the white-tailed deer. I come from a long line of hunting people on my mother's side. I quite enjoy hunting. But I absolutely refuse to shoot any creature with the ingenuity, not to mention the sense of humor, to stand on its head!"

"You refuse!" Lofton was red with anger now. His face contorted and he pulled at his collar, as if to let out steam. He stalked forward, suddenly unmindful of the nearby bruin. "Refuse! What did you come here for, if I may inquire? What sort of big-game hunter are you?"

"Big-game hunter?"

"Indeed, I wonder what sort of Big Game Club it is that you purport to represent!"

"Big Game Club? I am afraid there is some confusion here."

"Confusion? I should say there is . . . !" Alfred Lofton paused, huffing not two paces from Mister Walton. Others of the company had closed ranks some yards away. Maude groaned from her upended posture and rolled onto all fours. "Do you mean to say that you are not a big-game hunter?"

"Why, no, sir," said Mister Walton. "I am nothing of the kind. Is that why you roused me this morning?"

"And you're not from the Big Game Club in Boston?"

"I do not have that honor, no."

Maude, a bear temporarily forgotten, grew impatient with the discussion and wandered down the bank to the river.

"You're not the hunter they promised to send up from Boston?" asked Sundry.

"No," said an amazed Mister Walton, "but it certainly clears matters up to discover that you thought so. Good heavens, I thought you the most singular fellows!"

"You're an imposter!" said Lofton with new venom.

"Not at all," said Mister Walton.

"A brazen charlatan!"

Mister Walton would not dignify this accusation with a reply. He merely adjusted his spectacles, looking slightly hurt, and passed the rifle to Lofton. "Your rifle, sir."

Lofton threw the rifle to the ground and took one step forward. The men behind him had gathered around, and as one they pressed forward menacingly. Lofton's fists were raised before him and he growled: "I have half a mind to teach you a lesson, sir!"

"Why don't you teach it to me first," suggested Sundry as he stepped between them.

"No, Sundry," said Mister Walton. "That isn't necessary."

"I beg your pardon, sir," said Sundry, "but I think you're too much a gentleman to swing first, and I think this fellow knows it." Sundry eyed Lofton carefully. "You're also a good ten or twelve years younger than Mister Walton, aren't you? Perhaps you and I are a closer match."

"Stand aside," said Lofton, and he lifted his arm to push Sundry away.

Sundry swept Lofton's arm back and raised his fists. "Come on," he said. "Maybe that stuffed shirt will give you some padding." As one the company leaned forward, and Sundry took in each of them eye by eye. "Come on—one at a time, or all at once."

"All right, gentlemen," came a new voice. "What seems to be the problem?"

The tension snapped like a stick, and the assembly broke in two so that three official-looking men might stride into their midst. "Sundry, what is this all about?" demanded the tallest of the newcomers.

"This *gentleman* here was just about to teach someone a lesson, Sheriff." Neither Lofton nor Sundry had backed down from their threatening postures.

"In boxing?" Sheriff Piper, rangy of limb and long of jaw, eyed Lofton with curiosity. "Mr. Lofton, isn't it?"

"Yes, my name is Alfred Lofton."

"You were making some noise about the escaped bear, if I remember."

"I complained that nothing had been done."

"I do remember," said the sheriff, and the glint in his eye indicated that the memory was not a pleasant one. "Well, Mr. Lofton, in all my years I've only known Sundry to be in one scuffle; and with the outcome of that particular case as evidence, I'd guess that he didn't need any lessons. But if you consider yourself a master of the art, you are welcome to proceed."

"I wouldn't dirty my hands," said Lofton. He snatched the rifle from the ground at his feet, gathered his company together with a haughty scan of their faces, and led the way back to the road.

"Sundry," said the sheriff. "Were you really going to punch that nice gentleman in the nose?"

"If you had given me half a minute," said the young man, "I think I might have."

"Well," admitted Piper, glancing after Lofton and his becalmed hunting party, retreating up the field, "perhaps I was half a minute too hasty. Now," he said. "It's not an original turn of phrase, but if someone could explain to me what this was all about . . ."

25. The Extraordinary Befuddlement of Mr. Thump, the Singular Distraction of Mr. Eagleton, and the Superior Determination of Mr. Ephram!

MR. THUMP HAD QUITE LIKED HIS ROOMS on Portland's India Street before his Fourth of July holiday, but they did not seem to satisfy him now. He was, these days, in something of a funk. His friends Ephram and Eagleton had not been unaware of this melancholia of his as they traveled home by rail on Sunday the fifth; nor were they unaware of the reason for his bewilderment.

Ever since his collision with Mrs. Roberto (in her attractive suit of tights) the substantial world had grown hazy to Thump. It was not the bump, taken on the forehead from one of her black high-heel boots—the bruise from that portion of the impact was well on its way to disappearing. No: it was the softer shock of waking in that striking lady's compassionate lap, and the continued shock of gazing past her ample charms into her lovely (and extremely frank) brown eyes.

The force of this experience had been amplified that very evening at the Fourth of July Ball, when Thump so manfully led a conversation with the attractive Mrs. Roberto into an invitation to dance that she could not refuse. Their conversation (presented here for those studying the art of masculine charm) followed this course:

MRS. ROBERTO (*spoken in a hushed and husky whisper just a fraction of an inch from the back of Thump's ear*): Ah, my darling sir! How I hoped to reacquaint myself with you under less trying circumstances!

(THUMP, *who has felt as much as heard* MRS. ROBERTO's *sweet speech, says nothing, but looks as if he has tried unsuccessfully to swallow a large marble.*)

MRS. ROBERTO (*her lips closer to* THUMP's *ear, her voice huskier*): When I first gazed down upon your magnificent beard and your noble brow and saw how gallantly you attempted to break my fall, tears rose in my eyes!

(THUMP, *now convinced that he has accidentally ingested several large marbles, all of which are lodged somewhere between his jaw and his shoulders, says nothing. The ploy is effective.* MRS. ROBERTO, *sensing his manly reticence, moves to the fore so that she can speak to him face to face.*)

MRS. ROBERTO (*her dark hair gorgeously frames her exotic features; décolletage is the watchword of her gown, she wags a tapered finger at him*): You thought to have me at a disadvantage, leaving me without your name.

(THUMP *says nothing.*)

MRS. ROBERTO (*one dark eyebrow arching luxuriously*): But I have inquired and found you out.

(THUMP *says nothing, but does grow pale. It will be remembered that* THUMP's *friends* EPHRAM *and* EAGLETON *have left the scene in order to socialize with two young women on the other side of the hall. In the absence of his friends, his erudition and virile flair are all the more remarkable.*)

MRS. ROBERTO: I must properly introduce myself and express my—

(THUMP *hiccoughs.*)

MRS. ROBERTO: —admiration. (*Here her hand finds itself in his and is raised to his lips.* THUMP *is so artful in his paralysis that it would seem to anyone watching that she alone has motivated this intimate action. She says:*) Please call me, as my late husband did—

(THUMP *hiccoughs.*)

MRS. ROBERTO (*forming the word as if she were expressing the essence of chocolate*): —Dorothea . . .

(THUMP *says nothing.*)

(MRS. ROBERTO *looks at* THUMP *as if he were the very confection she has seemed to have been describing.*)

(THUMP *says nothing, but looks rather as if he might melt in a particularly warm hand.*)

MRS. ROBERTO (*though no invitation has been heard by our ears*): Oh, I would love to dance. (*And being an athletic woman, she is able to lift him briefly from his feet as they are swept onto the dance floor.*)

(THUMP *is silent, but slowly his lessons from Mrs. De Riche's Academy of Ballroom Sciences begin to take effect. Once his limbs actually begin to move, their steps take on something like grace.*)

Thump had always respected the opposite sex to an extreme degree and done so from a safe distance. That distance had been uncannily shortened, and he was not yet in the way of recovering. His rooms, as a result, seemed rather empty of a sudden, and what had given him immense comfort only three days ago now evoked little pleasure for him.

He had first taken these rooms seven years ago, in 1889; it was the year of the Oklahoma Land Rush and the Johnstown Flood; Benjamin Harrison was President. He had been a good deal younger then—his beard was not so extraordinary, and his world view (he liked to think) was not so . . . well, worldly as now.

On the day that he first occupied his rooms, he bought the inaugural volume of Theodore Roosevelt's *The Winning of the West* and spent the evenings of the next several days ensconced in his new den, marveling at Mr. Roosevelt's strenuous prose. Inspired, he took several long walks.

Thump was fascinated with the vigorous life and often read about it. The shelves of his den were lined with the adventures of great travelers and explorers. He was especially interested in sailing, and always knew when high and low tide could be expected.

His rooms (the den, a parlor, a bedroom, and water closet) reflected this robust outlook—the furniture was large and dark and masculine, the doilies and antimacassars were plain, and the curtains were serious and contemplative. The few knickknacks that he had collected were of a nature wild and foreign; he had a teak elephant on his parlor mantel and a pair of unidentified antlers on his den wall, both items bought (with the encouragement of his friends Ephram and Eagleton) from a local merchant.

The routine of his life had seemed pleasant as well, before the Fourth of July: his Thursday-night dinners with Ephram and Eagleton, the days that he looked in on the family shipping firm and chatted with the clerks, reading, walking in the park, visiting his uncle in Exeter. It is true that he had quietly yearned for female companionship (as had his friends) and (with his friends) had cultivated the necessary talents with dance lessons and art-appreciation seminars and concerts.

But until his Fourth of July holiday he had not felt truly dissatisfied with his lot. His rooms seemed empty now, his way of life uneventful. By Tuesday afternoon, drastic action seemed required and, bracing himself, he took a walk almost an hour earlier than he had originally intended.

Mr. Eagleton had grown as restless as Mr. Thump over the last day or so. The problem, of course, with a successful holiday is that it may very well cast a cold light upon the mundane progress of a normal day; and when you are wealthy in a worldly sense, and therefore wealthy in time, it takes some ingenuity to make such a normal day pass quickly.

The term *hobby-horse* had been coined, sometime in the seventeenth century, to describe the eccentric enthusiasms and whims of the well-to-do classes; by the end of the nineteenth century that term had been shortened simply to "hobby" and given the respectable attention of all the better periodicals and many seemingly rational people. It was near the turn of the century that the collecting of stamps and coins, abetted by increased travel, first took hold of the idle imagination. The breeding of horses and dogs and cats, not strictly for practical purposes, was imbued with sudden importance. Some eccentrics with time on their hands began to write books!

Eagleton's own hobby was the prognostication and comprehension of the weather. He often looked at the weather. His friends Ephram and Thump admired the way in which he clasped his hands behind his back, squared his shoulders, and tilted his head ever so slightly, the better to contemplate some atmospheric phenomenon. Eagleton observed the skies with the eye of a man whose cerebral faculties were wholly concentrated upon the object of his attention; and he could gaze at a cloud with a degree of seriousness and candor that encouraged others to believe that he saw with a deeper vision than they.

One of Eagleton's favorite haunts was Portland's beloved observatory on Munjoy Hill, and from its top (when the wind wasn't blowing too stiffly) he was alert to the widened horizons and a great deal more weather than could be observed upon the ground. There was no place of greater altitude in the environs of the city, and Eagleton thought highly of it.

But even the observatory held no fascination for him today. He had attempted to wrest himself free of his fitful state by taking his lunch to the top of the tower, but could not focus his mind upon the sunny weather at hand. He thought only of the rain on Saturday night when, under the protection of his umbrella, he had escorted a lady by the name of Ophelia to her family's carriage.

He was in his own carriage now, being driven back to his home on

Chestnut Street and thinking of that charmed evening. It was fortunate (and more fortunate than he knew) that Ophelia and her friend, Sallie, were masterful conversationalists. He and Ephram had said little more than what you would expect to hear from a guard at Buckingham Palace (having adopted a similar posture). But the course of the one-sided dialogue (and the men themselves) had been thoroughly captivated by Sallie and Ophelia's easy chatter and contagious laughter.

Ophelia, thought Eagleton, sighing as his carriage trundled down Middle Street. At about this juncture, he did unknowingly pass Thump (who was, when we last saw him, moving on foot in the direction of Eagleton's house). Eagleton sighed again, thinking: *She laughed so prettily.*

Ophelia and Sallie had laughed heartily that evening, saving their strongest gales of amusement for those moments (which fell every ten minutes or so) when Ephram announced the time and Eagleton the weather. Ophelia was sure that she had never met anyone who could make her laugh so, and said as much. She had even touched Eagleton's hand during this communication—a gesture that had shot through him like a bolt of lightning.

The very recollection gave rise to a sudden need to exercise himself, and Eagleton told the driver to let him off. Patting the side of the carriage to indicate that the driver should move on, he walked for a while without conscious direction. He had not gone very far, however, when it occurred to him that he needed company in his distraction—and no one he knew, at this point, was more distracted than his good friend Thump.

Eagleton turned about on his heel with the intention of walking to his friend's apartment and very nearly knocked Thump over in the process.

"Thump!"

"Eagleton!"

"Extraordinary!" said Eagleton, retrieving his fallen hat.

"I *am* amazed!" said Thump, picking up his walking stick.

"Meeting on Middle Street."

"In the middle, as it were."

"I couldn't have expected it."

"I certainly didn't."

"I was only just going to your house."

"And I to yours."

"This is remarkable."

"A coincidence."

"I can't say how happy I am, running into you like this."

"And I you, old friend."

"I must admit, a certain melancholia has haunted me these few days."

"I am similarly beset!"

"Oh, my friend," said Eagleton. "A man needs purpose!"

"He does indeed!"

"The very distraction from which I seek relief hinders my ability to seek a remedy!"

"Good heavens! How similar to my own quandary!"

"It is said that two heads are better than one, and it is with this in mind that I have come seeking you, hopeful that our combined faculties might solve my dilemma."

"Eagleton! Our motives are but mirror images of one another!"

There and then, upon the sidewalk, the two of them stood and thought. No verbal communication passed between them, as if physical propinquity alone might foster a cure for their distracted minds. So intense was their thinking, so deep was their involvement with their problem, that passers-by paused to regard them with interest and curiosity. (Several people would mention the sight when they sat down to dinner that evening.)

For several minutes Eagleton and Thump remained in their thoughtful postures, peering one at his feet, the other at the sky; and it would seem finally that Eagleton's theory concerning two heads would not be borne out this day, when a sudden and simultaneous light radiated from their noble faces.

"Ephram!" shouted Eagleton.

"Yes!" agreed Thump with equal force.

"Each on our own would never have thought of it!"

"I'm sure you are right!"

"It is his magnificent reason that will free us of our melancholia."

"Of course."

"Ephram is a very straightforward thinker, Thump."

"He is indeed!"

"My weather is variable. It is mercurial and hardly predictable beyond a day or two. Even your tides differ from day to day, ruled by a varying moon. But Ephram's time . . ."

"Yes?"

". . . marches on unchanged!"

And so they marched themselves, not realizing for at least a block and a half that they had set off in separate directions.

"To our chairman!" announced Ephram. This was, in fact, the third time that he had communicated this opinion—first uttering it in the parlor of his own home, seconding it on the sidewalk of Danforth Street outside his house, and voicing the thought a third time while racing with his friends in a hired cab toward Spruce Street.

From the very beginning, Eagleton and Thump could not have agreed with him more, and yet they seemed to do just that with each repetition of the phrase.

Ephram had been out of sorts before his friends had arrived. The cruel vicissitudes of time were the theme of his uneasy thoughts—the very time that Eagleton had deemed unchangeable. But Ephram, who carried three pocket watches and whose house snicked and ticked with clock gears and rang with gongs and bells at every quarter, knew that time was an entity relative to the happiness of the individual experiencing it.

At the Fourth of July Ball he had more or less conversed (actually rather less than more, since he had been dumbfounded and she bright and talkative) with an attractive young woman for one hour and forty-seven minutes and time had flown. Now, the prospect of ever conversing with that particular female (or even seeing her) again was dim beneath the pall of his own uncertainty and social inexperience—and time dug in its claws to slow each moment into an hour, and every hour into a day. The very ticks and bells that normally caused him so much pleasure now pained him like cruel and tiny darts . . .

. . . until, that is, he was rescued from this chronic torture by the sudden and unexpected arrival of his friends Eagleton and Thump!

"A man needs purpose!" announced Ephram, when the three had shared their similar states of distraction.

"My words exactly, Ephram!" said Eagleton.

"Hmmm!" said Thump, though it sounded as if he were clearing his throat.

"Gentlemen!" said Ephram. "We must have a mission!"

"Yes!" exclaimed Eagleton, quite excited now. "It is extraordinary how completely we think alike. Isn't it, Thump?"

"Hmmm!" from Thump again.

This universal agreement was pleasant to Ephram and he began another pronouncement when it become clear that Thump was actually trying to dislodge something from his throat. Ephram banged the man violently between the shoulder blades and a wax grape, taken from the arrangement on a nearby table, shot across the room.

"Never fear, Thump!" said Eagleton, mistaking the reason for his friend's watery eyes. "We are a club, are we not?"

"Yes!" said Ephram, as if the thought had just occurred to him.

Thump went into a fit of coughing.

Ephram gripped Thump's shoulder. "All for one and . . . everyone . . . together. . . ." He knew that this declaration lacked the ring he was wanting, but the sentiment was there. Unfortunately, there was no name for their club yet, so there was no grand entity to specifically invoke; the purpose and intent of their club was also amorphous, but this did not deter Ephram's train of thought.

"We need a mission, to be sure," said Eagleton. "But I am hanged if I can think of one!"

Thump waved a hand in the air, a gesture that his friends were sure betokened agreement, when actually he was hoping for a glass of water.

"The answer is simple, Eagleton," said Ephram. He paused so that the sequel to this statement would not be drowned out by Thump's renewed hacking. "To our chairman!" he said.

The fact that Mister Walton as yet had no idea that he had been voted chairman of their nameless club seemed no obstacle as they waited for a cab.

"To our chairman!" said Ephram, and this was the second instance above mentioned.

Thump had, by now, gotten his drink of water, but was still rubbing the tears from his eyes. Ephram patted him sympathetically on the back and said something about Mrs. Roberto.

Eagleton almost smiled to see one friend comfort another so. "I was quite down before Thump arrived," he admitted.

"Melancholy was my companion," said Ephram. He hailed an approaching carriage, shouted the address of Mister Walton's home, and the three of them piled in. "Spare nothing, man!" said Ephram to the driver. "Time is of the essence!" The great detective himself could not have put it better.

The driver frowned down from his seat and said something monosyllabic and unintelligible. Ephram waved an impatient hand at him and the fellow simply shook his head and eased the cab into traffic.

"Expected fine today," said Eagleton. "Increasing clouds possible tonight."

"Low tide at 3:13," said Thump, more like his old self again.

Ephram consulted a pocket watch. "It is twenty-two minutes past one," he said, and after a long pause he added: "To our chairman!"

It was a fine day to begin an adventure. The sun was dazzling, and a sea breeze rose as the afternoon wore on, moving through the great oaks and elms and maples that lined the handsome streets of Portland. Ephram, Eagleton, and Thump said little; little needed to be said, and, after all, they felt it was important not to second-guess their chairman—that grand man of action, Mister Walton.

They made a dapper trio, their coats finely cut, their hats crisp with recent fashion and worn at carefully studied inclines. Eagleton alone affected the use of a cane, but Ephram sported a new watch fob, and Thump's beard had been trimmed just the day before. They looked stoically ahead (or in Thump's case—who sat opposite—stoically behind) and only began to take notice of their surroundings when they reached Spruce Street, which had become famous to them as the home of their gallant (if incognizant) leader.

"I believe this is the correct place," said Eagleton, the first to climb down from the cab. He pointed to the brick domicile with his cane, while Thump paid the driver.

Ephram held the card that Mister Walton had given him in front of his nose and matched the street number on it with the cast-iron numbers visible beside the front door. "Right as usual, my friend," he said.

"Oh," said Eagleton, raising a hand to ward off this embarrassing praise.

"Shall we?" suggested Ephram. He opened the gate and led the way up the walk to the front door.

When they knocked, the echoes within the house had an unoccupied quality, and they waited on the top step for some minutes before turning away in disappointment. They looked to one another, hesitating on the top step, their backs to the door, each hoping that one of his friends might have a second course of action to suggest; none of them, unfortunately, had thought the matter any further than finding Mister Walton.

They were startled, then, by the sound of the door swinging open and Cedric Baffin inquiring if he could be of service.

"Yes, certainly," said Ephram, brightening. "We hoped for an interview with Mister Tobias Walton." He handed the retainer a card with the name *Matthew Ephram, Esq.* printed in bold letters upon it.

Mr. Baffin glanced at the card with courteous interest. "I am sorry," he said. "Mister Toby is not at home."

"Has he not returned from Freeport, then?" wondered Eagleton.

"He hasn't, actually. He has gone on to Wiscasset. I am not sure when to expect him back."

"That is unfortunate," said Ephram. He exchanged serious looks with Eagleton and Thump. "We did want to speak to him, you see. We have elected him to the position of chairman of our club, and we hoped—in the spirit of that station—he might favor us with his advice."

"Well put!" said Eagleton with obvious admiration for his friend's elocution.

"That *is* news!" said Cedric, pleased for his employer. "He will know what club I speak of, if I tell him?"

"Oh, yes! Assuredly!" said Eagleton.

"We haven't a name yet," said Thump with great dignity.

This seemed to surprise Mr. Baffin. He had collected cards from each of the men by this point, and none of their names were familiar to him. "You've known Mister Toby for some time, I gather?"

"Not at all," said Eagleton.

"Just met him," said Ephram. He looked to Thump. "Was it the day before yesterday?"

"It was Saturday," corrected Eagleton. "Fourth of July."

"Ah, yes," said Ephram. "Appropriate, that."

"We're not sure what sort of club, you know," added Thump.

"Yes, well," said Mr. Baffin. "I certainly will inform him as soon as I am able."

"Wiscasset, you say," said Ephram. To Eagleton and Thump's ears some new purpose was lurking in the voice of their compatriot.

"Yes, sir."

"North and east of Portland, I think," said Ephram, almost to himself.

"I do believe," said Cedric.

"Gentlemen," said Ephram as he returned his hat to its perch; Eagleton and Thump followed suit. "Much obliged," said the trio in chorus, retracing their steps toward the street.

"It is a lovely evening," said Mr. Baffin, who stood in the doorway, somewhat perplexed. The three men turned.

"Fair and warm tonight," said Eagleton. "Increasing clouds tomorrow with a chance of showers."

"High tide at 8:47," said Thump.

"It is 8:14 presently," informed Ephram from one of his pocket watches as they waved to Cedric.

Cedric Baffin watched them disappear in the twilight, glanced at the cards again in the light from the hall as he shut the door, chuckling to himself.

Back on the street, Ephram halted for a moment and looked industriously pensive. Eagleton and Thump waited in silence, knowing that he was in the throes of an idea. "Eagleton," he said.

"Yes?"

"Thump."

"Hmmm?"

"I am thinking," said Ephram, and Eagleton and Thump shook hands, they were so pleased with one another for having guessed that this was the case. "Mister Walton, I suspect, has ventured by himself upon some new exploit, and just as we feel the need of his leadership, he no doubt would find invaluable the presence of . . . his club!"

"Good heavens!" said Eagleton. Thump harumphed with great feeling. "You don't mean?" added Eagleton.

"Yes, my friends: I propose that we follow our chairman . . . to Wiscasset!"

Thump nodded vociferously.

"To Wiscasset!" cried Eagleton.

26. A Shaggy Bear Story

SOME MAY HAVE THOUGHT IT ODD that James, a veteran of the Navy, preferred to travel by rail, but he had spent so much of his youth gazing out over ocean expanses that he found the variety of sights offered up by the land to be of constant interest and comfort. From his seat in their private compartment he would often gaze out over the changing landscape, a book or a newspaper held open but unread upon his lap.

Mercia was better able to concentrate on a good book or a bit of needlework, while keeping up her end of a conversation with Cordelia, who found the relative solitude of the private compartment less tolerable.

While passing through Wiscasset, however, they were in the dining car, an environment more suited to Cordelia's sociable frame of mind. Those passengers who had not heard of the town's fugitive bear were quickly informed as they approached the county seat, and Cordelia herself presented an entertaining and only slightly exaggerated version of the story. No sighting of Maude was made, though everyone in the car gazed out the left-hand windows for a glimpse of the celebrated creature. The passengers laughed at their own expense when Wiscasset and the Sheepscot River had dwindled behind the contours of land; their talk and chatter fell into separate pools again.

"Well," sighed Cordelia. "Now we have no bear to look forward to." She lifted the cozy from the teapot on their table and poured herself a cup.

"Are you fond of bears then, miss?" asked an elderly gentleman at the next table. He was a small fellow with a deep, resonant voice and a pleasant face that peered out from a mass of white beard and mustache. His white hair had thinned considerably, so that the dome of his head shone with the light from the window behind him, but his blue eyes, set among crow's feet and crinkles, gleamed clearly through a narrow pair of spectacles. He turned in his chair so that he could look admiringly at Cordelia.

"I have never had the pleasure of their acquaintance, sir," she replied.

"Ah, well then, don't worry. There is always another bear to look forward to in this life."

"I am glad to hear you say it." Cordelia rewarded the man's kind assurance with a bright smile.

James turned away from his view of the passing scenery to consider the old man. "You've known a bear or two in your time then, Mr. . . . ?"

"Tolly," said the man, leaning forward to shake hands. "Isherwood Tolly."

James introduced himself and his wife and daughter.

"Yes," said Mr. Tolly. "Bears are an inevitability of life. But they don't have to be a misfortune. I had a farm, years ago, and it was a bear that saved it from ruin."

"The bear saved the *farm* from ruin, Mr. Tolly?" asked Cordelia.

"And myself."

"Do you still have the farm, Mr. Tolly?" asked Mercia.

"Oh, no, ma'am," he answered. "But I did once, years ago — mostly stumps and stones. I cleared several acres of land and built a little nook of a house back in '33. I was twenty-three years old, unmarried, with no family, and several miles outside the village. I didn't see people very often that summer and fall, so that winter, when the nights came early and the wind in the forest carried away every other noise, I was starved for the sound of a human voice and near foolish for the want of company."

Mr. Tolly shifted himself in his chair so he could more comfortably address his listeners, who, by this time, included more than just the Underwoods. "I may *have* been foolish, actually. For I greeted the first human creature that crossed my path like a long lost brother.

"He nearly frightened the wits out of me, to begin with, for he was standing a few feet away, knee deep in the snow and as quiet as an Indian, when I came out of the cow shed one morning. I spilt half a bucket of milk jumping back. He was a hard thing to look at in any circumstance. His hair was long and unkempt; to say that he wore rags would flatter his attire; and he had the largest, longest nose I had ever seen on mortal man. He was uncommon tall, and raw-boned, but his teeth were as fine and bright as if he had just cut them. If I hadn't been so lonely for the sight of another person I would probably have chased him off with a gun. And soon enough I wished I had.

"His name was Burl, and I invited him in for a bit of breakfast and a cup of coffee. He nearly took up the entire kitchen, sitting at the table with his legs stretched out, but he talked about seeing moose and trapping fur and where the best trout could be fished. I thought at first he was some mad hermit, living by himself in the forest, till he mentioned his brothers. I said to him that they must live a distance away, but a wave of a hand in the direction of the woods was the closest to an address I could get from him.

" 'I'm not very clever about keeping track of the days,' he said. 'What's the date today?'

"Well, I had an almanac hanging from the windowsill, in which I carefully marked each day before I blew out the light and climbed into bed every evening, just so I'd know where I was in the year. 'It's the twelfth of December,' I said, checking the almanac.

" 'Yuletide comes,' he announced, and he slapped a knee and nearly bumped his head standing up.

" 'If you're nearby come Christmas Eve,' I said, following him out, 'drop in and I'll fire up some rum and butter.'

"Well, he thanked me politely enough and trudged off. I stood at the door, watching him disappear among the trees, but he turned around two or three times and stopped, as if he didn't want me to see the direction he was going, so I went back inside."

Mr. Tolly was warm to his story now, his eyes darting from face to face in order to engage each listener. The rhythm of the rails beneath them, the warmth of the summer day and the bright sun had been enveloped in the snows and forests of his tale.

"Now, I hadn't exactly taken to the fellow," he continued. "So my only excuse for offering such an invitation is all that time I had spent alone. In fact, I had felt more than a little uncomfortable with him. It was almost as if I had been conversing with one of the trees that had decided to see what I was up to, or a piece of rock face, broke away from the hills looking for a fireside to warm his granite bones. I went outside half a dozen times that day, just to study his footprints in the snow and prove to myself that I hadn't dreamt the entire visit.

"More weather drifted over the farm and forests, the livestock were dopey with winter, and I nearly forgot Burl with all the work to be done. Christmas Eve came and I made myself a stew on the hearth and lit an extra candle when night came. There was a small item about Christmas in my almanac that I had been saving, so I sat down with a bowl of stew and the only bit of writing in the house that I hadn't read four times over.

"Suddenly there came such a bang at the door that I thought it would break in half. I flew out of my seat with a shout, and in the very same moment remembered my invitation. No other could have leveled such a thunderous blow. And when I said come in, the door swept open and in strode Burl.

"But he wasn't alone."

Mr. Tolly paused, turned to look for his cup, and found it empty. It wasn't three seconds before someone flagged down a waiter bearing a pot and got it filled for him. And as he recommenced, there was such a straining to hear his every word, and such a lot of earnest eyes watching his face, that if not for his voice and the rumble of the train itself the car would have been quite silent.

"But he wasn't alone," he repeated. "In came a brother, right behind him — Rulf was his name, and he was taller and shabbier, and his nose was larger and longer than Burl's. Then came a third brother — Gart, and he was wilder still. And a fourth and fifth, and they strode in with a horrible noise, whooping and hooting and shouting and howling like wolves, and flapping their arms. Thirteen of them squeezed into my humble little rooms, their heads bent and their elbows knocking things from the walls. Cairn and Stie and Nutt packed in, and each was more vast and vastly more unattractive than the one before him.

" 'Some coney stew, Wald!' shouted the seventh to the eighth. 'Well, Houth, let me fetch you a bowl!'

"In shouldered Chuff and Spank and Veer, and they decided there wasn't enough room, so they kicked out the table and chairs. Then came Terth and Runt, who was the biggest of them. Thirteen, and you have never seen such a fantastic assemblage, scraping the ceiling and stumbling into the fire and flattening anything underfoot. And the noise, the absolute din! I was buffeted about like a leaf in a storm, and they laughed and sang in voices like great rocks falling down a hillside.

" 'Where's the hot buttered rum?' shouted one of these giants, and soon they found the barrel and the butter, the nutmeg and the sugar, and things got wilder still. It was not long before I crawled out on my hands and knees, dragging along any bit of clothing or blanket I could lay hold of, and spent the rest of the night in the shed with the cow, who was restless with the clamor from the house.

"The next morning, I woke from a fitful sleep. The cow had settled down and my back was against her side. She'd eaten the sleeve off my coat, but I thought it small enough favor to ask in return for providing a soft pillow and a warm mattress. I clambered to my feet and threw open the shed door. All was quiet. Even the wind had silenced. It was Christmas Day and the forest itself seemed hushed and respectful.

"Except for the walls, very little in my house remained standing. What furniture had not been tossed into the snow was splintered, and what food had not been eaten was strewn about the place as if a pack of wolves had torn it apart. I was stunned, but I roused myself, only too aware of the long cold winter ahead of me; I could spend no time grieving over my situation.

"There was an Indian family nearby, the Weathertongues—'nearby' meaning within ten or twelve miles. They were masters of living off the land, and more than generous with the surplus of their larder. I would have had to abandon my poor cow, or slaughter her, if not for the Weathertongues. Able Weathertongue and the rest of his family listened to my fantastic tale and spoke seriously amongst themselves concerning it.

" 'There have always been rough characters living in the forest,' said Able, before I tied on my snowshoes to tramp home. 'Even before your people came. But when your people came, they brought their own rough characters, and I think your rough characters and our rough characters have gotten together and made themselves some sons. A little wild behavior is one thing, but this is . . .' and he shook his head, unable to conjure up the proper word.

"I was fortunate that spring came early in 1834. One of the Weathertongue boys saw after my livestock while I went into town for supplies. Through the winter I had thought of nothing but leaving farm, field, and beast behind and becoming a sailor, or hiring onto a mill, but with the warmer months I found myself appreciating the work I had put into my holdings, and by summer's end I had improved both house and tillage.

"Harvest came and went, and I gathered in for winter. Snow fell, and I marked off the days in my almanac. The Yuletide approached and an odd jumpiness came over me; my nerves tightened and the muscles of my back felt shrunken and too small for my bones.

"Christmas Eve came and I sat watching the door, listening, waiting. I had built a new shed that summer and spent the day putting my breakables and perishables into it. Night came, and the wind blew up and howled at the eaves. I sat in the dark, with no candle and only the smallest fire glowing in the hearth. Starting at every strange noise, I wished that I had accepted my neighbors' invitation to join them for the evening.

"Then came the blow at the door and I jumped to my feet. I waited, keening my ears for every sound. Another blow came, louder still. I said nothing. Awful rumbling voices conversed among themselves, muffled through the door. Another blow shook the hinges and rattled the sill; then a voice called my name.

" 'He is not home,' came one theory.

" 'But I smell a fire. He must have banked the hearth for us,' came another.

"That was all they needed. The door was thrown open and in they came, huge and ungainly, filling up my tiny home and declaring: Why hadn't I spoken when they called? Was I asleep? They laughed and roared and knocked the breath from me pounding my back.

"The noise they made was worse than I had remembered, and when they saw my cupboards almost empty and nothing cooking in the hearth, they roared louder still. Three of them ran out into the woods and came back a little later with a great black-staved barrel of rum and the carcass of a twelve-point buck. The hearth wasn't big enough for their purposes, so they made a great bonfire just outside the door that singed the sides of the house, and they clambered in and out, bumping their heads in the doorway and holding wrestling matches on the kitchen floor.

"I considered driving them out, but even with a shotgun in my hand I would have seemed puny to them. Upon my word, they would have laughed at me. I simply crawled into the cow shed with a blanket, and when I woke up the next morning the fire outside the house was still smoldering. The shed, where I had put in my winter's store, was emptied and flattened. The next year I planned to be away for Christmas Eve."

Mr. Tolly looked to his cup again, and someone asked a waiter to leave a pot of coffee at the old fellow's table. "Tea will do," said Mr. Tolly, and the waiter, who had been as intent on the story as any of the passengers, hurried off to fulfill his office.

"Who were these louts?" asked one young man pettishly, thinking perhaps that *he* would have done something about the situation.

"Beyond their names, I never knew," said Mr. Tolly. "And I never met another soul that had ever laid eyes on them."

"What was this about a bear, Mr. Tolly?" asked Cordelia.

"Ah, yes," he replied. "I was going to tell you about the bear." The waiter arrived with the tea then, and half the car joined Mr. Tolly in a cup. Their spoons jangled against china as they waited for his story to continue. With great method he sipped from his cup before obliging their curiosity.

"I managed, with help, to get through that winter as well, but I knew that the farm could not survive another visit from Burl and his kin. Then came December of 1835, and three days before Christmas a great blizzard bundled in from the coast, piling up snow past my knees, and blowing drifts over my head. I never left the house, except to tend to the livestock, and by the morning of Christmas Eve I was getting mighty anxious that I wouldn't be able to get away before my annual guests arrived.

"But the sky cleared in mid-morning and I packed my kit and strapped on my snowshoes. I banked the embers in the hearth and saw to the cows—

there were two of them by now. Then I turned my face in the direction of the Weathertongues' property and stopped in my tracks.

"A man—a normal sort of man, that is—stood at the brink of the forest, a pack on his back and a musket across his arm. He looked almost black against the trees, they were so laden with snow. 'Ho, there,' he called. 'Where am I, pray tell, and what day is it?'

" 'Shirley Mills, in the state of Maine, and it's Christmas Eve,' I called back.

"I advanced toward him a few steps and he said: 'Careful, careful. Old Benjamin here isn't used to any human creature but myself.'

"I halted, squinting my eyes against the glare of the snow. Then something white moved and let out a low throaty growl. It was a bear, a white bear, a polar bear! It was the biggest bear I had ever seen in my life, and it stood up on its hind legs and licked the snow from a branch that stood fourteen feet high if it stood an inch.

" 'He won't bother you,' said the man. 'As long as you don't come too close.'

" 'Great gee whillikers, man!' I shouted. 'What are you doing with that beast?'

" 'I'm bringing him to Washington,' he declared. 'As a gift to Andrew Jackson.'

"Well, I sincerely hoped that the President would know what to do with a polar bear, and said so; but I explained to the man that I was off to spend Christmas Eve with my neighbors, and regretted that I wouldn't be able to show him any hospitality. That was all right with him, he was too done in to appreciate anything but a bit to eat and a bed to sleep in, and he asked would I mind him staying the night if he left everything the way he found it.

"I did my best, then, to explain about Burl and his twelve brothers. I even admitted that I was spending the night away just to be clear of their roughneck celebration, and that I was seriously considering leaving the farm, lock, stock, and livestock, to anyone who wanted it. He wasn't to be daunted, however. Not at all. He'd been trudging for weeks with this bear at the end of a rope, and if I didn't object, he would take his chances. The day was getting on by then, so I wished him well, told him what he'd find in the larder, and headed out."

Mr. Tolly shifted in his seat, sipped from his cup, and said in a grave tone: "What I tell you next I only know from the bear catcher's own account.

"The bear catcher, whose name I never did learn, poked up the embers in the hearth and threw some logs on. Then he helped himself to some of the food which I had not bothered to hide, and settled himself down with my almanac. By his own reckoning, he had not slept under a roof, nor read a bit of printed word, for a year and half. Greatly obliged by his present circumstances, he quickly fell asleep at the kitchen table.

"It was the bear, tied to a tree outside, that woke him. He heard the sound of hungry growls and realized that he hadn't fed the creature, so he got his pack and went out to feed the polar bear the last of his pemmican, and while he was doing this, Burl and his brothers came galumphing out of the forest. Now it will say something about this tribe of wild men that a man who had subdued a polar bear found them singularly daunting. He watched in astonishment as they strode across the clearing in the moonlight and banged on the front door.

"He told me that the house shook with the blows, and deciding that he could spend another night without a roof over his head, he climbed the very tree to which he had tied the bear, quite happy to have escaped the notice of my uninvited guests.

" 'He is playing hidey-seek with us again,' shouted one of the brothers, and they threw open the door and tumbled in. Soon they had a great bonfire stacked outside the door. Irritated with the light, the polar bear dug himself into the snow, so that only his black nose was visible. The man in the tree climbed higher still, and watched as the brothers howled and sang and danced and fought and took turns throwing each other into the fire. Sparks and logs flew, and the smell of singed hair filled the woods.

"As they were digging into the larder, one of the brothers came out with a large sausage and proceeded to cook it over the bonfire on a stick. Two of the clan tried to wrest the meat away from him, but he staved them off with several powerful blows and wandered away from the fire to enjoy his repast.

"His path, as it happened, took him to the tree where the frightened onlooker was hiding, and to which the bear was tied. The great long-nosed roughneck chewed at the still sizzling sausage with a satisfied growl, then stopped to stare down at the polar bear's nose. The bear, smelling the sausage, had begun to sniff and snuff from under the snow.

"The ugly fellow called to his brothers and, already half-drunk with rum, they tramped over and watched the polar bear's nose wriggle and sniff, fascinated and puzzled till one of them declared that it was the farm's dog, hiding from them. 'He wants a bit of sausage there, Spank! Let him have it!' And with an evil laugh, Spank took the sausage, still hot from the fire, and laid it on the sniffing nose.

"If the earth itself had opened up at their feet and thrust forth a great spewing, spitting, frothing, enraged monster from its most terrible depths, they could not have been more shocked. The bear stood to its hind feet in one massive movement—fur bristling, muscles rippling, claws like daggers, teeth like jagged ice. A great mantle of snow covered the creature's shoulders and the crown of its head, making it more frightening and shapeless still. It let out such a roar that the brothers were knocked from their feet, and the bear leaned back into the tree with such force that the man sitting in it feared he would be shaken out.

"Several other trees in the vicinity suffered that night; in fact some were actually torn out by the roots or broken off at the ground by the force of the brothers' exodus. The man in the tree thought another blizzard had hit, the snow was flying so, and for some minutes he could hear the sound of thumps and crashings and curses in the forest.

"The bear, more angry than hurt, let out a growl and curled up in the snow again. He was still sleeping there when I returned the next day, after a night mixed with the pleasantries of the Weathertongues' hospitality and the understandable anxiety I felt over the fate of my farm.

"As it turned out, Burl and his brothers had not had the chance to do any great amount of damage, and I can tell you I cooked up a stew solely for that bear, I was so thankful. Before the afternoon was very old, the man gave his thanks and his goodbyes and took the bear south, toward Washington and President Jackson. I never saw or heard from them again, and I never knew if Old Hickory ever got his polar bear.

"But the next year, about a week before Christmas, I was bringing wood in from the shed when a familiar voice came out of the forest. 'Hey there, farmer! How's that dog of yours?'

"I looked into the woods but could see no one. 'Dog?' I said, sounding puzzled. 'Oh, you mean the puppy I had last winter. She's full-grown now, and had a litter of her own. They are somewhere in the woods hunting, I think.' I listened, but there was no reply. 'Are you and your brothers coming for Christmas Eve?' I inquired, but the woods were silent.

"And a breath of wind just touched my ear, like someone whispering: 'Gone!' "

Cordelia shivered, though the day was warm and sunlight streamed through the windows of the dining car. She was aware, once more, of the rhythm of the rails and the people around her. James had found his pipe and was smoking contentedly, leaning back in his seat. Others drifted back to their own tables or left the car.

"More tea, Mr. Tolly?" asked Mercia.

"No, thank you. I'm about washed out with all the tea and coffee I've had. The throat does get dry, though, ma'am."

"That is quite a tale, Mr. Tolly," said James pleasantly.

"It all happened sixty years ago. I am nearly eighty-six now, and it's the best this old head of mine could remember."

"You remember it vividly, it seems," said Mercia.

"The experiences of youth," said the man wistfully.

"One thing, though, Mr. Tolly," said Cordelia. "I understand polar bears are ferocious beasts, and hardly tameable. However did the man subdue such an animal?"

"In a fair fight, miss," said the elderly fellow with gentle gravity. "Two falls out of three."

"I wonder how Maude is doing," said James.

27. Chorus for Duck and Bear

DUCKY PLANKE HAD LIVED IN THE WOODS AND FIELDS of Davis Island, on the eastern shore of the Sheepscot River, for years. The Davis family, who had owned and would own the island for generations, tolerated his presence by ignoring him. Several members of the Davis clan, during the latter part of the nineteenth century, had seen Ducky's ambling, ragged figure traversing the meadow below the barn, and even crossed paths with the odd fellow in the "two-acre wood" once or twice. They seldom mentioned these sightings to anyone, and perhaps thought of Ducky as just another wild creature roaming on Davis land.

No one knew where Ducky slept, or what he ate, or how he survived winters, barely shod and dressed in ancient clothes. There was a list of things that people didn't know about Ducky; no one knew where he had come from, no one knew what his true Christian name was, and no one knew how his surname had been discovered—no one knew and no one remembered.

But people up and down the river, people from the surrounding towns, saw him occasionally from their boats and their dories and their canoes as he sat beside the water, clucking softly and meekly to himself.

"Hey, Ducky!" they would call to him, and he would toss a hand in the air for greeting. Several Samaritans, including certain members of the Davis family, had tried leaving food for the man by one or another of his favorite haunts, but as often as not they would return to find, from the telltale scat, that a raccoon or a fox had enjoyed it instead.

Ducky Planke was the *green man*, a spirit upon the island, and a bogeyman by which to threaten uncooperative children.

He was indeed like a natural creature of the wild, and stood for long hours when the sun had set, watching one house or another and the shadows of people passing the windows of lighted rooms. Other times he shuffled in the dark—pitch dark on moonless nights—through the woods to the river and admired the lights of Wiscasset across the water. Ships hulked against the wharves there, and once he had watched the highest flames of a fire several streets up from the waterfront.

The river was a fair highway for smugglers, and occasionally small boats passed him quietly in the night, signaling the transportation of goods not bearing the Custom House stamp. He listened to the scull of oars from the banks below Fort Edgecomb.

By day he went to the other side of the island and watched the traffic of the boats and the people on foot and on horseback and in rigs crossing the bridge to and from Wiscasset. Just past midday on Tuesday the 7th of July, 1896, he sat happily among the rocks by the waterline, not far from the bridge, filling his pockets with periwinkles and snapping seaweed pods between his fingers.

He clucked and quacked to himself in the bright sun and watched as a cormorant disappeared beneath the surface of the river, only to appear half a minute later and several yards away with a fish in its bill. The black bird brought to mind a bit of verse that someone had recited for him in his youth.

> *The cormorant is a homely bird,*
> *The common shag he's called sometimes,*
> *He's often seen, but seldom heard,*
> *And never répeats silly rhymes.*

Ducky repeated this silently to himself several times over, then cawed like a crow, and the cormorant took wing and disappeared upriver on the other side of Goose Island.

Looking in that direction, Ducky saw several figures, tiny with distance, on the Wiscasset shore, forming a line in a field. He watched them as they bunched up beside a stand of trees, and saw another figure scrambling down the riverbank just below them. Ducky's eyesight was sharp, but he could only guess that this lone figure was a large dog. He lost sight of the creature for several minutes, and had to climb to a higher venue before catching sight of a black head bobbing in the current of the river.

Fascinated, Ducky hurried to the northernmost point of the island, where a glacial boulder afforded him a place to stand. Here he watched with increasing excitement as the swimmer neared the Edgecomb shore. The bobbing head disappeared briefly behind Goose Island as the outgoing tide drew it downriver.

Arriving at the mouth of a little salt marsh that divided the Walker and the Smith farms, the black bear waddled up onto the flats and shook herself vigorously. There she played in the mud, clawing up mussels to break open with her jaws and eat, rolling on her back and groaning with pleasure.

Ducky was beside himself with happiness, and he jumped up and down on the huge boulder, clucking and quacking and flapping his arms. Maude sat up on her haunches and mooed at him. For a moment the riverfront sounded like a barnyard, till the bear tired of the conversation and waddled shoreward, disappearing in the marsh. For several minutes Ducky could discern her movements from the shaking reeds and cattails. Then she was gone.

Ducky couldn't remember when he'd had such a good time.

For her part, Maude slept the rest of the day away in the Smiths' rubbish pit, where she also managed to find a bite to eat. When night had fallen, she crossed through several backyards and frightened half a dozen dogs on her way to the Marsh River, where she found the fishing tolerable the following morning.

28. Colonel Taverner Proposes

KNOWING MISTER WALTON'S JOVIAL CHARACTER, the reader will not be surprised to learn that he dined that evening with the sheriff and his family. His extraordinary account of the upside-down bear would have, of its own, recommended him as a dinner guest, but upon learning of the portly fellow's acquaintance with Mary Moriarty—to whom the sheriff was distantly related (and for whom, if the truth be known, he had harbored a boyhood affection)—Sheriff Charles Piper insisted on playing the host.

The tale of the bear was wagged again for the sheriff's appreciative family, and no one enjoyed the telling of it more than Mister Walton. He outdid himself in expressing the confusion he felt when he discovered an inverted bruin before him, and was positively hilarious in his attempts to reproduce Maude's cowlike groans.

There were three children still living with the sheriff and his wife, Fawn. Jimmy, who was seven, was keen to know if a bear could indeed sound so bovine; Henry, who was ten, wanted to know if Mr. Lofton might offer to fight Mister Walton again; and Anne, who was seventeen, was interested in hearing more about Sundry Moss.

"Sundry was rather brave, I think," said Anne.

"He's a noble fellow," agreed Mister Walton. "Though I wish he had not felt it necessary to put himself between Mr. Lofton and myself. I am sure that Mr. Lofton would have cooled off, given time."

"Cooling off is not something for which Mr. Lofton is known," said Mrs. Piper. "Sundry was quite right in taking your part."

"You know Mr. Lofton, then."

"He and his wife, and several other families from parts south, rusticate at the Wiscasset House every summer," said the sheriff. He pushed himself away from the table so that he could lean back and stretch his legs before him. "Lofton's the type, you know, that gives folk from away a bad name. He thinks culture arrived in these parts with him."

"Social aristocracy is often confused with culture," said Mister Walton sagely. "And aristocratic breeding with good manners."

"That is very well put, Mister Walton," said Mrs. Piper.

"That is what my father told me. It was in the context of an admonishment, I fear, during my large-headed youth."

"Well, Sundry was rather brave, I think," said Anne again, who seemed to think that the conversation had wandered.

"He was indeed." Mister Walton waved away a third helping of roast beef. "He is a very likable fellow, though I do find his name a curiosity."

"Sundry *is* a curiosity," said the sheriff, with a quick smile in the direction of his disapproving daughter. "You have yet to meet his brother, Varius, I take it."

"Good heavens!" said Mister Walton.

Sheriff Piper chuckled; his wife smiled.

"He has a brother named Various?"

" 'Varius'—without an *o*," said the sheriff.

"A twin brother," said Henry.

"Sundry and Varius?"

"Their father is an eccentric," said Mrs. Piper, who began to clear the table.

"Not to mention that Dr. Cushman, who delivered Sundry and his brother, had a rare sense of humor," added the sheriff. "Wyman—that was Sundry's father—was arguing with his wife what the baby's name should be, and each of them had thought of half a dozen possibilities by the time the doctor was called for. It was a surprise, of course, when two boys arrived. When Mrs. Moss and her sons were sleeping, and the doctor was in the kitchen washing up, he told Sundry's sister—who couldn't have been more than six or seven at the time—to go in and ask her father if they had come up with any names, so that he could write out the certificate of birth.

" 'Have you come up with any names, Papa?' asks the little girl.

" 'Various and sundry,' says Wyman. So, thinking these are her brothers' names, she goes out and announces the fact to the doctor.

"Very carefully," said the sheriff, ghost-writing on the table, "the doctor entered the names, though by his own account he spelt 'Varius' without the o because he thought it looked Latin. He had every intention of making out a real certificate once everyone had appreciated the joke, but Wyman decided he liked the names, and they stuck."

"That's wonderful!" exclaimed Mister Walton. "All the more so since Sundry's name does him justice somehow."

"I'm not sure that I could explain it to anyone, Mister Walton," said Mrs. Piper, "but I think I know what you mean."

"What does the boy do, there at the hotel?" asked the guest.

"A little of everything," said the sheriff, with a wry expression. He pulled his watch from his pocket and consulted it. "I'm afraid I have to go up to the jail for my nightly inspection, Mister Walton, but if you'd like to take a walk, I'll give you a tour."

The day had not yet turned to gloaming, and a small breeze had caressed its way up Federal Street, skimming away the heat of the afternoon. Mister Walton and Sheriff Piper were greeted by several people who were also taking the air, and hailed from the porches of houses they passed.

The building that constituted both the jail and the jailkeeper's house was of two personalities. The keeper's house, on the left, was a handsome brick domicile with granite lintels and sills; the front door was painted a formal black, which varied nicely to the eye against beds of bright flowers ranked at either side of the front steps. Curtains hung in the windows, and trimmed shrubs stood at its corners.

The jail end of the building, however, gave every evidence of its use. There was little in its stark granite walls to interest the eye, except for stains of rust below the iron bars of its narrow windows. A fence separated the jail grounds from the keeper's lawn, and a general air of solitude and frost hung over that barren yard and the gray walls it surrounded.

A knock at the front door brought a young girl, who ushered the sheriff and his guest to the kitchen, where the jailer, Seth Patterson, and his wife, Laura, sat with a muttonchopped fellow at the table.

"Ah, *shehriff*," said this third person with a distinct burr in his voice, "I've been waiting *fohr* you," and he rose with his hand extended. He was a handsome fellow, perhaps fifty years old, not tall, but of such a hard and energetic build that he gave the appearance of a large man compacted into a small carriage. His hair had receded only slightly, but it was without the slightest hint of gray and allowed to grow full enough as to take years off his appearance. His clothes were sharply cut and dapper, and it was clear that he took pride in his aspect.

"Roddy," said the sheriff, shaking the man's hand. Mister Walton was introduced to the room, and while he exchanged greetings, Sheriff Piper said with only a dash of irony in his voice: "This is Colonel Roderick Taverner, Mister Walton, late of Her Majesty's army, who has kindly come to the colonies to assist our Customs Service in the apprehension of smugglers."

Mister Walton received this information with a bit of a jolt, as if the Scotsman might suspect that he had assisted in smuggling rum (however unwittingly) as recently as the week before. Taverner smiled, however, and shook Mister Walton's hand with feeling. "Pleased to meet you, *sir*," said the colonel, his burr from this point to be left to the imagination of the reader.

"Well, Roddy," said the sheriff. "I suppose you weren't waiting for me on social grounds."

"That would be pleasant, Charles," said the man as he reoccupied his seat at the table. "But you suppose correctly."

Room was made at the table for Mister Walton and the sheriff, and Mrs. Patterson put a kettle on the stove.

"What's smuggling tonight, then?" said Piper.

Taverner glanced briefly at Mister Walton, decided that the sheriff trusted the bespectacled gentleman, and said: "Of that I'm not sure. But there's been nocturnal activity observed on Davis Island, across the river, and I have reason to suspect certain sightseers to drop by for a visit near the fort this very night."

"The fort," said Piper, pulling a frown. "It's not a very hidden place, even at night. There must be half a hundred coves and inlets between Westport and Sheepscot Bridge that are better suited for sneaking goods in."

Taverner smiled, like a fox contemplating a hen. "That is precisely why it interests me so, Charles!"

"When are you setting up watch?"

"An hour or so after dark, I think. Mrs. Patterson is a brave hand at keeping jail, I'm told, so Seth is willing to join us. Perhaps Mister Walton would like to come along."

"I think Mister Walton may have had enough adventuring today," said the sheriff, but something in the portly fellow's expression must have told otherwise. "Would you care to join us? Strictly as an observer, mind."

"I'd be fascinated."

"Are we keeping watch from the blockhouse?" asked Piper.

Taverner lifted a large ring, from which depended three great iron keys. He shook them meaningfully.

"Well, Mister Walton," said the sheriff. "You said you wanted to see Fort Edgecomb. You didn't, perhaps, consider touring it by starlight."

"I am quite excited."

"Do you play cribbage, sir?" asked the colonel.

"Oh, most certainly," said Mister Walton.

"Ach! That's fine. If there's moon enough, we can have a pleasant game or two."

29. Captain Coyle's Riddle

THE STEAMSHIP which was the Underwoods' connection from the rail end at Rockland pulled up to the docks at Ellsworth when the last inkling of sunset had long since faded. Cordelia stifled a yawn as she stepped down the platform to the wharf, and since stretching in public was unheard of, she discreetly flexed her limbs as she waited for her parents to follow.

"It feels a bit like rain," said her mother as she joined her.

James had their baggage tickets in hand when he came down the ramp. The crew of the ship and the dockmen were working the loading platform, and already trunks and bags were being passed down to the wharf. A great gout of steam billowed from the stack with a loud hiss, and a tremor ran through the boat as if it were some unruly beast, vexed to be held still for even a moment.

"Ethan should be round about somewhere with the carriage," said James. "I'll see to our bags."

"It's such a nice night," said Mercia. "We'll wait up by the street."

James strode down the wharf, weaving through the small groups of arrivals and greeters, tipping his hat at the occasional bit of eye contact. Then a young face emerged from the darkness and the crowd.

"Uncle James!" shouted Ethan Morningside, who was twelve, towheaded, and short for his age.

"Ethan, how are you?" said James, and he shook the boy's hand warmly. "Your aunt and cousin are waiting up above."

"The carriage is just across the street, but I thought you might like a hand with the baggage."

"You're a good fellow, Ethan." James flagged a porter with a handcart and the three of them were able to locate the Underwoods' bags and load them.

They found the women where the wharf met Water Street. Cordelia hugged her young cousin happily and embarrassed him by declaring him handsome as she inspected him at arm's length. His aunt Mercia added to his troubles by saying how tall he had grown (an obvious bit of flattery) and ruffling her hand through his hair as she remarked how pretty it was.

"The carriage is over there," said Ethan, hoping to avoid any further admiration. He led the way and helped the porter secure the Underwoods' baggage on the Morningsides' rig. James brought up the rear, slowing his walk at the sight of a familiar figure.

"Captain Coyle," said James, approaching an older man who stood to one side of a carriage as a trunk was being loaded by two porters. The man raised his eyes at the sound of his name, and recognized James with the slightest change of expression.

"Ah!" said the captain. "Young Underwood."

"Not so young anymore, sir," said James as they shook hands.

"It's all relative," said Captain Coyle. He had never been a tall man, but age had stooped him further. His face had filled out since James had seen him last, but his hawklike nose was the same, and he still sported muttonchops that did nothing to disguise his lack of chin. The old captain's manner had not changed, either—impatient at the best of times, he spoke even now with a hint of irritability. "You're not sailing these days, are you?"

"No, I've been retired from the sea for some years now."

"More in your brother's blood than yours, I think."

"Yes, it was indeed. You've heard about Basil."

"I was sorry to read that he had passed on. He was the best junior officer I ever had during the war. Brave as a bulldog."

"It's good of you to say so."

"It's not good of me at all! It's the truth! Are you living here?"

"No, actually my wife's family hails from Ellsworth, but it's business concerning my brother that has brought us here. We received his sea trunk recently and found that he had bequeathed a large parcel of land to my daughter. We've come up to get a look at it."

"Just now, eh?" The captain tipped the porter and opened the carriage door to climb in. "He died in South America, didn't he? These things can take time finding their way home."

"Yes," said James. "A very fine fellow, Mr. Stimply, saw my brother's things all the way from Venezuela to the Portland Custom House."

Captain Coyle had found his seat in the carriage now, but he hesitated with the door and leaned forward to look at James seriously. "Charles Stimply?" he asked.

"Yes. Do you know him?"

"The Charles Stimply that sailed on Captain Underwood's last ship?"

"Yes, indeed."

"And he brought your brother's belongings home recently?"

"I spoke to Mr. Stimply barely a week ago. Why?"

"Well," said Captain Coyle. "I buried Charles Stimply at sea eight months past. Driver!" The carriage door slammed shut and the horses were whipped up. The rig had turned in the street and driven off before James was able to fully grasp what Captain Coyle had told him.

The noise of the riverside fell away as young Ethan Morningside shook the carriage reins and Faymar, the mare, clopped into a trot. Faintly, behind the sound of hooves and wheels, Cordelia could hear the *pee-ik* of a nighthawk from some nearby tree or rooftop. They crossed a bridge and climbed a side street, and as they approached the Morningside home they could see that every light in the house was burning cheerily. The glow from the windows cast crosshatched patterns upon the lawn and lit the walk like a full moon.

Priscilla Morningside was out the door before Cordelia could climb down from the carriage, and with delighted squeals the two young women dropped fifteen years from their apparent age and danced around the yard together. A toy fox terrier was close at Priscilla's heels and, sharing in the young women's excitement, the dog leaped about while emitting a series of piercing yelps.

"Priscilla," came Grace's voice from the front door. "Priscilla!" It was clear that she objected to some aspect of her daughter's behavior, but wasn't quite able to articulate it. Mercia wished that there were someone to welcome her as Priscilla had welcomed Cordelia, but it was pleasant to greet her sister with a simple hug when she stepped into the front hall.

"Mercia!" said Grace. "Whatever am I going to do with that girl?"

Mercia just laughed softly, saying: "Oh, Grace."

"James!" said Grace, when her brother-in-law came up the steps, and from her tone one might believe that seeing a robust adult male was akin to sighting land. She took his hand warmly and accepted a kiss upon the cheek.

Ethan clambered in with two large pieces of luggage, and the Morningsides' aging male servant came laden behind the boy. Priscilla and Cordelia brought up the rear, laughing and out of breath and still hugging one another. The terrier darted between them as they crossed the threshold and allowed Mercia to scoop him up.

"Teacup," said Grace. "You are quite as bad as the girls."

Cordelia's hair had come undone, and a fall of red tresses slipped forward to obscure half of her face. Something—possibly just seeing one another—had amused her and Priscilla so greatly that they burst into renewed laughter as Grace gave them her most exasperated expression. Teacup, wiggling in Mercia's arms, let out another of his sharp barks.

"Priscilla," said Grace tiredly. "It is not enough that you go out without a hat, but your sleeve has come unbuttoned."

"Aunt Grace!" declared Cordelia. "It's so wonderful to see you!" She hugged her aunt with rather more zest than the woman was accustomed to, but Grace was more tolerant of exuberant behavior in her niece than she was in most people.

"Cordelia, you are a whirlwind!" admitted the aunt, almost with a laugh. "Good heavens, look at your hair!" She went to work on Cordelia's emancipated tresses, brushing them back carefully so that she could gaze for a moment at her niece and say: "Dear me. Dear me."

It surprised most people when they discovered that Grace was five years younger than Mercia, but it is a mistake to equate gravity with age. A reader of tea leaves had once told Grace that she had an aged soul, and she took this to mean that she was in some sense older than her sister after all.

"Well, Mercia," said Grace once when they had reached one of their common disagreements. "I *am* older than you."

"Yes, I know," replied Mercia. "And it's a wonderful trick since I was born first."

"Never mind," Grace had maintained in all seriousness. "It was just a mistake our parents made, that is all."

Grace was a thin woman, more handsome than beautiful, with dark brown hair that she wore in a pragmatic bun. Not as tall as her sister, she stood stiffly erect (when she was not feeling faint) and gave the appearance of more height than was hers by nature. It was five years since her husband, Henry, had died; and though no longer in widow's black, she did still dress in somber shades which, contrasted with her pale complexion, gave her an ethereal quality. Standing in the hall, she touched her forehead with the tips of three fingers and briefly closed her eyes. With a deep sigh, she said

"There!" as if she had fought off an oncoming *spell*, then insisted that they not linger in the hall, since a late supper was waiting for them in the dining room.

It was during the meal that Mercia first noticed her husband's preoccupation. Teacup had placed himself by James's chair, where the dog reckoned he would receive the most generous, if surreptitious, portion from the table. This, as a rule, would have proved a worthwhile strategy, but Mercia—seated next to her husband—glanced down at the dog several times and saw that Teacup waited in vain.

There had been enough crises, large and small, in the Underwoods' lives for James to perfect an ability to hide his emotions when something was disturbing him; and similarly enough such plights for Mercia to develop her own ability to see through his dispassionate mask. She reached for a spoon beside her plate and managed to touch her husband's hand, lightly and with meaning. James glanced at her sideways and gave her a small smile that indicated he would explain when the opportunity arose.

As he raised a glass to his lips, he wondered for the hundredth time: If Captain Coyle had indeed buried Charles Stimply at sea last November, who was the man who had come to their house, and why? Why would a person assume a false identity to perform such an honest deed? Why the elaborate lie—and what else was not what it seemed?

30. Sundry's Change of Position

MISTER WALTON CHEERFULLY AMBULATED BACK to the Wiscasset House, where he readied himself for his night excursion with the sheriff and the colonel. He was greeted as he entered the foyer by Sundry Moss.

"Sundry, how are you?" said Mister Walton. "I want to thank you again for your action on my behalf this afternoon." He shook a finger in friendly admonishment. "I am not very sure that it was necessary, but it was quite laudable of you to take my part."

Sundry looked embarrassed as he waved the portly gentleman's thanks away. "Lofton went to Mr. Hubbard's office this afternoon and demanded you be thrown out of the hotel on the grounds that you're a fraud."

"Good heavens," said Mister Walton.

"He had Hubbard half-convinced, I think—Lofton's pretty well thought of here on account of his money—but some of the other guests insisted the whole thing was an honest mistake. Hubbard called me in and I told him you were having supper at the sheriff's. That brought him around."

"It is unfortunate," said Mister Walton, "but a comedy of errors rather than a tragedy. I don't understand how anyone could feel that their day has been poorly spent when it includes a full-grown bear standing on her head."

Alfred Lofton strode into the hall just then, attempting to look as if he hadn't been listening to their conversation from the next room. He stopped in his tracks when he saw them, and with his best expression of angered dignity he said to Sundry: "I thought you were told that your services were no longer required!" He threw back his shoulders, as stiff and sour as he could make himself.

"I had business with Mister Walton," said Sundry, who clearly did not like explaining himself.

"You may leave, then, if your business is over," said Lofton, ignoring Mister Walton's presence in the room. "You're not employed here anymore, and heaven knows you're not a guest."

"Not employed?" said Mister Walton. "Sundry, don't tell me . . ."

"He has been let go," said Lofton with satisfaction.

"Only because I didn't say 'I quit' fast enough."

"The result is the same. You don't belong here anymore, and you may leave."

"Sundry is working for me, Mr. Lofton," said Mister Walton without blinking. "So you won't have to concern yourself."

"Mister Walton," said Sundry. "You don't have to —"

"He's been given the boot!" Lofton insisted, directing his anger now at Mister Walton. "And I think it wise not to interfere!"

"I don't like to benefit from another's misfortune," said Mister Walton with a straight face, and never losing his peaceful demeanor. "But the hotel's loss, in this case, is my gain, I fear."

"Mr. Hubbard will be gravely offended!" said Lofton darkly.

"I can't imagine it," quipped the bespectacled fellow. "Only small people are easily offended."

Lofton, who until now had done his best to appear offended, found himself at a loss for a response.

Respecting Mister Walton's quiet way of dealing with the unpleasant Alfred Lofton, Sundry covered the lower part of his face with a long hand to hide an involuntary grin.

"This hotel, sir," said Lofton, "is not big enough for the two of us."

"If you can suffer the crowding another night, Mr. Lofton, I assure you that I will be leaving in the morning." When Lofton had stiffly exited, Mister Walton said, "What do you think, Sundry?"

"That was more than nice of you, Mister Walton, but I'll be on my way now."

"On your way? I thought you might not mind working for me."

"Well, of course not. But what would you want me to do?"

Here the bespectacled fellow was at a bit of an impasse. "I've always thought that traveling with another was a great improvement over traveling alone," he said finally. "Perhaps you would provide me with some company."

"I would have to do more than that, Mister Walton, if I was in your employ. But I'll tell you what: I think you are just the sort of gentleman who could find worth in a valet. A gentleman's gentleman, so to speak."

"Capital!" said Mister Walton. He held out his hand to seal the deal.

Sundry shook his new employer's hand thoughtfully. "I think I'm going to enjoy working for you, Mister Walton."

31. Night Watch at Fort Edgecomb

FORT EDGECOMB WAS A VISIBLE DARKNESS against the clouded night sky as Colonel Taverner's party approached by foot from the road. The night was unseasonably cool, and a suggestion of rain was in the air. They walked, when they could, in the grass for the sake of quiet, and dew collected on the toes of their boots. Somewhere, in a pond or marshy place behind them, frogs and peepers spoke. Ahead of them was the presence of the Sheepscot River—the smell of salt and seagrass, the sound of current against the rough shoreline, and the perception of open sky above the moving water.

They were prepared for certain eventualities, for three of the party were armed—the sheriff, Seth the jailkeeper, and the colonel, carrying a rifle, a shotgun, and a brace of revolvers, respectively.

They numbered five, which was the originally conceived force plus Sundry Moss, who insisted on accompanying Mister Walton and whom Sheriff Piper did not mind having along. Gazing up at the blockhouse from the side of the road, they numbered six if you counted Ducky Planke, who watched unseen from the confines of a small stand of trees behind them. Ducky did not follow them, however, when the small group crossed the parade ground and melted into the fort's encircling shadows.

Mister Walton felt like a medieval pilgrim before the gates of a sleeping castle, his imagination stretching the small blockhouse into parapets and bastions. He half expected Colonel Taverner to pound upon the heavy oak door to arouse sleeping watchmen, but the colonel instead produced his ring of keys, which clinked in the darkness as he fitted the proper one into its lock.

The door shuddered slightly on its hinges—a short chuffing noise, like the cough of some great animal; Taverner did not open it all the way, but produced a small can of oil from a satchel he had brought with him. "Now, Mr. Moss," he said in something below a whisper. "You look the most narrow amongst us. Perhaps you'd be good enough to pry yourself inside and pacify these hinges." He gave Sundry the can of oil, and the young man disappeared like a cat (if a very long cat) inside.

The door was not entirely silent as it swung open, and Seth Patterson took on the job of easing it back and forth several times till the oil had worked its way between the hinges. A cold atmosphere greeted them as they entered, and the colonel allowed a sliver of light from a storm lantern so that they could see their way to the second floor.

The great door was closed behind them and Taverner politely invited Sheriff Piper to go before him. "I'm not sure, Roddy," said Piper quietly, "if the ghosts in this place will favor the presence of a British colonel, however retired he may be."

"I don't think I believe in ghosts, Charles," said Taverner.

Piper's soft chuckle faded as he turned away and sneaked up the stairs.

The second floor of the blockhouse formed a ring around the stairwell and the ladder that continued to the small lookout tower above. Taverner thought that a person's silhouette in the tower might be visible from the water, and so he placed the first lookouts—himself and the sheriff—at the gun slots facing the river.

Benches lined the outer walls of the second floor, and the others sat between the sheriff and the colonel. There was very little moon showing through the clouds, so that Taverner's cribbage deck would stay in his satchel, but soft-voiced conversation seemed allowable, and the colonel himself began the train of discussion by asking about the origins of the fort.

"It was built during our last difficulty with you people," said Sundry.

"Ah, the conflict of 1812. I thought as much."

"It was meant to safeguard the river from the British, then?" said Mister Walton.

"To guard Wiscasset, actually, which is the important site," said the sheriff, a loyal member of the opposite bank.

Sundry, who hailed from the Edgecomb side of the river, said wryly: "Really? It's an odd thing they built it on Edgecomb soil."

"Well, it was garrisoned primarily with Wiscasset men," explained the sheriff.

"And the only shot they ever fired was over the head of a frightened fisherman," informed Sundry.

"Perhaps the fisherman was from Edgecomb," suggested Seth.

Mister Walton chuckled softly, and if any of them had been closer to the sheriff they would have heard him chuckle as well.

Taverner whispered in the silence that followed:

> "Rise, rise, ye clans, rise,
>   Rise, for your tartan, your wife, and your brother.
>   Rise in the morn and the dark of night,
>   'Gainst anyone else but each other."

"I suppose," said Piper with humor, "that we shouldn't be exhibiting disunity before a member of the British army."

"Ach, no worry," said Taverner. "You sound like good Scots. It is music to my ears."

"The truth is," admitted the sheriff, "the Union Jack gave our grandparents some uncomfortable moments. The British landed at Boothbay and on the other side of the river near Wiscasset, and I've been told that at least one man was killed, shooting from the porch of his house."

"As a boy," said Mister Walton, "I got a glimpse of war from a distance, while our regiment waited to be called into line, listening to Confederate guns and seeing the black smoke over the hills. But that was in Virginia. It is difficult to picture such a conflict here."

"The land forgets these things," said Taverner. "For good or worse, it's people that remember."

Conversation fell away with this thought and they listened to the night—tree peepers and frogs, the bark of a dog, the brush of a light breeze against the eaves of the fort. Dim bands of luminescence played across the faces of Colonel Taverner and Sheriff Piper as they peered through their gun slots. Even inside, one could sense that rain was on its way.

"We very nearly had a brush with the French here in Edgecomb a hundred years ago," said Sundry, his mind obviously turning upon the historical.

"Can that story be true?" wondered the sheriff.

"Have you ever been to Captain Chase's house and seen the furniture that is still there?" asked Sundry.

"I've never *been* invited to look at the Chases' furniture," said Piper, who wasn't sure that Sundry had, either.

"They say that the Clough family in Boothbay has letters sent by old Captain Clough to his wife, telling her to expect the queen," said Seth.

" 'Do not prepare to receive a queen, but only a very sad and broken-

hearted lady,' " quoted Sundry, who was perhaps not averse to a bit of romanticizing.

"You've read these letters, as well," said the sheriff dryly.

"My mother's family was very friendly with the Cloughs," said Sundry, unperturbed by the doubt in Piper's tone.

"The Chases? The Cloughs?" said Mister Walton, whose curiosity was greatly piqued. "You say a queen was expected here?"

"Marie Antoinette herself," said the sheriff.

"Ach," said Taverner, though whether from surprise or disbelief it was difficult to say.

"If we had gone past the Fort Road," explained Sundry to Mister Walton, "continuing along the eastern shore of the cove, we would have crossed an old wooden bridge and climbed a hill till the path took a severe turn to the left. About halfway up this part of the hill, there is a square two-storied house set back from the road. The Chases live there now, but a hundred years ago Captain Clough and his wife, Sarah, owned the place."

Mister Walton listened with a mixture of interest and amusement. Sundry sounded like a guest speaker on the lecture circuit (albeit one speaking *sotto voce*); his posture, however—seen dimly in the dark— indicated a person who was ready to fall asleep at any moment. Sundry was sprawled upon the bench, his legs stretched before him and his feet crossed casually at the ankles.

"So it is the Cloughs, in this case, who merit our interest," said Mister Walton, to indicate that he was paying close attention.

"Oh, yes," agreed Sundry. "Captain Clough, by all report, was as stiff-backed and salted down a republican as lived in these parts. He was not a lover of royalty by any means—he was in fact a former officer of the Continental Army. But like many of his peers he was more than a little horrified by the excesses of the French brand of revolution.

"Our merchant fleet was finding lucrative trade with France's new rule, but the revolutionaries were constantly suspicious of foreigners, so it is strange that old Stephen came into contact with royalty at all. Somehow he had communication with the queen's court, which was under house arrest, and she was able to gain his sympathies. Now Captain Clough," waxed Sundry in a poetical manner of speaking, "was a hard-shelled tight-fisted Puritan of the old school, and Marie Antoinette had lived a life of voluptuous luxury."

"Good heavens!" said Seth under his breath. The mere mention of such intemperance scandalized him.

But Sundry liked the phrase so much that he said it twice. "Voluptuous luxury."

"Good heavens!" repeated Seth.

Taverner gave a low hiss. "Keep it down or say nothing."

Elbows on knees, Mister Walton leaned closer to Sundry, encouraging him to continue speaking softly, but above all encouraging him to continue. "They make an extraordinary pair," whispered the portly gentleman with suppressed excitement.

"The queen's celebrated charms would have been lost on Captain Clough, but she was known as an honest talker, and greatly humbled by the fall of her house. Some sense of Christian charity, or chivalry perhaps, stirred within him, and he offered to help her escape to America."

"Somehow—" continued Sundry.

"There are a lot of *somehows* in this story," said the sheriff without looking from his gun slot.

"Well, *somehow* is all anyone knows about it," replied Sundry, as if that answered any doubts. "At any rate, the captain managed, by some means unknown to us, to get many of the queen's belongings—furniture, wardrobe, and jewels—aboard his ship, the *Sally*."

"He smuggled them, you're saying," interpreted Taverner wryly.

"Unfortunately, the queen's plans for escape were discovered, and Marie Antoinette, as you know, was subsequently beheaded."

Seth put an involuntary hand to his neck.

"And what happened to her things?" wondered Mister Walton.

"Many of them are still in the house, though other people own it now. One of the rooms is still decorated with faded French wallpaper that the captain brought back with him from the queen's court. He might have sold his unexpected cargo, but chose instead to bring it home with him, perhaps so that he might remember the brave woman whose life he had hoped to save."

"Extraordinary!" said Mister Walton.

"Who's to say he didn't dupe the queen?" said Sheriff Piper. "That he didn't reveal her plans to the revolutionary committee as soon as he had her belongings on board?"

This thought offended Sundry's faith in human goodness, and he let out a low sound of disgust.

"Ach," said Colonel Taverner. "You've dealt with too many criminals, Charles. Reputation is a powerful force, and if he hadn't been known as an honest man, I am sure that the prevailing legend would never have stuck."

There was a brief silence then, the sounds of the night reasserting themselves upon their conscious thoughts. Mister Walton thought he might hear the first sprinklings of rain upon the roof of the fort.

The colonel spoke again, as if the conversation had never stopped. "I am surprised, though, that some rumor of the dauphin escaping with your Captain Clough hasn't been intimated."

"Actually," said Sundry, "there are those who think it so."

"I'd wager there are, boy," said the colonel with a wink. His voice descended below a whisper, so that they could barely hear him, and he pointed at his horizontal outlook. "And perhaps these are the ghosts of Captain Clough and the dauphin I see now, sneaking into shore."

32. Voices in the Night

"I CAN HEAR THE FALLS," said Cordelia, lying back on her cousin's bed. The night breeze had stilled, and the roar of the falls drummed behind the voices of insects and peepers through the open window. Cordelia had herself wrapped in a blanket against the chill of the night; Priscilla sat at her dressing table with a shawl over her shoulders and combed her long dark hair. Both knew that Grace would heartily disapprove of their exposing themselves to the dampening atmosphere.

Priscilla paused dreamily as she contemplated Cordelia's romantic evening at the Fourth of July Ball. "I don't think I have ever had a stranger ask me to dance," she said wistfully.

"I wonder if there might be a waterfall on my land," said Cordelia.

"And to think of dancing with him all night. Mother would have been horrified." Priscilla gathered her hair over one shoulder and recommenced combing. Cordelia had always been envious of Priscilla's hair, which was black and hung down to her waist, but envious in a way that one can be toward a cousin who is also your best friend. Priscilla Morningside did not have Cordelia's fine features—the flat plain of her cheeks could have been less long, her nose a shade less prominent—but she had, in James's words, a fine chin, and it was commonly recognized that her dark eyes were beautiful and that she smiled easily despite her mother's serious example.

She was also extremely shortsighted, and her eyeglasses complicated an already interesting face. Cordelia thought they added charm. Priscilla was sure they added dowdiness, and would have wagered good money that they had contributed to the fact that she had never had a stranger ask her to dance.

"I do love your hair," said Cordelia.

"I know a hundred women with hair just like it."

"Not as full."

"Oh, yes. Every bit."

"Not as lustrous."

"Nonsense. *Your* hair is radiant."

"I'm a carrot top. Most people think red hair is an impediment."

"Every boy turns when you walk past."

"That is not to say which *way* they turn."

"Oh, for goodness sakes!" Priscilla leaned forward in her search for the right words. "You are a beautiful fall day," she said with a dramatic air, and almost giggled when she said it.

"You are the forest in winter," said Cordelia in a matching tone.

Priscilla laid her comb on the table and stood. "In your blue gown you are like red-gold leaves against the clear autumnal sky, unclouded and breathtaking, a hint of spring yet to come in the sunlit green of your eye!"

Still on the bed, Cordelia stretched out her arms in a gesture of unlimited generosity. "You radiate the warmth that waits beneath the cover of snow, and even dressed in summer white you are the mystery of starlit nights and the beauty of dark trees against the frost."

"Oh, please," said Priscilla. "You're embarrassing me. Don't feel you have to stop."

The two young women did their best to repress their laughter. "Which eye has the hint of sunlit green?" wondered Cordelia hysterically. The hour was late and they were silly with it—Cordelia worn out from the long trip north, Priscilla equally tired from anticipation. Unable to speak, Priscilla simply shook her head and collapsed onto the bed beside Cordelia.

A knock on the door momentarily stifled their hilarity and snapped them into a sitting position. "Priscilla!" came a nettled hiss. "Why aren't you abed? It's after midnight! You're keeping your cousin up."

"I'm sorry, Mother. I was just combing my hair."

"Yes, well, go to sleep."

"You comb your hair so noisily," said Cordelia when her aunt's footsteps had receded down the hall.

Priscilla drew the bedspread over her. "I'm glad she didn't come in and find the window open."

They lay at right angles to one another, looking at the ceiling, and said nothing for some time. They might indeed have been icons of autumn and winter: one exuding an enigmatic wit that matched her freckles and red hair; the other plainer in her beauty, her long hair shining in a black spill about her face. The clock in the downstairs hall struck some portion of the hour.

"Do you think my father had a sense of humor?" asked Priscilla after another span of silence.

Cordelia took several moments to answer. "I think so. I wish I remembered your father better."

"He was often away. Often, when you were here, he was away."

Cordelia reached out and gently touched her cousin's hand. Priscilla gratefully grasped Cordelia's fingers and pressed them to her cheek.

"I miss him," said Priscilla. "For myself and my brother, but mostly for Mother. Sometimes I think I hear him walking past the door, and I look up and it's Ethan. Do you know," she said, craning her head back to look at Cordelia, "I think that if he were still alive I would be married by now."

"Does your mother keep you so cloistered?"

"Oh, not really. We just seem to have less confidence without him. I suppose it would be much the same if Mother had gone."

"Do you want to be married?"

"It is what we do, isn't it?"

Cordelia recited with wry formality:

> *Whether you find him tall as a stack,*
> *Or low as a mine shaft, thin and musty;*
> *Toss over all others and set your tack*
> *For the potent Captain of Industry."*

"Goodness sakes!" said Priscilla with a short laugh. "Is Mr. Benning a captain of industry, then?"

"Less a captain, perhaps, and more of a pirate. Oh, not that he's dishonest or dishonorable," Cordelia explained when her cousin shot a wide-eyed glance in her direction. "There is something rakish about him, that's all."

"Don't tell Mother. She won't let him on the property."

"A pirate of industry," said Cordelia, liking the phrase.

"Well, I have never had a stranger ask me to dance, much less a *rakish* stranger."

"Probably I will never see him again."

"I shouldn't worry," said Priscilla. "He sounds quite smitten to me, and I wouldn't be surprised if he showed up at the front door, looking for you."

33. The Unexpected Effects
of Ducky Planke

DUCKY PLANKE BARELY NOTICED when the ragged clouds, with a single drop of rain, gave him a cold tap on the ear. From his hiding place among the scruffy trees and bushes that lined a small stretch of the Eddy shore he could see the vague movement of shadows as Colonel Taverner's company positioned themselves at either side of the short gravelly beach. The sound of oars, dipped carefully, and water scuttling along low gunwales entered the echoing perimeters of the cove as a dark mass emerged from the gloom on its way inshore.

Another rhythmic noise, like oars plying the wind, caught Ducky's attention, and he looked up in time to sense as much as see the lumbering shape of a great blue heron pass over him.

Hiding now among some rocks above the shore, Sundry Moss caught the sound of the heron as well, and for a moment it startled him. He did not have Ducky's immediate sense of what was flying past, but decided quickly that it was no phantom. Without having truly appeared, the heron was gone—banking through the darkness to the next head of land—and in its wake, the sound of the incoming boat was clearer still.

Having ascertained that the night runner was heading for a bit of strand just east of the fort, Colonel Taverner deployed himself and his men behind large rocks on either end of the beach. With rifle and shotgun, the sheriff and Seth took the furthest post, unknowingly creeping a mere yard behind the hidden Ducky Planke in their circuitous route to the cover of a large boulder.

Waiting from behind a natural buttress of rock overlooking the shore, Colonel Taverner, Sundry, and Mister Walton listened to the boat's progress. "Keep down, till we're sure they're not armed," had been the colonel's last hushed words to Sundry and Mister Walton as they had cat-footed out of the fort.

"It's probably just another fisherman from Edgecomb," had been Sundry's barely audible comment.

Now the colonel was featureless in the dark, but Mister Walton could see enough of the man's silhouette to know that he brandished a revolver in one hand and his shuttered storm lamp in the other. Their vigil was not altogether comfortable, unfortunately, for the ground was damp with a low mist and preliminary rain and they were quickly discovered by a small flock of hungry mosquitoes. Mister Walton's seat was wet as soon as he set himself down, but he dared not shift his rotund figure for fear of giving away their presence.

The rain came on in slow earnest to add to their troubles, and they turned their collars against the swarming insects and the cold drizzle.

The thunk of a bow against the shore and the muffled clunk of shipped oars charged them with expectancy, and all discomfort was forgotten. Mister Walton sensed Colonel Taverner stiffen like a dog on point, and they waited again for the sound of boots upon the beach, and the scrape of the boat being pulled up from the reach of the tide.

There was a small splash and two or three steps that sounded like careful shovelfuls of gravel, a second set of thumps indicating someone in the boat moving to the bow; then a voice on shore called: "Quack! Quack!"

He was so taut with excitement, and the unexpected voice was so incongruous with his expectations, that Mister Walton almost shouted with surprise.

"Quack! Quack!" came the voice again. It was really a very good imitation of a mallard. "Quack! Quack!" repeated the voice, and the figures on the beach, momentarily frozen, now clambered noisily back toward the water.

Colonel Taverner leaped up from his place of hiding and lifted the shade of his storm lamp. Across the way, Sheriff Piper followed a similar plan of action and the scene on the beach was captured by two pale shafts of light.

"Don't move!" shouted Colonel Taverner. "I am an agent of the Customs Service and I am armed!" He leveled his revolver just in front of the lantern so that those in the boat below him could see the truth of his words.

Mister Walton had been told to stay down till any possible danger had passed, but his overwhelming curiosity (and perhaps the damp seat of his pants) urged him to his feet, and he raised his eyes over the sheltering rock.

Two men were discernible: one, slight and bearded, stood in the aft end of a dory which was only three-quarters in the river; the other, built like a bull, was caught on the beach, frozen in the act of pushing the boat from shore.

On the other side of the small cove the sheriff and Seth could be seen as vague outlines, their weapons glinting in the light of their lantern. "Easy," said Piper, and he put a hand on Seth's shoulder to discourage the jailer from stepping out from behind his cover.

"You on the beach," said Taverner clearly. He winked away a drop of rain that had landed on the brink of his eye. "I want you to slowly pull that vessel onto shore. You in the dory—sit down and hands up."

Sundry took hold of Mister Walton's arm with the intention of pushing him out of harm's way. Nothing happened for a series of protracted moments; the boat rose and fell slightly with the movement of the tide.

"Quick now!" snapped Taverner, and as he said it the man in the boat sat down, dropped his oar, and lifted a hitherto unnoticed form from the bottom of the dory. With a snap of his arms he had pulled a child, a boy no more than four or five years old, up to his chest like a breastplate. His chin resting on the youngster's head, the man flashed a strange and discomforting smile. The boy gave no indication of fear, looking only confused and wide-eyed, as if he had just wakened.

Such a turn of events could not have been predicted, and even Colonel Taverner was at a moment's loss.

"Push, you fool!" snarled the man in the boat, and the bull-like fellow on shore propelled the dory, suddenly and powerfully, into the river.

Taverner could not shoot at the man in the boat for fear of hitting the child, but he fired a warning into the air. His plans, however, were to amount to all or nothing that night, and the Bull ducked his head again as he turned shoreward and bolted with surprising speed. Seth alone leveled his weapon, but a sudden sense of proportion stayed his hand. Having seen the huge fellow selflessly save his comrades, and not knowing the extent of his criminality, Seth simply could not bring himself to shoot the big man down.

"Get him!" was all that Taverner could think to shout, and Sundry hit the ground running, like an unloosed spring, charging down the bank of the shore.

With a crash the Bull was through the break of trees and pounding up the field that led to the Davis homestead. The dory was almost beyond the range of the lanterns now, pulled first by the tide, then by wiry muscle as the man pushed the boy from him and unshipped the oars.

Somewhere above them rode a half moon, and, though overcast, the sky reflected a strange gray clarification onto the landscape. Clouds showed beyond the great hole in the underbrush where the Bull had broken through; and, following him, Sundry bounded into the field, his long legs finding their true speed in the open meadow. The field was wet with rain, and he could hear his quarry shushing through the long grass. The Bull had shown extraordinary speed at the start, but his size began to tell in the long run, and at the top of a steep knoll Sundry narrowed the distance between them to a few feet.

The huge fellow, a good head taller than Sundry, paused at the crest of the rise, possibly to take his bearings, but more likely for the purposes of gaining his breath. He sounded like some large animal now, chuffing with his exertions.

Sundry had no plan. He was in fact propelled by several factors — youth, courage, a sense of duty, the excitement of the moment — none of which encompassed a single practical notion of how to subdue such an opponent. The Bull swung about just as Sundry leveled a flying tackle at his quarry's waist.

The thought occurred to Sundry, as he collided with the Bull, that he would have had similar luck attempting to pull down a large oak. A grunt exploded from the giant—not from the force of the attack, but from mere surprise. Sundry on the other hand let out a long sough, sure that he had done damage to every bone and joint in his body.

They remained there for a moment—the Bull unmoving as a cliff, Sundry grappling at the man to regain his knees. Then the giant took a step down the opposite side of the knoll, dragging Sundry with him, and slipped on the rain-slick grass. Halfway down the slope Sundry let go of the man, whose descent resembled that of a large boulder. Sundry finished the bottom of the hill on his stomach and found himself up to his elbows in a small stream.

With a startled gasp he sat up in time to see the Bull towering above him. The great chest expanded with a deep breath, the powerful arms rose, and the ham-sized hands brandished a rock the size of Sundry's head, which was the very object for which it was intended.

Sundry froze in horror. Then the Bull froze in horror. A sound reached them, rising and falling and wailing—a cross between the call of a loon and the hoot of an owl. An eerie figure plunged down the slope—arms waving, rags whipping in the wind of its movement.

"Owooo-uhhhhowwww-uhhhhowwww!"

The Bull let out a second grunt and ran, barely thinking to drop the rock halfway up the next ridge.

Sundry was on his feet and shaking his rattled brain when Ducky Planke hooted and *looned* past him and up the opposite slope, veering in a separate direction from the Bull.

"Sundry!" came a voice from the top of the ridge behind the young man. The outline of Sheriff Piper and the shine of his rifle's barrel appeared there. Mister Walton, puffing and blowing, appeared next.

"I'm down here!" called Sundry. "Stay there, I'll come back up."

"Good heavens, son!" declared Mister Walton when the young man reached the top of the hill again. They were shadows to each other, there in the dark, the rain cold on their ears. "Are you all right?"

"Now, what did you think you were going to do, once you caught that fellow?" wondered the sheriff.

"I did catch him, actually."

"The one that got away," said Piper wryly.

"Mr. Moss," said Colonel Taverner, who was calmly bringing up the rear with Seth. "I am not accustomed to having my orders obeyed with such speed and enthusiasm. Perhaps you'd like to work for the Customs Service."

"I have employment, thank you."

"Yes, well, it's probably safer for you. I didn't mean for you to take on the entire smuggling population of the state by yourself, you understand."

"You say that you caught him?" said Mister Walton.

"Sort of the way Napoleon caught Wellington. We went rolling down this hill, and I was still waking up from the fall when he offered to knock my head in with a rock. About then Ducky Planke came by and frightened him off."

"That's who the quacker was!" exclaimed Seth.

"Frightened him off?" said a bemused sheriff. "Ducky frightened that moose off?"

"He *was* sort of ghostly, hooting and wailing. He saved my life, I swear it!" Sundry raised his hand as if he were in the witness box.

"Ducky Planke?" asked Taverner.

"It takes a little explaining," said the sheriff. "But Ducky is what you might term a 'character,' who lives on the island."

"And he was the one who warned them of us?"

"No, no," said Seth. "Ducky just quacks now and again."

"He's *quite* good at hooting and loon calls," added Sundry.

They were walking back toward the fort now, their pant legs soaked and their hats drooping in the cold drizzle. Two or three houses in the vicinity showed lights, lit by those wakened when Taverner fired his gun.

"That's the last we'll see of them," ventured Seth.

"Don't be so sure," said Taverner. "There wasn't anything *in* that dory, that I could see, so they must have been picking something up. I'll call in some of the agents at Bath to help me search the shoreline tomorrow."

"I'm rather worried about that poor little boy who was with them," said Mister Walton.

"Just another dirty ragamuffin, Mister Walton," said Colonel Taverner. "Willing to help break the law and pick your pocket. He'll be dead or in jail before his time, but he's a bad one from the company he keeps."

"There are no bad children, Colonel," averred Mister Walton. "Only bad influences."

But the colonel had gone on to other things. It was his plan to keep watch in the fort the rest of the night, in case the man in the boat should return. Seth offered to stay with him, but to complete the illusion that their post was deserted, Sheriff Piper took Mister Walton and Sundry back to Wiscasset in the carriage. When they reached the rig, an owllike hoot rose from somewhere below them.

The three of them paused and looked down toward the water.

"That was real, I think," said Sundry.

Mister Walton hunched his shoulders and found no comfort in his wet collar. He waited willingly, however, staring into the rainy night. Soon they were rewarded.

"Quack, quack! Quack, quack!"

Book Six

JULY 8, 1896

34. Boothbay Harbor

NORTH EAST TELEGRAPH
COMPANY
OFFICE — WISCASSET, MAINE
JULY 8 PM 11:00
PORTLAND, MAINE
MR & MRS C BAFFIN
12C ADAMS ST

LEAVING FOR BOOTHBAY. WEYMOUTH HOUSE TONIGHT.
REGARDS.
    TOBY

THE WET WEATHER MADE SECTIONS of the road to Boothbay greasy, and the horse that Mister Walton had hired (along with a small trap) had a cautious air about her, so Sundry let her have her pace, which was moderate. The trap's fringed canopy kept a good deal of the intermittent rain from their heads, but their faces were damp with the shrouds of mist that blew across the fields and straggled against the treeless hills.

It was a pleasant journey despite the rain. The day was not particularly cold, and they were well dressed. Mister Walton nearly lost his hat in a sudden gust when they crossed the Sheepscot River from Wiscasset, after which he pulled it over his head so that the tips of his ears pointed at perpendicular angles.

Turning onto the Eddy Road, they met Colonel Taverner and Seth Patterson returning to their own rig from a night of watching and a morning of combing the shore for contraband. Seth was snoring in his seat, but the colonel looked as sharp as if he were fresh from a good night's sleep. Asked for the sequel to the previous night's excitement, the colonel regretted that he had nothing to report.

"They were fair frightened off," he said. "I expected better of them."

"They were the strangest smugglers I have ever heard of," said Mister Walton.

"I've been pursuing night runners for nearly twenty years," said Taverner, "and I wonder at nothing."

Mister Walton nodded, but the truth was that his own potential for wonder remained unhindered despite a life of travel and discovery. Perhaps Colonel Taverner had some innate *inability* to be surprised, and if so, Mister Walton thought it too bad. He liked the colonel, but would not care to be on his wrong side. He and Sundry wished the two civil servants good day (Seth was still asleep) and proceeded along the Eddy.

As with most of Mister Walton's movements during the past week, traveling to Boothbay was the result of a suggestible whim—this particular suggestion having been forwarded by Sundry. Boothbay seemed a fair goal to Mister Walton, since he had never been there.

Sundry proved an amusing guide; he drove well and he was filled with anecdote and legend, all of which he gladly shared as they passed particular homes or landmarks.

Climbing a steep hill through a small settlement of white houses, they passed Captain Clough's fabled home—a two-story Colonial structure some distance from the road that spoke no word to the unknowing traveler of its singular confluence with history. "It's difficult to comprehend that a queen nearly lived there," said Sundry.

"Not unlike people," said Mister Walton. "Some of the most remarkable I have known were the least remarkable to look at."

"Yes, and some are remarkable only to look at."

Mister Walton chuckled.

Once on the road to Boothbay the river valley disappeared and they were trotting slowly between stony fields and rolling knolls. Only an occasional house claimed the land. The wind which had been at their back drove light sprinkles of rain upon them. Mister Walton termed the weather "resolute in its dampness." It did not darken the general outlook for their day, however; for Mister Walton, the prospect of new sights and new acquaintances were enough to frustrate the purpose of any cloud.

Sundry, for his part, was born with philosophy.

They had not gone very far on this route when they came up behind a man wending his way shanks' mare. The rain had picked up a bit, and Sundry did not have to be told to offer the fellow a ride.

He was a broad, hefty sort of person, topped by a wide-brimmed hat that drooped over his ears with the rain, and somewhere between Sundry and Mister Walton in age. When he raised his head they could see an expanse of large unshaven features; when he smiled, several teeth were conspicuous by their absence. "Oh, I couldn't climb up there!" he said. "I'm soaked to the bone!"

"Nonsense," said Mister Walton. "All the more reason to get where you're going."

"Heading for Back River to see my uncle," said the man, and he clambered up into the trap, which sagged slightly as he settled himself. "I am very much obliged to you, sirs. Thaddeus Orne," and he offered his hand.

Introductions and handshakes were exchanged, and they sat back beneath the canopy as Sundry negotiated the trap around a boggy piece of road.

"I was just saying," said Mister Walton, "that the weather is very determined."

"It has a constant way about it," agreed Thaddeus. "My father says it will clear tomorrow."

"Does your father predict the weather, then?"

"No, he reads the paper."

The older man mouthed a silent O as Thaddeus nodded in a matter-of-fact way; but having been caught out, Mister Walton proved good for it, saying: "I do like the old way of doing things."

There was respect all around in the trap from that point onward, and Thaddeus didn't even blink when Mister Walton suggested that a person could "sing the clouds away."

"Do you think so?" asked Thaddeus.

"I am very sure of it. When I was a child, my mother and I would sing up the sun whenever the rain grew tiresome."

"I'm sorry I didn't know about it sooner," said Thaddeus, tapping at the brim of his sopping hat. "What did you sing?"

"Anything! Anything at all!"

Thaddeus put his head back, then, and a wonderful tenor voice soared out of him.

> "Diana, My dear!
> We've passed through another year!
> Our engagement drags on,
> And I try to be strong,
> But impatience is growing, I fear!

> "I'd marry you today!
> In my carriage we'd both ride away,
> And begin our new life

As husband and wife;
Who cares what your mother will say!

"Oh, give to me a sign,
And promise you'll always be mine.
It's been too long a wait.
Let's fish or cut bait!
This month you will turn fifty-nine!"

When he was finished, Thaddeus peered around the edge of the canopy at the sky. "That was marvelous," said Mister Walton.

Thaddeus pulled his head back in. "Nothing definite yet."

"Maybe it needs to be louder," suggested Sundry.

"Well, join me this time."

"My goodness!" said Mister Walton. "I'd much rather listen to you. Please, give us another."

"Not at all. Do you know 'Jenny Jenkins'?"

"I've heard two or three renditions," admitted Mister Walton cautiously.

"We'll sing one as won't embarrass us if we meet a lady," assured Thaddeus, and so they sang:

"Oh, will you wear red, oh my dear, oh my dear,
Will you wear red, Jenny Jenkins?
I won't wear red, it's the color that I dread,
I'll buy me a fol-de-rol cap
Play the fiddle!
I'll buy me a skirt and a blouse for the middle.
Fol-de-rol, fol-de-rol,
Roll, Jenny Jenkins, roll!

"Then will you wear green, oh my dear, oh my dear,
Will you wear green, Jenny Jenkins?
I won't wear green; I'm a fright to be seen.
I'll buy me a fol-de-rol cap
Play the fiddle!
I'll buy me a skirt and a . . ."

The distance to Boothbay Center, once known as North Boothbay, seemed too short, and Mister Walton was sorry that Thaddeus couldn't sing with them all the way to the harbor; but here he parted with them.

"I do think your method works, Mister Walton," said Thaddeus, though the rain hadn't even considered letting up.

"Thank you," said the portly fellow. "My mother knew what she was doing, I think."

"I bet she had a lovely voice."

"Indeed she did." They waved, and Mister Walton thought he could hear Thaddeus humming to himself as they drove off.

Boothbay was one of the more populated towns along the coast, and this was indeed its center, with a church and school and town house, a smithy and several stores. Traffic increased as they neared the common, as did the presence of the harbor, nestled beyond the next hill. The air had changed as they neared the end of the peninsula—not gradually, but in noticeable stages: the warmth of the day falling just a bit, the dampness of the rain giving way to the dampness of the ocean air, and the tang of salt reaching the nose like a tonic as they rounded a bend in the road or crested a knoll.

"I can feel the ocean!" declared Mister Walton, and he filled his lungs with a great invigorating draft.

Sundry slowed the trap to a halt so that a woman, umbrella held high, could carefully pick her way past the puddles as she crossed the road before them. A man standing in the doorway of a store—a butcher's apron about his middle—answered Mister Walton's cheerful greeting with a wave. A two-horse coach, coming from the harbor, passed them with a flurry of clopping hooves and splashing wheels, and Sundry tipped his hat at a pretty face that looked out at them as the coach trundled by. Then he shook the reins and they made the fairly marked descent toward the harbor.

At the top of the next slope the harbor became apparent in glimpses between buildings, then in longer views as they neared the wharves. Though as bound to the sea as Wiscasset, Boothbay was another sort of place altogether. Wiscasset was a town of merchant commerce, and great ships paid tribute to her navigable shore, snug within the body of the mainland. The railroad came there, and where the Sheepscot River and Wiscasset Station met, the cargo of the world passed, a prosperous transaction that was revealed in the town's handsome custom house and in the grand outlook of her wealthier homes.

Boothbay, in contrast, was of a dualistic nature. The first facet of her personality was immediately clear to Mister Walton as Sundry drove them past the closely huddled homes: here was a fishing village, classic in its tiers of buildings that faced like an amphitheater onto the constant drama of the harbor water. Gulls navigated the currents of air above the fishing vessels, the seine nets strung up to dry on sunnier days, and barrels of bait in the aft of lobster boats.

The major highway to Boothbay Harbor was traveled by steamships, and a degree of cargo did arrive in this fashion—generally to supply the many stores in the area. But no train came to Boothbay; she stood upon an outer reach of land, and the maritime traffic made her sister to the islands and other ports of call along the coast. Some of her people might feel closer to Boston than they did to the town of Edgecomb next door.

And there lay the second side of her nature, for the picturesque village, the rocky shores, and pine-clad slopes had long since welcomed the summer rusticators. Resort hotels and seasonal businesses thrived as Boothbay grew famous amongst those who sought a summer retreat. Fleeing the press of the cities and the heat of more southern climes, happy crowds arrived with the onset of the warm months, populating the verandas of her hotels, and charging the atmosphere of the otherwise quiet village with the excitement of new faces and amusing accents.

Mister Walton wondered aloud if Thaddeus Orne was still singing on his way to Back River, for when they reached the carriage drive of the Weymouth House the sun had found a break in the clouds and peered, as through a keyhole, upon the view it had been recently denied.

The manager of the Weymouth House was efficient in handling their bags and in stabling the rented horse and trap, so that it was not yet noon and they had the rest of the day to deal with at their leisure. A small restaurant closely overlooked the busy wharves, and here they had lunch.

The sun continued to assert itself, and soon it held a substantial portion of the sky. The effect was dazzling, with the rain-dampened wharves and boats shining with the obliging light. If cheerful in the rain, Mister Walton was positively jolly as the day brightened, and it was not long before he was happily conversing with those at neighboring tables. The talk centered mostly on a giant sea creature that had been seen off Monhegan recently, and some good-natured banter was had concerning the nature of the beast and the odds of its being seen again.

As a rule, Sundry would have enjoyed listening to this conversation, and perhaps joined in himself, but he felt a great need to stretch his legs after the morning's drive. A robust gentleman with a booming laugh was just suggesting that the sea creature's chances of being sighted again were in direct proportion to the amount of hard drink available, when Sundry excused himself from Mister Walton's side for the purpose of taking a walk.

Gravity and the fascination that water holds over mankind as a race drew the young man to the wharves, and he found a lonely post against which to recline his lanky frame. The breeze was in his face, the sun at his back, and the sound of the current rippling against the pilings below had a musical tone that soothed the ear. A steamboat, the *Nahanada*, pulled away from a nearby dock and swung its bow about for the trip through Townsend Gut and up the Sasanoa to the Kennebec and Bath.

Sundry was doing his best to concentrate on nothing at all, but a small scene developing on the next wharf drew his attention.

There was a small shack of a building there, where a crab picker plied his trade. Steam rose from holes in the roof and from a single window, billowing from the crab picker's great boilers. Sundry could see the crab man, a spindly fellow without hair or teeth, and two older women pass the window as they worked. Occasionally a bucket of crab shells flew from the window into the water, with some of the refuse not quite making it off the wharf.

A little ragamuffin of a fellow, no more than four or five years old, with nearly as many holes and patches in his clothes as he had clothes, was entertaining himself by pitching these shells into the harbor. Sundry watched the tyke with sympathy, thinking that a pile of picked crab shells was as close as the little fellow would ever come to a bag of toys. He wondered when the boy had eaten last and, seeing the tyke inspect the shells for meat that the pickers might have missed, decided it had been a while since his last meal.

Sundry was jingling some change in his pocket and had just determined to do something about this hungry state of affairs when two sharp young men, around eighteen or nineteen years old, came up to the little boy and began to praise his ability to throw.

It occurred to Sundry that these two were of a charitable disposition and he relaxed.

"I'll bet you I can throw one of these shells farther than you," said one of the young men. "What do you say, Garrett?"

"I don't think you can do it," said Garrett.

"Well, I bet you," said the first fellow to the little boy, smiling broadly.

Sundry smiled; here was a clever way to give the boy a bit of money without the appearance of charity.

"What are you going to bet, Bo?" asked Garrett.

"I am thinking. I will bet you five cents," said Bo to the little boy, "against your hat that I can throw one of these shells farther than you can."

The tiny fellow hardly understood what a bet was, but agreed to the wager with a silent nod.

"Go ahead," said Bo encouragingly. "Give it your best."

The little boy took up a piece of shell and gave it a toss in the direction of the water. It flitted out past the end of the wharf, stumbled in the light breeze, and plitted in the current barely a yard out. Sundry thought that Bo would have to be very clever in order to throw a shorter distance.

"Uh-oh!" said Bo.

"You've seen it now!" said Garrett, laughing.

Bo picked up a shell, weighed it in his hand, then flung it several yards into the harbor. Immediately the two began to laugh uproariously, and Bo snatched the hat from the little fellow's head. There was a sort of stunned expression on the child's face, and when he put his hand up to his bare head, Bo and Garrett went into new convulsions of laughter.

"Would you like to try and win your hat back?" asked Bo, when they had composed themselves.

"I think you boys have had enough fun," said the crab man, peering out his window. "Let him learn his lesson and leave him alone."

"I won it fair and square, old man," smirked Bo, waving the hat.

"You won it—though I would argue with 'fair and square.' Get!"

"I thought you were going to throw that shell," said Sundry, who had hurried back to shore and was now walking up the other wharf.

Bo and Garrett were startled by his approach, but relaxed when they saw him. Sundry Moss was tall, but his long limbs and slim frame did not present a particularly threatening appearance.

"I suppose you are going to show me how it's done," said Bo, not sounding as if he cared.

"Why, I could throw *you* further than that!"

"I don't think you had better try," said Bo, his false smile slipping into a threatening sneer.

Sundry stood almost toe to toe with the man. Garrett stepped up to his friend's shoulder, adding to the sense of danger directed toward the newcomer. Sundry winked at the little boy, who stood at the end of the wharf, trapped by the unfolding scene. "What are you, afraid of getting wet?" asked Sundry.

"I'm not afraid of anything you can do," said Bo, and Sundry had to admit to himself that the fellow did not seem the least bit daunted.

"You know, the other day," said Sundry, "I threw a fellow clear across the harbor to the east side."

Bo and Garrett laughed then, and some of the tension dissipated. "Clear to the other side?" said Bo.

"I'll bet you that I can do the same with you."

"You'll bet me, huh?" said Bo, still laughing.

Sundry made a soaring motion with his hand to indicate how Bo would sail to the eastern shore of the harbor. "I did it before."

"That's very funny."

"It is a wild ride, so he told me. Didn't even get his feet wet."

"What's the game?" asked Bo, a bit more seriously.

"Nothing. I'll bet you"—and here Sundry reached into a pocket and counted out several large coins—"I'll bet you twenty dollars against that hat that I can throw you to the other side of the harbor."

"You're out of your mind."

"I am quite serious."

Bo looked at the money in Sundry's hand, then glanced at his friend with a puzzled laugh, then turned to the crab man, who was watching all this from his window. "Are you hearing what he's saying?" Bo asked.

"I'm waiting to see it," said the crab man. The two women working with him joined him at the window. Several other people, including two fishermen from a nearby boat, clambered onto the wharf for a closer view.

Bo thought about the proposed wager and could see no hole in it. Then he weighed the discomfort of getting wet against the twenty dollars, stuck his hand out, and said: "You're on! I wager that you can't throw me across the harbor—your twenty dollars against this hat. Our friend the crab picker will hold them for us."

Sundry shook the young man's hand. "Agreed," he said.

But Bo felt suddenly cautious. "You're going to throw me across the harbor."

"Yes."

"To the other side."

"That's it."

Bo laughed. "You'll toss me and my feet won't even touch the water."

"They might sting a little bit."

Satisfied, Bo took off his coat and emptied his pockets, handing his things to Garrett. He walked up to the edge of the wharf. "I'll stand at the edge here and make it a little easier for you," he said.

"That's very sporting of you," said Sundry. He patted the little boy's shoulder, advanced to the end of the wharf, and without ceremony took Bo by the scruff of the neck and by the britches and threw him into the harbor. There was a loud round of applause, despite that Sundry had only gotten the fellow no more than three yards out.

It was obvious that the harbor water was cold, Bo was that anxious to be out of it, but he was laughing as he swam to the ladder, and sounded like his own personal rainstorm, dripping into the water, then onto the wharf as he climbed up. "Well, that was the easiest twenty dollars I ever earned!" he said with a look of contempt at Sundry.

"Not yet, you haven't," said Sundry. "I didn't say that I could do it the first time!" And without warning he took hold of Bo by the back of his shirt and britches and threw him in again. He dusted off his wet hands with several loud slaps, and said to the astonished crowd: "I sort of have to build up to it." A great roar of laughter filled the harbor and echoed from the eastern shore.

When Garrett saw that Sundry was waiting for his friend at the top of the ladder, he dropped Bo's things and closed in on him.

"I didn't make a bet with you," said Sundry. "But it'll be good practice." Seeing a hard look in Sundry's eyes, Garrett stopped just short of grappling with him.

Bo had reached the top of the ladder by now and was protesting as Sundry attempted to muckle onto him a third time.

"Don't worry about me," said Sundry. "I've got all day. Of course, you could always forfeit."

"I'll do nothing of the kind," hissed Bo. "You tricked me!"

"I would say it is just about as fair and square, me against you, as you against a four-year-old." Clearly Sundry was pushing, and a weathered old salt came up between them and suggested that everyone had had his money's worth.

"He's a cheat!" snarled Bo.

"You made a bet," said the fisherman. "And you have to allow him the opportunity to fulfill it. If you didn't stipulate how many tries he could have, you have no complaint."

Bo rubbed the water from his eyes, snatched up his things where Garrett had dropped them, and stormed off the wharf.

Sundry collected his twenty dollars from the crab man, then replaced the hat onto the little boy's head. "Remember," said Sundry. "When someone offers to bet you something, it is usually because they know they can win. Now, where do you belong?"

Having uttered not a single word, the little boy appeared hesitant, even fearful of breaking his silence. He stared at Sundry with large blue eyes, daunted perhaps by the young man's rough way of dealing with his tormenters.

"He came in on that toy steamer down by the mill," said the crab man, hooking a thumb over his shoulder. "Came in with Sir Eustace Pembleton." The name was delivered through the nose to indicate how Sir Eustace would say it.

Sundry looked again at the boy's ragged clothes—unable to believe that he came in with any sort of *sir* at all. "What's your name?" asked Sundry of the child, and for the first time since Sundry had seen him, the boy actually moved his lips, though little or no sound came from them.

"Bird," said the boy, when pressed.

"Bert?"

"Bird," he said simply.

"Well, Bird. Let us go see if Sir Eustace is at home." Sundry did not like the way that the boy tensed up when this course of action was suggested. He took the child's hand, however, and led him off the wharf.

Sundry had never seen anything quite like the vessel that had been dubbed, by the crab man, a "toy steamer." Barely thirty feet long, with a stack hardly taller than Sundry himself, it did indeed look like a child's version of the genuine article. The cabin, its trunk oddly slouched, was low and nearly as large as the boat itself, so that there was only a narrow deck to walk on. The forward section of the cabin was slightly raised to accommodate the pilot with a proper view, but Sundry couldn't imagine that any pilot would willingly take her out, she looked so unseaworthy. She was dirty, in need of paint, and laundry hung from her sides. The name across her bow was *Proclamation*.

Standing upon the run-down dock that served the *Proclamation* as a wharf, Sundry wondered how a boiler, which needs be so small, could render enough steam to put the boat under way. "You don't sail in this thing, do you?" he wondered aloud to the little boy.

"We don't sail," came a nasal tone from the direction of the boat. "We steam." A man emerged from the dilapidated cabin, ducking his head beneath the lintel, and steadied himself with one foot upon the shallow bulwark. "Do not be amazed," he said. "She is a prototype—the parent vessel of an entire fleet. She is, by my own coining, the first 'personal steamer.'"

"I see," said Sundry, hoping that some measure of apology sounded in his words. He was, momentarily, dumbstruck. The man before him was rail thin, and dressed in shabby attire that had, not so long ago, been fashionable and expensive. His dark beard was newly trimmed, but his hair was long and badly kept, and his eyes were bleary lights above sagging pockets.

It was the very man in the dory that had gotten away from Colonel Taverner only the night before; and Bird was the child—hardly seen in the shadows—that this man had used as a living shield in order to make good his escape. Having watched from the darkness along the shore that night, Sundry himself was in no danger of being recognized.

"Sir Eustace Pembleton, I presume," said Sundry, when he had recovered sufficiently from his surprise.

"I am," said the man, infusing the simple statement with an uncommon degree of hauteur. "What trouble has this urchin got into?"

With a hand on Bird's shoulder, Sundry felt the child tense again. "Not any trouble at all," Sundry replied. "He's a very good fellow. He seemed to be alone and I simply asked where he came from. Is he your son?"

"He can get inside," said Sir Eustace, without answering Sundry's question. He looked at the boy in a vague sort of way and jerked his head once in the direction of the cabin. "There is no reward, if that is what you are looking for. He wasn't lost."

"I wasn't looking for one," said Sundry as Bird climbed from the dock to the vessel's narrow deck.

Sir Eustace directed a weak backhanded slap at the boy's head, but missed, then looked up at Sundry again and blinked at the distaste he saw on the young man's face. "He is my charge," said the man. He glared then, toward the shore end of the dock, and Sundry felt a tremor in the boards at his feet.

Only then did it occur to him that the third member of that strange trio had yet to be accounted for, and looking over his shoulder with as much composure as he could muster, a sudden discomforting thought was unhappily confirmed. Trudging heavily down the length of the dock was the giant fellow who had nearly crushed Sundry's head with a rock the night before.

Sundry managed a weak smile that froze as the huge man halted several giant steps away and scowled at him, with less recognition in the expression than uncertainty. It had been dark, after all, during their pursuit and struggle, and Sundry relaxed ever so slightly as the man's frown drifted into perplexity.

The giant's hesitation was enough for Sir Eustace, however, and the bearded man shouted in a voice high pitched with nerves. "Well, come on, you idiot! I can't wait here all day! Get in and shove us off!"

Sundry stepped aside for the huge man, who lumbered past and lowered the near side of the miniature steamer several inches with his great weight as he stepped down. Sundry gave a wave that felt silly and looked in vain for Bird in one of the cabin windows. Then he turned up the dock and tried not to look as though he were hurrying.

Mister Walton had known Sundry Moss for only the better part of a day and a half, and yet was sufficiently impressed with the young man's characteristic calm to be surprised when Sundry met him on Boothbay's Main Street in a state of barely concealed agitation.

The sun won out as the afternoon began, and Mister Walton was on a leisurely stroll through the village, feeling somewhat sleepy with the warmth of the day and the effects of his meal. He was thinking on the curious events of the night before.

Sundry was not running, but there was a briskness to his step and a seriousness to his expression that suggested that all was not well. Mister Walton halted on the sidewalk and waited for the young man to catch sight of him. When they did meet, Sundry was brimming with urgency.

"Mister Walton, that man with the beard—the one in the boat, just the last night—well, I've seen him."

"The fellow with the boy?"

"Yes, *and* I've seen the boy. I spoke with them. Then the big fellow that I chased arrived, and I think he recognized me."

"Good heavens! Where are they?"

"On the oddest little boat I've ever seen, and heading out of the harbor even as we speak."

"My word! Colonel Taverner would like to know about this."

"I wish I could have stopped them!"

"Well, we have no proof that they've done anything illegal—except perhaps running away from Colonel Taverner."

"I'm more concerned about the little boy."

"Ah, yes. He's been on my conscience as well. Leaving the harbor, you say."

"Come this way. I think we can catch sight of them on the other side of this building."

Such was not the case, however, and they continued in the direction of the shore till they could see the *Proclamation* steaming its way toward the mouth of the harbor. Mister Walton agreed that it was a singular contrivance, and the two of them meandered toward the wharves, watching the vessel disappear, till Sundry found himself standing once again by the crab picker's shack.

"Who is this Eustace Pembleton?" asked Sundry of the crab man through the open window.

The picker's face appeared amidst a gout of steam. "*Sir* Eustace Pembleton, if you please—though I don't know where the *sir* is coming from. He's an out-of-work actor, if you ask me. I'm more royalty than he is—a direct descendant of Brian Boru!"

"Any idea where he's going?" asked Sundry.

"Anywhere he can cadge a dollar or two to get him to the next port. He'll scour every dump and low tide itself to fuel that contraption of his. He's a schemer, that one. A swindler."

"A confidence man, do you mean?" asked Mister Walton.

"Yes, he'll get a person's confidence, with his accent and his false title. Did he get something of yours?"

"No," said Sundry. "Just my curiosity."

"He is a curiosity at that. You're a bit of a schemer yourself, aren't you? That was a sharp one you pulled on that smart fellow, aye? Toss him across the harbor!"

Mister Walton felt he had missed something. He watched Sundry; and Sundry watched as the last sight of the *Proclamation*'s head of steam disappeared behind the western point of land at the harbor's mouth.

35. The Members Are Outraged

WEDNESDAY'S MID-MORNING TRAIN STOPPED in Wiscasset with no more fuss or fanfare than had the train before it, or would the train to follow. Familiar and unfamiliar faces came from or boarded her as the engine chuffed and voices—charged with command or cheerful in greeting—called out in the damp air. No one within sight or earshot of the station would have found anything noteworthy in the typical transfer of cargo, mail, and passengers— and yet three of those passengers, in their arrival, represented another step toward the birth of a glorious tradition!

Ephram, Eagleton, and Thump gazed up Wiscasset's steep Main Street, and the handsome aspect of the town, with ragged clouds tumbling behind the line of roofs and trees and steeples, seemed rife with dramatic possibilities; here they expected to reunite with Mister Walton, the chairman of their yet unnamed and undefined club.

They were a prepossessing trio, smartly attired, mustaches and beards (excepting Eagleton, who was clean-shaven) trimmed, newly minted luggage stacked about them in expectant pyramids. Eagleton took in the demeanor of the sky with the practiced understanding of a true meteorographer. Ephram checked one of his watches and announced that the train had arrived on time. Thump turned to look past the waterfront buildings at the Sheepscot River—making a mental adjustment in his mind to calculate the tide.

Several young boys gathered about them, offering their services in removing the mounds of luggage to their intended destination.

"Where are the best accommodations in town?" asked Ephram of one lad.

"I don't know of anybody who uses the stuff," said the boy with a smile—he couldn't have been more than ten or eleven years old.

One of the other lads playfully rapped the boy in the back of the head. "The best rooms are at the Wiscasset House, sir," said this older fellow. He pointed up the street.

"Fine," said Ephram; then to Eagleton and Thump: "That will be the establishment Mister Walton has patronized." He liked the fact that the inn bore the name of the town, since it would aid history in recreating this meeting with their illustrious chairman—as, indeed, it would have, had Mister Walton still been there.

"Ah, Wiscasset!" said Eagleton, as they strode up the street with their newly acquired entourage. "Noble borough, where proud meeting waits its consequent season!"

"My word, Eagleton!" said Ephram. "You must put that to paper for the club archives!"

"Hear, hear!" said Thump enthusiastically.

"Nobleboro is north of here," informed one of the boys.

"Ah, Wiscasset House!" intoned Eagleton, encouraged by his friends and unfazed by this new information. "Your walls yet bear no mark as home to institution's birth!"

"We've got a bear loose hereabouts," said the boy with the facts. "She hasn't been seen since yesterday, but a fellow from Portland darn near shot her."

"A bear?" said Ephram.

"Portland?" said Thump.

"Who was this fellow?" asked Eagleton.

"His name was Walton."

The trio came to a direct halt, and the boys carrying their trunks and bags paused in clusters above them on the slope of the hill as they realized they were leaving the men behind.

"Walton, you say!" said Ephram.

"Tobias Walton, hunting a bear?" wondered Thump aloud. It was too wonderful!

"That was his name," said the boy. "I carried his bags up the night before last."

"You say he *nearly* shot the bear," said Ephram, wanting to get the facts down cold. "Was he hurt?"

"No, he just got that bear to stand on its head."

Ephram, Eagleton, and Thump looked at one another, wondering what to think of this extraordinary news.

"Stood on its head?" said Thump in wonderment.

"We must hear about this adventure from the man himself!" announced Eagleton. "It's . . . well, it's . . . epic!"

"The bear stood on its head?" said Thump. He wasn't at all sure why Mister Walton would want a bear to stand on its head, but it was a marvelous thing nonetheless.

"Come, let us go meet with this remarkable man!" said Ephram.

He had not gotten more than three or four paces up the street, however, when the boy said: "But he isn't here anymore."

Ephram turned about on his heels and nearly fell over. "What?"

"Oh, no, sir. He left this morning."

"He left with Sundry Moss," said another boy.

"He nearly got in a fight with a dozen fellows from up at the Wiscasset House," said another.

The three men could not understand it; purportedly Mister Walton had been on a bear hunt, during which he did not shoot a bear, but caused one to stand on its head; he then came near to violence with a large group of men, and left town with a variety of mosses.

"Where did he go?" asked Eagleton of this fountain of knowledge.

The boy shrugged. "Maybe he *did* go to Nobleboro. He and Sundry Moss headed across the river in a hired rig this morning."

Thump looked distressed, but he was only thinking—attempting to picture Mister Walton in a carriage with stacks of assorted mosses on the seat beside him. "Perhaps they're for medicinal purposes," he ventured.

The proprietor of the Wiscasset House was pleased to discover three dapper gentlemen, surrounded by luggage, in the foyer of his inn; he was puzzled when they began to ask questions concerning the whereabouts of their chairman; and he was chagrined when the name of Tobias Walton drew the annoying Alfred Lofton from the parlor.

The tall Lofton chose Thump, the shortest of the three, as the man he would address, since he could more effectively look down his nose upon him. "Are you representatives of the law?" he asked.

Ephram, Eagleton, and Thump thought about this.

"I thought, perhaps," explained Lofton, "that you were here to arrest him on some charge of fraud."

"Fraud?" said Ephram, the first to find his voice.

"Now Mr. Lofton," said the proprietor. "I am sure the confusion was simply the result of an honest mistake."

"Idiocy, then?"

"Idiocy?" said Eagleton. His clean-shaven countenance gave him the look of youth and energy above his companions, though he was their senior by several months. "Are you using such terms as *fraud* and . . . well, this other word . . . in conjunction with the name of Mister Tobias Walton?" There was the hint of guarded outrage in his voice.

"If name and character are one and the same," said Lofton, managing to peer down his nose at Eagleton, though they were of a height, "in a gentleman they are the same of course. In the case of this . . . Walton . . . well, he has a name, I suppose—but character? I do doubt it."

"Ephram?" said Eagleton, as if calling for help.

"I am just speechless," said Ephram, and save for those words, this proved true. His mouth opened and closed several times without anything like a sound passing from it. When he did speak again, it was only to repeat himself. "I am just speechless."

"Thump?" said Eagleton, when Ephram proved stricken.

"He is the finest of fellows," said Thump, looking at his feet.

Lofton raised one eyebrow.

"He is a rare gentleman."

Lofton smiled with one side of his mouth.

"He is . . ."

Lofton chuckled nastily.

Thump looked up at the sound of Lofton's amusement. "He is our chairman!"

"I shall warn you," said Eagleton, pointing to his short friend, "this man is an expert in the ring!"

Thump's eyes bulged at this statement, and the expression of shock on his face, engendered by Eagleton's remarkable statement, looked very much like outrage.

Lofton looked less sure of himself now; Thump was shorter than he, but stockily built; and the man's massive beard lent him a wild and bristly look. Lofton's smirk sunk into a sneer, saying: "I suppose he uses you to protect himself much as he uses Moss."

Thump and his friends were mystified by the suggestion that Mister Walton had protected himself with a form of plant life; it was beyond their understanding, although several strange scenarios ran through their minds as they stared indignantly at Alfred Lofton. Had Mister Walton used groundcover to hide himself from the bear as a duck hunter uses a blind? Had their chairman used moss as a form of talisman? Did he have a botanical background?

Thump had had enough of Lofton's superiority, and what he said next was said with a most pugnacious tone of voice. "The gardener," he announced, "knows his blossoms better than the footman!"

There was an extended silence after this statement. Lofton looked vaguely confused. Ephram gave him a superior *take that* sort of expression and led the way from the foyer of the Wiscasset House.

Lofton, who realized that he might have queered business between these three men and the proprietor of the inn, looked suddenly sheepish.

Eagleton gave his short friend a proud pat on the back. "Come, Thump," he said. "Let us find our chairman." His expression towards Lofton was of the *he told you* variety.

Thump was the last to leave, followed by the entourage of boys with their trunks and bags. Ephram and Eagleton waited for him on the street; they each shook his hand warmly.

"You were a lion, Thump," said Eagleton. "A veritable lion. I can't tell you . . ." There were almost tears in Eagleton's eyes.

Ephram shared the sentiment. "I couldn't have said it better. Mister Walton himself would have done well to have said it better." None of them could have explained what Thump's statement had meant, but Ephram and Eagleton were sure it had served the purpose.

"It was something my mother used to say," said Thump quietly.

"She was a wise woman," said Eagleton.

"We must hire a rig and follow Mister Walton," said Ephram. "Perhaps he has merely gone to the next town."

"We must find out what the next town is," said Eagleton.

"The boy said 'sundry,'" said Thump, looking at his feet. "How many types of mosses do you suppose there are?"

36. An Unexpected Expedition

PRISCILLA HAD NEVER FELT SO PRESCIENT and Cordelia never so shocked as when John Benning appeared in the front hall of the Morningside home with Aunt Delia. Priscilla wasn't at all sure that she hadn't conjured up the man with her suggestion of the previous night.

The young women were in the arbor behind the house, and the last to know of the arrivals. Ethan came out to announce that Aunt Delia had arrived with a man, which was more than enough to pique their interest.

Grace and Mercia were the first to greet their aunt and the unexpected guest. Mercia offered her hand, which Mr. Benning took with quiet poise; Grace considered such intimacy with a new acquaintance to be improper and did not offer the same. John Benning met their eyes with something like frankness, and Grace considered his candid manner a touch audacious.

James Underwood came next, and one might have expected the younger man's self-assurance to wilt somewhat in the presence of Cordelia's father, but he shook James's hand and looked him in the eye as if he hadn't danced with the man's daughter an entire night.

Ethan Morningside, by this time, had been hugged and kissed by his great-aunt Delia, and he charged outside to spread the news of the new arrivals.

It took a while for Cordelia and Priscilla to reach the front hall—they did not want to arrive out of breath, and so appear too eager to see this unidentified man.

Priscilla was the first to see Mr. Benning, and though she had never met him, she instinctively knew who he must be. She was quite charmed before he ever spoke, but charmed further still when he introduced himself, adding: "You must be Miss Morningside. Your cousin spoke of you so glowingly that I could not mistake you."

The cousin in question entered then. Cordelia heard the man's voice before she saw him, and thought for a moment that her heart had constricted to the point of stopping. All eyes were upon her as she entered, and she had never done anything so difficult as to look at ease as she smiled her recognition of him.

"Miss Underwood," said John Benning with the most obvious regard.

"Mr. Benning," returned Cordelia. "I do meet you in the most surprising places."

This statement, along with the involuntary blush in Cordelia's cheeks, startled her aunt Grace like a whispered secret.

Priscilla was feeling giddy; and standing shoulder to shoulder with her cousin, she was able to drive an elbow into Cordelia's side while smiling beatifically for the rest of the gathering. Amongst the swirl of skirts Cordelia gave Priscilla's ankle a swift kick as she stepped forward to greet the handsome young man.

Aunt Delia had watched all this with amusement, and she alone guessed what the loud *thock* was, and why, when the gathering moved into the parlor, Priscilla limped slightly.

"It's so nice to see you again, Mr. Benning," said Mercia, "when there is no music to distract us from getting to know one another." She adroitly offered the young man her arm as they were directed to the parlor, saving her daughter the embarrassment over the proper procedure.

"I fear that your daughter's patience with me on the dance floor was more than I could resist," returned the man.

"Oh, dear," said Aunt Delia to no one in particular. "This *is* going to take a long time."

The Morningsides' toy fox terrier, Teacup, had made herself at home in John Benning's lap, and the young man had accepted this sign of tolerance from the household pet with aplomb. While Teacup's namesakes, along with attendant saucers and silverware, were being handed out to the gathering by the elderly butler, Merton, John Benning explained his arriving with Aunt Delia.

"When I found no one at your home, and no servants to tell me when you would return, I worried that something untoward had happened. Knowing your relation to Mrs. Frost," and here he nodded to Aunt Delia, "I returned to Freeport. I feared that she would think me forward, asking after you, but I inquired only as to your well-being and not your whereabouts."

Cordelia was not fooled by John Benning's formality of speech, for it was clear that he was gauging his words for the room's highest common denominator of propriety—Aunt Grace. Priscilla had giggled twice since they gathered in the parlor, and Cordelia gripped her cousin's hand with quiet meaning, but she nearly laughed herself at the frown on her father's face as he listened to Mr. Benning's stilted discourse.

Hoping to cut short the explanation, Aunt Delia said: "I thought it polite, since he had been invited to call on you, to explain where you had gone and what you were doing. John was very gracious, I thought, to offer his services as a surveyor when you go to view your land."

"Oh, dear," said Aunt Grace, her teacup poised inches from her lips.

Nothing else was said as they digested this. To Cordelia, the notion was thrilling, and more than a little daunting—to have someone so near to a beau, and yet a stranger, making such obvious advances toward her. To Aunt Grace it was improper, with no room for argument.

"Of course," said John Benning, "I would make my own arrangements, and arrive separately from your party." It was clear that Aunt Delia had startled him by introducing his proposal so early in the conversation. "I do understand that your land is situated in something of a rustic venue. I've had a bit of practice, in my line of work, with *roughing it*, and you might find my experience of some use."

"That's very generous of you," said Cordelia's father.

There was almost a tone of refusal in his voice, and Grace, approvingly, drew the cup that had remained hovering in the air to her lips and drank with the assurance that her brother-in-law would take care of the situation.

James glanced at his daughter, who didn't know if she wanted this impulsive young man along with them or not. Suddenly the idea of *not* having a suitor seemed very simple and pleasing. James himself was thinking of the complications that chaperonage would add to the trip.

"I think that traveling separately is rather silly," announced Aunt Delia. "I'm going with you, and I'm not traveling separately." This was the first anyone had heard of it, but it did put paid to further discussion. Clearly Aunt Delia had instigated the entire proposal in an effort to bolster Cordelia's social life, and it seemed that she had no intention of missing out on any further developments. "Priscilla, you shall go too."

"Aunt Delia!" said Grace.

Priscilla, who had nearly laughed out loud several times during the course of this discourse, was almost as shocked as her mother. She had intended to broach this very subject (or, indeed, to let Cordelia broach it) but had, like John Benning, fallen victim to her great-aunt Delia's precipitate method.

As was her wont, Great-Aunt Delia was having a good time upsetting the apple cart. "Grace," she said, as if she were talking to someone who would have difficulty understanding. "Priscilla needs an experience. She's altogether too pale, and Cordelia will perhaps want . . . the company. Certainly I am not able to gallivant over hill and dale once we arrive at some base camp." This reference to Cordelia's need for a chaperone was by no means artful, but it stumped Grace.

"Well," she said. "This is true." There was a moment's silence. Grace was of the opinion that a chaperone of the same age was no chaperone at all. She also realized that it was up to her to make the situation as proper as it could be. She knew her duty and she followed it. "I am in need of some fresh air myself, I think, so I too will go along."

"Yippee!" shouted young Ethan. He leaped from his chair and danced about the room. "Yippee! That means I go too!"

"Ethan!" said Grace in a stage whisper, as if his behavior wouldn't be noticed if she spoke quietly enough. Then she leaned back in the love seat she occupied, her hand to her breast, her eyes fluttering. She was having one of her faint spells. "Oh, Priscilla," she said mournfully. "Do you see what you teach your brother with your dancing about the yard?"

"Here," said Mercia, doing her best to hide her irritation. "Have a sip of tea, dear."

"Priscilla is pale, Lord knows," said Aunt Delia to a bemused James. "But Grace is death warmed over." She leaned toward John Benning, who had just finished pouring tea for Grace, patted the young man on the knee, and said: "I think you've come just in time."

"This was going to be a simple family outing," said James to his wife. "But I guess it's to be a major expedition instead. I'll wire ahead about the increased size of our party."

"Alert the newspapers," said Aunt Delia wryly. "Grace is leaving the house."

"Oh, Cordelia!" said Priscilla in a hysterical whisper. "It's going to be such a romp!"

Cordelia was stunned—Aunt Delia had just orchestrated an adventure, complete with her beloved cousin and a man who made no secret of admiring her. She looked over at John Benning and nearly flinched when he winked at her.

37. Damariscotta

EPHRAM, EAGLETON, AND THUMP had too much luggage, really, for the carriage they hired, especially when their own shapes were added beside and behind the driver. Thump was somewhat lost in the very back of the rig, his top hat just peeking above an upended trunk to either side of him; and Eagleton found it necessary to clutch at two or three bags every time the carriage rolled over a bump or lurched into a rut along the wet road.

They had inquired of the driver—an ancient fellow who was hard of hearing in one ear and completely deaf in the other—the name of the next major settlement, and after a very loud conversation in which there was more verbiage than meaning, they discovered that the next community along this road was embodied by the twin villages of Newcastle and Damariscotta.

There was something romantic in the meeting of these two names, for the one rang with the sound of the Old World and the other seemed to ring as loudly with the New. Oddly enough, their driver heard this portion of their conversation and offered his own thoughts.

"Ah, yes! Those Damariscotta Indians!" he said with great feeling.

Eagleton, as alert to the driver's impressive tone of voice as he was unaware of the mischief in the man's eye, expressed interest in this hitherto unknown tribe.

"Greatly feared amongst the Abenaki," said the driver.

"Were they?"

"Oh, my! Tore trees out by their roots and played at ninepins with boulders as big as your head. Their men were as tall as you like, don't you know, and their women taller."

"Taller than the men?"

"Taller than you like."

Eagleton frowned; he wasn't sure that he disliked tall women. "What made them so remarkable, do you suppose?"

"Oysters!"

"Oysters?"

The driver looked at Eagleton as if wondering which of them was hard of hearing. They drove for several moments before he spoke again. "You should *see* the oysters they ate!"

Eagleton wasn't sure how that was possible, and said so.

"Stacks and stacks of shells," explained the driver.

"I see."

"Piles of them!" The ancient man raised one hand high above his head. "Mounds! Hills of oyster shells!"

"Good heavens!"

"That's how they got their name."

"That is how the Indians got their name? What does *Damariscotta* mean?"

"*The tribe that fishes very little in the river.*"

"And did they fish very little?"

"They ate oysters!"

"Oh."

"You don't fish for oysters; you dig them."

"And these oysters," interjected Thump, the shortest among his companions. "They contributed to the vitality of the tribe?"

"Absolutely!"

"And what happened to this acme of indigenous aboriginals?" asked Ephram.

"Disappeared."

"The Indians disappeared?" said Eagleton, rather sorry to hear these tidings.

"No, the oysters disappeared. The Indians moved in with their neighbors."

"Assimilated in the end," said Thump. He had once read a social history of mankind.

"And these oyster shells," said Eagleton. "You can still see them?"

"Those that haven't been carted off or rendered down for lime."

"Once we have found Mister Walton," said Eagleton to his friends, "perhaps we should take in these artifacts."

They drove on in silence for several minutes.

"I quite like oysters," said Thump.

*　　*　　*

The road to Newcastle from Edgecomb (or, at any rate, *this* road from Newcastle to Edgecomb) was sparsely populated, given to fairly straight lengths on the horizontal, and anything but on the vertical. Some farms had fields stretching to the road, but in as many places trees had begun to take hold—white pine, jack pine, and the occasional maple or oak or elm. The weather had transformed from the uncertain to the promising (just as Eagleton had predicted), and the soft wind that drove the clouds before it ruffled the lengthening grass and rushed among the leaves.

They then drove for some distance with the only sight of man or beast being a wagon heading in the opposite direction. From one hilltop, trees and houses on the other side of the Damariscotta River were plain to them, though they yet could see nothing of the river itself. The roofs of houses on this side of the river were visible from this height as well, and a train was heard, then sighted on the next ridge of land to their left.

Soon they were taking gentle descents toward the water. Houses were frequent and finally numerous, and gathering prettily near this meeting point along the life-giving and occupational river.

There was something dramatic about the sharp corner leading onto Newcastle's Main Street; the sounds of a busy town rose up around them, and the beauty of the riverside was immediately apparent. Without discussion their patriarchal navigator took them over the last hill and across the bridge, trotting his rig faster than he perhaps should have. Eagleton took note of a sign before the bridge that promised a three-dollar fine to anyone who drove or rode faster than a prudent walk.

"That sign has been there forever," said the ancient fellow with a scoff and a wave of his hand. He was forced to slow the pace, however, as they trundled onto Damariscotta's tree-lined thoroughfare. Soon they were pulled up before a bank and the sign of the Maine Hotel, which occupied the brick building's second and third floors.

Eagleton paid the driver and thanked him for his dissertation on the Damariscotta Indians. "Nothing to it," said the fellow, his answer open to the interpretation of more suspicious individuals than were these three.

A broad stairway led to the upstairs lobby of the hotel, and there Ephram, Eagleton, and Thump met with disappointment to find no Mister Walton listed among the guests there. The management was obliging, however, and before they signed themselves onto the register, a boy was sent to the inns nearby to find whether their chairman had found other lodgings.

This seemed a very civil way of doing business to Ephram, and he said so, his friends echoing this sentiment. They chatted happily with the manager, but seemed to confuse him when they mentioned the Damariscotta

Indians. Ephram was eulogizing on that tribe's noble character and on the advantageous effects caused by the eating of oysters, when Thump made a sound of discovery that did not lose its dramatic force for being expressed without discernible words. He did in fact grunt, although with deep conviction.

A small bill was affixed to a board in the hotel lobby, and Ephram and Eagleton hovered over either of Thump's shoulders to read from it what had so caught his attention. It was a program of entertainment to be performed at the Lincoln Hall on Friday the 10th of July. Surrounded by numerous advertisements for local business was the following information:

> 1. *Overture,—The Fair Maid of Perth,—Bizet.*
>   ORCHESTRA
>
> 2. *Concerto for Two Cornets,—Schneider.*
>   *executed by*
>   D. H. CHANDLER AND J. TYLER
>
> 3. *Acceleration Waltz,—Strauss.*
>   ORCHESTRA
>
> 4. *Guest Speaker,—Notes on Ascension*
>   MRS. R.

And there they came to a halt, each expressing wordless astonishment in much the same manner as had their friend. Thump added another grunt to the dialogue, and though these communications were made in the most polite tones, they briefly lent the hotel lobby the atmosphere of a slightly restrained barnyard. The manager peered from behind his desk with great interest.

"Mrs. R.," said Eagleton.

"Hmm," said Thump.

"Notes on ascension," said Ephram.

"Hmm," from Thump again.

Who could this be, they wondered, but the extraordinary Mrs. Roberto, the ascensionist?

"Mrs. R.?" said the manager. "She's a religious speaker. I'm not sure why the initial instead of a name."

"Oh," said Ephram, hoping that a note of disappointment did not ring too loudly in his interjection.

"Religious, you say," said Eagleton. This seemed separate from Mrs. Roberto's area of expertise.

Thump, however, had experienced something very powerful when he wakened in Mrs. Roberto's lap, and he wasn't at all sure that the two things weren't connected somehow. "There may be something illuminating here," he suggested.

They perused the rest of the bill:

5. Selection,—I Puritani,—Bellini.
ORCHESTRA

6. Museum Piccolo Polka,—Beckett.
EXECUTED BY E. P. BECKETT

---

*Gentlemen are respectfully requested to abstain
from expectorating on the floor of the hall.*

"I quite like polkas," said Eagleton.

"Perhaps it would be wise for us to sit still a bit," ventured Ephram.

"I would like to see these shell heaps," agreed Thump.

The boy came back after half an hour to inform them that no Mister Tobias Walton had registered at any of the local inns or taverns, but that word would be sent to the Maine Hotel if such an individual appeared.

"I am sorry," said the manager. "Your friend doesn't seem to be any-where in town."

"Yes," said Ephram. "Thank you for your considerate help. By the way, where is the Lincoln Hall?"

The manager pointed. "It's just the next building, sir."

"Yes," said Ephram again. He glanced from Eagleton to Thump. "I think," he said to the manager, "you may register us through to Saturday."

The twin villages were singularly pleasing to the club members. The weather remained uncertain, but while the sun played in and out of a series of dark clouds they took in the local sights. From the bridge they admired the tree-lined Main Street and the steepled church upon the hill; and from the steps of the church upon the hill they admired the tree-lined Main Street, the broad river, and the rustic and melancholy aspect of old shipyards now fallen into disuse.

They were filled with great purpose as they walked, and never failed to tip their hats to whomever they met along the way. With some people—store owners leaning in the doorways of their establishments and young boys playing at baseball in an empty lot beside the Lincoln Hall—they stopped to talk. Inquiries concerning the Damariscotta Indians garnered two sorts of response: the first was characterized by a puzzled or blank stare;

the second, by an expression of great wisdom (especially among the young) followed by some fascinating bit of knowledge.

"They were such a short people," one lad informed them, "that they were seldom seen."

This surprised Ephram, since the driver who took them here had insisted that the Damariscotta Indians were exceedingly tall.

"They were very clever about their height," amended the boy, when informed of this discrepancy.

"See the wooden Indian here?" said Herman Sykes, standing outside his fruit, confectionery, and tobacco business. (A sign above his door apprised the reader of a *First Class Billiard Room in the back!*) The tradesman hooked a thumb at a nearly life-sized carving on the front step of his store.

The three men gave the impressive figure a careful appraisal.

"Yes," said Ephram.

"Nothing like that."

After spending several minutes inspecting the wooden Indian, to see what the Damariscotta tribe *didn't* look like, they continued their perambulations about the town.

In the evening, during dinner, a Mr. Buchanan regaled them with a tale concerning the Damariscotta Indians and his father, which included also prominent roles for a gang of cutthroats, a stolen pig, and a steam geyser.

"I do think I will put Mr. Buchanan's story to paper," said Eagleton later that night. "What do you think, Thump?"

"First-rate," said that worthy. Standing by a window, overlooking Damariscotta's Main Street, he turned slightly and raised his chin so that his prodigious beard preceded him slightly. "I was very fond of it," he continued, looking thoughtful, "and I am sure that future members of our club will be glad to have it passed on to them."

"Exactly!" said Eagleton. He had purchased pen and paper earlier in the day, while his ideas were yet vague. "What do you think, Ephram?" he said. "I am going to record Mr. Buchanan's remarkable tale."

"I understand that you are," said Ephram, "and it is a worthy notion. Perhaps," he added, looking wise, "we should record Mister Walton's heroic ride through Portland. Certainly we should include the newspaper description in our archives."

"Yes!" agreed Eagleton.

"And there is the courageous action of our own Thump—undaunted in the midst of two angered politicians, struck down by a parachutist."

This reference to the lovely Mrs. Roberto (in her attractive suit of tights) gave rise to a large sigh in Thump's breast, after which he informed his friends that any mention of that collision must in no way impugn Mrs. Roberto's (here another sigh) parachuting skills.

"Hear, hear!" exclaimed Eagleton. He sat at the desk in Ephram's room and peered at the first piece of blank paper, ink bottle set carefully to one side, pen dipped and poised.

There was a moment of silence. Forming the points of a triangle with him, Ephram and Thump stood at opposite sides of the room, shoulders straight, hands clasped behind them. They desired to record this event indelibly upon their minds; perhaps they would even write about it—this first writing-down of their experiences.

They continued to wait. Hand raised, Eagleton peered at the paper, as if words might fall upon it from his hovering pen. He was attempting to conjure a sentence deserving enough to inaugurate such a literary event. When a sentence did not present itself, he considered a simple phrase; when no worthy phrase came to mind, he attempted a single word. He shifted slightly in his seat, unable to decide between *The* and A.

He pondered the top of the page, breaking the silence and startling his friends by saying: "You know, I wish I knew what the name of our club was to be so that I might use it for a heading." He turned in his seat to look at Ephram, then Thump.

"Hmm," said Thump.

"A name," said Ephram gravely. This was a sticking point, no doubt.

"Perhaps I could simply write *the Club*," suggested Eagleton.

Ephram and Thump came over to the desk and peered hard over his shoulders at the blank piece of paper; *the Club* did not seem to answer.

"Hmm," said Thump.

"A name," said Ephram again. He shook his head.

"Perhaps, for now," said Eagleton, "I should leave it blank."

"Yes, yes," said Ephram and Thump, with such conviction that Eagleton found himself joining them. "Yes, yes, leave it blank for now. Only thing for it. Something will present itself."

38. A Message Decoded?

"WHAT DO YOU THINK OF THIS BENNING FELLOW?" asked James of his wife, when they had retired to their room at Morningside House that evening.

Mercia could smile at his choice of words—*this Benning fellow*—since she was looking away from her husband, letting her hair down at the dresser. "You mean John, dear?"

James knew what his wife was up to and he smiled himself. "Yes," he said, the word long and dry.

Mercia turned in her chair, letting her hair fall as she did—a precisely calculated movement. "He is rather taken with your only daughter, if that is what you're asking." She shook her head now, and her hair tumbled about her shoulders.

James laughed. In the lamplight, with her hair down like that, he thought that she looked twenty years old again. "So far we're on the same track," he said.

"Do you like him?" she asked, before he could.

He stood there in his stocking feet and shirtsleeves, one hand poised in the midst of loosening his tie. "I don't dislike him."

"That will be a relief to him."

"Don't you dare tell him I said so. I'm behind in this round so far, and a little fear of the old man might not be out of place."

"John Benning doesn't strike me as the fearful type . . . I'm afraid."

James grunted as he stepped into the next room in search of his pajamas. When he returned, he had them on, and he stood in the doorway, a piece of paper in his hand. "Of course, any fear I managed to invoke would be quickly dissipated by your aunt Delia. Or should I say: Cordelia's *great*-aunt Delia. There is an appropriate namesake, if ever there was one." The humor hadn't left his voice, however.

Combing her hair, Mercia gave him a raised eyebrow in the dresser's mirror. "She handled Grace very nicely, I think."

"She handled us all very nicely." He sat on the edge of their bed, tapping at the paper in his hand. "Clever, these septuagenarians."

"He's not a shy boy," said Mercia, turning to her husband with the belated answer to his question. "But then I wouldn't give him much credit with Cordelia if he were."

"No, *shy* is not a word that came to my mind."

"He's intelligent, he's well mannered, he seems to come from a nice family—if what we hear about him is true. He is very handsome. What do you have there?"

James looked down at the paper in his hand as if he had forgotten it. " 'Our Minmaneth,' " he read aloud from the piece of paper, " '*is a young goatt.*' "

"Ah, the note from Basil's chest." Mercia took the paper from him and looked at it as if something new might suddenly appear upon it. "I hadn't noticed this before," she said, pointing at a brown discoloration in the very middle of the paper.

"I was looking for invisible ink," said James, half amused at himself and half embarrassed. "You take lemon juice, you know, and write with it. Then the person receiving the note holds it up to the heat of a candle and the writing turns brown."

"Unless it disappears again, I would say that you didn't find anything."

He shook his head. Round about the middle of the day, Mercia had realized that something was troubling her husband. It meant nothing that he concealed his thoughts so carefully—that he smiled as easily, and behaved as evenly, as ever; she knew him too well. "You know," he said, "that I don't keep things from you."

"What is it, James?" She turned in her chair and placed a hand on his.

"Oh, nothing very serious, I think. Just puzzling." He shook his head again, then raised his eyes to hers. "Do you remember Mr. Stimply?"

"Why, of course. Here we are, because of him."

"Well, something odd happened last night, at the station."

"Here in Ellsworth?"

"Do you remember, I stopped to speak to an old gentleman on our way to the carriage?"

"Yes. Captain Coyle, you said."

"Basil's commanding officer during the blockade."

"I remember."

"Captain Coyle knew Charles Stimply." James said this carefully, as if laying out the boundaries of a logic problem—and, indeed, perhaps he was.

"Yes," said Mercia, when she thought she had considered this statement long enough.

"Charles Stimply sailed with Captain Coyle on his last voyage out." Again the pause, and Mercia's acknowledgment. "Charles Stimply died—"

Mercia's face fell. "Oh, no! He was such a nice old fellow! What happened to him?"

"—eight months ago." Now Mercia paused till James repeated himself. "Mr. Stimply died eight months ago."

"Eight months ago?"

"Captain Coyle buried him at sea."

"But how can that be?"

"If Captain Coyle is right, and this is the same Mr. Stimply who sailed with my brother, then the man who so nicely delivered Basil's sea chest was not who he claimed to be."

"But why . . . ?"

"Exactly! Why would he claim to be someone else if his motives were honest? And if his motives were not honest, why would he so conscientiously deliver Basil's sea chest at all? There was no fortune lying there, to be sure, but several of the items were of some value—the ivory figures, the brace of pistols."

Mercia thought back to the night of the old mariner's visit. "Mr. Stimply . . . or whoever he was, did say that Mr. Pue took charge of the chest when he tried to take it off the ship."

"There are ways around such things," said James. "He had to bring it aboard in the first place, and at some expense to himself, taking on extra personals. And why did he make such an effort to tell us about it, and that story about Basil saving his life? It might even make sense if he had expected some reward for his efforts, but he refused when I offered."

From behind drawn curtains came the muffled tap of light rain upon the windows. Mercia experienced a slight shiver. She took the shawl that she had placed on the back of her chair and pulled it over her shoulders. "He seemed so . . . right, *our* Mr. Stimply."

"I am not convinced that he wasn't, in his own way. Certainly he did us a good turn, delivering Basil's chest. The question, more than ever, is why?"

Mercia looked again at the piece of paper in her hand.

Our Minmaneth is a young goatt.

"So now you have returned to this," she said.

"It seems a difficult sentence to parse out, at first glance."

"But on the second glance?"

"The third or fourth, actually. I had a notion about it, even before I spoke with Captain Coyle. But his surprising news didn't make my speculations any more comforting."

"I've had a thought myself," said Mercia.

"I *thought* you might. What have you come up with?"

"Well, it occurred to me after you told me that this Minmaneth of yours was known for, among other things, burying treasure."

"Yes," said James, encouraging her to continue.

"A young goat, as Mr. Pue would tell you, is a kid."

"And . . . ?"

"The term *young goat* here is spelt with two *t*'s. It would seem that *kid* with two *d*'s would correspond nicely." James was nodding emphatically. "It sounds rather silly, really, but then you have *kidd* with two *d*'s, and when you connect the word *kidd* with treasure, you must think of Captain Kidd."

James slapped his thigh with satisfaction. "That is just exactly what I arrived at! And I felt just as silly."

"You mustn't feel lonely, then, for your daughter is feeling silly too."

"You told Cordelia what you were thinking?"

"No, she came up with it quite separately."

"But you see?" said James, taken by a wave of sudden enthusiasm. "This would make sense, not only of the sentence itself, but of Basil's reasons for writing such a cryptic note in the first place. So very few people have ever heard of Minmaneth, and only Basil and I ever heard our mother's stories about him. Without the notion of buried treasure the term *young goatt* gets you nowhere."

"And where does it get us?" wondered Mercia honestly.

"I'm not sure. But it puts an even darker shade to the motives of the fellow—whoever he is—that came to our house a week ago. And adds some mystery to this land Cordelia has inherited."

"I would still like to know," said Mercia, "why Mr. Pseudo-Stimply saw fit to do us a favor under a false name."

"We had better keep our eyes out," said James. " 'Peeled,' I think, is the authorial turn of phrase. No doubt it will fall out that Captain Coyle was mistaken, or that there is some simple, unremarkable explanation." James took the piece of paper again and let out a short sigh of frustration as he looked at it for the hundredth time. "My first thought may have been correct after all—that this is just a product of Basil's fevered mind."

"Well, I am just as glad that we're to be a large party. And this *Benning fellow* seems an able young man."

James gave no heed to her teasing. "Your sister, Grace, should prove a good deterrent, I think, to any rascals. And that's not to mention your aunt Delia. I'll feel safe sandwiched between them."

39. Thoughts on a Pirate

CORDELIA WOULD HAVE GONE FOR A WALK in the rain if her aunt Grace had allowed it. Priscilla, of course, was absolutely prohibited from such capricious behavior, and for Cordelia to walk alone at night in the rain was out of the question. In Priscilla's room, Cordelia sat at an open window, chin to hand, elbow to sill. The rain was fine and warm and the slight mist from it that reached her face felt soft and cooling.

She *needed* cooling, she thought. Her mind had been racing all day.

Fluttering behind Cordelia, her shadow dancing about like that of a moth in the gaslight, Priscilla made ready to leave in the morning. "Oh, I just can't believe it! It's so exciting! It's happened so fast!" she was saying over and over, with several variations and the occasional addition of: "Oh, Cordelia, we're going to have such a time!"

Cordelia's mind was occupied with other business; they were, after all, venturing out for the purpose of visiting *her* newly inherited land. She had certain convictions regarding this bequest; indeed, she was more convinced than ever that some sort of buried treasure awaited them within the precincts of her recent estate.

But to be perfectly honest, these considerations were greatly overshadowed by the sudden participation of John Benning. She had thought a great deal about Mr. Benning these last few days, and had even put herself to sleep with those late-night imaginings so conducive to pleasant dreams.

It is very well to dream, to be sure, or even to anticipate a romantic encounter when the time and place of its occurrence remain in the abstract; it is another hod of clams when that appointment is suddenly lurched into the here and now.

Cordelia considered sneaking out into the rain by herself, just to stand out on the lawn, her arms outstretched, her face lifted to the sky. She felt strangely heavy in her heart and knew that she was feeling something like fear. A sigh escaped her, and Priscilla stopped in her rotations.

"Good heavens, Cord, you sound just like my mother!"

"Do I?"

"Aren't you excited? I had hoped that you were pleased that I am going with you. Or are you less pleased now that John is coming along?"

Cordelia woke up to this accusation. "Of course not!" she exclaimed. "How could you suggest such a thing? I'm just not sure what it all means, that's all."

"Oh, you're nervous. I would be too." Priscilla took stock of her own feelings. "I *am* nervous!" she announced. "I almost laughed out loud when he winked at you."

"You did laugh out loud."

"Well, it was a quiet laugh."

"And I'm not sure what I think of being winked at."

"You *are* sounding like Mother!"

"He's so . . ."

"Handsome?"

Another sort of expression prowled Cordelia's eyes. "Yes, he is that."

"Intelligent? Witty?"

Cordelia could not deny this assessment.

"Genteel? Able to handle my mother?"

"He's very forward."

"Thank goodness! You're nervous, that's all. I am too. To go anywhere, but to make an expedition! And to have a prospective lover along! I hope you don't mind if I enjoy this romance a little bit alongside of you."

"Your chaperonage is required," said Cordelia gravely, not yet able to imagine herself alone with John Benning now that he had made his interest in her so obvious. She wondered what he might be doing, even now; no offer had been made to him for staying at the Morningside home, and he had not waited for one, curtailing any awkwardness over the question by announcing early on that he had rooms at the Ellsworth Hotel.

Cordelia thought of him perhaps thinking of her.

The afternoon and evening had been pleasant the way George Ferris's enormous amusement wheel might be pleasant if you weren't quite sure of heights; one doesn't court romance for its calming effect. After tea, John Benning had been invited to walk in the arbor behind the house; and Aunt Grace, despite Great-Aunt Delia's attempts at stalling her, advanced herself as a member of this party.

The arbor was a handsome little park of shade trees overhanging, in dual ranks, a circular footpath; and though the clouds greatly outranked clear sky that afternoon, it was refreshing to stroll aimlessly with congenial company. John Benning made himself extremely amusing to Grace, and soon she had his arm as Cordelia and Priscilla walked with them. Cordelia was almost grateful for the chance to observe him, as it were, from a distance.

Grace, despite her prim attitude and mature years, was pleased by John's attentions, but soon she insisted that she was feeling light-headed and that she must sit. A nearby bench was conscripted for this purpose and he retrieved chairs from a corner of the arbor for the two cousins.

From his place beside Aunt Grace, John Benning was able to speak to all three women while lavishing a certain sense of attention on Cordelia; and yet, he managed this so artfully that Cordelia alone was fully aware of it. While John managed Aunt Grace, Cordelia managed simply not to blush.

He had traveled a great deal, and seen much of life for a man of his years, but the tribulations of living at such a peak did not show upon his face. It was his self-deprecating humor that attracted Cordelia the most; he might have seemed too sure of himself, too forward in his desires, if not for this ability to churn the grandest of adventures into grist for the mill of comedy. And in the midst of a droll anecdote, he might turn a phrase or a word to double meaning.

Even Grace had laughed aloud as he demonstrated his attempts to survey a small island during a series of vigorous earth tremors. "Several major landmarks on the island did all but switch places," he maintained. "Before the worst of the tremors hit, my back was to the ocean; and when the ground had finished shaking my back was to the mainland."

"You had been completely turned around, Mr. Benning?" asked Grace.

"No, the island had."

"The experience seems to have shaken you, sir," said Cordelia, laughing.

"I have been shaken worse since," he answered.

Cordelia blushed even now, thinking of it.

A knock came at the door, and Ethan barely waited for his sister's "Come in" before bustling into the room with Teacup. Ethan was helping everyone to prepare for the *expedition*, as if any delay might cause the promised excursion to slip from their hands. "Can I help with anything? Can I put anything in the carriage?" he asked, keen on making himself indispensable.

Cordelia called to Teacup and lifted the dog onto her lap. "I've hardly started my packing," Priscilla was saying to her brother.

"Are you going to marry Mr. Benning?" asked Ethan frankly of Cordelia.

"I hardly know him!" exclaimed Cordelia as if the thought had never occurred to her.

"Ethan!" said Priscilla, nearly laughing.

"I think you might," said the boy. He laughed himself, pleased to have gotten a rise from both of them.

"Here," said Priscilla. "Take these bags and get away!"

"He's a nice fellow," insisted Ethan as his sister ushered him from the room. Priscilla shut the door and laughed conspiratorially at the expression on Cordelia's face.

"I hope he doesn't say something like that to your mother," said Cordelia.

"He knows better," Priscilla assured her.

Cordelia stroked Teacup's ears gently, thinking nervously of what the next few days might unfold.

"Well?" said Priscilla, and when her cousin looked up questioningly, she said: "*Are* you going to marry him?"

Cordelia threw a hairbrush at her.

40. Monstrous Rumors

NOT KNOWING WHERE COLONEL TAVERNER called home or headquarters, Mister Walton sent a telegram, regarding their sighting of *Sir* Eustace Pembleton and the *Proclamation*, to the customs agent by way of Sheriff Piper in Wiscasset, and might not have done that if not for the child on board the little steamer. "I have a suspicion," he told Sundry, "that we are not forwarding any very surprising news. The colonel has many eyes, I think, and no doubt a pair or two right here in the harbor."

All possible duty seemed done once the cable was sent, though they felt incomplete in it and the need, for the time being, of some new source of diversion. Some people are lucky in this pursuit, and Mister Walton, it seems, was one of them. Trouble is one form of diversion that follows or is followed by certain members of the race, laughter another; but the purest form of diversion must be the pursuit of *something new*—laughter and trouble sometimes being included.

Mister Walton (who had many adventures to tell of before this humble narrative commenced) understood that the surest way to experience something new is to meet some*one* new. Having sent his telegram from the service desk in the lobby of the Weymouth House, he obeyed this formula for divertisement by leading the way to the hotel's liveliest parlor.

The liveliest parlor, as it turned out, was actually a porch overlooking (if one looked over several roofs) the sunlit harbor. All adjectives are subject to relative interpretation, of course, *lively* not excepted; Mister Walton and Sundry had been in more spirited company in the past few days, but none more interesting to the student of human nature.

Some dozen or so people populated the porch, rendering but one chair for Mister Walton's occupancy and a railing for Sundry's leisure. An ancient woman held court there; her tiny wizened face nearly disappeared beneath the shade of a gigantic bonnet. "It was a very pleasant journal," she was saying. "I don't know why they ever stopped it. I still read the old numbers—I keep them at my table."

"What does she mean?" asked a thin bald fellow with large mustaches.

"It's not the paper they are talking about, Gran," shouted a young woman to the lady.

"*The Squid,*" said another person. "She's speaking of the paper they printed during the summer months—years ago it was. *The Squid* was its name."

"What are you saying?!" demanded the old woman.

"They're not talking about the paper, Gran," repeated the young woman. "They are talking about the monster that people have seen out to sea."

"Monster? I don't know about any monster!" Gran looked put out. "What conversation! We never talked about monsters in my time."

"It was a two-sheet paper," said a man with white whiskers. "I remember it. The locals called it *The Squint*. It's the *Squirrel Island Buoy* now, though not as well thought of among the older folk."

"Who's talking about monsters?" demanded Gran. "It's not proper conversation." One could see, however, that her interest was up.

"Some sort of creature has been sighted off Monhegan, Mrs. Eccles!" said the white-whiskered man in a loud tone.

"Oh?" She tucked a hand in her bonnet and cupped it behind one ear.

"A great shadow was seen in the ocean and a long appendage came out of the water and slithered onto the deck of a ship. Something like it has been reported several times in the last few weeks."

"That's all very well," replied Mrs. Eccles. "But should you be talking about it, is my point."

The young woman smiled at the assemblage apologetically; there were some quiet, if respectful, chuckles among the group, and two or three pairs of rolling eyes.

"In the interest of science, ma'am!" declared the bald man.

"Oh, science. I'm not sure that science isn't a lot of humbug. Germs and electric lights and ape men. In my day we had bad air, oil lamps, and a handful of dust—and I'm not sure that we weren't better off!"

Mister Walton, who couldn't have disagreed more, thought the ancient lady's opinion charming nonetheless. His pleasant smile caught Mrs. Eccles' attention.

"Who is this, Mary?" she asked impatiently. "You haven't introduced me."

Mister Walton rose and bowed gallantly. "I am to blame, ma'am," he said. "I have not yet introduced myself, nor my young friend here." And he proceeded to answer this deficiency.

"What is this creature they are talking about?" asked Mrs. Eccles, peering from the confines of her bonnet with rheumy eyes.

"I fear that I know no more than you do, ma'am," replied Mister Walton.

"The object sighted was estimated at twenty-five to thirty feet long," said the bald man, whose name was Hansbach. "Some think it was an enormous sea snake. Some say it was the tentacle of a giant squid."

"Good heavens!" said Mister Walton. "Is it possible?"

"There are strange things lurking with Davy Jones," said Mr. Berkeley, the white-whiskered man. One of the women shivered audibly, which encouraged him to tell of a small fishing vessel in Newfoundland that was nearly pulled under by a giant squid.

Three or four pools of conversation swirled about this topic; and several eerie legends, along with the opinions of local fishermen, were discussed. "My experience," said Mister Walton, "is that the truth, when discovered, is almost always more astonishing than the legend."

"Well said!" agreed Mr. Hansbach, and Mr. Berkeley added his support to this notion.

A woman of middle years came from inside the hotel, and she was brimming with such an air of business that she easily gained the attention of the entire group, including that of Mrs. Eccles, who held one hand to her ear and cried out "Eh?" every now and then.

"I am pleased to inform you," said this new arrival, brandishing an open copybook and a pencil, "that after some difficulties I have chartered a boat—the *Winter Harbor*—for the purposes of viewing this creature." ("Eh?" from Mrs. Eccles.) "There are only so many places available, but I am giving you the first opportunity to sign on." She raised a pair of spectacles to her eyes and peered at the group.

"I suppose the captain has guaranteed a close look at this phenomenon," said a young man at the other end of the porch. ("What did he say?" from Mrs. Eccles.)

"He has done nothing of the kind," said the woman, undisturbed by irony. "But he does know where the beast has been sighted. Any number of people have seen this creature when they weren't looking for it, so I see no reason why we shouldn't find it who are."

"Bravo!" said Mr. Berkeley with some humor. "Count me in." He raised a hand. ("Eh?" said Mrs. Eccles.)

Two or three other brave souls, including a husband and wife, asked to be included. "When do we leave?" came another query.

"Captain Pinkham believes that the direction of the tide is important. We will leave tomorrow at noon. Sir?"

This last was directed toward Mister Walton, who rose with great enthusiasm and introduced himself. "Tobias Walton, ma'am."

"Phileda McCannon, Mister Walton." She offered her hand and gave his a very firm and amiable shake.

"Your expedition sounds highly amusing," he said.

"I can count on you, then?"

"Oh, please do! And my friend here."

"Gentleman's gentleman," said Sundry, who looked anything but, lounging carelessly against the railing. ("What is that?" asked Mrs. Eccles. "Eh?")

"Really?" said Miss McCannon to Sundry with honest surprise. She penciled in Mister Walton and Sundry's names, then Mr. Berkeley's and several other people's. Some wanted no part of the adventure, and looked horror-struck with the very notion of such a "monster watch."

"You are going, aren't you?" asked Mrs. Eccles of her great-granddaughter, Miss Bishop, when all had been explained.

"Of course not, Gran," said Miss Bishop. "I wouldn't leave you."

"Well, you're going to have to leave me if you don't go," said the dowager simply. "Put us in your book, or on your list, or whatever it is," she ordered Miss McCannon.

"You're not going, surely, Mrs. Eccles!" said an astonished Mr. Berkeley.

"I certainly am!" snapped the old woman. "And Mister Walton here will hold my hand if need be, won't you, sir!"

"I would deem it an honor and a pleasure, ma'am," said Mister Walton with all sincerity.

"Oh, go away!" she said, waving a hand at him, but she looked gratified.

"Do you think this is wise, Mrs. Eccles?" wondered Mr. Hansbach.

"What? Do you think we'll see any silly monster? I daresay the chances are slim. But if we do I'll look him in the eye and we'll see who blinks first."

"There's something in that," said Mr. Berkeley, under his breath.

Book Seven

JULY 9, 1896

41. Fishing for Information

GRACE WAS APPALLED to discover that her brother-in-law had been serious about leaving on their expedition the next morning. James and Mercia and Cordelia were packed to go, of course; Aunt Delia as well; and foreseeing this possibility, Cordelia had supervised Priscilla's readiness. Ethan had his bag at the door. Grace was aghast at such precipitate behavior and staged a short and unsuccessful rebellion.

"For goodness sakes, it can't be done!" she pronounced.

"I will help you, Grace," said Mercia.

"Well, there is no help *for* it! Why didn't you tell me last night?"

"I was sure that I had," said James dryly.

"I suppose there are hotels in the middle of this wilderness," said Grace with more irony than he would have credited.

"To my knowledge, no," he said.

"And what are we to sleep in?"

"Tents and sleeping tackle await us at Millinocket. There is a flush business in the rustic amenities there. People use the town as a jumping-off spot for hunting and fishing. The lumberjacks provision there as well."

None of this sounded very promising to the decorous lady. "And food?"

"Taken care of. I wired first thing this morning that our party had increased."

Grace capitulated, but as she mounted the stairs—head erect, back stiff—it was clear that she had second thoughts about *roughing it.*

Young Ethan let out a slow whistle. It had seemed a near thing and it would be more than he could bear to miss this trip now. Priscilla and Cordelia also looked relieved.

"Please, Aunt Delia," said Mercia. "I think we'll need all the help we can get." The older woman followed her niece up the stairs to assist in Grace's packing.

All things considered, Grace did marvelously well, and they were no more than three hours behind James's timetable when they reached the station. They had missed two trains, and had to run only moderately fast to catch the third.

John Benning had been waiting for them at the station those three hours, but he greeted them happily and with admirable patience. He directed the stowing of their baggage; and Grace allowed him to find her a seat, softening slightly with his promise of protection. Cordelia thought him very funny.

The train itself helped to mollify Grace's overburdened sensibilities; the line to Bangor was as finely appointed as any in the country, and her delicate eyes were briefly soothed by the sight of finely polished brass and richly colored fabrics in the private cars.

Mutiny suffused those delicate eyes, however, when James ushered them on toward more public accommodations, and only the presence of several genteel ladies in the first-class riding coach convinced her to be seated there. The conductor spotted her as a needy customer almost immediately and let it be known amongst his subordinates that she was to be waited upon with the utmost deference.

Now, there is a great deal of difference between a person who requires assistance, or looks to be served, and one who is needy. The average person meets his or her fellow on more or less equal ground; needy individuals imagine their demands to be broadcast from a position of height, when in fact anyone coming to their aid usually views them as lacking in either intelligence or ambition—possibly both. The needy person, becoming a needy customer, is often the first to be waited upon and probably the first to be despised. Grace emanated such weary neediness; she would ask the price of an object without first scrutinizing the tag hanging from it.

"I really must have refreshment," she said before the train had started, as if the journey from Morningside House to the station had something in common with the Oregon Trail. The refreshment vendor, with his cart, was several coaches away, but the conductor sent for lemonade forthwith.

And so they were off—a jolly group on the whole.

Cordelia hid her childlike glee by turning her face to the window while the more populated section of Ellsworth fell away. By a trick of the light, however, she could see John Benning's reflection there. She watched him surreptitiously till he looked in her direction.

She was situated—by way of her aunt's careful seating arrangement— across the aisle from him, but they were facing one another, and she blushed to find him smiling at her.

"It was a lucky catch that I had on the wharf last Thursday," he said, his smile never losing its frankness, nor its appeal.

Priscilla, sitting next to Cordelia, cleared her throat, but continued to gaze innocently at the passing outskirts of the town.

"Did you catch something?" said Cordelia.

"Briefly, at any rate."

"Was it a *big* fish?"

"Not a fish, really." He glanced at Grace, sitting opposite him, but Cordelia's aunt was explaining some point of propriety to Mercia.

"Was it a cold, then?" asked Cordelia wickedly. "Did you catch a cold?"

"Not yet," he said, and the sight of a slightly raised eyebrow on that handsome face shot through her like a dart.

It was true: without being entirely shameless, she had encouraged him from the beginning. This was not a chase—or if it was, it was a mutual one. Cordelia possessed a mischievous wit, which was generally couched in a dry delivery. Once, when she had frightened off a prospective suitor with her droll repartee, her father had termed her *a saber rattler,* and she had thought briefly of letting her blade dull a little.

Some things are not to be changed, however, and Cordelia was one of them. She was rather glad now, for there is nothing more joyful to a good fencer than a worthy opponent.

"Well, you best be cautious," she said. "Especially if you're used to climates that are too warm. It can be chilly where we are going." Her eyes belied her words, for there were deep pools of laughter there.

"As I say," replied John Benning, "I'm used to roughing it. Quite relish it, actually."

"But you must be careful, Mr. Benning," said Aunt Grace, who had caught the tail end of this conversation. She was so forward as to touch the young man's arm. "Cordelia is right. It is easy to imagine that one place is as congenial as another, but I know from my reading that it is not so. You will think me rough around the edges, I am sure, but I have read Stanley's adventures—well, there were parts I did pass over—but I was impressed with how unlike two places can be. Boston and Ellsworth are much the same by comparison." A man arrived with her lemonade at this point and she accepted it with stately poise.

"I don't think you rough at all, Mrs. Morningside," said John Benning. "But only braver than some."

This was a new sort of compliment for Grace, but she was thoroughly pleased with it. "You are very kind," she replied. "It was a volume in my late husband's library, that's all."

Cordelia thought there was something very pretty about her aunt, just then, and imagined that John Benning saw it as well. He smiled winningly, first at the aunt, then at Cordelia.

Feeling a renewed streak of mischief coursing through her, Cordelia matched his smile. "I understand there is good fishing in the lakes around Millinocket, Mr. Benning."

"Yes," he replied. "But the water may be too cold for bathing," referring to her near-dunking off the Custom House Wharf.

Priscilla went into a sudden coughing fit that Grace concluded was brought on by leaving the house without a hat the night before.

James, who with Ethan and Aunt Delia sat a row away from the rest of the party, lowered his paper and exchanged an amused glance with his wife. "I'm not sure that we'll have time for either fishing or bathing," he said before disappearing again behind the newsprint.

Cordelia caught a glimpse of her father's eye and found herself blushing again; yet she was not finished—this new reference to the incident on the wharf brought to mind the lovely woman who had been John Benning's companion that day. The unnamed beauty had haunted Cordelia's natural optimism this past week whenever an opportunity to daydream about John had presented itself. Cordelia was not interested in vying for a man's affection, and having set this standard for herself, she half-dreaded venturing into this territory.

For it came to this: she liked John Benning more than a little. It did not harm his outlook that he was handsome, but Mr. Benning had other, more complex qualities that superseded (in her heart, if not in her eyes) his mere outward appearance. He had, to begin with, a definite *panache* about him without a jot of the foppishness that often accompanies such a degree of style and elegance. There was indeed something of the reckless about him, happily leavened with a strong measure of wit and humor.

He was perhaps attracted to similar traits in her, and certainly she covered her apprehension concerning his beautiful companion with a degree of boldness and wit. "I am sorry that I didn't have the chance to meet your . . . friend the other day," she said, and gave him a look that was particularly blunt. *Give the wrong reply*, her expression seemed to say, *and you might just as well get off at the next stop.*

It is fortunate that human ears do not independently cock toward interesting sounds, or those people in the immediate vicinity would have looked much like a kennel when the fox horn is blown.

"Ann, you mean?" said John Benning, once he had translated the message in Cordelia's eyes.

"I suppose, yes," said Cordelia, inwardly flinching at his use of another woman's Christian name. "Is that her name?"

"Ann—well, she's more than a friend, actually." John Benning's own expression was absolutely unreadable; he did not blink, but regarded her with a sort of steady candor.

Cordelia's mouth felt dry suddenly and there was an involuntary hesitation to her response. "Oh?" She hated how the word sounded, weak in the air.

Recklessness and humor: his expression was challenging, then suddenly droll. "Yes, she is my cousin."

Cordelia did not miss a beat now. "Well, I hope I have the opportunity to meet her someday."

"I hope you do, Miss Underwood," said he, his expression conspiratorial.

Cordelia found herself laughing quietly to herself. They had left Ellsworth behind, and Priscilla was doing her best to appear interested in the treeless countryside. They dared not look at one another. Cordelia reached for the bag that she had brought on board with her, and took from it the copy of *Tristram Shandy* that she had been reading.

And conversation ebbed for a while as they trundled northwest.

42. Briefly with the Club

"IT HAS BEEN A WEEK, THUMP," said Eagleton to his friend, who sat to his right at breakfast that morning. "Do you realize that it has been a week?" he said to Ephram, who sat to his left.

"A week?" said both men, more or less in unison.

"Well, a full week come this evening." Light dawned gradually upon the faces of Ephram and Thump as Eagleton spoke. "It was one week ago today, Thursday the 2nd of July, 1896, that our esteemed friend first conceived the notion of . . . our club."

"Hear, hear," said Ephram as if he were apprised of this intelligence for the first time. Thump appeared manfully embarrassed.

"Of course," continued Eagleton, "we have, as yet, no name for our order."

"True, true," replied Ephram.

"And we have not, as yet, gleaned a purpose for which this . . . club . . . might exist."

"Exactly so!"

"It seems we will not meet, as planned, upon the appointed spot—"

"No."

"—nor upon the appointed hour."

"To be sure."

"And we have no idea as to the whereabouts of our chairman, nor he that he *is* our chairman."

Ephram made no reply to this thought; it was singular, how unlike a club they were.

"I foresee great things!" declared Eagleton, undaunted—or perhaps incognizant—of the paradox he had so carefully proved.

"Hear, hear!" said Ephram with renewed vigor. Thump, oddly quiet throughout this discourse, cleared his throat—a sound meant to indicate concurrence with his fellows.

They were greatly affected by this conversation—Ephram, Eagleton, and Thump—and rising from the breakfast table, they did not say a word amongst themselves till they had reached Damariscotta's Main Street.

"I hesitate to say it," said Ephram hesitantly, "but there *is* a certain indeterminacy regarding our organization."

"It is true," agreed Eagleton.

They stood upon the sidewalk for some minutes, looking exceedingly indeterminate, and would have stood there longer, no doubt, if not for the rousing nature of Thump's vision.

"There is nothing to do but wait," he said. "There is no accomplishment to be had but mindful observation." He had read this pronouncement in *The Sister He Never Knew* by Mrs. Liliva Albright, and never had a borrowed phrase seemed to him so apropos. Eagleton was so moved he had tears in his eyes and was forced to march ahead of his friends to save himself embarrassment.

Despite Thump's brave words, one thought marred the tenor of the moment. "Oh, would that Mister Walton were here to advise us!" said Ephram gravely.

"Without the head," said Thump, "the body must act through instinct!"

"Good heavens, Thump!" said Ephram. "You are right!"

"We must make our chairman proud!" continued the man, his beard thrust forward, one finger in the air. They were striding now with observable purpose. "We must uphold the tradition!" he declared.

Eagleton brought them to a halt once again. "Is there a tradition?"

"There will be," said Thump, and hearing him say it with such conviction, they had faith that it would be so.

The three friends had already explored Damariscotta's Main Street to the minutest detail, so they retraced their steps slightly and climbed Elm

Street on the other side of the Lincoln Hall. They passed through the shade of the titular trees and admired the handsome homes on either side till they came to the house of Mr. Springer, who was out by the street painting his fence.

"We have been hearing about the Damariscotta Indians," said Eagleton, shrewdly altering the focus of their immediate thoughts.

"I have never heard of them," said Mr. Springer.

"Really!" said Ephram. He couldn't imagine a man living in Damariscotta and not hearing about the tribe that gave the town its name.

"They had a great sense of humor," informed Eagleton.

"Clearly someone does," said Mr. Springer.

"You missed a spot there," said Eagleton amiably, and they were content to stand and watch Mr. Springer paint for the better part of half an hour.

43. Cordial Mayhem

No place in the state of Maine was ever so tangled in contradiction as the city of Bangor. Incorporated in 1791, it had become by the mid-nineteenth century the major crossroad between the state's two great livelihoods, the sea and the forest; great trees were felled to the north and west, and within the city's precincts they were fashioned into some of the finest vessels the world has ever seen. Set upon the western slopes of the Penobscot, Bangor had the feel of an inland town, with the great woods nearby, and yet deep-water anchorage was only twenty-three miles away.

The river itself could seem like a forest for all the vessels anchored within sight of the city limits. Walking along the river after church one Sunday morning in 1883, Jobadiah Lincoln, vice-president of the railroad, and his family counted more than seven hundred masts.

Bangor was second to none, in Maine or anywhere else, for pure wild, caterwauling, fist-sweeping, rapid-riding, hard-swigging, swing-'em-from-the-yardarm-till-they-cry-uncle, and watch-out-you're-in-the-wrong-part-of-town! Great fortunes were made between the ship and the shore, and the private mansions and public buildings of the city were designed by some of the country's greatest architects; but from their third-story windows one could view the *Devil's Half-Acre*, a cauldron of dark taverns, grog shops, larcenous flophouses, and brothels exuberant with business.

There were merchants and tradesmen as well, of course, and their families; and churches, filled to the choir lofts of a Sabbath morning.

Bangor is said to have been named by accident. When the Reverend Seth Noble was registering the town in Boston, back in 1791, he was humming a hymn by that title, and thinking the clerk had asked him what song it was (when the man had actually asked the name of the town), the Reverend Mr. Noble said: "Bangor."

"If it didn't happen that way, it should have," said John Benning, having told this story to his fellow travelers. They had just made a stop at Ellsworth Falls, and Green Lake was sparkling to their right.

"Imagine if he had been humming the 'Hallelujah' Chorus!" said Cordelia.

"Here we are," said James, who was scanning his newspaper. "Do you remember that row at the Fourth of July picnic?"

"The one the parachutist landed in the middle of?" asked Cordelia.

"You should not end your sentences with a preposition, dear," instructed Grace. "And I am not sure that a *row* is a proper subject for polite conversation. Don't you agree, Mr. Benning."

"Well, Mrs. Morningside," replied the man, "a row of itself *might* be a proper subject, but I understand that this one was between two politicians."

James chuckled from behind his paper, though if his humor was the result of the written account of the epic battle, or Mr. Benning's reply, there was no telling. Mr. Benning, for his part, gave no indication that he had been signally responsible for the great Blithewaite–Van Smooten bout.

"Don't worry, Grace," said James. "It says here that *'the combatants maintained a dangerous distance from one another; dangerous, that is, to the crowd at least, for they were never closer than ten feet till the parachute caused them to disappear from sight altogether.'* "

"I wish we had been closer to it," said Cordelia. Quite innocently she turned to John Benning and asked him: "Did you see the fight?"

"Well, yes," he said, carefully. "I did happen to be there."

"I would have paid good money to see two politicians in the ring," came a familiar, though unexpected, voice. A balding head and a white beard emerged from behind the back of a seat several rows down from the Underwoods' party.

"Mr. Tolly!" said Cordelia, and indeed it was the same fellow who had beguiled their trip to Rockland with his story of the Christmas bear.

"At your service, ma'am," said Isherwood Tolly.

Grace peered at the man to see if they should be talking to him.

"What a pleasant surprise!" said Mercia. "Are you going to Bangor?"

"Yes, ma'am. Visiting my sister. I lived there once."

"I don't suppose politicians have fistfights in Bangor, Mr. Tolly," said James.

"Not the politicians, no; but I've seen some terrific jams in my time." James winked at his daughter, for like an expert angler he knew that he had used the right bait. "I saw, in my youth," reminisced Mr. Tolly, "the awfulest, sockingest, most thunderous, hair-singeing, eye-popping fight since Hercules tackled Atlas. I don't know but what it was the most extreme sort of powder-up since the history of man first said: 'What day is it?'! And there was I, barely big enough to straddle a cat and ringside for the whole event."

The *clackety-clack* of the rails sounded loud in the silence that waited for Mr. Tolly's story. Grace looked as if he had offered to personally explain to her the fine art of mule skinning—which, perhaps, he could have done. She was quite dumbstruck, and Cordelia wondered briefly if she had been frightened more by the subject of his discourse or by the grammatical genius with which he presented it.

"What happened?" asked Aunt Delia.

Mr. Tolly swung himself around so that his feet were in the aisle. He hung on the back of his seat with one arm and fished in his pocket for a pipe. "Well," he said. "It came about like this. . . .

"I was eight years old and my father ran a supply store by the waterfront. We weren't in the Half-Acre, but we were close enough so that you could smell a blast of rum every time someone opened a tavern door, and hear the revels at night like a great engine of destruction. We went to church twice a week, and I credit my survival to it." Mr. Tolly was searching for a light, and James obliged him with a pocket box of lucifers.

"There was a timber man in those days," continued Mr. Tolly, once he had fired up his pipe and drawn several satisfying puffs from it, "Daniel Hector Oakenspill was his name, and he wasn't the tallest jack and he wasn't the broadest, but somehow he was the biggest man I had ever seen, except for one. He rode those logs like his hair was on fire, and blasted into town like a spring flood whenever a drive came through.

"He patronized my father's supply store, however, and he always doffed his cap and spoke like a deacon to my mother. He knew my name and once gave me a baby crow called Applewood. But there was a wild look in his eye, and when he walked the floorboards cracked and the candy jars rattled. My mother assured me that I wasn't to speak to him outside the store.

"There were many establishments on the hard side of town, you see, courting many purposes, and his exploits in them all were legend. At eight years old I couldn't be expected to understand everything I heard about Dan Oak, as he was known, but it was clear just to hear his voice—like a tree falling—that he was the most drastic sort of man that ever set foot on shore—except for one."

Mr. Tolly's pipe fumed like a steam engine as he drew on it, the smoke catching in the breeze of an open window. He savored the pipe stem for a moment; then he said: "Now, as you have probably guessed, there was another man in those days—a seaman, Henry Goliath Stormthrew, and he was no taller than Daniel and no broader, but he was the other biggest man I had ever seen. He sailed the *Thinks-I-to-Myself*, which had been built at Bangor, taken by the British in 1813, and salvaged off the coast of Africa by a merchant-adventurer by the name of Ernest Polyscope. But that's another story.

"That ship ran the lumber line for more years than anyone could remember, and Hank Storm, as he was known, would come in on her like he was singlehandedly filling the sails, and once she dropped anchor, he'd tear through town like an unexpected nor'easter!

"He plied his custom at my father's store as well, and held his hat in his hand and spoke as softly as he could to the ladies. He had a voice like the crash of the surf, but he always called me Ish, and gave me a macaw once, named Mr. Feldspar, that he had bought in South America. He had the look of a barely controlled tornado, and if he moved too quickly the windows shivered and the pages of my father's ledger book fluttered out of place. He was not to be spoken to outside the store as well.

"For, you see, he cut a swath through the dark end of town like an act of violent weather, and they said that the fallen sort of women (pardon me for mentioning them) flocked to him with as much sense as moths to a flame. I couldn't be expected to know what that meant, all those years ago, but there was no mistaking him for anything but the other most drastic sort of man that ever put one foot ahead of the first."

Mr. Tolly couldn't have set up an entire war with more promise. The range of his voice went beyond the Underwoods' party and the entire car fairly rang with keening ears. True to his craft, he found it expedient just then to pause in his story. His mouth was dry, it seemed, and a young man who hadn't even been introduced to the speaker ran off in search of the lemonade cart.

Mr. Tolly was much obliged when the reviving draft arrived, and he smacked his lips with such vigor that a general thirst was realized throughout the car. The man with the lemonade cart, sensing a windfall business, appeared, and a picniclike atmosphere ensued that was very agreeable.

"So, Mr. Tolly," said James, "when did these two upheavals meet one another? I am supposing that they did."

"Yes, sir; but it wasn't at my father's store, and it wasn't in the Devil's Half-Acre. Strange as it sounds, in all the years they frequented those places, they had never so much as laid eyes on one another. More than once they had torn through town at the same time, but like similar magnets they kept apart. Some believed that they hadn't the slightest *notion* of one another's existence, and no one was very anxious to introduce them.

"They were like two natural forces, you understand, and the thought of them simply shaking hands caused otherwise stout men to shiver. It was pretty well agreed upon in the town of Bangor, when I was young, that putting Dan and Hank within reach of one other would more than double the danger—one might just as well introduce fire to oil, or water to electricity.

"Now, it is a verifiable actuality that any two men can talk politely and even become friends, given the chance; but put them in different uniforms, or train them in the use of different tools or philosophies or shaving soap, and you will have two men who are sure that the other lives primarily to contradict him. I did know a fellow once who insisted that reasonable men can disagree, but somebody knocked him cold with a cast-iron frying pan just then and I never did hear the remainder of his hypothesis.

"Differences ought to complement one another, of course, there being no better example than those lumberjacks and sailors who regularly dismantled each other whenever their paths crossed in the streets and taverns of the Half-Acre. It never occurred to them, I suppose, that the seaman needed the woodsman to bring the forest to them, and that the woodsman needed the seaman to take their forest all over the world. They had the most fantastic dust-ups whenever they met in the dim quarter of town, and the newspapers tallied the ongoing toll like baseball scores.

"But Henry Goliath Stormthrew and Daniel Hector Oakenspill never came face to face till one sunny afternoon on State Street—and I was there, almost responsible for it."

Mr. Tolly looked hungry at this point: an inward sort of expression apprehended him, as if he were taking a mental inventory of his physical condition, and the resulting information told upon his face with great eloquence. (It was either that or his stomach grumbling.) Clearly it required a certain amount of energy to recall the memories and he was in need of sustenance if he were to continue. Several hampers were cracked toward this end, and Mr. Tolly found himself regaled with any number of sandwiches and cold chickens and large helpings of sweet pastry. Everyone else followed his example, though it was early for the midday meal, and the sense of a picnic outing increased.

"Is there a woman involved in your story?" wondered John Benning. He, like everyone else, did not want to encourage Mr. Tolly to speak with his mouth full, but neither did he want the man to reach his destination before he finished.

"There is, sir," said Mr. Tolly in reply. "Though in a wholly innocent manner."

"You surprise me, sir," said James, who felt safe saying this out of reach of his wife's foot.

"She was my cousin," said Mr. Tolly.

"Ah, well then. One's cousins are often wholly innocent—especially the female ones."

"Ursula Dupré was her name; she was the daughter of my mother's sister and had come to stay with us during the summer months. A flaxen-haired beauty, my friends! Yet her eyes were brown! I quite loved her from the start. She was tall and lithe, and my father called her Sunflower. I cannot describe her further," said Mr. Tolly, almost with tears in his eyes. "She was too beautiful to me. She was eighteen that summer and absolutely bursting, though equally unaware of it in a dignified sort of way."

"Good heavens!" said Grace. "Whatever can he mean?"

Cordelia and Priscilla were each wondering if they were ever bursting in such a consummate manner. Cordelia had often thought that she *would* burst.

"It was the second day of July, and I was eight years old, when my mother sent me with Ursula to buy me some Sunday best, as I had outgrown my nicest shirt and trousers. Bangor hadn't reached its bustling height in that day, but the dirt streets and wooden sidewalks were charged with business, and dust was in the air from the traffic.

"We didn't do up the Fourth like they do these days, but we knew what it was about, and flags were flying from the storefronts and from the top of the courthouse. There was something of a festive air wherever we went, but I'm not so sure that Ursula didn't bring it with her, she was that charming, and everyone—man, woman, and child—smiled at us, and nodded, or doffed their hats, and every man took a sidelong glance as we passed them.

"We were on our way home, after a successful foray, with my new toggery wrapped in paper bundles and tucked up under my arm. With my other hand I held Ursula's, and I was not a little proud of the fact, basking in a sort of reflected glory, I suppose."

The train came to a whistling stop during this portion of the story and several listeners looked about apprehensively, for fear that this might represent their destination—a terrible fate in the middle of Mr. Tolly's tale. If any one of them had planned to debark, however, no one did so, though several people joined them and had to be shushed to silence.

"A solitary gust of wind," said Mr. Tolly as the train recommenced its journey, "can be a charmed thing, or a cursed one, or simply mischievous—but knowing where the wind blows is not a little talent, and had we a single inkling of an impish sprite of a breeze suddenly bold with the chance of chasing a hat from off a pretty head, we might have taken another way home."

"The wind blew her hat from her head, Mr. Tolly?" asked Cordelia.

"Yes, indeed. Without warning and without hesitation that breeze saw its opportunity and lifted her hat—a pretty little straw topper with a blue ribbon—off her head and into the street.

"I was on my way to retrieve it before it ever hit the ground; but Ursula was not the sort to stand on gallantry and held me back so that she could fetch it herself. She needn't have bothered, however, for I froze in my steps at the sight before me. The two biggest men I had ever known were closing in on that hat with identical purpose.

"It was ironic, really—Hank Storm, the sailor, was striding from the shore side of town, and Dan Oak, the lumberjack, was tramping from the river. They arrived at the hat like mirror images of one another, bending to pick it up and just checking themselves short of bumping heads. They straightened to their full heights then, and except for the color of their hair and the cast of their features and the cut of their clothes they were almost twins. It was an awful thing to see. Ursula stopped in the middle of the street, as struck by the sight of those two as I was—as anyone would be.

" 'Pardon me,' they said in unison—the words polite, but the tone in their voices like dire warning.

" 'Please, don't bother yourselves,' said Ursula, the way someone might speak at a church social. It was then, unfortunately, that those two men took a glance at the owner of the hat, and the fate of that day was sealed as tight as an acorn.

" 'You will forgive me, I am sure,' said Daniel Hector Oakenspill to Henry Goliath Stormthrew. 'I was just preparing to retrieve this hat for the young lady.' He spoke as quietly as he was able, and still you could feel the words vibrating beneath your feet.

" 'You will excuse me, I have no doubt,' returned Henry Goliath Stormthrew to Daniel Hector Oakenspill. 'But I myself was on the verge of fulfilling the very same duty.' He spoke in as soft a voice as he could, but the air hummed with his speech. A man observing the scene from the other side of the street groaned, it was such a horrible thing to watch.

" 'When I restore the hat to her,' said Dan Oak, 'I will certainly express your worthy intentions.'

" 'That is quite unnecessary,' returned Hank Storm. 'But I will assuredly explain to her, once I have given back her hat, how commendable were your designs.'

"With each new courtesy onlookers grew more terrified. Dan and

Hank stood stock-still, leaning toward one another like two trees, or two masts, in a self-contradicting breeze.

" 'I fear you misunderstand me,' said Dan, 'though I am sure it is due to my own poor elocution.' Someone standing beside me fainted dead away at this.

" 'I am almost certain,' answered Hank, 'that my poor rendition of the language has caused a misapprehension on your part.' The sound of someone running in pure terror caught my ear from behind. I myself was rooted to the spot and had not even the sense to pull Ursula from harm's way.

"Ursula alone was unshaken; she stepped between the two men and fetched her hat for herself. 'Gentlemen,' she said, and unhurriedly returned to the sidewalk. 'Isherwood,' she said, and tugged at my elbow as she passed by.

"Now I would have been relieved to think that was that," said Mr. Tolly. "But before I had taken two steps I was unnerved by some of the most frightening words I have ever laid an ear to.

" 'I am powerfully sorry to inform you,' said Hank to Dan, 'that this conversation, however pleasant it may have been, has impeded the realization of my purpose.'

" 'I can hardly explain the pain it gives me,' said Dan, 'to apprise you that our discourse, which otherwise has been thoroughly diverting, has managed to obstruct the futherance of my objective.'

"Their foreheads nearly touched, they were leaning toward each other so, and their smiles were so absolutely congenial that my face hurt to watch them. No one who was there that day could ever say who moved first—we were all so mightily transfixed by those handsome smiles. Ursula was just telling me to come along when it happened—a thunderclap, an explosion, a rush of displaced air—and when the dust cleared Dan Oak and Hank Storm were twenty yards apart, each at the end of his own skid marks, which had deepened at their extremities into three-foot trenches.

"Every other citizen within a hundred yards was on his or her back, except for Ursula, who looked as if a month of rain couldn't have made her angrier. I straightened myself onto my seat (pardon my mentioning it) in time to see what looked like two locomotives charging one another in the middle of the street.

" 'I am so sorry!' shouted Hank and he caught Dan on the chin with such a whack that the lumberman pirouetted on his toes and swung back around.

"Hardly fazed, Dan bellowed: 'I am sure you'll forgive me!' and took

Hank such a slam to the chest that the sailor somersaulted in the air and landed on his feet.

"Then, expressing further niceties, Hank picked Dan off the ground and drove him head first a good eight or nine inches into the street. (We measured the holes later.) Not one to be outdone when it came to common courtesy, Dan righted himself and, with a very polite turn of phrase that I can't recall just now, rendered the same treatment onto Hank.

"They continued to speak very highly of one another as they stood toe to toe and traded such blows that people in three counties thought a thunderstorm was on its way. Twice they found themselves worked into self-manufactured pits and were considerate in helping each other out so that they could begin again. They scratched so much dust in the air in one spot that they uncovered bedrock, and for three-quarters of an hour or so found this a congenial place upon which to throw one another.

"You can imagine that we scrambled out of the way pretty quickly, hurrying behind a blacksmith's shop, which did little good, since they knocked that structure down. If anything, their cordialities toward each other increased once they discovered the hammer and anvils under the debris. You have never heard such ringing in your life.

"In all, before mid-afternoon, they had partially or completely leveled seventeen buildings and rerouted one major thoroughfare. The dust and sand raised by their activity hung over the town like a dense fog and darkened the sky like an eclipse of the sun. Ursula dragged me home in a great huff and swore she would marry the next single Quaker fellow she laid eyes on, which is exactly what she did one week later, and moved off with him to Oregon, to my everlasting childhood sorrow.

"Things were far from over, however, for neither Dan nor Hank were run out of pleasantries, and by evening they almost had tears in their eyes, they were so fond of one another.

"Now, it was an odd business; people would be certain that Hank was getting the upper hand and they'd realize then that the battle had fallen closer to the river. Then it would seem that Dan was come ahead and someone would mention that the scrape had tumbled near the forest. The noise had grown deafening, and just about the time they had reached Humboldt's Livery Stable and were batting at each other with a pair of wagons, a town meeting was held to decide what could be done.

"A worse situation was narrowly avoided, for those who made their living from the woods had one idea of what was to be done, and those whose calling was the sea had another. The only thing that kept that discussion on track was the awful noise of that battle raging just a few streets away.

My father was there, and he said that every once in a while someone would have to leave because word would arrive that their store had been demolished or their house had been knocked down.

"Forester, seaman, or indifferent—it was plain that something had to be done, and quickly. Finally a plan was decided upon, and the assembly proposed to somehow lead the two combatants to a nearby gunpowder mill, lay down a good amount of fuse, and blow the two of them to kingdom come.

"And just as the unanimous *ayes* died away, it was realized that none of them could hear the sound of battle anymore. Holding handkerchiefs before their faces as they waded through the dust-filled air, holding lanterns that scarcely cut through the murk, they left the town hall and followed the trail of debris and litter to the very gates of the Devil's Half-Acre.

"There they lay, side by side, Dan facing inland, Hank facing toward the sea. They were not dead, but they were dead to the world—exhaustified, said one man, positively exhaustified. Those two giants were as fervent about unconsciousness as they were about fighting and good manners; they were out cold, done in, mutually untethered from the waking world. But nobody imagined this to be anything but a temporary state of affairs. Something still had to be done.

"My mother appeared just then, squinting through the dust. 'I hope they'll be pleased!' she said. 'Ursula is going to leave us the first chance she gets! Why don't you bury the both of them right where they lay!' When she was told they weren't yet dead, she said she didn't much care. Talk went around about what to do with the two men, and when someone mentioned how Hank seemed to thrive the nearer he got to the water and how Dan waxed strong the closer he got to the forest, my mother suggested that they switch places.

"Why, it was a stroke of sagacity! The men stood around and scratched their heads, they were so puzzled why they hadn't thought of it themselves. Water was to Hank and the woods were to Dan what hair was to Samson! What better way of spiking both these cannons by depriving them of their natural elements?

"And so, while still insensate, Hank was loaded onto the back of a buckboard and driven inland to a lumber camp in one of the territories; Dan was taken aboard a schooner and sailed out with the tide. It was melancholy really, each of them sentenced to prison of a sort, for neither of them ever came back—they were that weakened by their imposed conditions. Oh, they continued to do great things, for sure—especially when Dan was docked upon some forested island, or Hank brought logs down the Penobscot—but there were never such stories about them. I never saw either of them again, but I remember both of them as being extremely polite."

It is not a long journey from Ellsworth to Bangor, even with the occasional stop at small stations in between; it is shorter still when such a story speeds the way. Mr. Tolly finished his tale just as the outskirts of Bangor came in sight. People began to rouse themselves, as if from a dream. Hampers were packed and linen put away; the lemonade man had left to restock his cart; James folded his forgotten newspaper.

"Good heavens!" said Grace several times. She was looking very pale, and since her daughter's hand was not close enough to pat protectively, she patted her own. "Good heavens!"

"So she married a Quaker," said Aunt Delia, as if that were an exotic turn of events. "Not that it mattered to them."

"You are quite right, ma'am," said Mr. Tolly. "It is my experience, nine times out of ten, when fists fly, the cause has long since flown. It wasn't Ursula, and it wasn't her hat—those two sized each other up and their altercation was as sure as sailors' grog. But they were a polite pair of ruffians, and it was often remarked upon afterwards."

The engine ahead of them sent out a shrill whistle as they neared the platform on the east side of Bangor; the rhythm of the rails began to slow.

"What happened to Applewood and Mr. Feldspar, Mr. Tolly?" asked Cordelia.

"*Miss* Feldspar, as it turned out. For a macaw and a crow they got on exceedingly well. They flew off together one day and raised a batch of macrows. I never saw them again."

Cordelia had been here before with Mr. Tolly. "If you never saw them again, Mr. Tolly," she asked, "how is it that you know what they raised?"

"They still write," said Isherwood Tolly. He fished through his pockets, frowning with thought. "Got something from them just the other day. Now where is that . . . ?"

44. The Kraken Speaks

"Well, sir," said Mister Walton to Captain Pinkham. "I had a very odd dream last night, but I never dreamed that I would be steaming out to sea in search of a nautical monster."

"No man knows the day until the sun goes down," said the captain, a pipe clenched fiercely between his teeth. He was a husky sort of man, though no taller than Mister Walton, with spectacles that he squinted through and the slightest hint of stubble upon his face. His pipe seldom left his mouth, and when he spoke, he seemed to snarl around it, giving him the air of a practiced curmudgeon, though to the observant a glint of humor never left his eyes.

At fifty-five feet, Captain Pinkham's boat, the *Winter Harbor*, was longer than the vessel that Sundry and Mister Walton had seen earlier in the day, but still small in the way of steam-driven craft. Despite a healthy degree of skepticism regarding their mission, Mister Walton could not help but wonder if a larger boat might be more suitable for chasing sea serpents. He left the thought for others to voice aloud, however; and when someone did, Captain Pinkham had an answer.

"You're safer from these creatures in a small vessel, sir," he said. "Big boats just make them ugly."

"They must object to anything that challenges their extraordinary size," said Mister Walton, following the captain's logic.

"They are that jealous, sir," agreed the captain.

"What is he saying?" shouted Mrs. Eccles, who was being carried past them—chair and all—into the pilot house. The thrum of the steam engine, small as it was, did nothing to aid her in her deafness. This procession stopped briefly since the elderly woman insisted upon it by whacking one of her porters on the top of the head. "What is she saying?" she demanded of her great-granddaughter

"I didn't hear, Gran," said Miss Bishop. "He wasn't speaking to us."

"He was talking aloud, wasn't he?"

"The captain says," said Mr. Berkeley, "that these creatures are less apt to disturb a small vessel."

"Good heavens!" snapped the elderly woman. "Let's all row out in a dory, then!"

Mister Walton thought he heard a short laugh from the captain, who followed the woman's entourage inside. Other passengers began to drift down the wharf in small groups, and Miss McCannon, who had instigated the excursion, was counting off members of the party as they came on board. There seemed a round score of them altogether, counting the captain and his two crew members, and it occurred to Mister Walton that the lot of them defied the capacity of the *Winter Harbor*'s single lifeboat.

They set off just before the tide began to turn, and Captain Pinkham gave a couple of jaunty toots with his steam whistle to add to the excitement of their departure. Nobody (including Miss McCannon) really believed that there was any likelihood of seeing a sea serpent, but this did nothing to dispel an air of adventure from the outing. Most of them stood at the railing and waved to people on the docks and along the shore. The boat weaved its way among the anchored vessels and passed several craft coming in before it broke free from the constraints of the harbor.

It was half past twelve. A breeze met them as they steamed out, and Mister Walton reveled in the bracing air, his nose keen to the tang of salt. The sea was moderate and the boat pitched only slightly, but Sundry was not so familiar with the roll of the waves, no matter how gentle, and his employer was quick to notice the telltale signs of distress on the young man's face.

"Dear me," said Mister Walton. "We must get you something to nibble on. It's the only thing for it." Miss McCannon, fortunately, had foreseen such a problem and was already passing pilot crackers out to the more discomforted among them. Sundry seemed unsure of this tactic, but his trust in Mister Walton's judgment, not to mention Miss McCannon's insistence, won out. The effects were laudatory if not complete, and Sundry's face turned from a jaundiced yellow to a pale white.

As it turned out, he soon had the added pressure of being in the company of an attractive young woman, and though his complexion belied the attempt, he did his best to appear unconcerned with the movement of the boat. Miss Bishop joined them at the rail, reminding Mister Walton (on the orders of her great-grandmother) that he had promised to hold the elderly woman's hand if the need arose. Good-naturedly Mister Walton went inside the pilot house to fulfill this office; Mrs. Eccles sat majestically in the small room, her chair steadied by her two young attendants.

"What a lot of folderol!" she said when Mister Walton entered, but it was clear that she was enjoying herself. "Who is that young man with you?"

"A friend of mine, traveling with me," said Mister Walton.

"Yes, I guessed that, didn't I? I like him, though. He's not too handsome and he stands straight. I would like my great-granddaughter to marry someone who isn't too handsome. Her father was very good-looking and he slouched, and I was never very fond of him. He used to look at himself in the mirror, and he denied cheating at solitaire."

"Did he cheat at solitaire, then?" wondered Mister Walton cautiously.

"Of course he did! Everyone cheats at solitaire! Denying it, though, indicates a lack of character. Do you cheat at solitaire?"

"Well," said Mister Walton, chuckling heartily. "I have flipped an extra card now and then. It seems so much trouble to reshuffle the deck."

"There! Do you see? *You* have character."

"It's very kind of you to say so. I shall remember your rule."

Mrs. Eccles waved a hand impatiently. "Folderol!" she said.

They watched the two young people talking, and Mister Walton felt sympathy for Sundry, who was doing his best to ignore his seasickness. The young woman, for her part, looked as comfortable as she would on firm ground, but when Miss McCannon made the rounds with her crackers again, Miss Bishop gamely took one so that Sundry might feel less embarrassed in doing the same. They nibbled at their crackers, talking quietly—the wind blowing in their hair. Watching Miss Bishop, Mister Walton might have been recalling another young lady, known in his own youth, for he sighed deeply and turned to look out the pilot's window. It was not long before Mrs. Eccles was snoring loud enough to be heard above the engine noise.

The mainland diminished as islands rose out of the earth's curvature into crags of granite and scrub pine and brave houses standing against the weather. The mood of the ocean, which was almost playful after two days of storm, grew plain as the mainland disappeared from their port side. Captain Pinkham pointed to the east, where the last remnants of the morning's rain curtained a portion of the horizon in a dusty gray.

"Where is this prime site for spotting monsters?" wondered Mister Walton to the captain.

"Between Seguin and Southport, at the Black Rocks," came the reply over the engine noise.

"A descriptive name."

"They are not much to look at, it's true. There is one rock that only shows at low tide, or near it, which is why it was best to come this afternoon."

"And this is where our sea serpent lives?"

"It is where *I* saw him last."

Mister Walton mouthed an O in silence, eyes wide with surprise; then he caught what he thought to be a quick wink from the captain. Amused, and not a little bemused, he waited for the captain to tell his story in his own time.

Coastal lands are, on the whole, more mysterious than other places; the sea and the weather conspire to erase the works of man, so that the origins of words and phrases, as well as physical structures, quickly disappear with succeeding generations, leaving the puzzle of empty cellar holes, and riddles posed by the names that are left by forgotten people and events. Any place that men have long frequented must hold such secrets; the coast of Maine, older than most in its general settlement, is filled with them.

But the sea itself, in its depths, thrives with secrets. Flight is mysterious, but birds—plain to the eye—are not; the most diffident member of the forest may evade our direct knowledge, but we can see the sign it leaves behind and tread the paths it walks. Like night, the ocean reveals itself close at hand or not at all; human sight and (more significantly) human perception travel poorly within it.

This sense of mystery, of the unimaginable fathoms below him, was familiar to Mister Walton. He stood in the doorway to the pilot house, looking out over the waves, and though land was still visible, the stretch of ocean between their small craft and the jagged coast surged like a living thing, intimating the presence of great creatures and great schools of creatures to fill its vastness. The shadows cast by stray clouds were indistinguishable from the shadows of animate forms lurking just below the water's surface, and the waves themselves might roll from the movement of some monstrous leviathan. At the very least he understood that dark and teeming cycles of life flourished in the cold silences and terrible pressures below, and that the largest vessel man would ever build could hardly skim the smallest surface of such a measureless entity as the Atlantic.

It was not long after the craggy ledges known as the Cuckolds that the Black Rocks became discernible in the distance. Captain Pinkham gave the wheel over to his first mate and, reigniting his pipe, stood in the short companionway to the passengers' cabin, where groups of people stood and sat, conversing among their own circles. The captain watched for several minutes before one of them took notice of him and hailed him good-naturedly.

"How long before we see this sea serpent?" wondered the fellow with a laugh, which was followed by more happy laughter.

"Well, it's true," said the captain around his pipe. "I have been hired to show you some such creature, and I am glad you laugh and enjoy yourselves—it is a particularly fine afternoon for an outing, and promises to be a particularly fine evening. But I will be honest: if I thought there was some likelihood of finding this monster, I would not have taken you."

"You disappoint us, Captain Pinkham," said a middle-aged lady, barely concealing a smile.

"Then be disappointed, please, ma'am, and Lord bless you. I would not take you within reach of that beast, nor myself, either, for all the fame and fortune in the world."

"You've seen this creature yourself," said the first man.

"I have, sir. And if I cannot give you sight of her, I can give you report of her, and show you where I sat in terror of falling into those awful clutches." The captain stepped down from the pilot house and put a shoulder against the wall behind him. He blew smoke rings as he considered his tale, glancing at Mister Walton, who had taken his place in the doorway.

The captain's audience waited, and the sound of the engine's thrum took precedence, though behind it one was conscious of wind and waves and Mrs. Eccles' tinny snores from the pilot house.

"It was nineteen years ago this September," said Captain Pinkham. "I was a younger man in those days, and I daresay my heart was stronger, though a strong heart may yet feel fear. I was a first mate aboard the bark *Windward*, under the command of Captain Lewis, and we were coming down from Boston with a mixed cargo when we fell among great islands of fog blowing across our path, through our sails, and over our deck.

"It was early in September, but more like the very midst of August—hot and humid and still. The haze rolls off the ocean at times like these and blinds the coast and founders ships; sound carries unnaturally and sailors peer the harder for the sudden lack of sight. A small breeze coaxed alongside us, but the sails were laden with the damp and the shrouds dripped as from a rain. We planned for Wiscasset late in the afternoon, but Captain Lewis was uneasy with the fog and hoped to find anchorage that night at Five Islands.

"The fog was low and we saw Sequin occasionally, the lighthouse against the brief glimpses of sky, her light blinking, her horn lonely in the close air. You meet such a landmark, in such a mist, with gratitude, and leave it behind with regret until the next light, or the next bell, gives shape to the gloom ahead. The fog is a strange thing, and strangest of all at sea, and no sailor feels wholly at ease in its shadow.

"We first heard the breakers, almost gentle, against the Black Rocks. It was good to hear those waves—silent ledges are the killers, but noisy breakers are like a rattlesnake, warning. Here was another landmark passed safely. But then the fog parted and a cry of terror reached our ears that freezes my blood to think of it."

There was a silence among the listeners as the captain drew his pipe back to life with several deep puffs. There was a crafty look in his weathered face of which Mister Walton alone took note. Captain Pinkham might feel a chill in recalling that cry of terror, but he rather enjoyed giving a chill telling about it.

"I have seen curtains upon the stage part with less effect than did that fog," he recommended. "It fell aside from those black crags and hovered like a frame upon a startling scene. Two women clutched for life upon the rocks, burying their heads against the roar of the breakers, and raising their arms and voices betweentimes for help.

"Now there is a good deal of superstition among sailors, and a man need not be book-learned to know of the Sirens who lured ancient mariners to wreck and doom. On any coast there are tales of spirits and merfolk drawing incautious men to their deaths, even appealing to one's sympathy with cries of helplessness and distress. Our first emotion, I must tell you, was fear.

"But the cry of help at sea cannot be ignored; there is no plainer symbol of life's troubles than a human creature adrift upon the waves. A sailor hears such a call for aid and thinks to himself: There but for the grace of God go I.

"Action that follows hard on thought is another quality of the seaman's life; before a word was hardly spoke we shortened our already meager sail, dropped a drag anchor to slow us down, and Captain Lewis put the wheel about dangerously. I myself was one of the first into the rescue boat, but if I had known what else lurked ahead, besides those water-racked rocks, I might have hid in the hold rather than tender my assistance.

"We were bold that day, but approaching such a predicament requires consideration. We kept a line with us in communication with the ship, as much to keep us together in case the fog descended again as to serve in our rescue operation. The remnants of a boat, in which the women must have crashed, bobbed and scurried among the breakers, and the piece of a bow with the name B. *Audrey* bumped against us as we oared past the terrified women. We could hear their voices, but not their words as they shouted and waved—warning us, we thought, of such dangers as we already well understood.

"There were four of us in the longboat, and we made plans as we rowed against the waves. Could we bring ourselves up against the lee of the Black Rocks in these relatively gentle seas? Could we prevail upon these poor women, already exhausted, to swim some short distance to us? Could we reach them a line, or one of us swim ourselves with a rescue rope?"

Captain Pinkham stepped away from the wall and moved among his listeners, gazing out the windows of the passenger cabin as if he could see the scene even then. "A renewed cry of horror," he said, "sharpened our attention, and we stout men joined this particular chorus as we watched a long suckered arm rise out of the waves and grope searchingly only a foot or so from one of the women.

"I will never forget her face. She and her companion were dressed in white, their hats long lost to the sea, their hair and clothing soaked and dis-arrayed. Her face was gray with fear and disgust as this slithery arm—no less than thirty feet in length—felt its way to within inches of her clutching hands. She was near to casting herself to the mercy of the cold sea rather than suffer the touch of that pink tentacle, and we were frozen in abject horror hardly less than hers.

"We saw then what had not been plain to us before. Several powerful tentacles clung to the dark formation, and when the waves dipped into a trough, a single unblinking eye surfaced briefly.

"It was the Kraken! How often had I heard of her, of the great battles that men had fought against her—won and lost—of the terrifying struggles men had watched between her and the mighty killer whales of the northern seas! How little had I believed in her until that horrible moment!

"One of our crew was standing in the longboat, raising the line from the *Windward* above his head to clear the Black Rocks as the waves rose and fell. Another shipped his oar and brought it up like a club, his face rigid with the sort of detestation such fear can boil within the human breast.

"The scene was clear to us now—the two women clutching the safest ground against the breakers while shifting their place upon the crags as several snakelike limbs crawled along the jagged rocks and barnacles, searching for them. Up from the seaward side of the rocks a single arm lifted like a great worm above their heads.

"A wraith of fog obscured the rocks for several terrible moments, then the crack of a rifle was heard, and mist behind us was parted by the bow of the eighty-six-foot steamer the *Sasanoa*. I have never seen a vessel arrive with such heartening effect, for her purpose was immediately clear. Captain Lowe himself stood at her bow, levering round after round into the chamber of his rifle and shooting toward the shadow of the beast beneath the water.

"It is dangerous to fire over water; a bullet striking the surface can as likely come back and split your skull for your troubles, and even cannonballs have been known to double back upon the ship that fired them. To boot, a bullet is a poor thing once it pierces the water, and quickly loses its lethal energy. But we cheered, nonetheless, as the *Sasanoa* came as close as her pilot dared while Captain Lowe peppered the water with his fire.

"Our presence had been unknown to the crew of the steamer until she emerged from the haze, and her wake, as she was brought about, impelled us closer to the rocks. Some providential combination of wake and wave bumped us gently against the perilous island, and the man in the bow of our boat simply leaped ashore with the line in hand, held the bow firm against the rocks while the women fell into the boat in their hurry to join us. Then he shoved us away just as one of those tendrilly arms curled after him.

"The man with the oar nearly pitched out of the boat as he leaped forward and swatted the arm away. The fleshy suckers gripped the oar and ripped it from his grasp. The oar flailed above the water, then disappeared beneath the surface. When it bobbed into sight, shattered into several pieces, we shuddered to think that one of us or both our passengers might have been dragged to our deaths in just that manner.

"The crew of the *Sasanoa* drew the creature's attention with a hail of fire, and we made the best use of this borrowed time by rowing with our remaining oars back to the *Windward*. We had nearly reached the ship when a horrifying roar came across the water, our heads wheeling about in time to see a jet of water rising from the waves and the great tentacles disappearing.

"It was a nerve-torturing trip to the ship, knowing that the Kraken lurked somewhere beneath us, wounded perhaps, certainly enraged. I bent to my oar, fearing with each stroke to strike some large form beneath the water. That awful roar, which I learned later was the result of its form of locomotion, echoed through the drifting fog.

"Once aboard, our spirits were greatly improved. The women were remarkably sturdy about their ordeal, and effusive in their gratitude. They had been traveling between Salter Island and Todd's Head when an odd current caught them and dragged them away from land. No amount of rowing would alter their unwanted course, and soon they discovered that something more sinister than a simple riptide was dragging them to wreck upon the Black Rocks.

"The *Sasanoa*, heading from the Kennebec to Boothbay Harbor on its daily run, caught sight of the marooned women just ahead of us and was slowed in her rescue by a sudden thickening of the fog in the mouth of the Sheepscot as she turned about.

"The haze lifted while we pieced together this story and we saw the figure of Captain Lowe as he called out to us to ask if all was well. The *Sasanoa* steamed past us and we hollered back our thanks.

"The afternoon conjured a breeze from the south and with it we took into Five Islands. The Kraken—whose tentacles had each measured the length of five tall men, whose eye we had seen staring balefully from the waves, and whose incredible proportions we could only guess at—was not seen again, to my knowledge, until recently, perhaps.

"And here are the Black Rocks, my friends, the very scene of my tale."

All eyes came about, and the craggy outcropping of rocks rising from the sea was greeted with a respectful silence. The scene was simple enough, and innocent (if nature can be considered innocent), and yet their perception was suffused with Captain Pinkham's remarkable story, and seasoned (no doubt) by its three final words: *until recently, perhaps*.

Mister Walton was impressed with the tale, but also amused. The image of those two women, scrambling upon the slippery rock, the horrible tentacles groping for them, the longboat rowing in amongst the waves, the

Sasanoa bursting from the fog—perhaps, he thought, he should be writing some of these tales down.

The *Winter Harbor* turned away from the Black Rocks; which was a relief, if any of the passengers had admitted it. On their return, however, Captain Pinkham took the wheel and brought them closer to the scene of his story. The breakers crashed, the foam glistened. Again Mister Walton's imagination was able to conjure shapes beneath the water.

"There it is!" cried out one of the younger men, pointing. He led the wave of nervous laughter that followed, and those who had been most startled joined in at their own expense.

"Why did the captain refer to the monster as a she?" wondered one of the young women.

Her beau let out a puff of smoke from his cigar. "Predatory, grasping, unpredictable."

"The male sea monsters are apparently minding their own business at the bottom of the ocean," said Mr. Berkeley.

"The female of the species is more deadly than the male," said the beau.

"Then you had better be careful how you respond to such a query," said Miss McCannon, setting off another wave of laughter.

Several passengers, feeling brave, stepped out to the rail to watch the Black Rocks go by. The light of day began to evaporate Captain Pinkham's tale. Mister Walton accompanied Miss McCannon to the stern of the boat and they listened to the jovial conversation.

"Sea serpents!" said one fellow. "It's all rather silly, really."

"It wasn't a sea serpent; it was a giant squid, you know," said another as they neared the northern end of the rocks.

"Yes, well, while I was in Greece I got a taste for squid—calamary, they call it. I find it difficult to be in awe of anything that I have eaten."

The sudden explosive roar that emanated from the vicinity of the northernmost rock set them on their heels, brushed their hair back, and shivered the very deck they walked upon. Miss McCannon let out a whoop and retreated into the arms of Mister Walton, who was not averse to the unexpected comfort imparted by an adjacent body. The company froze in their startled attitudes and, as one, let out a second cry of alarm when a crew member appeared to tell them that Captain Pinkham was going to run full steam ahead and would they please not fall overboard.

A babble of chatter and speculation rose, and it was generally agreed that something had roared—almost angrily, according to the young beau who had expressed such caution regarding females.

"Thank you, Mister Walton, for your support," said Miss McCannon.

She pulled away from his arms and brushed at a stray lock, her smile quiet but becoming. "I was rather startled, really."

"As was I," admitted Mister Walton. "I can't imagine what it could have been."

She held a hand to her bosom, took a breath, and laughed. The steamer was making some headway now, and the Black Rocks were dwindling from sight. "Yes, well . . ." she said, awkward now that the brief crisis was done. She reached out and patted his hand gently. "I best go in and see how the rest of the party is doing."

"Yes, of course," said Mister Walton, blinking behind his spectacles. "Oh, dear!" he said. "Poor Mrs. Eccles! She must have been frightened to death!"

Mrs. Eccles was only just waking up. It was a great tree-felling snore from her own self that rattled her bony frame to the point of coming to. "Gnnnnng! . . . What, what?! . . . Oh, folderol!" She swayed in her seat, so that her attendants, who had been gawking through the window, were startled into action and jumped to catch her. "Get away! Get away!" she shouted, swatting at them. "What's to drink? Where am I? Good heavens, I've been transported!"

"Oh, no, Mrs. Eccles," explained Mister Walton. "We are on an excursion, looking for sea monsters."

"Yes, yes, of course! What do you think I am, dotty? What a lot of folderol! Did we find one?"

"Not exactly," said Mister Walton with a smile.

"Not exactly? How do you 'not exactly' find a sea monster?"

"You are right, of course."

"It's like more or less fighting a war, or sort of being kissed! Some things just aren't done in half measures!"

Mister Walton bowed to her wisdom, and she laughed.

"Did we hear the Bull?" asked the elderly woman.

"The Bull, ma'am?" He leaned closer to her to be sure that he had heard correctly.

"Yes, the Bull. Did we hear it?"

"I'm not sure. What does it sound like?"

"I heard it most of my lifetime ago, when I first met my husband. He took me in a sloop one summer's day and brought me alongside those Black Rocks outside Sheepscot Bay. Filled me with all manner of stories to get my nerves up. I had been cagey with him, you see, all season long, and he'd pressed himself fervently.

"There is a hole in one of those rocks, you see—worn there by so many years of waves driving upon them—and when the tide is right and just coming back in, a certain sort of wave will drive through that hole and roar like a bull. Of course, I knew all about it, but I liked him by then and jumped right into his lap when that thing set off. *He* was so startled, he didn't even know enough to kiss me!"

"Gran!" said Miss Bishop, who had entered the pilot house.

"Well, it is true! And if I hadn't been smart enough to instigate that kiss, your mother might never have been, nor you, either."

"Well, Mrs. Eccles," said Mister Walton, giving Captain Pinkham a sly look over his spectacles. "I think we did hear the Bull."

"Timed it rather nicely, I thought," said the captain without turning from his wheel.

"Oh, folderol!" said Mrs. Eccles.

45. Caught in the Act

FOUR PRESIDENTS, two royal princes, numerous statesmen, famed sportsmen, and dignitaries had stayed at the Bangor House, so Grace considered the establishment suitable for their patronage. The only blight upon the hotel's reputation was that Oscar Wilde once lectured in its ballroom, but Grace was of a forgiving nature and considered this to be an anomalous factor in the building's history. She did ask, however, which had been his room, only to be sure that none of *her* party was to be placed in it.

The hotel manager was familiar with this particular concern and he assured Grace that she would not so much as share a floor with that infamous bit of real estate. He had quieted many an anxious heart with this same assertion and, indeed, was so solicitous of his customers that he willingly shifted the location of the *Oscar Wilde Room* from moment to moment to benefit either their curiosity or their peace of mind.

The Underwoods and their party arrived in time for lunch, after which they found themselves with an afternoon to do with as they pleased. The young people were up for a tour of the city, and Grace felt it necessary to accompany them, since James and Mercia did not volunteer and Aunt Delia had gone to her rooms to rest from her travels.

A carriage was hired, and John Benning sat with Grace, opposite Cordelia and Priscilla, as they took in those instructive sights listed in the older woman's guidebook. When they returned two hours later, Grace was weary from the ordeal and insisted that her daughter and niece must be as well; Cordelia and Priscilla were duly ordered to follow her example by retiring to their rooms till supper. John Benning bade them good afternoon and was glimpsed, from the stairs, sitting with a newspaper in the foyer.

Neither of the young women had any intention of resting in the next few hours, and were planning to join forces in Cordelia's room when James appeared in the hall and asked to speak to his daughter.

"Did you have a nice jaunt?" he asked when Cordelia stepped into her parents' rooms, but the question was merely polite and required nothing more than the simplest reply. James nodded toward the door to signal that she should close it after her, and he drew up a chair so that they formed an intimate circle. He looked reflective as he asked her to sit; Mercia sat by the window, and Cordelia could not read her mother's expression. Cordelia was convinced that John Benning was to be the subject of their conversation, and her stomach tightened uncomfortably.

"I met an old acquaintance when we arrived at Ellsworth the night before last," began James without ceremony. "A man under whom your uncle Basil served during the war. Captain Coyle—you may have heard me speak of him. . . ."

"I don't think so," said Cordelia quietly, her raised eyebrows indicating both curiosity and trepidation.

"He thought highly of your uncle, and in discussing him I spoke of your bequest. One particular detail of the story rather surprised him, and he told me something in return that surprised me at least as much." James took a slip of paper from his coat pocket; he looked at it briefly then passed it to Cordelia. "I wired Maurice, who worked for me at the firm, asking him to seek this matter out."

Cordelia took the telegram and read it.

PORTLAND TELEGRAPH COMPANY
OFFICE — 54 KENNEBEC STREET

JULY 9 AM 11:00
BANGOR, MAINE
MR JAMES UNDERWOOD III
BANGOR HOUSE

TRACKED COYLES SHIP BETHEL TO CHARLESTON. CHARLES
STIMPLY ABS LISTED DEAD BURIED AT SEA 17 DEC 95 OUT OF
ANTILLES. WAITING FURTHERS.
    MAURICE

"I don't understand this," she said, after reading the telegram four times over. "It says that Mr. Stimply died last December."

"Yes, exactly," said her father.

"But what does it mean? We saw him barely a week ago."

"Did we?"

Cordelia had understood the implications of the telegram immediately, but her memory of the rough seaman was fond, and her expectations for her inheritance were so enthusiastic that she refused, for a moment, to consider anything that might dampen them. James knew his daughter understood and did not attempt to explain.

"But if that wasn't Mr. Stimply," she said at last, "who was he, and why . . . ?" She raised her hands, palm up, leaving the sentence unfinished.

"When a person pretends to be someone they're not, it doesn't bode friendly intentions."

"It does put a sinister color to the whole affair." Rather than appear disturbed by this communication, she looked pleased. Mercia leaned forward and touched her daughter's arm. "We are concerned about continuing this expedition till we know more about the man who visited us."

"Oh, but it's clearer than ever!" said Cordelia. "The treasure! Did Mama tell you, Papa? *Our Minmaneth*—that is the treasure you were always searching for. *Is a young goatt*—a young goat with two *t*'s is a kid with two *d*'s. Kidd. Captain Kidd. And whoever came into possession of Uncle Basil's trunk couldn't figure it out because they had never heard of Minmaneth. It was terribly clever of Uncle Basil!"

"Your father came to the same conclusion," said Mercia.

"Oh."

"But if all that is so," said James, "—and it is still, let us say, questionable—then it perhaps makes our position the more perilous."

To Cordelia it made their position the more exciting. "But Papa, we can't just turn around and go home."

James laughed softly.

"We simply can't! Aunt Grace says there is safety in numbers, though it's John she thinks dangerous." Both her parents noted the use of Mr. Benning's first name.

"We might be glad of Mr. Benning," said James. Then he corrected himself slyly. "*John*. There'll be the guide as well." It was clear to Cordelia that her father was game to continue, and that only a call to sober consideration was holding him back. "Perhaps we should see what—"

He interrupted himself to listen to the sound of scuffling feet in the hall, and they were startled by a crash against the door, followed by a long groan. By the time James was across the room, where he threw open the door, the scuffling had begun again.

Two men were poised as wrestlers—each with a single foot on the floor—then a sudden shift tipped them to one side and John Benning was revealed in the act of throwing his opponent to the carpet. James's tall presence caused the combatants to freeze in their struggle, and John released his hold on the downed man and sprung to his feet.

"What in the world!" said James, more surprised than angry.

"Forgive me, Mr. Underwood," said John Benning. "But I came up the stairs and found this fellow eavesdropping at your door."

"I did nothing of the sort!" declaimed the man as he tottered himself upright. "This madman tackled me like a ruffian ballplayer!"

"I kept you from running off, you mean," said John.

The irate man straightened his jacket and tie as he glared at Benning. He was a dark-haired fellow with a close-shaven beard, and though he was well groomed and well dressed there was something wild about him. "I am sorry," the man was saying to James. "But I mistook your room number for my own."

"He mistook your business for his own, that much is true," said John.

"I was preparing to unlock the door. . . ."

"Most of us put a key to a lock, not our ear!"

James patted John's shoulder to indicate that further explanation was unnecessary. "James Underwood," he said to the other man. "I am sorry for the trouble, but Mr. Benning is with us, and you will understand if he mistook your intentions."

"Percival Goodkind," said the man, shaking James's hand cautiously.

"My card, sir," said James, taking one from his vest pocket and proffering it to the man.

"Thank you," said Mr. Goodkind. "I am without my card at the moment."

James smiled and nodded that he understood, and Mr. Goodkind retreated down the hall, rubbing his head.

John appeared somewhat embarrassed. "I don't believe for an instant that that was a mistake," he said.

"I don't, either," said James. "But it is your word against his."

Everyone was breathing suddenly, and Cordelia laughed with relief that the scene was over. She waved a hand at John's apology, glancing down the hall to see that Mr. Goodkind had disappeared. Two doors down, Priscilla peered nervously into the hall.

"We must ask the clerk about him," James was saying. "In the meantime, John, I suggest you step into our rooms so that we can explain to you what this might have been all about." It was then that he noticed Priscilla; he crooked a finger at her. "Come on, my dear," he said. "We might as well get this out all at once."

46. Red-Painted Mystery

EVENING CAME UPON BOOTHBAY HARBOR like a gentle breath of wind; and indeed, the trees barely stirred in a warm breeze. A slight haze in the atmosphere, touched by the sociable glow of the lampposts, obscured the stars, but the streets were brisk with strollers and the benches and lawns along the water were dotted with the pale summer costumes of lovers and lone romantics.

It is to be imagined that many a profession of love was made on such a night, when Venus or Jupiter, bright in the reflected glory of the westered sun, shone more beautiful than the stars through the summery mists; the fragrance of the breeze, redolent with flowers and the tang of salt, a distant foghorn, or the sound of water upon the shore would fill all but the sternest heart with the desire for another heart close by.

Such effects were lost, however, in the vicinity of the Weymouth House, from whose parlor windows, open to the warm night air, laughter issued in a most steady flow. Were we to leave the street and ascend the sloping lawn of the inn to peer after this merriment, we would first see Sundry Moss holding forth before a knot of rapt listeners who roared with glee as he described his futile attempt to knock down a suspected smuggler.

Mister Walton, at a table in the opposite corner of the room, was playing at whist—partnering with Mrs. Eccles against Miss Bishop and Miss McCannon—while explaining to these women and several onlookers how he looked over the sights of a rifle at a bear as it stood upon its head.

"Her digits fidgeted," he said, and demonstrated with his fingers the precise manner in which an inverted bear might wiggle her toes.

Miss Bishop covered her face with her cards, suppressing a shriek of laughter. "She fidgeted her digits," said Miss McCannon, barely able to pronounce the phrase. There were tears in her eyes.

"Yes," said Mister Walton, who had to remove his spectacles and dab away his own tears with a handkerchief.

"Mister Walton, you're very naughty," said Mrs. Eccles with a smile. "You have made me forget what I was about."

"Miss McCannon led with hearts, ma'am," said he, still chuckling.

"Ah, yes." The old woman eyed the table sharply.

"Someday, Mister Walton," said Miss Bishop, "I would like to hear your account of *today's* adventure." She neatly played her side of the hand and gave him a wry look.

"In any proper version of the story, of course," he said, playing along, "we would actually see the monster. Perhaps it would attempt to climb aboard, till it collected a stern reprimand from your grandmother."

Mrs. Eccles seemed pleased with this image of herself, scolding a monster from the deck. "It wouldn't get its arms around me," she said bluntly.

Mister Walton and Miss McCannon glanced reflexively at one another, and as quickly looked away. However intentionally, the elderly woman's words had roused in their minds the moment when they had been frightened into each other's arms. He had the sudden urge to apologize again for his instinctive action, but obviously could not have done so in the presence of others.

But there was another hindrance to a second apology as well, and he was truly beginning to feel it as the day, and then the evening, wore on: the contradictory sense of apologizing for something that had been so pleasant.

He glanced again at Miss McCannon and felt a general and generally ignored sense of loneliness sharpen into something more specific. She was not a beautiful woman, but middle age and good humor had made her handsome. Her features were not fine, nor was she delicately built (she was, if anything, a little taller than Mister Walton); and yet she was filled with energy and intelligence, and there was something about her that appealed greatly to him. A certain regret was mingled with his admiration, since she had already made it known that this was to be her last night in Boothbay. It did seem too bad, to meet such an exceptional person so briefly.

He looked at Miss McCannon's hands, which he thought pretty; and catching sight of his glance, she turned her cards away, as if he were attempting to see what she held. He looked up, surprised and more than a little embarrassed, and met her soft smile. "I thought, several days ago, that my life was going to quiet down," he said before thinking.

"That would have been too bad," she said carefully.

It dawned on him that it was his play; befuddled, he discarded when he meant to trump. "Yes," he said. "I quite like to meet people and do things."

The table had grown quiet. Miss Bishop smiled again behind her cards.

A feeling of gratitude suddenly filled Mister Walton and he sighed happily. "Since returning home, I have had the most extraordinary adventures and met a great list of wonderful people. Until recently I have not properly appreciated the life and history of my own home state."

"If it's history that interests you, you should meet my brother, Jared," said Miss McCannon. The game recommenced as they spoke.

"Is he an historian then?" asked Mister Walton.

"Yes, of sorts. An antiquarian with the Peabody Museum at Harvard. He is working on a dig, right now, just a few miles inland."

"Then I could very well meet him, you're saying!"

"You must!"

"This is an Indian site, then?"

"At one time, actually," she replied. "But he is digging deeper, in hopes of finding artifacts of the Red Paint People."

"The Red Paint People," said Mister Walton, quietly trying the phrase. "I've read the name somewhere."

"We know almost nothing about them, but they are very ancient. Jared suspects they antedate the Algonquin tribes by a thousand years."

"Good heavens!"

"Is it possible," wondered Miss Bishop, "that just as we supplanted the Indians, the Indians in their turn drove an earlier race from the land?"

"Anything is possible," said Mr. Berkeley. "Irony is history's favorite form of expression."

"And who shall drive us out?" wondered Mrs. Eccles.

"I shouldn't worry about it," assured a young onlooker.

"Perhaps the Abenaki and the Micmac thought the same thing when they took possession of the land," said the old woman. She took possession of another trick and looked askance at the young man.

"Why were they known as the Red Paint People?" asked Miss Bishop.

"Actually, we don't know what they called themselves. We have named them so because of the stores of red ocher found in their graves."

"It's fascinating!" said Mister Walton.

"People have unearthed Red Paint sites for almost two hundred years now. It was generally thought to be a sign of bad luck, however; the red ocher made our superstitious ancestors think of devils, perhaps, and they often scattered what they found."

"Where is this place that your brother is digging?" asked Mister Walton.

"It is on the Damariscotta River, in the town of Damariscotta."

"The shell heaps," said Mrs. Eccles.

"You've seen them," said Miss McCannon.

Mrs. Eccles nodded and managed another trick.

"The shell heaps I have heard of," said Mister Walton.

"You must see them," said Miss McCannon.

"I will."

"I am going up the Damariscotta tomorrow," she informed him. "Perhaps you would like to accompany me, as I am planning to visit my brother. I am staying with friends tomorrow night, but there are two or three fine places in Damariscotta where you could stay."

Mister Walton was taken aback by this invitation, and yet flattered. "That's very kind of you." He glanced at the faces around the table, sure that everyone else was sure that something was going on between himself and Miss McCannon. Miss Bishop looked nearly as pleased as he felt, and at a brief glance from both parties in question, she put her cards up before her face a third time. *Well,* he thought (and the thought made him a little lightheaded), *perhaps there is something going on between us.* "I'll wire ahead," he said.

Book Eight

JULY 10, 1896

47. Composition

Aunt Delia had enjoyed fabricating their little expedition; but the masquerade was over, and the next morning she revealed that she would accompany it no further. The rest of the party—most particularly Cordelia—was disappointed that she would be dropping from their company, but in hindsight they understood that it was impractical for a woman in her late seventies to expose herself to the arduous pleasures of *roughing it.*

"You go and have a good time," she said, with a wave of one hand—as if encouraging them to have fun in the backyard.

There was some fear concerning Grace's reaction to this turn of events, but Aunt Delia sprung her change of plans even as they readied to leave the Bangor House, and was so hustly and bustly as she hurried Grace along that very little argument was had from that court.

Aunt Delia went with them to the station and walked up the platform to see them on the train. Whether the old woman had foreseen what happened next, Cordelia was never entirely sure.

The railway line that traveled to the interior of the state from Bangor did not generate a sympathetic reaction from Grace. She had never been to this end of the station and thought the platform, the train, and the people altogether too workaday.

The scent of lumber and raw timber saturated the warm air of the western platform. The cars looked secondhand, and even the engine had the appearance of hard work. The few passengers boarding this train were almost all of one working class or another—lumbermen mostly; but if certain subtle differences were obvious to you, you might pick out hunters, and fishermen, and guides, and adventurers.

Grace was horrified to discover that there were no private compartments on this train, nor even private berths, but only curtained bunks in the sleeping car. James explained that they would not be spending the night on the train, but Grace invoked *the principle of the thing* and looked as if her feminine virtue were under siege.

A sense of hesitation hovered over them as they waited for a porter to take their baggage; James and Mercia exchanged uncertain glances past Grace, and Aunt Delia gave her vapor-prone niece a sympathetic pat on the hand. A man stood nearby, dressed in rough clothes that must have itched in the warm July sun, for he scratched at himself with both hands as he walked down the line of cars.

"Do you know, Grace," said Aunt Delia soothingly, "I think you are looking peaked. Perhaps you should beg off with me, and we can spend another quiet day at the hotel. I could do with the company."

"But I mustn't," said Grace, with a tone in her voice that suggested that perhaps she could. "It's quite necessary that I come along."

"Not at all," said Delia, leading her niece away from the others and speaking in low tones.

"But Cordelia and . . . Mr. Benning. Mercia is so . . . *nonchalant*."

"Certainly you can't imagine that James will leave them alone for long."

"No, that is true. James is very levelheaded."

"And they will have Priscilla to accompany them. I know you think your daughter capricious, but you must trust in your own example."

Grace looked back at the train. The man they had seen scratching himself was still at it, and as she watched him he spat a wad of tobacco.

"Well, if Ethan comes back with us, I suppose . . ."

"Good heavens, Grace!" said Aunt Delia. "Can't you see that Ethan needs some time with his uncle, now that his father is gone? Look at them."

Grace did; Ethan stood beside James, looking tall and straight with James's arm upon his shoulder. The boy turned and smiled at his mother.

Tears filled Grace's eyes as it occurred to her just how desperately her son must miss his father. "You are right, of course," she said. "I think, Aunt Delia, you planned this all along."

"Come," said Delia, making no direct reply to this. "Before they load your bags."

In the eyes of her family, Grace Morningside was excessively prim, and this quality had only been strengthened by the absence of her husband. She knew that even her children thought her stiff, and that her daughter in particular felt constrained by her mother's straitlaced rule.

She was surprised, then, when her children expressed honest sadness at the announcement that she would not accompany them; and she was deeply touched when both of them offered to leave the expedition to accompany her home.

"You go and have a good time," she said to them, echoing Great-aunt Delia in word if not in meaning; an undertone of self-sacrifice ran through her voice that she could not contain. She hugged her children briefly and bade them spread their wings without her.

James wished to be on the train, and quickly, but he stifled this urge in order to acknowledge Grace's leave-taking. "You are sure of this?" he asked when he bent down to receive her kiss upon his cheek. The truth was that Grace's departure, once executed, would make the rest of their journey a good deal less complicated.

"Yes," she said as she turned to embrace her sister. "Please take care of the children." Then she added "All of them" as she hugged Cordelia. "And from you, Mr. Benning," she said, not offering her hand, "I expect the most proper behavior."

"I will do my best to meet those expectations," he replied with a bow.

"Do so," she said.

They were hardly seated before the train moved forward with a shudder; dust shook loose in the car, and a brief cloud of smoke and cinders blew in from the engine so that they were obliged to shut the windows. The wheels sounded roughly on the tracks and the train rumbled and tilted as they eased around a sharp bend.

It will be wondered what was said the night before, once certain members of their party were informed about the more mysterious aspects of the expedition. There was indeed a good deal of discussion, and it was generally agreed that something was up

Argument ran along the line of *what* that something was, however, but not once was it suggested that the expedition be canceled or postponed. Each understood the need to be alert, but no sense of danger clouded their hearts. The Underwoods were an active people whose recent generations had energetically vied for what they wanted, whether settling frontiers, political debates, or business deals; competition was expected and even welcome.

Only Priscilla showed misgivings, and they might be compared to the apprehensions of a person who, vaguely wary of heights, yet boards a Ferris wheel with a happy laugh.

John Benning—perhaps the most prudent of the lot—suggested that they pick their guide carefully when they came to Millinocket. "The agency in Millinocket has already hired a guide for us," said James.

"Perhaps we should find out, then," said John Benning, "whether he was picked, or whether he volunteered."

"Oh, my goodness!" said Cordelia, a happy thrill touching her spine.

"It's a shame that your aunt Delia hadn't caught that fellow peering through keyholes," said John, with only a hint of irony. "She would have boxed his ears more ably than I."

Cordelia half-expected to find Mr. Tolly on the train with them, and was rather sorry not to see his friendly face among their fellow passengers. She would have liked one of his mile-eating stories on this leg of their journey.

She had, instead, the miles themselves—eaten by track and coal and steam. Those regions northwest of Bangor had the grandeur of hard use; great expanses of cleared land—some of it farmed, some of it settled into tiny hamlets, but most of it rolling over distant hills with nothing but bare stumps, scraggly bushes, and scrub pine.

There was less said among the Underwood party today than yesterday; this train was noisier, and that in itself might have discouraged conversation, but there was more to the silence among them. Ethan alone was chattery, and John Benning showed him a magic trick or two, then produced a deck of cards and offered to play hearts with him—something he might not have done if Grace had still been with them. She would not have objected to cards *per se*, but would have been a little shocked that he carried a deck on his person.

James had serious thoughts as he watched the quiet land fall past them. Despite his outward humor regarding John Benning and Cordelia, he was not entirely comfortable with the young man's forward manner, but this could be ascribed to a common characteristic of fatherhood when it comes to daughters—in this case an *only daughter*.

John Benning was wise not to press himself upon Cordelia this morning—her aunt Grace had grown doubtful of his intentions the day before, and had been on the verge of making a case to Cordelia's mother. Today, with Aunt Grace gone, it seemed James's office to take up the staff of wariness.

But John Benning's circumspection was certainly most wise because of Cordelia herself, who began to wonder why he didn't pay attention to her despite what others might think. She answered his seeming indifference by not looking at him, and tried to appear interested in the copy of *Tristram Shandy* upon her lap.

The day was clear. Fat and amiable clouds populated the sky, and to the west there were mountains—an ancient blue ridge in the distance.

Upon a slope, barely a quarter of a mile away, a solitary horseman waved as the train passed, and Cordelia lifted her hand with such a soft and simple movement that—had he articulated her from all the other faces in all the other windows—he would not have seen her quiet gesture. The wave was for herself somehow, a gauge of where she was going and that she *was* going, like a dreamer who pinches himself in order to verify an unexpected reality.

It was noon by the time they reached the town of Milo, where the forests had begun to recover from the industrial and maritime heyday of the mid-nineteenth century. Here they stopped to stretch their legs while the train took on water. An eating house specializing in soup, pie, and strong coffee stood along the tracks, and Cordelia gamely led the way to its dark interior. Their boots and shoes clunked noisily upon the boarded walk.

The establishment was cleanly and expertly run by a large woman in a large calico dress who did not often sell pies by the slice but was politely willing to do so. They stood in the middle of the little room and peered into the shadowy corners where men in shirtsleeves ate with their elbows on the table, while James and John Benning negotiated the purchase of some refreshments. Cordelia found a map on one of the dark walls and traced their route from Bangor to Millinocket with the tip of a finger.

Three burly fellows rose from their table and passed while the proprietor waited upon the Underwood party. The youngest among them cast a glance at Priscilla as he went through the door and said something quietly in French.

"What was that?" said Cordelia, who spoke the language well enough to have understood the gist of the man's words.

"He was remarking upon your cousin," said John Benning.

"Good heavens!" said Cordelia, managing a fair imitation of Priscilla's mother as she cast a glance of mock indignation in her cousin's direction. "How impertinent!" Cordelia took hold of Priscilla's arm as if to protect her. Priscilla looked surprised to be the point of anyone's remark.

"He said that you have beautiful eyes," said John to Priscilla.

"We have heard enough, thank you," said Cordelia.

Priscilla wasn't sure she *had* heard enough, and said so.

The incident might have seemed a small business to anyone else, but Priscilla was oddly affected by it. A sadness washed over her as the train took them from Milo. She could not recall ever having been complimented by someone who was not safely related or distanced by age, and though she felt a sense of pleasure in having been admired, her overwhelming reaction was one of melancholy. It seemed such a nice thing to say, that she had beautiful eyes, and yet so hopeless somehow, that she felt like crying.

She sighed instead, and Cordelia turned from her window to watch her cousin carefully. No words passed between them, but Cordelia took Priscilla's hand and squeezed it, her eyes half questioning, half understanding.

"What do you expect your land will be like?" said Priscilla, gamely attempting to change the subject of unspoken conversation.

"Well," said Cordelia, "I have had the image in my mind of something that Uncle Basil gave me years ago." She rummaged in her handbag, producing after some work the brooch that he had given her.

"Yes, I remember," said Priscilla, taking it and finding new interest in the delicate cameo. She touched the face of the brooch, as Cordelia had done a hundred times herself, tracing the scene so artfully sketched there.

"I see my land atop a hill, looking down upon this lake." Cordelia indicated the same upon the cameo. "And these trees, and that bit of ledge by the shore. I am afraid my imagination has gone no further."

"I hope it is just like this," said Priscilla, and when she smiled, tears glistened in her beautiful dark eyes, so that Cordelia could not help but reach over and hug her.

Brownville Junction was their final stop before reaching Millinocket, a jumping-off point for loggers and sportsmen, quieter still than Milo, more roughly built, and more closely hemmed in by tall young pines. In the territories beyond, the forest increased in depth and darkness. The heat of summer met the shade of tree and thicket like a soft kiss, and a heady perfume of balsam and pine permeated the passenger cars. Cordelia leaned her cheek against her window and closed her eyes to savor it.

James folded his paper now, and his wife laid her needlework to rest upon her lap. The game of cards between Ethan and John Benning slowed to a crawl with waning interest as the woodland deepened its presence around them.

They had read of such places, of course, and dreamed of them in those early hours when sleeping visions are borrowed from unnamed and ancient ancestors. The treeless acres so familiar to them might give the impression—however false—of full disclosure, as if, looking over a field, the eye could command all life and thought sustained there; but forests practice no such deception. Deep woods are the very metaphor for secrecy, and peering into an immeasurable forest, the plainest imagination can conceive of teeming life beyond the veil of brush and branch, and even convince the passing glance of hirsute faces and wary eyes peering from leafy top-lofts and ferny underbrush.

And for those who cannot see the forest for the trees, that which conceals, conceals even itself.

The forest fell away again, in stages conspicuous to the eye. The train passed over a stretch of water, banked to either side two or three times, then made a final sharp turn to the right, leaning with the curve as open country swept into view like clear sky behind rushing clouds. Ahead of them, the rustic settlement of Millinocket came into view.

And here we are, said Cordelia to herself as the penultimate leg of their journey came to a slowly rumbling, whistling, brake-hissing halt.

The day was clear and fine as the Underwoods and their company stepped onto the platform; the street before them had left behind the muddiness of spring and not yet succumbed to the dustiness of late summer. Several locals were taking in the air, standing at their stoops or leaning against porch railings. Train arrivals were often good for business and always good for gossip. No one was disappointed by the Underwoods.

A small white-bearded fellow regarded them carefully. "You'll be Mr. Underwood," he said to James.

"Yes . . . Mr. Butler?"

"I am. I've stacked your things in the backroom over to the store. Your horses and buckboard are stabled across the street."

"We are obliged."

"Mr. Scott is down at Mrs. Cuthbert's, taking a bath." Mr. Butler tipped his hat to the ladies. "Pardon me for saying so."

"Mr. Scott is our guide?" asked James.

"He has been so hired, sir, yes."

"I trust his ablutions will not take long. We want to reach our destination before sundown."

"There is more of him than me," said Mr. Butler, interested in the question. "I can't exactly say how long it would take him."

"Does Mrs. Cuthbert have a place to sit?" asked Mercia.

"She has a porch, ma'am."

"Perhaps we can wait for him there," she suggested, and so they did—the women at any rate, while the men (including young Ethan) brought their animals and gear from the stable to the hitching post outside Mrs. Cuthbert's humble boardinghouse.

Cordelia had been sitting too long already, and she paced the length of the porch while her mother and Priscilla sat and watched her. Mrs. Cuthbert, pleased to have female company from more populated soil, was quick to produce a very civilized tea. She sat and chatted with Mercia about the women's vote.

The boardinghouse stood in the middle of town—a cluster of some twenty buildings or so along a single street—and from its front porch they could see Mount Katahdin looming in the distance over the stables across the way. A few houses and businesses were rustic in appearance, but most of them might have graced any New England street, their glass windows peering out from painted or whitewashed clapboards. Chickens scratched in the yard and a cat sunned itself in a store window just across the street.

"Children," said Cordelia. "I don't see any children." She paused by the porch railing and looked up the street to the railway station and, beyond that, a tall hill topped by three lonely trees.

"I don't see anyone to speak of," said Priscilla.

Indeed, they had trekked through some uninhabited spaces, but ahead of them was a vast territory of wilderness. The town itself seemed hushed and secretive—poised to take root at the edge of the great timberlands while it was yet too small to offer any threat or hazard to the wild acres within its reach. Cordelia and her cousin were gazing at the distant razor-backed hump of Katahdin when James arrived with the buckboard, Ethan at his side, and John Benning behind them expertly riding a black mare as he led another saddled horse along. The chickens scattered before them.

"No horse for me?" asked Mercia.

"No lady's saddle," explained her husband.

Mercia looked put out, and James apologetic. "There is nothing for it, I suppose," she said.

"It's the one thing I hadn't thought of," said James, accepting the blame.

"Ethan will want to drive the buckboard," said Mercia. "I will sit in the back and look balefully at you."

"It will probably be rough ground," said John Benning, attempting to put the best light on the subject. Mercia was an excellent rider and undaunted by rough ground, but she graciously nodded to him, as if this thought made her feel better.

Standing at the porch rail, Priscilla pointed, asking: "Are we going in that direction?"

"Towards Katahdin?" said James. "More or less. Does the old mountain look forbidding?"

"Not forbidding, perhaps, but a little watchful."

"That's just old Pamola, the thundermaker," he said as he climbed down from the buckboard. "But he's gotten sleepy in his dotage and doesn't come down these days, does he, Mrs. Cuthbert?"

"He still comes down, now and again, Mr. Underwood," replied the woman from her rocker. "Sometimes a cloud will appear over that mountain's back like a bad thought, and people are glad if they're indoors."

"I don't think I've ever seen anything so big," said Priscilla.

"The ocean," suggested Cordelia.

"It's not such a big mountain," said John Benning, tethering the horses by the porch. "There are peaks in the Rockies three times as tall."

"He is stooped with age," came a new voice, rich with broad vowels, and carrying with it the hint of a burr. "In his youth he made other mountains dizzy from craning their necks to look into his face." A tall man—as tall as James—stood at the front door; he had a large brow and rugged features, ruddy with weather; his hair was that indeterminate color that lingers between straw-blond youth and gray age; his hands were thick and his legs long. He was dressed in denim and flannel, his pant legs tucked into calf-high boots, and his sleeves rolled past the elbows.

"The Appalachians are old mountains," agreed John Benning.

"They *show the very age and body of the time,*" said the man, "*its form and pressure.*"

"Mr. Scott, I presume," said James, climbing the steps of the porch.

"Mr. Underwood," said the man, shaking James's hand. He took in the rest of the company, glancing only briefly among the women. Cordelia realized, in the quick scan of his gray eyes, that Mr. Scott was a good deal younger than she first thought. "Mr. Butler tells me that you want to leave this afternoon," he said.

"That would please us," replied James.

"Well, Dresden," said Mr. Butler, who was crossing the street. "I see you have met the Underwoods. Your horse and gear are ready at the stables." Cordelia glanced between Mr. Butler and Mr. Scott several times before it was clear to her that the name *Dresden* had been directed at the guide.

Mr. Scott could almost be seen to wince at the sound of his Christian name. He cleared his throat and tromped down from the porch, casting a sidelong glance at the stabler; then strode off to retrieve his horse.

"It's an unusual name," said Mercia. "Dresden."

"His mother was German," said Mr. Butler. "It's the town she came from. Well, here comes Mr. Cross. Prepare to have your likeness taken."

A man appeared with a camera slung over his shoulder: a local store owner who extracted a few extra dollars from passing sportsmen by taking their photographs and having the resultant prints ready by the time they returned from the woods. Here, it seemed, was the opportunity for an unusual composition, with the inclusion of three women; it pleased him to have something besides overly equipped hunters and fishermen to photograph, and the Underwoods were easily talked into posing. Cordelia later sent a copy of the picture to her aunt Delia with a letter, saying:

*Are we too well spruced up to look like homesteaders? I think so. I espe-
cially look elegant sitting among our gear in the back of the wagon. Papa
arranged things so that I could sit on the canvas tents, which were comfortable enough, though they smelled musty. Doesn't Priscilla look happy? And
Ethan, holding the reins? A breeze came up as Mr. Cross prepared his
camera, which is why mother is holding her hat—a difficult pose. I think
Papa sits like nobility on his horse—I do love this picture of him.*

*I wish John Benning had allowed himself to be part of this picture, but
he would have none of it—graciously insisting that an outsider should do
nothing to mar a family portrait. Oddly enough, Mr. Scott can be seen,
though I am sure he thought himself out of view. He is on the left, slightly out
of focus, his head down. He would be a handsome man if he would smile.*

The letter continues with an account of what happened next.

48. Walton from Walnut

MISTER WALTON STEPPED ONTO THE PORCH of the Weymouth House and
filled his senses with a host of satisfying adjectives. A dry breeze pinked the
surface of the harbor, dispelling the haze that often settles upon the
summer coast. The sun shone with a perfect intensity, inhabiting a sky so
blue it might have been imagined by a child, sharing that azure field with
great cumulus clouds set at full sail like fleecy airships.

What can be said about a perfect summer day on the coast of Maine? This
day fairly beamed with goodwill, and Mister Walton stood speechless with
gratitude before it. Others joined him on the porch and there was a great deal
of deep breathing and gusty "ahs" as they leaned against the porch railing.

A person of disagreeable nature is not often made less so by such conditions, whereas an amiable soul will find an extra measure of grace to celebrate the day. Sundry was so impressed by Mister Walton's joyous aspect
upon the porch that he nearly laughed aloud with a sort of gladness, just to
know that such a happy man existed.

"So," said Sundry, "we are off to Damariscotta this morning."

"Yes," replied Mister Walton. "And if the town is as picturesque to the
eye as its name is to the tongue, it will be a fine outing."

"It is a pretty town," said Sundry offhandedly; he was from Edgecomb,
after all, and not expected to praise other places too highly.

"I like Miss McCannon very much," said Sundry.

"Do you?" asked Mister Walton; he had come to value Sundry's opinion.

"My mother would say, she is handsome in her ways."

"That is very nice," said Mister Walton, as if he were thanking Sundry. "Yes . . . handsome . . . very nice."

Phileda McCannon joined them shortly thereafter, and though she greeted the sunshine with great pleasure, she did not indulge in the sensual flavor of the day; she was quite happy with the sun and the warm breeze, but it was no more than she had expected.

An hour after breakfast, they were seated upon the upper deck of the *Islesford*. Captain Leeman chatted with them as they waited for the final passengers to be boarded, and he helped Phileda list the sights they would be passing on the excursion.

"The fort at Pemaquid is gone, then?" asked Mister Walton.

"Oh, yes," said the captain.

"The Pemaquid settlement prefigures Plymouth by nearly fifteen years," said Phileda.

"Really," said Mister Walton.

"The famous Samoset first met English settlers here, and the colony at Plymouth was rescued in its first winter by supplies from Pemaquid."

"Then why the preeminence of the Pilgrims in our history books?" wondered Mister Walton.

"There was more hazard here," explained the captain. "Pemaquid was burned out several times. Fortunes were harder to carve this far north and this close to the French colonies. Certain Pilgrim descendants were powerful enough to convince that the nation began at Plymouth Rock."

Phileda looked conspiratorial. "Why, the first Thanksgiving feast wasn't even held at Plymouth."

"No!"

"Allen Island, in Georges Harbor, 1607," she said flatly.

"Then Plymouth is the younger brother!" declared Mister Walton.

"Rather than our Pilgrim Fathers," added Sundry, "those who stepped on Plymouth Rock are more rightly our Pilgrim Uncles."

"I will speak of them just that way," said Captain Leeman, "to a woman I know whose family stems from the *Mayflower*."

"Someone who wears her pedigree upon her sleeve?" asked Phileda.

"Yes—my sister."

"I am not sure why anyone *wants* respectable ancestors," said Phileda, when the captain had returned to his duties. "I myself rather enjoy a little associative disreputability. I really do."

"There must be a rascal in every family tree, I suppose," said Mister Walton with some humor.

"You spoke of someone," said Sundry to Mister Walton, "the first time we met—a grandfather, I believe—who was rescued from a profligate life by a hole in his boot."

"Well," said Mister Walton, with an air of disappointment. "He was a *reformed* rascal in the end."

Phileda shaded her eyes, squinting as the *Islesford* came about and swung with the channel current. "I would like to hear how a man was rescued by such a humble bother," she said. "Was he a Walton?"

"He was not born a Walton," said Mister Walton, eager to oblige. "His name was Walnut, you see—Elisha Walnut, the fifth child of a well-to-do family, though not in the habit of doing anything very well himself. It was in 1798, according to family legend. . . ."

It was a story that Mister Walton would tell more than once, since there is a written record of it amongst the archives of the Moosepath League. The hand that wrote this document has yet to be positively identified, and some debate among archivists and historians has taken place regarding it; but it is clear—as much from the tone of the piece as from the style of handwriting—that it was *not* written by Eagleton, the club's first historian.

The chronicle does not vary greatly from known fact, however, nor from Mister Walton's story as he told it to his companions. It is presented, therefore, for the delectation and enlightenment of the reader.

Elisha Walnut, fifth scion of a prosperous Cambridge family, found himself— in the spring of 1798—in extreme financial embarrassment, which was in consequence of such a dissipated style of life that he could expect neither monetary support nor familial sympathy from his long-suffering relatives. First and foremost among his creditors was the infamous Henry Steeple—a gambler, whose means of winning at cards was questionable, and whose manner of settling unpaid debts could be painful, if not fatal. Several people, suggested one of Elisha's waggish friends, had been buried on Henry Steeple's account. In answer to his peril, Elisha described the better part of valor—and left Cambridge by the first coach, which was heading north.

Elisha knew of a distant cousin in Maine—which was then still a part of the Commonwealth—who resided in the vicinity of Bangor, and he hoped, with his reputation left behind, that their kinship might bear upon this relative for a bit of hospitality.

But he was destined never to meet his cousin, nor ever to set foot within a hundred miles of Bangor. It is one thing to leave behind a reputation, and quite another to outrun one's personal disposition. So, when a certain female (whom some would disdain to call a lady) boarded the coach in Portsmouth and, from her seat, proceeded to smile upon Elisha in a suggestive manner, old and unadmirable instincts rose within him. After an evening stop at an inn, these two found themselves alone in the coach, and a good deal more than smiling found itself on their proposed itinerary.

Fate would have it otherwise, however—fate and Maine's spring (of which there is little) and mud (of which, that time of year, there is quite enough). Just as Elisha was shifting himself to the opposite seat the coach wheels on one side plunged into a morass of soft clay, the result of which was that the door to the carriage flung open and he was pitched from the vehicle into the night. The woman, now alone with the better part of his belongings, thought herself well ahead of the game and neglected to voice the alarm of man overboard. She shut the door, we are told, without a single backward glance. However many her faults, curiosity was not to be counted among them.

If the spring mud had compounded Elisha's woes, it also provided him with a soft landing. The breath was knocked out of him, and he was momentarily stunned, but beyond the soreness and aches expected from such an ordeal, he experienced no major injury. From his back he heard the clop and trundle of the coach as it disappeared into the darkness. He sat up with a groan, pushed himself to his feet, and shook the mud off himself as best he could.

The night was slightly overcast, and a middle-aged moon was well above the western horizon. Elisha looked south along the road, but did not take to the idea of retracing his path. He looked north, knowing that the relatively large town of Portland lay in that direction. A harbor town, he hoped, might be more amenable to his immediate needs—and so, shivering, he went north, dictating, however unintentionally, the fate of successive generations.

Trudging through the night—wet, cold, and eventually footsore—Elisha thought upon his misfortune, and came to the conclusion, as he reached the outskirts of Portland in the growing light of a false dawn, that he had only himself to blame. A small voice of self-recrimination, hitherto unheard from, spoke up within him, and with the expression of a beautiful dawn (the sunrise of which he viewed from a hill overlooking the sea) came a determination to apply himself to honest labor—the first honest labor, he decided, that would offer itself.

Once he reached the waking town of Portland, a hole in the sole of one of his boots sent him to the door of a shoemaker, Jacob Arbuthnot, who—it so happened—had recently lost his only apprentice to the adventurous life of a sailor. Intending to pay for the repair of his boot with some of the few coins left to him, Elisha listened to the troubles of the busy tradesman, and watched with interest as the fellow worked. It seemed a quiet, safe trade, this shoemaking; and Elisha breathed deeply the smell of leather in the shop. It looked pleasant, working with one's hands; people appreciated a good shoe—heaven knows Elisha did at this moment.

Elisha Walnut then became Elisha Walton—his family never again heard from him, and he never again heard from his past, his reputation, or his previous tendency toward dissolution. He was not young to be beginning an apprenticeship—but he showed a talent for the work. Indeed, he had such a mind for business, and such an eye for style, that trade grew and prospered. In eight years, the master retired, and Elisha purchased the business. Two years later he married Fanny Woolrich, the daughter of a local blacksmith.

In 1810 they had a son, christened Jacob Walton, who saw the family business grow, and move, and grow again—into a factory with workers and salesmen and the latest in shoemaking machinery—till they had a business that helped define the harbor town, while the Waltons became respected citizens whose favor was sought, and whose opinions were counted.

In the intervening years, father and son barely set foot from the city precincts, and the Waltons were famous homebodies until a third generation came into their own—Jacob the second, who was reportedly lost at sea off Cape Hatteras; Elizabeth, who married a missionary in Africa; and Tobias—born in 1849—who joined the Federal Army in 1865 and became the drummer-boy for a regiment that never heard a shot fired in anger.

Tobias had a great love of travel that his father dismayed of and his grandfather mistrusted. He was a jolly fellow and took after Josephine, his mother, who laughed easily and projected innocence upon everything she saw. Fascinated with the world outside of their native city, she encouraged his explorations. When the business was incorporated, and forty-nine percent of the shares were sold, a comfortable fortune was assured to as many generations as were willing to spend wisely. They invested in shipping, and did well; and Tobias became the family representative—traveling among the great cities of the eastern seaboard.

As his family passed on, Tobias had less and less reason to return to Portland, and when his mother's sister—the last of her generation—died, he came home to close the house in which he had spent an idyllic childhood.

Or so legend has it.

" . . . And so," concluded Mister Walton, "when my aunt August died, I came home to close up the family estate—a duty which I have dealt with by the utmost procrastination."

"Perhaps," suggested Miss McCannon, "the house does not want closing."

"Perhaps not," said Mister Walton quietly.

During the course of his tale they had steamed upriver, past islands and coves. A great marsh fell past them on the port as the pilot prepared to take them through the river's next meander.

On either hand, well-demarcated fields swept down to the banks, which as often as not fell into blunt ledge and precipitate cliffs. High above them, orderly farmhouses and the homes of mariners, marked by widow's walks and lookouts, dotted the landscape.

A breeze chased them, or passed them, or accompanied them, according to its gusts. Swirls of swallows flitted after bugs that hovered upon or above the water.

The noise of the *Islesford's* engines, and its passage, was at once agitating and hypnotic; the wind in the trees and upon the fields could not be heard from her decks, though the breeze's course was clear to see, like the wake of unseen runners through the grass, and the weight of invisible birds upon the leaves.

A happy and unspoken quiet fell upon the passengers as they rounded an island and the twin villages of Newcastle and Damariscotta could be descried between the next two points of land. There was an obliging symmetry between the two towns, with a bridge connecting them like the balance bar of a scale. The elevated sun shone upon the roofs of houses, and glowed upon steeples on either side of the river, and the haze of summer rose like a sleepy man's vision above one of the loveliest and most pleasingly assembled settlements that Mister Walton had ever seen.

"Yes, Sundry," he said. "It is a pretty town."

49. Alces alces with Undergarment

THEN CAME *the moose.*

Eagleton would refer to him as "that fateful moose!" and it was thought until recently that all reference to this cumbersome (if serendipitous) quadruped went no further than the immediate vicinity of Newcastle, so it was gratifying that a letter was recently found, the contents of which corroborates the written testimony of Eagleton and Mrs. Maloney.

I was repairing a fence at the northern border of my property the other day [wrote Captain John Taylor to his brother], *when a large animal on the slope below the Academy caught my eye. It looked to me like a horse, and I watched it for a good quarter of an hour before I realized my mistake. In another season I would have roused Benjamin and gotten my gun. It was a moose, brother! an unusual enough sight to halt my progress on the fence for another half an hour while it made its way toward the river and eventually* strolled from sight behind the next hill. He was quite racked out, but appeared to be minding his own business, so I minded mine.

Now let me tell you what happened that very evening at the Lincoln Hall, and you will think that things have grown rather wild hereabouts. . . .

It will be noted that Captain Taylor makes no mention of red flannel underwear.

It was oysters for lunch at the Maine Hotel that momentous day, and oysters that led to a conversation concerning the famous shell heaps on the shores of the Damariscotta River. All further events, you will see, stemmed from this fact; and so, without oysters, you would be reading a very different sort of account from this point on, or (most likely) no account at all. The Moosepath League has, ever since, celebrated July the 10th with toasts to (and dishes made up of) this marvelous bivalve.

It is difficult to eat an oyster from the half-shell with any degree of delicacy; one must approach the task with a rough-and-ready attitude, something that Ephram, Eagleton, and Thump had in good supply. Thump, in particular, covered himself with honor in this pursuit, and his friends were quick to praise his appetite.

"Ah, the oyster!" said a gentleman from the next table. "It fulfills one appetite and whets another!"

"Hear, hear!" declared Ephram, without the slightest notion of what the man was saying.

"We understand," said Eagleton, "that the Indians ate a great deal of oysters in their time."

"Oh, yes!" affirmed the man. "And possibly another race, that lived here before the Indians, feasted on them as well."

This interested the trio, and they said as much.

"Haven't you seen the shell heaps, then?" asked the man.

"We did hear about them," said Ephram. "Tell us, what are they?"

"See them for yourselves, gentleman. You will not be disappointed. It will make you a proper walk this afternoon, something for which you have sturdied yourselves with this potent meal. If you're not sturdy for something else, if you take my meaning."

They didn't, but laughed with him as he winked knowingly. "Go and see these shell heaps," said the fellow. "It's an inspiration how the Red Man put them away. I am part Indian myself, don't you know?"

An anecdote followed this declaration, the gist of which has been lost over time; but the three friends were duly motivated to view the fabled site, and the next half-hour found them walking jauntily down Damariscotta's

Main Street to the bridge. They were innocent, of course, without any notion of nearing an historic junction that would henceforth be celebrated by Moosepathians through the years.

At the bridge they saw the *Islesford* docking against the wharf just below them. Several people on the steamer's upper deck waved and, filled with a sort of *esprit de corps* with the rest of the world, Ephram, Eagleton, and Thump waved in return.

"It is a shame," said Ephram as they crossed over to Newcastle, "that we weren't able to locate our chairman."

"Who knows what adventure he has experienced since we saw him last," said Eagleton. "Eh, Thump?"

Thump stood some yards behind them, gazing at a maple tree as if he had never seen one before—head tilted back, hands behind him. Ephram and Eagleton joined him, looking as if they had lost a kite in the upper branches.

They were travelers, and everything, common or rare, was a curiosity to them. They had seen many a noble tree, maple and otherwise, in their native Portland; but this was Newcastle, and who was to say that they would ever again have the opportunity to view a Newcastle maple?

Their progress was not rapid, therefore; countless sights demanded their attention—trees and shrubs, houses and outbuildings, front yards and granite stoops. It was all extremely informative and uplifting. They greeted passersby and raised their hats to the ladies; they patted a friendly dog and observed two innings of a baseball match with four boys on one team and three on the other. The way was punctuated by a short hill, from the top of which they could see an array of beautiful homes on either side of the river. The day had reached an almost mythical sort of perfection for them, and they were nearly mesmerized by it, when they first heard a woman's voice calling: "You get back here, you miserable creature!"

They had walked some distance from the general press of human society. Nature had replaced the sounds of man with its own deceiving quiet—the trill of songbirds and the sift of an idle breeze through the grass. The club members had imagined themselves alone, in fact, and so their attention was quickly taken by this cry.

Thump saw the woman first and pointed toward a rise in the land, west of them. A small figure in a plain dress and apron stood looking away from them down the opposite slope, one hand raised in a fist, the other resting demandingly upon her hip.

"Drop it, I tell you!" came the voice again, and each of the men looked briefly at his own hands. A sound of disgust exploded from the woman, and she turned about, as if the sight before her was more than she could stand.

The three men might have been schoolboys caught in the neighbor's apple tree, their faces revealed such horror. There was an overwhelming sense that to fall under this woman's baleful eye was to be implicated in whatever had raised her ire. Thump wheeled about, still pointing, as if he had suddenly remembered a pressing engagement in the opposite direction; Ephram decided that the shell heaps could wait no longer; and Eagleton physically expressed a sudden desire to retrace his steps entirely.

If the woman had not already seen them, the sound of their foreheads colliding would have quickly marked their presence.

"You!" she shouted. "You, down there!"

"Yes?" said Ephram, facing the wrong direction and gripping his brow. "Yes? Where did you go?"

Thump, who had received a knock on the noggin from Mrs. Roberto's shapely heel only days before, was experiencing a sort of flashback. "High tide at eighteen past six!" he shouted. There was a beatific expression on his face. Eagleton, in an attempt to reverse his reverse in direction, fell over him.

Eagleton struck his chin, and the consecutive blows caused him to imagine that his mental capacities had been compressed somehow, a peculiar sort of perception oddly augmented by the foreshortened appearance of an ant at the end of his nose.

"I feel quite unusual," he said aloud to himself. "I really do."

Thump recovered quickly, all considered, and with Ephram's help he lifted Eagleton to his feet.

"What *are* you doing?" the woman was shouting throughout this display. "Come up here! Can't you see I need your help? Come up here now!"

Ephram, Eagleton, and Thump staggered hardly at all as they made their way up the short slope; Eagleton's path was a little circuitous, but he straightened his walk as he neared the top.

"Please, you have to get that pair of flannels for me," she was saying as the object of her difficulties came into view. And so that instant in time that club members often call *The Moment* came to pass.

They stood upon a rise of land, with an inlet of the river before them, and the view was picturesque in the extreme. Most of the acreage within sight was cleared of trees, though certain stands of birches did dot the landscape, their pearly barks glowing as with a light of their own. Where white clapboarded houses stood along the riverbanks there were often maples and oaks, or stands of lilacs and rosebushes. Everything between was lush with summer grasses and wildflowers; the river glistened in the sunlight.

But the only thing to impress itself upon them was that a moose was trotting about in the hollow below them, with what appeared to be a suit of red flannel underwear flying like a pennant from his antlers.

Eagleton concluded that his mental functions were still slightly abbreviated. He blinked several times, during the course of which neither the moose nor the red flannels disappeared. The moose did stop trotting, however, and stood for a moment to contemplate the people above him. Eagleton felt that a stationary moose with red flannel underwear was preferable to one in motion, and so continued to blink, hoping that he was causing the creature to go away. The moose blinked back at him.

A breeze came up and gently pulled at the red flannel sleeves. The suit had been caught by one of its legs so that it seemed to wave for help. The moose munched heartily upon a clump of dandelions, the flowers of which hung decoratively from the end of his bulbous muzzle.

A moose is a cumbersome beast without a pair of red flannel underwear, but with such an accoutrement it is almost impossible to look at politely. Mrs. Maloney, who had been looking at the creature for some time now, still gaped. "I don't know what I'll do if I don't get those back!" she declared. "My husband only has the one suit, and he won't get dressed without it!"

"Oh, my!" said Ephram.

"I had them out on the line, and that fool just walked through and picked them up as he went."

Ephram didn't know what unnerved him the most—the close proximity of this wild beast, or the prospect of discussing undergarments with Mrs. Maloney. She was daunted by neither moose nor underwear, and continued to remonstrate with the three friends for their failure to act upon the situation.

"You!" said she to Thump, gesturing emphatically. "Get those away from him!"

It was unfortunate that she singled out Thump for this dictate, since he was the shortest among them; but he had set a standard for himself and could not forsake a woman in distress. Ephram and Eagleton stood as still as trees, watching with amazement and admiration as he took a single step forward.

"Hmmm," said Thump cautiously. He waved a hand inconclusively at the animal. "Yes . . . well, come, come," he said.

"Good job, Thump!" whispered Eagleton.

The moose, below them on the slope, showed neither hint of compliance nor change of expression. The dandelions had vanished, and they could hear the animal chewing.

Thump's shaking was barely visible as he took a second step down the slope. "Here, Bossy-Bossy-Bossy-Bossy," he intoned.

The moose, if anything, looked confused by this mode of address. It paused in its ruminating and watched Thump, as if *he* were the one sporting a suit of underwear upon his head.

As the man progressed into the hollow and neared the level place where the moose stood, the difficulty inherent in his lack of height became clear to the onlookers. "Here, Bossy-Bossy-Bossy-Bossy." Thump drew near enough to the moose to smell its moosiness, which was rather more pungent than a cow in its stall. Once he was within a yard or so of the animal, his options seemed narrow; indeed, without a stepladder or a good running jump, he was reliant upon the moose to bend its head.

Something of an impasse occupied the next several moments as these two regarded one another with varying degrees of uncertainty. Those above them on the slope stood motionless; even Mrs. Maloney held her breath.

With an impulsive toss of its antlers, the moose broke into a short trot. Ephram and Eagleton let out shouts of surprise, and Thump was so startled that he regained the top of the slope before the moose had covered half the ground.

The moose paused again. Shaking its antlers had only tangled the red flannels further; they were wrapped about the animal's right antler like a great turban.

Mrs. Maloney scolded the men as they assisted each other to their feet. "Great goodness sakes alive!" she shouted. "You there!" she demanded of Eagleton. "You're tall! Now quick, before he's gone!"

"Yes, well . . ." said Eagleton. "A plan, I think . . ."

"Strategy," declared Ephram, a finger in the air to stress the point.

"Approaching a moose!" said Eagleton.

Thump had not yet fully recovered to participate in this Lockean association of ideas. His beard, disarrayed and splayed out in numerous directions, had picked up diverse natural objects during the course of his retreat, giving him the appearance of Rip Van Winkle after his twenty-year sleep.

Ephram and Eagleton exchanged several more fragmentary thoughts while Thump recovered. The moose watched them with kind attention.

"The obvious approach has not succeeded," stated Ephram.

"Obviously," agreed Eagleton.

"And this in no way impugns our friend's gallant effort."

"Assuredly not!" declared Eagleton.

"And without the obvious, there is . . . ?" Ephram looked about for the appropriate word.

"There is . . . ?" echoed Eagleton.

Mrs. Maloney had retied her apron, and was now stomping down the slope in the direction of the moose.

"There is . . . ?" repeated Ephram.

". . . that which is not obvious . . ."

"Oh, yes!"

"Diversion, perhaps."

"Bravo!"

"Diversion!" said Eagleton again with more confidence.

"We will divert the moose!" declared Ephram.

"Gentlemen!" said Thump, his faculties returned, his dander up. "We must not make the same mistake twice."

Mrs. Maloney was in the hollow, some distance away, shouting at the moose.

"Indeed," said Ephram.

"That would be repetitious," asserted Eagleton.

"Did we *make* a mistake?" wondered Ephram.

"It was myself," admitted Thump. "Ephram."

"Yes, Thump?"

"Eagleton."

"Yes?"

"It seemed—at first—fitting, and even sporting, to approach the problem by thinking like a moose."

"Indeed," chanted Ephram and Eagleton together; they had seen nothing mooselike in Thump's attempt to retrieve the prize, but were willing to take his word for it. They waited for his pronouncement, keen not to fall into the same miscalculation, but he did not immediately expound his theory. His bushy eyebrows bunched together in a thoughtful frown. Perhaps he was occupied by the sight of Mrs. Maloney clambering over a stone wall in her pursuit of the recalcitrant beast. "Hmmm," he said.

"Perhaps," suggested Eagleton helpfully, "perhaps we need to *out*think the creature."

"Exactly!" said Thump, and he waggled a finger in the air to indicate that he could not have said it more plainly.

"I think you have it, gentlemen!" announced Ephram, his expression enlightened, his voice filled with admiration.

There was another silence between them as they watched Mrs. Maloney's figure dwindle. Her voice continued to reach them intermittently as they strained to hear what she was saying.

50. History Beneath the Heaps

MISTER WALTON CAME TO DAMARISCOTTA with no suspicion that momentous circumstances awaited him. There *was* one strange phenomenon that he was able to recall years later, but too much should not be made of it. It happened upon the bridge, where he and his companions waited for the steamer that traveled to Damariscotta Mills.

It was a trick of the light, perhaps, or a condition of geometry—the product of a mind keen to observe and a personality fertile with enthusiasm. The sun had nearly reached its zenith, shining upon the objects of the day as if the works of God and man alike had been recently polished. People strolled by, or paused upon the bridge to peer out over the powerful current: women with their parasols and men in their straw boaters, parents grasping their children's hands as a cart or a carriage or a horseman clopped by. There was no shade at the end of the bridge.

The town of Damariscotta itself seemed almost of another world, its tree-lined Main Street stretching away to the church at the top of the hill. Shadows filled the atmosphere between the white houses and the brick buildings, and the relative darkness set the town apart so that he imagined it as a painting, a photograph, or a scene upon the stage.

Years later, he found it a difficult sensation to describe, but best approximated it by comparing Damariscotta's Main Street, at that moment, to the corridor Alice discovers when she falls down the rabbit hole. It was such a brief sort of main street, but rife with possibilities as it turned past the church and disappeared. Side streets beneath the boughs of leafy elms and maples and oaks called to the curious like paths in the forest, and he was not at all sure that—had he walked in the direction of the town—he wouldn't have run into a canvas or a stage flat.

It was a strange presentiment, but one that he enjoyed, and he was sorry when the vision ebbed away and the town was simply a pretty place to pass the time.

Sundry noticed his employer's momentary abstraction, and it occurred to the young man that Mister Walton was thinking how to politely leave him behind for a while, so as to have Miss McCannon's company to himself. Realizing that his presence might make a romantic afternoon less so, Sundry offered to leave the expedition and take their bags to the hotel.

"Oh, no, no," said Mister Walton, suddenly animated. "We will hire someone to take our things. This oyster bank sounds too fascinating to miss!"

"If you're sure," said Sundry. "I just thought that you might . . ." His voice trailed away with an uncertain wave of a hand. He looked at Miss McCannon, who understood quite well what he thought and questioned him mischievously with her eyes. Sundry's ears turned red and he quickly went in search of someone to transport their bags.

"He is a gallant boy," said Miss McCannon with feeling to Mister Walton.

"Yes," said the bespectacled gentleman, not understanding her entirely, but pleased to hear praise of a friend. "He is a wonderful fellow!"

It was not a long trip from the bridge to the shell heaps, where a crude dock—populated by a single rowboat—reached out from the bank. The shell heaps gleamed from both sides of the river, and upon the eastern shore they were shorn into small cliffs where recent excavation and commerce had taken tons of the ancient accumulation away. From the deck of the boat Mister Walton saw tall grasses waving above the middens, and dandelions bobbing their heads against the blue sky. Several yards north of the plundered heaps, and barely above the high-water mark, crouched a small hut.

The steamer pulled in to the dock, her stern coming about, her wake advancing before her and breaking against the landing piles and the shore beyond. A flurry of swallows swooped past the white banks and disappeared around the next bend with a sudden and unanimous change in direction. Two men stepped from the little shack, their sleeves rolled past their elbows, their wide-brimmed hats shadowing their faces. Miss McCannon waved, calling out her brother's name, and the taller of the men shouted happily as he hurried down the bank.

"Phileda!" he said as he met her at the shore end of the dock. He lifted her ashore and embraced her.

Jared McCannon brimmed with youthful intensity as he smiled up at his sister's companions. "Let me take that," he insisted, reaching for their picnic hamper. It was heavier than he had expected, and he laughed with a sort of *whoosh* as Mister Walton and Sundry passed it to him. "My goodness! Who else are we expecting?" he said with good humor.

The two men stepped ashore and Jared laughed again when he realized that he hadn't a hand free to shake with them. "Oh, scoot!" said his sister. "Find a place for us to eat. I'm hungry."

The second man from the hut arrived—an elderly fellow whom Mister Walton was surprised to recognize. "Professor Chadbourne!" he declared.

"Who's that?" asked the older man, lowering his own spectacles. "What? Toby Walton, is it? Good heavens!"

"What a great pleasure to see you!" said Mister Walton, grasping the professor's hand warmly.

"Toby and I know one another through a mutual acquaintance," explained Professor Chadbourne to Jared McCannon.

"And how is our friend?" inquired Mister Walton.

"Not well these days, I fear," replied the elderly man. "Old wounds haunt him still." Mister Walton's face clouded with this news, though it did not seem to surprise him.

Lunch was laid out upon the grassy bank, overlooking the shell heaps from the north. A bright red blanket made for a cheery tablecloth, and from her picnic hamper, Phileda produced plates and cups and silverware, boxes of sandwiches and bowls of cold salads and pitchers of tea and lemonade.

Before settling himself to their picnic, Mister Walton gazed about him, and Phileda pointed southeast at a farm beyond the neighboring fields. "It's named Round Top," she told him. "The two brothers who built it fought at Gettysburg with the 20th Maine, and they named the farm after the famous hill that they helped to defend there."

Mister Walton could not reconcile such a violent event with the peaceful vision before him. Sheep grazed on the near side of a low stone wall, and cows stood in sociable groups beneath the shade of the elm trees that flanked the barn. He turned back to his fellow picnickers and, catching sight of Professor Chadbourne, he smiled. "I could not have imagined, Professor, when I rose this morning that I would be sharing a picnic lunch with you this afternoon."

"The world turns on surprises, Toby," said the professor.

"Did you attend Bowdoin, Mister Walton?" asked Phileda's brother. He handed along a bowl of stuffed eggs.

"I did not have that honor, sir," replied Mister Walton. "Though I *have* had the pleasure of attending several of the professor's lectures years ago."

There was something wry in the bespectacled fellow's declaration, and Professor Chadbourne chortled to himself, but neither offered an explanation for their humor.

"His famous lectures on the folkways of the Micmac?" asked Jared.

"No, his famous lectures on political ethics." This topic surprised Jared, and Mister Walton looked abashed. "Please forgive a private joke between the professor and myself. It was not proper to bring it up amongst company."

"There is a story here," said Miss McCannon, dolloping her brother a large portion of potato salad.

"But one that Mister Walton is not at liberty to share, I fear," said her brother.

"Someday, perhaps," said Mister Walton, sorry to have been impolite. "Please, forgive me."

"Sometimes a little mystery is very attractive," said Phileda, herself sparking a humorous glance from her brother.

Mister Walton did his best to distract attention from his sudden blush by searching for a fork. Sundry, who was making good use of the fare set before him, said nothing, but it was clear from his expression that he did not find mystery all that handsome.

"And have you been studying Indian life here, Professor?" asked Mister Walton, hoping to relocate the focus of conversation.

"Professor Chadbourne was the first scholar to investigate these middens," explained Jared. "Or, rather, the middens on the opposite shore."

Mister Walton turned slightly to look across the Damariscotta. A fairly strong breeze, traveling upriver, nicely complimented the sunny day, brushing past his face and tugging lightly at his hat. On either shore the white heaps glowed in the sun, snowlike in contrast to the summer greens and variegated wildflowers that stretched in all directions.

The shell heaps were nothing more than their title purported—great piles of white refuse, accumulated over centuries through the industry and appetite of the river's indigenous people. The remains, of clams, mussels, and quahogs—but mostly of oysters—rose in mounds as high as sixteen feet along the shore. It staggered the imagination when one considered the span of time necessary to amass such a quantity of discarded shells.

Mister Walton visualized in his mind a plate of oysters that would constitute a meal, then wondered how many such plates were represented below him. "How long have oysters been eaten on this bank?" he wondered aloud.

"There are some who believe, sir," said Jared McCannon, "that the very deepest shells to be found were cracked open before the birth of Christ."

"And you believe . . . ?"

"I wouldn't be surprised, Toby," said Professor Chadbourne, "if those first oysters were taken from the river bottom while the Israelites were yet under the rule of Egypt."

"You can see them, can't you?" said Phileda to Mister Walton.

They were walking together along the foot of the banks, and he had paused to gaze up at the compressed levels of shell and soil, his head craned back, his hands clasped behind him.

"The people before us," she said. "They are still here, in a manner of speaking."

"Yes," he admitted. "I can see them. The smoke rising from the bank, the glow of their fires against the growing heaps behind them and reflecting from the water as night draws on. And the people themselves, speaking in their ancient tongue; reflecting upon their day, telling tales, singing, laughing."

Quite naturally, she put her arm in his as they recommenced their stroll. "You are a poet," she said pleasantly.

His laugh was gratifying to hear. They moved closer to the water, which reflected a darker version of the sky's piercing blue, the current jumbling its own image of the opposite shore. Swallows swept along the surface of the river, darting through the shade of the western bank in search of insects, vaulting and somersaulting through the summer air with unconscious artfulness.

Other birds sang in the meadow above, and they could hear Professor Chadbourne giving Sundry a tour of the oyster banks, with occasional footnotes provided by Jared McCannon.

Another human voice from across the river mingled unexpectedly with these more immediate sounds and carried with it enough distress to draw their eyes to the hill on the western bank. Several figures there were running in several different directions, pursuing a large animal. There was something droll in the way they chased about the field, and Mister Walton could not but smile to watch them.

"Is that a horse?" asked Phileda, shading her eyes with her hand.

"No, it's not," said her brother, who suddenly stood beside her. "It's a moose."

"No!" said Phileda. She adjusted her spectacles.

"It is a moose," said Sundry, who had joined them.

"There is something familiar about those people," said Mister Walton. One of the figures fell over a stone wall and slid on his stomach down the slope on the other side. A second man below him looked away from this event, but was soon aware of it when the involuntary traveler swept him from his feet. Together they proceeded down the slope in a tangle of arms and legs till their descent was halted by a stand of bushes. A third man appeared and attempted to extricate his fellows from the offending shrub.

Mister Walton's companions were quite astonished. "My goodness!" he said. "They do remind me of some fellows I met recently."

"Why should they be pursuing a moose?" wondered Phileda.

"It's carrying something on its antlers," said Sundry. "Can you see it? It's something red."

"There's a woman, too," said Jared. "Look!"

The figure of a woman appeared by the stone wall, and they could not tell if her high-pitched voice was berating the moose or the men struggling with the bush below.

"I've seen enough," said Jared. "My curiosity has got the better of me. Who's for taking the boat across? . . . Exactly," he said, when the show of hands was unanimous. "Quick! There is room for us all, if everybody sits tight!"

51. Formation

While toiling in my fields today,
I lingered on a treeless hill;
And there I stretched myself and lay,
And there my spirit drank its fill.

I heard the buzz of bees aloft,
And wild blooms brushed my form reposing.
The wind was light, the earth was soft,
And soon my drowsy eyes were closing.

Lazing on the summer grass
When work still called—the more fool, I;
For afternoon would quickly pass
Beneath the sun of warm July.

But how, a humble man, could I
Deny or denigrate the worth
Of smiling up at God's blue sky,
And resting there on God's green earth?

THESE VERSES CAME TO CORDELIA (herself drowsy in the back of the buckboard), and she did not quite know whose they were. But she was weary from her travels, from happiness and excitement, so she allowed herself to drift, and not even the wagon's occasional lurches could discomfort her.

The conversation did not lag, despite her disappearance from it, and she half-listened to her mother's childhood memory of family outings, to Priscilla's desire to see a white-tailed deer and Ethan's tale of his encounter with a fox. Her father and John Benning spoke occasionally from their horses; Mr. Scott not at all—he rode at the head of the party, and she could not see him from her seat among the supplies and tents.

She could see John Benning, however, past the rainbow cast against her half-closed eyes by the bright light of day. He rode well, as she imagined he would, his posture straight and easy with the animal's gait. More than once (though she could only see him in silhouette with her eyes closed) she was sure that he looked at her, surer still that he would not have been alarmed to know that she saw him watching.

Mr. Scott, on the other hand, had not given her a second glance (to her knowledge) since she met him. Cordelia noted this lack of interest, and suspected that Mr. Scott was the sort to look over the queen's head in order to talk to her chamberlain. She decided to be annoyed by him.

It was not long before the forests crept into view, stands of trees and dark lines in the distance like waiting armies. It was a young forest, with thickets of low-lying vegetation—junipers and scrub bushes. Alders stood in messy clumps where the land was wet, and pines and firs and hackmatacks grew alongside their predecessors' remains.

The way rolled with hills, and granite bones broke the surface of the earth in large and rugged outcroppings. Great slopes and low mountains hunkered beyond the forests, and Mount Katahdin ran like the moon upon their right hand, peering into valleys, and looming larger as they moved north and west.

The trees gathered about the winding path, darkening the atmosphere with a shade of hushed expectancy. Noises came from the deeper sectors of the forest—birdcalls or squirrels scolding—voices that sounded large and strange from the unseen places beyond the first line of trees. The way itself was damp with recent rain and mushrooms ranked in fairy circles amongst the dark trunks.

They traveled without hurry, stopping only to let the animals drink from a stream, or to choose the best way around a deep water or a fallen tree.

They broke from the forest where a vast field rolled away from them like the folds of a blanket. The scent of water and a patch of blue spoke of a lake beyond, but what caught their attention was the extraordinary green of the field.

"It's like a park!" exclaimed Cordelia.

Dresden Scott brought his horse's head around and rode back to the wagon. "It is a park, in a sense," he said, speaking directly to her for the first time. "When Europeans came here, they were amazed to find large tracts of fields and meadows, just like this. They looked for some natural reason for these treeless acres, but as it turned out the Indians were responsible."

"I never thought of Indians as great clearers of land," said James.

"Most of us don't," replied Mr. Scott. "We think of them as woodland people, pitching their homes where nature has left a clearing. But they had an agronomy all their own, and kept their fields clear through controlled burning. Of course it was important to have cleared land for crops, but the deep grasses also coaxed game from the woods and simplified the hunt."

"Are you saying," asked Cordelia, "that Indians are, to this day, burning this land every spring?"

"The man who bought these acres hired the Indians nearby to do just that." Mr. Scott led them down the slope of the field, drawing up where they might look down upon a long and fingery lake. Mercia suggested they have their meal here, and Cordelia jumped down from the wagon and half-ran to the brow of the slope.

The grassy banks were littered with wildflowers, and a breeze brought the scents of grass and pine and water like balms to the appreciative travelers. The lake reflected the forest that clung to its far side. A large section of gray ledge hung above one corner of the shore. Cordelia saw something familiar in that granite formation — certainly something dramatic — and she declared that it was in need of a name.

"It *has* a name, Miss Underwood," said Dresden Scott. "The old people around here call it Minmaneth Rock."

Priscilla leaned forward from her seat, her eyes wide, as if not sure she had heard correctly. Mercia touched her niece's hand lightly and John Benning tapped an admonitory forefinger twice against his lips. Cordelia stood looking away from Mr. Scott, and the surprise upon her face did not betray her. James coolly regarded the guide. "Minmaneth," he said. "Is that an Indian name?"

"It does have an Indian sound to it," said Mr. Scott, without commitment. He dismounted and began to look through his saddlebags.

John Benning walked to the brow of the hill, beside Cordelia, and trained his eyes upon the dark and distant overhang of rock. "Those glaciers were very distinctive sorts of carvers, weren't they," he said dryly.

"What a pretty lake," said Cordelia.

"It's all so beautiful!" declared Priscilla, hopping down from the buckboard. "Do you suppose, Mr. Scott, that Cordelia might hire the same people to clear her land?"

"Ma'am," said Dresden Scott. "This *is* her land."

"Goodness sakes!" said Mercia quietly, though she had half-suspected it.

"Very nice, Mr. Scott," said James sincerely.

"It's so beautiful!" shouted Priscilla again. "Cordelia!" she said, hurrying to her cousin's side. "Cordelia! Did you hear? This is your land!"

"I know," said Cordelia. She was holding the brooch that her uncle Basil had given her; looking not at the lake and the forest and the granite ledge below, but staring at the lake and forest and gray ledge carved upon the piece of agate in her hand. "Uncle Basil," she said, and Priscilla could not read the expression on her face.

52. No Longer Nameless

THE ROWBOAT TUNKED AGAINST THE SHORE and Sundry hopped onto the bank with the bowline in hand. The bank was steep above them, but an ancient stream bed conveyed them gradually to the meadows beyond.

Sundry led the way to where the stream bed broadened into a wet declivity. Mister Walton had no sooner reached Sundry's side than a well-dressed though hatless man with a large beard hurried by, not ten feet away. A moose, wearing a suit of red flannel underwear on one antler, followed this fellow at a trot. A second man hove into view, waving his arms and shouting a series of unconnected vowels, and a third man could be seen, some distance away, calling out: "Divert him! Divert him!"

In the center of this activity stood the woman they had seen from their vantage on the eastern shore; she watched this activity—men and moose— her feet apart, her hands on her hips, and did not give the impression of one who is gladdened by what she sees.

The participants in this strange chase stopped then, huffing and blowing with their exertions. It was clear that they had run themselves out. The moose had other difficulties; the red flannels had partially dislodged from their perch and fallen over the animal's face. The moose let out a snort that startled everyone and the garment shuddered like a window shade in the wind.

Several moments passed before the moose made a second uncultured sort of noise—a kind of honking bellow—and with a toss of his head, he flung the underwear into the breeze, which carried the garment to the feet of Mister Walton. The moose pivoted with unexpected grace, bowled over the bearded man, and disappeared amongst the nearest row of trees.

"Good heavens!" declared Mister Walton. "I *do* know these fellows!"

If an angel had appeared before him, Thump could not have been more thunderstruck. He was, to put it mildly, out of sorts—having nearly been run over by a large mammal—and he blinked up at a cottony cloud, thinking that it looked like a great round-faced man smiling down at him. And then that great round face was suddenly occulted by the familiar round and smiling face of Mister Walton.

"Mr. Thump," said the bespectacled man. "Are you injured?"

"It is very kind of you to inquire," replied Thump, who was not at all sure he wasn't dreaming. He looked for Ephram and Eagleton, but saw, instead, that Mister Walton held the very object of their chase!

Of course! he thought. *In the hour of our direst need, our chairman has come forth to lead us!*

"You have it!" he declared. Thump saw that other people were gathered about him.

"Shall we call for help?" asked Phileda.

"Mister Walton!" came a great shout, and Eagleton rushed into Thump's field of vision to shake hands with the great man.

"Can you move?" asked Sundry of Thump. He took the supine man by a hand and a shoulder and helped him up.

"My word!" Eagleton declared. "The suit itself!"

Mrs. Maloney appeared next, her hands out to accept the hard-won prize.

"I am not mistaken!" declared Ephram. "It is the chairman!"

Mister Walton gladly transferred the undergarment to Mrs. Maloney, who huffed once in the direction of Ephram and Thump and hurried off for home. (Mr. Maloney did go into town the next day to purchase a second suit.)

Eagleton shook Mister Walton's hand and congratulated him on accomplishing what they could not. "Brilliant," he was saying. "Brilliant."

Ephram took up the hand shaking when his friend left off. "The prize *and* our chairman, all in a single day! A singular day! Remarkable!"

Without explanation or introduction, Eagleton shook the professor's hand, then carried on to Sundry and Jared. Ephram followed Eagleton's lead.

"You can't imagine how far we chased that moose!" averred Eagleton.

"Miles," said Ephram. "We have chased that moose for miles."

"Oh, yes," agreed Eagleton. "Certainly miles."

"How many miles, do you suppose?" wondered Sundry.

"Two, three . . ." suggested Eagleton. "The animal did not move in a straightforward fashion. His path was circuitous."

"Three," said Thump, settling the matter. "Oh, yes. Three miles if a single step. Back and forth, back and forth. We covered this ground several times. I am sure that it was three miles."

"A league, in fact," said Jared McCannon. "A league is generally measured at three miles."

"A league, yes," said Thump, not knowing that a golden phrase was about to fall from his lips. "We were on the path of that moose for a league!"

"Do you think so?" asked Ephram.

"Oh, yes," said Eagleton. "Thump is right. We followed that moose's path a league, certainly."

"It was a *moose path league*," said Mister Walton with a chuckle.

"Pardon me?" said Thump, quite taken by the phrase.

"A country mile and a moose path league."

"Yes," said Thump, as if to himself. "A moose path league. . . ."

"Well," said Phileda McCannon. "Why don't you gentlemen come with us across the river? We can make two trips with the boat and you can help us finish what is left of our picnic."

"Well," said Ephram, "I'm not sure we should. . . ."

"Nonsense!" said Phileda. "I insist."

And as they were already moving in the direction of the shore, this argument won out. They picked their way down the field and, following the stream bed, disappeared behind the steep bluff of the western bank. Thump was the last of them, the straggler, walking abstractedly with his head down and his hands clasped behind his back. He mumbled to himself, his voice lost among the louder, happier sounds of conversation and discovery.

Then they were gone, their voices drifting, trailing away, covered by the breeze as it skimmed across the grass.

A bird called from a nearby bush, and something rustled nearby.

The breeze softened and momentarily died.

And from the direction of the river, clear and triumphant, came Thump's voice, filling the sudden void of sound.

"That's it!"

53. A Slip of the Thumb

THE SOUNDS OF CAMP BEING PITCHED found their way over the hill to James Underwood's unattending ears. As a former naval officer he found it natural to toss out an order or two and leave the duties of making camp to others.

And so, John Benning directed the raising of the tents, while Mr. Scott managed the animals and Mercia built a fire from wood that Ethan gathered. James rummaged through his haversack till he found a pair of binoculars, and walked over the brow of the hill toward the lake.

The sun stretched the shadows cast by Minmaneth Rock, and streaks of light penetrated the cavelike hollow beneath the massive overhang. James sat down on the slope, rested his elbows on his knees, and raised the field glasses. To the naked eye, the shore rose gently and disappeared in the gloom below the igneous formation, but his lenses revealed to him a damp, ferny place that gave no indication of human influence.

He was certain, however, that human industry had visited that forsaken place; felt sure, in fact, that his brother had stood beneath that giant rock. It was difficult, from this distance, to judge the dimensions of the granite outcrop, but he guessed that a dozen men could easily stand beneath it.

It occurred to him to investigate the perimeters of the lake; he had, after all, every indication that others were interested in the mystery surrounding his daughter's bequest. Who was to say that those *others* had not followed them, or even preceded them to these acres?

"So, Mr. Underwood," came a voice from behind him. "Do you think that your brother's cryptic note leads to that piece of rock?"

John Benning stood several yards above him on the slope. "Yes, son, I do," said James. He turned back to the view below them, indicating by his easy manner that John was welcome to join him.

"Have you learned anything about Mr. Scott?" asked John, plunking himself down.

"Not much. He is not a great talker, Have *you*?"

"Not really. But he was very quick to inform us about the name of that rock over there."

"Yes, he was," replied James. "And that leads me to believe that he can be trusted." He regarded John Benning's raised eyebrows. "If the false Charles Stimply, or the man whom you caught eavesdropping, or whoever is behind them was aware of a place named Minmaneth Rock, they wouldn't need us here to find what they're looking for. And if Mr. Scott knew anything about my brother's message, or the circumstances of Cordelia's inheritance, there would be little reason for him to point it out so quickly."

"You're right, of course," said John. "It's just that that fellow last night, spying through keyholes, has me nervous."

James smiled. "Well, in that case, do a bit of spying yourself." He passed John Benning the binoculars, raised himself to his feet with a minimum of creaking, and walked back up the slope in hopes of finding a crackling fire and a brewing pot of tea.

When John Benning reappeared in camp, the sunset glowing behind him, Cordelia almost resented his presence. How she would have basked in the revelation of this place—the beauty of it; even the mystery presented by the presence of Minmaneth Rock could not so complicate the pleasure of discovery as the exhilarating nearness of this handsome young man.

But matters of the heart will take precedence, and Cordelia's enjoyment was partially lost in the anxious attraction between John Benning and herself. She felt that her emotions were drawn too thin, and was exasperated, as one might be at the arrival of welcome company just as one has reached the last chapter of a good book.

The light of the campfire took over its tiny kingdom at the top of the hill, and more than one member of the party thought briefly that it was better than Morse code for announcing their presence.

Mr. Scott did not join the party, but sat on a box by the tent that he would be sharing with Ethan and John Benning. Seated beyond the brighter perimeters of the firelight, he pulled a small knife from one pocket, the beginnings of a wooden hand-carving from another, and proceeded to whittle. He seemed uninterested, even unaware, of the conversation around him, until Mercia drew him into it.

"And how long have you been a guide, Mr. Scott?" she asked.

He hesitated as he made certain that he had been spoken to, hesitated again as he calculated in his mind. "Nearly seven years, ma'am," he said.

"And do you enjoy it?"

Mr. Scott had gone back to his work, and so he paused again. "Yes, I suppose I do."

"But in the winter . . ."

"I have a place north of town," he said. "Simply keeping warm and fed in those months occupies a person."

"The woods must be beautiful in the winter," offered Priscilla.

"They are very . . . empty," he replied without disagreeing with her. "There are signs of life, of course—the tracks of mice and rabbit and deer, the sounds of the ravens and chickadees—but there is a particular stillness when there is only snow underfoot and the songbirds have gone."

"It sounds lonely," said Cordelia quietly, hardly aware that she had spoken. The proximity of John Benning had made her self-conscious, and she had said little since dinner.

"One can feel lonely in a crowd, Miss Underwood," said Mr. Scott.

Cordelia looked up and saw his eyes shining with the firelight in her direction. John Benning caught the subtle change of expression in her face and looked past his shoulder at the guide. "Dresden," said John. "Did I hear that correctly?"

The guide did not respond immediately.

"Your first name?"

"Yes."

"I have never heard it used for a person's name before," pressed John.

"My mother was born there, in Germany," he specified, since in the state of Maine there is also a town called Dresden.

"But you sound a touch of the highland," said Mercia, "which would explain your surname."

"My father was from Edinburgh," explained the guide. "They met on the passage over. We lived in Halifax when I was young and my mother insisted that I speak like a native." He looked as if he had said more than he had intended and he returned to his carving.

"Are you related to Sir Walter?" asked Cordelia, with such brightness and interest in her voice that Mr. Scott smiled.

"From some distance, I am told," he said.

"I greatly admire him," she said.

"I won't hold it against you," he replied, and if this was an attempt to be wry, it was an awkward one; if it was an attempt to put paid to the conversation, it was successful. Cordelia thought that he cut himself with his knife, but she could not tell for sure in the wavering light of the fire, and he gave no indication of it as he continued to work the small piece of wood. Once the conversation had turned to other topics, however, she saw him put the edge of his thumb to his mouth.

54. Mister Walton Proves His Mettle

THUMP'S VOICE CARRIED like a cry of "Eureka!" over the river, echoing from the bank of ancient shell heaps on the opposite shore, and the rest of the party turned to regard him on the slope above; he did look stimulated, almost like a prophet with that magnificent beard and the light of triumph in his eye.

"That's it!" he cried again. "I do beg your pardon," he added. "The answer to an old conundrum." He appeared embarrassed.

"It is remarkable how often we find answers when we are not looking for them," said Miss McCannon graciously. She held her hand out to Eagleton, who stood near to her. "I am Phileda McCannon."

"Good heavens!" said Mister Walton, realizing that he had been remiss. "I haven't introduced everyone!"

"Christopher Eagleton," said that man, taking Miss McCannon's hand. "This is my brother, Jared."

"Matthew Ephram," continued Eagleton. "And Joseph Thump."

And so went this mutual presentation, everyone standing upon the bank with one foot lower than the other. Mister Walton apologized for his oversight. "I don't believe you know Sundry Moss," he said.

"I am familiar with a moss or two, but not sundry," said Ephram. He shook Sundry's hand, waiting for Mister Walton to introduce the young man.

"Really," said Mister Walton. "Are there Mosses in Portland, then?"

"Oh, yes, I expect so," replied Ephram. "At Deering Oaks, certainly."

"Perhaps they are related," suggested Mister Walton, amiably.

"I suppose they might be," said Ephram, with great thought. He had never felt any noticeable enthusiasm for moss, but Mister Walton's interest caused him to wonder if he hadn't overlooked a subject of some fascination.

Eagleton and Thump also waited to catch Sundry's name. Sundry, for his part, was aware of the misunderstanding and prepared to enjoy it.

"I read somewhere," stated Eagleton, "in a book, I think, that all mosses are related."

"How many do you suppose there are?" wondered Thump.

The conversation had taken an odd turn, and Mister Walton was about to clarify matters when Sundry himself spoke up.

"There are eleven Mosses in Edgecomb," he said.

"In that town alone," said Eagleton, impressed by this firsthand knowledge. "Christopher Eagleton," he said, shaking Sundry's hand again in hopes of gaining his name.

"I am glad to meet you," said Sundry. "Yes."

"I am sure that you will find various moss in most towns," suggested Ephram.

"Actually," said Sundry, "you will find Varius Moss in Hallowell."

The three friends digested this in silence.

"At the lumber mill there."

Mister Walton cleared his throat. "Perhaps we should continue this conversation on the other side of the river." The look of pure innocence on Sundry's face made him chuckle.

"Certainly!" said Eagleton. He was thinking of Alfred Lofton's assertion that Mister Walton had used sundry moss to protect himself and was keen on knowing how it was done.

Thump again brought up the rear, wondering who this young man was, who was so knowledgeable about botany. It occurred to him, as he walked, that some inspiration had stopped him in his tracks, and it was a moment before he recalled it to mind. "Ah, yes!" he said to himself.

There it was, as Thump brought up the rear. And there it was, as they partook of the remainder of that well-stocked picnic. And it was still there when the steamboat came by on its last run of the day and picked up the increased party for the trip back to town.

Even if Thump had not cried out "That's it!" during their descent to the river, Ephram and Eagleton would have known that something was up from the glow of Aristotelian inspiration upon his face. As they waved with the rest of the group to the dwindling figures of Jared McCannon and Professor Chadbourne, Ephram and Eagleton wondered when Thump would share his revelation with them.

"And so," asked Miss McCannon of the members, "you haven't told me how you know Mister Walton."

"He is . . ." said Ephram haltingly, ". . . our chairman."

"Pardon me?" said Mister Walton, unsure of what he had heard.

"We have a club, you understand," explained Eagleton.

"How nice," said the woman. She glanced at Mister Walton, as if he might add something to this explanation.

"Have you a mission, yet, for your association?" he wondered.

"I do believe we are getting closer to that," averred Ephram.

"What is the name of your society?" asked Miss McCannon.

"We haven't actually got a—" began Eagleton, when Thump, quite uncharacteristically, interrupted him.

"The Moosepath League!" he declared bluntly.

One corner of Miss McCannon's mouth and an eyebrow rose. Mister Walton laughed delightedly. Sundry folded his arms. Ephram and Eagleton looked astonished.

"Thump!" said Ephram.

"My good man!" said Eagleton.

"The Moosepath League!" said Thump again.

"That's it!" shouted Ephram, echoing Thump's earlier declaration. It was so fitting, so tied up with their club's short history, so very rugged in its sound! "The Moosepath League!" said Ephram, trying the name in the air.

"My good man!" said Eagleton again, pumping Thump's hand ecstatically. "The Moosepath League!" It had such a ring to it, such an implication of adventure, such a clamor of the outdoors! "That's it!" he agreed.

"The Moosepath League," said Thump.

"Congratulations," said Mister Walton.

"My dear sir," said Thump with great formality. "It was your own self who put the words together."

"Indeed, it was!" remembered Eagleton.

"Good heavens!" cried Ephram. "It's true! Thump has named our club, but it was Mister Walton who provided the inspiration!" And another round of hand shaking ensued.

How glorious—in one afternoon their chairman had rescued them from a wild animal, recovered the object of their quest, provided them with a delicious meal (prepared by Miss McCannon, to be sure), furnished them with transportation back to town (perhaps a matter of accident to less enthusiastic minds), and now called into play the very name by which their club would be hailed throughout its splendid history!

Tears sprung to Thump's eyes, and Mister Walton laughed again as the bearded fellow embraced his chairman.

It is remarkable that so little remains to mark the evening of July 10th, 1896, in Damariscotta, Maine. There is a brief reference in a local journal that resounds with none of the excitement that must have been experienced by those attending the Lincoln Hall that night. There is, to be sure, Captain John Taylor's account to his brother. *Now let me tell you*, he wrote, *what happened that very evening at the Lincoln Hall, and you will think that things have grown rather wild hereabouts.* . . .

Most important, of course, is the inscription on the wall of the dressing room, stage left, of the Lincoln Hall itself—for it marks the camaraderie of the evening's adventures, the source of a local legend, and the beginning of a noble and long-lived tradition.

The inscription can be seen there still.

Looking from the dining room of the Maine Hotel, Mister Walton could see the town's main thoroughfare filling with carriages and traps as people gathered for the evening's entertainment. There was excitement and pleasantry in the dining room itself as the guests chatted over dessert.

It was in the course of dinner conversation that the term *chairman* was employed several times by the members of the club, and Mister Walton realized finally that they were referring to himself.

"Why, yes," said Ephram, upon questioning. "Didn't you know?"

"Know what, my friend?" asked Mister Walton.

"I suppose he wouldn't know," said Eagleton.

"We have perhaps been hasty in conferring this position without Mister Walton's knowledge," said Ephram to Eagleton.

"We have perhaps taken much for granted in imagining that he would accept," agreed Eagleton.

"Good heavens!" said Thump, looking discomforted. "Have we been impertinent?"

The three took on an air of uncertainty, and Ephram stood slowly, like a student ready to take the blame for a class prank. "Sir," he said, with great humility. "I do believe we owe you an apology."

"Certainly not," said Mister Walton. "Do I understand that you are offering me the chairmanship to your club . . . the Moosepath League?"

"Yes," said Ephram, his head hanging low. "I fear we have risen to extreme heights of presumption. A man such as yourself must have more lofty institutions than ours calling upon his time and his sagacity. We greatly regret attaching your name to our organization without your express consent."

"Ah, I would very much like to be a part of your order, but I fear I am not worthy of the honor you bestow upon me," answered Mister Walton.

"Certainly you are!"

"Nonsense!"

"More than worthy!"

"Well then, gentlemen," said Mister Walton, himself standing. "I must say that I quite enjoy your company, and if you will indeed have me as your chairman, I will gladly serve as such."

Ephram's eyes were misty and he had some difficulty speaking. "Gentlemen," he said finally. "This is a great day! I take extreme pleasure in handing over my temporary captaincy of . . . the Moosepath League to our chairman, Mister Tobias Walton!" And here they stood (Sundry included) and applauded.

"How many are in your organization?" wondered Sundry, when the applause had finished and the resultant rumble from the rest of the dining room had died away.

"We are all here," stated Ephram calmly.

"Would you care to join us?" asked a newly enthused Eagleton, leaning forward in his seat.

"Well, I'm not sure. Is it proper for the chairman's employee to be part of the club?" Sundry questioned the chairman himself.

"What are the rules?" wondered Mister Walton.

"There are no rules!" declared Thump happily, and there in the dining room of the Maine Hotel, one of the Moosepath League's most celebrated members was nominated, elected, and applauded.

Sundry took it all with great composure, raising one hand from behind his head to acknowledge his induction. "I do like an organization without rules," he said quietly.

And so the first official function of the Moosepath League was to attend that evening's concert performance. They made for a brave sight, walking the short distance to the Lincoln Hall. It was a handsome building with wide front doors and a broad staircase leading to a gaslit lobby. Glittering chandeliers hung in the hall itself, and the five members of the club could see the crowd gathering in clumps as they purchased their tickets.

The streets grew quiet as the last stragglers hurried through the wide-flung doors at the bottom of the stairwell; and from the open windows came the strains of tuning instruments, tremoling with the sleepy songs of birds in the warm evening air.

Hardly a breeze stirred the beautiful trees that lined the main street, so that a glimpse down the length of the town might have been like a photograph, painted with the colors of life—a postcard, perhaps, with the legend on its back saying "Damariscotta, Maine; July 10th, 1896." The sun pinked the horizon behind the buildings opposite the Lincoln Hall, and long shadows fell upon the storefronts and facades.

Applause sounded down the empty streets, the faint tick of a baton, then the opening bars of Bizet's Overture to *The Fair Maid of Perth*. Music emanated from the hall, as if it were a great brick bandstand; and across the small alley the employees of the Maine Hotel listened through their own open windows to the concert's first selection.

There was no one to see the large dark form padding its way down the back street from behind the Northey Square Livery Stable. Had there been, they no doubt would have conjectured about the presence of a medium-sized bear in the middle of town.

Students of the Moosepath League have attempted to trace Maude's path from the eastern shore of the Sheepscot River to the front entrance of Damariscotta's Lincoln Hall. Maude's path from the river to the hall was later discovered, from muddy paw prints, and a lay-down was found on the banks among a stand of birches. It is generally agreed that the bear was sleeping when her sensitive ears caught the first piece of the evening's entertainment. Possibly the noise of the instruments put her in mind of the small orchestra that traveled with Colonel Cobb's Wild West Show.

At any rate, her paw prints indicated that she did not linger at the foot of the stairs, but lumbered with her rolling gait up into the lobby, like any other patron of the arts. The ticket taker was in the office, counting the receipts; the manager was in the balcony.

There is some disagreement concerning the amount of concert that Maude took in before she was observed, sitting placidly at the back of the hall with her hind feet splayed out before her. Some people swore that they had heard a cowlike sound during the applause for the waltz, but they thought at the time it was the tuba player tuning his instrument.

It was time for the guest speaker, and the master of ceremonies appeared on stage from behind the curtain. "Many of you have heard," he said, "or even read about the Ascensionist movement, and there has been much discussion concerning it and its adherents. The belief in physical ascension before the moment of death, the deferment of personal distinction through the dropping of Christian names for single initials, and the use of spontaneous singing in their rituals—these and other unusual aspects of this movement may seem strange to us; but the people of this grand state have long enjoyed a reputation of open-mindedness, and I know that it is an interest in new things that has drawn many of you here tonight."

He paused in his speech and squinted past the footlights to the back of the room, then shook his head. "And so, I ask you all to welcome Mrs. R., who will answer questions for fifteen minutes after her talk. Mrs. R."

Mrs. R. came from behind the curtain amidst polite applause. "Thank you for your kind welcome," she said. "Let me tell you of my dream of ascension, that first taught me . . ."

There was a polite silence as she leaned forward slightly to squint beyond the footlights. ". . . tell you of . . ." She leaned further and shaded her eyes. Now curiosity got the better of much of the audience, and people were craning their necks to see what had caught her attention. There was a collective gasp in the back of the room; then Mrs. R. said something in a small voice and fell in a heap upon the stage.

The next moments were filled with great confusion. Some people stood to see what had happened; others continued to look to the back of the room for the source of the woman's agitation. Several men appeared from behind the curtain or climbed onto the stage from the audience. "She's fainted!" came the call. "Water, bring water!"

"A bear!" shouted someone. There were several screams and a panic among the back rows. People were climbing onto their seats, or attempting to crawl over their neighbors—anything to get away from the back of the hall.

"A bear?" said Mister Walton. He stood, an odd thrill running through him. Thump—that man of action—had run halfway up the aisle in the direction of the stage; he then turned about in a sudden change of mind and came to a halt after two strides.

More screams, from men and women both, echoed from the lofty ceiling, and a commotion of movement and shouts filled the air.

"Good heavens!" Eagleton was saying. "It's a bear!"

"A bear?" said Mister Walton again.

Sundry, standing on his seat several places down, could see the round ears and broad back of something making its way down the center aisle.

"Sundry?" called Mister Walton.

"As I live and breathe, Mister Walton!"

The portly fellow leaned around Ephram to get a better view, and soon a familiar ursine face hove into view. "Maude!" shouted Mister Walton, and somehow the sound of her name pierced the chaotic voices and movement to reach the creature's furry ears. Maude swung her large head in the direction of the gathered Moosepath League and Eagleton half leaped into Ephram's arms, causing a near chain reaction of human dominoes.

"Stop!" shouted Mister Walton, catching Ephram with one shoulder and throwing his arm out in the bear's direction.

The babble of frightened voices quieted; the press of bodies shifted; shouts turned to hushed exclamations of disbelief. Mrs. R. revived on the stage; she sat up and took the glass of water offered to her, but only gaped over it when she raised it to her lips.

The general retreat had halted; near silence fell over the hall. The men on stage followed Mrs. R.'s startled gaze. Halfway down the center aisle, a bear was standing on its head.

Maude mooed in recognition as Mister Walton emerged from the row of chairs. He inched around her, his hand out. "Maude," he said sternly.

"Toby!" said Phileda McCannon in a stage whisper.

The bear let out a groan; her inverted hind feet waved in the air, then she dropped to the floor with a weighty bump and the swish of claws.

"Maude," came Mister Walton's voice. He was several paces toward the back of the room and he beckoned gingerly to her. "Come, come," he said. He was rather astonished at his own actions, and more than a little relieved when Sundry Moss appeared at his side.

"What are we going to do?" asked Sundry.

"I think we are going to walk her from the building," said the chairman of the Moosepath League. He moved with Sundry to the door of the lobby. "Maude," he said with some conviction.

The bear bawled like a recalcitrant child, and a ripple of shudders and half-bitten exclamations ran through the crowd.

"Maude!" said Mister Walton with more severity in his voice. "Come now."

The bear shambled slowly, grunting like a farm animal that has been called away from the feeding trough.

"Come, Maude." Mister Walton and Sundry were in the lobby now, at the head of the stairwell. The bear fell into her rolling gait, and as she left the hall a huge sigh of relief expressed itself from the crowd like a single puff of wind.

Mister Walton and Sundry walked slowly down the stairs with Maude two or three steps behind. Mister Walton felt as if he were exercising a dog.

They reached the bottom of the stairs and stepped aside, making room for the bear as she shouldered herself out onto the sidewalk. The sky was gray. Evening had fallen. They paused to listen to the chirp of early crickets and breathe the cooler air.

Then there came a resounding applause, spilling from the open windows above. Shouts of "Bravo! Bravo!" and wordless cheers punctuated the ovation.

Maude grinned, happy to hear again the sound of an appreciative crowd.

"What do we do now?" wondered Sundry, feeling remarkably calm standing next to the large beast.

"We should wire Sheriff Piper, I think. He will know whom to contact. Perhaps the man from the Wild West Show will have arrived. Come, Maude!"

They walked down the alley to Main Street, where they rounded the corner. As they proceeded, a ripple of tension swept down the line of horses tethered along the way. A young man, sweeping the door stoop of the Maine Hotel, caught sight of Maude and froze, wide-eyed and open-mouthed.

"Good evening, son," said Mister Walton easily.

"Good evening, sir," said the boy.

"Where will we find the telegraph office, if you please?"

"Two doors down," said the fellow, pointing. The wary snort of a horse startled him.

"Thank you," said Mister Walton.

"You're welcome, sir." He peered after them in the twilight as the three companions ambled down the street.

Sundry could not resist looking back over his shoulder and tipping his hat. "Nice night," he said.

55. The Writing on the Wall

IT IS ONE THING TO HEAR (or even sing) the deeds of Hercules; it is quite another to see for yourself as he wrestles the Erymanthian Boar!

How inspired, therefore, were Ephram, Eagleton, and Thump to see their stout and stouthearted chairman call forth his powers of authority, take command of the situation, and quell the wild nature of a full-grown bear!

The surrounding crowd was hardly less astounded, and the applause that broke out was spontaneous; half believed that they had witnessed a remarkable act of bravery, and the other half were as convinced that they had seen nothing more than a remarkable act.

The three men bathed in the ovation—as proud of their chairman's deeds as if they had performed them themselves. Thump raised his hands in the air and bowed slightly (a mysterious gesture to those who did not know him), accepting praise for the absent Mister Walton.

"Thump! It is amazing!" cried Ephram.

"I am agog!" declared Thump.

All about them islands of conversation ebbed and flowed, while the orchestra leader and the manager of the Lincoln Hall discussed how they would conduct the remainder of the evening. The word came down from the dressing room that Mrs. R. felt too airy to continue, but much of the evening's music had yet to be performed.

"Do you know," said Eagleton, "I must confess to a certain degree of disappointment. Despite having been informed that Mrs. R. would be a religious speaker and not the Mrs. Roberto who immediately came to mind when we first saw the word *ascensionist* in the same citation, I was half hoping, when the curtain parted, to see that noble lady whom we met upon the field of Freeport."

"Ah, well," was all that Ephram could think to say. Thump could think of less. Clearly they each had been affected (and Thump not the least) by a similar unspoken hope.

"And yet," said Ephram, after some thought, "it remains a singular coincidence, to meet two Mrs. R.'s within the space of a few days, who each describe themselves as Ascensionists."

"It is not a common term," agreed Eagleton.

"However separate these two Mrs. R.'s are in expertise," continued Ephram, "it seems almost fateful that we should cross paths with *both* of them in such a short while."

"Indeed," said Eagleton. "It is deep."

"Hmm," said Thump.

"I wish," said Ephram, "that Mister Walton were with us now. I can't help but think that he would have sage words regarding this mystery."

"How extraordinary," added Eagleton. "To be drawn away by a bear. And the young man too."

"It is, perhaps, a test," said Ephram, in such a small voice that his friends read, rather than heard, what he had said.

"A test," said Eagleton.

"In the absence of our chairman," said Thump, "so early in his chairmanship, we are perhaps called upon to prove ourselves worthy of him."

"My goodness, Thump!" said Ephram. "You may be right!"

"Yes," said Thump. "We must follow his example!"

"Shall we?" suggested Ephram.

"We must . . . act!" Thump turned to the front of the hall and began to press through the crowd toward the stage. "We shall interview this Mrs. R.!"

"Good heavens!" cried Eagleton, as he and Ephram followed.

"To the backstage!" cried Thump, and all heads turned to see what new excitement had occurred.

They hurried past the manager and the orchestra leader, excused themselves past the matrons and town fathers sitting in the front rows, and Ephram shouted apologies. Their ascent of the stage was more dramatic than graceful, and their disappearance behind the stage-left curtain raised the level of conversation and speculation in the hall to a new height.

To this day the immediate backstage of the Lincoln Hall—now known as the Lincoln Theater—affords a challenge to anyone of standard size, and offers no room for flown sets or hidden choruses. The three friends found their progress halted straightaway by an inconsiderate wall. Upstage, however, there was (and is) a door on either side, and they quite naturally spilled through the nearest.

Thump half ran, half tumbled down a flight of stairs to a little room below, where several stagehands were discussing the evening's unprecedented events. Ephram and Eagleton caught themselves and each other at the head of the stairs, while Thump attempted to articulate something to the young men.

"Mrs. R.," he said uncertainly.

One of the stagehands hooked a thumb over his shoulder, and following his gesture, Thump saw that there was also a flight of stairs leading up from the stage level. He hurried back to his friends and led the way in a scuffling run up to the stage-left dressing room.

The term *dressing room* occurred to Thump just as he reached the top of the stairway, and his sudden check—caused by the implications of this term—precipitated a painful sort of three-way collision, which ended in a tangle of club members upon the floor.

"What is the meaning of this?" demanded an angry male voice.

Each of the members attempted to help his friends to their feet, despite that a body should himself be *on* his feet before performing this kindness. A good deal of confusion was had concerning who was helping whom, and the outcome was that Thump fell over (or was knocked down) several times again before solidly regaining his feet. Continued bewilderment was the result of the three gentlemen brushing the dust from one another's shoulders;

Eagleton had his hat knocked from his hands, and Thump accidentally cuffed Ephram on the side of the head.

"Who are you?" demanded the voice.

As one the three men straightened up and regarded the pair before them. The frail and fey Mrs. R. sat upon a short bench looking alarmed; the man standing before her was bald, mustachioed, and irate.

"Do pardon us," said Ephram to the man.

"We are," said Thump with obvious pride, "members of . . . the Moosepath League."

Eagleton stepped forward. "We are acquaintances of Mrs. Roberto."

"I know no Mrs. Roberto," said the man.

"She is an ascensionist of another sort," explained Ephram.

"What is it that you want?" demanded the man. "My wife has had a very frightening experience!"

"Ah, yes," said Ephram, his hat over his heart. "Our condolences."

"Mrs. R.'s carriage is here," came a voice from down the stairwell.

Mr. R. took his wife's hand gently. "Come, dear," he said. "You," he directed toward the three men. "Stand aside!"

They did. Mrs. R. rose tentatively and allowed herself to be led to the stairs. Mr. R. turned a glare upon the three members as he passed them. Then the couple were down the stairs and out of sight. A small round of applause drifted up from the hall as Mrs. R. and her husband moved through the audience. Soon the orchestra could be heard, tuning up again.

"This has been inconclusive," stated Ephram.

"What could it all mean?" wondered Eagleton.

"It is all very uncertain."

"Perhaps we were meant to wait for Mister Walton after all."

This dialogue was conducted during a general and circuitous investigation of the small room, a sort of unhurried caucus race, during which they noticed many signatures and dates upon the walls. Eagleton stopped to peer at a name, scribbled in ink at eye level; he could not read it. Other graffiti boasted the titles of familiar speakers or musical talents who had prepared themselves in this space. "It has been a remarkable day," said Eagleton, and he could be said to have indulged in understatement here.

Ephram sat upon the short bench and thought: A *moose, red flannel underwear, shell heaps . . . a bear; and of course, Mister Walton, gloriously taking each situation in hand; yes, here is grand understatement!* He respected Eagleton for it.

Thump continued to stalk the room like a caged lion.

Eagleton peered down at a low table at the end of the bench; there was an inkwell and a sheaf of writing paper. He opened the drawer in the table and found writing implements—several pens, a small brush, a bottle of ink. He took no more than a moment or two to settle his mind upon his next course of action. He opened the bottle of ink, selected the brush from its brethren, and scanned the walls for a spot that was more or less clear of writing.

Ephram leaned back on the bench and watched him. Thump ceased his pacing and stood at Eagleton's shoulder, making noises of approval.

Eagleton worked with utter concentration. He did not pause or reflect until he was finished; and when he was finished, he stood back to take the measure of what he had done.

Some, of course, wonder to this day why a more specific date was not attached; but they are, perhaps, missing the point. The single record of the year is a statement in itself—in fact, a statement of a state of mind. One day alone was not enough to encompass what they had seen, and what their recent experiences meant to them.

The omission of Sundry's name disturbs others, but Eagleton can be excused for this, considering the circumstances of the day. He was perhaps thinking that the three of them and Mister Walton formed a quadrumvirate of charter membership.

Nevertheless, it stands there to this day—on the wall of the stage-left dressing room of the Lincoln Theater, in Damariscotta, Maine:

THE MOOSEPATH LEAGUE
1896

M.E.   **C.E.**

J.T.   **T.W.**CHAIR

Thump could find no words. He patted Eagleton's shoulder.
Ephram spoke for them all, quietly, saying only once, "Bravo."

56. Design

A NIGHT BREEZE CHUCKLED AGAINST the tent where Cordelia and Priscilla slept; and the moon splayed soft shadows across the grassy hill, where all colors were some shade of gray in the light of the night's rising lamp.

Cordelia slept the sleep of the exhausted, deep and dreamless. Their entire party—perhaps Mr. Scott excepted—had been torn between excitement and fatigue as the evening wore on; and to the surprise of everyone (herself included) it was Cordelia who initiated the call to bed.

Camp had settled down quickly; the fire was leveled and banked to a dull glow. Priscilla and Cordelia had talked in low voices while they retired (hardly less dressed for bed than for the day); then they climbed beneath their respective blankets and dropped off in the midst of conversation.

The night cooled as the breeze came up, and the moon in the smallest hour silvered the line of hills in the east.

Cordelia did not waken all at once; there was only the realization that she was not asleep, that she had been asleep, that she wanted to roll over and drift off again. The shuffling sound in the tent she thought was Priscilla, who was often restless in her sleep; then there was a dull moment when the shuffling ceased to sound commonplace or natural, and her half-blissful desire to float softly back to that dreamless state was replaced by an irritation at being wakened altogether.

There was a light in the tent when she opened her eyes, and a startling shadow that fell across her and climbed up the near wall and a large rough hand suddenly covering her mouth. Cordelia found no scream within her, only a terrible panic for an unrestricted breath. She was lurched to her feet and held in a solid grip, the sharp smells of tobacco and sweat and damp wool rising to her nose.

Other shadows lurked before her, and a sliver of light from a partially opened storm lamp cut across Priscilla's empty cot. Cordelia forced herself to fall limp in the arms of her attacker, then with one whiplike snap of every muscle in her body she nearly broke herself away.

The man behind her grunted angrily; a shadow dislocated itself from the corner of the tent, the beam of lantern light pivoting, and the gleam of a pistol that rose to kiss Cordelia's forehead coldly. A pair of feverish eyes glowed on the other side of the pistol, and Cordelia had the image of a gaunt and unshaven face, a hawklike nose.

But fear had dropped out of her, replaced by a bitter and overwhelming anger, and she met those eyes without flinching. The man with the pistol was no fool; even as Cordelia prepared another defensive assault, he turned the lantern back to a bound and gagged and weeping Priscilla and, more important, turned the pistol upon Priscilla as well. His face did not turn, nor did his gaze leave Cordelia's.

Suddenly the horror of the situation penetrated Cordelia's anger, and the pit of her stomach was touched by ice.

"Quietly," came a voice, itself so quiet that she could not be sure if it came from the man before her. Barely lowering his gun, he snatched up some clothes at the foot of her cot; then he did relax long enough to peer out from the flaps of the tent.

With a violent wrench, Cordelia was out of the rigid hold and, flinging herself horizontally over her cot, she reached beyond it for the porcelain cover to a chamber pot. It was a bulky broad-shouldered man with a large beard who lunged for her as she swung herself and the stonelike lid around, catching her attacker full in the face. There was a silence-piercing crack and a low grunt. The man fell to his knees, and Cordelia barely avoided his grasping hand as she jumped to her feet.

The size of the tent, however, constrained her retreat, and she found herself off balance as she ran into the back wall. The stricken man rose like a surge of ocean above her; rage animated the jerky movements of his limbs, and a fist shot out and popped against the side of her jaw.

Cordelia did not lose consciousness, but that state of half-dreaming returned to her. She endeavored to regain her feet, but could only make her hands and knees. A string of whispered curses, excuses, and invective hissed in the close air of the tent. She was lifted roughly and carried as dead weight from the tent. Riding bumpily over a broad shoulder, her breath whooshing from her with every second step, she thought she glimpsed the form of Mr. Scott stretched upon the ground—then silvery moonlight on the grass, a descending slope, horses, men moving with increasing noise, the sound of a pistol shot, two more shots from another direction . . .

Her wrists were trussed behind her, and she was lifted over the withers of a horse. Hard language carried over the sound of men climbing into their saddles.

"You ignoramus!"

"I didn't mean to hit her so hard!"

The gaunt man stuck his sharp nose into the larger man's face and hissed beneath his breath. "Do you know what the boss will say? Do you know what he'll do to you if she's hurt permanent?"

"Well, the boss didn't have the lid of a thunder jug broke in his face!"

Another pistol shot heralded the arrival of a third man, who neatly mounted his horse and led the way toward one end of the shore. Cordelia endeavored to understand how many there were—at least four, she was sure, but darkness covered their movements and hoofbeats confused the ear.

"You'll get away lucky if he doesn't put a rope around your neck and hang you by degrees!" spat the hawk-nosed man, who disappeared from the circle of Cordelia's consciousness.

The ride was bruising, the man behind her holding her firmly over the back of the horse. They rode past the lake and over a hill; then the way darkened among trees. They slowed, one horse clopping ahead of them and three more lagging behind. She was lifted down and steadied onto her feet.

"I don't know anything," she said.

"My goodness," said the hawk-nosed man. "We must have made a mistake." He held her things out to her. "The boss thinks you might want to be properly dressed, so you can ride like a lady in your clothes, or you can ride like a saddlebag."

"I don't mind wasting a little of your time. . . ."

"You'll be quick about it. Behind the horse."

Cordelia's tongue discovered several loosened molars on one side of her face. She had taken the clothes, and she turned now to send a withering gaze in the direction of the man who had hit her. There was enough moonlight to see that he was ill at ease. "It's not your boss you have to worry about," she said.

"Oh, I'd expect your rescuers any minute now," said the leader. "We only laid out your guide and scattered the horses. Of course, it's a simple thing to follow a trail through the woods at night."

There was a chill among the trees, and Cordelia simply pulled the dress over her nightclothes. She stood for a moment behind the horse, feeling shaky and sick. The shadows of men and horses moved restlessly in the dark; but more than seeing them, she could hear where they were—almost hear their shapes and sizes—as they hunched upon their mounts, waiting for her.

Astonishment over what had happened gave way as fear caught up with her; breathing was difficult and her heart pounded large and erratic within her. She touched her aching jaw carefully, trying to think without the muddling effects of fear and anger. Losing whatever was buried beneath Minmaneth Rock gave her little pause, but the thought of her parents, most especially her father—who would never forgive himself if something happened to her—caused her to reconsider her false bravado.

She appeared around the front of the horse. "I *do* know something," she said.

The hawk-nosed man simply said, "Tell it to me."

"On the shore of the lake, opposite where we camped . . ." Cordelia spoke slowly and with care. "There is a large rock formation there, called Minmaneth. All I can tell you is what I suspect."

"And that is?"

"That what you are looking for is buried somewhere beneath that rock."

Even in the relative dark, there was an odd glint in the man's eye. "And how do I know you are telling the truth?" he wondered quietly.

She was puzzled by the look—even a little fearful, as if she had just made a very bad decision. "You know I am," she said, with more conviction than she felt. "Now you can let me go."

He laughed—an unnatural sound on that dark trail.

"I'm no danger to you," she insisted. "I can't tell you any more. You can leave me on foot."

He laughed again.

"I have no shoes," she said.

"Well, you're barefoot, then."

Cordelia had come close to pleading, which itself might be dangerous; a disquieting sensation ran down her spine. She took a breath and forced herself to speak with more calm. "Which horse is mine?" she asked.

"Do you see an extra horse?" said the leader. "You will ride with your friend. I promise he will be docile." Then he reared a foot back and drove the toe of his boot into the bearded man's knee. The stricken man hardly dared to complain, but groaned softly and grimaced. The smaller man had smarted his own foot in the process and, cursing beneath his breath, he limped back to his horse.

Cordelia allowed herself to be lifted up and held herself stiffly, stanchioned by the man's arms as she rode sidesaddle. The outriders returned, and two lanterns were hung on short poles and carried like cavalry banners so that the road ahead of them was lit by more than streaks of moonlight through the trees.

They traveled briskly, but without a sense of hurry or fear. Cordelia noted the way as well as she could, her vision distracted and her sense of space and distance baffled by the shadows of trees upon trees rolling past them in the lamplight. Even touched by the moon, the dark beyond their tiny island of illumination seemed large and substantial.

It was barely half an hour since she was wakened, and the situation began to settle upon her, first with slow deepening dread, then with shock. Her jaw ached. "My God!" she said, half in prayer. "Priscilla!"

"We left her behind," came the voice of the band's leader in front of them.

The memory of Priscilla, tied and gagged and terrified, welled up within Cordelia, and outrage drove away all other emotions. "I may hang you myself," she said with such cool pragmatism in her voice that the hawk-nosed man turned in his saddle to glance back at her. "And your boss," she added.

This made him smile. "Yes, he may hang yet," he said.

They moved steadily along a tote road, taking careful cuts through the forest where the way doubled back on itself. The trail was marked by pieces of birch bark tacked against the dark trunks of pine or fir, and these blazes were taken down and tossed into the trees once they had served their purpose.

They traveled for several hours with little rest; the moon told the passing of time by commanding the height of the sky and peering down at their backs. They were heading due north. The moon began its descent to the west, even as the eastern horizon, seen occasionally from a tall hill, glowed with the coming dawn.

Eventually they came to a fork in the road, and here they stopped to discuss the boss's orders. Cordelia had the opportunity now to consider the faces of her kidnappers: the leader; the bearded brute who had hit her; a younger face in the periphery of light; a sour-faced man chewing and spitting tobacco; another man who spoke with a Southern, rather than a Yankee, drawl.

The leader laid out "the boss's" orders, with a particular emphasis in the direction of the man behind Cordelia. The conversation was in half-statements and incomplete sentences, however, and difficult to follow. They spoke almost in code, around her; but one thing was clear: she was not to be harmed in any way.

The leader gave a quick wave of his hand and he and the younger man turned down one side of the fork, eastward. The remaining men continued with her down the opposite path, the moon behind their left shoulder, and dawn rising beyond the piney forest.

57. Pursuit

JAMES UNDERWOOD WAS NOT TO BE DAUNTED by pistol fire aimed so obviously above his head, even before he knew that his daughter had been kidnapped. The great crack of the chamber pot lid against the skull of the largest abductor had wakened him immediately, and he stepped from his and Mercia's tent not half a minute later in an unbuttoned shirt, breeches, and boots.

The moon outlined dark figures in a silvery light as they scuttled over the hill. Mercia appeared from beneath the tent flap and reached for her husband, but he was gone, hurrying after the intruders.

The brow of the hill fell away to reveal the lake below and the presence of the forest beyond, a great wall of trees, like a palisade guarding the further perimeters of the water. Partway down the slope the forms of men and horses roiled in shadow. The first shot hardly startled him and he continued his pursuit. Two more shots rang out, further to his right, but these were distinctly meant as warning and he, conversely, was not to be frightened away.

He slowed his pace once the figures were mounted, knowing he had no hope of catching them. The horsemen broke into an easy lope down the hill, and it was then that James first caught the glimpse of white, thrown over the withers of one of the animals, that told him just how wrong things were.

Mercia, in the meantime, ran to the tent where the young women had retired. She nearly fell over the prostrate form of Mr. Scott, but did not stop to see if he were alive, injured, or dead. The pistol shots whined over the hill as she stepped into the tent.

Struggling in her bonds, Priscilla lay in a corner where she had been dropped, but in the darkness, Mercia did not see her immediately.

"Cordelia? Cordelia?" Mercia called. Dim illumination from the moon shone past her shoulder onto the empty cots. The light of a lantern bobbled and wavered against the side of the tent, then shot past the raised flap as John Benning entered behind her. The next moments were a jumbled nightmare of realizations as Ethan, then James, arrived at the tent; Priscilla was loosed from her bonds and Mr. Scott came to.

The guide was standing uncertainly at the brow of the hill when

Priscilla was half led, half carried from the tent and into the night air. For the lack of a better place, they brought her to the center of camp, where the remnants of the evening's fire glowed dully. They listened to the disturbing tale of her waking to rough hands and Cordelia's subsequent abduction, told between the sobs and wheezings of near-hysterics.

Before she was finished, James sent Ethan off to find the horses, which had been scattered. "Keep your ears and eyes open," said James. "I'm sure they're long gone, but shout out if you hear or see anything."

"I know she saved me, hitting that man," said Priscilla. "They were so silent till then. They didn't dare take the time with me, once you were roused."

"Who?" said Mercia, the fright in her own voice barely controlled. "Did you see any of them? Did Cordelia seem to recognize anyone?"

"It was so dark. . . ."

"Perhaps someone will kindly tell me what I've hired into," said Mr. Scott, who—ignored up to this moment—stood outside their circle. He pressed the back of his head with one hand.

"It is my fault," said James, his face grim as his eyes looked into the darkness beyond the guide. Priscilla was crying now, and he reached down to touch her shoulder. "I am so sorry, my dear. Forgive me." But he gazed out at the night, and might have been speaking to his daughter.

"And where were you?" asked John Benning of Dresden Scott.

The night was cool and Mercia had stirred the coals, raising flames, the light from which revealed anger on Mr. Scott's face. "I might ask the same of you, sir," he said, the address more authoritative than deferential. "I nudged you when I first heard sounds in camp, but you sleep deeply, it seems."

"You nudge lightly, it seems," said John Benning, his tone flat with suppressed hostility.

"I was struck from behind, outside the ladies' tent," said Mr. Scott, indicating the place on the back of his head with another rub.

"That is easy enough to say," continued Benning.

James stepped up to the guide and felt for himself; there was no intimacy in the gesture, only the privilege of command. "He has a lump the size of an egg back there," said the retired naval officer.

"Easy enough to take a lump for the sake of appearance," said Benning.

"I haven't been told what this is all about," said Scott, ignoring him.

"It's that rock, isn't it," said Mercia. She held Priscilla's quieting form, rocking the young woman gently. "It's Minmaneth Rock."

"What about it?" asked Mr. Scott.

James spoke up. "We have reason to believe that there is more to my daughter's inheritance than simply this land. Perhaps something buried. Perhaps beneath that rock. And we have had reason to believe, these past few days, that someone else knew something about this as well."

"And you brought these people here with you?" There was the look of disdain growing in Mr. Scott's eyes.

"I never imagined anything like this," said James, with such a note of self-recrimination and bitterness in his voice that Mercia let out a single sob before stopping herself from breaking down entirely.

"Well, your daughter is gone, and we must get her," said Mr. Scott simply.

"Ethan has gone to look for the horses," said James. "Perhaps we should help him. I will follow them. If you would loan me your rifle . . ."

"I think you should stay with your family," said Mr. Scott.

"Perhaps you should tend to your own affairs," said John Benning.

"She is my daughter, Mr. Scott."

"And your ability to track . . . in the moonlight?"

"I think I can follow several horses," said James.

"I'm sure that I could navigate a ship, Mr. Underwood," said the guide.

"Your point is taken," said James, after a moment's thought.

"Are you suggesting that we let *you* follow these people?" asked John Benning of Mr. Scott.

"I am *suggesting* nothing. I am telling you that you have little choice." Scott never took his eyes from James's face. "You can wait till morning, but I think you should be able to follow the road back to Millinocket in this moonlight. There you can raise the alarm, and soon the woods will be thick with searchers. Send a telegram to Old Town for the nearest law. You will want to ask for help down at the Indian settlement as well."

"And what are *you* doing?" asked John Benning.

Dresden Scott was already gathering food and water, a bedroll, his rifle, and binoculars as he spoke.

"I will at least find out where they are going with the young lady, and meet the rescue party on my way back."

"*If* you come back."

Mr. Scott stopped to regard John Benning carefully. Motives and emotion were not easy to read in the moonlight and the wavering glow of the reawakened flames. "I don't understand this sudden suspicion—after all, I was the one struck over the head—but if we can catch a second horse quickly, Mr. Benning, you are welcome to come with me."

"You couldn't stop me, Mr. Scott."

"I think you would do well to stay with these people, in case they are threatened again, but it is your decision."

Benning looked to James, who nodded. "You go with him."

"Let's find the horses," said the guide.

Dresden Scott pulled up at the edge of the lake and dismounted quickly to cast about, crouching in the wild grass.

"What's the delay?" said John Benning. "I thought you could track in the moonlight."

"There have been deer down to the water, and the trail is lost a bit, but I suspect they're skirting the shore here." Leading his horse, he hurried along the edge of the water till the sign of the riders once more rose out of the confusion of prints. Then he was mounted and off in one easy motion.

The tracks became difficult to follow on the forest road, in the shadows of the trees and along the harder surface of a worn trail. Several times Mr. Scott doubled back to discover a shortcut taken through the brush to avoid a switchback in the tote road. "Someone has thought this out very carefully," said the guide at one point.

"Someone," said John Benning. Whenever they turned from the road, he insisted on being shown the tracks they were following, as if fearing that the guide might lead them purposely astray.

It was long since light when they came to the fork in the road. Mr. Scott was familiar enough with the way that he slowed his pace in anticipation of it. He rode several yards to the left, turned his horse around, and followed the right-hand path a similar distance.

"They've taken her that way," said the guide, pointing down the left-hand road.

"How can you say?"

"There is one horse making more of a mark than the others." He dismounted and led the way to one of the prints in question. "I suspect that the deeper prints tell two people on one animal."

"Perhaps it is a larger horse."

"She's gone this way," said Mr. Scott quietly. "They stopped here to talk about something. See the prints shifting about. The horses are shuffling. This fellow over here is a nervous rider. Then they split up for some reason." He looked up at John Benning. "These two heading toward the right may have doubled around to catch anyone following them."

"I'm not worried," said John Benning. "I'm armed."

"I know."

"What if you're wrong?"

Mr. Scott stood up from his demonstration. "She is a very pretty young woman, Mr. Benning."

"And what does that mean?"

"I am guessing that you came with the Underwoods for something other than business purposes."

"Tread lightly," warned Benning.

"You are furious with yourself for allowing such a thing to happen to Miss Underwood, and you're looking for anyone to take the blame."

"I don't trust you."

"At this juncture, you have little choice."

"Little choice again, eh? That's where you are mistaken, Mr. Scott. I am going that way." John Benning pointed down the right-hand road.

"And what is your reasoning there?"

"Simply this: if you *are* trustworthy, then you're following the proper trail and you will locate Miss Underwood. If you are not trustworthy, and you are trying to send me down the wrong path, then *I* will find her in that direction."

"Very elegant," said the guide, obviously impressed. "And you think that you can follow a trail by yourself?"

"You forget, I am a surveyor by trade. I am used to reading the land, and following old signs."

"And you *are* armed."

John Benning had his hand in his jacket, gripping the pistol there. "Why don't you start down your road, Mr. Scott, so that I can take mine. I don't like turning my back on you just now."

There was more than idle threat in Benning's gesture, and the guide lifted himself into the saddle with a sort of cautious ease. "I am reminded," he said, "of something my mother used to say."

"Your mother from Dresden."

"*Suspicious is what suspicious does.*"

"If you are trustworthy, Mr. Scott, then you will find her, and I will be in error. In that event, I will tender my apologies."

The guide half-smiled, turned his horse down the left-hand track—and there they parted, with caution on both sides.

58. Below Minmaneth

ANCIENT, CRACKED, AND MOSS-COVERED, Minmaneth Rock stood out from the hillside, a great gray heap on the northern end of the lake. Centuries had passed since human imagination first made of it a petrified behemoth—ossified and earthbound, the forgotten creature of God risen from the dark forest to be pounded by rain and touched by the sun. In the moonlight, it seemed to shift unnaturally: phosphorescent tendrils of quartz swimming within the granite face, and flakes of mica sparkling like shards of polished glass.

Since the last glacier put its finishing touches upon this place, wild creatures had rested beneath it for shade and shelter, and the first men had watched it as they passed near, certain that some sentience, however slow and geological in its processes, lived within that hard brow. The Indian people identified it with the wandering dog of Pamola, the stormy god of Mount Katahdin, till a displaced Scotsman entered the history of the tribe and (because of some long-forgotten event) the granite mound was given the name of Minmaneth.

Nothing within sight of Minmaneth Rock was as primeval as the rock itself—not the trees, not the lake, certainly not the man crouching atop it.

The man himself was hardly visible to those waiting anxiously below; only the occasional blink of the moon, reflected off binocular lenses, expressed his presence and occasional movement. Once in a great while, a low muttering reached the ears of those upon the ground. Then a stone the size of a thumbnail banged against someone's cheek and the resultant outrage, though whispered, sounded like a shout over the lake.

Several voices hissed for quiet, but the man atop Minmaneth Rock chuckled heartily. "Pardon me. Must have knocked it loose with my shoe." The stricken man rubbed his cheek and growled invective. The voices hissed again.

"They're gone," said the man atop the rock. He raised the field glasses to his eyes for another look, the lenses magnifying light as well as distance. The entrance into the forest, where he had last seen the remainder of the Underwood party, was empty—they were gone. "I thought for a while," he said, scanning the hill across the lake, "that the boys had done their job too well. It took them almost an hour to catch the rest of their horses."

He chuckled again, then got to his feet and walked and dropped in stages down the granite side. On his way he stopped to pull at a length of coarse twine, which he had hung by a thick knot from a burr of rock. Years past, human hands had neatly chiseled a thin vertical wedge in the face of the stone brow, and the twine had been let down through this. The climber wrapped this twine around his palm as he reeled it in and was rewarded finally by a brass plumb bob. Then he continued his descent, jumping the last few feet to the shore, where his companions were already bending to their spades and picks.

Some digging had been accomplished, since the "Morse" flash of a mirror told them they were in the right place, and it was careful work timed with the height of the wind in the trees and illuminated by the rising moon; now lanterns were lit and the work begun in earnest. The hollow beneath the rock and the surface of the lake formed something of a natural amplifier, and the racket of spades crunching through soil and screeching against stone stung the nerves, after such a long self-imposed silence.

The lantern glow threw back the limitless night, but also formed fantastic and distracting silhouettes against the rock, so that the men themselves were dwarfed by their own shadows. Seen from a distance, they might have been gnomes or troll folk come aboveground to labor upon the earth.

The man from the top of the rock took his turn, falling in beside his comrades with a sort of fierce glee. "How deep do you suppose Captain Underwood dug?" asked the man, who passed his shovel on.

"Deep enough," came the short answer.

"If you want anything to stay buried," said another, "you put it six feet under."

"How do you mean?" asked one fellow, pausing at his work.

"Things'll get up and walk around if you don't bury them proper," said the sage, a white-bearded fellow with a pipe clutched between his molars.

"I buried men in a lot less, in the war," said a man with a pick.

"Aye," agreed the man with the pipe. He took the stem from his mouth and blew a column of smoke. "And those are fields I wouldn't care to visit on a night like this."

"You're giving me the shivers," said a narrow fellow on the other side of the deepening hole.

"You're turning up more air than dirt," said the lookout.

There was a pause, each man waiting the length of time that would allow him to continue without the others imagining he had been bullied into it.

"So six feet it is," said the man with the pick, returning to his work. "We'll have her out before daybreak."

"If I knowed old Captain Basil, he dug her down twenty feet," growled one rugged fellow as he drove his spade down with a heel. "And all by hisself."

"Six feet," said the older man. He clamped the pipe between his teeth again and spoke from the other side of his mouth. "A smart man digs six feet down. Any further and things move about down there like moles."

"Now you're talking nonsense."

"Am I? How do you think this was so hard to find the first time we dug it up? Captain Kidd buried it to one place, and Captain Basil and us—a hundred and more years later—found it thirty feet inland."

"I imagine," came the voice of one who couldn't.

"How'd they know to find it, if it weren't where it was put?'" asked a skeptical fellow outside the circle of diggers.

The man with the pipe paused then, and leaned on his spade. "Well, I'll tell you, since I was there. We dug where the map told us, and it was hard going. And we dug six feet, and we dug ten feet, and we widened the trench and we dug fourteen feet, and we found something like a pocket in the ground and a run of loose dirt heading inland, directly north by the compass. 'It has moved,' says the captain, and doesn't waste another minute but sends the Dutchman—Pete was his name—to find the nearest apple tree. And Pete was a water witch in his time and he doused her like a well. And we hit it, too."

"But what's it doing here, after all these years? Why didn't it get divvied up?" wondered the thin man, his shadow like a stick behind him on the wall of rock.

"If you're not going to work that spade, pass it over," said the lookout to the bearded fellow. "But let's hear it from you, how it happened."

The older man passed the implement on with unstated philosophy. A small breeze had picked up from the east, and he moved beneath the shelter of the rock where he could rest a shoulder. He snapped a lucifer into flame with a thumbnail and put the lit match to his pipe. "Well [*puff*] we were all expecting [*puff*] shares, of course. [*Puff.*] Ah! But we felt the need to hurry back into American waters, which we did. And we came up the Penobscot to the home of a family named Verrill, on the shore of Bald Hill Cove. And there we were taken in, and a celebration was ready for us."

"I know the place," said a man just outside the circle of light. "I don't know the people. Bald Hill Cove—that's in Orrington, or nearabouts."

"Yes, though the family is gone from there now. They had a daughter, you see—pale blue eyes and dark, dark hair. A very fine young woman. She'd look you straight on, honest enough to shame you. Her name was Elizabeth, and Captain Basil called her Beth, if you take my meaning.

"Now the captain and the boss's father—we called him the colonel— were like this." The man raised two crossed fingers and turned them about for all to see, like evidence at a trial.

"Till a woman came between them," said one of the diggers.

"Not at all. There was never a more honorable soul than she, unless it was the captain—or the boss's father. Why, there was a bride and groom and a best man to be had in that dining hall that night—*and* lifelong friendship. We were all feeling pretty kind to one another, I can tell you. It isn't often that men do what we had done—dodging the British Navy, playing at smuggling to mask our real purposes. . . .

"It was in the midst of our celebration, between the soup and the fish, that news arrived by way of the Verrills' son. It was April the 13th of '61."

One young digger paused and contemplated this date without success.

"The day after the 12th," said one of the older men.

Another reached over to cuff the back of the youngster's head. "Fort Sumter, you divot."

"Oh," said the confused fellow, returning to his labor. The men were up to their knees in the hole and the dirt continued to fly.

"The boss's family were South Carolinians, of course. Everyone aboard ship knew about the secession—we'd heard it from a passing merchantman out of Boston—but there was talk of some sort of agreement to keep it all together, and the captain and the colonel went on with their plans, ever hopeful, you see. . . .

"But Sumter was fired on and the war begun, and the colonel, who had his own bottle of wine at his elbow, says the South will need real funds to carry on a war, and he knows where his share of the treasure is going."

The old man looked past the overhang of rock, past the lake to the east, and saw the first hint of dawn lining the tops of trees with a gray light. The spade work slowed, then stopped. Several men there knew about such moments, and even the hardest among them had a respect for the decisions made when that news came.

"It was a good deal quieter after that, and no one was any quieter than Captain Underwood. Miss Verrill held his hand in plain sight, but he looked like the good stuff had just been taken out of him; hardly a bone left to keep him upright. And his face was pale, and he kept blinking, and finally he rose from the table and said good night.

"And the next morning, he told his best friend that he could not, in clear conscience, allow what we had uncovered to benefit a cause so detrimental to the safety of his country. They argued for the first time in their lives; almost came to blows. And the crew split, with about twenty of us standing by the captain, and five or six with the colonel. There were hot words that day, more painful to those two men, I think, than knife wounds.

"But old Captain Underwood was as honorable as the day is long, dear man that he was, and he decided that if he couldn't let any *one* man have his share, he couldn't let *anyone* have his share."

"And you went along with it?" asked someone incredulously.

"It was a bitter pill, no doubt, but the captain was not a man you crossed in such matters. We were all feeling like patriots, on both sides, in those days, and we stuck by his decision—right down to his personal secret regarding the place of reburial."

"But after the war . . ."

"Hard things happened in that war; and though the colonel accepted the captain's decision, the situation ate at him as the war progressed. The captain served in the blockade—Yancy was there with him, weren't you, son." A man nearly as old as the storyteller grunted and gave a short nod.

"The colonel served on the staff of Jefferson Davis himself. And the story goes that near the end of the war, when the Confederacy was on its last legs, he promised his president enough funds to payroll half the army. The colonel, you see, was convinced that the captain would never have risked the secret of the new burial place dying with him. And the colonel was more than a little convinced that Miss Verrill was a likely source of information, so he attempted to kidnap her, right out of her own home, so the story goes."

"Like father, like son," they say, said the man with the pick, climbing from the hole.

"Do you think?" said the old fellow, with an odd look in his eye.

"You say 'attempted.' "

"Not successful, however. He escaped with his raiders, but was wounded—almost mortally. Shot in the lung. It was that wound, actually, that was blamed for his death about ten years after the war."

"He lived, then, to fight again, eh?"

"No, he never served after she put that bullet in him." The pipe came out for inspection again. He tapped it against his boot heel, emptying the bowl before searching his pockets for more tobacco. "Ah, the war brought some hard things."

"Better bitter enemies than bitter friends," said the lookout. He handed his shovel over and retrieved his field glasses.

The forest woke with a breath from the southwest, a shifting wind that hushed through leaves and needles. The first songbirds replaced the call of night peepers; a crow's harsh cry carried like laughter through the trees.

The lake and the land, the great dark pines and the bulk of rock were black and inscrutable against the increasing light; then the hill across the water took on color and the ripples on the surface of the lake became visible as dark wrinkles. A chipmunk scolded from atop Minmaneth Rock, and an acorn bounced down the stone brow and into the hole.

In daylight the crew looked like any other band of laborers; some wore beards, some simply had not shaved for some time; their faces were weathered and their hands were hardened according to age and experience, their sleeves rolled to reveal sinewy forearms. Many wore their hats throughout their exertions—bowlers or curl-brimmed felts pulled down to shade the eye from the dazzle of the brightening atmosphere. As the hole deepened and the piles of dirt around it rose, even the hats disappeared, and only the blades of their shovels could be seen in dark flashes of thrown soil and gravel.

The excavation was some ten feet in diameter, and seven feet at its deepest, when the object of their search came to light.

The size of the box, as they scraped the dirt from its lid, astonished them. This was no strongbox, no drawer-sized coffer to be lifted by one man, or even two. Here was an old sea chest, banded in iron, covered in a thick layer of pine tar and wrapped about with ancient chains. The farther they dug, the more amazed and excited they became, laughing and shouting in triumph. Twice they attempted to pull the chest free, but it was firmly packed in its burial place, and patience was required as they continued to delve around it.

The third attempt to pull the box from the hole was being readied when the sound of horses brought the proceedings to a halt. Heads turned, and several men moved unhurriedly to retrieve a rifle or a shotgun.

Two riders appeared from the northwest, picking their way through the trees and around deadfalls and boulders. The hawk-nosed man led, looking worn and weary. Behind him, the young man nearly slept in his saddle.

They pulled up several yards from the hole, but from the height of their mounts they could see the chest, black and bound in brown rusted chains. One of the men stood proudly upon the box, hands on hips, as if displaying the fruit of his own solitary labor.

The weariness and the sleepiness, respectively, lifted from the riders, and the older man even smiled from one corner of his mouth. He dismounted and tossed the reins to someone standing nearby, then approached the hole.

"Well, boys," he said with a short laugh, "this is the second time I have seen that chest uncovered."

"Third time's a charm, they say," said the bearded fellow who had told the history of the box.

"Bite your tongue!" said the man at the edge of the pit.

"This time we'll see what's in it, Benjamin."

The hawk-nosed man nodded. "Aye."

"How'd you find us so quickly?" asked one of the men.

"He read the boss's message, just like we did," answered the white-bearded historian.

"I thought old Underwood was in cahoots," said the lookout. "He handed over his glasses and left the boss on the side of that hill to flash a signal to us."

"It's just like the boss says," intoned Ben. "Go easy about things and people put what you want right in your lap." He gazed up at the massive overhang of granite. "So this was the place."

"Half of us were camped right next to it," said the lookout. "When everybody was to bed across the way, we allowed ourselves a little light. Chester climbed up and found chisel marks in the face of the granite, so we dropped a plumb bob through and found the spot like mother found the button."

"He surely didn't expect us to have it raised this quick!" exclaimed one of the younger men.

Ben strode down to the shore of the lake. "What's gone on over there?"

The lookout hurried up with his binoculars and handed them over. "They've been gone for hours now. We didn't know what to think after you were gone. We counted six people and figured you only got one of the girls."

"We would have had both of them, but Miss Underwood proved a bit of a handful." Ben glanced back at the line of men gathering behind him. "Took the lid of a chamber pot to Ernest's head."

This brought both exclamations of surprise and hilarity.

"Did he feel it?" asked someone dryly.

"Put him on his knees. I'm glad it wasn't me. And I'm glad I'm not him," he added. "He busted her in the chops."

Now there was real astonishment. "He hit her?" asked half a dozen men.

"Took her right out, square in the side of the jaw."

Numerous deprecations of Ernest's character rose from the gang, though more than one quietly expressed what he'd do if someone broke a stone lid over his head.

"What's the boss going to say?" wondered one of the young men.

"The boss'll toast him over a slow fire," suggested someone.

"The boss will be here soon, so look lively," said Ben. "The sooner we have that chest raised and out of here, the better for all concerned—Ernest possibly excepted."

While the crew returned to the pit to raise the chest, the white-bearded fellow stayed behind with Ben. "Ernest hit the young lady," he said, shaking his head.

"He did indeed."

"That's a shame. She was very pleasant to me when I came to their house."

"You deceived her, didn't you?" said Ben without a lot of concern. "And I helped nab her. So knocking her senseless was just the next thing."

"I don't like to think of us mistreating the captain's niece," said the old fellow.

"It's been a long hard slog between digging up that chest thirty-five years ago and digging it up again today."

"Old Charlie Stimply must be rolling in his grave."

"What's left of him. Henry! You and Ames get the horse and wagon."

The white-bearded fellow, who had once played the role of Charles Stimply, followed the hawk-nosed Ben to the edge of the pit, where a concerted effort was lifting the huge chest from its resting place of three and a half decades. In another moment the box was resting beside the hole, and the men stood about it, gazing at it with wonder and satisfaction.

"What do you suppose is in there?" asked one man aloud. The horse and wagon was led out of the woods and drawn up to the side of the pit, but no one made a move to lift the chest onto it.

"What do you suppose we open her up and take a look," said the white-bearded man to Ben in a quiet tone.

"These men have behaved very well, under the circumstances," said Ben, under his breath. "You open that chest here and it'll be every man for himself. Come on now!" he shouted. "Let's get her aboard! She's not going to climb on there by herself."

"Good work, gentlemen!" came a voice that startled them all. Heads turned to see John Benning astride his horse, not ten yards away. He held a pistol, which was leveled into their midst, carefully covering the entire company. "Good work, but you make a little too much noise," he said.

There was a prolonged silence. "It won't happen again," said Ben, with that strange half-smile. He stepped forward slightly.

"See that it doesn't," said John Benning sternly. He slipped the pistol back beneath his coat and eased himself out of the saddle. Ben snatched up the reins. The band of men stepped aside for Benning, making an avenue to the object of their labors.

He stood then, poised not unlike a mountaineer with a flag, and looked down at the ancient artifact.

"Who could have thought it would have been so simple, boss?" said one of the younger men. "To find the spot so quick and dig it up so easy . . ." His voice trailed off, silenced by fierce looks from the false Charles Stimply (who knew much more concerning the history of the chest than he had told) and Ben (who knew more still).

The false Charles Stimply—one Samuel Adams, by name—thought on the real Charles Stimply and how the two of them had tended the malarial Captain Underwood in a hut on the coast of Venezuela, and how they fended off John Benning's band of armed men, whom Charles would later dodge and Samuel join.

Ben was thinking on the death of Colonel Benning, and how Mrs. Benning had cursed the name of honor, which had pulled a man between his best friend and his sovereign state.

"And how is Miss Underwood?" asked John Benning in an expressionless tone. He turned to Ben when no answer was immediately tendered.

"There was an altercation," said Ben uneasily.

"I thought there must have been. Miss Morningside was not clear about details, but the fact that you didn't take her indicated something went awry."

"She broke a stone jar lid over Ernest's head."

"I saw the pieces in the tent. That's what woke everyone."

"I think so."

"And?"

"Ernest hit her."

"Ernest Davies hit Miss Underwood." It was a flat statement, chilling for its lack of emotion.

Ben barely dipped his head to one side and shrugged. "She was fine when I left her, sir. A little shaken, of course."

After some thought, John Benning said: "I don't like it, but if you roughhouse with people, you have to expect someone to be roughed up."

"That's what I thought, sir. But it is unfortunate."

"I'll deal with Mr. Davies. Did she tell you anything?" asked Benning.

"I thought we were going to have to scare her, at first," said the hawk-nosed Ben, "but we gave her a moment to think about it and she did the wise thing."

"She told you where to look."

"Did everything but make a map."

"Good. Then they have no reason to suspect me. Now I can catch up with Mr. Underwood and help organize his daughter's rescue. You know the way out of here?"

"I do."

"It has gone rather simply, hasn't it," said John Benning, looking across to the young fellow who had spoken earlier. There was something in his tone that allowed the men to relax. Some of them let themselves smile again, feeling the sense of celebration rise once more within them. "We've been up against some very smart and determined people from the start," he continued, returning to his horse. "But leave the eternal verities of honor and duty aside, play what cards are handed to you, and few will have the wherewithal to foul you up."

59. Reprise the Overture, Please

I CAN'T HELP BUT THINK," said Ephram to Eagleton and Thump, "that it is fortunate we crossed paths with the moose before the bear."

"Yes?" said Eagleton.

"Do say," encouraged Thump.

"I think that *the Bearpath League* has not the same ring to it."

"Exactly!" said Eagleton. "Exactly! Thump?"

"I couldn't agree more!"

Besides this colloquy, the ride back to Damariscotta from the station in Newcastle was a quiet one. Mister Walton, sitting by the driver, closed his eyes and listened to the sounds of late evening, breathing the cool night air, feeling the slight wind of their movement in his face. Maude was gone, and he imagined (however sadly) that quieter times were pending.

It had been pleasant to see Charles Piper again. As representative of county law, the sheriff had accompanied the bear's trainer to the station. "Who is attracted to whom here, Mister Walton?" asked Piper good-naturedly.

"I think the feeling is mutual between us," answered the bespectacled gentleman, unperturbed. "But I fear our luck in this matter has run its course, and I am happy she will be returning to her audiences. I trust you feed her well," he said to the man from Colonel Cobb's Wild West Show.

"She's the baby of the troupe, sir."

"Very fine," said Mister Walton.

It had been late in the evening when they saw Maude off. Sheriff Piper waved from the train, and Mister Walton laughed.

The laughter returned to him as they rode across the bridge to Damariscotta. Ephram, Eagleton, and Thump heard his quiet chuckle and found themselves smiling at one another; without knowing the source of their chairman's laughter, they were yet willing to join in with it.

Ephram looked down at his own feet, perhaps pondering some pleasant memory; he laughed quietly, his shoulders shaking. "Ah!" said Eagleton, as if catching his friend at something; his grin spread wide across his face. "Oh ho!" said Thump, looking sly. Ephram and Eagleton turned to their friend, eyes large, brows raised. "Oh ho!" said Thump again.

Then the three of them laughed uproariously. Mister Walton turned to see them; just the sight of their good humor brought forth from him a delighted shout, and before they reached the door of their hotel even the driver had tears in his eyes from laughing so hard.

Sundry—his long form crammed into a corner of the carriage, his legs stretched out in the opposite direction—was asleep. When the carriage drew to a halt, it took them some moments to wake him up so that he could go to bed.

Eagleton, before he retired that night, wrote a series of brief notes in his newly begun journal; but when he attempted to record the hilarity they had experienced in the carriage, he could not recall what had caused it. Finally he decided that the effect was the important thing, and he wrote upon the page: *Had a moment of great glee on the way home.*

It was mid-morning before Mister Walton appeared in the hotel dining room, searching for breakfast. There the charter members of the club and Sundry Moss occupied a table by a window and they hailed him cheerfully. Pulling up a chair, he apologized for keeping his companions; but his apologies were met with much gracious insistence that a good sleep, in the light of his recent adventures, was no more than his due.

The rest of the table had already consumed a large breakfast, but the club members were unwilling to let their chairman eat alone, and they thoughtfully ordered another round of eggs and ham and potatoes with sauce and herring and scones with jam and a very large pot of coffee for themselves. Sundry thought these good manners laudable and emulated their example.

It was almost noon before breakfast was finished, and there seemed a great need to get up and move about. The members considered one another with the sort of uncomfortable satisfaction that accompanies an excessively full stomach. Thump let out a groan of overindulgence disguised as a sigh, startling himself.

"Oh, dear!" said Mister Walton about nothing in particular.

Sundry looked like he might fall asleep again.

Ephram glanced at Sundry, wondering how he and his friends—after all this time—could gracefully inquire about the young man's name. Eagleton was thinking that their breakfast deserved a mention in his journal.

"I should cable the Baffins," said Mister Walton. "They take care of me at home," he explained. "I should really let them know where I am. Then, perhaps, I might look up Miss McCannon, and hear her impressions of last evening's entertainment." This last thought was expressed with a smile. He rose from his chair, feeling like a newly loaded freighter that must be navigated with extra caution. After standing for a moment, he thought he could walk, and he invited the others along.

The suggestion cut through their torpor slowly, but they rose in his wake and followed him down to the street.

The receiver was clicking at a steady rate when they entered the telegraph office. Several men stood about, their eyes intent upon the operator, who scribbled upon a large pad of paper. Most of these men recognized Mister Walton as the man who had tamed the bear at the Lincoln Hall; and each acknowledged this newsworthy person with a nod or a silent word, but the previous object of their attention quickly drew them back.

Mister Walton had seen such a gathering before, when he was a youngster at the beginning of the War Between the States—men tense with concentration upon the ticking of the telegraph receiver, waiting for the verbal translation of the operator to tell them the outcome of an engagement between armies.

The tableau stopped him from approaching the counter at first, and when he did rest an elbow there, he waited for the talking clicks to pause and the operator to look up before tendering his message.

"Just as soon as the line clears," said the operator. The machine began to dance again and he turned back to his pad. "There's a fairly large party organized at Millinocket," he said. "The first of them have already taken up the search."

Mister Walton glanced at his companions, then at the other bystanders in the room. A man took a pipe from his mouth and said, in a puff of smoke, "A young woman was abducted."

"Good heavens!"

"Happened last night," said another man. "Rode right into the family's camp and snatched her from her tent."

Mister Walton and his friends unconsciously imitated the attitudes of those who came before, listening with uncomprehending ears, half-convinced that a note of dire necessity, or even peril, could be heard in the staccato *knacking* of the telegraph receiver.

"This is much of what we got before," said the operator. "It's all over the wires. They're asking for any information that might help to find her." He read aloud from the audible code as he wrote. " 'Miss U.'s father . . . *requesting information able seaman . . . Charles Stimply.' "

Mister Walton's friends were mystified by this communication.

Miss ewe's father? mused Ephram.

Miss you, Father? thought Eagleton.

Misuse Father? wondered Thump, somewhat aghast at the suggestion. Even Sundry pictured the father of someone named *Miss Yew*.

"Excuse me," said Mister Walton slowly, "but did you say 'Miss U.'?"

"Underwood," said the operator, scanning the message. "Yes, it's all the same. Wire's jumping with it." He turned in his chair. "Of course, I can't blame them. What do you suppose—?"

"Miss Underwood?" said Mister Walton, the general sense of anonymous horror crystallizing into something more personal. A sharp twinge plucked at his heart. "Is her name Cordelia?"

"Yes," said the operator, and while he continued to read the chatter of the line with one ear, he looked with renewed interest upon Mister Walton. "Do you know her?" The other men in the room drew closer.

"I certainly do," replied Mister Walton foggily. He was picturing the lovely young woman, red hair gleaming in the sun, snatching him from a fall into Portland Harbor, lending a discreet shoulder when he had injured his ankle. He remembered how she had laughed, how prettily she had danced at the Freeport Ball. "Dear me," he said, barely above a whisper. "What could have happened?" His heart fell at the thought of her parents.

Sundry was at his elbow, his face dark with concern. "Is there anything I can do for you, Mister Walton?"

"No, Sundry, thank you. . . ." Mister Walton removed his spectacles and rubbed his eyes with the back of his wrist. "Yes," he said, as if only now understanding Sundry's question. "Yes, Sundry." He replaced his glasses and straightened with sudden resolve. "You can do me the favor of accompanying me to Millinocket."

"I'll get our things," said the young man. He touched the portly fellow's shoulder, as if to shore him up. Then he was out the door.

"Forgive me, gentlemen," said Mister Walton to Ephram, Eagleton, and Thump. "I had hoped to continue our acquaintance—may I say friendship—and perhaps take our league on a scenic tour on the way home to Portland. But you will understand when I tell you that though I have not known the Underwoods long, they have been very kind to me; especially Miss Underwood. I don't know what help I can be, in this terrible situation, but I must offer anything I can."

"Of course, of course!" said Thump manfully.

"Couldn't be clearer!" said Eagleton, looking as if he had suddenly joined the military service.

"We would expect nothing less, sir!" declared Ephram, and he began a round of shaking hands.

"You're very good," said Mister Walton. "I will look you up then, when I return home."

The club members gaped at one another as if there had been some gross misunderstanding. "Mister Walton, we will accompany you!" said Ephram with great force.

"But I couldn't impose upon your—"

"Nonsense!" said Eagleton, who felt there was no other choice but to disagree with the chairman.

"A friend of yours, Mister Walton . . . !" said Thump.

Mister Walton was at a loss. "Thank you," he said. "I am sure they will be glad for every able-bodied man."

The members had never thought of themselves as able-bodied (or not in so many words), and they looked at one another with a sudden and renewed respect. Thump was so moved that he attempted to leave the telegraph office without first opening the door.

"Good luck!" shouted the operator as they helped Thump outside.

The bystanders looked out the window as the group of travelers followed Mister Walton up the street. "Who were those men?" asked someone.

"Don't you know?" said another, who had held conversation with Eagleton the night before. "That's the Moosepath League."

Heading up the street, Eagleton had something in particular on his mind. "The young man," he said to Mister Walton.

"Sundry?"

"His name . . ."

"Yes?"

"Exactly."

60. Moose Manor

MORE THAN FORTY RIDERS were checking their gear and mounting up on the dusty Main Street of Millinocket when John Benning galloped into town. He was hatless, his expression grim and weary. James Underwood separated himself from the crowd of horses and men and took the bridle of Benning's mount as the young man pulled up. "Did you find her?" asked the father.

"I didn't, sir," gasped Benning. "I'm sorry. The trail went in two, and so Scott and I split up as well."

"Then he'll have found her," said James, more definite than he felt.

"I have to confess, Mr. Underwood," said Benning as he dismounted. "I didn't trust him. When he insisted that Cordelia was taken in the one direction, I left him and took the other. I was wrong."

"That's all right, John," said James. "It was your concern for my daughter that made you do so. I thank you. Now turn that poor horse in and find a room at Mrs. Cuthbert's and get some rest."

"I couldn't. I'll get a fresh mount and come with you. Go ahead, I'll catch up with you."

"I won't have it, John." James handed Benning's reins back to him and walked to his own mount. "You've done all anyone could expect of you. You won't be any good to Cordelia if you're worn down to nothing."

"You've had no rest, I warrant."

"I'm her father." James swung up into the saddle and scanned the riders about him. "Sheriff?" he said to a heavyset man on the next horse.

"Gentlemen," said the sheriff. "We will ride to the site of the abduction, then take the several roads to the interior. Let us pace ourselves. This could be a long search."

The sheriff led the mass of horsemen down the street. Mercia appeared, reaching up to touch her husband's hand before he was gone. "Rest up, as well as you can," he was saying to John Benning. "Then go down to the telegraph office and see if any answer to our inquiries has come back. Anything we can find about these people might help in catching them. We'll leave plenty of sign, with this crowd, to follow if you learn something." James leaned down to kiss his wife, then was gone. On Mrs. Cuthbert's porch, Priscilla and Ethan watched him go.

"Come inside, John," said Mercia as the thunder of hooves died and the street became still, the dust of the pack drifting northeast with the wind. "Mrs. Cuthbert has dinner ready. You look famished. We just have to trust that Mr. Scott has found her."

"Yes, ma'am," said John Benning. "I trust he has."

Cordelia realized that she was dozing (despite her aching jaw), and she shook herself, the unexpected movement translating itself to the man behind her with a start, and thence to the horse, so that the animal drew up to the edge of the road.

"What's the matter?" asked the man with the Southern accent. He turned his horse about and the other rider halted some distance ahead.

It took a moment for Cordelia to think of something. "I need a drink. I'm very thirsty."

The Southerner weighed her request. He was not unlike her father in some way—thin, gray-haired, a strong jaw and straight nose—but the elements had worked longer (or harder) upon his features, and his skin was weathered and ruddy. He reached behind him and felt out a canteen from his saddlebags. Cordelia took the canteen suspiciously, opened it, brushed the rim with her palm, sloshed the water in it, smelled of it experimentally, then took a small sip. When this did not prove harmful, she essayed another drink, and then another, keeping each draft small and taking her time.

It was the first time that he had stopped to look at Cordelia, close up and in daylight, and she felt uneasy when she passed the canteen back to him and saw his look of frank approval. She met his gaze without blinking and ended the uncomfortable moment with a stern "Thank you."

"Is there anything else?" he asked, with barely concealed irony.

"Yes," she said, as if trading small talk. "You can take me back."

He made a small sound, like a short laugh, then wheeled his horse about and led the small band on.

As midday progressed, the tote road became a trail. The trees grew older and larger and further apart, and there were long slopes with little descent upon the opposite side. It was a hilly and glaciated country, with great boulders and shoulders of granite to skirt. At each corner and split in the trail, the Southerner stopped to be sure of the way. There were no blazes here, and several times he took a paper and a compass from a pocket.

Cordelia was reminded of a story she had once heard of a fellow who was lost in the middle of Boston. *I know where I'm going*, went the end of the tale. *I know how to get there, I just don't know where I am.* Perhaps she laughed, because the man glanced in her direction and tucked the compass back beneath his coat.

If she did laugh, it was out of a giddy weariness. She no longer held herself so stiff between the arms of the man behind her. She had done her best to ignore his presence, despite the occasional bump against his broad form, the smell of sweat, and the sound of his breathing—somewhat labored with his size. Slowly she ceased to care. They had been riding since before dawn, and now it was mid-morning to be sure.

Then the trail became a path, the nature of its direction more specific as it wound toward the top of a ledgy hill. One winding brought a low building in sight; a cabin, rough-hewn from logs, with no porch or front steps. The path stopped below the cabin door.

As they drew closer, Cordelia could not help but take interest in the building. Its log walls were covered from sill to roofline in bas-relief carvings—primitive figures of animals and men engaged in mythlike struggles and dances, great trees spread out like the roots of life and filled with the simplified representations of apples and birds and squirrels.

The window and door frames were carved into long fish, or snakes, or several surprised-looking bears perched on each other's shoulders, or wolves hanging to one another's tails. The front door presented a large rendering of a moose, sitting back on its haunches. Above the door was a sign that said: *Moose Manor Kindley Wipe Your Feet!*

The inside of the cabin was cool and dark. The Southerner stepped in first and called a greeting, standing in the doorway. The sour-faced fellow stood by their horses. Cordelia could hear his stomach grumbling; she realized she was hungry herself. No answer came from within, and the Southerner told the sour-faced fellow to deal with the horses.

There was one room, with a thick-legged trencher, a stone fireplace and chimney opposite the door, and several chairs, including (surprisingly enough) a Boston rocker. There was even a shelf of books beside the chimney, tilted precariously. The walls within were dressed like those without.

"Carved inside in the winter, outside in the summer," said the Southerner in his drawly accent.

"Who did?" wondered Cordelia, her curiosity getting the better of her.

"Old man lived here. I don't know his name. The old man of the mountains. It's a hunting lodge now, or a spot to spend the night between places. Can you cook?"

Cordelia was so sore and weary, the idea of even eating seemed like too much work. "A meal doesn't come with the room?" she said.

"There are some cots in the corner there," said the man. "I'd shake them out first, but you might want to lie down a bit. Ernest here can scratch up something to eat."

"I thought we weren't supposed to use our names?" said the big man.

"Who's to say that's your real name?" asked the Southerner.

"Oh."

Cordelia hardly heard this exchange. She staggered over to the cots in the corner, brushed at one of them two or three times, then rolled onto it and plunged into an exhausted sleep.

When she woke, the sun had shifted to the other side of the cabin. It was no shock to wake up and find herself there; the whole ordeal had surged through her dreams, rushing and eddying around the images of loved ones and friends like an unwelcome flood tide. She did not feel very rested, and she thought it wise to feign sleep while listening to the comings and goings of her kidnappers.

A fire had been lit; she could smell pitch and smoke and hear the snapping of sappy wood. The smell of cooking stirred her stomach into a growl. Barely peering past the rainbow of refracted light in her eyelashes, she could see Ernest peering into a pot that hung in the fireplace. The sour-faced man stood in the open doorway. The Southerner sat with his feet on the trencher, reading from a large blue book.

"It says here," said the thin fellow. " *'Every lineament of his body indicated strength. His stature was rather above six feet; his chest broad; his limbs sinewy, and remarkable for their symmetry. There seemed to be no useless flesh upon his frame to soften the prominent surface of his muscles; and his ample thigh, as he sat upon horseback, showed the working of its texture at each step, as if part of the animal on which he rode.'* "

"Who is it?" asked Ernest, rather taken by this description.

"Horse-Shoe Robinson, we are told," said the reader, glancing at the cover of his book. "But that is not all. Listen to this. *'His was one of those iron forms that might be imagined almost bullet proof. With all these advantages of person, there was a radiant, broad, good nature upon his face—'* well, so there would be upon mine if I looked like that, and bullet-proof to boot!—*'the glance of a large, clear blue eye told of arch thoughts, and of shrewd, homely wisdom.'* Well, of course," he added, looking up. "He's from Virginia."

"I'm going out back," said the sour-faced man.

The Southerner took his feet down from the table and sat up. "What have you been eating? Apples out of season?"

"A man does what he has to do," answered the man. There was more humor in the thought than Cordelia would have credited.

"Better watch the door," said the Southerner to Ernest, feet back up, book once more raised.

Ernest got up and stood at the door. Cordelia felt her stomach contract and wondered when dinner would be ready. Ernest was a brute, no doubt, but from the smells he knew how to cook. She thought of sitting up, but caught sight, beneath lowered lids, of the Southerner watching her from over his book. He seemed to drink her in, thinking about her the way a person thinks about a feast laid out before a hungry stomach. She shut her eyes, but found the blindness worse. She opened them slightly again and he was still watching her.

An odd sound came from outside—a dull thump, as if a door had been pounded by a heavy fist. Cordelia's eyes opened wide. The Southerner dropped his book and looked toward the door. "What was that?" he asked Ernest.

"I don't know."

The Southerner got to his feet. "What's that?" he said again.

Ernest frowned, cocking an ear. A muffled voice could be heard, like someone shouting down a barrel. The Southerner snatched up a shotgun and shouldered past the larger man. "You stay here." He dropped down from the stoop and Ernest watched him disappear around the corner of the cabin.

Cordelia was sitting up now, her mind spinning with hope and dread. "What are you cooking?" she asked.

Ernest was startled. He peered into the dimness of the corner where she had lain down, his eyes blinded from looking out into the daylight. "A stew, I guess."

"It smells good," she said, sounding cheerful. "Shall I go stir it?"

"Yes," he said, pleased that she didn't seem angry with him for hitting her. "That would be fine."

Cordelia stretched carefully, taking note of all the sore spots. She walked stiffly to the fireplace and bent over the stew, stirring it slowly with the iron ladle.

61. Tipping the Scales

AT THE HILLTOP WHERE CORDELIA HAD BEEN SEIZED, James explained how their camp had been laid out. Several men in the party were guides, and it was no more work than a glance for them to pick up the trail first taken by the kidnappers, then by Dresden Scott and John Benning.

From the brow of the hill, James's unaided eye could see that the ground beneath Minmaneth Rock had been disturbed. "That's the rock you were speaking of," said the sheriff, pulling his mount up beside James.

"Yes. Mr. Scott called it Minmaneth Rock."

"That's it," said one of the guides. He held a pair of binoculars to his eyes and scanned the other side of the lake. "There's been some digging over there."

"Yes," said James, the expression in his voice vague with thought.

"Something buried, you say," said the sheriff.

"Something my brother put there years ago." James turned to the sheriff after a protracted moment of silence and found a host of curious faces. "I can only guess," he said.

"Something stolen?" asked the sheriff—smiling quietly, as at a co-conspirator.

"Not in this century."

"And they took your daughter to find out where it was."

"We hadn't a clue ourselves, until we heard the name of that formation."

"And taking her," continued the sheriff, "had the added benefit of driving the rest of you away while they went to work."

"I'm almost surprised that Cordelia told them," said James. "Though I am glad she was sensible, and gave them what they wanted." He only hoped that she was sensible enough to have given it to them quickly.

The sheriff sent half a dozen men down to the site, then led the rest of them down to the lake. Soon after they reached the place where Dresden Scott had seen deer sign mixing with the kidnappers' trail, a rider from the excavation site came up.

"They've certainly dug something out of there," he declared. "Must have been a dozen of them. They didn't like digging, I guess—left every shovel and pick right where they dropped them."

"And where did 'they' disappear to?"

"Some of them into the forest. North. But there are tracks heading in this direction along the lake; a wagon as well. You'll cross those tracks up ahead of you here."

The sheriff sent another half-dozen of his men to follow the diggers north; and while this detachment skirted the perimeter of the lake, he picked two other details—one to follow the chain of ponds and streams that led to the larger lakes in the west, and the other to head northeast to the Millinocket River.

"Unless they plan to go all the way to Canada, they must be circling to get behind us. This may be the longest path to your daughter, sir," he said to James, pointing at the trail leading down to the western end of the lake. "But it is also the surest."

"I'll go with you," said James.

"Very good." The sheriff wasted no more time in leading the pursuit along the original trail. "I trust, sir," he said to James, as they rode together, "that we will meet with Dresden soon, and that he will have news about your Miss Underwood."

James said nothing—both praying for and dreading such a meeting.

From a vantage on the eastern face of a forested hill, Dresden Scott could see one wall and the roof of a cabin—old Pete Stem's Moose Manor. The chimney was smoking, and Scott thought he caught a glimpse of a horse beside the cabin. His own mount nickered below him on the slope, and he glanced down to see that she was all right. Then, taking up his rifle, he scrambled down from the bit of knob where he had been crouching and picked his way around to the other side of the hill.

From a second outlook he identified the three animals he had been tracking since before dawn. He checked his pocket watch, unconsciously testing it against the sun. It was just past two.

Dresden Scott had been a guide for most of his adult life, and a guide is a watcher, and a tracker, and a hunter—a Maine guide, which, as Teddy Roosevelt said, was different from any other sort of guide he had ever met. *Never,* wrote the President-to-be, *have I known men so honest in the pleasure of their occupation, and so unassuming in their triumphs!*

It would be a romanticism to say that Dresden Scott read the woods and the rivers and the lakes as a city dweller reads the sign on the street and the number on the door. The deep woods can turn even the wiliest, most experienced woodsman back on himself; but if a Maine guide doesn't know exactly where he is, it won't take him long to figure how to get where he wants to be.

Dresden Scott did not learn these things like blessings at the foot of some aged trapper or sage Indian, or some legendary guide before him. Certainly he learned from these people—working with them, watching them. But most of what he knew came simply from living where he lived, and doing what he was doing that warm July day in 1896—picking it up as he went.

He had tracked deer, and moose, and bear, lost souls, and two fugitives in his day, and one thing he had learned was that tracking was more than simply following prints and spoor; real genius lay in knowing where the quarry was headed, sometimes before the quarry itself knew.

Some time mid-morning the whimsical image of Moose Manor sprang to his mind, and as the day progressed, that impression grew clearer—as he followed the three horses—till it reached the level of certainty.

Scott leaned the rifle against the base of an old birch and sat on his heels with his back to the tree; he considered the wisdom of waiting for help against the practicality of acting quickly. The men inside the cabin must know that a rescue party would soon be on its way; and whoever these kidnappers were (Scott wasn't sure he understood the situation yet), their motives must reveal themselves soon.

Scott scratched his beard, snapped a blade of grass from the base of the tree and chewed on it. He could stand to rest, he knew that; his stomach growled, and he realized that he was hungry as well as tired. Then a series of associations linked in his mind and the germ of an idea lifted him right to his feet.

He had been atop this hill before, had actually slept in the cabin, so he was familiar with the immediate surroundings. Now he traversed the crest of the hill, moving quietly among the trees, watching where each step was placed. In a few moments he was looking at it—Pete Stem's privy. Tall and ruggedly built, it was fashioned (in old Pete's simple but pleasing style of carving) into the image of a four-sided pointy-headed bear, the door of the privy forming the bear's abdomen.

Scott listened intently past the quiet hush of the southwestern breeze, then leaned into the path that led from the cabin to the privy to be sure that all was clear. Satisfied, he approached the outbuilding, attending to it with a very specific scrutiny.

The privy had been constructed with great care, and placed on a small foundation of stone—perhaps six inches high—to discourage rot in the lower sill. With numerous glances over his shoulder, Dresden Scott picked at the stones beneath the door and along the front of the structure, finally kicking at them with the heel of his boot in order to loosen them. They made a grating sound against their fellows, like the growl of an animal.

He slid the loosened stones back in place, then disappeared among the trees, where he sat in the fern and brake with his rifle across his lap, wishing he had brought something from his saddlebags to eat. From where he waited, he could see through the greenery if someone came to the privy, but was more or less invisible as long as he kept still.

He closed his eyes, relying on his ears to warn him, and then the sun in his face drew a yawn from him and he was roused from an unintended nap.

Scott blinked, his eyes dazzled by the sunlight through the leaves. At least an hour had passed, and he silently cursed himself for dozing.

Some sound, alien to this hillside, had pricked his consciousness; now he keened his ears and leaned forward. There was the tramp of feet, and the unpleasant squirt of someone spitting tobacco juice—one of the signs he had followed to this place, and probably the very noise that had wakened him.

A sour-looking fellow came into view, unshaven, wearing a slouchy felt hat; he stopped to peer at Pete Stem's bear privy, and found nothing in this eccentric work of art to relieve his expression of general dissatisfaction. Then he stepped inside and shut the door behind him. Scott could hear the snick of a latch—an odd precaution this deep in the wilderness.

The guide was on the path, silent and sudden, like a bit of wind; standing, listening, waiting for the man inside to put himself in one of the more vulnerable positions known to humankind.

The time he estimated to be enough; the sounds from within the outbuilding, to be expected. Scott quickly yanked at the upper row of stones beneath the front of the privy, the sound of them scraping free startling the man within into a worried "Huh?"

Then Scott was behind the outhouse and—without a bang, or a grunt or groan—he placed his hands as high as he could against it and tipped the whole marvelous contraption over, door first.

The shout from the man inside and the crash of the outhouse against the path came simultaneously, so that they rung out like a single noise. As the dust cleared, a second shout—muffled and hollow-sounding in the horizontal privy—and then a third shout carried out over the hill.

Once more Dresden Scott took up his rifle and, taking care not to leave any trace of his passing, vanished into the surrounding forest.

Even if someone had been near, the frightened and confounded shouts of the man in the privy and the din caused by his attempts to extricate himself would have drowned out the noise of the guide's retreat. This time Scott went further into the trees, toward the cabin, and waited, allowing his ears to direct his next movements.

Soon he heard the cautious tread of a second man, and the drawl of a Southern accent, calling quietly: "Duff? Duffer?"

Scott felt like laughing, as if this were some schoolboy prank; then he caught the flash of a shotgun's muzzle through the trees.

"Duff?"

"Wallace, I'm in here!" shouted the man in the privy.

"Duff!?"

"Help me, Wallace! Get me out!"

"What have you done?"

"I haven't done anything! The wind knocked me over . . . !"

"The wind?"

"Or an animal! I heard something, like a bear!"

"A bear?" Wallace peered about. "A bear?" he said again. "Maybe like that trained bear that got loose in Wiscasset?" Wallace laughed. "Maybe it's the bear you're inside of! Duff, did that bear eat you?"

"Wallace, this isn't funny!"

"No, of course not," agreed the Southerner, laughing. "Duff, you're supposed to sit in there, not dance!"

"Now stop it and get me out of here!"

Wallace laid down his shotgun and considered the best way of honoring Duff's request. "I don't think I can lift it upright with you in it, but I can probably roll it. Hang on." He scooched down beside the toppled outhouse and took a purchase with his hands.

The cold, business end of a gun barrel touched him at the base of his neck and he stiffened with sudden horror.

"Just take a couple of easy breaths," said an even voice behind him.

It was difficult for Wallace to comply with this suggestion.

"What was that?" asked Duff, sounding like he was shouting down a rain chute.

"Now, let go your hands, very slowly," came the voice again, "and take off your shirt and belt."

Moving with studied care, Wallace did as he was told.

"Who is that?" demanded Duff.

"It's the man who tipped you over, you bonehead!" growled Wallace angrily.

"Man? Tipped me over?" Duff mumbled to himself for a moment, then yelled out, "I told them not to take that young woman! But I went along to watch out for her!"

"Now lay down on your stomach with your hands behind you," said Scott, prodding the nape of Wallace's neck again to punctuate the command.

"I told them, 'You can't be taking people willy-nilly, like that!' " continued Duff. " 'That's a very nice young lady,' I told them, 'and you best think twice!' "

Every muscle in Wallace's body twitched as he lay facedown. Scott snapped up the shirt and, at a safe distance, twisted it into a serviceable cord; then he put a knee in Wallace's back, set his rifle atop the prostrated privy, and tied the Southerner's wrists tightly.

Duff's defensive summary continued. "I wasn't there when they took her! Didn't know anything about it!"

Scott used Wallace's belt to cinch his captive's ankles.

"You could have knocked me over with a feather when I saw her! But I knew I better go along just to watch out . . . !"

"Duff, shut up!"

"Now, Wallace, you tell him —"

"Duff, shut up."

"Wallace?" said Duff uncertainly.

"That wasn't me."

Cautiously peering around the front of the cabin, Dresden Scott was surprised to see Cordelia Underwood cautiously peering from the front door. She had a cast-iron ladle in her hand, raised in a vaguely threatening gesture.

"Miss Underwood?" he said quietly.

Cordelia's expression took on the amused look of someone who has witnessed a surprising (and pleasing) feat of agility. *Well, if it isn't Horse-Shoe Robinson,* she thought, and very nearly said it aloud. "Mr. Scott?" was what came out.

The guide stepped forward — still alert — his rifle in one hand, Wallace's shotgun in the other. "Where's the third fellow?"

"Oh, him? He's down here."

As he came closer, Scott noticed two large boots, toes up, in the doorway. He glanced from the boots to the ladle in Cordelia's hand. "Did you hit him?"

"Yes," she said, the way she might have admitted to baking a pie. "Twice, actually. The first time he only said 'Ouch,' so I hit him again."

He looked into the dimness beyond the door; stretched out on the floor, the large bearded fellow looked as if he were asleep.

"Do you think I killed him?" asked Cordelia, in a softer note.

"It would serve him right if you had," said Scott, though it pleased him, somehow, that the notion of killing one of her kidnappers disturbed her.

Ernest let out a snore.

"Oh, good," she said, but she raised the ladle again. "What about the other two?" she asked.

"They're set for a while. Let's gather the horses and get while we can."

He saddled one of the animals, while Cordelia came out with two saddlebags. They combined the foodstuffs into one of them and tied it to the saddle.

"There's stew cooking inside," she said.

"Can you eat and ride while I lead you to my horse?"

"I would like to try," she admitted. "I haven't eaten since last night." At his nod she hurried inside, then came back out with two steaming bowls, two spoons, and a blue book under her arm.

"I'm glad you had time to read," he said, but she made no reply, and he held her bowl as she climbed into the saddle.

They were an odd sight as they descended in a careful sweep down the hill—he with a rifle and shotgun slung over his shoulders, she being led on the horse, both of them sipping from their bowls of stew.

"Didn't my father come with you?" she asked, suddenly alarmed at James's absence.

"He had to stay with the rest of your family," said Scott.

There was a pause; then, "And Mr. Benning?"

"Mr. Benning didn't trust my sense of direction."

"Oh."

"I'm sorry if I disappoint you."

"Not at all. It was very good of you to come."

62. The Villain Among the Victims

SUNLIGHT FELL IN SPARKS AND FLASHES through the upper branches of the forest, dappling the way and glinting upon the wings of dragonflies or bits of mica or the occasional stream that crossed the trail. Tall and many-tiered clouds loomed overhead like becalmed ships; but a wind breathed within the trees with enough briskness to carry the call of birds and the scent of wood blooms, while keeping away the mosquitoes and black flies.

Cordelia was too tired or too distracted to feel the glory of the day. The excitement of her escape and a bowl of stew were enough to greatly revive her; but now that she was reviving, the presence of Dresden Scott was enough to make her feel awkward, costumed as she was with a dress pulled over her nightclothes.

He offered to take her off the trail so that she could rest without fear of anyone catching up with them, but she was anxious to reach her family. She hardly knew this man and felt strange riding beside him.

Scott, for his part, was solicitous at first, then curious, and finally a little cross as the initial pleasure from his victory over Duff and Wallace fell away. "So your uncle buried something beneath Minmaneth Rock," he said, when neither of them had said anything for several minutes.

"Did he?" asked Cordelia, honestly wondering.

Scott imagined she was being evasive. "That's what your father said."

"Oh."

There was a new, rockier silence; Scott, feeling the need for—not to mention the right to—an explanation, scowled at the young woman. "Well?"

She caught the dark look. "You probably know as much as I do," she replied.

"I doubt that." He had never objected to guiding a party that included women, but now he was beginning to think that he did. He had liked Miss Underwood—the presence of a pretty young woman in his line of work was a considered treat—and he was grateful that she had taken care of the third kidnapper for him. But he was tired now, and a little irritated that she made him nervous. "I'm not in the business of tracking armed men," he growled.

"I'm very sorry that you did, then," said she, her voice high.

"You'd be a long time waiting for Mr. Benning. He's off in the wrong direction."

Cordelia was disappointed that John had not been in on her rescue and did not like to be reminded of it.

"And I would rather not do business with people who falsify their intentions," he added, when she made no reply.

"We did no such thing," she snapped. "We asked you to show us to my property, and anything else was our own affair."

"It is my affair when my well-being is threatened!"

Cordelia bristled. "Well, they took *me*, didn't they! And no one forced *you* to come after me!" The moment it left her mouth, she hated herself, she sounded so ungracious.

"And no one forced me to be knocked cold with the butt of a pistol, I suppose!" he demanded, pointing at his skull. He nudged his horse ahead of hers, putting his back to her and (he hoped) an end to the conversation. He thought he must sound as ungracious as she.

The unpleasant awareness of being terribly wrong stunned Cordelia. She remembered that Mr. Scott had been stretched out in front of her tent when Ernest carried her off. "That *was* you, wasn't it?" she said, sounding small and far away.

He said nothing.

"I am sorry," she said. She felt exhausted and worthless.

He rode ahead of her, his back stiff and his shoulders straight.

She thought of asking him if he had been hurt, but that was too little, too late. "We couldn't be sure that there really was anything buried," she said. "Not until you told us about Minmaneth Rock. Then we were sure, but we had no idea—I *have* no idea—what it might be."

"Well, whatever it was, it's gone now."

"Do you think?"

Scott slowed his horse and turned to regard her with less severity. "That was why they took you, wasn't it? To find out what you had learned and where it was?"

"Yes, and I'm afraid that I did tell them."

"You were very wise to do so."

They rode on in silence—down a gully, around a leafy bend, and up a stony slope; the horses carefully picked their way. At the top of the hill, Cordelia said, "Thank you." The trail was straight and level for twenty or thirty yards, then dropped to a small stream, where the horses paused to drink. "Do you think whatever it is has been taken already?" she asked.

"The field was clear," he said, "once you were taken and the rest of us split in different directions."

Scott prodded his horse forward again. When he looked at her, he was so sorry to have behaved badly—after what she had been through—that it hurt, and so he faced forward and away. She was a bit disheveled; her hair was in a tangle, but it glowed like copper in the sun, and her freckles stood out in a perfect dusting across the bridge of her nose. Perhaps it was just that she was so pretty that hurt.

"I will be sorry not to know what was buried there," said Cordelia, but she was sorrier still that she had let her exhaustion overcome her good manners. She had hoped that he had relented in his anger, and was struck with disappointment as he turned his back again.

Scott hardly heard her. He was remembering how she stood over the prostrate form of Ernest, brandishing a cast-iron ladle like a club. It had been an appealing sight, her peering out into the sun and smiling at the sight of him. Her bare feet would have been scandalous in town, but here they were merely charming. He decided to look straight ahead and not think about them.

Coincidentally, Cordelia was thinking about that very same moment: how clever he had been in her rescue and what good humor he had exhibited when he saw that she had made short shrift of Ernest.

This sudden trouble was a poor showing for both of them, and they rode in silence for several miles.

"Do you hear that?" asked Scott. He pulled up at one end of a forest corridor. Cordelia unexpectedly found herself so close to the man that their knees touched. Scott had his head cocked to one side, turning an ear away from the breeze in order to hear something ahead of them. "Do you hear it?" he asked again.

She was distracted, at first, by the opportunity to regard his features from such an immediate perspective; then the sound did reach her ears. It was not quite like distant thunder, nor yet quite like an approaching locomotive.

"Horses," she said. "How many are there?"

"Several, anyways," he said. "Let's hope it's the rescue party, but just in case . . ." He nodded once toward the trees and waited for her to disappear among them, but the rumble of approaching hooves was suddenly louder, and three riders appeared down the trail.

Scott took his horse several lopes toward the newcomers while dragging his rifle from its scabbard. More riders appeared, the first three pulling up thirty or forty feet away. Scott fixed himself squarely in the path between Cordelia and the oncoming horsemen, a shell levered into his rifle before a word could be said or another step taken. He did not aim, but pointed in the general direction of the riders, who piled up and ran into one another.

"Dresden!" came a familiar voice, and he found himself staring down the barrel of his rifle at Irving Johnston, the sheriff of Penobscot County.

Even then, it took a moment to drop his guard. He was angry at himself for being careless, for allowing such a large force to come up on him so quickly—and he had been a little frightened.

Behind him, Cordelia had unsheathed Wallace's shotgun and was breaking the breech with the intention of loading it. Then her father pulled up beside the sheriff and she almost dropped the gun where she was.

"Daddy."

James Underwood jumped to the ground, and halfway between Scott and the sheriff, Cordelia met him and he threw his arms about her, his face grim with tears and a fierce joy. Cordelia too was crying—and for the first time since her abduction she yielded herself to a series of great sobs that shook both of them.

Dresden Scott was thunderstruck by the scene—the absolute and honest love between the parent and the child. A vision of a much-loved but long-departed face—some scene from his own past—rose up to obliterate the one before him and he looked away.

"Mr. Scott," said James. "I am at your service." He reached out his hand.

Scott did not know how the man had approached him, but tears still ran down the father's face, and the guide looked instead at the hand. Scott dragged the back of his own hand across his eyes, as if he had been at hot work; then he took James's hand and shook it firmly.

There was a lot of sentiment on the other end of the small stretch of path as well. Several men had taken off their hats, and more than one found the need to clear his throat. "Good work, Dresden," said the sheriff. He had taken the shotgun from Cordelia and checked to be sure that it was not loaded. Cordelia discovered that she was gripping two shells in her other hand, so hard that her palm hurt, and she passed these to the sheriff.

"And you knocked him right over the head?" said one of the men who were returning with Cordelia and her father.

"Three times!" declared another. "She hit him three times!" Clearly the story was going to be a popular one.

"A chamber-pot lid and a cast-iron ladle," said a third man.

Nine men had gone on with the sheriff in hopes of catching the three kidnappers at or near Pete Stem's cabin. This left five men in all (counting James and Dresden Scott) to accompany Cordelia back to Millinocket.

It had been suggested that they camp where they met (the father and the guide, as well as the young woman, were exhausted), but Cordelia hoped to make their original campsite before nightfall, to ensure that they reached town the next day. She could not help thinking of her poor mother, and Priscilla and Ethan, *and* John Benning, waiting to hear of her fate.

James explained with a good deal of feeling how John Benning had wanted to go with the search party after riding all night. He passed on to Dresden Scott, also, John's regret at having mistrusted the guide.

This news was received with little enthusiasm, probably due to

Cordelia and Dresden's weariness. Cordelia considered the excuse a bit flat, no matter how tired Mr. Benning was; after all, Dresden Scott had ridden all night and morning as well.

But she felt shameful thinking such a thing, and it caused her to wonder if, after all, she were a shallow sort of person. Perhaps she was seeing how little she knew John Benning—he had proved himself to be charming, it was true, but charm itself need not be a quality of great depth. He was amusing, and his frank admiration had been exciting, but it occurred to her that he had revealed very little of himself. She looked at Dresden Scott, who rode in front of her, and hoped that he had forgiven her for her ungracious words.

Regarding John Benning's regrets, Dresden Scott was neither impressed nor glad to hear of them; it annoyed him that he might have to think well of the man, which made him think less well of himself. For some reason, since rescuing Miss Underwood, he had behaved poorly, and he hoped that she would only remember that he had come to help her, and not that he had sounded angry about it afterwards.

"I think that John is a very good fellow," said James, hoping to make his daughter feel better.

The thought irritated her, but she smiled warmly, understanding what her father was attempting to do. "Yes, I think he is," she said.

Mr. Scott seemed to have seen something ahead of them on the trail and hurried off to look at it. Once he reached his object (unseen by the rest of the party) he only glanced at it cursorily and continued riding beyond the circle of conversation.

"Hit him three times!" said the first man again, with an appreciative whistle.

The wind fell to nothing that night, so that the smoke from their fire rose in a twisting column toward the vault of summer stars. Sparks were lifted with the currents of heated air or spun above the flames, erratic as insects.

James stared into the flames, and past them, into the events that had taken him here. Several feet away, Cordelia lay with her back to the fire, a blanket pulled up to her chin, her red hair the only part of her visible in the glow.

Dresden Scott, too, sat considering the fire, and neither man could have said why exhaustion hadn't taken them. The truth was that Cordelia afflicted them both, the father with guilt and the younger man with regret. The two men commiserated without understanding, and when the need to speak forced itself to the surface, they behaved as if it were the abandoned pit beneath Minmaneth Rock that troubled them so.

"Do you have *any* idea what was buried across the lake?" asked Dresden Scott quietly.

James looked up, wondered if the question was outside of Scott's legitimate concern, then thought of the man rescuing his daughter and said: "As to its exact nature, no; though a clue left by my brother, who buried it there, leads me to believe that it had something to do with William Kidd."

"The captain?"

James gave half a smile. "Yes."

"The pirate?"

James's laugh was short and low.

"No wonder you kept it to yourself," said Scott.

"I think I would give whatever those scoundrels dug up just to know what it was," said the father. "If it were mine to give. But curiosity can demand a high price."

"*Men prize the thing ungain'd more than it is,*" cited Scott.

"That's the second time I've heard you quote the Bard," said James.

"Is it?"

"Or the second time I recognized it. Is fluent Shakespeare to be expected among men of your trade?"

"I don't know. . . ." said the guide. "A book may be more highly prized in a place like this. More rare and, therefore, better remembered."

"Are you carrying *Hamlet* in your saddlebags, then?"

"*Much Ado About Nothing*, actually." Scott chuckled. He glanced past the fire at Cordelia, wondering if she were asleep. "It was my mother who filled me with words. Her English was not perfect, and she was conscious of it in public. But she had read Shakespeare in her own language, as a young girl, and was under the impression that a complete knowledge of him was necessary to anyone functioning among Anglo-Saxons. My father might have mitigated this opinion, but he died before I was old enough to remember him."

James took advantage of this unexpected reminiscence by observing Dresden Scott closely, peering past the beard and the wavering shadows to those gray eyes. There was something about the guide that he liked very much—not just that the man had rescued his daughter, but that he had done it so simply, and referred to it (when asked) with such little fanfare.

"And your mother?" asked James, more to keep the man talking than for his own curiosity.

"When I was seventeen."

James calculated that this event must have taken place a decade and a half ago, though for the look in Scott's eyes, it might have been yesterday. "I am sorry," said the father, and Scott straightened his posture, where he sat on a log, as if he had been caught at something. There was an uncomfortable silence that James attempted to fill with another question. "Were you raised in Millinocket?"

"Down on Pleasant River, near Brownsville. My mother cooked, and sewed, and did laundry. We were more fortunate than a lot of people."

"And your education never tempted you from the woods? You never went out into the world?"

"The world?" Dresden Scott spoke as if this were a matter of semantics. "The book in my saddlebags is proof that the world will come to me, Mr. Underwood."

James wasn't so sure, but he did know men who lived unhappily in the very press of things. For himself, he liked his city street and was glad for carriages and trains and steamboats.

"I'm afraid I spoke some angry words to your daughter today," confessed Scott suddenly.

"You did?" said James, almost amused. His tone was wry. "I can't imagine it. Did she take you to task for dawdling?"

"Not at all!" insisted the guide. "It was my fault entirely."

James found that hard to believe, and almost said so. He looked over to his daughter, who was indeed asleep, and a great rush of gratitude, relief, and love filled him. Had Mercia been there, sitting about the campfire, she would have told Dresden Scott to apologize, if he felt badly, and be done with it. James simply said, "I'm sure it was nothing."

After another silence, Scott asked, "What will your daughter do with her land, do you think?"

"I wouldn't hazard a guess. Certainly she was taken with it. She might pitch a tent or build a castle." James yawned, and suddenly he felt as if he might not make it to his bedroll. His last glimpse before closing his eyes was that of Dresden Scott staring into the fire. *He's younger than I*, thought the father. His last thought was of his wife, who did not yet know that their daughter was safe.

The lights burned late at Mrs. Cuthbert's. Little was said at dinner, though John Benning was asked to give a more detailed account of himself. Ethan, piqued at not being allowed to accompany his uncle, made himself the prime questioner. Mercia said little. Priscilla was timid and apologetic, as if she had caused it all somehow; she sat like a ghost at the table.

Mrs. Cuthbert presided over her table with calm and dignity.

"And you lost all sign of the two riders?" asked Ethan, and Mercia's eyes lit up at the annoyance in the boy's voice.

"Yes," said John Benning, patiently. "I got off on the wrong track, I'm afraid, and couldn't find my way back."

"So Cord could be with the men you were following after all."

"Ethan," said Mercia. "I think John has answered enough questions."

"You are right, of course, Ethan," said Benning. "I couldn't be sure. But before I lost it, the trail was moving back in this direction, so I suspect not."

Ethan looked as if this did not satisfy him, but let it go.

"I'm sorry," said Benning to Mercia. "I think bed probably is the best thing for me."

"Please, John, get some rest. We will let you know as soon as we hear anything."

He stood from the table, looking as if he might collapse before he mounted the stairs. "I am so sorry about this, Mrs. Underwood."

"I know you are, John. Thank you."

Looking embarrassed and impotent, he left the table and disappeared upstairs.

"It seems I should have been able to do something," said Priscilla—the first words she had spoken in an hour.

"Nonsense," said Mercia. "What would any of us have done?"

"Cordelia was so brave." Tears coursed down the young woman's cheeks. "When she saw me, she looked as if she could have driven off the whole lot of them. I suppose she did in a way."

Ethan smiled, but there were tears in his own eyes, and the expression had a ferocious quality to it. "I wish I could have seen it—her knocking that brute over the head!"

Mercia looked as if she wished for some silence and space around her, but Priscilla was beginning to tremble.

"Let's go to the front room, then," said Mrs. Cuthbert, taking command. "I have a jigsaw puzzle there that I've been working on for three weeks, and I can't seem to get anywhere with it." She stood at the head of the table and pronounced the meal over. "Dishes can wait. Come now." She scooped up her three guests in the breeze of her passing and situated them at a card table in her cozy, well-lit parlor. "It's Benjamin Franklin with the kite. The box is here somewhere. At any rate, I've got the kite, and there's a dog here, I think, but I can't make heads or tails of Ben himself."

Ethan was glad for something to occupy him. Priscilla and Mercia shuffled some of the pieces about absently. By the time Ethan had grown tired enough to lie down on the sofa and go to sleep, Mercia had hold of her niece's hand on the table.

Another hour ticked away, and Priscilla's head had come to rest on her aunt's shoulder. Mercia held her while the young woman slept, fitfully, nervously. Mrs. Cuthbert came into the parlor at quarter to eleven and found Mercia herself asleep, sitting up in the chair. The landlady turned down the lamps and went to bed.

Book Ten

JULY 12, 1896

63. The Man Himself

MERCIA WOKE SOME TIME PAST MIDNIGHT and insisted that Priscilla and
Ethan go to bed in proper fashion. She herself went to her room and sat up
in the dark, gazing from the window out into the moonlit street, listening to
the midsummer crickets and peepers. Once the sound of a horse brought
her closer to the screen, but the rider passed by to the other side of town.
She lay down on the bed, then, and waited.

Birdsong woke her, and sunlight warming the bed where she lay. She
sensed movement in the house, smelled biscuits and bacon, and realized
that she was hungry, and yet almost sick at the idea of eating.

Where could her daughter be? What sort of night had Cordelia passed,
and in what sort of company?

Steps sounded on Mrs. Cuthbert's porch. Mercia sat up and could see
herself in the mirror above the commode. "Good heavens," she said. Her
first inclination was to hurry downstairs, but seeing her like this would not
be a comfort to her sister's children. Outside Mercia's door, Mrs. Cuthbert
had placed a pitcher of water, still tepid from the stove. Mercia was grateful
for this small amenity and soon, with the help of a brush and a change of
clothes, felt more or less ready for whatever the day had in store.

She stopped at the head of the stairs to get the shivers out of her sys-
tem, then descended to the front hall with great calm, and even the look of
optimism.

Breakfast had been set and Priscilla and Ethan sat at the table. Ethan
seemed as ferocious as the night before, with an appetite to match. Priscilla
worked admirably at her meal, though each mouthful was a chore. John
Benning stood at one of the windows overlooking the porch and the street.

"Good morning," said Mercia, like a teacher greeting her class.

Her niece and nephew returned her greeting with a weak smile and a
determined smile, respectively. "Mrs. Underwood," said John Benning.

It took some courage and a deep breath to ask the first question. "Has there been any news?" She knew that she would not have been allowed to sleep had there been.

"Not really," said John. "I went down to the telegraph office, as your husband requested, but there has been little response. Several people have wired information concerning Charles Stimply, but it does nothing more than confirm what we already know about him—that he served with Captain Underwood, and that he died several months ago at sea."

There was a silence as Mercia took her place at the table; then John said, "I should have gone with them."

"We all wish that we could be with them, John," said Mercia.

"I wish I could be with Cord," said Ethan. "Wish they'd taken me instead." And he meant it.

"I'll go back down to the telegraph office in a little while," said John. "Then perhaps I should ride out and try to catch up with them."

Mercia decided that this was not the moment to dissuade him. Mrs. Cuthbert arrived with a pot of coffee and John sat down.

James sent the youngest of their party to Millinocket at first light. The fear and anger over his daughter's mistreatment had turned (now that she was safe among them) simply to anger. He wandered the hilltop and walked partway down the slope while the dew was still upon the grass and a low mist hung over the lake. He turned to peer at the campsite above him, half-convinced that the men who had abducted his daughter would come again. He was glad when he saw Dresden Scott standing at the top of the hill; the presence of the guide, young as he was, gave James a sense of security.

"I have to say that I'm curious about that digging," said Scott, when James returned to the camp. "If you don't mind, I think I will ride over there and have a look."

"Perhaps you should wait," suggested James, "and we'll all go. I think Cord deserves seeing what's left as much as any of us."

They did not begrudge Cordelia her sleep, and it was nearly mid-morning before she emerged from her tent. She was greatly revived, her red hair and white dress brilliant in the sun. Two men from the search party were still with them, and Dresden Scott was not the only one who had difficulty keeping his eyes off her.

Together they broke camp, packed their things, and rode down the long slope to the lake. On their way, James told Dresden Scott more of what he knew concerning the ancient adventurer Minmaneth.

Skirting the eastern perimeter of the shore, they came to Minmaneth Rock, the base of which began some thirty or forty yards from the water.

The men who had dug the hole were not expecting to labor for their fortune any time soon, it seemed; picks and shovels lay where they had been dropped the moment the great chest was uncovered.

James looked down at the shore, and at the forest and the massive formation of granite. He envisioned his brother here, wishing there might be some clue to reveal Basil's motive for burying something in such a wild and remote place.

He was impressed by the ancient aspect of the rock itself. The soil had accumulated over millennia, the lake (the work of beavers, perhaps) might be only a century or two old, and many of the trees about them were no older than the span of a man's life; but that great mass of gray stone towering over them must have been formed before any human had ever set foot upon this land. Once, in Boston, James had seen the reconstructed bones of an iguanodon, said to be one of the oldest creatures and long extinct (perhaps destroyed by the Great Flood); and he had experienced a similar feeling gazing upon its ancient remains.

A puff of wind skittered last year's leaves into the hole. They could see where the ancient box had been laid; and scattered about were the footprints of at least a dozen men, the tracks of horses, and the ruts made by wagon wheels. "Whatever they found," said one of the men, "they must have taken it down along the shore."

"Did they miss something?" wondered Scott. His sharp eyes had caught a flash of white in the dirt, where the hole was the deepest. He jumped down into the pit and kneeled beside the object. James hunkered down at the edge of the hole, and Cordelia leaned upon his shoulder, peering after him. On the opposite side, the two men who were left from the search party mirrored their interest.

Scott knew what he had found before he had completely uncovered it, and he worked with care, brushing the loosened dirt aside. The ground was compacted and peaty, but he quickly exposed the desiccated bones of a human hand, held together by tendrils of ancient plants and the pressures of rock and soil.

But as soon as the bones came clear of the surrounding dirt, they sprung apart like a broken toy, giving everyone the eerie impression of life being relinquished even as they watched.

The guide reached into the dirt to one side of the disintegrated hand and touched the surface of something hard, which proved (after further excavation) to be a wide, flat rock. One of the men joined Scott and helped him push over this smooth plate of stone.

Death, however old, can raise human sympathy, and an involuntary sound of pity escaped from Cordelia as the figure beneath was revealed.

"My word!" said James. "Do you suppose that's the old boy himself?" He slid down into the pit beside Scott. A thrill traveled through him as he looked into the ancient eye sockets. "It is very well preserved, considering how old it must be," he said.

"Perhaps it is just an Indian burial," said Dresden Scott. He was taking note of the arrowheads and beads, the slight remains of some garment, possibly buckskin; animal bones lay about the human remains, indicating to the guide that game, or perhaps a favored dog, had been buried with the warrior to accompany him to the next world.

James reached into the barrow and took from it a small object. He peered at it for a moment, rubbing it with his thumb and forefinger. Then he passed it to Scott, who stood and held it to the light. Scott reached the object up to Cordelia, who took it almost fearfully.

The ring was of gold and had fit a man's finger. It was a signet ring with several small designs, one being the Scottish lion, rampant.

"This pit has some story to tell," said Cordelia.

The other men were given a look at the ring; then James replaced it in the grave and Scott, with some help, gently settled the great stone back into place. It was an hour's hard work to fill the hole in again.

"We should go, before it gets much later," said James. "Your mother will know by now that you're safe, but she will be anxious to see for herself. Unless someone has caught up with our burglars, whatever else was in this hole is lost to us, I fear."

They returned to their horses and rode slowly along the shore toward the forest road and Millinocket. Cordelia and her father caught each other looking back, as they mounted the slope to the trail. Then they disappeared among the trees, and Minmaneth Rock continued its gray and ancient vigil.

A crow called from deep in the forest.

64. A Deed Nearly Done

IT WAS MID-AFTERNOON when fourteen men and a large tar-covered chest in three boats came through the narrows between Quakish and Ferguson Lakes. Some of the men slept, stretched against the gunnels, their hats pulled over their eyes; some hunched wearily in their seats. Those whose shift it was to row viewed the final three-quarters of a mile to the landing at Millinocket with relief.

The hawk-nosed Benjamin Hasson lifted the brim of his hat, yawned long and wide, and watched as the farther shore drew near. This leg of their enterprise, he knew, was uncertain, and he was apprehensive as the buildings beside the lake, along with the public dock, took shape in the waning distance.

The boats schooled toward a point south of the dock, where a man stood on a ledge, several feet above the water; and Ben's craft was the first to bump quietly against the rocky shore. It was a young fellow who waited for them, hardly more than a boy, but tall; and he craned his head to see the chest in the second boat.

"Is the word out about us?" asked Ben.

"There are rumors going around, but half the men in town are still on the trail looking. The girl's father didn't explain much, I guess, or the sheriff didn't pass it on. Somebody said there was a lot of activity down at the telegraph office, but Mr. Benning has been down there three or four times, so I guess there's nothing to be concerned about. All anybody's talking about is the girl."

It took a good deal of effort, and some precarious moments, to shift the chest from the second boat to the shore. Ben supervised the situation, and cursed when he was certain that their prize was going overboard. Somehow the trunk managed to stay dry, though several of the men did not.

It was not far from the lake up a bank to a narrow path, but the way was steep in places and the unwieldy trunk seemed to fight with them. They were glad, when they reached the path, that a cart was waiting for them.

"The boss thinks of everything," gasped one of the men gratefully.

They could hear the whistle of a train coming from the northeast, then the engine, and the rumble of the wheels. "Like a clock!" exclaimed the young fellow who had met them on the shore.

"Not yet it's not!" growled Ben, thinking of the distance to the siding.

They took turns pushing and pulling at the cart, and the fabled treasure chest traveled still closer to its final destination.

It *was* like clockwork. In the mill yard they waited behind an outbuilding while the engine backed several cars onto the siding. Two railroad men joined the crew, and the chest was loaded onto the back side of the only boxcar in the link. Then the two linemen returned to their legitimate occupation, and the crew hurried to the station on the other side of town.

Nerves were high, driven by exhaustion and exultation over a job nearly finished. The bulk of the gang bought their tickets and dispersed throughout the passenger cars as soon as the train was coupled back together and pulled up to the platform.

Ben watched from outside the station as a second train, arriving from the south, drew to a stop with a chuff of steam and the deafening rumble of the braking engine. Several porters and an unusual number of passengers, including two newspapermen, stepped down to the platform; one man boarded. The porters made piles of baggage and boxes, while two of the arrivals stepped into the stationhouse.

Soon the train had pulled out of the station, and three of the arrivals stood in a small cluster, peering in unison at the disappearing train, then at the dusty street beyond the tracks, then at the rough-hewn barn looming opposite them. There seemed to be but one stimulus among them at any given moment, or a single string pulling all three heads at once.

"It is rustic, don't you think, Thump?" said Eagleton.

"I do," said Thump. "I certainly do think it is rustic. But I would be very glad to hear Ephram's point of view."

"Oh, yes," said Ephram. "I think your estimation quite . . . estimable."

"Good heavens!" declared Eagleton. It was not usual for Ephram to forward such a jest, and it *quite* took his friends by surprise.

Ephram seemed pleased with himself. He put his hands behind his back, attempting to look casual.

"Now there are three likely sportsmen," said one of the gang to Ben.

Ben smiled. It was true—the club members looked nothing if not well-to-do, and innocent as babes. Most people, even from the city, appeared at such an outpost as Millinocket in sportsman's clothes, but these three looked as if they were waiting for the theater to open.

"I hope no one offers to put a gun in their hands," said the gang member wryly.

Ben frowned; the three men had turned in his direction with a unified look of unexpected recognition, and it startled him.

"Gentlemen!" came a familiar and (to Ben Hasson) commanding voice. John Benning stepped past him, clapping Ben upon the shoulder, and approached Ephram, Eagleton, and Thump as if they were his oldest friends. "Gentlemen!"

Eagleton was the first to react, putting a hand out. "A pleasure . . . a pleasure," he said several times. He had recognized the man as he approached the station platform, but could not recall his name.

Ephram came to his friend's rescue, shaking the man's hand next. "Mr. Benning," he said.

Thump was the least enthusiastic; it was John Benning, after all, who had picked him to referee the great Blithewaite and Van Smooten bout, and the shock of that event had never completely left him. Benning, however, provided all the locomotion needed for a vigorous handshake.

"Gentlemen, gentlemen!" said Benning again, smiling broadly. "Ben," he called. "Let me introduce you to some old acquaintances. Gentlemen, Benjamin Hasson." Benning very deftly allowed the members of the club to introduce themselves, since he had never learned their names.

"We are beginning a club, you know," said Eagleton, carried away by Benning's enthusiasm.

"Really?" said the hawk-nosed Ben.

"Looking for members," said Ephram to Benning. "Ground floor."

"A club?" said Benning. "He says a club, Ben."

"Yes, boss . . . I mean, Mr. Benning."

"How are things?" inquired Benning of his subordinate easily. He might have been asking after the health of Ben's mother.

"As we've been saying, Mr. Benning," said Ben proudly, "like clockwork!"

"The deed is nearly done, Mr. Hasson," said Benning. "Congratulations."

"It seems the members of the club have an acquaintance here in town," said Sundry to Mister Walton. The young man watched the unexpected reunion from the stationhouse; with daylight reflecting against the window, he was no more than a silhouette to anyone outside.

Mister Walton, who had been garnering information from the ticket-seller, came up behind Sundry and squinted into the brightness. "My goodness!" he said. "That's Mr. Benning. After Miss Underwood saved me from going overboard, Mr. Benning saved *her*. Then, on the Fourth, he turned up at the Freeport fairgrounds, and at the dance that night. It was plain that he was quite taken with her. . . ."

Outside, Thump was saying, "The Moosepath League."

"I quite like that," said Benning. "Perhaps you will sponsor me, Mr. Thump." He gave the short fellow a friendly whack on the back.

"Yes, well . . ." Thump looked embarrassed in a manful sort of way. It was all very masculine and jolly, and just the sort of robust conduct he had hoped for in the life of a club member.

Some of the gang gathered close, drawn by the laughter and the presence of their boss.

"Do you know the other men?" wondered Sundry, inside the stationhouse.

"I don't think so," said Mister Walton.

"They're a rough-looking bunch," said the young man.

There *was* the quality of a gang about the men who surrounded John Benning and the three members, and yet they seemed deferential to the handsome young man; some appeared tentative about him, as if Benning's presence made them nervous. None of the men were familiar to Mister

Walton, but they put him in mind somehow of the smuggling crew who had loaded Horace McQuinn's wagon at the Mariners' Hospital.

"Well, I must get back to the telegraph," Benning was saying, with a wink in the direction of Ben Hasson. "I'm waiting for information regarding Charles Stimply," he added playfully, speaking directly to the white-bearded Samuel Adams, who had played the part of Charles Stimply at the Underwoods' nearly two weeks before.

Mister Walton and Sundry could not hear what was being said, but there was something odd about the scene, and even something wrong. If John Benning was in Millinocket, it seemed that he must be here for the same reasons as they—to render whatever aid he could to Cordelia and her family. And yet, Benning appeared too jolly, too satisfied—and too much in charge.

"Perhaps she's been found," said Sundry hopefully. He started for the station door just as Benning was leaving the group of men with a friendly wave.

"No word yet, then?" called one of the men.

The hawk-nosed man who had been nearest to Benning gave the fellow a quick, almost startled look; but Benning called back, "Not yet." The men were speaking at some distance from each other, and these were the first words that Mister Walton and Sundry could hear.

Mister Walton stopped Sundry with a gentle hand on the shoulder. "Wait a moment, Sundry," he said, and they watched Benning enter the telegraph office. "Is there something peculiar in all this?"

"If *you* think so, I'd say sure there is," replied Sundry. "I just thought it was my naturally suspicious nature. If he was here to help Miss Underwood, it seems that his bearing would be more solemn; and if his bearing wasn't solemn, it seems he wouldn't be here."

"That is it exactly, my friend," said Mister Walton. "Sundry?"

"Yes, Mister Walton."

"I am going to employ a bit of subterfuge."

"Really?" Sundry couldn't imagine Mister Walton doing such a thing.

"It is not very gentlemanly, I'm afraid. I'm sure there is an explanation, but I marked that fellow for a rascal the first time I met him. It's not fair to judge a conversation you can't hear, but the circumstances are so strange. If I am in error, and I certainly hope I am, I will very gladly tender an apology to the man."

"I'll come with you."

"No, you wait here with our friends. I'll be back after I have an *unexpected* meeting with Mr. Benning."

* * *

Ephram, Eagleton, and Thump were waiting with Sundry in the station-house when the chairman returned, looking darker than Sundry had ever seen him. The three companions took no notice of Mister Walton's somber aspect. Thump was missing a button and he was staring at the empty spot on his jacket, as if the button would rematerialize. Ephram and Eagleton commiserated with Thump regarding his loss.

"It's quite mysterious, actually," explained Ephram to Mister Walton. "It was there the last time he looked."

"Did you meet anyone at the telegraph office?" asked Sundry.

"Yes, I did," replied Mister Walton. His manner was abstract, and it was clear that his mind was racing. "Mr. Benning was very surprised to see me, and quite grim. Miss Underwood has not been found yet. He was, in fact, in the camp when she was taken. He was traveling with the Underwoods."

Thump had stopped a passing porter and was showing the man the mates to his missing button. The train, linked up now, chuffed into the station yard, and the weary crew on the platform began to board her.

"Mr. Underwood is out with the search party," Mister Walton was saying. "But Mrs. Underwood is with her nephew and niece at a Mrs. Cuthbert's boardinghouse. Gentlemen," said Mister Walton, with more authority in his voice than was his usual wont. "I have a favor to ask of you—not in my capacity as your chairman, but as a friend."

Ephram and Eagleton's attention turned from the missing button to Mister Walton's face; and after a moment or two, Thump (who was bent over, searching the floor) straightened himself and regarded the chairman of the Moosepath League with surprise and gravity. The very thought of being called upon as Mister Walton's friend filled them with a great deal of pride and not a little purpose. Even Sundry Moss was impressed.

"My dear Mister Walton!" said Eagleton. "We are at your service!"

"We must fashion some excuse for your returning on this train," explained the portly chairman. "Mr. Eagleton, your mother has taken ill."

"Good heavens!"

"Your friends will return with you."

Ephram, who appeared to understand Mister Walton better than did his two friends, said, "Are we acting in the nature of . . . detectives, Mister Walton?"

"Yes, in fact."

"Good heavens!" said Eagleton again.

"Do you remember the sharp-nosed man who was speaking with Mr. Benning?"

"Yes!" said the three men as one.

"I want you to stay close to him, but not to let on."

The three men looked ready for the task, even eager. Sundry hurried to buy tickets for them, while Mister Walton explained that he needed to know where the sharp-nosed fellow and his compatriots were going. "I would almost go myself, but Mr. Benning expects me at the boarding-house. Now, don't put yourselves in any danger—but find, if you can, where they are going. Wire me here in Millinocket when you have the chance."

"Quick!" said Sundry. "The conductor is making the last call."

The three men snatched up as much of their baggage as they could carry and hurried out, Thump making a more circuitous route to the door as he searched for his lost button. A porter was called and the conductor watched as the baggage was put aboard; then the three men clambered into the nearest passenger car, where the hawk-nosed Ben Hasson's face could be seen resting by a window.

Suddenly Thump appeared at the door of the station. He put his head in, out of breath, his eyes alight with excitement.

"What is it?" asked a startled Mister Walton.

"I found my button," announced Thump. He waved the object in the air, then hurried back to the train.

"Dear me!" said Mister Walton. "What have I done! Sundry, perhaps you had better go with them."

"Yes, Mister Walton," said Sundry, almost with a salute.

The train took its first lurch forward.

"Quick, quick!" said the portly fellow, eyes wide with sudden panic. "You need a ticket!"

Sundry raised a ticket, already purchased for himself, with a wink. "Just waiting for the order, sir," he declared, grabbed his bag, and was gone.

"I'll wire ahead when I learn something!" shouted Mister Walton.

Sundry caught the third passenger car as it rolled slowly past, and he waved as he was trundled out of sight.

By the time that Ephram, Eagleton, and Thump had gotten their bearings, the swift and efficient Sundry Moss had found them.

"Sit right next to the man," said Sundry.

"Really?" said Eagleton.

"Yes, just be very straightforward about traveling with him. Tender your excuse when he asks you, and he will suspect nothing. Act mysterious and he will think you are mysterious."

"I think he's right!" said Ephram to Thump. "We must be very straightforward."

"Straightforward it is!" announced Eagleton.

"Yes," said Sundry. "Straight"—he pointed down the aisle in the direction of the man they were to watch—"forward."

Ben Hasson was perplexed to see the three men (who had just arrived in Millinocket) on the train, and not a little troubled to see them sit near him. "Aren't you making a short visit of it?" he asked.

"We are supposed to stay close to you," said Thump. This seemed as straightforward as he could get.

Sundry very nearly buried his head in his hands.

"What?" said Ben, sitting up.

"Oh, and Eagleton's mother is ill," added Thump.

"I don't like that part," admitted Eagleton.

Ephram had the look of a man who knows something is wrong, but can't quite put his finger on it. "Oh, and we're not to let on," he said. This made him feel better.

"What is this?" demanded Ben.

"Mr. Benning sent us," said Sundry, hoping to save the situation.

"The boss?" said Hasson, without thinking.

"The boss," agreed Sundry. *I've got you*, he thought, but added aloud, "I've always known him as Mr. Benning, of course."

The hawk-nosed man had seen the other three fellows talking like great chums with the boss, but he had never laid eyes on this younger one. "I haven't met you," he said to Sundry. "Perhaps you had better explain yourself."

"These gentlemen are eager to learn how to play cards," said the narrow young man. His wink was slow and crafty.

"Are they?"

"Are we?" wondered Eagleton.

"Our friend Mister Walton is very fond of card playing," continued Sundry.

"My goodness," said Thump. "We should learn posthaste!"

"The boss, you see," said Sundry, "thought you might enjoy teaching them."

"Did he?" said Ben Hasson, with a chortle and the barely concealed look of a shark smelling blood. "He does think of everything, doesn't he." A deck of cards was produced from some pocket on the man's person, and Sundry knew he had successfully marked his man. The deck slipped from its case and was shuffled with remarkable acuity. "We just need a proper surface to deal on," said Ben.

Sundry was looking for a piece of luggage. "Yes," he said. "The boss is a very intelligent fellow."

65. The Man with the Silver Lining

MERCIA WAS ON THE PORCH of Mrs. Cuthbert's boardinghouse when Mister Walton came up Millinocket's dusty main thoroughfare; her hands were folded calmly on the porch railing, and she was looking away from him, gazing up the street. He stopped for a moment, bag in hand, and took his hat from his head. She did not see him, turned away as she was, but she looked very striking and very sad, and Mister Walton suddenly feared that he was imposing.

"Mrs. Underwood," he said from the street.

Mercia looked around slowly and recognized him immediately. "Mister Walton," she said, with great regard. One would not have guessed that she had met him only twice before.

The portly fellow walked up the steps to the porch. "Please forgive me, if I am intruding, Mrs. Underwood. I heard about your daughter, and she had been so kind to me that I could not stay put."

"Mister Walton," said Mercia. She took his hand warmly. "Cordelia is so fond of you. She has spoken of you often since our day together."

"I really don't know what help I can be, but if another search party is sent out, I am a fairly agile horseman, despite my girth."

"I am so glad you came," she insisted. "Cordelia's cousins are as worried as I, and my reserves of tranquillity are near an end. A new face, and such a welcome one, will help immeasurably."

And she was ushering him into Mrs. Cuthbert's front hall when the staccato beat of hooves—the sound of a rider in a great hurry, the sound that she had been waiting for—brought her up short.

The rider reined in before the boardinghouse, a cloud of dust catching him as he dropped from his mount. "Mrs. Underwood?" he inquired of Mercia, who met him at the foot of the porch steps. "I'm sorry it took me so long, but my horse went lame and I had to borrow—" He stopped himself and took a breath. "Your daughter's fine, ma'am."

Mercia began to tremble, and Mister Walton hurried down the stairs to her side. She could not look at anyone, and Mister Walton found his eyes welling up in sympathy as she cried and shook.

"She's fine, you say?" he said to the messenger.

"She's with her father. Mr. Scott found her. He trapped one of the kidnappers in a privy!"

"Good heavens!" said Mister Walton.

"He's a clever one, our Mr. Scott. And Miss Underwood stretched one of them out with a ladle."

"Thank you," said Mercia. "Please, I'm sorry . . . I'm exhausted, is all."

"Nothing to it, ma'am," said the young fellow, taking off his hat.

Mister Walton led Mercia back up to the front door. Ethan and Priscilla hurried onto the porch to hear the news, and John Benning came up and listened to the messenger repeat his tale. Benning tried to give him something for his troubles, pressing several generous bills in his hand, but the young man refused.

Mercia took Mister Walton's hand again, and as this did not seem to serve the purpose, she embraced him. "Oh, Mister Walton! You are a good-luck charm!"

Mister Walton turned red to the ears.

Mercia talked to John Benning about riding to meet her husband and daughter, but decided to help Mrs. Cuthbert prepare a meal for their return. The notion of Mrs. Underwood riding out with Benning worried Mister Walton, and he considered getting a pistol, as well as a horse and saddle, to accompany them; though he did not voice his suspicions. Benning had been willing to go if Mercia wanted, but did not press her either way, and she decided in the end to be patient.

Late in the afternoon a young boy came on a mule, waving his hat and calling out that *they were coming*. The northern end of Mrs. Cuthbert's porch filled with people, and Main Street of Millinocket was suddenly so populated that one would have thought a parade was on its way.

Tired but happy would describe the small group that appeared north of town. Tired and relieved and mostly happy would describe Cordelia as her horse pulled up to a halt. John Benning helped her down, and the boy with the mule took her reins.

Mercia met her daughter at the bottom of the porch steps and embraced her with all her might. Applause broke out along the street.

Cordelia looked up, past her mother's shoulder, at her cousins. Priscilla looked thoroughly miserable, she was so happy; she shook with sobs. "I heard you conked one of them with a ladle!" shouted Ethan, proud as he could be.

"Mister Walton!" exclaimed Cordelia, when she caught sight of the man. She was pleased and mystified to see him.

"But where is Mr. Scott?" asked Mercia.

"He left us a mile or so outside of town," said James. He swung down from his horse and wearily handed his reins over to the first person who would take them.

"He sent his best regards to you, Mama."

"I wish he had brought his regards himself. It's a terrible thing if I can't thank him."

"If I know Dresden Scott," said Mr. Butler, who had first met them at Millinocket two days before, "he'll wander into town when he thinks the fuss is over. He gets embarrassed easily."

"Well, I am very put out with him," said Mercia. She appraised her daughter at arm's length. There was an expression of great failure or disappointment in Cordelia's eyes. Mercia took a long, measured breath that filled in nicely for a direct question.

"I'm just tired," said Cordelia.

"Let's get you inside."

While the men congregated in the parlor, Mercia and Priscilla escorted Cordelia to a room upstairs. "Oh, my dear," said Mercia when she was sitting on the side of the bed beside her daughter. "I am so sorry. And your father, of course, blames himself."

"It wasn't anybody's fault except for . . . those men. And I don't know what I would have done if Mr. Scott hadn't come when he did. I was so frightened."

"And he wouldn't come into town with you?" Mercia asked.

"Oh, come sit," said Cordelia to her cousin. She took Priscilla's hand and pulled her to the edge of the bed. The gesture was genuine—a way in which to surround herself between loving ramparts, and also to let Priscilla know how much she was needed—but it doubled nicely by drawing attention from her own distress.

Mercia was not to be fooled; that same sense of personal failure in her daughter's eyes was again too obvious. "Cordelia, what happened?"

"I was just terrible. I shouted at him." Her freckled complexion was red with suppressed tears.

"You did what? Cordelia, you'd hardly known the man for a single day!" Mercia almost laughed.

"Oh, I know! But it isn't so easy to be rescued like that. If it had been Daddy, I would have just hugged him till he yelled."

"Well, Mr. Scott is a very hardy young man," said Mercia, "and he might not have yelled so quickly."

Cordelia did not hear her, or chose not to. "He was good-humored about it all, at first, but then he acted a little piqued—as if we had kept something from him."

"We did, rather," said Mercia. "Dear, they knocked him over the head with the butt of a pistol, and they were armed men he was trailing. It's a remarkable thing that he didn't wait for the search party with your father to catch up."

"I know, I know, I know. . . . I just feel terrible, because he was so nice to me. And I think I hurt his feelings. . . ."

"My word, you're tired," said the mother, cradling her daughter and suddenly feeling like she hadn't since her children were young. "One just doesn't know." She thought of Mr. Scott. What would he do? What does such a man do when his feelings are hurt, or when a pretty young woman such as her daughter pricks at his heart? Mercia imagined him making camp in the forest, lying awake at night, looking up through the branches at the stars; it *was* very melancholy. "One just doesn't know," she said again.

Priscilla hadn't said a word, but only held her cousin's hand.

"No, one doesn't," said Cordelia, and then she was asleep like a child, and they eased her onto a pillow and pulled a quilt up beneath her arms.

Downstairs, Ethan sounded authoritative as he said that with one of the kidnappers knocked cold, one tied up, and one caught in a privy (and since Mr. Scott had taken their horses), they were as good as caught. "And won't they talk!" said the boy. "Since they're caught and they won't get a penny of anything their friends dug up, won't they just talk!"

"No honor among thieves, do you think?" said John Benning easily.

"Maybe their friends will plan an escape for them," suggested the boy, himself awed by this construction.

They sat in the parlor—James Underwood, young Ethan Morningside, and John Benning; Mister Walton stood by a window, worrying about the men he had sent back on the train. What had he been thinking? He had picked up on a pack of scoundrels in a minute, and sent his friends after them. Sundry he didn't worry so about; Sundry radiated a certain native ability to take care of himself, though he also radiated a hastiness to action that bothered the portly fellow the more he thought of it.

But what had he been thinking, sending the Moosepath League after treasure hunters and kidnappers?

Mercia and Priscilla came into the parlor and everybody rose. Mister Walton turned, but stayed by the window, unwilling to take his scrutiny—his carefully hidden scrutiny—from John Benning.

"She's asleep," announced the mother. "She's exhausted, poor thing—and so, my dear, are you," she added to James.

"I must leave, I'm afraid," said John Benning. "I am sorry not to say goodbye to Cordelia," he explained. "But while waiting for telegrams at the office I received one of my own. Family business."

"I know Cordelia will be sorry to have missed you," said James. He put out his hand when it was clear that Benning meant to leave even as they spoke.

"I am sure we will meet again," said the young man, with one of his winning smiles. "Mister Walton, I trust I will see you again. We do manage to meet in surprising places."

"Yes. The wharf, the fairgrounds, the telegraph office . . ." Another person might have detected something cautious in Mister Walton's handshake.

Mercia gave John Benning a motherly embrace and a kiss on the cheek. "Thank you, John, for everything. I hope your family is well."

"Oh, yes," he said, as he was followed to the front hall. "Nothing to trouble yourselves about." He did not linger at the door, but raised his hat and hurried down the porch.

"That's very disappointing for Cordelia," said a concerned father.

"Mr. Benning leaving?" said Mercia. "It would be very awkward if he didn't. I wonder if he knows it."

"Why would you say that?" James wondered, a little perplexed, and even a little shocked.

"Because, my dear, he is very much out of the running."

"With Cordelia?"

"Oh, yes."

"Do you mean Mr. Scott? Just because he rescued her? I mean, he's a fine fellow and I couldn't think better of him, but just because he rescued her John's out of the running? That doesn't sound like Cordelia at all."

"It happened before that—didn't it, Priscilla?"

Priscilla, who had appeared not to hear this conversation, was briefly startled.

"Well, *I* thought so . . ." she stated quietly.

"It was when he told us about the woods in the winter, I think," said Mercia, leading them airily back to the parlor. Enjoying her husband's confusion, she added, "I suspected something was in the wind before that."

"Good heavens," said James. "You mean to tell me that the color of my grandchildren's hair might be dictated by a passage of well-worded description?"

"The color of your *children's* hair was decided by a glance, my dear," said Mercia. And looking remarkably saucy (and sure that he had an overwhelming desire to at least touch her hand), she smiled and slipped out of reach. "Mister Walton," she was saying. "I can't tell you what it meant to me to see you this afternoon."

"Mrs. Underwood, I am just happy that your daughter is safe. I must say, I hope I have the opportunity to meet this Mr. Scott."

"You may yet," said Mercia.

Mister Walton wondered whether to tell them of his suspicions concerning John Benning. He decided to wait. "Please forgive me if I am overly inquisitive," he said. "But did all this really have to do with . . . a buried treasure?"

66. Further Wit in Evidence

"How about five-card draw?" proposed Benjamin Hasson.

"Excuse me?" said Ephram. Eagleton and Thump too were curious.

"Poker," said the card shuffler simply.

"Oh, dear," said Eagleton.

"Poker?" Thump looked like a minister to whom drunken revelry has been suggested.

Ben Hasson attempted to mitigate the suggestion, and while this task commanded his attention, Sundry studied him from across the aisle. Had this fellow indeed helped to kidnap a young woman? What a desperate act that seemed, and yet how calm the man.

Ephram was leaning forward, so that his whisper might be heard above the rails. "Isn't poker a form of gambling?" he asked the hawk-nosed man.

"Gambling?" said Ben.

"I am sure that it is!" said Eagleton; he had read about gambling once in a gripping novel—*What Drove Him Mad!* by Mrs. Melody Clydethrope.

"Gambling?" said Ben again. He could not have been more puzzled if someone had objected to silverware at the dinner table. He flashed a glance in Sundry's direction and Sundry smiled to indicate amusement rather than observation.

"Poker doesn't *have* to entail gambling," said Sundry wisely.

"It doesn't?" said Ben Hasson.

Sundry tapped the side of his nose. "I am sure that our friend would never suggest such a thing. Would you, sir?"

"I wouldn't?"

"Please forgive me," said Ephram. "I did not mean to cast aspersions."

"Never," agreed Thump.

"Ephram never casts aspersions," informed Eagleton.

"A certain amount of money does change hands, however," continued Sundry. "It is a tradition of the game, not to mention a social nicety, for each player to pay the dealer a predetermined sum."

"A tradition, you say," said Thump. He was fond of traditions.

"Yes, that is nice," concluded Ephram.

"And you see," said Sundry, "the dealer is whoever has taken the previous hand. Isn't that the best way of explaining it?" With raised eyebrows, he appealed to the man with the cards.

Ben thought this through, and a smile like a beam of light brightened his features. "I've never heard it explained with greater delicacy, sir."

"Sundry," said the young man, holding out his hand. "Sundry Moss."

Presented with such an obvious alias, Ben felt at home with the fellow. "Ben Hasson," he said.

"Matthew Ephram," said that gentleman, adding his hand to the round of shaking. "It *is* a very . . . traditional sort of thing, isn't it." Eagleton and Thump introduced themselves, adding their high regard for custom and social niceties.

"How much would you suggest paying the dealer today?" wondered Ben Hasson. "Twenty-five cents?"

"Fifty," said Sundry.

Hasson glanced at the three neophytes.

"Oh, yes," said Thump. "I'm sure that it is only fair. This dealing seems a complex thing."

"I am sure that you will get the hang of it," said Ben.

The conductor came by, just then, and turned a tolerant (if somewhat envious) eye away from the unfolding game of cards. Sundry watched as Ben Hasson produced his ticket, and caught enough of a glimpse to see the city of Bangor marked as his destination.

Sundry and the members of the club had tickets that would take them all the way to Portland. While their tickets were being punched, he did his best to distract Ben Hasson by accidentally knocking the makeshift table, and therefore the cards, into the aisle.

Sundry stepped off the train at Brownville Junction. It had been many hours of riding for him since this morning, and he had a legitimate need to stretch his long legs; but he was also hoping for communication from Mister Walton at the telegraph station.

He had only known Mister Walton for the better part of a week, and yet he admired the man enough to obey his wishes without question, and cared enough about him to wonder if he should be serving directly at his side. It disturbed Sundry that his portly friend was dealing with the head of the snake, while Sundry himself kept watch over the body; and he might have hastily retraced (re-retraced, as it were) his path if not for the members of the club, who so obviously required his chaperonage.

He had hoped for a word from Mister Walton to assure him that all was well, and he returned to the train unsatisfied and a little troubled.

"Those are very good hands," said Ben Hasson. He was helping Ephram, Eagleton, and Thump with their card playing. It was very nice of him, they thought, to look at their cards and coach them, when he had his own cards to worry about—not to mention the dealing, which had been his responsibility since they began. "Those are very nice hands, Mr. Moss," he said.

"I think they are learning quickly," said Sundry.

White-bearded Samuel Adams had scented out the odd game, much to Ben's dismay, and social niceties dictated that he do his best to help the three men as well. Sundry was introduced to Mr. Adams as a friend of the boss's, and when a third member of the gang lighted upon this diversion, Sundry was introduced as a *good* friend of the boss's. He leaned back, smiled upon the members of the club, and conveyed vast pleasure, as if he liked nothing better than to see three innocents hoodwinked with such ease.

For their part, Ephram, Eagleton, and Thump seemed well stocked with the necessary funds for such a fleecing, and quite cheerful to part with them.

At Brownville Sundry inquired, in vain once again, for any message, and upon his return he raised a questioning look from a naturally suspicious Ben Hasson. "Business," said Sundry, thinking that a fully articulated excuse might be as suspect as nothing at all. Others of the gang had gathered around the game by then—a rough-and-ready-looking bunch—and it occurred to Sundry that Miss Underwood might be secreted away on the train itself.

He rose from his seat after what he hoped was an appropriate interval, and made a cursory tour of the train. There were no private compartments, however, in which a person could be held against her will; and if she were being kept in one of the freight carriers behind them, there was no way—outside of walking the tops of cars—for him to continue his search.

It was in the window at the end of the last passenger car that he caught the reflection of someone peering in behind him, and it was all he could do to stop himself from looking quickly over his shoulder. Instead, he stood for a moment, looking out at the boxcar that followed, and the flash of passing forest to either side. He turned away deliberately, as if lost in thought, but knew before looking that the person tailing him would be gone.

At Old Town Mister Walton caught up with him in a telegram. Sundry read it several times over with a mingled sense of relief and regret. He was certainly glad that Miss Underwood was safe, but Mister Walton had spoken of the young woman in such glowing terms that a young man could not be blamed for hoping to be the author of her rescue.

Standing on the platform, he thought for a moment that his friend had left behind some of his luggage, but realized that Mister Walton would have wired the railroad if he had been missing something. No — the *large chest* was not missing, but stolen! Here, perhaps, was the actual motive for Miss Underwood's kidnapping.

It did not occur to Sundry to speak to the local constabulary; Mister Walton himself had said nothing in his telegram about alerting the authorities — he simply said, *Please take no risks.* Sundry read the telegram again, grateful for the final message — *Will follow* — though he feared that Mister Walton could not follow soon enough.

He found a deep pocket for the telegram, but changed his course in the midst of boarding the train. He returned to the telegraph office, took a form from the counter, where a number of pens and an inkwell were provided. Here he paused for thought, then carefully wrote:

To: MISTER TOBIAS WALTON
      CARE OF MRS CUTHBERT
      MAIN STREET
      MILLINOCKET

      PLEASE SEND URGENT WIRE TO BEN HASSON BANGOR
      STATION SAYING . . .

The train increased its passenger list as they traveled south. Sundry picked his way through the aisles, past outstretched feet and bags and unfolded newspapers. *Kidnapped Woman Unrecovered,* read a headline.

"How is business?" asked Ben Hasson, as Sundry took his seat again.

Thump had actually won a hand and was thoroughly embarrassed to receive fifty cents from each of his fellow players. "Good heavens!" he said with a laugh and a blush. He shuffled the cards nervously. His friends were proud of him, and Ephram patted Thump's shoulder with comradely affection.

"Business is fine," said Sundry.

"That's good," said one of the gang. "We thought you were going to wear yourself out."

67. No One Knew the Day Until the Sun Went Down

THE CONDUCTOR'S VOICE RANG OUT with the litany of stops, and Bangor loomed early in the call—large and daunting in Sundry's mind. His nerve froze somewhat as he reassessed his intentions, and briefly he regretted sending that telegram to Mister Walton. But just when his heart was gripped, he took a breath, and felt suddenly giddy as he considered how much he was going to enjoy himself. It has been said that the devil is a collection of virtuous qualities put to bad ends. So it might be imagined that Sundry Moss had many of the traits of a true rascal, and was only waiting for the chance to employ them in a good cause.

The perseverance, meanwhile, of Ephram, Eagleton, and Thump was heroic, considering that between them they had only realized two hands in all the distance from Millinocket to Greenbush. Once Thump was in the position of dealer, however, he had an odd run of luck that could not be broken by either Ben Hasson's machinations or bad advice. Ephram and Eagleton were fascinated (and not a little awed) by their friend's sudden command of the cards. Thump was embarrassed and apologized several times.

From up ahead, the engine whistle pierced the air and the conductor came through the car announcing Bangor as the next stop. Sundry felt his stomach tighten. Ben Hasson found this an auspicious moment to call it a game and shuffle away the deck. Thump was pleased (he dreaded winning another hand) and he offered to give back the money he had won. Ben Hasson looked as if he had swallowed something wrong.

The outskirts of Bangor rose up around them—lumberyards and a brick factory, a sawmill on the river, and the aged constructions of the Devil's Half-Acre. The steam whistle shrieked among the buildings; the rhythm of the tracks slowed; the brakes clashed and rang. The trail of ash and steam caught up with the cars as knowledgeable passengers shut the windows; a billow of white and gray obscured the station briefly, like a passing bank of fog.

Then they were stopped; the brakes and the chuff of steam and the rumble of the tracks fell away to the babble and commotion of a busy railway station. "Well, gentlemen," said Ben Hasson to the club members, "it has been a pleasure." But doubt showed in his expression. "I will tell the boss how entertained we were."

"Certainly," said Ephram.

"We can't tell you how much we appreciate your instruction," assured Ephram.

"You're sure you won't take your money back?" asked Thump.

They extended their hands as they rose, but Ben Hasson was down the aisle with the rest of the gang, none of whom looked back.

"A laudable company," said Ephram. "I hope they will consider our club."

"It will be delightful to report our newly acquired expertise regarding the playing of cards to our chairman," considered Eagleton. "Aces high!" he added as a sort of farewell to the men disappearing in file from the car.

Sundry watched from the window as several of the gang dispersed from the station platform, while others gathered about Ben Hasson, who seemed to be reading something.

"It has occurred to me," said the ever-astute Thump, "that we were supposed to *stay close* to Mr. Hasson."

"Good heavens, Thump!" said Eagleton. "I do believe you are correct!"

"In the excitement of the cards," said Ephram, "I quite forgot, but those were precisely Mister Walton's words."

"I have received a further communication from . . . the chairman," said Sundry, halting a sudden rush down the aisle, "and if you will follow me, we will execute his wishes."

"*And* there is the problem of our tickets," said Thump, still brimming with revelation.

"Good heavens!" said Eagleton again.

"Our tickets *are* for Portland," said Ephram. "It might be improper to get off at Bangor."

"It *is* impolite not to inform people of a change in plans," agreed Eagleton regretfully.

"I fear my knowledge of railroad etiquette is lacking," admitted Ephram. "Where is the conductor?"

Sundry herded the club members up the aisle of the passenger car and away from the station. Outside the compartment, he led the way down the steps on the river side of the train, so that the locomotive and its line of cars would screen them from the platform.

It was while passing through the car that Ephram discovered the previous day's edition of the *Portland Courier*, a copy of which was abandoned on one of the seats. It is true that the *Eastern Argus* was Ephram's journal of choice, but the very sight of a paper from home (after being deprived of such for three days or more) was enough to drive all other considerations from his highly occupied mind. The paper was folded open to one of the middle pages, and Ephram held it up before him as he fell down the steps.

"Good heavens!" he said, as he got up from atop Thump. "There has been an incident at Leith and Gore's Refined Soap Company!"

"An incident!" declared Eagleton as he helped Thump to his feet.

Thump, who recognized immediately his own favored organ, barely gave notice to the altered condition of his hat. "What has happened?" he wondered.

Details are as yet not forthcoming, read the item, *but we have been informed that an incident has occurred at Leith and Gore's Refined Soap Company. Our readers can rely on us to report any further particulars.*

"Good heavens!" said Eagleton.

The engine and the passenger cars had been disengaged from the freight cars and now were trundling out of the station. Fearing that they would be seen as soon as the train had pulled away, Sundry suggested that they turn slightly so that the raised newspaper concealed them from the platform. Truth to tell, this was not an ideal solution, and if any of the gang members at the station had not been distracted by other matters, they might have found the sight of a newspaper with four pair of legs worthy of closer inspection.

Clumping down the steps of the car, Ben Hasson heard his name called from the platform. A boy in the official livery of the North East Telegraph Company stood there, and he called for Ben with a sort of authoritative query. The hawk-nosed man was startled to hear that his arrival was anticipated, and the reverse nod he gave the boy was curt and wary. "What is it?" he growled as the boy approached.

"Telegram, sir."

"I know that! Give it here!" Ben snatched the paper from the boy's hand, and when the boy did not immediately make himself scarce, he tossed him a small coin and a glare. Standing amidst the ebb and flow of people, he read the telegram.

"What is it, Ben?" asked Samuel Adams. He and several of the gang were standing about, like actors in a play who have forgotten their lines.

Ben looked sharply about him. "Get!" he said in a harsh whisper to the man nearest him. "You're not to hang about. Come back tonight, as the boss ordered." He glanced at Samuel. "It's from the boss. I'm supposed to meet a fellow named Leach outside the seminary."

"The seminary?" The idea seemed a little frightening.

"The cemetery?" wondered one of the other men.

"Get!" Ben stalked a few feet away, rubbing the stubble on his chin as he reread the wire. "Wait," he amended. "Better you stay here after all. But don't make a scene of yourselves."

"What is it?" asked Samuel again. Hasson tipped the telegram slightly so that Samuel, and only Samuel, could read it.

NORTH EAST TELEGRAPH
COMPANY
OFFICE—MILLINOCKET, MAINE

JULY 12 PM 6:15
BANGOR STATION
MR BEN HASSON

CHANGE IN SITUATION. CHANGE IN PLAN. WAIT OUTSIDE SEMINARY IMMEDIATE TO ARRIVAL FOR PARSON LEACH. DON'T ALARM THE MEN.
    THE BOSS

"You're supposed to wait for a preacher?" said the white-bearded fellow incredulously.

"Yes, and you're coming with me."

"But why did he sign it 'the boss'?" wondered Samuel.

"If the situation has changed, he may have good reason not to use his real name. I don't know. How should I know?" Hasson considered this unexpected twist while a second engine backed up to the freight and lumber cars, prior to pulling them onto a siding that overlooked the river. "Stay here, but . . . spread out," Ben said to several of the men.

"What is it, Ben?" asked one of them, wide-eyed.

"I don't know yet. It's nothing. Just a little change. I'll be back." He made a gesture to Samuel and they disappeared around the station house.

The rest of the men—those who hadn't quickly scattered—stood about, looking more than ever like forgetful stage players. They glanced at one another, exchanged shrugs, whispered in huddles. A hay wagon loaded with sheep was drawn up above the station, and as the freight engine pulled away, the sound of the animal's bleating took precedence over the platform.

"Is he gone, then?" inquired someone.

"Gone?" asked one of the men. He and his fellows nearly jumped out of their skins at the sight of Sundry and the club members amongst them. The men backed away in an irregular and widening circle.

"Is he gone?" demanded Sundry.

"Ben?"

"Yes, Ben!"

"He just left. And Samuel with him."

"Hmmm," said Sundry. "The boss said that Samuel would go with him. He said to me, 'Sundry, just you wait and see if old Samuel doesn't charge off with him.' "

"He did, did he?" One of the older men approached Sundry with a dark look in his eye. "And why did he say that?"

"According to the boss," explained Sundry, "it was all the proof he'd need that they were in it together."

"Maybe you had better explain yourself," said another in the now constricting circle.

"They've double-crossed you, boys," announced Sundry.

"Who?"

"Who do you think? And why do you think we're here?" Sundry swept an arm out to incorporate Ephram, Eagleton, and Thump. Thump, who had a certain precedence when it came to the *Portland Courier*, had been given command of the newspaper and he was reading to his friends. " '*Mrs. De Riche is beginning a new instructional on the season's most popular dances,*' " he was saying. Sundry looked back at the gang members; he hooked a thumb over his shoulder at the club members. "They're a cool lot, aren't they? Now Hasson and Adams are not alone in their little scheme, so we had better move quickly."

"Doing what?"

"Why, getting the chest and getting it out of here, of course."

"But we weren't supposed to move it till after dark."

"I don't like this," said one of the gang, a large black-bearded fellow, who stepped forward. He poked a blunt forefinger in the vicinity of Sundry's nose. "And I don't know who you are, but—"

A collective gasp from Ephram, Eagleton, and Thump brought a halt to the man's final pronouncement. Thump had folded the paper back to its original shape, and some communication there had shocked them terribly. " '*Young woman abducted near Millinocket!*' " he read. The three members looked up in unison, expressed their horror to Sundry, then swept the stricken faces of the gang members with their wide eyes.

"Why . . . it's . . . it's *illegal!*" asserted Ephram.

"I don't know what your game is," said the large man, his finger hovering an inch or so from Sundry's nose, "but you're sailing dangerous waters."

"Easy there, Ollie," said another fellow. "He's a good friend of the boss."

Ollie stared down the length of his finger, then slowly dropped the threatening digit.

"Why do you think Ben just left?" wondered Sundry. "Where do you think he went?"

"The seminary, he said," said one of the younger men.

Sundry raised an eyebrow. "Did he? I *thought*, when I first met him, that he had a certain theological inclination."

"He got a message from the boss," said another.

"Did you see it?" asked Sundry.

The members of the gang inquired silently of one another.

"He only showed it to Samuel," said someone.

By now Sundry, the members of the gang, and the members of the club were conspicuous for being the only people on the platform (save for the sheep farmer), and Ollie and his fellows were beginning to feel the heat of scrutiny, real or imagined.

"I think we should wait till dark," said someone.

"I think you should," said Sundry. "And that will give Hasson and his cronies a good long time to get there before you."

The paralysis of indecision hung over the gang members. The farmer paced the platform. The sheep bleated in the afternoon heat, glad perhaps for the river breeze. Thump read aloud from the article concerning the abduction of the young woman.

"Good heavens!" said Eagleton suddenly. "We left Mister Walton in Millinocket!"

"And Mr. Benning!" added Ephram.

These pronouncements induced a series of nervous flinches from the small crowd.

"Hey, be careful there," said Ollie.

"I told you they were cool," said Sundry. "Just the men for the task ahead. You've gone this far in secret and under cover of night; let's finish the job in broad daylight and under the nose of the law."

"That sounds like the boss," said one of the men.

"It was the last thing he said to me before I boarded the train."

The door to the freight car swung wide on grumbly hinges, and the walls of the car vibrated like simmering kettledrums. Several members of the gang cast discomfited glances about the freight yard. "Don't look so mysterious," said Sundry to one of them. "Isn't that right, Mr. Ephram."

"Hmm?" said that man, looking up from the paper. "Oh, yes," he said, remembering now. "Act mysterious and you will appear mysterious."

"A very wise man said that," informed Sundry.

"I'm still not sure why you've changed your plans," said the railroad man who had opened the door. "Mr. Benning said expressly, 'After dark.' "

"We're not entirely sure ourselves," said Ollie, his voice growling on a note in sympathy with the complaining hinges. He climbed into the car with the railroad man and waited for his eyes to adjust from the brilliance of the day. "Someone better climb up and help us. And bring that wagon up."

Sundry was among the three men who pulled themselves up into the shadows. Ephram, Eagleton, and Thump—who had experienced some trouble crossing the tracks while reading—took note that something was happening and looked up in unison from their newspaper.

Ollie loomed like a bear when Sundry stepped into the dark. He leaned with both hands on a large trunk, the whites of his eyes showing as he studied Sundry. "That was a very good act, letting Ben take those fellows at cards . . . I think."

"I take no credit," said Sundry truthfully.

"Well, take warning, then," said the black-bearded fellow. He glanced from one to another of his comrades and back to Sundry. "I am watching you, *and* those three out there."

"You know, the boss wasn't too sure about you, either," said Sundry.

Ollie looked daggers, then barked, "Lay hold of her!"

Sundry was astonished at the weight of the chest, and conscious, as they moved it, that a certain degree of care was warranted. He felt a weakness in its sides, as if it might break in half as they slid it across the floor of the car. Once it stood in the light, its age became apparent to him; and what felt soft and leathery he found to be a thick and ancient coat of tar.

And he realized that this was not some bit of stolen luggage or a recently purloined cache of valuables. The wonder of the chest was that it looked so exactly like its fictive counterparts—a pleasing vision to the average observer, but worrisome to anyone hoping to secrete it past the rest of the observing world.

There was no way for Sundry to know the history of this artifact—that it had sailed upon the *Adventure* with Captain Kidd and been buried on an island off Nova Scotia; that it had been dug up by a crew of American adventurers more than a hundred and fifty years later, but that honor and war had led to its reburial in the heart of the Maine wilderness—there was no way for Sundry to know these things, but he could easily construct something like them while his palms rested upon the time-cracked surface of tar and his eyes scanned its black, burly, and mysterious bulk in the light of day. The chest was consecrated, not just with age, but with human effort and motive, and perhaps with human blood as well.

"The boss didn't tell you everything did he?" said Ollie, the look of wonder was so clear upon Sundry's face.

The chest had drawn the interest of everyone; even Ephram, Eagleton, and Thump allowed themselves to be distracted from their newspaper.

"Gentlemen," said Sundry. He had no idea how to proceed, and hoped that his three companions, at least, might understand the necessity of paying attention. A horse and wagon was drawn up to the freight car and from the plank seat the man driving spat a stream of tobacco juice to punctuate the fact of his arrival. "Perhaps you would help lift this into the wagon," said Sundry to the club members, ready for opportunity to render inspiration.

There was a general milling about; some of the gang wished to put their hands upon the object of their labor, some did not trust the newcomers with it, and others had no desire to heft that great weight again.

Thump seemed the most game of the club members; he endeavored to climb into the wagon but found that the newspaper hindered him. He passed it from hand to hand, lifting first one leg, then the other, and looking somewhat like an instructor of calisthenics. Finally, he handed the paper to Eagleton, who thus burdened found it difficult to help his friend into the wagon. The problem was studied, and it was agreed upon that Ephram should hold the paper while Eagleton lent his assistance to Thump.

"What are they doing?" asked Ollie.

"There is no quick way to explain it," answered Sundry. Any advantage he had hoped to gain by filling the wagon with his supposed accomplices was undone by the delay; three of the gang had climbed up and hoisted the chest down before Thump had even gotten to his feet in the conveyance.

The wagon shivered slightly with the weight of the box, and the horse jerked ahead a foot or so, throwing the men in the back off balance and Thump onto his seat. Somehow he had contrived to land on his hat, and he was pulling it out from under him when Ephram let out a cry of amazement.

"Good heavens, gentlemen! The object of our admiration is to be in our own fair city!" It was difficult for those outside the club to interpret Ephram's words, but the subject was somewhat clarified as he read aloud.

" 'Those fortunate enough to have attended the ascension and parachute jump of the lovely Mrs. Roberto at the Freeport Fourth of July Festivities this season will be disappointed, no doubt, that a pair of politicians is not scheduled to box in the vicinity of her landing path when she repeats that brave performance at Portland's Deering Oaks on the thirty-first of this month. It must be agreed, however, amongst those who have seen her famous descent *that she makes a picturesque figure in her attractive suit of tights, and that the promise of this remarkable act will make the trip to the park well worth anybody's while.' "*

Indeed, all the men did agree that this last assertion had some merit to it. Several were familiar with Mrs. Roberto's act, and the driver of the wagon (smiling mysteriously) expressed knowledge of the woman.

Thump was taken with the paragraph, and rose to his feet with an expression of inspired abstraction. "You've met the lady in question," he said to the driver.

"*Questionable* might be the better way to put it," said the driver with a friendly wink.

While the other men climbed down from the wagon, Thump approached the driver. "You do say." It was clear that the fellow was ready to impart some important information. The driver waggled a finger to indicate the need to communicate in a whisper, and Thump eagerly leaned forward.

Nobody actually saw which portion of Thump struck which portion of the man in the driver's seat; but there was the sound of a blow from the former and a colorful expostulation on the part of the latter, who struck the horse's flank on his way to the ground. The horse, taking this blow as a signal to move, broke into a slow trot, and the driver was barely pulled away before the wheels of the wagon rolled past.

Thump stood, looking triumphant . . . or, rather, he would have stood looking triumphant if he hadn't been so indignant . . . or, rather, he would have looked indignant if he hadn't been so puzzled by the fact that he was in the back of a moving wagon, watching his friends and associates dwindle with distance.

Several of those associates (the more recent ones) were chasing the wagon. "Pardon me?" inquired Thump, who had difficulty making sense of their cries over the rumble of the wheels. The wagon hit a bump and he disappeared briefly behind the chest.

The reins had been looped over a hook at the side of the driver's bench and they hung loosely over the horse's back, occasionally and lightly slapping the animal with the jogging of the wagon, so that by the time Thump's head reappeared, the creature had increased its speed to a fast clip.

"What is this?" demanded Ollie. He made a grab for Sundry, who stepped back and threw his hands up in honest (if pleasantly surprised) confusion.

"I only said . . ." the driver was saying, but the remainder of his complaint was lost in the chorus of angry shouts.

"I am a bit taken aback," admitted Ephram.

"I didn't know Thump could drive," said Eagleton.

Passing the station house, Thump found that several people were watching him with a very polite sort of attention, and he waved to them. It occurred to him then that no one was piloting the vehicle, and he was put in mind of Mister Walton, who had experienced a similar sort of adventure. He felt a touch of apprehension mixed with a degree of pride (in being so connected with their grand chairman), and he decided that he should sort through these emotions before acting upon the situation.

Before this task was accomplished, however, the shrill whistle of a train, coming from behind, encouraged the horse to still greater speed, and with the wagon's sudden surge forward, Thump performed something like a somersault over the chest and struck his head. His hat flew from the wagon.

The horse, in its dedication to confusion, crossed the railroad tracks and entered Bangor's infamous Devil's Half-Acre, where illegal liquor was peddled, where sailors and coarse landsmen and hard women caroused, and where well-meaning people did not linger.

Sundry's long legs brought him to the head of the pack, where he was one of only half a dozen able to cross the tracks before the oncoming train swept by in a frenzy of its screaming whistle and clanging bell. The street beyond the station house was busy, but the horse and wagon had sped through a break in the traffic and was now charging down the Half-Acre's main thoroughfare, which commanded the right of way.

The Half-Acre (which, in fact, covered several acres) was not a thriving place by day; some stray characters populated the streets and alleyways, a woman of suspect virtue might pace a few hundred yards of territory, but the streets themselves were not busy, since the sort of business most commonly taking place upon them was best conducted under cover of night. The street turned to the left and dipped so that Sundry lost sight of the wagon. He glanced over his shoulder at the other runners closest to him and wondered if his own designs were better suited the farther the horse went. If he outstripped the gang, he could simply leap aboard the wagon, once he did catch it, and be gone.

But further back than anyone else were Ephram and Eagleton, holding their hats to their heads, their free arms swinging and their legs stiffly pumping as if they were in a walking race. Sundry knew he could not abandon them.

Then he caught sight of the police.

Sundry ignored the people who peered from their rooms or stepped out onto front stoops to see what the commotion was about. He imagined that certain denizens, fearing a raid, were retreating through back doors.

"Run, kid!" someone shouted; another offered a side door to duck into, sure that he was running from the law.

Cresting the small rise in the street, he was surprised and distressed to find the horse and wagon (and therefore Thump) to be nowhere in sight. He pulled up, gasping, heard the sound of running footsteps catching up with him, and sprinted forward again.

"What are you running from, young fellow?" asked a gray-haired man on a little ragpicker's cart.

"I'm chasing after a runaway wagon," gasped Sundry, his lungs burning with the unaccustomed exercise.

The old man looked a little worse for wear, leaning from the seat of his cart, but he smiled cordially; his nose was red and his eyes were nearly squinted out of sight by his large red cheeks. "Oh, that," he said. "Went roaring down the street just a moment ago. Someone stopped her and pulled her into an alleyway down yonder."

Sundry was already on board the ragpicker's wagon. He took the reins, saying, "Take me there," and proceeded to carry out the directive himself. The pony was hardly in better shape than the ragpicker, but she made better time than Sundry could have after running so far.

He cast his eyes from side to side, glancing down the lanes and alleys leading to darker and less reputable places; and just as he feared that horse, wagon, and Thump had been spirited away altogether, he caught sight of the three of them resting peacefully in the shadow of a stairway; or horse and wagon were resting peacefully, at any rate.

Sundry leaped to the street, barely waiting for the cart to draw to a halt, and dashed up to the wagon, where Thump was sleepily rubbing the back of his head.

Besides that honorable soul, the wagon was empty.

The chest was gone.

It seems the season for rampant vehicles [read the *Portland Daily Advertiser* two days later]. *Last week we were interested to inform you of a runaway horse and wagon, which traversed our city from end to end under full steam, only to disappear from public sight and slip from the long reach of authority. It seems, however, that the problem of precipitate conveyances is not limited to our own city limits.*

Word from our sister-city on the banks of the Penobscot has it that a similar incident occurred on the 12th of this month. Chief Constable Alfred

Creamer of the Bangor Police Department was apprised of some possible rascality occurring near Bangor's South Station, and had dispatched himself with two subordinate officers to that district, when the sight of a recklessly charging horse and wagon drove away all other considerations.

A substantial body of men was already in pursuit, but the fugitive conveyance vanished within that section of Bangor commonly known as the Devil's Half-Acre. As if this were not enough to raise Chief Creamer's constabulary suspicion, the wagon produced, once they caught up with it, a hatless and semi-conscious fellow who proved to be a member of our own community.

It was Mr. Joseph Thump, of the Exeter Thumps, who recently has been connected with the chartering of a new club, dedicated we trust to something other than runaway wagons. Mr. Thump's presence in the wagon has not been explained, nor was the attendance of two fellow club members pursuing him with the large body of men on foot.

The affair deepened in mystery when a man who remained unidentified declared that something was missing from the wagon, but beyond the fact that it was a large chest, Chief Creamer could elicit no further details. It was imagined that a denizen or denizens of the Half-Acre kindly relieved the wagon of said item for the purpose of safekeeping, and that Mr. Thump, in his dazed state, was unable to recall the address to which said item had been taken.

A great deal of emotion was exhibited regarding the lost object, which one suspects might have been in the form of a barrel rather than a chest, but as the participants in the little drama seemed unwilling to burden Chief Creamer with further information, he declared the case closed and escorted Mr. Thump and three of his companions, upon request of one of them, to less precarious surroundings.

JULY 27-31, 1896

1. July 27, 1896

DRESDEN SCOTT'S DELIBERATE PROGRESS on horseback along the forest path was instinctive rather than intentional—he was neither hunting nor tracking this day—and the crow that had been heralding his movements to the surrounding woods all morning was more like a fellow traveler than a nuisance. The bird was often out of sight, but would inevitably return to flicker among the trees, or goad him from a safe branch, peering down with strange intelligence.

Some time near mid-morning, the sky appeared from behind a screen of oak and maple, and he broke from the trees onto the prospect that overlooked the now familiar lake and Minmaneth Rock. He drew the mare up and regarded the rise of land about him. The mare nickered, as if in recognition.

It was a warm day, with little wind; the trees were still, the lake glassy. There was nothing to stop him here except the memory of Cordelia Underwood running to the brow of the hill, her back to him, her red hair brilliant against the blue and green of the sky and the trees.

Though alone a good deal of his life, Dresden Scott had never (or seldom) been a lonely man. His only family had been his mother, and he *had* known loneliness after her death. Often he missed her still, though the woods filled him as conversation might other people. He had always enjoyed his life, enjoyed the work to which he bent himself, and enjoyed the people for whom or alongside whom he worked. His bachelorhood had grown around him till it had become what he was and how he accepted himself.

Now he stared from his mount at the uninhabited brow of a hill and thought of a young woman who once had stood there. The strangest thing about this longing was that he had known the object of his thoughts for hardly more than a day, and had spent a good deal of that time feeling irritated with her—or at least he had spent a good deal of that time fearing that she was irritated with him, which was not quite the same thing.

He thought again (for the thousandth time) of his abrupt departure, of how he had told James that he was leaving them, and how Cordelia—Miss Underwood—had looked regretful and had reached out for him as he turned his horse's head, though she was too far away, and of how he regretted that there was no graceful way to change his mind or take back his words.

It had been more than two weeks since he parted company with the Underwoods on the road to Millinocket, and the rush of longing and regret whenever he thought of that moment (which was often) was as strong as that very night after leaving her, when he sat at a lonely campfire with the great back of Mount Katahdin masking an entire quadrant of stars.

She wasn't the first pretty woman he had ever met, but she was the first *something* that he had ever met, and he had a great desire to understand what that something was, and he certainly couldn't understand it without her being close at hand. It wasn't the act of rescuing her, he knew; she had half-rescued herself, which, when he thought of it, made him . . . long for her the more.

Dresden Scott did not dislike people, though he seldom felt a great need for their company. People came and he appreciated their talk and their presence; people went away and he appreciated the quiet that returned. But Scott sat on his horse and looked about Cordelia Underwood's land, wondered if she would come back someday, and finally came to the conclusion that he was in need of distraction.

From a stand of birches, the crow cawed.

With one last glance toward the Cordelia in his mind who stood at the edge of the rise, he turned his horse's head in the direction of Millinocket.

Mr. Kelleher had the look of a once handsome man long gone to seed, rather like the establishment he ran in the city of Bangor, in the midst of the Devil's Half-Acre. He ushered John Benning and Ben Hasson past the small tables and chairs and the bar and the stools to the backroom, which smelled even more of stale beer and tobacco smoke. "Come in. Come in. Sit down. Sit down," chanted the proprietor of the Sleeping Dog. "Please, tell me your business and to what I owe the pleasure."

John Benning did not flinch at the dirty accommodations, but chose a chair that looked the least ready to fall apart, folded his arms, and sat back. Ben Hasson eased into a creakier seat. Behind a wide-topped desk, which might have seen legitimate business in its day, Mr. Kelleher gave his best impression (and a somewhat unsettling one) of a friendly smile. "Please," he said again, "tell me what I can do for you."

"You may remember," said Benning, with no preamble, "the incident of the runaway wagon. . . ."

"Oh, yes," said Kelleher. He ran a hand over his pink pate, as if he had hair to smooth back. "I read of it in the papers." He gave Ben Hasson a moment of polite attention. "All the papers, you know, remarked upon it."

"The wagon was discovered just outside of your tavern here," continued Benning.

"Imagine my surprise," said the proprietor. "Was that really a week ago? *Tempus fugit*, gentlemen, *tempus fugit*."

"And in the space of five minutes," said Benning, "an item in the back of that wagon was spirited away."

"Just the phrase the newspapers used—*spirited*."

"I could make it worth someone's while to find that item."

"That's very generous, of course, but you know I told the chief of constables everything I know, which I'm afraid amounts to very little."

"I see." Benning's expression (or lack thereof) remained unchanged. "There is another possible course of action."

"Yes?"

"If pleasure can be demonstrated, Mr. Kelleher, so can displeasure."

"That would be in the nature of a threat, wouldn't it?" said Kelleher, never losing the lilt of polite conversation.

"It would."

"It's very good of you to be so straightforward."

"I find it the best way."

"Of course, you're right. It certainly is." Kelleher continued to smile agreeably upon them. "Are you sure that there is nothing I can do for you, then?"

Benning rose and gave the slightest bow of the head. "Thank you for your time, Mr. Kelleher."

"Please," said the man. "Don't mention it."

Ben Hasson glowered angrily as he followed Benning to the door. The hawk-nosed man let himself be ushered into the hall beyond, but the younger man hesitated, as if remembering something of importance. "Mr. Kelleher," he said. "In case you do hear something about the missing item, you might warn people that a very ingenious sort of trap has been laid for anyone who doesn't know how to open it properly."

"Really, Mr. Benning?" said the bald fellow. "Aren't things odd!"

"I am still not sure what to think," said Benning, once their carriage was under way. In the opposite seat, Hasson looked worried, though it would have worried him to know it. He had realized, with a sudden and unpleasant shock, just the day before that the boss might ultimately suspect his involvement with the disappearance of the treasure, and it was of great importance to Hasson to avoid even the *appearance* of guilt.

The carriage driver brought them out of the Devil's Half-Acre in the direction of the riverfront. Benning watched, without seeing, the rows of warehouses and wharves. "I still can't imagine them as anything but the most hopeless of innocents—Misters Ephram, Eagleton, and Thump."

"They did seem hopeless at cards," admitted Hasson. "Perhaps too hopeless. I should have suspected. . . ."

"But it was this other fellow—this Sundry—who offered them up?"

"He was a sly one, make no mistake." Then, "Do you want some of the boys and I to visit Mr. Kelleher tonight?"

"No," said Benning, tiredly. "He's right to be unimpressed by our threats. He's a respected businessman in an illegitimate business, which means his friends and his thugs are one and the same, and he'll have plenty of them. In the end, of course, he may know as little as he claims. His eva-sive tactics may simply be a dodge contrived to get something from us."

"And everything was coming around so well."

"Yes. I suppose we were getting a little too sure of ourselves." The car-riage turned onto a wharfside alley where the bowsprit of a schooner reached over the cobbles like a flagpole, the ship itself looming huge in its close berth. "I would give the treasure itself," said Benning, "to know what happened to it . . . or simply to know what was in it."

Ben, perhaps not feeling so generous, said nothing.

John Benning turned to the hawk-nosed man. "I wish I was a fly on the wall of Mr. Kelleher's backroom right now, don't you, Ben?"

"Yes, boss, it might prove instructive."

The carriage came to a halt beneath the bow of the *Elaborate*, and the two men climbed out, taking glances up and down the alley before moving to the gangplank. Their plans had deteriorated to the point where Benning himself felt anxious, as if the authorities might descend upon them at any moment.

At the top of the gangplank they were met by the captain, who greeted them with an official air.

"Captain," said Benning.

"Mr. Benning," said the man. "There's a gentleman waiting for you in your cabin."

"A gentleman?"

"I didn't ask his name, sir."

There *was* a fly on the wall of Kelleher's backroom—several, in fact—and the proprietor of the Sleeping Dog swatted at one of them with a rolled newspaper as he leaned back in his chair.

"I think they know more than they're letting on," said Kelleher to the other man in the room. "But I'm hanged if I know what their dodge is."

"Why would they come looking for the chest if they knew where it was?"

"I don't know," said Kelleher. "All I know is that when I came back here that day, it was gone." He glanced at the floor beneath the other man—some associate, some partner in shady business deals. The other man took the glance to indicate where the chest had been left by the several men who had carried it from the wagon.

"I don't know how it could have been moved so quickly," said the other man.

Kelleher was actually glancing at the oak floor and thinking of the trapdoor cleverly built into it.

"And quietly," said the other man. It had taken four strong men to maneuver the large box up the side steps of the tavern and into this backroom. It had been, in fact, this other man—one Henry Bergen—who first caught sight of the runaway wagon, and who, in less than two minutes, called forth and organized the removal of the chest, once he had corralled the horse and wagon into the alley beside the Sleeping Dog.

Kelleher shook his head. "I'd like to know what was in that box," he said. This was true, though he didn't dare find out till he was sure that the affair was all but forgotten. "I was only out of the room for a quarter of an hour."

"Well, you couldn't have moved it by yourself," said Henry Bergen.

Not very far, thought Kelleher. The trapdoor was fashioned to work as a chute, and he had had only to shoulder the massive chest a foot or so before it tipped onto the wooden ramp and slid of its own accord into the hole below. There had been a loud scraping and an impressive thump in all this, but Bergen and his cronies had already scattered (most to the front of the tavern to feign interest in what was going on), and the approaching crowd of gang members, club members, and police raised enough of a ruckus to cover the noise. Kelleher laughed at the notion of moving the chest by himself.

Bergen chuckled softly. "You can't trust anyone these days."

Kelleher shook his head and laughed more heartily. He felt a twinge in his back from his exertions, which made him laugh the more. *Blast*, he thought to himself, *I'll have to wait a year before I can open that trap again.*

Bergen continued to laugh, but it was the laugh of a man who knows that he might have been duped; the laugh of a man who has laughed more than once in the face of bad luck—even his own.

John Benning paused in the companionway, inclining his head slightly so that he could see into the dimmer precincts of the *Elaborate*'s main cabin. A familiar figure of medium height and portly frame stood at the only window in the small room, unconscious of the young man's arrival. "Mister Walton," said Benning; he took the two steps down into the cabin.

The portly gentleman turned from the window, which afforded a view of little interest, and eyed the younger man sternly.

Benning put out a hand, but dropped it before Mister Walton had actually the opportunity to refuse it. Benning had experienced several surprising moments in the course of this affair, but none that so very nearly thwarted his ability to appear unsurprised as this one; he could not imagine how the fellow had found him. The presence of Mister Walton altered his perception of an entire chain of events, like the slight push that triggers the trail of falling dominoes.

"Mr. Benning," said Mister Walton, his voice even, his hands clasped behind his back. "I have come to ask you only one question."

"Please, feel free," said the younger man. He indicated a chair for his visitor's comfort, but the offer went unnoticed.

"Are you the author of all this commotion?" asked Mister Walton. "More importantly, were you behind Miss Underwood's abduction?"

"Yes," said Benning without hesitation, and though caught by surprise he was not caught without his wit. "To *both* questions."

"I feared as much," said Mister Walton. His head dropped slightly; then he took a breath and renewed his narrowed gaze into Benning's eyes. "One of your . . . gang . . . *struck* Miss Underwood."

"I am sorry for that," said Benning. "And he's not to get away with it." It was strangely difficult for him to meet the bespectacled gentleman's gaze.

"You are right there, I think," said Mister Walton. "He and two of his associates have been taken by the authorities."

"That isn't what I meant, actually. If you read the newspapers tomorrow, I believe you will discover that they are no longer in custody."

Mister Walton thought on this. "So, you shall punish the man for striking Miss Underwood."

"I will indeed. And he knows it."

"And who will punish you, Mr. Benning?"

This was the tougher question, and John Benning was not very pleased to hear it. Outwardly he lost none of his composure, unless by his absolute lack of answer—witty or otherwise. There was a soft rap upon the cabin door, and the voice of Ben Hasson calling after him. "It's all right, Ben," said the boss.

"Well," said Mister Walton. "I've asked more than the one question, haven't I?"

"Three, actually."

"And the chest?"

Four, thought Benning, and was annoyed with himself. The encounter had unsettled him to the point that his mind had divided into several voices, each speaking of its own volition. "I don't know where the chest is."

"Yes, Sundry thought that some third party had made away with it."

"Sundry? The man on the train?" A new set of dominoes began to fall in line. How had he misread this seemingly simple fellow so completely?

"I have said nothing to Miss Underwood concerning your involvement in this unhappy business," said Mister Walton. "I trust I will not have to."

"I am called away," said the young man. "I plan on writing to Miss Underwood my regrets, though I fear she may be disappointed."

"Not so much, perhaps," said Mister Walton, and a steely wit glinted briefly in his eyes. "She may be a better judge of character than you suspect."

"Nothing would surprise me concerning Cordelia," came Benning's honest reply.

Mister Walton nodded in agreement with this assessment of someone he liked and admired. He had not stirred a foot since he turned around, but stood like an uncompromising rock where Benning had discovered him. "I have a suspicion, Mr. Benning (and perhaps I prove my naiveté), that more than simple greed was involved in this business."

"Had I kept possession of the treasure, sir, Cordelia would have come into her share of it."

"And you would not have trusted her to do the same?"

"I didn't know her, Mister Walton."

"Yes, well, naive or not, it's the only reason that I am here instead of the police."

The door to the cabin opened then, without a knock or any other warning, and an exceptionally beautiful woman stepped into the small room. Nearly as tall as Benning himself, she was as dark as he, and in fact bore some resemblance to him. Mister Walton recognized her as the woman who had accompanied Benning upon the wharf at the very beginning of this affair.

"John," she said simply and softly, communicating both affection and a certain degree of command.

"Ann," said Benning. "This is Mister . . . Tobias Walton. Mister Walton, my cousin, Ann Benning."

Cousin Ann slipped a hand into Cousin John's arm, and though she smiled cordially as she took Mister Walton's hand in a brief but firm grip, there was a graceful warning in both her smile and her handshake. "I am very pleased to meet you, sir."

"Miss Benning," said Mister Walton. He glanced from the eyes of the young man to those of the young woman, and thought that the remainder of his questions had been answered. "I was just about to say that I must be going," he added, with no sense of retreat in his voice, but only the authority of having finished his business.

They followed him onto the deck, and stood together in the slight breeze by the cabin door. At the head of the gangplank he found he did have one question more.

"That first day, on the wharf—clearly your plans had been hatched by then—how did you manage to be there when Cordelia nearly fell overboard?"

"That, Mister Walton, was a happy accident."

"Hmmm," replied the portly fellow. "Perhaps." And suddenly a scamp of a breeze swept from the alley, up the gangplank, and picked Mister Walton's hat from his head. Just as he was turning away, his hat flew off, and John Benning snatched it from the air as it passed him—like a hawk snapping a sparrow from flight.

"Your hat, sir," said the handsome young man, when the moment of surprise had passed.

Mister Walton's smile was wry as he took the wayward article. "Good-bye, Mr. Benning," he said, and he trundled with a very real and unpracticed dignity down the plank.

Late in the afternoon, when Mrs. Cuthbert was taking down her laundry from the line in her backyard, she heard boots on her front porch and a knock on her screen door. The back door was open and she called a "Yes, yes" through it as she picked up the basket, tottery with folded clothes. "Yes, yes."

She was almost blind, coming from the sunshine into the shaded house. The front door opened directly to the parlor and, standing in the middle of the room, she considered the silhouette on the other side of the screen.

"Mr. Scott," she said, upon recognition. "Good heavens! Don't stand on ceremony. Come in."

Hat in hand, Scott opened the screen door and stepped inside, a looming presence in her low-ceilinged home. He often took a room when waiting in town for clients, or came by with the price of a decent cooked meal and a hot bath. Mrs. Cuthbert was not surprised to see him. "How are you?" he asked.

"No better," said the landlady, without indicating if this was a statement of physical or moral condition. "You've been scarce," she said, and when this elicited no explanation for his scarcity, she offered him a cup of tea and a piece of pie. He surprised her by accepting, though she didn't show it, and she led the way into the kitchen, warning him, "The strawberries were too late and too sweet for my taste, but next to a cup of strong tea the pie goes down easy enough."

"Thank you," said Scott, and he sat down at her kitchen table, looking weary, and laid his hat on his knee.

"What, are you going to eat and run?" she asked, snapping up the hat and finding a hook for it by the back door. She made a pleasant clatter with the kettle on the stove and the pie plate from its cupboard and the plates and cups. "That was a piece of work you managed, rescuing Miss Underwood," she said.

"She would have rescued herself, I think, given the time," he answered.

"I daresay you're right, though her family was glad enough not to wait. They'll be talking about that trick with Pete Stem's privy from now until the cows come home."

Scott made a sound like a laugh, and Mrs. Cuthbert had more hope for him. It seemed unsensible not to enjoy your own cleverness just a bit.

"Willy, over at the livery," she said, "says he's going to fix his outhouse down before one of the boys gets a funny idea."

"How was Miss Underwood?" he asked suddenly.

Mrs. Cuthbert never hesitated in her movements—slicing the pie, easing the pieces onto the plates. "She was pretty shaken, still, when she got here. She went upstairs and fell asleep in her mother's arms like a child. But she came down the next morning, and it looked like excitement more than fright, now that she knew it was all over. Her jaw was still a little sore." The landlady laid a large piece of strawberry pie before the guide. "Just as pretty as ever," she added.

He glanced up at her, then took the fork that she handed to him.

"She was sorry that she couldn't thank you again before she left. They all were. You didn't meet Mister Walton, did you?"

"Mister Walton?"

"Well, you should," she said, without explanation. "Oh, and I have something for you. . . ." She scurried into the parlor and returned with an envelope. "Well, take it," she said, when he didn't immediately do so.

Scott looked at the envelope and saw James Underwood's name in one corner. "What is it?"

"It's payment for work, I imagine."

"But Mr. Underwood and I settled up before we left." He peered at the enclosure, as if it might divulge its contents out of fear from a hard look.

"You'll know more about it if you open it up," suggested Mrs. Cuthbert, who was not above admitting that she was curious.

He hooked a big thumb into the envelope and tore it open. Several slips of paper fell out onto the table. The first bore James Underwood's handwriting:

Dear Mr. Scott [it read],
I hope that someday you might know how precious a child is to his or her parents, and if ever that child is in peril, I hope that someone like yourself is nearby to lend a hand.

James Underwood

The next piece of paper unfolded into a banknote of embarrassing proportions. Mrs. Cuthbert's eyebrows arched when Scott looked up. "I can't accept this," he said, holding up the banknote.

"And why not?" she asked.

"I just couldn't, is all. You contract out to guide people, you don't take money for . . ." He was almost angry at Mr. Underwood for his generosity.

"He knew you didn't expect anything, which is probably why he left it."

"Well, he shouldn't have. I can't accept it. I'll send it back to him. Is there a return address?" He couldn't find one on James's short letter, so he opened the third piece of paper. A handwriting that he had never seen, but immediately recognized, unfolded before him. It read:

Dear Mr. Scott,
I do hope you will understand how truly grateful I am for your troubles on my behalf. I have seldom felt myself in such capable hands, and was never so glad to see someone as I was to see you when you arrived at the cabin where I was being held.
I fear that my behavior on the trail home showed little graciousness and I can only plead exhaustion in hopes that you will forgive me.

I would like someday to return to my land near Millinocket, and I would be thankful for any advice as to what I might do with it. I promise, there are no more buried treasures, as far as I know, and a visit there would surely prove less eventful.

My mother asks me to tell you that she is perturbed with you for not letting her thank you personally for my rescue.

And I thank you again.

With fond regards,
Cordelia Underwood

At the bottom of the page, deliberately (some might say boldly) written, was the Underwoods' address in Portland. Scott stared at the letter for some minutes, forgetting his pie.

Mrs. Cuthbert could see the feminine hand through the paper from her seat opposite Scott. "She was worth the trouble, I think," she said.

Scott looked up, looking as if he would have liked to agree with her, but only took a deep breath before saying, "I can't keep this banknote."

"You're supposed to cash it in, not keep it."

Scott pulled a frown. "I'll send it back to them."

"*Send* it?"

"Yes." He began to fold the papers back into the envelope.

Mrs. Cuthbert didn't seem to hear the teakettle whistling. "*Send* it?" she said again. "You don't send something like that back, like a badly tailored suit! You deliver it personally!"

"Take it myself?"

"How else?"

"Hand it to Mr. Underwood myself?" Scott's ears grew red, just thinking of it.

"You couldn't send it in the mail. It would seem like an insult."

"Nonsense!"

"If you give it back, which you say you must, you have to deliver it yourself and inquire after Miss Underwood."

This gave Dresden Scott pause for thought.

"It's really the only way to soften the act of returning their gift to you."

It all sounded sensible to Scott somehow, but he shook his head. "I don't think she wants to see me again."

"And why not?"

Scott hesitated, shrugged, then said, "I spoke some harsh words to her, out on the trail."

"Did you apologize to her?"

"Not exactly," he answered, then shook his head. "No, I didn't."

"Well, then you *have* to go down there, don't you."

"I can't go down there. Mr. Benning will just think that I've gone down there to lord it over him, after he thought so poorly of me."

"Mr. Benning?" asked Mrs. Cuthbert, pausing on her way to the stove. "What makes you think you'll see Mr. Benning?"

"He and Miss Underwood were obviously . . ."

"Good heavens!" said the landlady again. "What you know about it you could fit in a thimble and have room for your finger!" She picked up the kettle and poured the hot water into the teapot. "Mr. Benning is long gone, I can tell you."

"How would you know?"

"I talked with her mother."

"Well, it certainly looked to me —"

"Looked to you! What did the young lady say in her letter?"

Scott looked uncomfortable.

"Did she thank you?"

"Yes, she did. . . ."

"You say you had words. It takes two, you know, to have words. Did she apologize?"

"Actually, yes. . . ."

"Did she say she hoped to see you again?"

Scott was beginning to wonder if the woman had read the letter herself. "Well . . . she did, in so many words."

Dunking the tea ball in the kettle, Mrs. Cuthbert leaned forward for the *coup de grâce*. "Did she leave her address?"

This was all a little too fast for Scott. His head was spinning. He scratched at his beard. "Yes. . . ."

"Ha!" said the woman in triumph.

"What are you saying?" he asked after she had poured out the tea.

"You can't win her up here in the woods, can you. Not when she's home in Portland."

She looked him squarely on, and he decided that the only way to confront his own sense of awkwardness was to look her squarely back. "Win her," he said, so far beneath his breath that it sounded like nothing more than a quick exhalation.

"*Faint heart never won fair maiden*," she intoned, which almost made him laugh.

"How did you know that I had any feelings for her at all?"

"Eat your pie," said Mrs. Cuthbert.

2. July 30, 1896

THE LATTER HALF OF JULY 1896 proved to be a model of changeable weather across the coast of Maine, with thunderstorms and showers hard upon the heels of sunny humid days and gentle western winds. Clear skies would break behind the rain, till the heat and humidity closed once more as the cycle began anew. The thermometers in Portland reached eighty-eight degrees on Wednesday the 29th of July, a day of heavy air and little wind. Mister Walton mopped his brow as he and Sundry left the waterfront in an open carriage, and the breeze from their movement was welcome.

For two weeks they had taken up the pursuit of the treasure, carefully treading the sometimes narrow path between the authorities in Bangor and the wary denizens of the Devil's Half-Acre. The authorities themselves were on the prowl, and John Benning as well.

But the treasure had disappeared, vanished from common knowledge, though Mister Walton demonstrated powers of detection that quite impressed his young friend, and even posited a theory that (though unprovable) was close to the truth. He also sensed, wherever they went, the presence of John Benning before them; hence his search for Benning himself, and (with the help of a certain fellow who walked in suspect circles) his visit aboard the *Elaborate*.

They had taken some leisure in returning to Portland, but having arrived at the western end of the waterfront, they felt that their immediate duty was to pay their respects to the Underwoods.

Sundry sat across from his employer and friend, his long legs stretched the limit of the carriage floor, his arms folded and his eyes nearly closed. One would think, in the close air and in so nearly a supine position, that the young man's perceptive faculties were at best vague; but there was something in Mister Walton's manner, an air of quiet distraction as the bespectacled fellow gazed upon the passing city, that caught Sundry's attention. He said nothing, but when Mister Walton's gaze rested briefly upon him, Sundry raised a nimble eyebrow to indicate a wordless question.

"I have been thinking of Miss McCannon," said Mister Walton, almost with a sigh.

"I liked her very much," said Sundry, suggesting perhaps that thinking of her was not a waste of his friend's time.

"Yes." Mister Walton almost sighed a second time. "We left rather precipitately."

"You had no chance to say goodbye."

"Exactly. It seemed necessary, of course, to hurry, but I fear she may have felt it odd, after our pleasant two days together, that I simply left without a word."

"I sent word to her from the hotel before we left," said Sundry.

"Good heavens! Did you?" Mister Walton suddenly sat very straight in his seat. "My good friend, how efficient of you! And how considerate!"

"All in the day of a gentleman's gentleman," returned Sundry with a negligent wave of his hand.

"Oh, my! I am much relieved. I am only sorry not to know where she lives, and where she was going from Damariscotta. We never did exchange addresses."

"I sent her yours with the message," said Sundry, never stirring from the horizontal.

Mister Walton let out a delighted laugh then, which turned the head of the carriage driver and those of several nearby pedestrians. Sundry did not smile, but he shook slightly with a suppressed chuckle.

"Thank you, Sundry," said Mister Walton.

They were on High Street by then, and it was not long before they reached the junction with Spring Street, on one corner of which stood the Underwoods' home. The driver was asked to wait for them, and he stood in the shade of his own rig while they advanced along the walk and mounted the steps to the door.

Grace Morningside generally approved of her brother-in-law, and so was sorry that he had allowed so much trouble to occur; James himself had seemed sufficiently apologetic for his part in the affair, so she said very little about it.

The Underwoods spent only a single night at Ellsworth on their way home to Portland, but in that short time Grace was convinced that her presence was required to rehabilitate them after their traumatic experience in the wilderness. The day after their departure from Morningside House, she decided to follow them. Priscilla and Ethan were ecstatic, though careful to hide from their mother such a superfluity of emotion.

Convinced that hasty preparation had led to the downfall of the Underwoods' expedition, Grace took several days to ready her own excursion; one could not, after all, be sure to find in Portland those amenities so taken for granted in Ellsworth. Priscilla and Ethan were mad with impatience, and just as careful to appear otherwise.

Grace and her children arrived with a small mountain of baggage, which was brought to the gate by two heavily laden carriages and labored into the Underwoods' house by a horde of porters. James and Mercia were pleased to see Grace, and grateful for her efforts; they were more than a little sobered by their recent trials, and welcomed even Grace's officiousness as a means of distraction.

"Don't concern yourself," said Grace to Mercia about one domestic chore after another. As it turned out, it was the best thing for Mercia to be so completely inactive, because she grew so completely weary of inactivity that much quicker.

James wisely took Ethan fishing, where silence and philosophy have always reigned.

Cordelia was of course pleased to have Priscilla close at hand once more, but that did not prevent her from spending a good deal of time by herself—lost in a haze of melancholia. Priscilla—understanding, if a little disappointed—took her cousin's inherited copy of *Tristram Shandy* where she thought her mother wouldn't find her and wended her astonished way through it in three days. She was closing the book and saying to herself "Good heavens!" on that third day, when the bell at the front door was rung.

Cordelia was roused by the bell at the front door.

Fully clothed on her bed, one arm draped over her eyes to bar the distracting light of day—she had lain there for an hour or more, having wandered the house all morning and part of the afternoon like a discontented ghost. Through the window screens she could hear the soft rattle of leaves in the slight breeze, and the *ha! hee-hee-hee-hee* of a robin in the oak outside her window. Her thoughts, predictably, were of the forests she had briefly visited, and of a certain man whose home they were.

The hours of her abduction and rescue seemed hardly believable to her, and by now she had spent more hours thinking about those two days than she had living them. Certainly she had spent more time talking to Mr. Scott in her mind than she had in person.

And there was the rub, for she could not regret what had happened, even though the thought of it could make her angry still. Conversely she thought she *should* regret having met Mr. Scott, the days since their parting had lingered so. But she had only to recall the humor that had spread across his otherwise serious features when he caught sight of her—barefoot, ladle in hand—standing over Ernest's unconscious form, and she would almost laugh with a quickening and painful pleasure.

"I will go back," she said to herself a thousand times, but it was not enough. The bereft heart must feel on good terms with the object of its affections, and she could not imagine that Mr. Scott had much use for her. Her poor showing on the trail back to Millinocket haunted her out of all proportion to the real event; and even the knowledge that this was probably so was small comfort. "I can't go back," she said to herself a thousand times.

And before she had the opportunity to say either of these things to herself a thousand and one times, the bell at the front door rang and she was gratefully startled from her regrets.

Her heart raced with the absurd notion that Mr. Scott had come to call, and she allowed herself this illusion for the brief moment it took to smooth down her skirts and hurry into the front hall. Voices carried up the stairs—her aunt Grace greeting someone with formal cordiality, and a male voice responding with a courtly manner that Cordelia found pleasingly familiar.

Mister Walton had not met Grace Morningside and thought that they had come to the wrong door; clearly, from her dress, this was no servant.

"Pardon us," he said with a deep and expressive bow, his hat in his hands. "We were looking for the James Underwoods."

"I am Grace Morningside," she said, responding to Mister Walton's unstudied charm with elegance; she returned his bow with the smallest inkling of a curtsy. Mister Walton could hear in her voice who she was before she had further introduced herself as Mercia's sister.

Clearly he was charmed. Even Sundry straightened his already straight posture, though Grace was of a generation with his parents. James entered the hall then and greeted the visitors with undisguised pleasure.

Then Cordelia appeared from above, and there was more lilt in her step, when she reached the bottom of the stairs, than she had exhibited in a week. She did not accept a simple bow from Mister Walton, and certainly not a handshake, but embraced him as she might have a beloved uncle. He reddened from ear to ear with pleasure. Even Grace appeared content with this display.

"I trust you are much recovered," he hoped aloud.

"Sir," said James to Sundry, when the young man was introduced, "I am very pleased to meet you. We are in your debt."

"My word," said Sundry, sincerely taken aback. "How could that be?"

"Why, for your efforts on our behalf," said James.

"I would hope for more success the next time I offer help."

"Nonsense!" insisted James half an hour later when, at a celebration over tea in the parlor, Sundry apologized again for his failure to rescue the treasure. "Mr. Thump's story alone is nearly worth it. I am convinced that nobody could have done more. Am I correct, Mister Walton?"

"I agree completely," said the portly fellow, with pride in his young friend.

"I think it very brave of you, Mr. Moss," said Priscilla, surprising even herself. She had not said a word since the two men arrived, and now she glanced from Sundry to her mother to her own hands, folded upon her knees, with sudden embarrassment.

"I was about to say the same thing," said Mercia to cover her niece's discomfort.

It was Sundry's nature to deprecate any honor directed towards himself, but such a tack seemed ungallant in this instance. "Thank you, Miss Morningside," he said simply, thinking that he could have fought Benning's entire gang for that single bit of praise.

This exchange delighted Cordelia more than anything else since she returned home, and she was not careful in hiding her pleasure.

Ethan was impatient to hear the details of Sundry's story, and said so.

The entire saga was retold from numerous points of view as the afternoon wore on; the Underwoods recounting Cordelia's abduction and the adventures leading to it, while Mister Walton and Sundry informed their hosts firsthand of the tail end of the tale—of the curious card game, the false telegram, and the runaway wagon. They told of their search through Bangor for the past two weeks and the little they were able to ascertain.

And the only element left out of their story was the name of John Benning.

Cordelia had seldom seen her aunt Grace so at ease as in the presence of Mister Walton. The gentle fellow's sense of decorum was more the result of a sweet nature and an innate kindness than it was of social study, and it was this that lent him such a gentle force. Erudite, traveled, and (above all) interested, Mister Walton had the power to dismantle the walls of stiff propriety by respecting them, and having none of his own. The gentlest rain, it is said, can break stone; and Cordelia was beginning to think that her aunt was not as stony as she had come to believe.

Grace responded to Mister Walton with interest, with a soft dignity and an uncharacteristic smile. In the front hall—while Mister Walton and Sundry said their goodbyes—she startled the Underwoods (and her own children) by insisting several times over that the two men visit her home in Ellsworth.

Mister Walton seemed taken with the idea; and Sundry, who thought there was a great deal to admire in the daughter, wondered aloud if Priscilla might care to show him about her hometown.

Priscilla managed a "Yes, of course!"—a short sentence, propelled in part by a moderately subtle jab in the ribs from Cordelia.

Once Mister Walton and Sundry were descending to the front walk—turning to wave and say goodbye at every second step—Cordelia felt that she could watch no more. She gave one last wave and returned to the parlor, where an overwhelming sense of sadness welled up within her. The sight of the empty, scattered tea things made her feel like crying. Instead she began to pick them up, their clatter sounding unnaturally loud.

"There are some very nice people, aren't there, Cord," said Priscilla, standing thoughtfully in the doorway.

"Yes," agreed Cordelia with some difficulty. "There are."

"I do think Mr. Moss was very brave."

"I know you do. You said so."

"Oh, dear! Did I make a fool of myself?"

Cordelia paused in her gathering to look up at Priscilla fondly. She smiled, but there were tears in her eyes. "No, quite the contrary," she replied.

"Cordelia," called her mother. "Could you come out here?"

Mercia too had felt a certain sadness to see Mister Walton and Sundry leave, as if their stories had diverged for the final time. *I shall have to look for mention of the Moosepath League in the papers*, she thought as she watched the two men reach their carriage.

A second vehicle had pulled up before the Underwoods' lawn, and a tall man stepped from it and inquired something of Mister Walton. He held flowers in one hand—not as some men do, like a truncheon, or as others, like a dying bird, but with a decisive authority.

"Hmm," said James, beside his wife.

The man shook hands with Mister Walton and Sundry, then looked up the walk and strode in the direction of the house. He was dressed handsomely in a dark suit and top hat, his frock coat opened to reveal the silk-faced collar and *revers*, the patterned vest and gold watch-fob. He wore a dark, neatly trimmed beard and mustaches.

"My goodness," said Grace. "Another visitor."

Halfway up the walk, the man officially took note of the people in the doorway and took his hat in his free hand.

"Cordelia," called Mercia again. "Could you come out here?"

There were several moments before Cordelia appeared in the hall from the parlor, her arms filled with tea things. Looking past her parents and her aunt Grace and Ethan, into the bright light of the summer afternoon, she felt a sudden shock as the newcomer mounted the steps.

He stood just outside the doorway, looking past the parents and the aunt and the young boy. Cordelia stood at the end of the hall, a blue silk flower in her red hair, her arms filled with cups and saucers, her expression startled . . . though, he hoped, not dismayed.

"Miss Underwood," he said, his voice large and resonant in the hall.

"Mr. Scott," said she, clearly not dismayed.

"Please come in," said James, after a brief silence.

Mercia deftly lifted the disarray from her daughter's hands as she passed. "I will put on the kettle," she said calmly.

And walking into the kitchen, the mother thought that some stories might *converge* a final time, as well.

3. July 31, 1896

INSPECTOR PUE STOOD at the Commercial Street entrance to Portland's Custom House and took a moment from his busy day to peer out over the crowded wharf, hoping to pick out the indolent figure of Horace McQuinn.

It had been warm in his office, even with the windows open; hardly a breeze stirred, though thunderstorms were expected. The sky was gray-blue, with a muted haze, and the day glared brightly, so that he squinted from one cluttered end of his view to the other. Those men whose employment took them to the wharves mixed darkly with the white dresses and summery jackets of languid strollers who came here simply to gain the benefit of whatever breeze the harbor could offer. Inspector Pue would welcome the storm.

Five men stood several feet away, gazing up at the Custom House with admiration. Inspector Pue was gratified by their respectful attention, but a little embarrassed as well, as if they were gazing at him with such interest, and he was about to turn back inside—back to his duties—when he recognized one of them.

"Mr. Pue," came a voice.

"Mister Walton," said the inspector, and he reversed his steps so that he might greet the portly fellow and shake his hand.

"Good heavens!" said Mister Walton. "It seems a year since we met!"

"Does it?" The inspector was slowly remembering the circumstances.

"A great deal has happened, sir, I can tell you," continued Mister Walton.

"Has it?"

"And to the Underwoods."

"Ah, yes." He recalled it all now. "Captain Underwood's sea chest."

His interest was sparked now, but Mister Walton was introducing his companions.

"Mr. Pue, this is Sundry Moss, who has been very much responsible for my staying in one piece these past few weeks."

"Indeed?"

"And let me introduce to you the inaugural members of the Moosepath League!"

"Oh, yes," said the inspector. "I have read something in the papers. . . ."

"Mr. Matthew Ephram, Mr. Christopher Eagleton, and Mr. Joseph Thump. Gentlemen, Mr. Pue, our customs inspector, who more or less saw me off on the very start of my recent adventures."

If the members of the club had shown extraordinary interest in the Custom House (which they had each seen a hundred times before), they were absolutely fascinated to meet the inspector who dwelled therein, the more so since he had played some mysterious part in their chairman's story. They took turns shaking the inspector's hand with a collective gravity and curiosity that very nearly made Mr. Pue smile.

"I can't say how pleased I am," said Ephram.

"It was very good of you," said Eagleton.

"We're quite grateful," said Thump.

Mr. Pue was not used to losing control of a conversation. He hadn't the slightest idea what these men were talking about, but he was more amused than annoyed. He glanced past Thump at Mister Walton, who was gallantly trying to summon up an explanation.

"There's weather on its way," said Mr. Pue, kindly alleviating Mister Walton of his burden.

"Yes," said Mister Walton, grasping at this straw. "It does feel thundery."

"Had a cow tethered in the backyard when I was a boy," said the inspector. "A storm came along suddenly and the cow was struck by lightning. Loudest crack I ever heard in my life. Didn't singe a hair on her hide, but we found her tethered on the other side of the barn, chewing her cud as if she hadn't been moved. She seemed none the worse for wear, but she gave sour milk for three weeks." He felt better, having said this.

"Good heavens!" said an astonished Ephram.

Thump gasped and looked about, as if the cow might be on display nearby.

Eagleton had pulled a small book of blank pages from his coat pocket and was furiously writing. "Sour milk!" he said.

"Well," said Mr. Pue, now that he had the situation in hand. "You gentlemen are on an outing."

"Our chairman is taking us for a turn about town," said Ephram.

"We are going to Deering Oaks, in a bit," informed Eagleton. "Mrs. Roberto is to perform her ascension and parachute drop, if the weather permits."

"I have read of her in the papers," said the inspector.

Thump, who had grown defensive on this subject since the incident in Bangor, looked wary.

"Inspector Pue," said a young man, holding open the door to the Custom House. "Colonel Taverner has wired for information concerning the items recovered from the *Castalanara.*"

"Yes, Mr. Prie, I'll be right in. Gentlemen." The inspector nodded to Mister Walton and his companions.

"You're acquainted with Colonel Taverner, Mr. Pue?" said Mister Walton.

"I am, sir."

"Please remember me to him. Sundry and I had a small adventure with the colonel."

"Did you?" said the inspector, more curious than ever. He must return to work, however, and he opened the door, pausing only to ask, "He didn't get you to play cribbage with him, did he?"

"Very nearly," said Mister Walton.

"Oh-ho!" said Mr. Pue, before disappearing into the Custom House. "He's a demon at the board, Mister Walton. A veritable demon."

"We are always looking for new members!" shouted Eagleton, when it was too late.

Climbing the stairs to his office, Inspector Pue wished that he had thought to ask after Mister Walton's valise.

Of the three original club members, only Thump had ever been out onto the Custom House Wharf. (He had told his friends many times of the experience.) The wharves had a singular reputation, even by day, as hotbeds of intrigue, thievery, and pandering; but with Mister Walton leading them they felt stalwart and invulnerable, though they did cast their eyes about in hopes of seeing some sign of dubious activity.

Sundry had never seen so many people, and did his best not to show it. Mister Walton, for his part, beamed—as if the energy and excitement around him were the battery and he the incandescent lamp.

There was much to see: dock workers and sailors, peddlers wandering the crowd, a man selling Italian ices, fancily dressed young men, and elegant women in summer white. Eagleton was nearly lost in the crowd when he stopped to observe Lyman Peabody tie knots with the stumps of his arms, and Ephram was brought to a momentary halt when a woman with unnaturally red cheeks and lips winked in his direction.

"Good heavens!" said Ephram. He held on to his hat, as if it might fall off with his astonishment.

"Ah, here we are," said Mister Walton happily, when they had come near the end of the pier. It was satisfying to see Horace McQuinn, leaning against his favorite piling, and Maven Flyce, his cowlick standing up from his head as if testing the breeze.

"Well, I never, Hod!" said Maven, his face a picture of surprise and wonder. "It's that fellow who lost his hat!"

"Yes, and he's still got it," said Horace, who looked as if he had expected Mister Walton's arrival that very instant.

"He's got people with him!" shouted Maven, as if this were the most incredible thing in the world.

"Oh, I don't doubt it," drawled Horace. He did not offer his hand as Mister Walton approached, but half-smiled as if he knew something amusing and possibly scandalous. "You're looking fit," he pronounced as the portly gentleman approached.

"And yourself as well," said Mister Walton cheerily. There was something in Horace's manner that made him want to laugh out loud.

"Oh, I'll make it," said Horace, which did make Mister Walton laugh. Horace sounded as if he were getting ready to sneeze, but he was only snickering at the pleasing absurdity of life. Maven had no idea what his friend was laughing about and was struck with wonder. Ephram, Eagleton, and Thump were as puzzled over their chairman's humor, and it looked for a moment as if they and Mr. Flyce might be related.

Their wonderment reached greater heights, however, when—before Mister Walton had the opportunity to introduce the club members— Horace leveled upon them his version of a serious stare and declaimed the following couplets:

> "The month of July, in '96,
>   Will be known for many a thing;
>   But of the distinctive Moosepath League,
>   Is what men will choose to sing.

> "Whether ranging far in the hinterland
>   Or foiling the aim of foul intrigue
>   There shall never be an order so rare
>   As the one that is known as the Moosepath League."

The Moosepathers could not have been more astonished if Homer himself had walked down from the hazy sky and recited the entire *Iliad*. Thump took a great breath and his broad chest inflated so that his chin looked in danger of being bumped. Ephram, astounded that the fame of their society had reached so far so quickly, looked away for fear that his deep emotion would betray him. Eagleton spoke the single word "Marvelous" in a breathless whisper as he quickly put Horace's verse to paper.

Horace appeared slightly suspicious of this last response, but few things troubled him for very long, and he looked out over the harbor, taking a long draft from his pipe.

"Gory, Hod!" said Maven, vastly amazed. "I don't know how you do it!"

"Very nice, Mr. McQuinn," said Mister Walton. Horace waved a negligent hand; he considered the moment (as well as the verse) forgotten. "I appreciate your help in tracking down Mr. Benning," continued Mister Walton.

"I said I owed you one," reminded Horace. "I liked your telegram." He reached a tobacco-stained hand into a pocket and pulled from it a wrinkled and dirtied slip of paper. He flattened it out as best he could, peered at it, and chortled. Eagleton drew close enough to read the message.

BANGOR TELEGRAPH COMPANY
JULY 23 AM 9:10
CUSTOM HOUSE WHARF — MIDDAY
MR HORACE MCQUINN

NEED HELP IN LOCATING JOHN BENNING POSSIBLY IN
BANGOR. REGULAR CHANNELS UNHELPFUL.
  TOBIAS WALTON

"I did think you might be here rather than elsewhere," said Mister Walton.

"Oh, I was here."

A low concussion—felt as much as heard—punctuated the hot summer day, and the crowds of people paused in their activity or (as the case may be) their inactivity to take stock of the coming storm. Dark clouds were gathering against the haze, rising like towers above the rooflines to the west. The club members were a little uncertain, standing out on the wharf as the possibility of rain and lightning increased. Mister Walton seemed undisturbed; he was introducing them and Sundry to Horace and Maven.

"I've read about you," Horace said to Sundry, with the light of humor sparking his eye.

Another roll of thunder broke over the bustling pier, and the sightseers were hurrying now to their carriages and shelter.

"I fear this does not bode well for parachuting this afternoon," said Eagleton regretfully.

"Going to see Mrs. Roberto, are you, lads?" asked Horace, and he winked. "I might come with you." There was a certain light in his eye.

Thump cleared his throat and looked serious.

Horace puffed carelessly at his pipe for a moment before expressing an appreciative sigh. "She is a fine sort of lady, to my mind."

"Well, Mr. McQuinn," said Thump, the clouds clearing from his expression, "we would be pleased if you accompanied us."

"Maven?" asked Horace.

"Good heavens, Hod!" shouted Maven, astonished by his friend's sudden suggestion of mobility.

Mister Walton seemed reluctant to leave, however. "I fear our adventures are over, Mr. McQuinn," he said.

"Probably," said Horace. He was gazing once more in the direction of the harbor.

Puffing under the glooming sky, the toylike steamer *Proclamation* was chugging past the Custom House Wharf.

Horace let out a grunt of amusement, and Sundry followed his gaze. Moving with sudden purpose to the end of the quay, the young man watched as the eccentric vessel steamed in the general direction of the harbor's mouth. The little boy named Bird stood in the stern, and he seemed to recognize Sundry. A small wave passed between them.

Further down, past the less reputable end of the waterfront, the *Proclamation* disappeared, and the smoke from its miniature stack dwindled into the approaching clouds.

AUTHOR'S NOTE

I AM NOT THE FIRST TO SPECULATE that Edgar Kelleher, the proprietor of the Sleeping Dog, knew the whereabouts of Captain Kidd's fabled treasure chest; Tobias Walton and John Benning, of course, were speculating sixty years before I was born. Many others have speculated since.

Fate continued to intervene in the tale of the treasure, however. The incident of the missing chest, so dramatized in the papers of the day, raised a certain public awareness regarding the Devil's Half-Acre, and in the midst of a civic-minded *housecleaning*, Edgar Kelleher was arrested for promoting several forms of vice. In January of the next year, he died in jail of pneumonia.

In February of 1897 the Sleeping Dog burned almost to the ground, despite the best efforts of the local volunteer fire department. A man was severely injured while attempting to climb into the cellar of the still-smoking ruins, and city officials declared the site a public hazard. The remains were filled in with several tons of dirt and gravel.

After a good deal of research, I believe that I have located the very place where the Sleeping Dog once stood. It is a parking lot now, and pavement covers the possible answer to many a riddle and the proof of one of our oldest legends.

Or maybe not . . .

An acquaintance of mine, an historian by avocation, claims to have seen a photograph (which he has since been unable to locate) of that very site and the adjacent buildings, dated sometime in the 1920s. Just south of the empty lot there was a dry goods store, and beneath the name of the establishment (he claims) was the following legend:

John Stewart Benning II, Proprietor

The reader may be curious about the several locales of this story and gratified to know that many of the buildings and landmarks described remain to this day. Portland's handsome Custom House is open to the public during business hours and is one of the jewels of that burgeoning city. The Mariners' Hospital at Martins Point is now a clinic.

The Harraseeket Hotel in Freeport burned in 1909. The Wiscasset House is better known these days as the Nickels-Sortwell House and is open to the public during the warmer months.

Fort Edgecomb occupies a point of land jutting into the Sheepscot River, and is as picturesque a place for a picnic as I know. The block house itself is open to the public during the summer and the grounds are wanderable year-round. The Marie Antoinette house is privately owned but visible from the Eddy Road in Edgecomb.

What remains of the Shell Heaps on the Damariscotta River have been preserved by the farsightedness of property owners. There are paths to these ancient middens, approachable from Route 1, and a respectful public is welcome.

The Lincoln Hall, site of the great bear scare, has been known for years as the Lincoln Theater. It has been the center of local culture for the past 120 years—it has variously been a town meeting place, a concert hall, a bowling alley, and a basketball court. It has seen live acts, vaudeville, and for the last several decades housed a movie theater. It is now being refurbished by a local group and doubles as movie house and stage for live theater.

On the wall of the stage-left dressing room, the legend *The Moosepath League* and the initials of its original members are still prominently displayed. A donation may get you in to see it!

On the subject of landmarks, the reader may be pleased to know that Mrs. Roberto did indeed make a career of parachuting from an ascended balloon "in an attractive suit of tights"—and was well thought of for it.

The Moosepath League continues quietly to this day, and its members carry on the club's tradition of civility, kind interest, and undaunted curiosity. Their creed includes *the Waltonian Principles* (named after our hero Mister Tobias Walton); and those principles are Tolerance, Compassion, Curiosity, and Humor. If Ephram, Eagleton, and Thump seemed a little too befuddled to possess a sense of humor, it is also true that they were quick to catch Mister Walton's laughter after the incident of the bear in the Lincoln Hall, and so we hold out hope for them. Certainly Mister Walton himself was a man to admire.

Though the club's involvement with the Underwoods was minimal, the culminating events are spoken of (in Moosepathian circles) as "the First Adventure," "the Minmaneth Adventure," or "the Adventure of the Underwood Treasure." There were many such adventures, not the least being the one that followed, which involved the social columnist Mollie Peer, baseball player Wyckford O'Hearn, Sir Eustace Pembleton, and the little boy named Bird with whom Sundry and Mister Walton were so concerned. This was one of the most dangerous enterprises involving the Moosepath League, which did not entirely come to a good end, and is thought of (in Moosepathian circles) as "the Adventure of the Wooden Indian" or "the Adventure Underground." Someday it may be told.

For now I must thank those who have been so supportive throughout the writing of this tale. At the top I must thank Joan Grant for her unwavering support. Thanks to Kris Ferazza for her kind article; to Emily Johnson for her accuracy; and to Bob Dolan for his keen eye for detail. Thanks also to David and Susan Morse for their belief in this project, their enthusiasm, but most of all for their friendship.

Thanks also to Carol Brightman for her enthusiasm and guidance.

I would also like to thank Carol Aigner, Jet Aldrich, Maureen Ferguson, Dominic Garvey, Pat Ginaty, Darryl Hubbard, Mary Beth Owens, Sumner Richards and Pam Richards of Fernald's Country Store, and Scott Silverman; this book is the better for the interest and energy they so generously gave. Thank you to marine historian Nick Dean for all his help and clarification. Also thanks to my cousin Stanley Coffin.

My fond appreciation to two of my finest teachers — Miss Yansick of the fifth grade (I hope I spelled your name correctly), and Larry Murphy.

Thanks for the encouragement and support of Jane and Mark Biscoe, Susan and Barnaby Porter, Penny and Ewing Walker, Pat and Clark Boynton, Joanne Cotton, Lynne Norris, Jessie Kirchner, Curry Tinkham, Hester Stuhlman, Helen Sampson, and all my friends at the Maine Coast Book Shop in Damariscotta.

In the "without whom" category, I would like to thank my friend and mentor, Michael Uhl, to whom I owe more than I can say. His encouragement, support, and endorsement have been unstinting and selfless. "Without whom" also includes my agent, Barbara Hogenson; her assistant, Sarah Feider; and my editor at Viking Penguin, Carolyn Carlson.

Greetings and thanks to my Norwegian friend and brother, Bjorn Guulvik.

I thank my parents, my brother, Rick, and my sisters, Terri and Cassie; my mother-in-law, Marjorie Hunter; and friends Kathleen Creamer, Les Harris, Karol and Gordon Clark, Barbara Daiute, Brian and Rosa Redonnett, and Ron and Patty Aho in more ways than I can count. Most particularly I thank my brother-in-law, David Hunter. David, much of this has been written with you (who have been so appreciative and insightful) as the reader I had in mind.

I would like to acknowledge the often anonymous writers for the *Eastern Argus*, the *Portland Daily Advertiser*, and the *Portland Courier* for reporting so vividly the events of July 1896; also Eliza Dennison King of Freeport, whose poem concerning the *Dash* Dr. Moriarty quotes in a slightly altered version. Mr. Tolly's "polar bear" story is adapted from a Norwegian folktale.

Thanks are due, of course, to the present-day members of the Moosepath League for their cooperation and participation.

But my greatest thanks go to my wife, Maggie, and our son, Hunter, who constantly remind me of that world of decency and kindness, goodness and laughter represented by Mister Walton, Sundry Moss, and the honorable members of *the Moosepath League*.

Van Reid
Edgecomb
September 26, 1997

MOLLIE PEER

The adventures of the
Moosepath League continue. . . .

Many of the characters found in *Cordelia Underwood* continue their rollicking adventures—and meet some new, unforgettable faces along the way—in the second Moosepath League novel, *Mollie Peer, Or the Underground Adventures of the Moosepath League*. For those who can't wait here's a sneak peek at what Van Reid has in store for Tobias Walton, Eustace Pembleton, and many others.

For more information on *Mollie Peer*, including discussion questions for readers groups, look in the Penguin Readers Guide to *Cordelia Underwood* that follows the *Mollie Peer* sample chapter.

Prologue: The Nightrunners
SEPTEMBER 28, 1896

THE BLOCKHOUSE AT FORT EDGECOMB, on Davis Island, had presided over another summer of picnickers and squealing children. Young boys had fired at the ghosts of British invaders (who had never actually ventured so far upriver). Rusticators had paced the embankments, and lovers occasionally found an unescorted moment in which to steal a kiss in the cool shade of the wooden fort. Names were carved on the blockhouse walls and upon the benches that lined its upper story. Sometimes an old salt, living nearby, would climb to the lookout and watch an afternoon pass over the Sheepscott River.

But the warm, often humid days of summer proceeded into fall. Crickets filled the air with their chirr, and sometimes a screech owl could be heard at twilight from the few wooded acres on the southern end of the island. The nights cooled quickly, and the stars shined more brightly.

Two nights before the end of September, however, clouds quilted the sky, obscuring all but the most indirect light of the moon, and a north wind brought little squalls of rain that watered the meadows and rippled the river.

"Woke early this morning well before sunrise and worried over Caleb," wrote Sallie Davis in her journal on the twenty-ninth of September 1896. *"Raining. Heard oars on the water, rubbing in the locks. I went to the window and caught the briefest glimpse of a lantern. Nightrunners, I suspect. . . ."*

By night, the river was a fair highway for smugglers, and small crafts passed quietly in the dark, signaling the transportation of goods not bearing the Custom House stamp. But only recently had a boat disturbed the shore of the island once the sun was down. A vessel had come several times in the past few months—an odd little novelty, hardly twenty-five feet from stem to stern but supporting the fuming stack of a steam engine—and as on this night, a dinghy would venture forth, and the creak of its oars would round the southern tip of the island as the boat entered the small backwater known as the Eddy.

"What are you at?" rasped one of the dinghy's occupants on this particular night. "Get me closer to the fort, you imbecile!" They were several yards from shore, the oars, like the stiff legs of a water bug, radiating dark ripples that touched the near bank and disappeared in the current of the river. Then the boat chuckled against the strand as a broad-shouldered man shipped the oars and clambered to his feet.

"You *are* an idiot!" hissed the still-seated man. "Is this as close as you can get us? Well, you're lugging him, not me. Haul us up further! I'm not catching my death because you can't master a pair of oars!"

The other man, who proved tall as well as broad when he straightened to his full height, splashed up to his calves in the cold water, grasped the gunwale of the boat, and leaned into the shore. The boat came easily, scraping lightly on the pebbly beach.

A third figure—a child of no more than four or five years—was lifted onto dry land, and the seated man, small and narrow in his voluminous coat, looked up at the banks rising to either side of the little cove. "Well, tie it off!" he insisted. "We haven't got all night! Now get his head. I'll help you get him out of the boat, but you're lugging him the rest of the way."

The larger man waded back to the floating end of the boat and raised from it the head and shoulders of a stiff form. The other lifted the feet into view, and with the child looking on, they carried the still shape to land. A sound came from the nearby woods, a long, vowelly yowl that was not completely distinguishable from a human wail. Residents hereabouts would recognize the voice of a bobcat—one lived on the island—but it seemed that nobody in the small group had ever heard such a sound, for all talk and movement came to a halt.

"Quick, quick!" demanded the smaller man in a strangled whisper, and in a moment they were climbing over the bank, in the direction of the fort, the largest member of this strange band laboring beneath the weight of the unmoving figure. They crossed the parade ground, glancing up at the old blockhouse and over their shoulders in this exposed place. They might have imagined that the octagonal walls, looming in the dark, opened a shuttered eye to watch them pass. Crossing a corner of the island, they came to a steep bank where brick and stone embankments rose above granite ledge. The larger man laid down his burden, and the smaller man leaned over the banquette to look for a shelf of rock. He let the larger man dangle him down over the side till he had his footing there.

Then the man at the top of the bank (a great bull of a man, really) took up the stiff figure and climbed over, leaving the child to crouch in the intermittent rain and cool air of the predawn. The wind rippled and tugged along the edge of the parade ground.

In her journal, Sallie Davis wrote, *"Lay awake till dawn. October coming."* Perhaps she was superstitious, for she added in the margin of the page, *"Soon I suspect other things will be wandering the night."*

Book One

OCTOBER 8, 1896

1. Out of the Fog

IT WAS DIFFICULT TO SAY NO to Mollie Peer, especially knowing she had spent an entire day at her typewriter, working on her columns for the *Eastern Argus*. It had been a lovely day, despite prognostications, and Hilda hated to deny her friend and fellow boarder a few minutes' walk before the sun went down. Besides, Mollie was never so ready to listen as when she had just finished her society column, and Hilda, as always, had much to say.

Stepping onto the porch of Makepeace's Boarding House, they were taken by how dark it had grown so early in the day. Signs of last night's storm spotted the lawn—leaves and twigs and smaller limbs strewn beneath the maples on either side of the walk.

The newspapers had warned against a hurricane, reporting telegraph messages of death and damage up the eastern seaboard (a ship was missing off the coast of Virginia), though later editions predicted merely a gale. From Portsmouth to the Maritimes, the coaster fleet sought shelter, and many of them had come into Portland the day before, so that the harbor was a thicket of masts and spars, and there was concern that the ships and schooners—so densely anchored in a high wind—might do damage to one another. But the storm that arrived on the seventh of October, though strong enough to warrant caution, had mostly blown itself out by the time it reached the Portland waterfront, and the eighth had come off cool and clear.

Mollie was glad that the trees had held on to their foliage; the maples and oaks along the street were red and yellow—looking purple and brown now in the gloaming. The air was colder than she had expected, and she considered going back for her wool cloak; but fearing to discourage Hilda, who had not been so keen for a stroll, she pulled her shawl closer about the shoulders of her jacket and led the way down the walk.

Hilda chatted, as she always did, discussing the private lives of her fellow workers at the rope factory and her flirtation with a packer who worked near her station. Mollie made the perfect companion for such talk; Hilda thought her friend overly secretive about her own affairs, but she knew from experience that Mollie would hear every word she said. Arm in arm, kicking at the fallen twigs, they let the path of least resistance draw them downhill in the direction of the harbor.

It was well past five o'clock and the streets were strangely quiet, as if an autumnal stillness had arrested the movements of homecoming shop-keepers and businessmen. Mr. Duncan, Plum Street's lamplighter, was mounting the hill, raising his long staff and fiery wick to the gas lamps as he approached them. He recognized Mollie and Hilda and tipped his hat when they passed, then turned and looked after them.

Hilda, with her light brown hair and plump figure, was an attractive enough girl, but the lamplighter's eyes lingered on Mollie before he turned back to his evening's chore.

Mollie was tall and moved with an assurance that one might suspect was developed through physical (even athletic) activity. She had strong shoulders and was considered large-boned for a woman. Though only twenty-two years old, she seemed, at first glance, more matronly than youthful. A second glance, however, often merited a third one—and the third, a fourth. Some men's heads would rise and fall as their attention grew increasingly distracted by what they saw, like a person who slowly be-gins to realize that he has misread an entire page of text.

As for her features, they were somehow more than the sum of their parts: Her nose had an Irish lilt (like her father's) and may have been a shade too small, and surrounding it her mouth and eyes (taken after her Italian mother's) seemed exaggerated and overprominent; and yet to-gether with the intelligence in those eyes and the wry set of that wide mouth, those strangely matched features conspired to make her beautiful the more one considered them.

Hilda chatted. They breathed in the crisp air, spiced with the scent of dry earth and leaves and wood smoke. Mollie kept her friend to a brisk pace, arms swinging with pleasure—not the picture of demure femininity but of glowing suffrage.

Then Mollie saw the boy walking uncertainly in their direction; a waif, a ragamuffin, four or five years old, his clothes barely holding to-gether. *He must be cold*, she thought. When he was within a few yards of them, he looked as if he might cross the street, and so she said hello to him.

He stopped, looking more uncertain still. Hilda ceased her gossip for a moment to consider the child, considered him of little interest, and recommenced her story.

"What's your name?" asked Mollie.

Hilda came to a second halt and looked put out. "What is it?"

"It's a little boy," said Mollie, approaching him.

"I can see that, but why are you talking to him?"

"Because he interests me." Mollie leaned down with her hands on her knees. "What's your name?" she asked again.

"Everything interests you," said Hilda with some irritation.

"It's my business."

"I dare say *he* won't make the society pages."

"I don't know. There have been millionaires who started with only a penny." She addressed this to the boy with an encouraging smile. "My name is Mollie." She held out her hand.

He put his hand in hers, as if he were giving her something rather than shaking it. He said something in a small voice.

"Bert?" said Mollie.

Only slightly louder, he said, "Bird."

"Bird!" she said, as if the word gave her great pleasure. "What a fine and unusual name! Where do you live?"

This was more problematic. Confusion and possibly even guilt swept past his face. "With Mr. Pembleton."

"Bird!" came a harsh croak, and the boy's eyes went wide. Hilda jumped with a little shout.

Mollie had seen the man coming in the periphery of her vision. She looked up and smiled, saying, "Mr. Pembleton," as one would greet a friendly neighbor.

The man gave her a sharp look. He was a scarecrow; ragged, thin, and dirty. He wore an ancient hat and a long, pockety coat, and even his blond hair—long and thin and hanging at all angles from under his hat—lent him the appearance of something standing in a field. He dropped his gaze to the little boy and swung an arm. "Come here! Where were you going?"

The boy had no answer but obeyed the command quickly, shoulders hunched as if in expectation of a blow.

The blow was aimed—the girls saw the man's muscles tense—but he shot a glance backward and lowered his hand to the boy's shoulder. His grip went white. "Come, come. We've been looking for you. Did you get lost?"

Behind the two young women, past the houses and through the trees on the street above them, the clouds glowed with a last purplish grandeur.

Ahead of them, in the direction the raggedy man and the raggedy boy disappeared, murk and shadow rose like an incoming tide.

Mollie took Hilda's arm and tugged; there was only a moment's resistance before Hilda fell in. "Goodness, he frightened me!" said Hilda.

"He likes to frighten, is my guess."

"Well, he can frighten someone else, thank you." Hilda was beginning to take note of the gathering gloom. They were alone on the street. "Haven't we come far enough? It's getting dark."

"So, what did Mr. Court say to you when you remarked how strong he was?" asked Mollie, looking avid to know the answer.

"Oh, he blushed!" Hilda laughed. "I like a man who can blush, don't you?"

"A man who can't blush has no shame, my mother used to say."

Hilda's chatter filled the air once more as they descended the hill with more of a fast walk than a leisurely stroll. Bits of lamplight appeared ahead of them, glowing bowls in islands of gathering fog through which the silhouettes of Mr. Pembleton and Bird rose and disappeared.

Hilda was still extolling Mr. Court's virtues, as well as the virtue of young men in general, when it occurred to her that Mollie was tiring her out. "What is the hurry, dear?" she asked.

"No hurry," answered Mollie. "I'm feeling energetic."

"*That* can't be healthy. Let's go home. It's getting dark."

"The lamps are lit."

"We have to walk *up* this hill?" exclaimed Hilda, as if suddenly realizing that what went down must go up.

"We're nearly to the foot of it. We might as well say we went the entire way."

"Mollie, what are you about?"

"About? I'm about nothing. I'm going for a stroll, is all."

"You're following that man and that boy, aren't you."

"Now, why would you think that?"

"You said yourself, it's your business."

"And you said yourself, they won't make the society pages."

"Then let's go back."

Mollie glanced anxiously down the street. The shadows of the two ahead of them were hardly discernible near the bottom of the hill. "Oh, come! Where's your sense of adventure?" She pulled at Hilda's arm with sudden urgency, her voice lowered to a whisper.

"Sitting next to my bed, in Mrs. Randolph's latest novel!" Hilda was hurrying with her despite her protestations.

"But aren't you concerned for that boy?"

"He's with his father."

"He wouldn't call his father *Mr.* Pembleton."

"Mollie!"

Mollie Peer stopped to look at Hilda standing just above her on the sidewalk. "I am going alone, then," she said simply, and hurried off.

"You most certainly will not!" exclaimed Hilda, and hurried after.

They slowed their pace near bottom of the hill, where Plum Street emptied onto Commercial Street. At the brick building there, they stopped to creep up to the lamp-lit corner. There were no shadows to hide in, but Mollie stayed close to the cold brick as they peered out at the wide street and the warehouses and waterfront beyond.

Fog rolled in from the harbor, billowing about the bows of great ships that loomed above the cobblestones and shifted between the buildings with the movement of water like stirring creatures in their berths. There were footsteps in the gathering atmosphere, ringing on the pavement in the dampness; hoofbeats and wheels railing out of the dark beyond the limits of the lamplight. Hilda held her breath. Mollie leaned away from the corner of the building, searching for the figures of the man and the boy.

A hand gripped her wrist with sudden ferocity; Mr. Pembleton was dragging her from her cover. "Feeling interest, are we?" snarled the man as he drew her close, and though she was as tall as he, he seemed to tower over Mollie with his dark anger.

Hilda let out a frightened wail.

"Let go of me!" demanded Mollie, doing her best to sound unafraid, though his clutch on her wrist was painful.

He focused a hard eye upon her, gritting his teeth as he bore down. Mollie cried out, and when Hilda stepped closer to the struggle, he stopped her with a single glance. "You must have something you care to ask me!" he was saying. "You've taken such care to follow me!" The night mist rose up from around their feet.

"Let me go!" Mollie said again.

Hilda had only gotten hold of the man's ragged coat when some dark force lifted her into the air and dragged her several feet away. A great bull of a man held her as she would the smallest child, and in his unyielding clench there was no sign of her struggling against him. For a moment she and the large, silent man disappeared as the fog blew past in an unexpected gust of wind and a man's voice from around the corner shouted out a surprised "Whoops!"

A homburg hat floated into Mollie's view, spiraling on its own axis to land not six feet away.

"Where did it go?" came the voice.

"I think it went round the corner," came another.

Mollie feared that Pembleton and his associate would make short, nasty work of her and Hilda, but then they were gone, vanished in the gloom and haze.

A tall, young man hurried onto the side street and found the hat. "It's here, Mister Walton," he called. The women were still frozen against the brick wall, and when he straightened up with the hat, he caught sight of them with a small start. "Hello," he said in such a friendly, straight-forward manner that, conversely, tears came to Mollie's eyes. He tipped his own hat.

"Hello," she said with surprising conviction.

There was laughter again and a jolly voice declaring that hats some-times showed as much a mind of their own as the heads on which they sat. Then a portly gentleman wearing spectacles and without a hat (or hair to speak of) appeared. "Have you found it, then? Sundry, thank you! I am re-minded of the day I came back to Portland and met Cordelia Under-wood. . . ." He caught sight of the two young women then, paused, and reached to tip his hat before realizing that his friend was in possession of it. "Good evening, ladies," he said with a cordial smile.

"Sir," said Mollie, standing straight now.

It was clear that the portly fellow thought they had surprised two women of the night and was politely ready to allow them to go their way; but then a look of concern fell across his face, and having retrieved his hat from his friend, he stepped closer. "Is everything all right?" he asked, di-recting his question toward Mollie.

"Well, to tell the truth," she said, feeling an unaccountable sense of se-curity with this man, "to tell the truth, we've had a bit of a fright."

Hilda let out a sob, and Mollie took her under one arm.

"How can we help you?" asked the bespectacled man, hat in hand as he stepped forward. "My name is Tobias Walton." The young man who had retrieved Mister Walton's hat was at his side with the readiness of a squire. "This is my good friend Sundry Moss," said Mister Walton.

Mollie stepped forward, albeit shakily, and offered her hand. Mister Walton's grip was firm, but it conveyed a gentleness that worked like a salve on her rattled nerves. He did not ask what had happened, demon-strating a degree of circumspection that she herself would not have pos-sessed. The young Mr. Moss peered into the rolling mist, up Plum Street, looking for the who or what that had frightened the young ladies.

"May we take you somewhere?" Mister Walton was asking.

Mollie thought of Mr. Pembleton and his large associate waiting above them in the fog. "Yes, that would be very kind of you."

"Our carriage is just down the street."

"We would be sorry to inconvenience you."

"Not at all," said Mister Walton as he led the way. "We were just going to the Shipswood to meet friends—a weekly sort of thing we do—and they will forgive us for being a few minutes late." The horse, then the vehicle itself, loomed out of the fog, and a driver dropped down from his seat to turn up the lanterns and open the door. "Mr. Griggs," said Mister Walton.

"Mister Walton," answered the driver, surprised to see his recent fare so quickly again. He glanced at the women curiously.

"Good heavens, child!" Mister Walton said as he handed Hilda into the carriage. "You're shivering." He insisted that she take his coat.

Mollie explained where she and Hilda lived. "It's only straight up on Plum Street," she said, "but if you could take a round way about—" She was thinking of Mr. Pembleton watching from somewhere on the hill.

Mister Walton caught a raised eyebrow from Sundry Moss, then looked up and down Commercial Street. "Of course, dear. We'll go to Middle Street by way of Market and circle around."

Mollie rested a hand on his. "Thank you."

There was silence between the two parties as the carriage got under way, during which they attempted, in those darkened confines, to size one another up without appearing to do so.

"If there is anything else we can do . . . ," Mister Walton began, his expression composed but his eyes filled with what Mollie had long ago termed (in her own father) an *unassuming concern*.

"Thank you," said Mollie. "We will be fine." Hilda, who had not said a single word since the attack, looked ready to belie this, and Mollie laid a hand on her friend's lap.

"The fog is quite thick tonight," said Mister Walton.

He did remind Mollie of her father—not physically (her father was large and muscular; Mister Walton, barely of medium height and portly), but there was a gentle vitality to both men. Watching Mister Walton, who smiled placidly as he peered out the window, she realized that he was not as old as she had first imagined.

The younger man wore a bemused expression, his arms crossed, his legs stretched where he could find room for them. He was not handsome, exactly, but pleasant enough to look at, with a wide nose and a square jaw. He was long and wiry, his manner courteous, if reserved. "I always thought a thick fog more like chowder than pea soup," he said to no one in particular. He seemed gratified by an expression of mystification on Hilda's face and a small smile from Mollie.

"There were two men," said Hilda suddenly.

Mister Walton glanced from one to the other of the young women. "Are you sure you're all right?" he asked.

"Yes," said Mollie. "You came just in time." She felt it necessary to say as little about the incident as possible; her landlady already thought her more adventurous than was becoming to a young woman. Mister Walton, she was sure, sensed (in a general way) the reason for her reticence and was debating how far he could, in good conscience, honor it. "I write for the *Eastern Argus*," she said, as if this would clear the matter.

"Really," he said, then, to the younger man, "Mr. Ephram will be very pleased. A fellow club member," he explained to Mollie, and she could see a delighted amusement enliven his eye. "Mr. Ephram is a great reader of the *Eastern Argus*."

"How nice," said Mollie, at a loss for further response. "A fellow member, you say."

"Yes," said Mister Walton, and this, too, seemed to amuse him. "You may have heard of us—the Moosepath League. Several members were in the newspapers last summer."

Mollie had heard of them. "Was that the buried treasure?" she asked, and sat forward, curiosity overcoming her recent fright.

"It seems very *much* buried at the moment," said the man. "But my friend, here, came very close to recovering it."

"A miss is as good as a mile," said Sundry Moss with good-natured self-deprecation. It was clear, however, that he was still thinking about Hilda's single comment.

"And there was a woman kidnapped," continued Mollie.

This was a subject about which Mister Walton could not jest. "There was indeed," he said, his expression serious again. "Though it all turned out well, I fear she had a very frightening experience." And this train of thought led (quite unintentionally) back to the two young women and their own recent fright.

"Did these men . . . accost you somehow?" asked the younger man.

Hilda only looked to Mollie, who said, "The fog makes everything so much more frightening, of course."

They were pulling up to the address Mollie had indicated, and she quickly took advantage of the distraction, opening the door before Sundry could reach it and expressing her gratitude.

She stepped onto the street, and Mister Walton appeared from around the horses. "Are you sure there is nothing else we can do for you?" he asked, his hat in hand, his balding head shining beneath the streetlight.

"Thank you, but we're really fine now," said Mollie, though Hilda did not look so sure of this. "It's been so nice to meet you." But by the time she had given her hand to both men, the door to the boardinghouse had opened, and Mrs. Makepeace was peering out at the assemblage. "Oh, dear," said Mollie. "This will take some explaining. Hilda, you'll never walk with me again."

"Would it ease matters if I went in with you?" asked Mister Walton.

"Oh, Mister Walton," said Mollie, "we've kept you away from your friends far too long already." She was shaking again, suddenly, and needed to use the distance between the street and the boardinghouse porch to gather herself for the inevitable round of questions from an inquisitive, if well-meaning, landlady. "Thank you so much," she said again, putting off any further offers on the part of Mister Walton, and taking Hilda's arm, she deliberately led them away from the carriage.

2. At the Shipswood

SMOKE AND VIOLIN MUSIC similarly drifted through the atmosphere of the Shipswood Restaurant, and if the members of the Moosepath League did not indulge in the Luciferian practice (any more than they played the stringed instrument), yet they were accustomed, here in their weekly meeting place, to the smoke of other men's cigars and pipes and felt invigorated, in a manly way, by the blue haze, even if they did not contribute to it. The violin music was nice, too.

The Shipswood was a fine establishment, with pleasant round tables and brightly lit chandeliers. The tablecloths were always clean, the service was friendly, and the tall, many-paned windows gave view during the hours of light to the business and hurry of Commercial Street and the better section of the waterfront.

Mr. Matthew Ephram, Mr. Christopher Eagleton, and Mr. Joseph Thump (of the Exeter Thumps) were old hands at this sort of thing. They had been meeting weekly at the Shipswood for more than twelve years, but that was before the fateful night when they were inspired to form a club. That was, in fact, before they had met and admired Mister Tobias Walton, whom they elected as their chairman; and it was well before they experienced several exploits in several other parts of the state while forming the Moosepath League!

During the past weeks they had had a succession of breathless escapades, taking tours about the city and even dining at Mister Walton's home. They had celebrated Eagleton's fortieth birthday, on which occasion Mister Walton had introduced them to the glories of baseball. They had observed a bicycle race at Deering Oaks and become subscribers to Portland's telephone service. They had made several telephone calls to one another.

Despite these wild sprees, Ephram, Eagleton, and Thump had not lost their sense of wonder; in fact, they continued to wonder a good deal, and on the evening of October the eighth they were wondering very specifically as to the whereabouts of their chairman.

"I do not recall," said Ephram, "that he has ever been late to one of our gatherings."

Eagleton, the club's self-appointed historian, gazed into the middle distance and considered this. "I myself have no recollection of any such tardiness and in fact rather consider him a man of admirable promptitude." It was well said, and Eagleton was feeling the effect of his own words when he realized that the particular middle distance in his direct line of sight consisted of a striking young woman who was returning his gaze with a good deal of interest. Thinking that he had collected more than was his share, Eagleton averted his eyes, sat straight in his seat, and raised his menu.

Ephram glanced toward the entrance of the Shipswood Restaurant. "What do you think, Thump?" he asked.

Thump looked up from his own menu and said, "Hmm?"

Ephram did not repeat his question, for it was then that a general hale-and-hearty welcome arose from the fore of the restaurant, and the three Moosepathians knew, from recent practice, that their chairman had arrived.

Other folk dined at the Shipswood of a Thursday night, and in the past several weeks they had come to recognize Mister Walton, who was able to spread cheer simply by passing their tables. His face beamed with sincere interest and pleasure in his surroundings as he entered, his manner was gracious as he stopped at one table to say hello, and his sense of humor was ever ready to appreciate a quip from this group or further a running jest with that.

Ephram, Eagleton, and Thump watched with pride as their chairman found his way to their table, followed by Sundry Moss. (A trusted companion and something of a gentleman's gentleman to Mister Walton, Sundry had been inducted as the fifth member of their society.) "Gentlemen, gentlemen," said Mister Walton when he arrived. "Forgive our tardiness."

"Good heavens!" said Ephram. "Never tardy! I would never say tardy! Would you, Eagleton?"

"Certainly not tardy!" agreed Eagleton. "What do you say, Thump?"

"I'm sure we were early," insisted Thump.

"You are very kind," said the portly fellow as he found his seat. "Sundry and I came upon two young women who had had a recent, if unspecified, fright, and we were pleased that they accepted an offer of a ride home."

"A fright?" said Ephram. The chairman was always in the middle of things, it seemed, and they greatly admired him for it.

"Young women?" said Eagleton.

"Hmm?" said Thump.

What had amounted to a slight digression in Mister Walton and Sundry's evening was viewed by their friends as a full-scale adventure. The members of the club were not a little taken with the description of the young women (Sundry's memory was especially glowing), and Ephram was very much amazed to hear that one of these ladies was a columnist for the *Eastern Argus*.

"Good heavens!" he said again. "And I a subscriber!" as if this were the most astonishing coincidence.

The conversation continued while dinner was ordered, waited on, and served, but Ephram found it difficult to immediately separate himself from thoughts of attractive young women and the *Eastern Argus*. Eventually, however, he rejoined the flow of discourse just as Sundry was informing them about his father's uncle, who had predicted the weather with great accuracy for twelve years, claiming all the while that he garnered his prophetic powers by milking a particular belted Galloway named Temperance. Certain anatomic features of the cow (which Sundry delicately left to the imagination of his listeners) were alleged to represent the four winds, and the difficulty or ease with which the milk came was given to foretell the corresponding variations of oncoming weather.

Ephram pulled at his fine mustaches.

Thump stroked his prodigious beard.

"I hope I do not sound precipitous," said Eagleton, who was fascinated with the weather, "when I say that I would like to look at this cow."

"I fear it is unlikely," said Sundry. "Both uncle and cow have long since departed." He raised his hands to stem the condolences; it had all happened long before he was born. "She lost her oracular powers, at any rate, before her demise. As a prank, one Halloween, some boys—or, rather, a crew of men behaving like boys—kidnapped her and bought her a ticket on the night train from Wiscasset. It wasn't till the train had nearly reached Bath that the conductor discovered her, but she was never the same again."

This seemed a sad end to a noteworthy career. Ephram, Eagleton, and Thump looked solemn. Mister Walton could not suppress a chuckle.

"But for ten years," added Sundry by way of consolation, "the village of Sheepscott hayed without fear of rain and canceled long trips before any blizzards hit."

"Ten years?" asked Mister Walton. "I thought your uncle predicted the weather for *twelve* years."

"Yes, but for two years nobody believed him."

"Ah!" Delight twinkled in Mister Walton's eyes.

"The Portland Bantams are playing an exhibition game against Lewiston tomorrow morning," said Eagleton, who had stolen a glance at the newspaper beside his place at the table. Mister Walton's enthusiasms were of great moment to the members of the club, and through him the local baseball team had garnered their fierce loyalty, though the game itself was still something of a mystery to them. "The paper looks to Mr. O'Hearn for some feat by which the year, if not the season, might be made memorable."

Ephram made a sound of interest and leaned over to see the headline indicated by Eagleton's index finger. Thump frowned down at his hands, which were open before him. He was considering the mysteries of bovine anatomy.

"I'm sorry to miss that," said Sundry. "But I think we will be preparing a way north tomorrow morning."

"My word, yes!" said Ephram. "The Hallowell Harvest Ball!"

"We have been forgetting your impending rendezvous with Miss McCannon!" said Eagleton to Mister Walton.

"Hmm," said Thump. He seemed to be counting something on his fingers.

Mister Walton smiled. "The ball isn't till Monday night," he announced happily, "but Sundry and I will be leaving tomorrow."

Several weeks before, Mister Walton had received a letter (which even now resided in his breast pocket) from Phileda McCannon, whom he had met during the previous adventurous summer. Though he had been forced by circumstance to leave her side more quickly than he would have wished, they had kept in communication ever since by post.

His friends, all of whom had been greatly impressed with Miss McCannon, could not have been happier if they themselves had been invited. Sundry, who had detected a bit of loneliness in his employer of late, was perhaps the happiest of all.

"Wonderful!" said Eagleton.

"Bravo!" said Ephram.

"Hmm," said Thump.

"Twenty past nine," said Ephram, consulting one of the three or four watches that he always carried about his person. They had stopped outside the Shipswood to take stock of the night and those noises intrinsic to the waterfront.

"High tide at eleven forty-eight," announced Thump, though he was somewhat distracted. He was musing again over the anatomic structure of cows. He had never been very close to one.

"Some chance of ground fog this evening," assured Eagleton. "Though this should be cleared by a wind changing to the southwest and brief showers before dawn." The ground fog was, in fact, all about them, and their carriage, some lengths down the glistening street, was nearly obscured by the mists that slunk from the alleys and drifted along the cobbles.

"The fog does make things *sound* very much closer, doesn't it?" said Ephram, adding, "Or perhaps I am mistaken. Perhaps the things we hear actually *are* near at hand and it is the fog that makes us think they are distant." He deferred in this question to Eagleton, whose great love, if not métier, was meteorography.

"I hadn't considered," said Eagleton carefully. "But it is a very remarkable effect."

Thump was looked to next, but he was still thinking about cows. "Hmm?" he said.

"I know that when my room is dark," said Sundry, "the foot of my bed is often not where I think it should be."

Ephram petitioned Mister Walton for his opinion on the subject of fog and its effects upon human perception. Eagleton attempted to explain to Thump the two theories that had already been expounded. Thump realized, with a start, what portion of the cow Sundry had been speaking of.

"I trust you will be back in time for next Thursday's meeting?" ventured Ephram.

"Oh, yes, surely," said Mister Walton.

Sundry, who had less confidence in human design, simply said, "Barring unforeseen incident," which comment they would all remember when next they met, at another time, in another place.

Mister Walton's late aunt August had always said, "Young Toby has a traveling bee," and it was perhaps not far from the truth, since he had spent many years away from the state of Maine. Recently, however, he had, with the help of Sundry (and his family's elderly retainers, Mr. and Mrs. Baffin), settled nicely into his family home and had remained more or less a constant inhabitant of Portland since the end of July. He had reacquainted himself with his neighbors, looked up old friends, and attended two or three concerts and a play.

He had, in fact, resituated himself from the outside in, spending his first month back in Maine traveling the state. August brought greater introspection, and he was seen less outside his house as he explored the family treasures and heirlooms from attic to cellar, reading old letters and much-beloved books, growing misty-eyed over brown photographs and silvered tintypes, tenderly brushing his father's suit or refolding his mother's wedding dress before putting them back into their trunks.

One day he took inspection of his parents' room and came across a small, stoppered vial of his mother's perfume. Sitting on the edge of the bed, he lifted the opened vial to his nose; the lily-of-the-valley scent had lost some of its vigor, but the ghostlike fragrance was all the more potent for its subtlety. Mister Walton felt as if his mother had walked into the room, and he was filled with an astonishing assemblage of emotions, wrapped up in affection and warmth. He was almost shocked to see his own face reflected in the mirror; he had not realized that he looked so much like her.

It was then that he forgot, for a moment, that he had made friends everywhere he went, that somewhere in the house Sundry was mending an old chair, Mr. Baffin was polishing the banister, and Mrs. Baffin was cooking supper. He forgot the members of the Moosepath League, who would have come running at the merest hint of his melancholy. He could only think of his parents and his brother, who were not here anymore, and of his sister, who was (the last he knew) in Africa. Sunlight fell through the window beside the bed and struck the waving shadows of an oak tree in the boundary of a skewed rectangle upon the carpet.

He was thinking of that patch of sunlight as the carriage rolled home that night. Ephram, Eagleton, and Thump had gotten off before their respective doors (with many a lifted hat and hearty handshake). "Miss Greenwood was wearing lily of the valley," he said, so quietly that Sundry had to think a moment before realizing what had been said. Sundry was attempting a reply to this when the older gentlemen looked up and smiled. "My mother wore lily of the valley," he explained.

Sundry nodded his understanding. "She made me think of my sister."

"They are lovely girls," said Mister Walton.

This fact had not escaped Sundry. Hilda had reminded him a little *too* much of his sister, but Mollie had struck him as a very handsome young woman.

Oh, Aunt August was saying in Mister Walton's mind, *young Toby has a traveling bee*. He could see the trapezoid of light on the carpet, the shadows of leaves and limbs waving.

"It will be good to see Miss McCannon," said Sundry.

Mister Walton nodded and smiled.

When they had paid the driver, bid him good night, and walked through the gate, the old house rose up before them—a welcoming presence in the evening air. A breeze ruffled the trees on either side of the house; crickets sounded a slow cadence. They mounted the steps, opened the door, and stepped into the hall. The smell of something baked filled the house, and they followed it to the kitchen, where one of Mrs. Baffin's apple pies awaited them in the warming oven.

A PENGUIN READERS GUIDE TO

CORDELIA
UNDERWOOD

Van Reid

An Introduction to
Cordelia Underwood,
or the
Marvelous Beginnings of the Moosepath League

In the idyllic summer of 1896 in Portland, Maine, several residents are embarking on adventures of a most audacious and entertaining nature. The young, redheaded Cordelia Underwood has inherited from her uncle Basil a large tract of land in northern Maine. In a chance but portentous meeting, she crosses paths with Tobias Walton, a wise and adventurous gentleman whose portly stature is dwarfed only by the size of his heart, and John Benning, a dashing bachelor with designs on Cordelia and her gentle character. It's the first of many encounters they will have with one another and with a wealth of Yankee originals.

At the Shipswood Restaurant near Portland's bustling waterfront district, we are introduced to Ephram, Eagleton, and Thump, the bumbling founders of the Moosepath League. Awed by a newspaper account of Mister Walton's extraordinary (if seemingly incidental) exploits and by his amiable character, the members unanimously nominate him as leader of their club—shortly after the incident of the moose and the red flannel underwear—and a small but intriguing piece of Maine's history is born.

Soon the Underwoods are off to explore Cordelia's inheritance, and accepting Mr. Benning's generous offer to accompany them, they head north while quietly entertaining hopes of deciphering the cryptic message that Uncle Basil left with the land deed: "Our Minmaneth is a young goatt." Busy with escapades that include a haunting deathwatch, a lady's parachute drop in her "attractive suit of tights," and a boxing match between two aging politicians, Mister Walton enlists the clever and talented Sundry Moss as his assistant and traveling companion. Upon learning that Cordelia and her family have found Uncle Basil's legacy to be more perilous than at first it seemed, the Moosepath League's chairman leads his exuberant cohorts to the Underwoods' aid. At the story's climax, all parties play crucial roles as they attempt to unravel the riddle of the sea chest and discover what elusive treasures may be hidden within.

Van Reid's tale is a classic story of generosity versus greed, honesty versus deception, good versus evil. But more than a captivating narrative, *Cordelia Underwood* is a stylistic achievement that harkens back to the works of Charles Dickens. Like its Victorian antecedents, the novel was originally serialized in a local newspaper, forcing the author to keep the action moving and the characters memorable so that the readers would await the story's continuation with eager anticipation.

Beyond simply the circumstances under which the story was originally published, *Cordelia Underwood* shares certain character-istics and plot devices with many nineteenth-century novels. It's peopled with good-natured characters, eager to lend a hand at the first sign of someone, preferably a complete stranger, in need. Even the villains seem to elicit the occasional sympathetic response from the reader. Digressive storytelling was prized in Victorian fiction, and the many anecdotes shared by Van Reid's characters—tales of ghostly apparitions, grizzled woodsmen, and bears of various sizes and temperaments—give the book a folklorish quality that sets it apart from much of today's fiction. This style, so appropriate given the characters and events of which Van Reid writes, complements his unrestrained enthusiasm for Maine's history. The result is a novel that brings to vivid life an arcane and wonderful piece of Americana that otherwise might have been forgotten.

In Van Reid's sequel to *Cordelia Underwood, Mollie Peer, or The Underground Adventures of the Moosepath League*, a throng of Moosepath originals return, from the wise, courtly Tobias Walton and the exuberant founders of the Moosepath League to the furtive Eustace Pembleton and his ragamuffin ward. New to the saga are baseball player Wyckford O'Hearn, spiritualist Madame Blinsky, and the remarkable Quibbling Society. They all cross paths with feisty young social columnist Mollie Peer, whose pursuit of smugglers (and a good story) leads them from the resonance of an unexpected kiss to a perilous October chase on the coast.

ABOUT THE AUTHOR

A lifelong resident of Maine, Van Reid writes about what he knows. *Cordelia Underwood* takes place in his home state, as will further installments of the Moosepath League series, including the next volume, *Mollie Peer*. Reid always knew he would be a writer, and decided to skip college in favor of the education he received working at various jobs near his home. "I was afraid I'd lose my individuality. I just had a feeling I could live here and learn what I needed to know and develop my own style." He currently lives (and for the foreseeable future, most likely will live) in Edgecomb, Maine, in a house that he and his brother built, on land that his family has owned since the 1800s. He and his wife have a four-year-old son and a newborn daughter. In addition to writing, Reid works as an assistant manager at the Maine Coast Book Shop in Damariscotta.

A CONVERSATION WITH VAN REID

In Cordelia Underwood, *historical fact and your own fictional inspiration seem to merge seamlessly. Did you undertake the writing of the novel hoping to bring to life Maine's colorful history, or was history more of a vehicle, or starting point, for the telling of your own tales?*

If history and fiction do merge seamlessly—which, of course, is greatly to be hoped for—then perhaps that is because my motives, even to myself, are difficult to separate. What is most conscious, however, and what I tell people is that I hope to create something of a "Northeastern myth." United States destiny and legend almost always point west, and in the process much has been left behind, even forgotten. Storytelling has always been an important aspect of my family's interaction, and the tales about my parents' childhoods and of the lives of my grandparents would fit right in with some of the adventures under discussion. It is here that my vision of people who are good and decent and wise finds its foundation.

Two separate works might also exemplify this point of view. The first is a history by Elizabeth Ring entitled *Maine in the Making of the Nation*, which was published while my book was in the midst of its serialization, and which corroborated a lot of personal feelings I had which were drawn from my own researches.

The second is a movie that I first saw when I was thirteen or fourteen. It was a western entitled *The Big Country*, which stars Gregory Peck as a sea captain from the East who goes out west to marry his fiancée. Peck's character was a great inspiration to me as an easterner who loved westerns and yet felt a little left out, and certainly his civilized manner, under which lies the tough nature one would expect of a seafaring man, must be an antecedent to the decent individualists—whether Mister Walton or Dresden Scott—in my own work.

Critics have likened your writing to that of P. G. Wodehouse, Mark Twain, and John Irving, but perhaps the most acute and frequently mentioned comparison is to Charles Dickens. How has his writing influenced your own work?

You are what you eat, they say, and that goes for what you read, I suppose and hope. It has also been said that one should write about what one knows, which must include people, environment, learning, and also the books in which you have lived. Dickens's works have certainly afforded me a lot of room and board, and perhaps the literary elements I loved the most—the panoply of characters, their range and dichotomous nature, the headlong rush of events, the digressive nooks, and what I call left-handed comedy. There is a passage in *Oliver Twist* in which two servants are described in heroic language as they do their best not to catch a group of fleeing thieves. It is brilliant and hilarious, and I must have read it twenty times before I entirely understood how Dickens did it.

Like much of Dickens's work, Cordelia Underwood *was originally published in weekly installments in a newspaper. How did this affect the evolution of the story? Will the same technique be used for future books in the Moosepath League series?*

There is indeed a rhythm to the events in *Cordelia Underwood* that was encouraged by its having been constructed in weekly installments. Fortunately, this same rhythm continues to work when the book is taken as a whole. The sequel, *Mollie Peer*, developed a rhythm of its own that I think is very compatible with, if different from, the first book's. Reader reaction also had, in a couple of instances, some effect on the proceedings.

The tall tales and anecdotes that various characters relate through-out the novel keep the listeners within the story captive, and work the same magic on the reader as well. Can you discuss the origin of these tales, and your thoughts on how they contribute to the novel as a whole?

There are really three levels in these books—represented by the ever-present three plot threads—that yet inevitably verge and entwine. There is the comic level of Ephram, Eagleton, and Thump. There is the Cordelia/Mollie level of everyday people thrust into extraordinary events. And there is the level occupied by Mister Walton and Sundry Moss, who always have one foot in the land of legend. Cordelia may hear a tall tale from Mr. Tolly, but Mister Walton is witness to the manifestation of a ghost ship.

The tales we tell are as important as the history we know, and Mister Walton in particular I think understands how much might be learned about his people and his home by the stories they choose to impart. Laurence Sterne said about his extraordinary novel *Tristram Shandy* that the best part of any story is the digression, so his must be a great story since it is all digression. I love digressive stories, and these side tales gave me the perfect opportunity to indulge this propensity; people have responded with great fondness for these tales.

Throughout the story, Tobias Walton is reminded time and again of the humble delights and unexpected intrigue that Maine offers—a sharp contrast to his previous misconceptions of his home state as a sleepy cultural backwater. Does his enlightenment reflect a similar change that occurred in your own relationship with your home as you've come to know Maine and its history more deeply?

What might be represented here is a lifelong awakening and education to the extraordinary people who have lived and the remarkable things that have happened in the state of Maine. In a conscious manner, the conversation with Captain Leeman in chapter 48 of *Cordelia Underwood* just touches this subject, but much more could be said about the effects of Maine and its people upon, among other things, Indian affairs, the Civil War, the arts, the history of technology and invention, and American politics.

The historical background that permeates the novel (i.e., social conventions, details of travel, styles of conversation) is effective at re-creating the environment of late-nineteenth-century Maine. Was this detail something you picked up naturally, or did you actively research the cultural particulars and social mores of that era?

In some ways, much of the Victorian milieu was not very far from my childhood. I was surrounded by many of the daily objects and, by the way of the old folk I knew, observed much of the social manners characteristic of that time. My reading, again, must have some proper effect upon my vision, and the newspapers of the day helped to top all this off, giving me a source by which to gauge the attitudes and concerns of the 1890s.

Like many of the players in Charles Dickens's novels, the characters' names in Cordelia Underwood *are memorably distinctive, and often lend insight into their habits, morality, or demeanor. Can you comment on the significance of these names, and how you came up with them?*

The redheaded Cordelia's name was inspired by Anne of Green Gables, who wishes she had been named Cordelia. (Perhaps this was my humble literary equivalent of granting her wish.) Tobias Walton's name came from Uncle Toby in *Tristram Shandy* and Izaak Walton, who wrote *The Compleat Angler.* Sundry Moss's name just happened in the process of writing, and when the sheriff informed Mister Walton that Sundry had a brother named Varius, I was as surprised as anyone. Then, quite naturally, the tale of how they came to be named was expressed from the mouths of my characters. It was all news to me.

As was the case with Sundry, many of the characters were named as they stepped upon the stage, though Dresden Scott—the name and the character—had buzzed about in my head for years. The names Ephram, Eagleton, and Thump have to me the rhythm of something falling down stairs—but where the names came from (outside of Thump's, which seems somehow obvious) I couldn't tell you. Wait'll they meet Durwood, Waverley, and Brink.

The Maine you depict in Cordelia Underwood *is an irresistibly charming one. It is perhaps testament to the effectiveness of the writing that the reader can't help but long for some aspects of that time and place that are missed in society today. In what ways is your conception of Maine at the end of the twentieth century similar to, and different from, the Maine of Cordelia Underwood's time?*

There is a great deal more ethnic and experiential diversity in Maine these days (obviously a positive trend), and yet the geography and the climate can have their effects so that many people, those who care about what went on before they arrived, often develop certain Yankee characteristics. There are those, of course, who come to Maine thinking it merely quaint, a condescending and uninformed attitude if there ever was one; these are the folks who believe that culture arrived with them, and they will probably never grasp how late and mistaken they are. They will always be "from away." Dialect and folkways are disappearing here as they are everywhere, and I can only hope that there have been enough people recording what passes away before it is entirely gone. African-American culture has been wise enough to nurture and respond to the oral tradition, saving that which is above value. I fear Maine's culture has not been so discerning.

In the second Moosepath League novel, Mollie Peer, *you introduce several more eccentric characters, including the spiritualist Madame*

Blinsky. How and why did you light upon the famous historical figure Madame Blavatsky for the creation of this new character?

The character Madame Blinsky was indeed inspired by the historic figure of Madame Blavatsky. I have always been fascinated and amused by Victorian spiritualism, and I reveled in the tales my father told about an elderly woman named Etta Place (rumored to be the Sundance Kid's widow) who lived in Wiscasset in the 1930s. She owned two monstrous black cats and held séances and "tabletippings" that my grandmother sometimes attended. I owe some of my inspiration for Madame Blinsky to Peter Washington's fine work on this subject entitled *Madame Blavatsky's Baboon.*

Can you give us a hint of what to expect from the next Moosepath League novel? Will it be the last?

I often tell people that *Cordelia Underwood* is the Fourth of July: fireworks, bright sunshine, and happy crowds; *Mollie Peer* is Halloween: rustling leaves and bare trees, people masquerading, and dark deeds accomplished in the shadows. The next book seems to be developing its own personality, but will, I believe, center around Christmas, with whatever that might entail. Mister Walton celebrating Christmas seems particularly pleasant to me.

When I first spoke to Carolyn Carlson, senior editor at Viking Penguin, I had three stories concerning the Moosepath League and attendant matter in my mind, and fully expected (and rightly, as it turns out) that more would be suggested during the process of writing. Certain side stories have suggested themselves as well. Much depends upon what bubbles to the top.

QUESTIONS FOR DISCUSSION

1) Horace McQuinn and Maven Flyce appear only briefly in the novel, most notably at the story's beginning and end. What is their significance in the book, and why do you think they are positioned as such within the narrative?

2) How does Cordelia herself stand apart from the many other protagonists of *Cordelia Underwood*? In the larger sense, what does her character represent, and why do you think the book was named in her honor?

3) While many characters play important roles in the story, the three founders of the Moosepath League seem to appear at many critical junctures in the book, and the name of their club provides the foundation for what will unite the Moosepath League series. As a group, consider their words, deeds, and intentions. In addition to being merely players in the unfolding of events, what does their presence add to the book?

4) John Benning appears early in the story as a suitor to Cordelia Underwood, but by the end of the book, his relationship to the other characters has changed greatly. Considering his character throughout the course of the novel, how did the author's handling of John Benning differ, markedly or subtly, from that of other protagonists?

5) Besides treasure, what does the mastermind of the plot to steal the sea chest have to gain? In what ways does he get his comeuppance? In what ways does he not?

QUESTIONS ON *Mollie Peer*

1) The weather is almost a character in its own right in *Mollie Peer,* as the story takes place in the particularly tumultuous month of October in Maine. Using descriptive passages from the novel, discuss how seasonal qualities of autumn play a role in the story. How does this setting create the tone for the action?

2) Discuss Mollie's motivations throughout the novel. Is she a woman ahead of her time? In what ways does she achieve success? In what ways is she hindered? How do her goals differ from those of our last heroine, Cordelia Underwood?

3) While Sundry is a loyal sidekick, he is also a powerful figure in the novel. Consider his relationship with Mister Walton. How does Sundry influence the outcome of events?

4) The theme of family is very important in *Mollie Peer,* notably because many of the characters—Mister Walton, Mollie Peer, Bird, and others—have lost those most important to them. How does this sense of loss affect the characters?

5) Describe the development of Mollie Peer and Wyckford O'Hearn's relationship. What is the source of their difficulties in getting along? How is their complex relationship resolved?

6) As the author indicates in his note, Amos Guernsey is a controversial figure in Moosepath history. In this retelling of history, is Amos a villain? Or is he an honest man just fallen on hard times?

For more information about other Penguin Readers Guides, please call the Penguin Marketing Department at (800)778-6425, E-mail at reading@penguin.com, or write to us at:

Penguin Marketing Department CC
Readers Guides
375 Hudson Street
New York, NY 10014-3657

Please allow 4–6 weeks for delivery.

For a complete list of Penguin Readers Guides that are available online, visit Club PPI on our Web site at:
www.penguinputnam.com

FOR THE BEST IN PAPERBACKS, LOOK FOR THE

In every corner of the world, on every subject under the sun, Penguin represents quality and variety—the very best in publishing today.

For complete information about books available from Penguin—including Puffins, Penguin Classics, and Arkana—and how to order them, write to us at the appropriate address below. Please note that for copyright reasons the selection of books varies from country to country.

In the United Kingdom: Please write to *Dept. EP, Penguin Books Ltd, Bath Road, Harmondsworth, West Drayton, Middlesex UB7 0DA.*

In the United States: Please write to *Penguin Putnam Inc., P.O. Box 12289 Dept. B, Newark, New Jersey 07101-5289* or call 1-800-788-6262.

In Canada: Please write to *Penguin Books Canada Ltd, 10 Alcorn Avenue, Suite 300, Toronto, Ontario M4V 3B2.*

In Australia: Please write to *Penguin Books Australia Ltd, P.O. Box 257, Ringwood, Victoria 3134.*

In New Zealand: Please write to *Penguin Books (NZ) Ltd, Private Bag 102902, North Shore Mail Centre, Auckland 10.*

In India: Please write to *Penguin Books India Pvt Ltd, 11 Panchsheel Shopping Centre, Panchsheel Park, New Delhi 110 017.*

In the Netherlands: Please write to *Penguin Books Netherlands bv, Postbus 3507, NL-1001 AH Amsterdam.*

In Germany: Please write to *Penguin Books Deutschland GmbH, Metzlerstrasse 26, 60594 Frankfurt am Main.*

In Spain: Please write to *Penguin Books S. A., Bravo Murillo 19, 1° B, 28015 Madrid.*

In Italy: Please write to *Penguin Italia s.r.l., Via Benedetto Croce 2, 20094 Corsico, Milano.*

In France: Please write to *Penguin France, Le Carré Wilson, 62 rue Benjamin Baillaud, 31500 Toulouse.*

In Japan: Please write to *Penguin Books Japan Ltd, Kaneko Building, 2-3-25 Koraku, Bunkyo-Ku, Tokyo 112.*

In South Africa: Please write to *Penguin Books South Africa (Pty) Ltd, Private Bag X14, Parkview, 2122 Johannesburg.*